Praise for JUDITH MERKLE RILEY

THE ORACLE GLASS

'Chilly, witty and completely engrossing. With a cheerful skewering (historically grounded) of the sheer, cretinous awfulness of the Sun King's satellites, plenty of skittery action, and a wisp of the supernatural. Great good fun'   *Kirkus Reviews*

'For readers who enjoy an exotic setting with a celebrity slant, the novel offers an intriguing vacation read'   *Publishers Weekly*

A VISION OF LIGHT

'A wonderful read and a gorgeously detailed picture of life in Medieval England'   *Rosemary Sutcliff*

'A most entertaining novel'   *The Times*

'[Margaret of Ashbury is] a delightful character and somebody one would be delighted to meet'
Rosamunde Pilcher

IN PURSUIT OF THE GREEN LION

'Even more delightful than Riley's *A Vision of Light*'
Kirkus Reviews

The Oracle Glass

Judith Merkle Riley

CORONET BOOKS
Hodder and Stoughton

First published in Great Britain in 1994
by Hodder and Stoughton
A division of Hodder Headline PLC

A Coronet paperback

10 9 8 7 6 5 4 3 2 1

British Library Cataloguing in Publication Data
Riley, Judith Merkle
Oracle Glass
I Title
813.54 [F]

ISBN 0 340 60993 1

Typeset by Keyboard Services, Luton, Beds
Printed and bound in Great Britain by
Cox and Wyman Ltd, Reading, Berks

Hodder and Stoughton
A division of Hodder Headline PLC
338 Euston Road
London NW1 3BH

**for Parkes
with love**

KING, COURT, AND CITY
IN 1675

Historical Figures in *The Oracle Glass*

Louis XIV, the "Sun King", King of France
Marie-Thérèse d'Austriche, Queen of France
Philippe d'Orléans, "Monsieur", younger brother of Louis XIV
Elizabeth Charlotte of Bavaria, second wife of "Monsieur"

Official Mistresses of the King

The Duchesse de la Vallière, former mistress, retired to a
    Carmelite convent. Three children by the King, one dead
    in childhood.
The Marquise de Montespan, current mistress. Her children
    by the King:
        Louise, dead at three
        Louis Auguste, Duc du Maine
        Louis César, Comte de Vexin, dead at eleven
        Louise Françoise, Mademoiselle de Nantes
        Louise Marie, Mademoiselle de Tours, dead at
        seven
        Françoise Marie, Mademoiselle de Blois
        Louis Alexandre, Comte de Toulouse
    In her household:
        Mademoiselle des Oeillets, confidential maid. Chil-
        dren by the King: possibly two, unacknowledged.
    Other family members of Madame de Montespan:
        The Duc de Vivonne, her brother
        Madame de Thianges, her sister
        The Abbess of Fontevrault, her sister
Mademoiselle de Fontanges, the soon-to-be favourite

The Marquise de Maintenon, at this time governess to the Marquise de Montespan's children, later to become the last official mistress

The Mancinis, relatives of the late Cardinal Mazarin

Philippe Julien Mancini, Duc de Nevers, patron of the arts and dabbler in the occult
Marie Mancini, Princess of Colonna
Olympe Mancini, Comtesse de Soissons
Marie Anne Mancini, Duchesse de Bouillon

Working Officials

Colbert, Jean-Baptiste, Secretary of Finance
Le Tellier, François Michel, Marquis de Louvois, Minister of War
La Reynie, Gabriel Nicolas de, Chief of the Paris Criminal Police, subordinate to Louvois
Desgrez, Lieutenant (later Captain) of the Watch, subordinate to La Reynie

Fortune-tellers, Witches, Magicians, and Poisoners

Primi Visconti, the King's fortune-teller
Madame de Brinvilliers, a celebrated mass poisoner
Catherine Montvoisin (La Voisin), society sorceress
Antoine Montvoisin, her husband
Marie-Marguerite, her stepdaughter
Margot, her maid
Adam Lecouret (Le Sage), magician, her lover
Catherine Trianon (La Trianon), sorceress, compounder of substances magical and pharmaceutical, an old friend of La Voisin
La Dodée, La Trianon's associate
La Lépère, abortionist and midwife, associate of La Voisin's
Marie Bosse (La Bosse), sorceress, rival of La Voisin
Marie Vigoreux (La Vigoreux), wife of a ladies' tailor, associate of La Bosse
The Abbé Guibourg, purveyor of Black Masses

Fictional Characters

The Marquise de Morville, Geneviève Pasquier, society
    fortune-teller
Sylvie, her maid
Marie-Angélique Pasquier, her sister
Étienne Pasquier, her brother
The Chevalier de Saint Laurent, her mother's brother
Matthieu Pasquier, failed financier and philosopher, her father
Marie-Françoise Pasquier, her mother
Grandmother Pasquier
Lorito, Grandmother's parrot
Mustapha and Gilles, the Marquise de Morville's bodyguards
Astaroth, a demon
André Lamotte (later de La Motte), incompetent poet and
    competent social climber
Florent d'Urbec, amateur mathematician, builder of mechan-
    isms, card shark, and sometime spy
The numerous and tumultuous d'Urbec family

ONE

"What, in heaven's name, is *that*?" The Milanese ambassador to the court of His Majesty Louis XIV, King of France, raised his lorgnon to his eye, the better to inspect the curious figure that had just been shown into the room. The woman who stood on the threshold was an extraordinary sight, even in this extravagant setting in the year of victories, 1676. Above an old-fashioned Spanish farthingale, a black brocade gown cut in the style of Henri IV rose to a tight little white ruff at her neck. Her ebony walking stick, nearly as tall as herself, was decorated with a bunch of black silk ribbons and topped with a silver owl's head. A widow's veil concealed her face. The hum of voices at the maréchale's reception was hushed for a moment, as the stiff little woman in the garments of a previous century threw back her black veil to reveal a beautiful face made ghastly pale by layers of white powder. She paused a moment, taking in the room with an amused look, as if fully conscious of the sensation that her appearance made. As a crowd of women hurried to greet her, the Milanese ambassador's soberly dressed companion, the Lieutenant General of the Paris Police, turned to make a remark.

"That, my dear Ambassador, is the most impudent woman in Paris."

"Indeed, Monsieur de La Reynie, there is obviously no one better fitted than you to make such a pronouncement," the Italian responded politely, tearing his eyes with difficulty from the woman's fiercely lovely face. "But tell me, why the owl's-head walking stick? It makes her look like a sorceress."

"That is exactly her purpose. The woman has a flair for drama. That is why all of Paris is talking about the Marquise de Morville." The chief of the Paris police smiled ironically, but his pale eyes were humourless.

"Ah, so that is the woman who has told the Queen's fortune.

The Comtesse de Soissons says she is infallible. I had thought of consulting her myself, to see if she would sell me the secret of the cards."

"Her mysterious formula for winning at cards – another of her pieces of fakery. Every time someone wins heavily at *lansquenet*, the rumour goes about that the marquise has at last been persuaded to part with the secret of the cards. Secret, indeed . . ." said the chief of police. "That shameless adventuress merely capitalises on every scandal in the city. I believe in this secret about as much as I believe her claims to have been preserved for over two centuries by alchemical arts."

Hearing this, the Milanese ambassador looked abashed and put away his lorgnon.

La Reynie raised an eyebrow. "Don't tell me, my dear fellow, that you were considering purchasing the secret of immortality as well?"

"Oh, certainly not," the ambassador said hastily. "After all, these are modern times. In our century, surely only fools believe in superstitions like that."

"Then half of Paris is composed of fools, even in this age of science. Anyone who loses a handkerchief, a ring, or a lover hastens to the marquise to have her read in the cards or consult her so-called oracle glass. And the damned thing is, they usually come away satisfied. It takes a certain sort of dangerous intelligence to maintain such deception. I assure you, if fortune-telling were illegal, she's the very first person I'd arrest."

The Marquise de Morville was making her way through the high, arched reception hall as if at a Roman triumph. Behind her trailed a dwarf in Moorish costume who carried her black brocade train, as well as a maid in a garish green striped gown who held her handkerchief. Around her crowded petitioners who believed she could make their fortunes: impecunious countesses, overspent abbés and chevaliers, titled libertines raddled with the Italian disease, the society doctor Rabel, the notorious diabolist Duc de Brissac and his sinister companions.

"Ah, there is someone who can introduce us," cried the ambassador, as he intercepted a slender, olive-skinned young man on his way to the refreshment table. "Primi, my friend here and I would like to make the acquaintance of the immortal marquise."

"But of course," answered the young Italian. "The marquise and I have been acquainted for ages." He waggled his eyebrows. It was only a matter of minutes before the chief of police found himself face-to-face with the subject of so many secret reports, being appraised with almost mathematical precision by the subject's cool, grey eyes. Something about the erect little figure in black irritated him unspeakably.

"And so, how is the most notorious charlatan in Paris doing these days?" he asked the fortune-teller, annoyance overcoming his usual impeccable politeness.

"Why, she is doing just about as well as the most pompous chief of police in Paris," the marquise answered calmly. La Reynie noted her perfect Parisian accent. But her speech had a certain formality, precision – as if she were somehow apart from everything. Could she be foreign? There were so many foreign adventurers in the city, these days. But as far as the police could tell, this one, at least, was not engaged in espionage.

"I suppose you are here to sell the secret of the cards," he said between his teeth. Even he was astonished at how infuriated she could make him feel, simply by looking at him the way she did. The arrogance of her, to dare to be amused by a man of his position.

"Oh, no, I could never sell that," replied the *devineresse*. "Unless, of course, you were considering buying it for yourself..." The marquise flashed a wicked smile.

"Just as well, or I would have you taken in for fraud," La Reynie found himself saying. Himself, Gabriel Nicolas de La Reynie, who prided himself on his perfect control, his precise manners – who was known for the exquisite politeness he brought even to the interrogation of a prisoner in the dungeon of the Châtelet.

"Oh, naughty, Monsieur de La Reynie. I always give full value," he could hear her saying in answer, as he inspected the firm little hand that held the tall, black walking stick. A ridiculous ring, shaped like a dragon, another, in the form of a death's-head, and yet two more, one with an immense, blood-red ruby, overburdened the narrow, white little fingers. The hand of a brilliant child, not an old woman, mused La Reynie.

"Your pardon, Marquise," La Reynie said, as she turned to answer the desperate plea of an elderly gentleman for an appointment for a private reading. "I would love to know where you are from, adventuress," he muttered to himself.

As if her ear never missed a sound, even when engaged in mid-conversation elsewhere, the marquise turned her head back over her shoulder and answered the chief of police: "'From'?" She laughed. "Why, I'm from Paris. Where else?"

Lying, thought La Reynie. He knew every secret of the city. It was impossible for such a prodigy to hatch out, unseen by his agents. It was a challenge, and he intended to unravel it for the sake of public order. A woman should not be allowed to annoy the Lieutenant General of the Paris Police.

TWO

My first appearance in the world gave little hint of the splendour that I was to attain as the Marquise de Morville. At the very least, there should have been a comet or a display of Saint-Elmo's fire. I have, of course, remedied this defect in my official biography, adding as well a thunderstorm and an earthquake. In the narrative before you, however, the truth will have to suffice. My birthday was, in fact, a very ordinary grey winter's morning in Paris, early in the year 1659. My mother had laboured the day and night previous, and her life was despaired of. But at the very last minute, when the surgeon had already removed from its case the long hook by which, as a last resort, the mother alone might be saved, his midwife-assistant cried out. Inserting her hand, she brought forth the shrivelled product of the premature labour, gasping at the blood that poured on to the sheets.

"Madame Pasquier, it is a healthy girl," announced the surgeon, peering severely at the tiny cause of his difficulties as the midwife extended me, howling, for my mother's inspection. My foot was twisted; I was covered with black hair.

"Oh, God, but she's ugly," replied my mother – and, with that, she turned her pretty face to the wall and wept with disappointment for the next two days. And so, within the week, I had been bundled off with a cartful of howling newborn Parisians to be nursed in the country near Fontenay-aux-Roses. I was not to return for the next five years, and then, only because of an accident. I had remained at home just long enough for my father to remark that I had grey eyes.

When I had just turned five, a great coach, all shining black with gold trim and high red wheels, arrived in Fontenay-aux-Roses. In those days, when coaches were less common even in Paris, an elephant could not have aroused more interest in the tiny village. Heads peeped out of every window, and even the village priest came to stare. The carriage was pulled by two immense bays in jingling, brass-trimmed harness. There was a coachman on the box with a long whip, three men behind in blue livery with bright brass buttons, a maidservant in a snow-white cap and apron, and also my father, grey faced and bent with worry. A letter addressed to Mother had come into the hands of his bankers, demanding more money for my care, and now he had come to fetch me home. He knew me right away because of my bad foot. The black hair, they tell me, had fallen out within a few weeks of my birth. He pointed me out with his walking stick as I scuttled along with the running children who had come, shouting, to admire the stranger's carriage. Then the maidservant leaped out and washed me and dressed me in fine clothes brought from the city, and my father gave a purseful of coins to Mère Jeannot, the baby-nurse, who wept.

The coach was hot and uncomfortable inside. The leather seats were slippery, and the fine clothes stiff and scratchy and tight. Mère Jeannot was gone. The strange man in the old-fashioned travelling suit and wide plumed hat sat on the seat opposite me all by himself, looking at me. His eyes were full of tears, and I imagined at the time that it was because he, too, missed Mère Jeannot. Finally he spoke.

"And your mother told me you had died," he said. He shook his head slowly, as if he couldn't believe it. I stared at his sad face for a long time. "I am your father, Geneviève. Don't you know me at all?"

"I know you," I answered. "You are the kindest father in the whole world. Mère Jeannot told me so." Then the tears ran down his face and he embraced me, even at the risk of spoiling the beautiful embroidery on his long-sleeved vest.

"What a cold-hearted little thing you've brought to me," said Mother, fixing me with a sharp glance from her china-hard green eyes. She was sitting in an armchair in her reception room, dressed in a *sacque* of yellow silk, inspecting samples of material sent by the ladies' tailor she frequented. Fresh from my trip, I stood across the room and looked at her for a long time. She was very pretty, but I remember that I did not wish to touch her. The fires were out and there was a chill in the tall, blue-and-white panelled room. I didn't notice for several years, until it was pointed out to me, the barrenness of the parquet floor, where the carpet had been removed, or the light squares on the wall, where the paintings by Vouet and Le Sueur no longer hung.

The house to which my father had brought me was an old mansion built in the days of Jean le Bon, located in the Quartier de la Cité in the heart of Paris. Above a reception and dining room rebuilt in the new fashion, its narrow old rooms were compressed around a courtyard with a tower at one corner and a well at its centre. On the ground floor, the kitchen and the stable led into the courtyard. There César and Brutus, the bay geldings, put their long faces out into the sun, dogs and cats lounged in the muck and searched for scraps, and cook shouted insults at the kitchen maid as she dumped dirty water out on the cobblestones. Above was the elegant floor, with gilt-panelled walls and nymphs painted on the ceiling, from which the music of violins could be heard when Mother entertained. Beyond this lay all that was ancient and unplanned, curious rooms of various sizes running almost at random into twisted staircases, and a maze of interconnected chambers.

The front of the house, a wide, low Gothic arch and heavy door to the street, revealed little of the complex life within: the maids kneeling to dust the heavy furniture while my mother locked the silver-laden sideboards; the manservant lowering the chandelier to replace the candles; my older sister playing the clavichord; Father's valet hurrying upstairs with a cup of cocoa; and high, high above, Grandmother's parrot pacing and squawking while the old lady read the court news in the *Gazette de France*. Above this all-concealing door were carved in the stone arch those little Gothic grotesques called *marmousets*; and from this, not only was the house known as the House of the Marmousets, but the narrow winding street beyond it, which ran from the Rue de la Juiverie to the cloister of Notre-Dame itself, was called the Rue des Marmousets.

Father, as I was to learn much later, had risen rapidly as a financier under the protection of Nicolas Fouquet, the *surintendant des finances*, only to lose his fortune and his freedom in Fouquet's fall. Father's face never lost the pallor of the Bastille, nor his heart a disgust for the court and its intrigues. He had been forced to sell his offices and now had only the income from a tiny country property left to him by an uncle. His years in prison had left him caring only for philosophy and with no interest whatsoever in returning to high finance. Rumours abounded that he had hidden money abroad, safe from Colbert, the King's *contrôleur-général des finances*, but Father kept his secrets.

Mother had had several horoscopes cast indicating the return of good fortune, but it was not returning fast enough to suit her. She still resented the fact that the royal pardon had not returned Father's fortune, which had been gobbled up into the maw of the ever-hungry Colbert. The King, she said, should have taken into account the fact that she was practically a Matignon on her mother's side and granted her an allowance.

"After all," she would announce, "it is inconceivable that a family such as mine, no matter in what straits, would have arranged my marriage to a *poor* man of your name, and now your mismanagement has left me in *most* inappropriate circumstances. It's entirely improper for a Matignon to live this way. I deserve to live better. Besides, you have quite spoiled my Wednesdays."

"What's a Wednesday, Grandmother?" I asked some weeks after my arrival, when I had climbed the stairs from the kitchen to Grandmother's room. Grandmother was always there. She never left her immense bed, all hung about with heavy green curtains. Whenever I knocked at the door, Grandmother's parrot repeated her "Come in!", stepping back and forth on its tall perch with its dry, yellow feet and peering at me over its curved orange beak with its little black eyes. If it had had a pink face instead of a green one, and wore a little cap, it would have looked not altogether unlike Grandmother.

"Ah, you've brought my chicory water, have you? Come and sit here on the bed and tell me what's going on downstairs." The walls of the room were painted in the old style, in dark red, the colour of dried blood, with geometric designs in gilt around the edges. The curtains were always pulled across the windows; Grandmother thought the sun unhealthful.

"Grandmother, why does Mother say she has a Wednesday, when they belong to everybody?"

"'Wednesday', *ha!* That's the afternoon that whorish

daughter-in-law of mine displays her bosom to the world and flirts with strangers. She calls it her 'salon' and demands that people call her 'Amérinte' instead of by her Christian name. Genteel, indeed – it's nothing but cards and court gossip . . . that, and an occasional bad poet who can't make a name for himself somewhere better. Oh, it was a ruinous day when that poverty-stricken family of parasites attached themselves to my son! Hand me my Bible from that nightstand, Geneviève, and I'll read to you about Jezebel, and what happens to wicked women." And so I heard something very interesting and lurid from the Bible, about the dogs eating up Jezebel except for her hands and feet. For Grandmother had been a Huguenot before her family had been forced to convert, and she'd kept the Protestant habit of Bible reading – to the scandal of the rest of the family.

On my way back downstairs, I crossed through Uncle's room, where he'd been sleeping all morning because he never went to bed at night. I saw his head and a strange woman's peeking out from under the covers. Uncle, my mother's brother, called himself the Chevalier de Saint-Laurent, although Grandmother always said the title was as false as he is, and it is what one could expect of a worm who made his living sinning at the gaming tables and borrowing from women. Uncle was accounted handsome by many, but there was something about his narrow foxy face and arrogant pale eyes above the high, slanting cheekbones that I did not like. Still, women thought him dashing.

So I peeked into the tall, gilt reception room on Wednesdays, hoping to see some interesting sinning like Jezebel and the hands and feet, but it was just grown-ups calling one another by pretend-names and saying sharp things to one another and drinking from the good glasses, while Mother laughed her special, silvery little laugh that she saved for Wednesdays. She wore her tight dress in violet silk that was cut very low in front and her gold bracelets with the diamonds on them. This was the time she would glance sideways under her lashes at the men, who would praise her green eyes and perhaps recite an impromptu verse on the subject of her nose or lips. There were only a few ladies, and those not as pretty as she was, and a lot of men who dressed like my uncle in baggy pants with lace hanging down their shins and embroidered doublets and short jackets all in silk. They talked a lot about luck at *bassette* or *hoca*, and whom the King had looked at last Friday, and pretended to be interested in Mother until, at a signal from her, my big sister, Marie-Angélique, would glide through, blushing. Then she was the only person they'd look at. Everyone knew she had no dowry because Father had no money – or, rather, had to save it so that my older brother, Étienne, could stay at the Collège de Clermont and become an *avocat* and get rich again for the sake of the family. But Mother hoped my sister might "meet someone important" on her Wednesdays, someone who could launch her into society on account of her beauty.

On Wednesdays Father shut himself up in his study to read about the Romans. That, and take snuff from a little silver box Monsieur Fouquet had once given him. He never really wanted to talk to anyone, except sometimes me.

"Why the Romans, Father?" I asked him one afternoon.

"Because, my child, they teach us how to bear suffering in a world of injustice where all faith is dead," he answered. "You see here? Epictetus shows that reason governs the world, being identical with God." He pointed to a place in the Latin book he was reading.

"I can't read it, Father."

"Oh, yes, of course," he answered in that distant, absent-minded way he had. "No one has seen to your education. I suppose I shall have to myself. Modern education is nothing but fables anyway, fit only to enslave the mind. Look at your sister – nothing but the most fashionable empty-headedness. She embroiders, tinkles at bit at the clavecin, and knows two dozen prayers by heart. Her mind is entirely formed by the reading of romances. And your brother, memorising legal precedents. He learns precedent instead of logic, and law instead of virtue. No, far better to learn about the Romans." Telling me that the rational discovery of truth was the highest activity of the human mind, he then gave me his own little leather-bound notebook to write down my thoughts to make them more orderly and arranged for a Latin tutor.

And so it was that I was educated according to my father's eccentric plan by a series of starving abbés and penniless students who exchanged lessons for meals until I had sufficient knowledge to be able to discuss the Romans and especially his beloved Stoics with him.

Very soon my days fell into a pleasant routine, although one utterly abnormal for a child. In the morning, I studied whatever my current tutor was interested in: fragments of Descartes, the Epicureans, the question of proof in geometry, the new discoveries in physiology of Monsieur Harvey, the English doctor. In all this, they were guided by Father, who believed that new minds should be trained for the new age; that science and rationality would drive away the superstition of the old era.

In the afternoon, I ingratiated myself with my mother by running confidential errands for her. From her I had three petticoats my sister had outgrown, an old comb, and the promise of a new dress at Christmas if I kept her secrets. Although Mother left me unkempt and untaught in matters feminine, still, I learned a great deal from her indirectly. It was on my afternoon errands that I learned where love potions, hair dye, and wrinkle creams could be bought, how to make change and tell false coin from good. I found out where to buy the best illegal broadsides for Grandmother and that Mother received letters in secret with heavy wax seals on them. It was not at all the proper training for a young lady of good family, who should never be seen outdoors without a lackey, but my twisted body and wild, untutored manners exempted me from all rules, just as they prevented me from receiving the benefits of my birth.

In the evenings, when Mother entertained the delightful Monsieur Courville, or the divine Marquis of Livorno, or the charming Chevalier de la Rivière or some other *poseur*, I discussed the rules of logic and especially the Romans with Father. I loved the way he would read, in his calm, deep voice, and then peer over his little reading glasses to make some comment on the text. Then I would display my small learning of the morning and be rewarded with his narrow, ironic smile. It was the perfect arrangement; I wanted no other life.

THREE

It was in the summer of my twelfth year that fate and my mother's ambition brought me to the attention of the most powerful sorceress in Paris. It was at that moment that the most devious mind in that devious city hatched the plan to create the Marquise de Morville. For the fashionable fortune-teller whom Mother chose to consult about the mending of her fortunes was, unknown to her, the brilliant and malicious queen of the witches of Paris, and it was she who discovered that I had been born with the power to read the oracle glass. I still remember how her eyes glowed when she recognised the gift and her quiet, possessive smile – the smile of a connoisseur and collector confronted by a rare vase in the hands of a fool. And because the sorceress was ingenious, determined, and as patient as a spider in the centre of a web, it was only a matter of time until I tumbled into her hands.

I remember the day well. It was a hot day in midsummer; that winter I had just turned twelve.

"Mademoiselle, did you put the bottle from the Galerie on my dressing table?" It was Mother's morning *levée*. Not much by the standards of the court, I suppose, but she was attended in her bedchamber this day by several servants, my latest tutor, and a man she had engaged to paint Marie-Angélique's portrait in miniature.

"Yes, Mother, right at the back, by the mirror. See there?" Mother eyed the spot suspiciously and turned so suddenly that the maid who was brushing her hair dropped the hairbrush.

"And the change? You've brought it all?" I held it out to her and she counted it carefully before putting it away. "And the note?" A note with an address on the Rue Beauregard from her *parfumier*. I took it out of my sleeve and gave it to her. "You haven't shown it to anyone, have you?" she asked, her voice sharp. I shook my head.

I didn't tell her that I'd tried the perfume on the way home the afternoon before. I had long ago discovered how to reseal a vial so Mother couldn't tell it had been opened, just so I could try out anything that looked interesting. The woman at the *parfumerie* at the Galerie du Palais supplied all sorts of things Mother needed: hair dye, rouge, and now a new scent with something extra having to do with incantations that would make the wearer irresistible. No better trial than on me, I'd thought. It's not much to make a good-looking person irresistible, but an ugly girl who can't walk right and who is as skinny and small as a monkey – why then, it would be really powerful. So I'd doused myself in it and hidden myself from Mother for the rest of the day.

First I'd gone to the tower room where the old clothes, mouse-eaten cushions, and furniture in need of mending are kept, and taken out my secret book. There I wrote the date: *20 July 1671*, and beside it: *Irresistible perfume – trial number 1*. Then I'd slipped out for the afternoon – something my sister was never allowed to do. But there is a freedom in ugliness: Mother did not care what happened to me, and Father never noticed I was gone, unless it was time to discuss the Romans.

Reeking of Mother's perfume, I entered the Street of the Marmousets as one would a river, drifting and bobbing among the crowds of merchants and urchins, the little knots of respectable women out shopping with their laden servants behind them, the occasional *avocat* or notary hurrying to the Palais de Justice with papers in a leather case under his arm. Here and there on the river bobbed a sedan chair, its white-faced, powdered occupant staring into space above the sweaty backs of the bearers. The river joined the main stream pouring towards the Pont-Neuf, and I slipped unnoticed, a pale, twisted little girl, limping sideways like a crab, among the mass of humanity. It was a fine day for a scientific trial; the bridge was crowded with beggars, players, peddlers, and little booths selling trinkets and illicit publications.

I started by purchasing a most satisfactory *libelle* for Grandmother, from a peddler of religious tracts who kept the best things hidden under his cloak. A bargain, newly smuggled in from Holland, where they print all the finest illegal pamphlets: *The Scandalous Life of Louis, King of the French*, in which it was explained that it was only natural that the King should repeatedly break the sacred tie of marriage, because he was in fact the natural son of Cardinal Mazarin, who had had an affair with the Queen. Of course I hid it away, because reading it was very nearly as illegal as publishing it or selling it, and joined the crowd of watchers and cutpurses around an impromptu stage, where several players in masks were shouting filthy jokes while a man who represented the wife's lover hit the cowering cuckolded husband over the head with a bludgeon made of stuffed leather. I passed on when they made their appeal for money, because mine was gone. A charlatan in a wide, battered felt hat with a case of medicines was singing about their virtues: a cure for pox or ague, boils or plague, come buy and be sage, live to a happy old age. He had a monkey on a leash, dressed in satin like a little man. It came up and touched my hand with its tiny brown palm and looked at me with its mournful, glittering eyes.

Fact number 1: the irresistible perfume attracts monkeys.

I felt a tugging at the back of my cloak. A dirty cloak robber, I thought; you'll get nothing of *mine* without a struggle. I clutched my cloak so hard around me that the thief's big hand actually lifted me up into the air. But I didn't let go, I screamed, "Help! Murder! Thief!"

"Not so fast there!" A boldly dressed young man in a short cloak, at least a dozen bunches of ribbons, and wide grey hat with a white plume put his sword to the robber's ragged doublet. The ruffian dropped me and fled, threatening to return with his friends.

Fact number 2: the irresistible perfume attracts robbers.

"What's a little girl like you doing here unescorted? Don't you know you could be killed? Let me take you home. Haven't I seen you coming out of the Maison des Marmousets?" My rescuer knew where I was from. Was he a fortune hunter or a hero?

Fact number 3: the irresistible perfume attracts fortune hunters.

"Hee, hee," the blind beggar at the end of the bridge laughed. "I saw it all. Very funny, very funny indeed, Monsieur Lamotte."

Fact number 4: the irresistible perfume makes the blind see.

Lamotte, I said to myself. Not a distinguished name. A

fortune hunter should at least have a "de" in his name. My heart still pounding, I looked up at my rescuer and saw beneath his hat brim a pair of glorious blue eyes, the profile of an Adonis, and shoulder-length brown curls that glowed in the sunlight. Looking back on it, I think now he must have been all of sixteen. I could tell by the look on his face that he had noticed my blush, and at the very same time my ugliness. My face turned hot. I couldn't decide at that moment which of us I hated the most: him, because he would never see me as I saw him, or myself, for having lost all ability to speak, even to thank him. As my white knight sauntered casually off down the Rue des Marmousets, I watched him go with a strange, new, painful sensation inside. I resolved to pinch it out as soon as I could.

Father had explained to me that a disciplined mind is the most important possession a person could have. That evening we were resting from the Stoics and reading Monsieur Descartes's *Discourse on the Method of Properly Conducting One's Reason and of Seeking the Truth in the Sciences.*

"Now, begin where we left off, at the Fourth Discourse," said Father, "and then explain what is meant."

"'But immediately afterwards I became aware that, while I decided thus to think that everything was false, it followed necessarily that I who thought this must be something; and observing that this truth: *I think, therefore I am*, was so certain and so evident that all the most extravagant suppositions of the sceptics were not capable of shaking it, I judged that I could accept it without scruple as the first principle of the philosophy I was seeking,'" I read. "That means," I said, "that according to the geometrical method of proof—"

"*Snf, snf* – What's that abominable scent? It smells like a whorehouse in here."

"I've no idea, Father."

Fact number 5: the irresistible perfume has no effect on people with clear understanding.

I had finished the day before by writing in my secret book by the light of a bit of candle end: *This perfume is well suited to Mother, but I shall not use it again.*

To return to Mother's *levée* on the morning of the day she changed my life: Having anointed herself with the irresistible perfume, Mother reviewed the address on the little note. It was the celebrated fortune-teller's address, and her advice would not come cheaply. Mother looked agitated, then stuffed the note in the bosom of her gown. Then she hunted here and there, in the old glove she kept under the mattress, the lacquered box on her dressing table, and the little coffer in the back of her armoire. All empty, courtesy of Uncle. At last she produced eight of Grandmother's silver spoons, which had vanished from the sideboard, and sent me to pawn them with the wife of the ladies' tailor on the Rue Courtauvilain, where gentlewomen in distress got cash on their silk dresses.

Thinking over the matter on the way home, it seemed entirely fair that I hold back two francs as my share of the spoons that Grandmother would have left to me anyway and go to the Galerie in the Palais, which was very close to where we lived. There at a stationer's stall I bought another little red notebook. The stationer was also selling from a well-hidden box an excellent *libelle* with a goodly number of pages for the money, entitled *The Hideous Secrets of the Papal Poisoners*. It told in some detail all the methods used by the ambitious Italians of olden times to get rid of rivals and explained how the Italian queen had brought them into France. Printed in Holland, best quality. I bought it for Grandmother.

Grandmother was delighted with this new addition to her collection of scandal. She was happily sitting up in bed, rereading about the destruction of Sodom and Gomorrah when I brought the *libelle* to her.

"Don't forget this, Geneviève, this is how the wicked are punished. With *fire* and *brimstone*." And her little black eyes glittered with pleasure while her parrot croaked out "Fire! Fire! Fire and brimstone!" and bobbed his green head. She put the *libelle* under her pillow, to save for later.

That afternoon, Mother had the horses harnessed and took us both across the Pont-Neuf, past the Halles and the Cimetière des Innocents, to very edge of Paris, directly under the ramparts near the Porte Saint-Denis. There we passed into a neighbourhood composed mostly of tall, graceful villas surrounded by large gardens. Mother had the driver stop in the Rue Beauregard, where we watched a masked lady slip furtively from one of the houses to a waiting carriage. Eight horses, attendants in full livery, and what looked at a distance like a ducal coat of arms painted on the door. The lady gave orders, and the carriage started away at great speed, barely missing a knot of lounging porters waiting by a pair of empty sedan chairs for the return of other clients of the fortune-teller. Mother looked satisfied: she liked doing business where the clientele were numerous and chic. And so, without even realising it, she stepped over the invisible border into the kingdom of shadows.

After a brief wait in an anteroom, where Mother sat fanning herself in the heat, the yellow from her damp hair trickling down her neck, we were shown by a well-dressed maid into the fortune-teller's reception room. The walls and ceiling were painted black; it was dimly lit by candles that flickered in front of a cluster of plaster saints in a corner. The shutters had been closed against the heat, but the heavy black drapes were pulled back from them. In the other corner was a statue of the Madonna in a blue robe, with a heavy candle burning before her and a vase full of flowers that gave off a sickly scent. A cabinet with open shelves beside an armoire displayed a row of assorted statues of china angels. In the dim light their faces took on a menacing aspect. A rich, heavy carpet covered the floor, and a small, elaborately carved table stood in its centre. On one side of the table was an armchair for the *devineresse* and on the other side, a wide, cushioned stool for the client. We sat down on chairs arranged beneath the china angels to wait.

"She'll be a hag," whispered Marie-Angélique to me, her blue eyes wide and her thick golden hair all piled high, a shining halo over her beautiful face. "I just know it. And, oh, what will I tell Père Laporte? He doesn't approve of fortune-telling." And I don't approve of having a confessor instead of a conscience, I thought. I was quite proud of mine, which had been produced through the discovery of the laws of virtue by the use of reason.

But the woman the maid ushered through the inner door was nothing like what Marie-Angélique had expected. She looked like a lady, dressed in dark emerald-green silk over a black embroidered petticoat. Her black hair was arranged in curls and decorated with brilliants in the latest court style. Her face was pale and elegant, with a wide forehead, a long classic nose, and narrow, delicate chin. Her smile was curious, narrow, and turned up at the edges, like a pointed V. I could tell that Mother and Marie-Angélique approved of her appearance. She makes good money in this business, I thought.

I studied her closely as she took her seat, for as one of my tutors had explained, the science of physiognomy allows people of education to discern the character of persons from their features and carriage. The fortune-teller looked about thirty; her air was self-assured, and her eyes, sombre and black, seemed all-knowing, almost mocking. Her whole presence had a sort of brooding intensity, and her posture as she sat in her brocade-upholstered armchair was regal, as if she were the queen of this secret world, temporarily admiring petitioners from a lesser place. Let's see what she has to say, I said to myself. We'll see how clever she is.

"Good day, Madame Pasquier. You have come to discover what fortune your daughters will have in marriage." Mother seemed impressed. Her fan ceased its motion. A logical conclusion when a woman comes in trailing two daughters, I thought. The woman is shrewd. After a number of flattering compliments were exchanged, Marie-Angélique was pushed to take her seat by the table directly opposite the fortune-teller. The most celebrated pythoness in Paris took her hand.

"Your family has suffered reverses," the fortune-teller said, running her fingers over my sister's palm. "You have been brought home from . . . Ah, yes . . . a convent school for want of money. The dowry has . . . ah . . . diminished. But you will fulfil your mother's greatest dream. A lover of the highest rank – a fortune. But beware of the man in the sky-blue coat. The one that wears a blond wig." Bravo, well done. Half the most fashionable men in Paris must have a sky-blue coat and a blond wig.

Mother's smile was triumphant, but Marie-Angélique burst into tears. "Don't you see marriage and children for me? You must look closer. Oh, look again!" Clever, I thought. Satisfy the one who is paying first. But how will she evade this problem?

"I don't always see the entire picture," the fortune-teller said, her voice soft and insinuating. "A child? Yes, I think. And there may be marriage beyond the man in the sky-blue coat. But just now I cannot see beyond him. Perhaps you should consult me again in a few months' time, when the farther future will appear more clearly." Very shrewd. Marie-Angélique would be back secretly before Christmas with every sou she could beg or borrow, despite all the admonitions of Père Laporte.

Mother was so impatient to hear her own fortune now that she very nearly pushed Marie-Angélique off the seat in order to hear the words of the oracle. In a confidential tone that I wasn't supposed to hear, the sorceress whispered, "Your husband does not understand you. You make a thousand economies for his happiness and he doesn't acknowledge one of them. He is without ambition and refuses to attend the court and seek the favour that would restore your happiness. Never fear; new joy is at hand." An odd, pleased look crossed Mother's face. "If you want to hasten that happiness" – the fortune-teller's voice faded out – "more youthful . . ." I heard, and I saw her take a little vial out of the drawer in the table. Mother hid it inside her corset. Excellent, I thought. When had Mother ever refused a remedy that promised to restore her fading youth? Now if all those creams actually worked, judging by the number of people selling them, all of Paris would have faces as smooth as a baby's bottom. "If he remains hard and indifferent . . . bring his shirt . . . a Mass to Saint-Rabboni . . ." Fascinating. One trip multiplied into several, with corresponding payments.

"And now, for the cross I bear daily," said Mother, getting up and pushing me forward. "Tell us all what will happen to a girl with a heart as twisted as her body."

The fortune-teller looked first at Mother, then at me, with an appraising eye. "What you really want to know," she pronounced coolly, "is whether this child will inherit money – money concealed in a foreign country." This was not what I'd expected. I looked at the fortune-teller's face. She was looking me over carefully, as if taking my measure. Then her dark eyes inspected my sweaty little palm.

"Unusual, this . . . ," she said, and Mother and Marie-Angélique crowded closer to look. "You see this line of stars, formed here? One indicates fortune. Three – that's entirely uncommon. It is a very powerful sign." Even the fortune-teller seemed impressed. It was quite gratifying.

"A fortune, an immense fortune," Mother hissed. "I knew it. But I must know. In what country is the fortune hidden? Can you use your arts to divine the name of the banker?"

"Stars formed on the palm never indicate what sort of fortune or where it is located, only that it involves great changes, and that it's good in the end. You will need a more specific divination to answer your question – a divination by water. There will be an extra charge for the preparation of the water." Mother's mouth shut up tight like a purse. "Very well," she said, looking resentful. The fortune-teller rang a little bell, and when the maid appeared she consulted with her. "The gift of water divination is a rare one, usually found only in young virgins – and so, of course, in this wicked world, it does not last long, does it?" Her sharp, sarcastic laugh was echoed by Mother's silvery "company" laugh. I wished we could leave now. This was quite enough.

The maid reappeared with a glass stirring-rod and a round crystal vase full of water on a tray. She was accompanied by a neatly dressed girl my own age, with brown hair combed back tightly and a sullen expression. The fortune-teller's daughter.

The fortune-teller stirred the water with the rod, chanting something that sounded like *"Mana, hoca, nama, nama."* Then she turned to me and said, "Put your palms around the glass – no, not that way. Yes. Good. Now take them away." The little girl peered down into the vase, which was all sticky with my palm prints, as the water became smooth again.

They had done something very interesting with the water. A tiny image seemed to form out of its depths, clear and bright like the reflection of an invisible object. It was a face. The strange, lovely face of a girl in her twenties, grey eyes staring back at me, black hair blowing about her pale face, the wind whipping a heavy grey cloak she held tightly around her. She was leaning on the rail of a ship that bobbed up and down on an invisible ocean. How had the sorceress made the image appear? Mother and Marie-Angélique were watching the fortune-teller's face, but I only had eyes for the tiny picture. The fortune-teller spoke to her daughter:

"Now, Marie-Marguerite, what do you see?"

"The ocean, Mother."

"But how did you make the little face appear?" I asked without thinking. The fortune-teller's dark, heavy-lidded eyes turned on me for what seemed like ages.

"You see a picture, too?" she asked.

"Is it a mirror?" I asked. There was an acquisitive glitter in the fortune-teller's dark eyes. Suddenly she turned her face from me, as if she had made up her mind about something.

"The fortune comes from a country that must be reached by crossing the ocean," the fortune-teller addressed Mother. "But not for many years."

"But what does the face mean?" interrupted Marie-Angélique.

"Nothing. She just saw her reflection, that's all," said the fortune-teller abruptly.

"Many years?" Mother's silvery little laugh tinkled. "Surely, I'll choke it out of her much sooner than that. Dear little wretch," she added as an afterthought, giving me a mock blow with her fan to let everyone know it was all in good sport.

Late that night I wrote in my little book: *21 July 1671. Catherine Montvoisin, Rue Beauregard, fortune-teller, trial number 1.*

Marie-Angélique – A rich lover, beware man in sky-blue coat and blond wig, perhaps a child.

Mother – Youth cream. Measure lines over next three weeks. Large joy soon.

Me – There is money in a foreign country. A thought: Beautiful women fear old age more than ugly women. When I am old, I will buy books, not wrinkle cream.

That evening, after discussing Seneca with Father, I asked him what he thought of fortune-tellers.

"My dear little girl, they are the refuge of the gullible and the superstitious. I would like to say, of women, but there are plenty of men who run to them, too. They are all fools."

"That's what I think, too, Father." He nodded, pleased. "But tell me, is it possible to see pictures in water, as they describe?"

"Oh, no. Those are just reflections. Sometimes they can make them seem to shine out of water, or a crystal ball, or whatever, by the use of mirrors. Most fortune-telling is just sleight of hand, like the conjurors on the Pont-Neuf."

"But what about when they seem to know people's secrets and handwriting?"

"Why, you sound as if you'd made a study of it. I'm delighted you are applying the light of reason to the darkness of knavery and superstition. But as for an answer, you should know that fortune-tellers are a devious race, who usually cultivate a network of informers, so that they know the comings and goings of their clientele. That's how they astonish the simple."

"Why, that settles the point perfectly, Father." He looked pleased. "But I have another question, a ... philosophical question..." He raised one eyebrow. "Which do the Romans say is better: to be clever or to be beautiful?" My voice was troubled. Father looked at me a long time.

"Clever, of course, my daughter. Beauty is hollow, deceptive, and fades rapidly." His gaze was suddenly fierce. "The Romans believed that a virtuous woman had no other need of adornment."

"But, Father, that was about Cornelia, whose sons were her jewels, and don't you think that she had to be at least a bit pretty in order to be married and have the sons? I mean, isn't virtue in a plain girl considered rather unremarkable?"

"My dear, dear child, are you comparing yourself to your sister again? Be assured, you are far more beautiful to me just as you are. Your features are exactly my own, and the only proof I have of your paternity." The bitter look on his face shocked me.

But for days afterward, my heart sang, "Not pretty, but special. Father loves me best of all." My secret. Nothing could take it away. I didn't even need to write it in my little book.

FOUR

"Come here and look, Geneviève. He's out in front again."
Marie-Angélique lifted the curtain of her bedchamber and
beckoned to me. I put down my sketch pad, and together we
peeped out into the misty spring morning. Heavy-budded fruit
trees, all ready to burst into bloom, lifted their branches above
the high garden walls opposite. And there, concealed in a
doorway across the street, stood the figure of a man. "He's
there every day. What do you think he wants?" Marie-
Angélique's face was pink with pleasure. She wanted me to say
again what she already thought.

"I imagine he's in love with you. Everybody is, sooner or
later." Poor man. It was early in the year 1674, and he had
hundreds before him. The heavy scent of narcissus in the vase
by Marie-Angélique's bed filled the room with spring. Beside
the vase on the little night table lay a copy of *Clélie* with an
extravagantly embroidered bookmark in it. Marie-Angélique
loved romances. They were her measure of life; a scene in
reality was judged by how well it matched up with the scene in
which Aronce declares his love for Clélie, or Cyrus abducts
Mandane in his luxurious ship. "Suppose, Marie-Angélique,
that Cyrus had a shabby little boat. What would you think
then?" I had once asked her. "Oh, Geneviève," she'd
answered, "Mademoiselle de Scudéry could not even *imagine*
such an unromantic thing." Poor reality – it always came off so
badly by comparison to the silly things she read. I was, at the
time, reading Herodotus with Father.

"Oh, do you really think he's in love?" she fluttered. "How
long has he been there? Three days?"

"No, more like a week."

"Oh, that's terribly romantic. Tell me, don't you think he
looks nice?" It must be the spring, I thought. In spring,
everyone falls in love with Marie-Angélique. I peeked out
again for her. He stepped out of the shadowy doorway, and my

heart died a little as I recognised his face. He had on high boots, a short embroidered jacket festooned with ribbons, an épée with an embroidered baldric, and a short cloak dramatically thrown back. His hat was tilted jauntily over his lean face, and he had managed to grow a moustache since I had last seen him. It was my white knight, André Lamotte, but now no longer mine, not even in imagination.

"Who do you think he is?" Marie-Angélique said dreamily. "He doesn't have any lace . . . Oh, is that a ring I see? No . . . but perhaps he's in disguise." Marie-Angélique was always hopeful.

"I saw him once when Father took me to the Luxembourg Gardens. He was reading," I said.

"Oh, a student." Marie-Angélique sounded disappointed. "But perhaps he is a prince, who is learning responsibility before he takes up his title."

"I think his name is Lamotte."

"Oh dear," responded Marie-Angélique. "You had better put down the curtain at once, Geneviève. Mother doesn't approve of staring at strange men." I dropped the curtain and picked up my sketch pad. There, amidst the dutifully copied flowers assigned by the drawing master, I sketched in Lamotte's handsome young profile. Beneath it I wrote, "Do not look at strange men," and showed it to Marie-Angélique, who burst out laughing.

"Sister, what *shall* I do with you? You will never learn the proprieties!" she cried.

"Come, come, Mesdemoiselles, what are you waiting for?" Mother bustled into the room in her cloak, with a basket of cakes, fruit, and pâtés over her arm. "Don't dawdle. You aren't children any more. It's high time you learned Christian responsibility." No, we were not children any more. I had turned fifteen, and Marie-Angélique was nineteen, and old enough to be married if she had had a proper dowry. Mother looked terribly businesslike. Charity was a new thing she'd taken up, between her visits to the fortune-teller. Now she made weekly visits bringing alms to the sick poor at the Hôtel-Dieu, the charity hospital that lay on the square near the Cathedral of Notre-Dame. Lately it was all the rage, and Mother loved to be fashionable. Besides, one could meet ladies of the highest rank bandaging sores and dispensing sweets in the vast stone *salles* of the Hôtel-Dieu; it was the next best thing to a visit to Saint-Germain or Versailles, and far more convenient.

The charitable fit had come on shortly after Father's creditors had seized our carriage and horses. At first, it seemed to me to be quite unlike Mother, who usually turned up her nose at beggars and gave very poor tips. But then again, it was fashionable, so she embraced her missions of charity with the same tenacious energy that preserved her salon. To still the rumours of a declining fortune, she made sure that the women of the Pasquier family were seen well dressed, with heavily laden baskets, murmuring benedictions from bed to bed with the other aristocratic angels of mercy.

Each of us found something worthwhile in these trips. For days after, Marie-Angélique would feed on the glimpse of the Marquise of So-and-So's beautiful ribbons, or the new hair-style of the Countess of Such-and-Such, and I would write in my little book. I was, at the time, testing the validity of religion by using the geometric method of proof to assess the efficacy of prayer. First I wrote down the illnesses and injuries of those we visited and the likelihood of recovery of the sick persons we had seen. Then, through ingenuous questioning, I attempted to ascertain how many prayers had been offered in each case. This I did by multiplying the number of relatives by a figure of one to five, depending upon how well the person was liked by his family. Then I would write down whether or not the person outlived his prognostication. The project kept me totally content. After all, the use of ordered thinking to discover the truth is the highest occupation of humankind.

Charity did Mother good and made her calmer. The day the carriage was taken, she had rushed shrieking about the house, then battered open the door of Father's study, where he and I were discussing Seneca, and covered him with abuse. He looked up at her, where she stood before his armchair, and his eyes moved slowly, so slowly, with a look I'll never forget.

"Madame, I leave you to your infidelities; you leave me to my philosophers."

"Your— Your stupidities, your lack of ambition— Your

refusal to be seen at court, to carry my petitions . . . your *Romans* have reduced me, Monsieur. They have brought me to *this*, and it is beyond my endurance."

Father spoke with utter calm: "The day I appear at court it will be to petition the King to have you shut up in a convent for your scandalous life. Go, Madame, and do not interrupt me again." He opened his Seneca again to the place where he had left his bookmark.

Mother stood still, all white, her eyes half closed. Then she spoke. "You are utterly *tiresome*," she said in a cold voice and withdrew from the low, book-lined room, holding the train of her pale green silk morning gown in her hand. Father sat still in his armchair, book open on his lap, and looked over his little reading glasses to watch her go with exactly the same expression with which one would regard an insect disappearing into a crack in the wall.

After that she had vanished in a hired chair for the rest of the day. Then it was not long before she discovered charity, and all was calm again.

But to return to our hospital visit. André Lamotte, bold and poor, swept off his hat for my sister with a flourish as we passed.

"Don't nod to him," said Mother, turning her face away. "He is without fortune. I'll not have you encouraging such people." As we turned down the Rue de Saint-Pierre-aux-Boeufs, I turned back to look at him. He was holding his hat over his heart, with a yearning expression on his face. When he saw me peeking at him, he grinned, and I thought I saw him wink.

We crossed the Parvis Notre-Dame, Mother looking to the right and left to make sure that we missed no one of consequence. "Ah, isn't that the Comtesse d'Armagnac I see arriving there?" she observed. "Walk a little slower Marie-Angélique, so that we may greet her as she passes." We entered the low, Gothic portals of the Hôtel-Dieu and were greeted by a novice, who preceded us down the long *salle* Saint-Thomas. As we paused at each of the massive curtained beds to offer sustenance to the sufferers lying within, Mother questioned him as to the fate of those who had partaken of her bounty the week before.

"I miss the patient sufferer on the right in bed number eighty-six – Monsieur Duclos, was it? Who loved my little cakes so. And, see here, I brought his favourite ones—" Mother's saintly tones showed only a hint of disappointment.

"Regretfully, Madame Pasquier, his sufferings on earth were ended shortly after your last visit."

"I shall miss him. He had such wonderful wit, even in suffering." Mother passed her handkerchief before her eyes and continued down the second row of beds, offering cakes, words of encouragement, and here and there a prayer. I noted it all. Days lingered, estimated number of prayers. So far, prayer was losing.

I left with ten cases. Two, to whom Mother had not given any attention, were getting better. Of the other eight, five had died despite a plentiful dose of prayers and Mother's little pâtés, and two more had turned that interesting greyish colour that precedes death. Writing in my book that night helped clear my heart. If I had a daughter, I would not take her to hospitals.

A thought: perhaps the geometric proof of the effectiveness of prayer has been measuring instead the evil effects of rich food on the sick? I went through my notes that night by the light of a guttering candle. I counted, I counted again. Yes, there it was. *Just to take an example, everyone who has eaten mother's pâtés and candied fruit has died, whether prayed for or not. Devise another proof. Surely God is not concealed in a pâté.* I paused, lifting my pen. Was it something Mother was doing? No, surely it had to be coincidence.

"Where are you going, all by yourself like that?" I'd come from our back door out of the garden gate with the remains of the hospital food in a basket.

"Rue de la Licorne, and what business is it of yours?"

"You know, I never suspected until this morning that you were a daughter of the house. I thought— Well . . . you know, the way you wander out by yourself and all . . ." André Lamotte was still haunting the street. I stormed past him, nose in the air, insulted that he'd ever taken me for a servant girl.

"You thought I was a paid companion, didn't you?"

"Wait, now – you can't carry that. I'll accompany you." He had a certain breezy charm, but I knew instinctively that, like the sun, he beamed equally on everyone, and it didn't mean anything. It was that egalitarianism of charm that offended me even more than rudeness would have.

"Just because I can't walk straight doesn't mean I'm weak," I said. "Besides, I should inform you right away that we have no inheritance, my sister and I, for all the house is so grand. So you may as well save your efforts for someone more promising." He laughed and continued to follow me shamelessly.

Having abandoned the basket at its destination, I turned to him and said fiercely, "Now, Monsieur Lamotte, tell me why you are following me." He made a leg in the mud of the alley, right there, and swept off his hat in a grand gesture worthy of the palace of Saint-Germain.

"Mademoiselle Pasquier, I, André Lamotte, of poetic soul and gentle manners, am at your service. I am not following you but escorting you. And I am doing so in order to ingratiate myself with the sister of the Divine Angel of the Upper Window."

"That's exactly what I thought," I sniffed, and I limped on ahead of him without looking back. He hurried ahead of me, and before I reached the corner he blocked my way, bowing again, and flourishing his hat. People were staring. I was humiliated.

"Mademoiselle, I will block your way for ever, unless you grant me your favour." A woman came out of a shop front hung with plucked chickens and geese, wiping her hands on her apron. She laughed.

"Nonsense," I snapped. I stared at them both and fled in the opposite direction. He replaced his hat and sped ahead of me in great leaps, confronting me at the next corner.

"You stop this!" I cried. He swept off his hat again. A gaggle of little boys playing ball stopped to watch. "Cruel woman," he declaimed, in the voice of the professional tragedian, "say yes, or I'll die of grief on the street."

"You quit this," I hissed. "You're humiliating me on purpose."

"When I die, Mademoiselle, it will be all your fault. The world will mourn yet another victim of woman's coldness." He clutched his hat to his heart.

"Tell him yes, you foolish girl!" shouted a woman's voice from a window.

"Yes, do it! He's very handsome!" cried another. Soon the cry was taken up. "Do it, you hard-hearted girl! Yes! Why, I'd do it!"

"If you die here in the street, your relatives will be disgraced," I announced, trying to ignore the gathering crowd.

"Ah, but I have no one – no hope but you." He wiped a pretend tear away. The gathering crowd shouted encouragement, and he bowed genteelly to them.

"Quit mocking me, Monsieur," I cried, stamping my foot as I felt my face turning hot.

"Heartless woman!" shouted a voice from the crowd.

"Stop it now. You take me home." I burst into tears of rage.

"Yes, yes, take her home!" was the joyful shout of the crowd. He replaced his hat.

"Very well, then, if you insist," he said, addressing the crowd and taking my arm with an elaborate gesture. Even then, Lamotte was a favourite of the mob. He nodded and grinned to the gleeful group of ragamuffins that seemed determined to follow us all the way to my doorstep. As he led them roundabout through the alleys and streets, they seemed to grow in number rather than diminish. Still raging within, I heard a cry. "There he is! The Grand Cyrus at the head of his troops!" It came from the open door of the Pomme de Pin, that notorious gathering place of would-be playwrights and authors of satirical pamphlets. It was often visited by the police in search of the authors of forbidden works, because folks like that have no fixed address. In short, it was a writers' den, a tavern of the lowest reputation among proper people. The ragamuffins gathered in a cluster behind my escort as he halted to address the source of the voice within the door.

"And like Cyrus, I carry off the prize," Lamotte announced calmly, addressing the swarthy, dark-haired young man in the open door. He was of medium height, slightly stoop shouldered from too much study, and unfashionably dressed in plain black.

"*Ha!*" responded the black-clad man, emerging from the mysterious opening with a taller friend. "To think that until this very moment I thought the unknown angel was blonde."

"Truly, love is madness to so change the colour of the adored's hair," agreed the tall, shabbily dressed fellow that appeared beside the first man.

"Her sister," announced my escort with a flourish, "the gateway to the adored, the artisan of my happiness – or despair – Mademoiselle Geneviève, may I present to you two of the companions of my life's journey: this honest-looking fellow in the threadbare coat is Jean-Baptiste Gillet, better known by his imprimatur as the Griffon. He is soon to grow celebrated as the publisher of my collected works, when I have written them." The tall fellow with the droll face bowed by way of an answer.

"Now, this soberly clad fellow beside him is neither a widower nor a Jansenist divine, but Florent d'Urbec, called Cato the Censor by those who know him best. He understands everything and approves of nothing. He believes in the universal applicability of the geometric method of proof, applying it equally to the fortunes of the state, the playing of cards, and the courting of young women."

The dark-haired young man in the ill-fitting provincial suit bowed deeply, with a flourish of his untrimmed, broad-brimmed hat.

"The geometric method?" I asked, somewhat taken aback.

"It is irrefutable," he announced, staring at me with impudent, intelligent black eyes. "From the geometric method, I intend to create a universal science of prediction." He had a fiercely aquiline nose, intense, serious brows, and black curls that fell about his ears in anarchic disarray, as if he had simply clipped them off himself with scissors to save the cost of a barber. But it was his smile that annoyed me most: a wicked, lazy, arrogant smile, as if he were the only clever person in the world. I'll show him, I thought.

"Oh, are you Cato?" I addressed the arrogant young man. "Author of *Observations on the Health of the State*? I'd always imagined you to be a gouty old gentleman."

"Mademoiselle, it is a mark of the frivolity of the times that you should imagine only the elderly capable of seriousness of purpose," he said, mocking me with his dark eyes. I was furious at his condescension.

"But really," I said aloud, "do you think it appropriate to

argue so consistently by analogy to the body in the case of an entity so very different in composition as the state? For example, the functions of the heart as discovered by the Englishman Monsieur Harvey are not at all those previously attributed to—" Monsieur Lamotte drew back and stared at me as if he had discovered a viper underneath his pillow.

"Ha, Lamotte, you've found another learned lady. I thought you were done with *précieuses*," the Griffon broke in.

"Monsieur Gillet, I am no *précieuse*, for I call everything by its right name and not by flowery disguises, Monsieur printer of scurrilous pamphlets."

"Please, Mademoiselle, you have wounded me. I spread enlightenment." Griffon put his hand on his breast.

"The Sign of the Reading Griffon? Supposedly printed in The Hague? The griffon of *The Hideous Crimes of the Abbé Mariette*? *The Unspeakable Acts of the Possessed Sisters of Loudyn*? And *La Putaine Errante*? Those you call enlightenment? Surely, then, it is you that is the *précieux*." D'Urbec turned and looked at me appreciatively, then looked back at his friend, the printer, and laughed.

"So, Gillet, you must cry '*touché!*' She has caught you fair, this excessively well-read little lady!" exclaimed Cato as he clapped the Griffon on the shoulder. "And you, poor friend, I see by your eyes you fear the divine sister may also be corrupted by the possession of a mind. Consider this, my friend – honest speech is to be commended in a woman, it being the rarest of feminine virtues." He folded his arms and looked me up and down with a sarcastic eye. I glared at him. He saw my glare and laughed again. "Mademoiselle, I must inform you that an intelligent woman has the key to my heart. Especially one who has, of her own volition, read my treatise on the salvation of the state through fiscal reform. Were it not so muddy, I would kneel before you and declare myself, O perceptive, grey-eyed Athena."

"You are all mockers, and I am going home. I am sure my Mother would not approve of your acquaintance." I turned to leave. The ragamuffins had given up and departed.

"Then we will accompany you, to help our dear friend Lamotte press his case – as well as to protect you from the sort of riff-raff one finds in taverns," the Griffon announced.

"Griffon, back off; you hinder me," growled Lamotte.

"Then don't expect me to print your next volume of sonnets," Gillet announced.

"When my plays are famous, I will have another printer publish the complete edition and grow wealthy in your place," Lamotte sniffed.

"Calm, calm, Messieurs. You have reached an impasse where only philosophy can resolve your differences." Cato caught up with the bickering party on my heels.

"*Political* philosophy? When have political philosophers failed to stir up trouble and sedition? Wars have been fought because of political philosophy," Griffon replied.

I turned the corner into the Rue des Marmousets so quickly that they had trouble keeping up with me, involved in their quarrel as they were. Then Cato stepped adroitly in front of me, striking a classic pose, with one hand over his heart and the other outstretched as if for oration.

"I appeal to you, Athena. They have wounded me to the quick. Defend me, a poor philosopher, and my works." The speech was mocking, but something quite different flickered deep in his eyes. It frightened me, and I fled from it. We had reached the little door beside the heavy carriage gate into our courtyard.

"You all embarrass me on my own doorstep. Good day, Messieurs."

"Oh dear," said Griffon, looking up and down our house. "It's the Hôtel Pasquier. They're very rich here. Petronius, you haven't a chance. Write all you want, you'll never even get an invitation to put your nose in the door." Of course, Petronius. What else would a fellow like this, all ribbons and fancy buttons, call himself but after the *arbiter elegantarum*? But the moustachioed cavalier had pulled a letter out of his shirt front, which he pressed into my hand.

"Mademoiselle, I beg you by all that is holy. Transmit this message to the Beloved Angel Above."

"To Marie-Angélique?"

"Marie-Angélique— Oh, I always knew she was an angel. Tell her I'm perishing."

"That's what they all say."

"All? I have a rival? Who is he?"

"Well, the latest one was my tutor. He languished considerably."

"With what result?" cried Petronius, suddenly fierce.

"By mutual agreement, he was sent away to make his fortune selling a scheme of memory training."

"Heart broken, I suppose?" He had regained his lightness of tone once more.

"Oh, I suppose. But he is now tutoring the bastards of some provincial count and paying his court to Mademoiselle du Parc, the actress."

"Then he was not worthy of her. I, on the other hand, am deeply worthy. Take my letter, I pray—"

"It will cost you." It was only fair I be repaid for all this public embarrassment.

"Isn't love worth more than mere money?"

"That isn't what I had in mind, Monsieur Petronius. I do you a favour ... one that isn't entirely proper ... and so you should do one for me in return. And I've been wanting a copy of the *Satyricon* for a long time, now. It would only be appropriate—"

"Oho, you are a bad girl, Mademoiselle. Anyone caught purchasing the French translation will spend a fine long time in the Châtelet," said Griffon.

"I had in mind the Latin. I can't purchase it myself, you know. I'll even pay you back."

Cato had been looking at me intently, all the while. "And I suppose you read Greek as well, Athena?"

"A little. My last tutor left too soon."

"Then consider that you might graciously offer Petronius here your assistance on account, lest he languish and die on your doorstep. I'll undertake to get you your naughty book, though it may take a while." Something about his sardonic smile made me confused and angry. I snatched the letter and slammed the door behind me, all in a moment.

"Oh, what is this?" Marie-Angélique took the note with some surprise.

"Another love letter, I think."

"So now even you are carrying them. Is it from that lovely young man who greeted me from his carriage?"

"No, the one with the ribbons and boots that stands in front of the door."

"Oh, him." Marie-Angélique glanced over the letter then crumpled it and threw it into the cold grate of the fireplace. "Tell me, Geneviève, how does it sound . . . to be a duchess?"

"Why, it sounds very good. Who is the duchess?"

"Mademoiselle de la Vallière became a Duchess, for being the King's favourite and bearing his children."

"The Romans believed the highest adornment a woman could have was her virtue. The noble Lucretia killed herself rather than suffer the stain of dishonour."

"But we are not ancient Romans, Geneviève. They're all dead. And we're French. Things are different in these modern times."

"They certainly are."

"My, you're sour today, Sister. Don't you believe in the power of love?"

"I believe in the power of logic, Marie-Angélique," I answered curtly as I left the room. I waited until she was gone and then returned to read the crumpled letter in secret. It was poetry, written late at night with drops of candle wax on it. I folded it in between the pages of my Cicero, where no one but me could ever find it.

FIVE

In the first weeks of September, Father fell ill with a mysterious stomach malady. The doctor pronounced it to be an overt balancing of the bilious humour, but after a series of strong purges, his condition worsened. Mother became most solicitous, cooking for him herself and even washing out his shirts and linen. To cheer him up and speed his recovery, I read to him aloud for hours every day. But with all Mother's care, Father still seemed to grow weaker. Sometimes I didn't think he was even listening, but then he'd turn his head and say, "Daughter, your presence is a stay and consolation to me. Begin again in the Tenth Book; tell me, how does Aristotle define true happiness?"

"Father, he tells us that true happiness is found in contemplation, whereas the common idea of happiness as pleasant amusements is fostered by the courts of tyrants."

"Daughter, you are quick to learn; read on." And so I continued to read from the *Nicomachean Ethics* concerning the foundation of happiness in virtuous activities, as he nodded in agreement whenever I reached a passage he especially liked, and smiled his ironic smile when I read that slaves could enjoy bodily pleasures, but were not accounted happy. I never quite understood what he meant in those days, though now that I have grown older I understand all too well how clearly he saw the world.

"So, *ma petite*, what's going on out there? My son ought to be recovering by now." Grandmother seemed to have shrunken visibly over the last few weeks, like an apple that is gradually drying out. The autumn rain battered at the window of her room, and the closed curtains smelled dank, even though the fire had been built up to keep the chill out. She put down her Bible on the bed, the pages open to Revelation.

"Grandmother, he's not better at all, even though Mother

has taken over nursing him. Even the Romans don't cheer him up the way they used to."

"Herself? The Whore of Babylon, nursing my son? 'Can the leopard change his spots, or the Ethiopian his skin?' Tell me of what this nursing consists."

"She does everything, Grandmother. She is quite changed."

"Everything?" The old lady looked suddenly sly. "Tell me, does she cook for him? Does she wash his shirts herself?"

"Why, yes, of course, Grandmother – and his sheets and bandages as well."

"Bandages? They never told me he needed bandages; they told me he was getting better."

"Oh, no. His sores would break your heart, Grandmother." Grandmother's white, wrinkled face turned even whiter, then her little black eyes blazed from beneath her cap. "It is in the soap," she muttered. "I have read of this." Struggling, she sat up in bed.

"Get me my stick, Geneviève, and my best black dress, there, in the armoire. Then assist me to dress. I am getting up." I couldn't have been more astounded if she had announced that the Seine had turned to wine. I brought her her stick and pulled her up until she was sitting on the edge of the bed. She gasped as she rose, then set her mouth tightly. Grandmother dressed in the old style of Louis XIII, without corsets, in heavy black widow's weeds, all embroidered in black thread and jet beads. Her feet were very tiny – the last vestige of her once-famed beauty, and she smiled as I pulled the little black slippers over her black woollen hose. When she was dressed, leaning heavily on my arm, she tottered to her ancient armchair and sat down, puffing.

"Now," she said, "I want you to get me pen and ink. I must write something. You must go, and without telling a soul, get a hired carriage. Remember, tell no one, and return as quickly as possible." I moved her little writing table to the armchair and set out pen, ink, paper, and sand before her.

As I opened the door of Grandmother's room, I thought I heard the rustling of clothing and swift, soft steps. I started, every nerve taut. Grandmother seemed so alien, all shrunken and frail, propped up in her chair, but with something strange blazing inside her as she wrote intently, her pen rapidly traversing the paper. I sent a boy to the carriage stand, then rushed back to Grandmother.

She was seated in her chair, her head thrown back, her body in convulsions. The little desk had toppled to the floor and the ink bottle rolled, unstoppered, spilling its contents in a semicircle of black on the sand-spattered carpet. Frantically, I called for help. Her parrot, screeching, fluttered to the curtain rod. Servants clattered into the room. Mother, holding a handkerchief, exclaimed in horror. Marie-Angélique stood behind her, white with shock. As the servants lifted the dying woman to her bed, the bird fluttered to the canopy, screeching "Drink, drink, old monster! *Awk!* Fire and brimstone!"

"For God's sake, strangle that dreadful thing!" cried Mother, and the servants added to the cacophony by pursuing it about the room as it flapped wildly above them and Marie-Angélique wailed, "Oh, don't! The dear, sweet bird! It doesn't know any better!" as she wrung her hands.

"Grandmother, Grandmother, don't die! Oh, please, you can't, can't die!" Even as I held Grandmother's clenched fist in my own two hands, I could feel her body grow icy and limp. I never even heard Uncle's soft, slippered step behind me.

"Well, here's a touching scene," he said, in a voice as cold as ice.

"Call the priest." Mother turned to me, her eyes flat and dead with hate. "It is you who have done this, Mademoiselle. It is all your fault. You have killed her by getting her up." As she swept from the room on her brother's arm, I was left alone with Grandmother's corpse, all dressed in the finery of olden days.

For what seemed like hours, I stared at Grandmother's stony face while the rain rattled against the windows. How could she have died so suddenly – she, who could have defied death for decades more? I heart a soft "*Urk. Urk,*" from above the bed canopy and looked up. The parrot, triumphantly uncaptured, was clawing his way across the canopy, making noises in its stomach, as that sort of bird does. I looked down at Grandmother's hand where it lay in mine and realised that folded into it was a crumpled scrap of paper. I took it up and smoothed it out. The letter she had been writing. It had been torn off, leaving a bit in her hand. I turned the fragment over. A name was written on it – a stranger's name. "M. de La Reynie," the paper said. Just that. Nothing more. But where had the rest of the letter gone? I hunted about her chair, where it might have fallen. Her empty cordial glass rolled by one gilded claw-foot, but there was no letter. I put the glass back on the nightstand, beside the little cut-glass bottle. If only I hadn't helped her up, I grieved. If was all my fault.

But Mother was at the door, with the priest and the men to lay out the body.

"Still here, are you?" Mother spoke in a cold voice, but her mouth was twisted in an eerie, triumphant little smile. "You should be ashamed." I bolted from the room, weeping.

As I left Grandmother's room, I saw that my brother had been summoned from the College. Short and square, he already showed signs of growing the righteous jowls and cold, fishy eye of a magistrate. He stood there, stiff and pompous, the soon-to-be heir of the house of Pasquier, condemning me with his eyes. An *avocat* in the making. Perhaps, if enough came to him in Grandmother's will, the purchaser of a minor office – the first step on the ladder. A quiet little wife with a big dowry. The Hôtel Pasquier refurnished in a more respectable style. I could see it all in his eyes. He would not be a fool, a speculator, a loser like Father.

"Geneviève, I know it wasn't really your fault." Marie-Angélique embraced me. "I don't care what Mother says." She steered me into a private corner of Mother's gilded reception room, near one of the tall, brocade-draped windows. "Now, you mustn't cry so. It will make Grandmother sad in heaven." She took out her handkerchief from her sleeve and dried my face. She looked worried. "Besides," she added, "you must think of Father. You must be cheerful for him, so he'll recover. You can talk with him about all those things he reads. It will make him better."

"Better? But— But suppose, Marie-Angélique, that he doesn't get better?"

"Oh, that can't be. It just can't." Marie-Angélique looked pale and agitated. There were circles under her eyes. "Without Father, I haven't a prospect in the world. There's nothing left,

nothing for any of us. They'll seize the furniture, the house—
What will become of us? Uncle has nothing, and Father's family
is dead. Étienne isn't finished with school yet. But Father can
still save us, Geneviève, once he's better. Make him cheerful,
Geneviève; make him well." Her voice faded to that conspiratorial whisper that everyone uses when talking about sick
people. "We've all decided we won't tell him about Grandmother until he's better, and can bear it."

I couldn't tell Marie-Angélique that I had seen the ghastly
grey colour creeping into Father's face, the colour that signalled
the inevitable end. That was the disadvantage of having studied
the sick people in the Hôtel-Dieu, rather than the clothing of the
fashionable visitors. A question for my notebooks that evening:
*Is truth always good? Devise a method to balance the temporary
pleasure given by well-meant falsehood against the shock of bad
news poorly prepared for.*

"Oh, I do wish black weren't so unbecoming to me," said Marie-
Angélique inspecting her face in her dressing-table mirror. In
the required weeks of mourning following Grandmother's
funeral, Marie-Angélique had undertaken to lighten the
heaviness that filled the house by having me read *Célinte* to her
while she tried out new hair-styles and altered her dresses by
the addition of braid and little rows of tucked ribbon. And
although I was ashamed to say it, I found the smell of illness and
the clouds of dark sorrow and regret in Father's sickroom more
than I could bear. Her mindless romances were a welcome
distraction.

"My, what a lovely sentiment Mademoiselle de Scudéry
expresses in that passage. How wonderful to be so in love," said
Marie-Angélique with a sigh.

"I'm not surprised you like it – you liked it just as well when
she used the selfsame passage in *Clélie*, if I'm not mistaken. If
seems she saves herself the trouble of writing anew in this
place."

"Oh, Sister, surely you are mistaken. Why, the characters
are entirely different."

"Well enough," I answered and continued reading the long
conversation in Cléonime's palatial mansion, in which the
company determines that the vice of secretly opening the

letters of others is sure to lead to cheating at cards and end in the final depravity of desiring to know the future, and so of becoming enmeshed with astrologers.

"Mademoiselle de Scudéry is very opinionated." Marie-Angélique looked annoyed. "After all, it is only natural to want to know the future. And I never cheat at cards." She had finished her hair and now took up her sewing. "Oh, do pull back the curtains, Sister – I just can't stand all this gloom . . . Oh, you are so indiscreet— Who is it that you're looking at down there?"

"Lamotte is back, Sister, and he's brought a friend to give him courage."

Having marked my place in the book, I had looked right out of the middle of the window. The sky, heavy and dark with coming rain, seemed to touch the tall, narrow housefronts across the street. There, wrapped in a long cloak against the cold wind, stood André Lamotte, alias Petronius, pretending to be deep in conversation with Florent d'Urbec, the censorious Cato.

"A friend? Does he look like someone of substance?"

"No, he's a philosopher—"

"And you *know* such people? Sister, you are impractical."

D'Urbec, dressed in a vast and shapeless Brandenburger overcoat and his wide, flat black hat, nodded in response to Petronius's flamboyant gestures, looking up at the window every so often. The Brandenburger had large pockets. Big enough for a book, I imagined. I caught his eye and waved. He pulled Petronius by the sleeve and pointed to the window. Then he pulled the book from his pocket, and the two of them pointed to it as he brandished it aloft. I gestured back, silence, and then pointed in the direction of the courtyard gate.

"Surely, Sister, you are not going to speak with them." Marie-Angélique put down her sewing and looked at me disapprovingly.

"Of course I am. They've brought a book. For . . . ah . . . Father." I found the two of them looking most pleased with themselves outside the narrow portal by the great barred carriage doors.

"We have it here," Lamotte announced grandly. "Acquired at untold cost and suffering, rarer than even the golden apples of the Hesperides."

"As Hippomenes tempted Atalanta, I throw it at your feet," announced d'Urbec. I blushed as I saw his knowing little half-smile. I had a terrible urge to grab the book away and run.

"Ah, no, greedy sister of the divine Marie-Angélique. First, a letter," announced Lamotte, pulling a folded, sealed sheet from his bosom and thrusting it into my hands.

"You do presume, Monsieur Lamotte."

"But surely your gracious favour... Oh, pardon. Have I been too unseemly in your hour of grief? I see you are in mourning. My ardent flame has blinded me to the social decencies. I hope your father did not suffer too much."

"It's not Father, it's Grandmother who died. But how did you know Father was ill?"

"I make it my business to know everything that's going on in my dear angel's house."

I turned on him resentfully. "Which one of the servants have you paid?" I queried. He blushed.

"Oh, so you didn't pay – I should have guessed. It's a woman you sweet-talked. Who?"

"I'll never tell." He laughed – but then he looked up to the house, and his face grew pale. "Can't you tell me if I even have hope? Won't she even speak to me?" he cried out, his voice anguished.

"You know the answer to that. Mother heard your name. She made inquiries."

"And she found out ... everything?"

"Enough to make her shut the door. You cannot be received here, Monsieur Lamotte." Lamotte seemed distraught. D'Urbec, always in control of himself, took his friend by the elbow.

"Bear up, Lamotte. There will come a day when you are received everywhere." When *I* am received everywhere, he seemed to mean. I wanted to answer, Monsieur Provincial, recognise truth: society makes little boxes for us, and we cannot escape them. You can no more be received in the house of Pasquier than a Pasquier can be received at Marly. Just because you know everything does not mean you can change it.

"But she is not promised to someone?" he asked, sounding desperate.

"No," I answered, annoyed at myself for the sudden spasm of

envy that passed through my heart. Meanly, I added, "Her marriage portion is not large enough."

"Did you hear that, d'Urbec? No secret dowry in Amsterdam, no private negotiations with some stuffy family of the robe." He slapped his friend on the back. D'Urbec winced. "I have hope! My poor, golden-haired angel! It is I, I, André Lamotte, who will rescue you from your cruel fate."

"You seem young to be insane, Monsieur Lamotte," I said, my voice waspish.

"Mad, oh yes. Mad with love. A thousand, thousand thanks!" He began to caper like an imbecile, right there in the street.

"Is he often like this, Monsieur d'Urbec?"

"Only when confronted by an unattainable pair of blue eyes, Mademoiselle," responded d'Urbec. "I myself, not yet having attained celebrity and wealth, avoid sorrow by refusing to pursue that which is beyond my means. Logic must always rule the heart." He looked at me a long time, his dark eyes regretful. I changed the subject.

"The book – it's really the *Satyricon*?"

"That it is, and let me inform you that you have very naughty tastes, for all that you read Latin." I could feel my face turn all hot.

"It's not that wicked, is it? I was just so curious, you understand."

"Curiosity. A great vice. It leads to opening letters, from there to peeking at cards, and thence to the astrologer's," he said, placing the book in my eager hands as he cited Mademoiselle de Scudéry's opinion.

"Surely, a philosopher should never lower himself to reading a trashy romance like *Célinte*," I observed. His eyes glinted, as if he had judged some secret test correctly.

"It is the duty of philosophers to know everything. Especially philosophers who have grown up reading aloud to elderly female relatives. But I must inform you, Mademoiselle, you blush very nicely." He turned away suddenly and, head down, his hands thrust into his pockets, followed his madly dancing friend down the narrow street.

SIX

Monsieur de La Reynie's secretary had shown Inspector Legras into the immense old Hôtel La Reynie, the centre of the newly reorganised Paris police. Legras looked around uncomfortably at the clumsy, dark furniture of a previous century. Why had he never noticed before how vaguely menacing it seemed? Those rows of law books, lined up like soldiers in the bookcases built against the panelled walls: a rank of silent witnesses against him. The chief was leafing through a little book. His face, even in repose, looked cold, civilised, and hard. A merciless face, thought Legras. The nose, too long and arrogant. The lines between the eyebrows and around the pale eyes, sinister. A dark moustache could not hide the odd sensuality of the mouth. Beneath it, the chief's chin was just beginning to show the effects of too many formal dinners. Legras resented that, too. A man who lived like that could not understand his struggles.

Spring sunlight fell in a golden stream across the heavy old desk and the open pages of the book. That damned book, his one failure. Why should one little book risk a man's career? Legras shifted on his feet and clutched his bound ledger to him.

"Legras. I want you to refresh my mind concerning this press – the Sign of the Reading Griffon." La Reynie's cold eyes looked up from the book. He did not invite Legras to sit.

"Monsieur de La Reynie . . ." the Inspector of the Book Trade could feel his knees faintly trembling beneath him. Oh, God, if not a chair, at least a stool. Standing would surely betray him. Legras could see the chief watching his knees with a sort of detached, professional interest. La Reynie, the interrogator, who could terrify a confession out of a suspect long before he was stretched out on the narrow table in the basement of the Châtelet.

"The . . . the Reading Griffon, publisher of pornographic

trash and *libelles* of distinguished citizens and officials, a propaganda press located in The Hague, undoubtedly supported by the treacherous William of Orange—"

"And yet," broke in La Reynie, we have searched every conveyance coming into the city, every load of wood or fodder . . ." Legras felt somehow less than human, under that unpitying gaze. "Legras, have you yet to consider the obvious? Illegal works, circulating in Paris as freely as if they were printed here . . ."

"An illicit press? Oh, no. How could that be, Monsieur? I assure you, under our new programme of inspection, nothing so large as an illicit print shop could escape us."

"Legras, you must broaden your mind. Consider a licensed shop, printing by day, say, religious tracts . . . or a portable press mounted on a cart, moved from stable to stable. I imagine another man might do better. Or, perhaps you have accepted payment from this Griffon?" La Reynie's voice was silky and menacing. Righteous son of a bitch, thought Legras. It's only human to take a little something, if there's no harm in it. But in this affair, Legras felt as clean as if he were newborn. Even he had recognised the danger of the little leather-bound book on the chief's desk. But if only Monsieur Louvois's secretary had not found the first copy – Louvois, the minister of war to whom La Reynie, as chief of police, reported. Louvois, the vengeful, the merciless, who never forgot a slight or an enemy. The Terror of the Netherlands had sent the little volume straight to La Reynie with a sarcastic note: "So this is how you keep the peace in the King's capital?" It was that note that would ruin him, Legras knew. Inadequate attention to duty. "You have brought your records with you?" The chief's voice called him back to the matter at hand. Here was the moment Legras dreaded. His records: every author in Paris from the highest rank to the lowest. Addresses, works, evaluations of reliability. Legras took pride in his records. Or, rather, he had taken pride in them. No matter who wrote what, a play, a sonnet, or just an epigram, they did not escape the indefatigable Legras's records for long. Except for one.

"You have seen this work, doubtless, Legras?" asked La Reynie, tapping the little book he had been reading with a forefinger.

"Monsieur de La Reynie, it has just been brought to my attention. *Observations on the Health of the State* – a malignant little work. I saw at once that it should be banned." Now Legras felt his knees firmer, but his hands had lost their steadiness. He clasped them beneath the ledgers to still them, then squirmed internally as he watched La Reynie's pale eyes take note of the gesture. The shadow of the galleys, the noose, seemed to be reflected in them.

"A work of treason, Legras. It advocates the elimination of the exemption of the aristocracy from taxation and proposes instead a replacement of all taxes by a single tithe proportional to income."

"Unheard of – preposterous," Legras managed to interject.

"This . . . ah, Cato . . . produces mathematical calculations to predict the collapse of the state due to fiscal insolvency. Listen to this: 'While it may be truly said that His Majesty is the head of the body politic, and the lower orders the limbs, nevertheless, will not the head suffer if the feet become gangrened? Thus have we overburdened the peasantry, who create the wealth of the state through agriculture. And when the rot reaches the heart, the body must die.' It is clear: 'Cato' advocates the destruction of the monarchy under the pretence of reform. This so-called geometric method is nothing but a disguise for treason. No wonder he conceals himself. Your records, Legras. I wish to discover who this Cato might be."

"I – I have not discovered precisely, but there are several possibilities— Here . . . and here—" Legras had opened his ledger on the desk, and he pointed to various entries with a trembling finger. La Reynie looked at the pages with interest, uncapped his inkwell, and took note of several names and addresses.

"Possible, but not probable," La Reynie observed tersely. He gestured to his secretary. "Take this to Desgrez," he said. "I want them brought in for questioning." As the secretary left, La Reynie turned again to Legras. "And you, Legras – I want you to bring me a little more respectable list than this. See? I have already obtained the *lettre de cachet* from His Majesty for this Cato." He indicated an open document lying on the desk, the seals already in place. "'Life in the galleys.' I need only to fill in the blank space beside the pseudonym. Now consider, I would hate to see this order gather dust. Find me the man who calls himself Cato, Inspector."

"Monsieur de La Reynie, it will be done. I guarantee it. I have an informant at the Pomme de Pin . . ."

SEVEN

"What is that they gave you?" Marie-Angélique met me at the foot of the courtyard stair, looking about her to make sure no one overheard.

"A letter for you and a book in Latin, that . . . ah . . . Father might like. Do come with me today and help me read. It gets so long, sometimes, and my voice tires." I handed her the letter, and she crumpled it into her bosom.

"It's much too depressing to sit with Father, and I'm sure I do it badly. I can't make him happy. Not half so well as you, Geneviève. Besides, the smell is so horrid. When you've read to him, why don't you come and help me distract myself? There's a dear little lace collar in the shop under the arch in the Galerie, and the sight of it quite cheers me up. Once I'm out of mourning, I could have the bodice of my dress remade in the new fashion, and it would go splendidly. The Chevalier de la Rivière admires me in lace. I'm sure Mother won't mind letting me have Jean to carry my train."

"Then let Jean accompany you, Marie-Angélique. The sight of lace collars and silver buckles doesn't cheer me up at all, these days."

Father's room smelled of medicines and illness. The windows were closed and the curtains pulled shut, to keep out the harmful air. Even the walls, dark green, seemed to be the colour of an old medicine bottle, and the great dark bed, its curtains pulled back, seemed like the skeleton of an ancient behemoth. He lay in his shirt and nightcap, too weak even for his dressing gown. On his dressing table, his formal and day wigs sat on a row of wooden stands, like so many disembodied, faceless heads, witnessing his painful struggle to leave the earth. The open door of his book-lined cabinet stood beside the bed. I tiptoed in and got Seneca, then sat in the straight-backed chair beside the bed to read. But after only a few words,

Father seemed too weary to listen. He reached out and put his hand on mine. He could not lift his head from the pillows.

"Geneviève, before we die, we must confess and make amends. I have done you a disservice."

"Never, Father. I can't imagine how."

"I educated you to suit myself, Geneviève, and not the world's ways. It was selfish, now, I see."

"Father, never so. You are the best, the kindest father in the world."

"But a foolish one. Do you understand, Geneviève? I never imagined dying. I thought I might enjoy your company and conversation much longer. What a selfish man I was! But now – now I see all. I didn't fit you for the cloister, my daughter. I had you taught the truth instead of superstition. Science, geometry, the new thought. Now what will become of you? You are fit neither to become a nun nor a wife. I beg your forgiveness, my daughter."

"Father," I answered, trying to ignore the pricking feeling in my eyes, "there is nothing to forgive. You've given me a home, your regard, and my own mind, which is the greatest treasure of all."

"Yes, the greatest treasure of all. Though notoriously hard to eat or wear or keep the rain off with, my daughter." His old wry smile flickered and faded. "Yes, the greatest treasure of all, and rarer than you know."

"I must interrupt." Mother had entered the room silently through the open door. She stood watching as Father fell into a fitful sleep, then turned to me impassively and said, "Geneviève, it is time to fetch the priest. He will not last the night."

Father sank rapidly in the next few hours. I showed in the priest, still brushing the first snowfall of winter off his biretta. The family stood at the head of the deathbed, with the servants weeping at the foot. I found that for myself, not a tear would come. Father was gone. Outside, the white flakes fell silently through the grey sky; inside, they were droning prayers. I seemed to hear Father's mocking laugh, a freethinker's laugh, rolling through the room as he discovered the universe beyond the body. Did Mother hear it too? Her eyes rolled suddenly toward the ceiling, she paled and clasped her hands, before she regained her composure. Oh, Monsieur Descartes, you do not have all the answers.

"An orderly mind can solve all problems," I could hear my father's voice repeating patiently in my head. My little book, you have another problem. When the priest had departed I wrote beneath *M. de La Reynie*:

The body, the mind, the soul – how connected? Method of trial; to be discovered.

"And now, Mademoiselle, you will tell us where it is." It was midnight; Father's corpse was still laid out on the bed in the room beyond, candles burning at its head and feet, as if to disperse the external darkness. I had been brought out of bed, still clad in my nightdress, and was backed into the windowless inner corner of Father's cabinet. Every drawer was opened in his desk, the books lay in heaps on the floor, having been methodically searched for scraps of paper between the leaves. A little coffer lay overturned and empty on one of the bookshelves. My uncle was tapping the panels and the furniture for any hollow sound that might reveal a hidden compartment. Before me was my mother, my brother standing behind her. They looked grimly conspiratorial.

"Where what is?"

"Don't play the innocent." Mother's voice was hard. "You know where the foreign account is. The money he hid from Colbert and the King. He told you where the treasure was before he died. I heard him whispering to you: he said 'treasure'. Don't think you can hide my son's inheritance to your advantage. Tell it now, or I assure you, you will not live to enjoy it."

"He never told me anything of the sort. There's no such thing."

"My brother, she is obstinate, as I predicted." Uncle turned from his work of vandalising father's library and fixed his narrow, calculating little eyes on me.

"I have your permission, Monsieur?" He turned to my brother, the new head of the house of Pasquier. Grown stolid and old with his new elevation, my brother nodded formally. It was then I saw my uncle pick up the long ash rod.

* * *

The next few days were spent in the company of the mice in the locked tower room. They sent Marie-Angélique to whisper through the door, "Geneviève, Sister, we've always been friends, haven't we? Just tell them, and everything will be all right again." But I could hear Uncle's heavy boots on the stair behind her.

"Sister, there isn't anything. Father told me he'd left me with the treasure of philosophy."

"Oh, Sister, then there's no hope," I heard her answer, sobbing.

Then one evening, when I had lost track of time, the door swung open. My uncle stood stooped over in the low door, his walking stick under his arm, a candle in his uplifted hand. His shirt was hanging open out of his unbuttoned doublet. His breath was heavy with wine. His eyes glowed with menace.

"Tell me," he said, in a heavy, intimate tone. "You're wise to keep it to yourself. What has your mother ever done for you? It's me – I'm your friend." No one's friend, I thought, repelled by him. "Dear little niece, how will you get it if you have no man to travel for you? Share it with me, and it will only be divided two ways." He set down the candle and moved toward me. I backed away into the corner. He pressed me against the wall and began to paw at my breasts. I couldn't escape the disgusting smell of his breath. "Tell me, tell me. We'll share the fortune, we two." Oh my God, I thought. He thinks that lovemaking will make me tell. I was horrified. "Come now," he said. "You know you want this. All women do."

"There's no secret, Uncle. There never was," I said, trying to push him away, turning my face from his. "Can't you understand?"

"There must be. There is! You're hiding it!" he cried, holding me tightly as he fumbled at my dress, as if I had somehow concealed the money in there.

"What are you doing?" I cried. "I have nothing. Can't you see?"

"There must be a paper. You have a paper with the name of the banker," he said, his voice slurred as he tried to force his hand into my dress.

"Get off. There's nothing!" I shouted, as I tried to push his hands away.

"Quit hiding it, you little bitch! I have to have it!" He grabbed at my throat and tried to batter my head against the wall, but I hit him in the face with all my strength and wrenched away. As I tried to flee, he clutched at my dress and it tore to the waist. The sound seemed to send him into a frenzy.

"Nothing, nothing! There's nothing after all! You deceived me! She deceived me!" I made a dash for the open door, but he overtook me in a few quick steps and threw me to the floor.

"Let me go, for God's sake. Let me go." My voice was strangled, his hands were pressing my throat shut. Dear God, I thought, he'll kill me here, and all for a fantasy of that ghastly money.

"Let you go? Let you go? You cheat—" His eyes were distended, insane. "Oh, yes, I'll let you go— Cheat— Liar— Thief— Devil's spawn—" As I struggled against him, his repulsive heavy body pressed me into the floor. "I'll let you go," he panted, "when ... you've ... repaid me—" My screams made his eyes glitter with pleasure. I was smothered in the foul breath that came from between his wolfish yellow teeth; the pain seemed to split my body in two. "Snotty bitch— Steal my money—"

When at last he got up, he buttoned his breeches and said, "Quit snivelling. You ought to be thanking me. Who else would bother to have an ugly freak like you?" Bruised and battered, clutching my torn dress to me, I could feel the hate rising up in me like a tide.

"I swear, I'll pay you back for this," I whispered. He laughed.

"A woman's vengeance? And just whom will you tell? I'll say that you begged me for it. Begged me, you ugly slut. You'll be a laughing-stock. Keep silent or be ruined, dear niece. There's not a soul will ever believe you."

The cold grey light of a winter's dawn had filtered into the tower room. A light snow had sifted on to the tall, peaked roof-tops of the Rue des Marmousets, so that they looked like peaked cakes covered with powdered sugar. I opened the tiny tower window and looked down. Below, the street was silent and white under the grey sky, with the first tracks of morning cutting through the white to the black frozen muck beneath. I tried the door. This time it clicked open. Uncle had slammed it when he left, but he must have forgotten to lock it. Very well, then, it was fated. Silently, I put on my cloak, then retrieved my little notebooks from their hiding place and tucked them into the remains of my dress. There was only one way left to silence the echo of Uncle's evil laughter in my head. Lucretia's way.

I crept quietly down the long, winding stair into the maze of rooms below – through Grandmother's tall red room, where the parrot moped in a covered cage. Around the corner and down, through a servants' antechamber, then through a door past Father's empty bed. Then through Mother's sitting room, downstairs, and through the dining room and the tall reception room, now cold and still. Goodbye, goodbye. They were up in the kitchen below the stairs. I could hear the clatter of pans. I limped, all hunched over, to the front door. Lifted the latch on to the icy street. Goodbye, house; goodbye, street.

Turn at the Rue de la Lanterne. Ah, there it is. The old friend. The Pont-Neuf, with the cold wind whistling across it, the cakes of ice floating in the brown water beneath it. The players were gone. The charlatan with the monkey, the portable booths with the pretty things, the mountebanks, the pamphlet sellers. The first beggars were out. Legless. Armless. A woman with a maimed child. Old soldiers. An old woman stumbled across the slushy tracks left by the first carriages. Cries. Wagons loaded with firewood crossing. Make way, old woman!

I stood a long time at the bridge rail. The sun rose higher, a faint circle of white in the slate-grey sky. It looked dark and cold, the river. The Romans knew how to do it better, I thought. A hot bath, perfumed. Open a vein. And as the red stained the water, lean back and fall asleep slowly to the lulling music of harps. We are not yet as civilised as the Romans . . .

The rattle and clatter of an approaching carriage barely interrupted my reverie. I was shivering terribly. There was no other way. After all, what was the difference? I was born a mistake. Well, the mistake would be put right now . . . But the cry of a coachman and the sound of stamping hoofs and champing bits broke into my thoughts like shards of ice.

And then I heard a voice behind me, from the carriage window: "It's cold, the river. I'd think a clever girl like you could do better than that."

It was the fortune-teller from the Rue Beauregard.

EIGHT

"Get in," said the fortune-teller, "or would you rather finish what you'd intended?" Her lackey had opened the door of her carriage, a discreet vehicle painted rather sombrely in black with red and gold trim. A handsome pair of matched chestnuts in brass-trimmed harness breathed steam into the icy air. I could see where she sat inside, in a heavy cloak trimmed with silk cord and broad hat over a woollen scarf that hid most of her hair. A fur-lined lap robe was thrown back to reveal her feet, in red leather boots, resting on a little metal box full of warm coals. She gestured to the seat opposite her, where a similar robe lay. "I have in mind to make your fortune, if you wish – unless, of course, you have a deep desire to join the other drowned corpses laid out in the cellar of the Châtelet. Most damp and unattractive."

"I don't deserve to live." My voice sounded faint.

"No more or less than anyone else in this city," she said in a careless tone. "What is it this time? Murder? Rape? Blackmail? Incest? Trifles – the commonest of the common in this great capital. What makes you think you can set yourself above everyone else, wringing your hands and flinging a perfectly good life away in a nasty, chilly river?" I stared at the padded brocade interior of the coach. It looked cozy and warm. Then I looked back over the snow-covered rail of the bridge. "Who are you to judge yourself?" she went on persuasively. "God gave us all life, and the judgment is His. But it is I who will give you fortune and happiness, if you will get in and hear what I have to say." She leaned forward to inspect me, as if she could spy out from my dishevelled appearance all that had happened. Then she gestured impatiently. "Make up your mind, and be quick about it. You're letting the cold in. I don't like weak people who can't make up their minds. Jump or get in." I got in.

"Now," she said cosily as the carriage rattled off into the

tangle of narrow houses beyond the Quai de Gesvres, "isn't it excellent that fortune caused us to meet this way? I have an outstanding business proposition for you." Fortune, indeed, I thought, for the habit of logic was strong in me. It is a strange coincidence that would provide two lap robes at this accidental meeting. But how could anyone know the mad rush of horrors that had swarmed over the Maison des Marmousets, or the exact time I might appear on the bridge? Clearly, I had gone insane. The idea that I might somehow engage in business confirmed it. It was impossible. A delusion. However, it was certainly a solid sort of delusion. The fortune-teller looked at me and spoke again:

"You're Geneviève Pasquier, the little girl who reads water glasses and speaks in great long words and learned phrases, like a little old man."

"I have studied philosophy with my father."

"My, my, such a strange thing for a little girl to do. You were smaller then, but you're exactly the same now. The limp. The way your back is all hunched over and twisted to the side. How old are you now? About fifteen? Yes, I think." She was looking me over closely with her calculating black eyes. "And, oh, yes, my condolences about your father. That was very sad." She had an eerily sweet little smile, pointed at the centre. Her figure was going just a bit to plumpness, but still quite elegant. And such friendly sympathy, when she hardly knew me. It didn't make sense.

"Now," she said, smiling her peculiar smile with the little steel barb inside it, "I imagine that you think I don't make sense. But I am a businesswoman and always make sense." The carriage had slowed almost to a stop as the coachman tried to make his way through the crowds of basket-laden market women and heavy carts that made the area around Les Halles almost impassable. A cacophony of voices, singing and shouting their wares, invaded the carriage.

"I don't know anything about business."

"Look out there," she said, pulling back the carriage curtain. "That's business – buying and selling. People want things; if you sell them what they want, you become rich. If you persist in trying to sell them things they don't want, you starve. Remember that; listen to those people out there, and you will create a fortune, as I have, starting out from nothing. Those people, there, have one thing in common – they all want to know what will become of them." She waved a beautifully manicured hand, decorated with several costly rings, to dismiss the hurly-burly outside. "How fortunate for me, and for them, that through my knowledge of the arts of physiognomy, of chiromancy, of horoscopy, I can provide them with such satisfactory answers. As my reward I have become rich. And now I wish to assist you to do the same." She seemed so reasonable, and so pleasant, that I found myself listening to her in spite of her obvious lunacy. She pulled from a little sack she had hidden beneath her lap robe a clear, stoppered jar of water. "Now, my dear little philosopher, tell me what you see here."

The glistening colours of her clothing and the interior of the carriage shone in distorted reflection in the jar.

"I just see reflections – that's all anyone sees." I looked at her and spoke firmly, as one rational being to another: "The pretence of reading fortunes in water, mirrors, and cards is superstition. The unfolding of the laws of nature follows the rules of logic; according to Monsieur Descartes—"

"Oh, my," she interrupted. "Are you quite sure that's all you see? Well, my goodness, if that's the case, our ride will certainly be shorter than expected. One more try, my dear." She halted the carriage just beyond the Cimetière des Innocents to still the vibrations in the water. "Now," she said, "hold it between your hands . . . yes . . . this way . . . look down through the water . . . now . . ." She chanted the odd words I'd remembered. "Tell me what you see about me in the water." Her voice was very soft and slow. "Tell me, tell me – just let the picture come up like a bubble in the water." I felt a sort of weakness and warmth go through me, and my stomach felt queasy as I saw the little figures start to form up, all rippling at the edges.

"I see – I see a well-dressed woman with dark hair, wearing a mask, coming to you. You are wearing a green dress with a red quilted petticoat and a lace collar. You take her to . . . the oddest little cabinet . . . it's all furnished with gilded, inlaid wood cupboards, and has a little window in the corner with tiny panes of glass and a seat beneath it. You open a door in one of the cupboards and there are shelves inside it . . . you take out a green glass bottle and give it to her."

"Yes, that's what I thought," she said quietly. "You see too much." Then her voice became energetic, and she was all business. "You are fortunate to have fallen into my hands. Others might have exploited you instead of assisting you to make something of yourself. Drive on, Joseph – Yes, where was I? Oh, yes. What is a gift without training? Nothing! Gold in a rock in the forest. It is artifice, artifice, my dear, that makes a gleaming jewel. Remember that." The carriage lurched forward, and I nearly slid off the seat.

Recovering myself, I answered, "I still don't understand." It is, after all, always best to appear stupid around people that have hidden purposes. It lures them into the open.

"My, you are slow today, for all that you've studied. Well, know this, Geneviève Pasquier. I make it my business to help people. Women, in particular. I intend to help you the same way." Her voice was warm and persuasive. I looked at her face, but her features were an enigma.

"After all," she went on, "what can an honest woman do, when she has fallen upon hard times? A new widow – the sole support of a brood of little ones. Laundry, mending, even prostitution wouldn't bring in enough to fill their dear little stomachs. But oh, she makes lovely rose water . . . knows how to compound lip rouge from an old family recipe. I hear of her . . . I pay her rent, buy her children a lovely dinner, and then I lease her a nice little booth in the Galerie, or maybe a little shop on the Pont Notre-Dame, I arrange things a bit with the powers that be and *voilà!* She's a fashionable *parfumier,* or a seller of elegant perfumed gloves from Italy, and no longer poor. She repays me with interest, helps me out a bit – from gratitude, you understand. We both benefit. You see how it works? Who else would help a poor woman down on her luck? The priests? The bankers? The King? All they offer is the debtors' prison, the Salpêtrière, transportation for life. How different it is when a woman has me for a friend." She looked at me benignantly, expansively, as a woman would look at a particularly nice piece of china she was acquiring to complete a collection.

Outside the carriage window a group of beggars stood

shivering in the snow. Among them was a blind woman and another covered with hideous sores. "See all those people?" she said, gesturing out of the window. "That's what happens when you haven't the craft to earn a decent living. I imagine the police will be rounding them up later today." I shivered. It could be me, standing there in rags. And now I'd lost my courage for the river.

"But you see," she continued, after the carriage went over several jolting ruts and we had to steady ourselves, "I offer more than the King – wealth, independence, happiness. Don't look at me that way. I'm not stupid, you know . . . Oh, my, yes, I can't count the help I've given. I buy lovely little houses, rent apartments, find sweet orphans positions as ladies' maids, or, if they're wellborn, companions to the very highest aristocracy. And they're all, all my friends and helpers. How grateful they are! And how happy I am! Yes, we must all help one another and become rich. So you see, I am a philanthropist." She gestured grandly out of the window to the long, narrow street, where ancient buildings closed in like walls on either side of the slow-moving carriage, as if she somehow possessed the world. "I am a philanthropist of women. I bring them all fortune while I bring fortune to myself. And I can bring you fortune, too."

I was more convinced than ever that I was entirely demented, and listening to the ravings of a madwoman in the bargain. Still, it sounded good. Suicide began to recede in my thoughts as the puzzle of the fantastical creature sitting opposite me began to pique my interest.

"But you have just said that people only buy what they want, and though my father left me the treasure of philosophy, as he called it, no one wishes to buy it – it can't even be given away. And besides, I have no knowledge of business."

"Ah, but my dear, you have the talent! And – lucky you! – the way you are, you will doubtless remain a virgin forever, and we shall do such wonderful business together, not like that silly Marie-Marguerite, who has spoiled her future already—" She broke off and looked at me closely. I must have looked very odd, for I was thinking of Uncle. "Tell me," she said, peering at me up and down, "you are still a virgin, aren't you?"

"Not any more," I said, staring resentfully at her. She took my hand and patted it. There was something almost commercial about her sympathy. Still, I hadn't had any lately, commercial or otherwise. Besides, she had an excellent carriage. I could feel myself warming toward her.

"Why, my— That's very interesting. All the better. Yes, so much the better. You and I, we'll be in business a long time. I'll teach you everything you need to know, establish you, and then we shall work out a plan of repayment. You'll soon be wealthy – fine wines, beautiful gowns, a carriage of your own . . ."

"What good does money do for a person like me? I don't want all those things! I want . . . I want . . . I don't know what I want." I knuckled my eyes fiercely to keep the stupid tears from welling up. Here I'd just been planning to commit suicide, and she told me a new dress would fix everything; the insult to my intelligence, on top of everything else, proved entirely too much to bear. Did she think I was an ordinary idiot female to be bought off with a lace collar or string of beads? I watched the look in her dark eyes shift as she spoke again, leaning forward to touch my knee.

"Believe me, my dear. Say yes, and I can give you what you dream of: beauty—" I looked up. Her face seemed perfectly normal as she spoke. Her eyes were a little intense, but not demented.

Look at me. Are you blind? I thought. You can't tempt me with the impossible.

"Impossible? Not for me," she answered my thought. "I can create you anew, and with my powers, make you desired by any man you dream of. Surely, a girl like you must have seen someone she fancies? He's yours, my dear, if you join me. I've done as much for ever so many grateful ladies." For a moment, I remembered beautiful André Lamotte, the cavalier of the window. And then I remembered the light in his eyes when he spied my sister. What a stupid fantasy.

"I don't want any men," I said, but the fortune-teller only gazed at my face and nodded ever so slightly.

"Come now," she said, "everyone has a heart's desire. Tell me what you crave, and you shall have it. Consider nothing beyond me. Now, do confess. You've thought of something, haven't you?" I could see her watching the play of emotions on my face as it all came back to me, my vow in the tower room, the hate, the fruitless rage bottled up like poison.

"I want revenge," I said.

"Revenge?" said the fortune-teller, and then she gave a little laugh. "Why, my dear, what could be easier for me? I am a specialist in revenge."

"He said no one would believe me, no one would listen..."

"Why, *I* listen. So many ladies come to me. What man listens to women? But I, I am the ear of Paris. Just think of me as Justice."

"I told him he'd pay, and he laughed at me—"

"Ah, you dear, talented child. Say no more. Join me and you shall have vengeance: bloody, satisfying, overflowing. Believe me, there's hardly anything as fulfilling in life as the destruction of an enemy."

"I want him ruined. I want him dead."

"Good," she said as she leaned back in her seat. We had reached the Porte Saint-Denis, that vast imitation of a Roman triumphal arch in yellow stone, dedicated to the glory of Louis the Great. "We understand each other now." The carriage turned to the left, into the long, narrow streets of Villeneuve and entered the Rue Beauregard. The street was lined with recently built, medium-sized villas of two or three storeys, widely spaced, with high walls between them over which peeped the barren branches of trees in hidden gardens. Big arched gates indicated that there were coach houses and stables behind the walls. Maids were throwing open the heavy shutters of the front rooms of the houses, and the first hopeful street vendors had made their appearance. A shabby man in a dilapidated hat and ragged leggings cried, "Flints and steel, flints and steel!" while another, carrying dead rats tied to a stick by their tails, offered up rat poison by shouting, "Death to rats! Death to rats!"

The fortune-teller looked at him and snorted with a brief, silent laugh. "No business here," she chuckled. To the curious look on my face she responded, "Oh, it's nothing. Just a private joke in the neighbourhood."

We halted in the snow, now turning to slush, as the lackey leapt from the carriage to open the coach doors of her garden villa's inner court.

"Do you see this house and the elegant garden behind the walls? It's all frosty and bare now, but so lovely in the summer – so green, and I have my little fêtes out by the pavilion, with charming striped silk tents set up for the refreshments. I'm thinking of ordering some dear little cupids from Italy for my fountain. Won't that be exquisite?" How did common sentimental turns of speech manage to sound vaguely sinister when they came out of her mouth? We were handed out of the carriage at the stairs. I almost slipped on the slushy steps, but she took my arm to help me to the door of the living quarters of her house, behind the formal reception parlour. Then she paused, fumbling for the key in an inner pocket in her cloak, while she scraped the slushy snow off her boots.

"Now that we are friends, my dear – think of me that way, won't you? Patroness and protégée sound so cold – you shall come to some of my lovely winter suppers with violins, as soon as you are *polished* a bit. I entertain witty people from all the best circles." She fitted the ornate key into the lock of the high carved oak door and pushed it open, leading me inside. A maid in a neat cap and apron came to take her cloak.

"And would you ever suspect that my husband failed twice in business?" she went on, pointing to the handsome chamber we had entered. "He lost two jewellery stores. Debtors' prison – ruin. Oh, I've seen the worst. What was I to do? After all, I have a taste for nice things. But thanks to the arts I learned at my mother's knee, I feed a household of ten mouths and do exactly as I please."

The rooms behind the dark, draped reception room were not at all mysterious, but homey and comfortable. From the snow-heaped courtyard we had entered into a sitting room warmed by a roaring fire in a big fireplace with a carved marble mantelpiece. The floor was covered with a cosy Turkish carpet. A heavy table with carved legs covered with a long brocade cloth stood in the centre of the room, surrounded by a veritable company of tall, heavily carved chairs with dark velvet seats. In between the massive armoires that stood by the walls was a pair of sumptuous tapestries depicting the repentance of the Magdalen and the presentation of the infant Jesus at the temple. Two infants, just more than a year apart in age, were playing on the carpet with their nurse, and I could hear the shouts of older children beyond the door. Several large cats lay somnolent on the hearth. Lying equally somnolent in an armchair near by was Antoine Montvoisin, her second husband – a pale, haggard man in a head napkin, dressing gown, and slippers. He did not wish to be introduced.

From the kitchen beyond came good smells, the shouting of serving maids, and the rattle and crash of dinner on the way. Suddenly, I remembered that I was famished. The luxury, the lavish use of firewood impressed me. This is a household with money, I remember thinking. It was not until some time later that I knew my patroness well enough to begin to guess at her income: more than all but the wealthiest of the aristocracy, about the same as a minister of state. The girl I remembered, Marie-Marguerite, the daughter of her husband by a previous marriage, now taller than I was, crossed our path carrying a cup of chocolate for her father. At that point, I would have signed over my soul for a cup of chocolate. Madame Montvoisin, whose sharp eyes never missed anything, smiled as she saw the look on my face.

Wordlessly, she led the way into her cabinet, and I recognised the little room I had seen in the glass. It was lined with locked cupboards, and the heavy red curtains were pulled back to reveal the little window, all white with frost. On the opposite wall, a warm little fire sat behind a pair of soot-blackened andirons that were made like cats. In one corner, an ornate writing desk was covered with odd things: a half-drawn horoscope, a little hand made of silver, an ink pot shaped like a satyr, and, amidst a rubble of loose papers, a little cat's face carved in amber that seemed to glow with light reflected from an unknown source.

"Sit down here." She pointed to a cushioned stool beside the writing table. I hoped she could not hear my stomach growl. Sensible of the drama of the moment, I didn't want to spoil it with such a common noise. "We need to have an understanding before we begin." Good. She hadn't heard. "For the first year, I will provide you with bed and board, clothing, instruction, and a little allowance for necessaries. You will return to me all that you earn." She took out a little key from her bosom and unlocked the door of one of the tall cupboards that constituted the little cabinet's chief furniture. I saw inside on the shelf a row of green ledgers, each labelled with a letter of the alphabet. She took down the *P* ledger, and a folder tied with string labelled "contracts", and turned again to me.

"After the year of training, if you show enough aptitude, I will set you up in a nice little establishment of your own, for which you will repay me over the next five years out of your income, plus twenty-five per cent of your overall income." She took a sheet out of "contracts" and laid it on the table. It was already written up in a legal hand, with blank spaces in it for appropriate facts. I remember being impressed with her foresight and organisation. Even though she was dealing in superstition, she did it like a lawyer or an important merchant, not like an old crone in an attic. She looked up from the contract and smiled, that odd little V.

"You will also perform certain little ... professional reference services for me, carry occasional messages or packages. After that, our partnership will include reference work alone. I will offer you my standard agreement, a fee based on a percentage of a referred client's payment. And, of course, I will continue to offer you whatever assistance and consultation you need, absolutely free." She sat down, took out a pen, uncorked the satyr ink pot, and queried, "Your full baptismal name, dear?" Squinting slightly, she filled in the first blank space in the contract. Then she looked up at me as if she had just remembered something. Later I realised that she never forgot anything. But she believed that everything must be presented correctly, like an important dish by a great chef. She raised a finger and cocked her head slightly.

"Ah, yes," she said, "but first, before we go any farther, you must swear to keep secret our agreement, and whatever you hear in this house or during your training." I was very hungry. My hands started to shake, and I could feel the blood leaving my face.

"Nervous?" She laughed. "Perhaps you imagine you must sign the contract in blood? No, the time to be nervous was when you were standing on the bridge. Don't you know the penalties for suicide? Did you really want your corpse to be exposed in the basement of the Châtelet for identification, then hung by the leg from the gibbet until nothing but bones were left? Why, that would make *me* nervous. Instead, you will be part of my secret family." She leafed through the green ledger labelled *P* until she found a series of blank pages. At the top of the first one, she wrote "Pasquier, Geneviève," and the date, 10 December 1674. Then she leaned forward confidentially.

"A family requires loyalty ... gratitude ... discretion. And in our trade, we hear so many secrets. It is a kind of confessional; we are almost like priests. People bring their little tragedies to us – often different people want the same thing, and we mustn't reveal it. Confidentiality, you must understand, is part of the fortune-teller's trade—" I started to slump off the stool. She looked at me with renewed interest.

"Why, I do believe you must be hungry. Just look at your hands tremble, and you've turned altogether pale. Let's have the oath now, and we'll celebrate with a bit of something." I was so hungry, I would have sworn to anything at that moment. But as the oath rolled on, conjuring by the puissant prince Rhadamanthus, by Lucifer, by Beelzebub, by Satanas, by Jauconill, and an infinite catalogue of infernal powers, I thought I would faint face down in her cloven-hoofed censer. Oaths, in my opinion, infernal or not, ought to be short.

Rummaging in one of the cupboards, she produced a large box of fancifully shaped marzipan, a bottle of sweet wine, and two glasses. "You know how it is," she apologised, "I have to keep it locked up from the children in here, or I simply wouldn't have *any*. Now, now, not so fast, or you'll get sick. Four pieces are entirely *enough*." And, refilling my glass, she took away the box and locked it up again. "Any more, and you'll spoil dinner." The wine had trickled into my insides like liquid fire. I could see two of everything now. The two La Voisins raised their glasses in a toast; I raised my two, as well. We drank to the ancient art of fortune-telling.

"The art of the fortune-teller!" she exclaimed. "Pleasing, profitable, and entirely legal! Ah, how lucky you are nowadays; the King's own law has declared superstition obsolete. No more trials for witchcraft, no burnings. Ours is now a new world – of science, of law, of rationality. But even in this new world, men must allow women their little ... aberrations, because we poor creatures are too simple to manage without."

She got up and put away the bottle and glasses in the other cupboard, and I could see that the rest of the shelves were lined with strange glass vials, all neatly labelled. She locked the cupboard again, turning to look at me from where she stood. What was in that cupboard? Something about it made my stomach feel queer.

"What's wrong? You're looking a bit green around the mouth. Oh, dear me. I shouldn't have frightened you with all that talk of burning. Don't worry; my arts have been judged entirely legitimate by the highest court of heresy, the doctors of the Sorbonne. I defended them myself. I was much younger, but even then I knew the power of an elegant gown and a handsome bosom over elderly divines! *Pooh!* Such prejudice! I imagine they expected some dismal, stupid old crone. I merely pointed out to them that I could hardly be faulted for using the arts of astrology when they taught it on their own faculty. After that, the Rector of the University himself invited me to call on him, and my persecutors in the Company of the Holy Sacrament were foiled. I still dine with the rector every so often – what a dear old pet! And what a table he spreads! Memorable!" I couldn't help but be impressed by her knowledge of the world. I wanted it for myself. What a dull thing I'd been, just living in books!

She reached into her desk and pulled out the contract. She pushed it towards me and pointed to the place I should sign. I could hardly read it, it moved about so, but I managed to hold it still long enough to dip the pen in the inkwell and splatter a signature across the bottom. She took up the paper, looked at it, and laughed.

"I see a splendid future for you," she said. "Water diviners are all the rage right now and travel in all the best circles. Of course, by themselves the images are not worth much; you must learn the art of interpretation from me, the study of physiognomy, the oracular pronouncement. But with your educated speech, you will be able to go – anywhere. And I do like a fashionable clientele; they will pay us both so much better." She got up and poked the fire. I wished very seriously that she would open up the cupboard with the marzipan in it again, but she didn't.

"Now, in the course of your work, you will hear very sad

stories: a cruel, unfeeling husband, a little, ah, embarrassment, on the way, the desire for a lover who is indifferent.
These you will send to me. Your glass will reveal that in the
Rue Beauregard they may find assistance for their problems.
Luck at cards, enlargement of the bosom, cures for the
diseases of love, the preservation of the body from wounds on
the field of battle. I offer a number of little confidential
services, without which the world of fashion, of culture, could
not flourish."

"Oh, I see," I said to be polite, but my mind was working
about as well as my eyes, and I hadn't taken anything in.

"I doubt that you do, just now." She chuckled. "Just do as I
say, and we'll be very happy with each other. Now, here is the
sign by which you will be known as one of us – the ring finger
and thumb together, palm up. Can you do it, or will I have to
show you again later? Just remember, you are very far from
being initiated into our true mysteries, so don't get proud – and
don't try to outguess me, will you, dear? Yes, that's right.
Now, let me take your elbow and we'll have dinner served. No,
the door's over here, remember?" And so it was all in a
morning that I was swept into a secret world that I had never
even suspected lay outside my own doorstep.

That day, she saw to everything, disarming my confusion
with a large and excellent midday dinner and the ordering of
the mending of my dress, which she pronounced much too nice
to discard, being a rather handsome light mourning gown in
fine grey wool, all trimmed with black silk ribbons. All
afternoon, somnolent with food, I languished upstairs in one of
her immense, tapestry-hung bedrooms in my petticoats,
awaiting the return of my dress. These were her hours for
receiving clients, and I was not to be seen in her house. I leafed
through a dull religious book prominently displayed on the
nightstand, *Réflections sur la miséricorde de Dieu*, and then,
rather daringly, searched the drawers, to be rewarded with a
more interesting volume entitled *Les amours du Palais Royal*,
a vial of what I took to be sleeping medicine, a number of
curious iron implements made like long pins or hooks, and a
heavy steel syringe with a long, slender tip. There was a pile of
clean, folded linen napkins and a roll of sheep's wool. I couldn't
imagine what it was all for. I was about to reward myself for my

stay with the excellent book about the Palais Royal when a noise made me start, and I hurriedly put back everything as it had been.

My heart stopped pounding when I saw it was only another of my hostess's ubiquitous cats, a big striped tom, leaping from his perch on top of the armoire, where he had been sleeping. He jumped gracefully onto the huge, curtained bed where I was sitting, purring and rubbing his head on my hand, demanding to be petted. As I played with the cat, I couldn't help noticing how warm the room was on this cold winter afternoon, even though there was no fire in the bedroom grate. Surely there was a stove hidden somewhere. What a clever way to keep a bedroom, ordinarily so frigid, cosy! I got up and looked about the room, hunting about the heavy, dark furniture. I lifted the rich green drapes that kept the cold from seeping in the frosty window and peeked out into the barren garden. Rows of neatly planted, winter-bare trees rose from the snow, and in the centre, a classical grotto with Greek columns and a fountain held up by nymphs made an ice sculpture, white on white, in the frozen landscape. Incongruously, a narrow chimney rose from the back of the grotto. Even Madame Montvoisin's garden folly was equipped with every comfort.

Giving up my search, I decided to return to the interesting book in the nightstand. But crossing by the great tapestry behind the bed, I felt an unusual source of warmth and smelled something odd. I lifted the tapestry, and there behind it was a little iron oven set into the stone wall, still giving off a fading warmth. An odd place for an oven, I thought, dropping the tapestry as I heard a knock on the door. It was the fortune-teller's stepdaughter, Marie-Marguerite, just my age but rather taller and straighter, and, as I looked her up and down regretfully, prettier, too. She had a tray with biscuits and chocolate sent up by her mother.

"I'd rather be here than downstairs just now," she said cheerfully, licking the brown off the corners of her mouth preparatory to devouring another biscuit. "All those dull masked ladies— 'tell me this, tell me that.' When I marry Jean-Baptiste, we'll live above his *pâtisserie*, and I'll do nothing but drink cocoa and play with my babies all day. You won't find me travelling all over the countryside incognito and letting strangers in my house! I'm going to live the way a real woman should, with my man taking care of me."

"Nice work, if you can get it," I answered, annoyed at her pretty brown curls.

"Oh, well, don't feel bad. You can't help it if men aren't interested. You'll do well enough reading water glasses, I imagine, though I thought it was awfully boring, myself. Want to play cards?" And she took from her apron pocket a pack of well-thumbed playing cards wrapped in a scrap of silk scarf. "Here," she said, dealing them out in an elaborate pattern like a star between us where we sat on the bed. The cards were like nothing I'd ever seen before. They were painted not with hearts and clubs but with knives, towers, faces of the sun, hermits, kings, and queens. "Why, that's a very nice one!" she exclaimed.

"Nice what? How do we play the game?"

"It's not a game, silly; it's your fortune. See the sun there? That's good luck. And that one there means money soon. Now, who else shall we do?"

"What about the cat?" She laughed and dealt the cards again. "Oh, puss, a death's head for you, you old thing. Best not go outside, or you'll be made into stew by the assistant gardener's family!" So we spent the remainder of the afternoon quite pleasantly, casting fortunes for various family members and grandees at court. "Only you mustn't do it for the King," she cautioned. "That's treason, and they will draw and quarter you in the Place de Grève for it." Clearly, becoming wealthy in the fortune-telling business had more pitfalls than her stepmother had made out.

NINE

"So, Mademoiselle, let's see how quick you are. Here are three cards: ten, queen, king. Now, I lay them out in order on their faces. Where's the queen?" I pointed to the place where the queen lay, face down, on La Voisin's great dark dining table. The winter rain rattled at the windows, in a way that made the tall tapestry-hung room and leaping fire seem all the more cheerful and delightful. "Wrong! Try again! Ha! Wrong again! Look sharp!" The magician's hands, smooth and deft, flashed across the cards. Another of La Voisin's lovers, but one of the chief ones, as far as I could tell from the comings and goings in this most complex of households. An older-looking, rumpled sort of fellow in a rusty wig and homespun, the man who called himself Le Sage seemed almost deceptively clumsy, until you looked into his shrewd eyes and caught sight of the smooth-moving, swift hands, so curiously white, which he usually kept protected in gloves.

"Your eyes need glasses, Mademoiselle— Why, here's the queen, hidden up your own sleeve." The white hand flicked past my own, as he produced the queen with a flourish.

The false shuffle, the break, the false cut, the force, I had learned them all, and now the desired card would slither invisibly to the top of the deck under my hands. Invaluable knowledge for a fortune-teller. But always, Le Sage was the master. Now he shuffled the three cards back into the deck, and the cards leaped between his hands like liquid.

"Show me that, Le Sage," I begged.

"Foolish again, Mademoiselle," he announced. "A card reader should never look too adept at the shuffle. A certain naive sincerity is important. Intensity. Survey each card slowly, as if you were spying an oracle of doom. Watch Madame through the peephole next time she reads for a client." Then, as if to prove his point, he shuffled the cards again, this time with one hand only.

Madame Montvoisin's house was a veritable factory for deception, with peepholes behind tapestries, a speaking tube between the dining room and the reception room, and oiled pulleys in the ceiling that could be worked from the floor above. In the days I had been there, I had already seen a séance at which a ghostly white hand had appeared, conveniently lowered on a black thread. Yet even then I sensed there were things I was not allowed to see. There was the masked woman, pale and frightened, who was shown upstairs for some unknown purpose. The smoking stove in the garden pavilion and Madame's study with its strange cupboards remained under lock and key. Sometimes Madame would silence jesting among the members of her household with a dark look, saying, "If you understood my powers, you would never say that in my presence."

But for the most part, I was too busy to wonder about the deeper mysteries in the house on the Rue Beauregard. I had been plunged into a round of instruction: the signs of the zodiac, the lines of the palm, the interpretation of blobs of candle wax dripped into a bowl of water. Then there was the deciphering of signs and portents and the study of objects, such as stones, and the memorisation of which of them restored health, brought luck, or protected against poison. All must be learned, if I were to impress my new clients, for most of the aristocrats who consulted fortune-tellers were themselves students of the occult, and quick to spot an amateur.

"So, Adam, how is the progress? Didn't I tell you she was quick?" La Voisin had bustled in from the reception parlour after the last of a long series of consultations.

"As usual, right, my love. Your powers of discovery are undimmed. And your idea – purest genius. The way she talks – all purse lipped and sharp, with those long words! Marvellous! Who would ever believe she was anything less than a century old?" La Voisin looked pleased with herself. Then nothing would do but to demonstrate my new skills. La Voisin ordered a bit of wine and a plate of cakes from the kitchen and then seated herself in her armchair at the head of the table.

"Ah, excellent," breathed the sorceress. "But you, Mademoiselle, what is this sour look I see? Where is your gratitude for the treasures of knowledge showered on you?"

"I thought I agreed to be transformed into a beautiful object of desire, not a card sharp," I answered. La Voisin laughed.

"All in time, you spoiled little miss. Why, I've already made the arrangements. It's about time you boarded out, anyway. I don't want to risk my clients getting a glimpse of you before you're done."

"Done? Like a roast?"

"Done like a masterpiece. You will be my crowning achievement."

"*Our* crowning achievement, my sweet," corrected the magician, finishing his wine. "Have you seen Lemaire yet?"

"Yes, it's all arranged. Consultation with Lemaire, then the dressmaker. Bouchet has been slow with the genealogy – he says court business is so heavy these days. I reminded him of his little . . . ah . . . debt to us, and that did seem to make him considerably more attentive."

"Bouchet, the genealogist?" I interrupted. "The one who improves people's ancestors when they want to rise at court?"

"Bouchet, the genius, my dear. You see? I've spared no expense. You must admit a title will enhance you. Besides, it opens so many doors. I wish you to have a well-placed clientele. Yes indeed, you'll enjoy your new self – that I can guarantee. How do you like the title of the Marquise de Morville, eh? Elegant, isn't it? Get used to the sound of it."

"But . . . but . . . I will be pretty, won't I? Like other girls? You promised." La Voisin and Le Sage exchanged glances.

"My dear," responded the sorceress," I promised to make you beautiful and desired, but I did *not* promise to make you like other girls. A fortune-teller must *never* be common. You must have that air of mystery – a goddess-like distance from all that is ordinary. Adam, did you bring the book?"

With a flourish, Le Sage produced from his pocket a little volume bound in calfskin. I leafed through it. A volume of manners from the time of Henri IV.

"Now, you can study that this evening," announced La Voisin, "after our lesson at the glass. I want you to pass for a creature from another century. The Marquise de Morville is a *very* old lady."

"But I don't want to be old," I protested.

"Not old. Preserved in eternal youth. By the secret arts of

alchemy." She waggled her eyebrows humorously. She didn't need to go further. I saw it at once. Mystery. Magnetism. A rare joke. Aristocratic households that would never have considered receiving the financier Pasquier, even in his days of favour and fortune, would vie with one another to receive the most outrageous charlatan ever conceived. Such are the penalties of wealth and boredom. It was delicious.

That night I wrote in my book:

12 December 1674. The great Plato says that the masses are not fit to govern by reason of their gullibility. But what shall we say then of the first families of France, who are equally gullible? How I wish I could discuss this point with Father. I believe he would find the Marquise de Morville as splendid a prank as I do.

The very next evening, after a hilarious celebration in which far too many toasts were drunk to my splendid new career, I was bundled off in a carriage to a concealed location, where I might regenerate like a caterpillar in its cocoon before I burst on an amazed world.

I awoke in an alien country. Winter light was shining through the open shutters of a narrow little room and making shining patterns on the bare wooden floor by the bed. Repetitive bouquets of stencilled flowers brightened the yellow-painted walls under the slanted eaves, and the tiny attic chamber smelled of fresh linen. The pillow felt as if it were filled with bricks. The featherbed weighed a thousand pounds. I had an awful headache. I turned my head. My clothes were hanging on a peg, my notebooks piled neatly beside my shoes. Someone had put a nightgown on me and put me to bed. Why, as long as I don't move my head, the fortune-telling business isn't bad, so far, I thought. There was a knock on the door, and a busy, buxom young woman in a cap and apron entered the room, allowing the smell of chocolate to float up from somewhere in the bowels of the house. I groaned.

"So, finally up, are you? How does it feel to be one hundred and fifty years old?"

"Exactly like being fifteen. But I've got a terrible headache."

"As well you might expect. I've never seen anyone drunker than you were last night when they delivered you here. I've brought you a headache powder. I compound them myself, and they are excellent. Here, drink this and dress. You have a busy day ahead of you. You're consulting Monsieur Lemaire today and being measured for a new gown at the tailor's. Up! Up! Yes, you have to drink it. And let this be a lesson to you. If you're to be a great fortune-teller, you must never lose control again. Leave wine alone, or you'll betray yourself in company."

I looked at the disgusting brew in the goblet. Reason enough to leave wine alone, if this were the cure. I drank it. It tasted like something dreadful scraped off the river bottom in summer.

"Ah, good. That's it. Now, if I could only give it a better flavour, I'd make my fortune," announced the woman. "Now, come downstairs when you're ready. We've made cocoa especially in your honour."

The headache was already passing. I got up, felt my limbs cautiously, and found them still attached, got dressed, and descended the narrow staircase. The large room downstairs was quite astonishing. It was part kitchen, part apothecary's shop. I'd never seen anything like it. There was an oven built into the wide brick wall of the huge fireplace and a tall, strange-looking stove with a tower beside it that contained charcoal, so cunningly built that the fire in the stove could be fed continuously for many days. There were long workbenches against the wall covered with curious glassware and sealed jugs. Two little girls who looked to be about ten and twelve were filling rows of small green glass vials with a funnel and ladle under the supervision of a tall older woman who held a copper vessel full of something mysterious. A kitchen maid in apron and cap, having stirred some eerily sweet-scented brew in a little pot beside the great soup kettle on the hearth, was now engaged in renewing the wood in the oven, from which a strange acrid smell came and mingled with the appealing scent of chocolate. There were boxes and bales of who knows what piled in the corners, and on shelves were ranged an array of strange, globular animals folded up and preserved in jars like pickles. Above everything, suspended from the ceiling, was a fantastical production of the taxidermist's art, a hairy creation with four legs, each ending in a huge stork's foot. The creature possessed feathered wings spread wide and a sort of human face compounded of plaster and what appeared to be goat hair. On the odd stove, a pan of cocoa was warming, while beside it on a little shelf sat a heavy earthenware plate of rolls, fresh from the baker's, all covered with a napkin.

"Ah, so you like our harpy. Nice, isn't she?" The older of the two women had turned around to address me. She was tall and thin, with greying hair tucked in a little cap above her pale face. She had a shrewd look to her, as if she had seen too much and made the best of it. She had introduced herself as a widow, Catherine Trianon, and people knew her as La Trianon. The little girls laid down the funnel. "Now, now," she admonished, "you must wash your hands before you eat anything. That's a rule, when you're learning this trade." Daughters? Apprentices? And just what trade was it? Alchemical? Pharmaceutical? I couldn't tell. The girls scampered off to set a bowl beneath the tap of the immense kitchen reservoir that stood in the corner.

"How do you know it's a she?" I asked, continuing to look up at the creature's curiously nondescript underside. The taxidermist had provided the thing's belly with a discreet covering of iridescent duck's feathers.

"Because everything in the house is a she. We wouldn't have it any other way." The shorter, pretty woman that I'd first seen upstairs, who was known as La Dodée, had fetched cups from a shelf and set them out on an empty worktable.

"*Hsst* now," warned her older companion, "I wouldn't be so ready to gossip until I'd seen the sign." She turned to me. "Are you one of us?" I made the sign I'd been shown. "One of us, and not one of us. How long since you left the other world?" Somehow, I knew what she meant.

"Four days ago," I said.

"My, what a change. What were you doing two weeks ago before it all began?" La Trianon queried.

"I was planning to drown myself, but instead I'm here," I said, in a matter-of-fact voice. Somehow they didn't look as shocked as most people would. I took another sip of their excellent chocolate.

"Was it a man?" asked the shorter woman called La Dodée. "It usually is. You aren't pregnant, are you?" What a ghastly thought. Suddenly the chocolate tasted like dust. The women saw the look in my eyes and nodded to each other. "Don't worry," answered La Dodée. "You're with us now. That's not a problem in our world. Though I can't say they don't try to make trouble for us. Men, I mean. They can't bear the thought of women running a business on their own. 'Where's your licence?' 'Who owns the building?' 'Are you sheltering felons or escapees here?' 'Surely you don't live entirely without men!' 'Surely we do, Monsieur Police, and our papers are all in order. We're respectable widows, following the trade left to us by our dear, departed husbands, distilling perfumes and medicines.' We wipe a tear from our eyes. We offer a bit of rose water for the wife or girlfriend. 'Have a drink on us, Sergeant; we know you're only doing your duty.' And, of course, influence helps. The influence of La Voisin. We can live as we wish. Without men."

"She says you've studied," interrupted the first woman. "So when she asked us to help you out, we said, 'good, if she can read and figure she can help us straighten out our records.'" I looked at the untidy piles of slips of paper everywhere. I was annoyed. This was not like a cocoon waiting to hatch a glamorous butterfly at all. La Trianon continued: "The business has got a little ahead of us lately. We've been so successful, you see – deliveries all over Europe. It's our quality. We guarantee quality and have never had a disappointed customer. So people rely on us. Good. I knew you'd help. We look after you, you look after us, La Voisin looks after us all. Why, we're almost a philanthropic society. Yes, welcome to our society. Do good, and you'll always do well, as my mother used to say."

Again, philanthropy. Surely, I had never met so many charitable souls in my life as in the last two days. We were interrupted by a silvery tinkle of a bell, from the front room, which was actually a shop front, done up as an occultist's parlour and decorated with astrological signs. La Dodée hurried through the parlour to the front door. "Oh, that must be Monsieur Jordain, the apothecary, with his delivery," I heard her cry as she vanished into the front room. "Thank goodness. We were all out, and we have so many orders."

She came back escorting a benign-looking elderly gentleman carrying a number of carnation pots all tied up with twine, which he put on the biggest of the worktables.

"Here you are, ladies – still fresh and lively. What's that I smell? Chocolate?"

"It's all gone," snapped La Trianon, cutting the twine and peeking into one of the pots suspiciously to judge the quality of the merchandise. I couldn't help getting a glimpse inside myself.

The pots were full of live toads.

My transformation was accomplished in a series of visits to the back room of the shop of a fashionable *coiffeuse-bouquetière* near the Porte Saint-Denis: yet another establishment tied to Madame's "philanthropic society". There I was poked and prodded and passed judgment upon until I wept: my face, my walk, my posture were unforgivable in a woman of fashion. A failed ballet master in Madame's debt was consulted and found that one leg was shorter than the other. He sent for a shoemaker, to make a padded shoe with a built-up sole, then squinted down my spine and sent for the *corsetière*. This worthy constructed to his order a hideous instrument of torture with steel stays than ran straight up to my shoulders.

"There," he said, as I was sewed into it so tightly that the tears squeezed from my eyes. "'Change her so her own mother wouldn't recognise her.' That's what the old witch said, and by God, that's what I'll do!"

"But how do I get out of it?" I asked desperately.

"You don't," he said calmly. "All of my pupils are sewn into their corsets night and day until they achieve court posture. Don't worry – the bones are still soft."

"Your eyebrows – ugh, they grow like weeds," said the *coiffeuse-bouquetière* as she plucked the hairs from the bridge of my nose.

"Why can't you do anything that isn't painful?" I asked, my mind on my aching back and sore ribs.

"Haven't you ever heard the old adage 'One must suffer to be beautiful'? You're lucky to have good skin. Not marked by the smallpox, though in a man a little marking is considered distinguished. The King, for example, is marked by the smallpox, and he is the *model* of elegance."

It made a certain sort of bizarre sense. What is a flaw in a common person is merely spice in an aristocratic one.

Suddenly I knew that the Marquise de Morville, if she became rich enough, powerful enough, could redefine beauty. That was La Voisin's trick. She had no magic potion to make me truly beautiful. She would simply change the way the world saw me. It was brilliant, like a magician's illusion.

The same dilapidated hired fiacre that always took me to and from these appointments was waiting to return me to La Trianon's establishment. I'd grown used to the idea that the coachman, a one-eyed man in a rusty black cloak, never asked for payment. But this afternoon, something splendid happened. The one-eyed man hesitated to help me into the little carriage, squinting up and down as if I were a stranger.

"Well, well, well," cackled the ancient driver. "Same clothes . . . must be the same girl, after all. Looks considerably less like a gargoyle." As the old horse ambled off, I could hear him muttering to himself, "Not bad, not bad at all."

But at the cross street, we had to pull suddenly to a halt at the cry of the postilions of an elaborately painted and gilded heavy carriage, drawn by six horses at a fast trot, whose passage sent pedestrians scampering and splattered slushy mud on everything near by.

"Make way! Make way!" We could hear new voices from the opposite direction as a second equipage, pulled by four heavy bays at full speed, careened out of the narrow street opposite. There was a scream of horses, wild oaths, and a crunching sound as the fast-moving carriages locked wheels and the lackeys from each equipage swarmed down to avenge the insult done to their masters' honour.

"Well, here's fun," grumbled the driver. "We're trapped here until they clear the street." The uniformed lackeys had drawn their swords, and we could hear them shrieking insults as they attacked each other. Then a cheer went up from the gathering crowd of gawkers, as the master of the first carriage leaped from his vehicle and forced open the door of the second carriage, pulling out its occupant to give him a good drubbing with his walking stick.

"You fool, you'll pay. I am the English ambassador," gasped the second man.

"Then take that, treacherous English," we could hear the first man cry as he struck a heavy blow with his stick. Both were soon lost to view amid their struggling servants, and interspersed with the cries of "*A moi! A moi!*" and "Damned lunatic!" we could hear the slither of drawn steel.

"Oh, my God, the police," said my driver. "And we're wedged in here tight. Draw the curtain." I saw the driver shrink into his cloak and pull his old, wide-brimmed hat low. Sure enough, peeping from behind the curtain, I spied the baggy blue suits and white-plumed hats of the Paris police. Their sergeant, distinguished by his red stockings, ran behind them as they waded into the mêlée. As they cleared a path to the wreckage, a wiry dark man of medium height with a sharp profile, wearing the decent suit of a bourgeois of good standing, moved towards the carriages with a commanding air. He doffed his hat humbly and bowed low before the wrangling gentlemen, one of whom, in his foreign-cut doublet and expensive-looking but provincial coat, seemed somewhat the worse for wear. In the fashion of such quarrels, they both turned on the newcomer and threatened him. The wiry gentleman beat a hasty retreat, bowing backward, leaving his police to take care of the lackeys.

"Driver, driver, are you free?" a man's voice enquired from the crowd. It was the police officer. I dropped the curtain.

"I've got a passenger just now."

"Then he can walk home. Desgrez of the police requires your services."

"It's a lady," said my driver.

"Oho, a lady, Latour?" The policeman had recognised my driver. "Then I'm sure your 'lady' won't mind a detour by the Châtelet now, will she?" The rickety little carriage swayed as he stepped in.

"Well, well – a lady, indeed; quite a pretty little lady, too. Not your usual type, eh, Latour, to judge by her blushes? Mademoiselle, may I present myself. I am Captain Desgrez, of the Paris police. I trust your detour will not be too far out of the way. Just where were you bound?"

Without a thought, I answered in the patois of the Paris shopgirl apprentice. "I'm returning to my mistress, Madame Callet. You know 'er, don't you? Fine linens for the gentry? I was makin' a delivery to the Hôtel Tubeuf." As the fiacre finally jolted into motion, he took out a notebook and a little pencil and began to write up his report of the accident. Once finished, I saw he was inspecting me closely.

"That's a rather handsome dress for the apprentice of a *lingère*," he remarked in an offhand way.

"Ain't it fine, now? I got it hardly worn in a used-clothing stall at the Halles." I was no fool. I knew where the servants and the poor of Paris get their grand, grimy, and mismatched things.

"Do you remember which *fripier* it was?" The quiet voice sounded definitely sinister. Squashed into the tiny carriage with him as I was, I feared he could hear my heart pounding.

"Why, the one near the column, with the sign of the monkey and the mirror." He looked a long time at my face. I opened my eyes and looked back. He had a narrow, intelligent face with dark, severe eyes. He wore his own black hair, cut short at the collar. If I had not known him for a policeman, I might have taken him for a seminarian – or an inquisitor.

"Might be true," I could hear him mutter to himself. "It doesn't seem to fit well. Still, light mourning, grey with black and grey silk ribbons . . ." He inspected the dress carefully. I could feel him looking at the long mended gash to the waist, where the ribbons and trim had been moved to conceal as much of the neat patching as possible. Aha, I thought. A man of logic. The most dangerous kind. We were approaching the judicial side of the great prison-fortress by the Rue Pierre-à-Poisson, where the long tables of the fish sellers that were built against the fortress wall were covered with thousands of goujons, carp, and other river fish. An army of fish sellers gutted fish and shouted their wares to crowds of customers who pressed around the carriage, oblivious of it in their search for the perfect fish. The stink was unbearable. Heaps of rotting fish offal lay beneath the tables, and rats ran freely through the foul mounds of garbage.

"Tell me, Mademoiselle. Did it show signs of having been damp when you got it?"

"Damp? Oh, no. Dry as a bone. See? The ribbons ain't run a bit, and the wool's not stained." I held out a sleeve to him. My God, I thought. They gave my description to the police when I vanished. Famille Pasquier – important enough to be a scandal, to be remembered by the police. But somewhere inside me, a voice was singing, "He doesn't recognise me; I look different; he called me pretty."

"Hmm. Interesting..." he said, as the little carriage pulled up in the great courtyard of the Châtelet.

"Is there somethin' wrong with my clothes?" I asked, making my voice sound alarmed.

"Why, not at all," Desgrez replied smoothly. "They are absolutely perfect. *Au revoir*, little *lingère*. Perhaps I will have the pleasure of meeting you again some day."

TEN

Captain Desgrez strode purposefully through the guardroom of the Châtelet to the inner door at the far end of the great stone hall. He scarcely acknowledged the greeting of the group of officers who stood as he passed, laying aside the muskets they were cleaning.

"What's wrong with him?" asked one of the officers, putting aside his long brush and pulling a pack of cards from his pocket.

"Don't bother him. When he's got that look on his face, he's on the scent of something," replied the sergeant.

"On the scent? Then too bad for the something," announced the first man, as he shuffled and dealt the cards.

Through the open door, they could hear the captain shouting at the chief records clerk in the rooms beyond the guardroom. Presently, Desgrez came out with a folder tied with string under his arm and vanished in the direction of Monsieur de La Reynie's chambers.

"Ah, Desgrez, do come in. I was about to send a boy in search of you." The Lieutenant General of Police, wearing his crimson robe of office, was as courtly as always, although he did not rise from his seat. Behind him the wall was lined with law books. Before him on the desk lay the transcript of the confrontation of two false coiners, who had previously been interrogated separately. La Reynie had marked the conflicting testimony and made note of it in the little red notebook that never left his side. It was a big case, one that involved the treasury and possibly even treason. Louvois, the royal minister to whom he reported, would be impressed. Desgrez removed his hat and bowed.

"Monsieur de La Reynie—"

"I can tell by the look in your eye, Desgrez, that you are on the track of something. Tell me, does it relate to the papers under your arm?"

"Monsieur de La Reynie, Latour the forger is back in town."
La Reynie put aside his notebook.

"That gallows bait?" the chief of police responded.

"And he was driving a girl wearing a dead woman's dress."
Desgrez opened the folder: "Pasquier, Geneviève, Disappear-
ance of." A scrap of costly deep grey wool fluttered out as
Desgrez laid a dressmaker's sketch before his chief. "The
identical garment, badly torn, neatly mended."

"The case is closed, Desgrez. The body was found in the
river."

"But the dress, Monsieur, showed no signs of ever having
been soaked. The braid had not run. It could have been new,
apart from the mending."

"And so you have come to request that the case be
reopened, as—"

"As murder, Monsieur de La Reynie. Relatives disappear
entirely too easily in this city, especially when an inheritance is
involved. As I recall, the girl involved had just been left a rather
choice country property the son had expected to come to him.
I wish to make further inquiries."

"Very well; your zeal is commendable. But I will have to
request that you delay your work on this case in favour of a
much greater matter. I have just received word that Madame
de Brinvilliers has fled from her hiding place in England at last.
The scandal of her escape from France was laid at our door,
Desgrez . . ." La Reynie looked suddenly bitter.

"But . . . her rank . . . surely Louvois knows . . . she was
assisted at the highest level . . ."

"They are blinded by rank, Desgrez. They believe there
should be two laws, these courtiers, one for them, one for
everyone else. But rank does not dazzle *me*, I assure you. This
kingdom must have one justice, or perish. Her rank does not
change the facts; the woman poisoned her family systematically to get money to support her lovers. If she were a
commoner, her ashes would already have been blowing in the
wind. I want you to find her, wherever she is, and bring her
back for execution."

"Where was she last sighted?"

"At Dover," answered the Lieutenant General of Police,
handing Desgrez the report of his English spies that he had

taken from the desk drawer. "I have here the name of the ship. You can begin by questioning the Master of the *Swallow*. There are also the names of several passengers here. My suspicion is that she will go to ground in a convent – foreign, but French-speaking. In which case we will eventually receive notification from the church authorities. The King himself has ordered that the most notorious poisoner in the history of the kingdom cannot be allowed to escape us."

"There is, however, the matter of religious asylum . . ."

"A small matter for a man as skilled as you, Desgrez. Just leave no traces – nothing that would embarrass His Majesty. I am putting you in charge of the case. You must bring her back here at any cost."

Desgrez bowed in assent, but deep in his memory he filed away the image of the shopgirl in the grey dress. And before he returned the folder to the records room he scrawled on it, "Callet – *lingère*" to remind himself of where to begin the inquiry anew.

ELEVEN

"My God, yer the cool one," said my driver as he handed me out of the fiacre and assisted me to the door of La Trianon's little laboratory. "You led him off this house as if you was born to it. You even sounded just like a little bit a girl from a linen shop in the Rue Aubry-le-Boucher. Now I know what she sees in you. Keep it up, keep it up, and you'll be Queen yerself some day." Queen? Queen of what? I asked myself, storing away the information for later use.

The news did not please my hostesses, who wrung their hands. "You'll have to tell *her*, she has to be moved at once," wailed La Dodée. "She may have brought us straight to – great God – Desgrez himself!"

"*Shh*. No more than necessary," whispered La Trianon fiercely, with a glance in my direction.

"Calm yerselves, I tell you. She led 'em off. He took her for the apprentice of a *lingère*. I'd swear to it on the cross. She's a clever one, she is."

"I suppose we'll have to take his word for it," said La Trianon glumly over a cold supper that evening.

"We'll know in a few days. La Reynie never lets things drag out. They might even be here tomorrow. From the arrest to the gallows – it can be only a matter of days with him."

The name I had copied into my notebook from Grandmother's dead hand. La Reynie. "Who is La Reynie?" I asked.

"La Reynie?" La Trianon answered. "Why, he is the new Lieutenant General of Police. The most dangerous man in Paris, because he is the most incorruptible. He answers to Louvois and to the King only."

My mind raced in several directions at once. Grandmother had written a mysterious letter only moments before her death. She had written to the head of the Paris police, and the letter had been torn out of her hand and destroyed. What had happened to Grandmother, there in that room alone? I tried to remember any strange detail, but I could think of nothing, except the remembered rustle of taffeta outside the room as I entered to find her dying of a seizure. What were my hostesses doing, that they knew so much of the mysterious La Reynie? Surely, it must be more than brewing love potions and telling fortunes. I had to find out what it was.

". . . it's not as if a person could earn an honest living in this city," La Dodée was complaining. "But at least rounding up beggars and imprisoning prostitutes keeps that policeman much too occupied to bother *us*. But still, why shave a girl's head and lock her up for doing just what the great ladies do and get rewarded for? The King's whore lives in splendour, and her children all have titles. What gives *him* the right to be keeper of morals for the nation?"

"The King does, my dear," responded La Trianon, "and never forget that."

"Then we must be grateful for the royal family," announced La Dodée, "especially Monsieur." Monsieur, the Duc d'Orléans, the King's younger brother. Monsieur wore rouge and patches and went to balls dressed as a woman; his male lovers had poisoned his first wife. While Monsieur lived, the King did not dare to carry out the law and execute those who lived like him. The hint was enough. I looked at my hostesses with new eyes. So that was it. A single word from a passing stranger could betray them to their deaths for the way they lived together. It was almost disappointing that they were so ordinary. From all the tales I had heard, I would have expected them to have beards, or wear strange clothes.

"You're . . . um . . . ?"

"Nice girls don't know about things like that. I thought you were better raised," sniffed La Trianon.

"I wasn't raised to be a nice girl. You're thinking of my sister, who's pretty and blonde."

"Isn't that always the story, now?" said La Dodée. "My, you're looking odd. Is there something you want to ask us?"

"Well, um . . . ah . . . is it true that h—, well, you know, can have babies without, well, a man?" Both women broke into shouts of laughter.

"Only the Blessed Virgin did that," said La Dodée.

"Yes, it's all just lies, you know. Just because they call us hermaphrodites, it doesn't mean we are made in some strange, abnormal way. We're really just women who can do without men, and that does upset them! Have another boiled egg. You're looking rather pale, for all that those people across town painted you up."

"It's the corset they sewed me into. My back feels as if it's on fire. And I'm so stiff, I'm afraid of falling and breaking my bones."

"Well, it does look much straighter already. Definitely an improvement," said La Trianon.

"Yes, we would have said so before, but we didn't want it to go to your head," added La Dodée.

"They said I'd have to sleep in them, and I swore I would. I'd do anything to be pretty like other girls, but now I hurt so much I wish you'd cut me out." It had been a hard day, with many shocks. I found the tears running down my face for no reason at all.

"Oh, don't do that. Give it a try. We make something right here that ought to put you right to sleep. Just promise you won't take it in the daytime. She would never forgive us if it spoiled your talent for water reading." La Dodée always seemed sympathetic.

"Tell me— You asked a question, now I get one," said La Trianon. "You speak so well, you must come from a good family. Why are you here alone? What makes you want to suffer pain and dishonour to join a world you know nothing about? You could be reading to your old father, or embroidering in one of those comfortable convents for rich girls . . ." Her words brought it all back to me, and I couldn't answer for a while. Then I looked at her – her stiff, narrow face, her hair pushed under her white cap – and into her dark, too-old eyes.

"Revenge," I said. "There is a man I hate. *She* has promised to make me strong enough to destroy him."

"Only one?" observed La Trianon. "My, you are young."

After supper, they compounded something from several of the bottles on the shelves and poured it into a glass of cordial. Seated in their little reception parlour, among the astrological charts, I felt the stuff go to work. A delicious limpness crept over my body; my brain felt all damp, and my thoughts became slow and dreamy. The pain left as if it had all been a fantasy.

"How are you feeling now?" they asked.

"Lovely. What was in that stuff?"

"Oh, this and that. But mostly opium. Remember, not in the daytime."

"I never noticed before . . . your parlour looks so nice. See how the candle flames each make a little circle of light around themselves . . . almost like faces . . ."

"And that's the girl who talked Desgrez out of following her home. She certainly seems different now." ·

"Desgrez. Who is he, really?"

"Him? He's the head of the officers of the watch, and La Reynie's right hand, but La Reynie doesn't mix in with the lowlife. La Reynie gives the orders; Desgrez does the arresting. Beware of him, if you ever see him again. Of course, he may not look the same. They say he's fond of disguises." La Trianon's face looked serious.

"Just see the way the smoke goes up, like a little blue thread. The candles could be hanging; perhaps you should put garlands in your parlour. They'd look so festive – black is so plain."

"It's not our business to look festive. It's supposed to be mysterious in here. That's what keeps the clients coming back, buying our potions and horoscopes. That little *frisson* of fear, that they are stepping into another world, the world of the occult. What we really need is a skull. Or maybe a skeleton. Yes, a skeleton would give the place a certain tone. It would add to business no end." La Dodée looked speculatively at a somewhat barren corner beside a little niche with a curtain drawn across it, which a skeleton might fill nicely.

"Tell me," I asked, feeling all warm and lazy inside, "is La Voisin secretly one of you – a hermaphrodite?"

"Her? Hardly." La Dodée snickered. "A new man every day, that's what she has. Picks 'em up like melons in the market and parades them home in front of that silly old husband of hers. Everyone, from titles down to nobodies. Just now she likes magicians, but for a while it was alchemists – and then she has an affair going on with the executioner. But I suppose you'd count that as business..."

"You should show more respect," La Trianon interrupted her. "Her ears are everywhere." She looked at me and seemed relieved to see whatever it was she saw in my face. "If you were not already aware, you soon enough shall be. We all belong to one great society, but not all are chosen for initiation into our true mysteries. Some remain for ever in the outer circle, weaklings who are content to eat the scraps from our table. But *she* has placed her hand on you, and so this I can tell you. We of the Ancient Ways are rulers of life and death in this city, and Catherine Montvoisin is the greatest of the witches among us. She is our queen." La Trianon's face grew hard, exalted, with these last words, and I felt suddenly that I had been drawn into a whirlpool of insanity. My little notebooks, a frail raft of reason, could never save me from drowning in it.

That night I had strange dreams. I dreamed I was being pursued by a faceless man. Mother was in it somehow, but she had become huge and hideous. The streets of Paris had twisted into an endless maze, and I ran frantically through them in search of something precious I had lost, the faceless man hard on my heels to steal it from me if I found it. Just as it was there – what was it? A house? I turned to see the faceless man looming above me, a knife in his hand. As I shuddered and my eyes fluttered open to stare into the dark, I realised I was lying on iron bars, strapped in tight. The pain was soaking through my crushed bones like acid. I fumbled by the bedside and found the half-full bottle they had left me and slid back into the sea of eerie dreams.

The next day I was delivered by La Voisin's own carriage to a new address, where I should stay for a week or so until my patroness was sure that Desgrez had been thrown off the scent.

"After all, my dear," La Dodée said as she bundled up my notebooks with a generous-sized jar of the sleeping syrup, "you are not really one of us yet. *We* have taken a blood oath and trained ourselves against torture, so that we will not betray one another. But *you* can't even stand a tightly laced corset." It was true. The dull ache spread through my body, sitting or standing. The tall shoe wore blisters on my twisted foot, and the muscles of my legs, unaccustomed to the new way of balancing, burned like fire.

The new place was a room under the eaves of a big old house in the Faubourg Saint-Antoine. There I was to stay with a dismal old sorceress called La Lépère, whose occupation had something to do with whatever unsavoury activities went on downstairs. I never saw the one-eyed coachman again. Later I heard he'd been sent out of town and established with a concession in hired chairs at Rouen. A seamstress visited me in the new rooms with a second-hand gown in bottle-green wool with vulgar yellow-satin trim more suited to the Italian comedy than the street. I hated it beyond measure. This she altered to fit me, and the telltale grey dress vanished. La Lépère observed it all, saying, "My, she does set a store by this venture, Madame High and Mighty! Playing games with the gentry. High-class customers she wants; more, more, more! And me, I work so hard and never make a penny at it. I sez a prayer for every one of 'em, and pays the sexton a bit of something to see them rightly buried in a corner of the church yard. But her – everything she touches turns to money!" She squinted at me as the seamstress knelt at my feet, marking the hem of the hideous gown for turning up. "At least she's paying me proper for keeping *you*, Miss Fancy! Where you from, that you speak so high, and look so low?"

"From out of town," I said, annoyed at her.

"That's what they all say. Don't see why you'd be any different, now that I think about it."

It was a great relief to at last escape the complainings of the most unsuccessful witch in Paris and to be out again, under the high, clear December sky, bundled into a *vinaigrette* with the unspeakable green-and-yellow dress decently hidden beneath an old homespun cloak. The cold wind whistled between the buildings on the narrow streets and rattled at the chimneys. With one hand I clutched a bundle of my few possessions and with the other I held on to a vast hat, which, with a heavy scarf that muffled my face, was sufficient to maintain my anonymity. The man in the shafts of the *vinaigrette* had the family shoes on; his wife, who pushed from behind, her skirts tucked up about her powerful calves, had wrapped her feet and legs in rags.

Beggars who staggered across the frozen cobblestones to extend their hands were stopped by her pungent string of insults, which always ended with "Why don't you try working for a living, eh, you street louse?" The streets were full of women with baskets and servants in livery, for there were feasts to prepare, candles and wood to be bought, messages and invitations to be extended. Now and then a passing carriage would push everyone to the walls, for there was no place in the narrow streets to walk safely. Chairs were popular in this season, for the bearers could carry them straight up the stairs and into the house, so that callers did not have to risk their satin slippers in the icy mud.

As we passed Saint-Nicolas des Champs, I saw a man in a fur-trimmed suit emerge from the church, in pursuit of a lady in a scarlet cloak with a white fur muff. A carriage drew up, and the lady, without a backward glance, allowed herself to be assisted in. As the carriage pulled away, I recognised the arrogant profile of the Chevalier de Saint-Laurent. Uncle. Monster. Oh, if there were a just God, He would have blasted him there where he stood! Uncle turned on his heel, and for a moment, his scornful gaze rested on the *vinaigrette*. I turned my head away, but for a moment our eyes met, and fear and humiliation raced through me. Stop this, I told myself fiercely. He doesn't recognise you. He can't. When I looked back again, he was gone.

"So, it is Madame Pasquier's daughter, the little girl who doesn't believe in the Devil, grown large. What is a girl like that doing, having a gown made for her at La Voisin's expense, eh?" La Vigoreux, the tailor's wife with whom I had once pawned so many things for Mother, had exchanged the secret sign and shown me into the well-remembered establishment on the Rue Courtauvilain. A fire was leaping on the hearth in the workroom that stood behind the front door. An apprentice was stitching horsehair into the hem of a vast gown of burgundy-coloured satin. Measuring tapes, pincushions, and scissors lay upon the immense cutting table. Mathurin Vigoreux was due to return any moment from the Marais, where he was delivering a Christmas gown.

"I'm learning to make my own living," I answered as she

helped me out of my cloak and hung it on a peg. Spying the hideous dress, she burst into laughter.

"Not in *that*, I hope, unless she is planning for you to open a mummer's booth at the Foire Saint-Germain."

"There was an accident to my own gown," I sniffed.

"Yes, I imagine there was, since when the daughter of *feu* Monsieur Pasquier vanished right about the time the contents of his will became known, the police were here to get a complete description of her mourning gown. I was relieved when they identified her body on a slab in the Châtelet. That looked like the end of it. Suicide of despair, they said. She was devoted to him. Good, I said. The police will clear out of it. But then they were back. Worse than rats in the kitchen! The gown, it seems, was not found among the victims' clothing that is hung on the hooks above the bodies. After seeing a scrap of material I'd had made into a little reticule, they decided the dress had simply been too valuable, and someone had stolen it from the Châtelet." She looked at me speculatively.

"You look different from when you were last here. Thinner. Older. Straighter. She's done something with your face. I almost didn't recognise you for a moment there. What's her plan? She wouldn't go to this trouble if you didn't have . . . a use."

"I'm going to go into business," I said, careful not to reveal too much.

"And disappear from your loving family, eh? Clearly, you are a girl who loves life – and is far cleverer than the ordinary sort. Tell me, what sort of business? Surely, you're not going to distil rose water – not in a gown of black silk costing a thousand *écus*."

"I'm going into fortune-telling. I can read water."

Her laughter rang through the little fitting room, and the apprentice, an ill-favoured youth badly marked with the smallpox, looked up. Then, apparently used to her fancies, he appeared to go back to work. "And you, not even a believer," she said, looking at me speculatively. "The little girl who once looked me in the eye and said all fortunes were false. This is a rare joke on all of us. To think, even I never suspected, and I have watched you grow up."

I had much to ponder as the measurements were taken and

the fabric laid before me for my inspection. Even the quaint drawing of the gown, with its Spanish farthingale and little ruff, scarcely distracted me.

When faced with the illogical, one must expand the sphere of logic to include rules of logic for that which is not logic. This is the only possibility in a world that works according to the rules of rationality.

"Well now, look in the mirror. What do you think of yourself?" La Voisin's voice sounded jovial and expansive. It was the afternoon of Christmas Eve, and her house was already filling with members of the "philanthropic society". The excellent smells of an immense dinner were driving me mad, for we had begun our fast in anticipation of communion at the midnight Mass. For you must know that in those corrupt times, when libertines confessed only on their deathbeds, and soldiers and freethinkers almost never, the witches of Paris were devout Mass goers. Only the King and his court equalled them for regularity of observance: both were equally ignorant of Holy Scripture, and both believed more in the Devil than in God. But because without God there is no Devil either, the witches regularly paid the Being above His due, while they looked to the being below for their livelihood.

So the entire company had already confessed to Father Davot of the little church of Bonne Nouvelle that stood at the corner of the Rue Beauregard and the Rue Bonne Nouvelle. Then that worthy would join us when, after midnight Mass, we would all fall upon the splendid things that were now tempting us from the kitchen. In the meantime, my new gown had been delivered, after a frantic effort involving the hiring of three temporary assistants to help with the sewing, as well as the engagement of one of the best-known professional embroiderers in the city. It really did feel like Christmas, after all.

"Not bad, not bad at all," pronounced La Trianon to La Dodée, as I stood before the rectangular glass in the tapestry-hung bedroom. The mirror was set in a frame like a picture. I emerged from the chiaroscuro like an ancient portrait. I was dressed in rich black, with velvet trim, all embroidered with black silk thread and jet beads, like a nobleman's widow of times gone by. Beneath the little starched ruff that covered my neck, a heavy silver crucifix – on loan only until I could afford to procure my own – shone against the black. My hair had been done in the style of an old portrait of Marie de' Medici. I had thrown back the translucent black veil attached to the tiny black beaded cap the better to see my face. All pale and strained with the pain of the heavy corset beneath the gown, it floated above the antique lace like an eerie, disembodied mask in the dark. It was an alien face, one that I hardly recognised beneath the white powder and high, artificially arched eyebrows: the look of extreme age hidden in the mask of youth. Beautiful, in its own way, and entirely unexpected. My back, still shrunken against the long iron rods that barely held it upright, looked somehow shrivelled with age. A tall ebony walking stick, nearly my own height, trimmed with a ring of silver and a bunch of black ribbons, finished off the picture as well as preserving my balance and disguising the last of my limp. I looked exactly as if I had stepped from a previous century, an ancient woman preserved by hideous secret arts that had given her the semblance of eternal youth. I was totally enchanted with the dramatic effect. A woman of mystery. A new person.

"Unbelievable." Le Sage, the magician, shook his head, looking first from me to La Voisin, and then back again, as if he couldn't get over the change. The sorceress's black eyes shone as she inspected her creation.

"I told you. I saw it from the first. Now it's perfect. Have you made the arrangements?"

"Yes, I called on the Comte de Bachimont yesterday. Told him I'd found her as a boarder in a tiny attic room in the Convent of the Ursulines – nearly starving, of course. He said I must bring her to him immediately, before you heard of her, or you'd surely snatch her up to make your reputation. He's desperately in debt and thinks he can use her to gain entrée into circles he hasn't yet borrowed from."

"Brilliant. Now remember," she addressed me, "not a word to the count or countess of your connection to me. They are not *of us*, you understand. They are connected with the Chevalier de Vanens and his crowd. Alchemists, with a laboratory in Lyons. Possibly false coiners, as well, if my suspicions are right. Once they have introduced you into better circles, drop them – but gently. You don't want to arouse suspicion—"

Her little speech of advice was broken into by the sound of a racket from downstairs. "Damn him, he's at it again!" she exclaimed as she bolted down the stairs, followed closely by Le Sage. "Don't!" I could hear Margot shrieking. There was the sound of children wailing, a crashing and a banging. La Trianon and La Dodée followed down the narrow stair, and I trailed behind them, cautiously feeling my way down each step, for stairs posed the ultimate danger to my new equilibrium. By the time I arrived, the quarrel was deep in progress. The cupboard doors of the witch's little cabinet room hung open, their locks pried off by force. Books with odd diagrams were strewn about, and stoppered bottles rolled underfoot. Antoine Montvoisin, still clutching several books to his skinny chest, was being beaten insensible by Le Sage, who battered at the frail-looking man with his walking stick while Marie-Marguerite tried to pull Le Sage off her father.

"And just what do you think you are doing?" shrieked La Voisin, white with wrath.

"Burning them. Burning the filthy things. I'm sick of this dirty business. Better a crust of bread in honour than a feast that comes straight from the Devil."

"You're eager enough to eat the feast when someone else provides it. Who got you out of debtor's prison, you mewling baby? I support ten mouths, and the biggest of them is yours. What have you ever done for me but fail in business? And now I've made a success of my business, you can't stand it. Put my *grimoires* back or, I swear, you'll not live until tomorrow."

"You think I don't know what you do, you with all your fine talk and society friends? The stove behind the tapestry? The ghastly pavilion in the garden? When they come to your garden parties, they dance on corpses, those society ladies. And they are gilded monsters, just like you."

"Put them back," she said coldly, towering over him as he knelt on the floor, her eyes blazing. The thin little man in the dirty dressing gown crawled along the floor, picking up the spilled books, as his daughter averted her eyes. Suddenly La Voisin turned and saw me standing in the open door.

"What did you hear?"

"Nothing," I answered. How desperately annoying. I had traded one maniacal household for another. Didn't anyone live decently in this benighted city? And, after all, if one is taken up by the greatest witch in Paris, one expects better. Grandeur. Mystery. No sordid domestic conflict.

"Good," she answered. "You learn very quickly. Margot, see to the dinner. I will not have my perfect evening spoiled by any *man*." She looked disdainfully at her husband, who was wiping his nose on the sleeve of his dressing gown.

I have long since been asked what dinner among witches is like. Do they feast on human flesh? Do they arrive on broomsticks? These are the prejudices of the uninformed. The witches arrived on foot, fashionably gowned, cloaked, and hooded, having strolled from midnight Mass at Notre-Dame de Bonne Nouvelle the few blocks to La Voisin's elegant little residence. The company that joined the witches there was cultivated and distinguished – *avocats*, an architect, and various priests and abbés, both frocked and unfrocked. Father Davot, the family confessor from Notre-Dame de Bonne Nouvelle, joined us, as did Le Sage, the magician, who was also La Voisin's latest lover.

On a well-set table, masses of candles, white, not black, were burning in handsome silver candelabra. There were hams smoked with anise, capons and ducks in savoury sauce, rich soup and pastries and sweets of extraordinary delicacy. The service dishes were of silver, with the exception of several huge tureens of exquisitely painted porcelain. There was, of course, a tiny *contretemps* during the soup course, when Margot jostled Monsieur Montvoisin's arm just as he was about to lift the spoon to his mouth, causing him to spill upon the lovely white tablecloth. His wife gave him an evil glare, as he looked up at Margot, and then, glancing at the puddle on the cloth, he ordered the maid to remove the soup plate with its contents untasted. "I'll just put it out in the kitchen for the rats," Margot said saucily, as she removed the offending dish.

Aside from that, the evening went perfectly. Father Davot ate second helpings of everything, and Le Sage drank too much wine and began to sing. As the guest of honour in my new persona, I picked at the capons stuffed with oysters in caper sauce and pronounced the dish "too modern", comparing it unfavourably to the simple and healthful dishes served in the time of Henri IV, when everything was boiled in the same pot. I deplored modern manners and the decay of the times with a fervour that would have delighted my grandmother. I tried out antique gestures and turns of phrase, to be met with awe and applause at the table. I found it infinitely gratifying to be the object of admiration. How interesting and amusing the witches are, I thought as I let them fill my glass again. How much more delightful and variegated their lives than those of ordinary women! And as I spoke, I remembered Grandmother. In fact, I became Grandmother. I took her inside of me, as it were, and she consoled me by her presence. It was lovely. I shall buy myself a parrot at the first opportunity, I thought to myself.

That night was the first of many triumphs for me. The candles were not burned down, the last song sung, or the last bottle emptied until the hour before dawn. The last of the stars had faded, and rosy light was chasing the black from above the Porte Saint-Denis when I departed in a chair. A new day. I felt content beyond words when a stray passer-by, still drunk beyond words from the night that had just passed, stopped to stare with awe at the mysterious veiled woman in black.

TWELVE

The following week, all eager to try out my new self, I dove into the society of impecunious nobles and shady foreigners that infested Paris, clung to the fringes of the court, and jostled unceasingly in competition for favour in this world, everything was for sale, nothing incapable of being traded on the market for personal advantage. The luckiest farmed taxes or courted heiresses, the less fortunate sold their possessions or informed to the police for money while awaiting the coming of better times. Gentility of manners and the ability to put up a good front were one's ticket of entrance, but to advance in the game more was necessary. A nice figure or pretty profile, in either a man or a woman, was counted an advantage, but a small one; rumours of an inheritance or a lucky streak at the gaming tables were better. A connection with the King, no matter how tenuous, was best of all. In this struggle to be seen, to have something about oneself worthy of gossip for at least five minutes, it was a great advantage to be a hundred-and-fifty-year-old woman who read the future in water glasses and could be persuaded to part with a jar of her youth ointment for the skin.

"It's a terrible curse, eternal youth. I wouldn't wish it on anybody," I told the Comtesse de Bachimont over the remains of the *ragoût*, as her maid, who was also her cook, housekeeper, and go-between to the pawnbroker, cleared the dishes for the next course. "Besides, the formula was made up over a hundred years ago. I have no idea whether it will work any more."

"But your skin – so unlined, so pale . . ." She couldn't resist passing her hand across my cheek.

"It is but the pallor of the tomb, Madame. I have lived beyond my time. But it is well my dear husband, the Marquis, never lived to see the corruption of this age." I dabbed at my eyes, but carefully so as not to disturb the sooty stain that made them look so interestingly sunken. She bought a jar.

"You read the future in water glasses, I hear," rumbled the

Comte de Bachimont as the candles burned low and the last of the supper was taken away. The dim light concealed the oddly barren look of their rented rooms. At the rate the furniture was being sold, I calculated they'd be back in Lyons before the turn of the new year. I'd need to work fast. Monsieur le Comte tried to put his hand beneath my skirt at the table. I didn't need to move *that* fast.

"My dear Marquise," – another guest, the physician Dr Rabel, leaned forward across the table – "isn't this gift, ah, usually confined to young girls?"

"Dear Doctor Rabel, after the age of ninety one loses all interest in sex . . . entirely . . ." I pushed away the count's hand. ". . . and, as it were . . . um, re-virginises. It was after that that the talent appeared."

"*Hmm*," he said in a learned voice, "yes, definitely. That would account for it. But tell me, the formula didn't work uniformly . . . that is to say, you are not fully youthful, um, all over? That is to say, when the abbé purchased the formula from Nicolas Flamel, didn't you then drink it, once it was made up?"

"It is a grief to me to lay open a sin for which I so long ago obtained absolution, but the formula was an ointment. The abbé used up most of it on himself, being too selfish to think of me first, even though I had sacrificed my hope of Paradise for him. When he applied the remainder of the formula to me, he started at the top, but there wasn't enough" – I dabbed at my eyes again – "and the second batch, you understand, was never as strong as the first . . ." I was pleased with my artistic embellishment of the skin-cream story. Creativity is, after all, the greatest satisfaction of the human mind. I composed my face in a distant, tragic look.

The company clucked in sympathy. What a selfish fellow, to leave a nice girl like me only half eternally youthful! I was planning how to expand the tale in the most interesting fashion, when Rabel broke in with a request for a reading. I was in my element. "I must have absolute quiet," I pronounced in an oracular voice. "The candles must be placed at equal distances around the vase, so as not to disturb the image." I sent them hustling about on little errands, adjusting the cloth, fetching the strange black bag in which I kept my round glass vase and its stand. I knew I required no picture at all to give a lovely reading.

La Voisin's intelligence network, and the training she had given me in the science of physiognomy, or the reading of features, were quite sufficient. If the pictures came up, it was a bonus; something to embellish my creation.

I spread a blood-red cloth, covered with cabbalistic designs, under the globular vase. I demanded "absolutely pure" water to fill it, and the cook, in awe, filtered the water through five layers of cheesecloth before I poured it through a decorated funnel that looked like solid silver into the magic vessel. I spent a long time selecting the correct stirring rod. The glass? The dragon's head? The serpent? I could feel the intensity of their gazes all directed at me, me. At last, I was popular and admired, just as the witch had promised. I was intoxicated with it.

I chanted, I stirred, and then, odd as it always was, I felt the eerie relaxation, the strange feeling of the nerves of the body vanishing, and a picture started to come up.

"How interesting, Monsieur de Vanens. You are in the image with Monsieur de Bachimont. You are selling something . . . ah, it looks like an ingot of silver . . . to an officer of the crown. Hmm, now he is signing a paper." Is it alchemist's false silver, being sold to the mint as real, or is it real silver, and stolen? I couldn't tell what kind of transaction it was, so I left the interpretation of the image to my watchers.

"It worked," breathed the Countess, leaning so close that she fogged the glass.

"Success. By God, the formula worked. The mint," said the Chevalier de Vanens. Well, well, false coiners after all. And probably going to jail for a nice long time, too. But they didn't want another reading, and I didn't want to offer to look for bad news. That was the problem with the little reflections. Their meaning was never completely clear. It was like looking through a window into a room where people came, went, and spoke unheard to the watcher. What were they saying? What had gone on before? What did it mean? Interpretation was everything. People think it's easy, seeing the future; you'll know everything, win bets, move before your house burns down, speculate in land. Well, it's not that way at all. Most people don't even understand the present. Why should they understand glimpses of the future?

That evening I sat up alone with a candle, cataloguing the

latest images according to the date seen, persons involved, and estimated time of fulfilment. Even visions require rational analysis.

The images pose an interesting problem, I wrote. *Precisely how are they related to the future? Either*

(I) they represent the actual future, which is absolute and immutable,

or

(II) they represent a probable future, if events continue as they are now going. If (I), then God has determined the future of the world at its beginning, and there is no free will. I stopped and looked at what I had written. It looked handsome there on the paper, all laid out with rational structure, like Euclid's geometry. Order and logic, taming the unknown.

Subconclusion (I.A.): God may have created the world and abandoned it to its own workings, like a piece of clockwork.

(I.A.i.): If God cannot interfere in the world, then God is not all-powerful. But God is by definition all-powerful, and so therefore if (I) is true, then (I.A.i.a.) there is no God according to our current understanding and definition of the term. If God exists but chooses never to intervene (I.A.ii.), then effectively (I.A.i.a.) is also true. The position of the libertines, I thought. Do as you wish. It makes no difference.

Now I turned to the analysis of position number (II): *If (II), then God allows free will, or human choice, to reshape the future. This occurs either because God is not all-powerful (I.A.i.) and the rest follows, or because (II.B.): Grace exists, and so does God.* This conclusion was a great puzzlement to me, because rationality should lead us to arrive at truth. I decided on the only reasonable test that I could observe and catalogue:

Test: 1. Bring up image of my personal future.

2. Create through free will actions that will change the image.

3. See if the image is modified.

But try as I might, I could not bring up an image relating to my own future.

THIRTEEN

Inspector Moreau was taken aback when he saw the cluster of carriages and chairs crowded in the street around the widow Bailly's modest establishment. He had spent the morning checking the new residents of the boarding-houses and rented rooms of his quarter for escaped criminals, soldiers absent without leave, and foreigners of dubious occupation. But interviewing this new resident would obviously take much longer. The respectable widow had notified him immediately of her mysterious new resident. Enquiries of the neighbours and of the widow's sullen, spotty-faced younger daughter had assured him that the mysterious woman was not a prostitute. In fact, she had no after-hours male visitors at all, and those who did consult her were confined to the parlour, their privacy barely assured by a screen that concealed two chairs and a large, ornate water vase that the widow referred to with great respect as "Madame's oracle glass".

As long as it was only fortune-telling she was doing, it was legal. But Inspector Moreau carried concealed in his coat a half-dozen spoons ornamented with the crest of a prominent family and had omitted to wear the blue suit and white-plumed hat of his police livery.

After a long wait, during which he occupied himself by inspecting the ghastly coloured tumours on the screen, which some amateur artist had obviously considered to resemble towers, he finally was able to take a seat beside the table with the oracle glass. The woman opposite him was tiny, neat, and expensively clad in a black silk mourning gown.

"You, too, have experienced a tragic loss?" he began, taking out his handkerchief.

"My dear husband, the marquis, in a hunting accident. It seems like only yesterday, but it was, in fact, August sixth. The day is burned into my grief-stricken memory." Her accent was refined, her mode of speech, educated. She could only be from the upper classes. But it was impossible to have been both married and a convent boarder this past August. Moreau felt it was time to make subtle enquiries.

"So recently? How stricken you must be to lose your beloved life partner only this past August." The marquise looked at him from behind her long dark lashes. Her face was quite white with heavy makeup. It was hard to tell how old she was. Her grey eyes glittered:

"Monsieur Moreau, my profound sensitivity leads me to feel as if it were only yesterday," she sighed. "But my poor, dear Louis met his unfortunate end on 6 August 1548." She dabbed at her eyes delicately with a lace-embroidered handkerchief. Moreau was impassive, but inside he had a powerful desire to chuckle with appreciation. A magnificent charlatan, this fortune-teller. He unfolded a lengthy false tale of woe, pausing at those places where the more sinister sort of fortune-teller might offer a quack potion, an illicit and criminal Mass, or, possibly, worse. Madame de Morville heard him out, her eyes sympathetic, and then went into an odd sort of semi-trance, staring into the depths of the glass. She seemed to be amused at what she saw, then looked at him with the oddest smile and said,

"Monsieur Moreau, all these troubles you are burdened with will soon vanish as if you had only imagined them. You will receive a commendation from one you respect and experience an increase in your income."

"But I need the money now," insisted Moreau, feigning a desperate tone. "If I can't repay the loan, I'll be imprisoned. Tell me, can you recommend someone to pawn these?"

Madame de Morville looked over the obviously stolen spoons.

"You are required by fate to take them back to where they came from," she said in a quiet voice. "If you succeed in pawning them, your fortune will take a very negative turn."

True enough, thought Moreau. So far, her advice has been eminently sensible and quite within the law. He paid her fee and departed to write up his day's report.

Marquise de Morville, Rue du Port-aux-Choux at the house of the widow Bailly. The marquise is a woman of indeterminate age and good understanding, who dispenses intelligent advice to

*the besotted and the silly for a modest fee. She does not sell love
powders, deal in substances passed under the chalice, or provide
referrals for other illegal activities. Safe.* As he poured sand
across the paper to dry it, he couldn't help wondering, even
though he knew it was foolish, just when he would receive that
commendation from Monsieur de La Reynie.

FOURTEEN

I was, at this time of my first prosperity, living in a furnished room in a boarding-house in the Rue du Port-aux-Choux. The mistress of this modest but eminently respectable abode was convinced that I had come fresh from boarding at the rather too austere Convent of the Ursulines upon the receipt of a small inheritance. The splendours of her cook and her excellent featherbeds accounted for the change. My rank and a fortuitous reading concerning her elder daughter's marriage had filled her with awe; thenceforth I ranked above her previous star boarder, a snuff-taking abbé with mournful, brown, spaniel eyes, who supplemented his tiny income by doing translations of Italian pornographic works.

For a small consideration, I was additionally allowed to receive visitors and clients in her little parlour behind the clumsily hand-painted screen produced by her second daughter, the unmarriageable one. My landlady acquired yet another small sum by reporting my presence to the police, who investigated my business and found it honest, at least insofar as deceiving the gullible is legal, though not meritorious.

The greater sorts of clients I visited in their houses, tipping the widow's little kitchen boy to retrieve a chair or fiacre from the hiring stands, depending on the distance and the weather. Within scarcely a week I had been to three unimportant salons and referred two ladies with unfaithful lovers to La Voisin as well as a man in search of a buried treasure hidden by his great-uncle during the Fronde. I was beginning to be able to compare the merits of the kitchens of several great houses. I felt like quite the woman-about-town. Yet though my life was in many ways mending, I still avoided public places where I might encounter my uncle or brother, who could unmask me and, as my male relatives, claim everything I had, even my freedom.

By the end of January, I found I had cleared the substantial sum of thirty-eight *écus*, which was not bad for a beginner. And so on a chill, misty morning in the beginning of February, I went to meet La Voisin on a Sunday after Mass to give her the proceeds of my first real work and my accounting.

The cold sun had just broken through the heavy morning mist, and the bells were still reverberating through the narrow streets of Villeneuve as the modest portals of Notre-Dame de Bonne Nouvelle swung open to disgorge a stream of jostling, gossiping Mass goers. Pushing my way through the dispersing crowd, I found I was following in the wake of a large, hunched old woman dressed in a flowing black cloak and an extravagantly overdecorated hat, who cleared her way by prodding the slow or unwary with an immense, gold-trimmed staff. Her face was heavily painted, and there was a malign glitter in her eye. Another witch, I thought; I'm getting to recognise them. Who could this one be?

My patroness, elegant in a fur-trimmed hood and well-cut, narrow-waisted jacket, had flung back her handsome embroidered mantle while she paused before the church door to pull on a pair of scented kid gloves. She looked up to see the gaudy old thing approaching her like a galleon in full sail; an expression of intense annoyance crossed her face. The old woman's heavily painted face broke into a knowing grin.

"And how is La Voisin today?" I heard the old woman ask. "Well, I trust? And how is the husband? Still alive?" She cackled uproariously at her own joke as La Voisin pursed her lips with disgust and walked quickly away without answering. The old woman continued to push her way into the church, where she evidently had business. My patroness, still icy with distaste at the encounter, spied me at a distance of several paces and made a hurried little gesture that I should meet her around the corner, away from the strolling, chattering crowd of Mass goers.

"That ghastly woman. I wish you to stay away from her. What on earth brought you here now? Go to my house by the side door and meet me there."

Offended, I walked the little way to her house, where the

door was opened by her husband, still clad in his old dressing gown. He seemed to be the only member of the household who had not gone to the late Mass.

"Come in," he said, as he shuffled back into the house ahead of me, trailed by an orange cat and her two half-grown kittens. "I suppose you'll want a seat," he added as he sat down in an accustomed armchair and one cat leaped on to his lap. A second took a perch on his shoulder.

"You look well," he said, after a long silence. He inspected me as I sat on the little straight-backed chair he'd pointed out to me. "Prosperous." He stroked the big orange cat on his lap. A rumbling purr rose from beneath his hand. "Less like a drowned rat than the first day I saw you." I didn't say anything. I was offended. Geneviève Pasquier could never have looked like a drowned rat. It's not a proper way for a person from a good family to look, no matter what circumstances they find themselves in. The silence sat very heavy among the brocade chairs and dark, ornate furniture that crowded the long, high-ceilinged room.

"Of course, when I first met *her*, she was the most beautiful woman in the world. I was madly in love. Can you imagine? Madly in love." He stared at the wall for a long time, as if the tapestry could answer. I couldn't imagine it. Gaunt, unshaven, and frail, he didn't look like a lover, a man who could whisper gallantries, or sing to the music of mandolins.

"I had a ring made up – of emeralds and pearls. How her black eyes flashed when she saw it! She was made to wear emeralds. It is the tone of her skin. You . . . should not wear them. They will make your skin look sallow. No . . . for you, a necklace of sapphires. Sapphires and diamonds. Your skin will look like the snow. The eyes will pick up the colour – the grey take on a bluish tint."

There was something eerily repulsive about all this. He sounded as if he were half asleep, talking in a dream. I could hear pattering on the floor above, the sound of something rolling, and the cries of children.

"The creditors . . . put the children into the street . . ." he went on in the same dreamy voice, like a sleepwalker. "As they were taking me to prison, they saw the ring on her hand. 'Hand it over,' they said and tore it from her finger. Her eyes flashed black, like wells of poison, like night storm-clouds that contain deadly lightning. 'I will repay,' she said, and her voice was steel. They laughed. They are all dead now, Mademoiselle. All dead. And she has sucked away my vital essence. I am dry. A shrivelled leaf. A withered apple—" There was a bang as the front door was flung open, and La Voisin entered by the black parlour. At the same time, Margot, Nanon, the cook, and assorted members of the household rattled into the kitchen door at the back of the house.

"Antoine, I will not have you boring the little marquise. Come, Mademoiselle, into my cabinet. Have you brought a full accounting?"

"Of course, Madame," I answered as I followed her into her little cabinet. The fire was out; she left on her heavy cloak but drew off the high gauntleted Italian gloves, finger by finger. They were dyed an exquisite deep blue. The scent of them filled the cold little room.

"That Antoine. As useless as my old tomcat. Can't catch rats, can't make kittens. And yet I keep them both on, though I can't imagine why..." She unlocked the cupboard door, hunted among her ledgers, and took down the volume *P*.

"Thirty-eight *écus*," she said, her black eyes glowing at the sight of the gold. "My, my. You do well so quickly." She stared at me suddenly, her eyes trying to pierce me through. "You haven't held any back, have you?"

"No, Madame. Here is the accounting. Paper, pen, and ink. Transport, and a pair of heavy stockings because the shoe was making blisters." She looked fondly at the pile of coins on the table, and then back to the sheet with my account.

"And what is this payment to La Trianon?"

"A sleeping draught. The corset is painful."

"Painful? Of course it's painful. You need the pain. It will harden your resolve to become rich. Give up the opium. Steel your mind with hate and revenge instead. Remember that it is *him* or you. Opium will undermine you." She struck her pen through this item. I resolved to hold back a portion of my next fee and to keep my purchase secret. I needed opium now. It drowned pain and stifled night terrors. It was the only cure for remembrance and grief. I was sure La Dodée would find it in her interest not to tell. After all, I was now a good customer.

My patroness looked up at me, for I still stood as she sat, making entries in her ledger. Her voice was calculating and her smile false as she said, "A lady such as you should not be without a maid. Who is lacing you up now? A servant of that silly widow?"

"Her youngest daughter helps me dress."

"Let me see those stays. *Hmm.* You are still bent. She isn't strong enough to tighten them right. You're still sleeping in them, aren't you?"

"I wouldn't have needed the sleeping draught if I weren't," I answered in a sarcastic voice. She smiled in return, but too many teeth showed.

"Just keep them tight, and soon you'll be out of them at night. I think I know just the maid you need . . ." I didn't like the sound of this. A spy to keep me in order. She must be afraid I would grow independent. I changed the subject.

"That woman who greeted you," I said, "who is she? One of us?"

"One of us, I suppose, in the larger sense," La Voisin sniffed, distracted by her memory of the offence. "That is Marie Bosse. You won't find that she's your type. Entirely illiterate, and adds on her fingers. She practises the Old Arts, but she has no business talent. Of course, she envies me. She wanted to be Chosen, instead of me. But who would have her? She's careless, and a drunkard. Besides, she was married to a *horse dealer*." La Voisin's voice dripped snobbery. A good thing La Voisin had raised the profession of witchcraft to be so elegant, I thought. I certainly had no desire to be associated with the vulgar widow of a *horse dealer*.

"Madame should not grieve for ever over a husband so long dead. How much more youthful you would look, my dear Marquise, were you to robe yourself in the fresh colours of spring." The elderly, snuff-taking Provençal abbé leaned his face so close as he spoke that I could feel his breath on my neck. Across the table, the widow Bailly abruptly ceased dishing out the soup and stared disapprovingly at him.

"I am too old to concern myself with the vanities of this world," I sniffed. But spring was in my heart. For the first time in my life, I wanted a new dress. A pretty one.

"Even the vanities which lead the multitudes to gather behind that screen every day in ever greater numbers?" The abbé's voice was lazy and knowing, as he gestured carelessly to the screen in the corner of the room which was both Madame Bailly's salon and dining room. Horrible man. Provençals never stop chasing women. It's a habit with them. On their deathbeds, they proposition their nurses.

"That is my charitable work, Monsieur. I spend my days helping others." I pretended to be busy breaking a roll.

"Madame la Marquise is a miracle worker, a miracle worker. A draper with his own shop and assistants. My lucky, lucky Amélie. And it all has come to pass just as she said," Madame rushed to my defence. Amélie looked at the table and blushed at the thought of her impending marriage. Brigitte, her younger sister, dowerless, sullen, and spotty faced, stared at her resentfully. The other boarders, a collection of impecunious foreigners and provincials, looked annoyed at the interruption of the meal.

"Surely, I cannot but accept the word of a hostess so charming," oozed the abbé. Madame Bailly blushed with pleasure and resumed serving the soup. The steady click, clank of soupspoons resumed. Monsieur Dulac, the notary, took up again telling of the scandal at the Foire Saint-Germain, which was only newly opened for the season before Palm Sunday.

". . . and when we arrived at the Rue de la Lingerie, all was in turmoil, stalls smashed, and a lemonade seller with a broken arm, I swear, and her whole stock spilled upon the ground. It was some young vicomte and a companion, dead drunk. They had pushed their horses into the fair and ridden them at full gallop through the alleys, waving their swords and overturning the stalls. I had narrowly missed being killed, being *killed*, if you may imagine!"

"Monsieur Dulac, you should confine yourself to the evening, when the *quality* attend, after the opera," Madame Bailly observed as her maid of all work removed the soup plates.

"As if *you'd* know," whispered Brigitte spitefully.

"And the prices are doubled, Madame Bailly," answered the notary, "and then I should have had to confine myself to looking only. Whereas today I saw a most marvellous creature for only two sous. A rarity from the far Indies – a raccoon."

"Oh, what was it like? Was it like a dragon?" queried Amélie.

"No, it was entirely covered with hair like a wolf and had an immense tail, quite striped. They are said to be as venomous as a serpent. But then, the Indies are a place of great danger. They say that there are carnivorous vines there capable of crushing a man to death and drinking his blood with their long, hollow tendrils." The company shuddered.

"*Ooo!*" exclaimed Brigitte. "Do they have one of those on display as well? It would be splendid to see it at feeding time!"

So nothing would do but that we would get up a party to go and inspect both the raccoon and the gentry that very evening, in a hired coach procured by the generous Marquise de Morville, whose charitable works had brought her ever-increasing prosperity.

"Oh, how I do love to ride in a real carriage!" enthused Brigitte, as we set off in the twilight for the grounds of the vast Abbey of Saint-Germain on the left bank of the Seine. Amélie shot her a withering glance.

The draper, a ponderous middle-aged fellow, who sat crammed beside his fiancée and her sister, announced, "When we are wed, you shall always have a carriage at your disposal, my dear Mademoiselle Bailly. Your dainty feet shall not touch the earth." Her mother sighed.

"What touching, what elegant devotion! Oh, Monsieur Leroux, you are so gallant!"

"How could it be otherwise with such a charming young person?" said the abbé, who, squashed between the widow Bailly and myself, had not yet decided behind whose waist his hand should creep. On my side, he encountered frost and hard steel, on hers, squeals and giggles. He withdrew to the more favourable side.

"Oh, look, they're lighting the street lanterns!" Brigitte pointed to a man on a ladder at the corner near the police barrier.

"Monsieur de La Reynie's finest invention," pronounced the draper. "Soon all of Paris will be as safe at night as your own bedroom, Mesdames. He has increased the watch and soon will have swept away every last beggar and thief that has disgraced our great city. Ours is an age of marvels . . ."

Our carriage had halted to let a grand equipage pass at the intersection. Its coat of arms was painted over and it was full of masked ladies and gentlemen on their way to the fair. The opera had let out. Beneath the newly lit lamp, a public notice newly affixed over several old ones caught my eye. The latest books banned by the police. Illegal to possess or print, purchase or sell, strictest penalties, etc. My scandal-loving eye searched for something interesting: *La Défence de la Réformation* – dull Protestantism. *Philosophical Reflections on Grace* – even duller Jansenism. *Observations on the Health of the State*, author unknown, pseudonym "Cato". D'Urbec, Lamotte's friend, the scholar. So this is what has become of your treatise on reform. The geometric theory of state finance has led you to the stake, if you are not in exile already. Somehow, I felt as if I had just come from a funeral.

"Banned books make the best collector's items, Madame la Marquise," the abbé remarked offhandedly, inspecting the place where my gaze had fallen. You ought to know, you old reprobate, I thought, since they are your trade.

"A man who would own such things is no better than a traitor who would undermine the safety of the state," announced Monsieur Leroux, the draper.

"They broke a traitor on the wheel last week by torchlight on the Place de Grève," interjected Brigitte. "Everyone says it was lovely, but *Mother* wouldn't let me go."

"It's not proper for a girl to go to night executions unescorted," announced her mother.

"A woman of a certain position should always go escorted to executions. I would of course always escort my wife to such commendable moral exhibitions personally," said Monsieur Leroux, clasping Amélie's hand.

"Of course, there's a great deal of money to be made in banned books," suggested the abbé wickedly, for he had observed the draper closely during the ride and had taken his measure.

"Money?" Monsieur Leroux's interest was aroused. "Why, surely, not very much," he added hastily.

"Oh, when *Le colloque amoureux* was banned, the price

went from twenty sols to twenty livres. And now there's not a copy to be had anywhere. It might well fetch thirty or more livres if a person could get hold of one." An ironic smile played across the face of the abbé.

"Twenty ... thirty livres? Why, that's astonishing. As a return on capital ..." The draper was lost in calculations.

"And then there's Père Dupré, who wrote anonymously to the police to denounce his own treatise attacking the Jansenists. A dull and unoriginal work; he had not been able to sell a single copy. Within a month, the entire edition sold out at ten times the original price." The abbé leaned towards the draper with a malicious smile and whispered confidentially, "Of course, it is important to have a powerful patron."

"Scandalous!" exclaimed the draper. "Still, it shows a certain commendable ambition. Far better than the disgrace of being a failure." Monsieur Leroux looked complacent. He, of course, would never consider being a failure. And to him, the patronage of the great could justify any enterprise.

We had by this time worked our way well across the Pont-Neuf, though our passage had been slowed by the crowds around a dentist on a platform, who was pulling teeth by the light of torches. But soon enough our carriage had joined the ranks of those waiting; in rows outside the fair precincts, and we had traversed the dozen steps down into the covered alleyways of the ancient fairgrounds. These were so old that they were sunken beneath ground level, as if pounded down by millions of feet over the centuries. Rows of booths, lit by thousands of candles, shone invitingly down the long alleys, which were called "streets" and named according to the goods sold in them. Vendors of lemonade, watery chocolate, and sweetmeats called out their wares. The smells of good things cooking wafted from the booths where food was sold. Many of them refurnished for the more elegant evening fair goers, had tables with white linen cloths and fine candelabra.

We strolled down the Rue de la Mercerie, to see the furniture and rare porcelains brought from Asia and the Indies. Amélie occupied her time happily exclaiming over what she would like to see in her house, once she was married. Placards announced a "*pièce à écriteaux*", one of the subterfuges by which the players at the fair evaded the official monopoly on the spoken word of the Paris theatres. The silent players could not be accused of speaking a word, for the dialogue was posted on large signs in each scene. We paused to watch two gentlemen elegantly dressed in pale silk bargaining for a vase. One of them looked so like Uncle from behind that it made me start. Surely he did not have a coat in that colour . . . The man turned, and I was relieved. No, not the Chevalier de Saint-Laurent. While my companions strolled on, marvelling at the jewels, the lace, the silver, the heaps of coloured sweetmeats and oranges, I felt cold all over, as if something I disliked might step from the shadows at any moment.

Men in strange costumes shouted the virtues of various gambling dens and tried to entice us to enter, and amid the cries of the vendors, we could hear the muffled sound of singing, accompanied by a clavier and flutes coming from one of the theatres. Why have I come here? I asked myself. They could see me, and take everything away. I walked on in a kind of trance, hardly noticing my surroundings.

A well-dressed gentleman followed by four servants in livery picked his way past us through the crowd.

"My," whispered the abbé to me, "the evening certainly does bring out a better class of people. Even the pickpockets appear to be of the upper class." His cosy, obscenely confidential tone brought me back to myself. I observed closely and, sure enough, saw a pale hand flash from its lace-decked sleeve into the pocket of a ponderous gentleman escorting two elderly ladies.

"*Ooo!* What divine earrings I see there!" cried Amélie, as she led Monsieur Leroux and the rest of us down the long, candle-lit alley called the Rue de l'Orfèvreries, where jewellery of all kinds was on display. Masked women in elegant incognito strolled with their gallants, pausing to point with a gloved hand.

"My dear friend, what a charming little brooch," we would hear in the high, cultivated voice of a court lady.

"My love, it is yours," and the gentleman would procure the desired object and present it to his mistress with a bow and a flourish.

"Ah, such pleasures; oh, my friend, I am fatigued."

"Allow me to offer you refreshment. The Duc de Vivonne

has declared that everyone must savour the new drink at the Turkish booth, which invigorates the senses most wonderfully."

"Oh, Monsieur Leroux," cried Amélie, "do let us stop there, too!"

And her affianced, anxious to distract her from the glittering display, agreed hastily.

We followed the masked couple to the Turkish booth, where we were seated near the door around one of the tables covered with fresh white linen that filled the large room. Above us stretched a vast, if rudimentary, ceiling hung with blazing chandeliers. Waiters in vast padded turbans and baggy trousers carried curious brass trays filled with tiny enamelled metal cups. A strange smell like burned cork filled the room – doubtless the Turkish beverage – but it was too late to leave gracefully.

"Surely, my dear one," I could hear the masked lady's high voice pierce the hubbub, "they should not have seated us so close to *nobodies.*" Madame Bailly and her daughters were too busy exclaiming over the lace and the coiffures of those at the neighbouring tables to notice, but the abbé shot me an amused look.

The masked lady's voice could be heard again: "That woman over there, for example, could be none other than Mademoiselle de Brie, the comédienne from the Théâtre de la Rue Guénégaud. I'm sure I recognise that dreadful dress and cloak with the train. I do believe they belong to the company – or maybe she bought them second-hand."

I shifted my gaze to the table in the more elegant section that contained the offending dress. A large woman in a black velvet mask, exquisitely gowned, was engaged in witty conversation with a gallant whose back was to us. His plumed hat was tilted rakishly over his own shoulder-length curls; his blue velvet mantle was carelessly draped over one shoulder, revealing its crimson satin lining. The woman seemed animated and fascinated by him. Even though her figure seemed past its prime, her mask could not conceal fully the remains of once great beauty.

"My masterwork, written entirely as a setting for your beauty and talents . . ." I could hear the man saying. What a marvellous little drama. An influential older actress, and the young playwright whose career she was sponsoring. How he flattered her!

The Turkish coffee that everyone had raved about so had arrived. We looked into the splendid little cups to see a thick, black liquid sitting like tar on the white enamel. How uninviting. No one wished to be so unsophisticated as to pronounce us gulled. After all, we had already seen the raccoon, which had unfortunately died and been replaced by a drawing, and the two-headed man, one of whose heads was wooden. None of us would ever admit the fair's most fashionable craze in drink to be nasty.

Monsieur Leroux lifted the tiny cup to his lips, while Amélie watched dotingly. "Most remarkable," he pronounced. "Somewhat like burned caramel," and he took another tiny sip.

Amélie lifted the little cup in the elegant way she had spied the lady lifting hers. "Why, Monsieur Leroux, you have said it perfectly. It is remarkable." But her face was puckered up.

". . . I see no one of distinction here. How can you say it is fashionable? Surely Monsieur le Duc meant another booth . . ." the lady's high voice floated to us. The rumble of her escort's answer was lost in the clatter of dishes. "Now, that veiled woman in the black silk over there, with the abbé, might be someone, were if not for the *impossibly* bourgeois people with whom she is sitting . . ."

I took my first sip from the tiny cup. Even the sugar, which made the drink as heavy as syrup, could not hide the bitter flavour of the stuff.

"Come, my love," said the playwright, his voice heavy with disgust at what he had just overheard, "the rustic nobility of the provinces have crowded out all of the court nobility from this place. There is no longer anyone of true fashion to be seen here." And with an elaborate gesture, he took the comédienne's arm. She swept her train up in her gloved hand, and together they paraded past the masked lady, then past us and out the door. I knew the man, from his waxed moustachios to the long brown locks that flowed over his lace collar with what appeared to be the aid of a curling iron. I recognised Lamotte, the beautiful cavalier of the Rue des Marmousets, made prosperous.

"My, that man is handsome," observed Brigitte, "although *she* is much too old for him."

"That is André Lamotte, the playwright," I said. Was it the dark drink that made my nerves tingle so in my body?

"My, to know so much of society," said Madame Bailly with a sigh.

"Lamotte . . . Lamotte," said the Abbé. "I know this name. I was at the Théâtre de la Rue Guénégaud before Christmas and I saw something— What was it called? It was quite the rage for several weeks. Oh, yes. *Osmin*. It was about a Turkish prince who dies of love for a Christian girl whose face he has only seen in a window—" He broke off to give me an intense, romantic stare. "Men die for love, you know," he added, trying to put his hand on my knee. I pushed it off.

"My, that's romantic." Amélie sighed.

"She was probably blonde and had a perfect complexion," announced Brigitte sourly. "They're all like that, those stories. No one dies for a girl with pimples."

I made myself busy sipping the rest of the bitter drink. My mind felt joyful; my thoughts flowed faster and faster. My senses felt acute. What a lovely drink, I thought. I must discover how to have it more often. Not much to taste, but what a splendid effect it has! Surely, a month at a spa could not give my body this strength, my thoughts this clarity. It was then that I knew suddenly that I must have André Lamotte. And cost what it might, I resolved to make him mine with the aid of the witches' art.

FIFTEEN

It was scarcely a week later that Dr Rabel, the society quack I'd met at the Bachimonts, came secretly to the little house in the Rue du Port-aux-Choux for a private reading. He had good reason to want to know his fortune; the first image in the glass showed me that he poisoned patients for money. I sought another image and saw him as the trusted advisor of a wealthy foreigner. I told him that he would have to leave the country suddenly but would become wealthy at a foreign court.

"Yes, yes. I know who that is – I recognise the description. It is the King of England. My reward – ha! Oh, fortune!" He looked at me with new respect. "And you. It is proof. The Devil does indeed work in the world, and you are in league with him. Why else would you appear in my life, so dark, so mysterious, to tell me the reward for my . . . my deeds?" Evil deeds, you mean, thought I, disgusted at his self-satisfied face. And now he wouldn't even be useful for my experiment in fortune-telling, because he wouldn't be at all interested in trying to change the picture in the glass. "The Devil . . ." he went on musingly, "when did you meet him? Can you reveal him to me? Did you have to sign over your soul for this supernatural gift?" I was beginning to find his twaddle repulsive.

"Not that I know of," I said airily, trying to rise above it. "I am simply the unfortunate product of alchemical science. An ordinary lady of good family . . . betrayed by love . . . an experiment gone wrong." He looked crushed. He'll leave, I thought. However, he does pay well, so I shouldn't discourage him entirely. "Of course," I went on, "I couldn't say that my former lover, the abbé, wasn't in league with the Devil when he made the ointment."

"Of course, of course," he muttered. "Most abbés are. It makes sense. What would a woman know? Still, to be

associated with the Devil even at second hand . . . yes, the duc
. . . my dear Marquise, you must allow me to introduce you
into a select circle . . . of people who will be very interested . . .
ha! You and I . . . I will astonish the world!" *Ouf*. First false
coiners, then poisoners, and now wealthy diabolists. But court
diabolists, powerful enough to be dangerous, even without the
aid of the Devil. Business was getting more complicated all the
time. It is just as well, I thought, that I have a woman of
experience to advise me. I must consult with La Voisin at the
earliest possible opportunity. I certainly don't want to wind up
as the sacrifice in some ridiculous satanic ceremony.

*5 March 1675. Why do people persist in dealing with the
Devil? If there is no God, then there is no Devil, either, and all is
waste and foolishness. If there is a God, why would anyone of
good sense want to deal with such a second-rate being as the
Devil? It not only defies logic, it is in bad taste.* The rest of the
page I filled with drawings of Lamotte's face.

"I wouldn't worry in the least, my dear," pronounced the witch
of the Rue Beauregard, stroking the little amber cat's head. A
chill spring fog swirled outside her window, but the leaping fire
on the two iron cats made the room almost too warm. I could
feel the sweat running down my back as I stood before her
writing table. She looked up at me from where she sat as if I
were being, somehow, difficult. "The sacrifice at a Black Mass
is, at the most, an infant, and often only an animal or a little
human blood would do. You are entirely too old. At most, you
might be asked to serve as an altar, but for calling the Devil, a
virgin is preferred. Now if the Mass is said on behalf of
someone, and she's a woman, she's usually asked to serve as
the altar herself, unless for some reason she requires a
substitute. A man, of course, needs to get a woman to serve.
But it's quite voluntary – otherwise, how would the chalice
stay put?"

She chuckled as she stared past me into the fire, as if
thinking of something else. Then she looked at me indulgently,
that strange little smile, all pointed at the bottom like the letter
V on her face. "No, you should have no troubles at all.
Whatever they do, just act bored, as if you'd seen it done
better before. You'll find your business rising by several

levels. Diabolism is all the rage in the highest circles these days. Our nobility grows tired of dancing, gambling, and making war. Novelty is everything." She put down the cat's head. Somehow, that made it clear the interview was over. As she got up from the little brocade armchair to leave, she turned and looked back at me, as I stood in front of her crowded writing table. The amber cat's head winked up at me from atop a stack of horoscopes in preparation. A number of little coloured bottles and one of her ledgers jostled for space with the vulgar little imp that held her ink. She paused at the door and looked back over her shoulder at me. "Ah," she said, as if she had just remembered something, "and if you see Père Guibourg, remind him that his last payment is overdue."

And so, newly fortified, I was introduced the following week by the celebrated doctor into the vast and luxurious hotel of the Duc de Nevers, a member of the influential Mancini family and nephew of the late Cardinal Mazarin. Nevers, I had learned, was a dabbler in magic who desired above all things to meet the Devil personally. Even among the noblesse, he was something of a celebrity. After all, it's not every day you meet a man who has baptised a pig. It was a small but interesting company present. Among the guests was the Duc de Brissac, an adept who spent a great deal of time talking about Paracelsus and *La Clavicule de Salomon*, which aroused interest only among the other alchemists present. I learned from Rabel that Brissac had thrown away his entire fortune in gambling and extravagant living and so had been reduced to living as a house-guest of the Duc de Nevers. Somnolent with boredom, I sat in the salon beside Rabel and the chattering Brissac and listened while the Duc de Nevers questioned an Italian fortune-teller – a fellow named Visconti, who was a favourite of the King – about demonic possession in Italy.

". . . extraordinary things are seen there, things one never sees in Paris. They are closer to the Devil in Italy . . . Tell me, is it worth a trip to Rome in this season?"

"It is simply that Italy is closer to the Inquisition, not the Devil, most illustrious Duke," responded the Italian coolly. "The Inquisition finds it supports their cause to accredit any fantastical tale. And thanks to the general imbecility of mankind, Italians will believe anything the Inquisition accredits. Thus are reputations made. No, Monsieur le Duc, if you wish to see the Devil you are just as likely to find him in Paris."

"But I have other wonders to show you. I want your opinion. Your opinion counts highly with me. Especially after you predicted His Majesty's latest victory against the Dutch so precisely! I have here in my very own household a phenomenon, the daughter of a *devineresse*, who can read your secret thoughts written in a mirror! And I have discovered a marvel even greater than that – that old woman there in black..." and his voice fell to a whisper as he talked about me. The cool gaze of the Italian fell on me. He was slender, olive skinned, about twenty-five, and dressed in the most elegant fashion. My face felt hot, and I was glad that my veil and a heavy layer of rice powder hid my features. So that's it, I thought. A fortune-telling contest. I'll best him, I told myself, fresh with the confidence of youth and my latest successes. They are all fools, these superstitious folk. Even the Italian.

The company crowded around as a pretty girl of twelve or so was brought out and a mirror set before her. But after a number of incantations and several false attempts to read in the mirror the word held in the mind of various of the noble onlookers, the girl burst into tears.

"You should have known the attempt would be futile," said Visconti, "since only virgins can read in mirrors, and the girl has been debauched in your household." He looked straight at Monsieur le Duc, who didn't even blink.

"But that does not take into account the phenomenon of re-virginisation, occurring in advanced old age," broke in Rabel in a learned-sounding voice.

"Re-virginisation?" The Italian laughed. "That is a secret that half the brides in Paris would like to know about." Snobbish Italian fortune-teller, I thought. I'll get you yet.

"This is my other phenomenon, discovered by the learned Dr Rabel. The Marquise de Morville, found living in poverty as a boarder in the Convent of the Ursulines. Over a century old, the victim of a hideous alchemical accident." The Duc de Nevers leaned over to address the Italian confidentially, "Tell me what you think."

"Madame la Marquise, your servitor," said the Italian, bowing extravagantly.

"I am pleased, Monsieur Visconti, to make the acquaintance of so distinguished a savant," I said, accepting his greeting in the old-fashioned way my grandmother used to receive her ancient callers.

"Your voice is that of a young woman," he said, "and if you would but lift that veil . . ." My moment. I lifted the veil slowly and dramatically, steeling myself against his ironic stare. The company gasped in amazement. Even Visconti's stare turned to a look of appreciation. I was wearing dead white powder and a dab of unbecoming bluish purple lip rouge, more or less the shade of a newly dead corpse. It was a lovely effect. I looked as if I'd just risen from the grave.

"Your face is . . . young . . . and beautiful," said the Italian softly, "though your walk and manner of speech are old." I couldn't help liking someone who thought I was beautiful. Our eyes met. "But the eyes – the eyes are ancient," he pronounced.

"Well?" broke in the Duc de Nevers.

"She is a fake," said Visconti. There were gasps in the room. You're on my list, Italian, I thought, I'll fix you for this. "She is not as old as she claims. Whatever the accident that preserved her face, she is not more than ninety or a hundred years at the very most." Good. First encounter, a draw. Now for the second.

"Her readings are extraordinary, extraordinary," proclaimed Rabel. I called for water, purified five times. Distilled water, not a difficult thing to obtain in a household of adepts, had been prepared in advance. The Duc de Nevers rang, and a servant brought a large pitcher of it. I sat down in front of a little table in the salon and spread out my things, making the most of each dramatic moment. I could feel Visconti staring at my neck.

"Now, Monsieur Visconti, I will read your fortune, and you will confess it's true." I chanted, I stirred, and cast darkly meaningful looks at the assembled company. The little picture emerged almost immediately: the darkened interior of a church. A masked woman entered from the street, glancing hurriedly behind her. She removed her mask, stopped briefly at the font to dip her fingers in holy water. She could not see the young Italian hidden in the shadows, his face a picture of yearning.

Luckily, I recognised the church. "You are in love with a beautiful woman you have seen praying in chapel in the south aisle of Saint-Eustache. You will lie in wait for her there, hoping just to catch a glimpse of her. She is married, and you follow her about disgracefully." It was his turn to be taken aback. I looked down at the glass again. Something very odd had happened. The little picture had changed, without my bidding. How curious, I thought. This isn't supposed to happen this way. Was my gift going out of control? What was causing it? Overuse? Opium? Never mind, I thought, as I looked closer at the image. It was amusing, indeed. I glanced up to find the company gathered around me, staring, breathing as one person.

"Beware, Monsieur Visconti," I said, wagging my finger in mock warning at his shocked face. "She will make an assignation in the Tuileries Gardens and send her maid to you, dressed in her clothes. Remember my warning and tell me if I have read the glass truly." The young man turned beet red as the company howled with laughter. "Very good, Primi." Monsieur le Duc de Brissac laughed. "You must admit she has hit the mark that time." But as I saw the look on his face I thought suddenly, I don't need an enemy at court. I'll give him something to make it even.

"Monsieur Visconti, I have heard you work wonders. It is only fair to ask you in return to read my fate and display your skill."

"Very well. First I shall describe your character through the science of graphology and then read your fate through the art of physiognomy, at which I am a master."

"That is true, true," murmured a woman. "I was at the Countess of Soissons's when he told the Chevalier de Rohan he had the scaffold written on his face. Madame de Lionne, who was in love with him, protested he had the most gallant face in the world, but Visconti was right."

I wrote on the scrap of paper offered for a handwriting sample: "Reason is the queen of all the arts of the mind."

Visconti looked amused.

"Madame la Marquise has a ready wit and has sharpened her mind with much reading in philosophy . . ."

"True, too true." I sighed. "If people could only comprehend the ennui of living one hundred and fifty years, they would never bother. I've had nothing to read for absolutely *decades*."

"She goes to Mass altogether infrequently for a devout ancient lady who has been a convent boarder for so long." It was my turn to be annoyed.

"Go on," I said. He inspected my face from several angles.

"The forehead," he said, nodding sagely, "is broad, showing intelligence. The nose, determination and pride. It is the nose of conquerors, of Caesars; I would say in this case, the nose of ancient lineage, the *noblesse d'épée*. The chin, however, too narrow – a vulnerable spot. Sentimentality, my dear Marquise, will be your downfall. The face as a whole – heart-shaped. The marquise was made for love, but pride keeps her from it. I suppose you are selling the ointment that preserved your beauty beyond the tomb?"

"Monsieur Visconti, how could you offer such an insult to my dead husband's honour? Trade, indeed! Think of your mother when you say a dreadful thing like that," I said, in my best owlish-old-lady manner.

"The rest," he announced, "I will tell her in secret, since it is not my business to embarrass venerable ladies. But from the lineaments of your face, Madame la Marquise, I will give you a warning: Beware the company you keep."

"Ah," sighed the onlookers, deeply impressed.

"And be careful of accepting food and drink from strangers." Well, that's pretty general, I thought. A triumph for Visconti. Now he won't be angry. Then he stood up and leaned across the little table and whispered in my ear:

"Little minx, I haven't the heart to give you away. I think I'm half in love with you already. And as a rule I prefer tall, golden-haired women, I'll have you know. But you – you're as bold a little girl as any cavalier who ever tried to seize a throne."

I could feel the blush spreading under my white powder and hear the company shout with laughter, thinking he had made an indecent proposition.

"This is a wicked world, a world of sinners nowadays," I cried, shaking my tall walking stick at Visconti.

"Why are old people always so ill-tempered?" he asked with a lazy smile. "Of what use is an alchemical remedy for the skin if there's none for bad humour?"

I told a number of fortunes that night and recommended to the mother of a girl who'd been made pregnant by her lover just before her engagement to the man the family had chosen that she go and consult with La Voisin. Just exactly what my patroness did with cases like that I didn't know, but I had begun to suspect of late that it might involve more than doling out talismans and powders made of dried pigeons' hearts. But just what went on with the tense, pale, masked women who avoided one another's eyes in her waiting room I could not imagine.

At the end of the evening, the Duc de Nevers had a purse of silver pressed on me in appreciation of my services. The servant who delivered it wanted some, Rabel wanted some, but there was still a tidy bit left, especially because I had tucked half of it away before he counted it. I wasn't surprised at all when I received a message a week later to attend Madame la Maréchale de Clérambaut, the governess of the children of Monsieur, the King's younger brother, and an astrologer of some repute, at the Palais-Royal.

"I am tired of black," I said to myself as I looked in the tiny square of a mirror on my dressing table that evening. Tired of playing at being an old lady, tired of peering in the water glass until my eyes ached, tired of telling lies. I could be pretty, I thought, if I had a dress the colour of springtime. The right dress – yes. Cut just so, to show an embroidered petticoat, but hide my shoes. These ladies of fashion, they weren't all so pretty, most of them. It was the clothes they had. And I looked almost straight, maybe even entirely straight in the dim light of the single candle that stood on the table beside the mirror. I wasn't that thin; I wasn't that small. Not really.

Now is the time I miss Marie-Angélique most, I thought. "You actually want a new dress, Sister?" she'd say. "Oh, do let's go and look at the fashion drawings at Au Paradis on the

Pont-au-Change. And they have the prettiest linens there, all made up. When I'm rich, I'll have a dressing gown from there, in that lovely painted Indian cotton, and some little velvet slippers just like I saw in the boutique across the way." Even without money, she lived for shopping. If I were with her, I'd feel the fun and excitement of new things and forget metaphysical worries. "Sister, you fret too much. A nice pair of earrings always makes a girl feel entirely new," she'd say if she were with me now. Maybe there was something to Marie-Angélique's philosophy of life, after all. I imagined her at home, playing the clavecin, admired by men. How lucky to be born beautiful, to have the luxury of carefree happiness.

The fatigue of an evening of readings made my bones feel all watery. I took a spoonful of my sleeping medicine and stared into the mirror again. Beware, said my mind. Remember the witches' warning. If you lose control of the images, they will possess you, and you will lose your mind. In the depths of the glass, figures seemed to be moving unbidden. But still I didn't look away. I wanted to drown myself in the shapes that had appeared. I could see Lamotte, sitting in his shirt on the side of a massive, brocade-draped bed. It was open at the neck, and I could see the white skin across his collarbone, the pulse of blood at his neck. He leaned forward and took off the shirt. God, he was beautiful. The fine dusting of hair across his chest, its rise and fall as his breath moved in and out. I put my face closer to the mirror, fogging it with my own breath. There was movement in the bed, and I could make out a strange woman's white arm, a round shoulder, a tumble of pale hair. Why did I need to know this? Is this how the images brought destruction, by breaking one's heart with the knowledge of what one was?

I could feel the tears making tracks through the heavy powder on my face. Had I frightened him that day, being too clever? Had he ever meant anything more than condescending gallantry, the way he had charmed me? Poor plain sister, what else could it have been? You were never anything but a means to get to the beautiful, unreachable face he saw in the window. Suppose I saw him again and I looked like a queen? Suppose I did get a *poudre d'amour* from La Voisin and put it in his cup? Suppose I laughed and chattered about charming nothings and rolled my eyes, like other women – oh, suppose on, Geneviève, you fool. André Lamotte will never be yours, no matter what you do. I took another big spoonful of the cordial, and the image vanished.

"Madame." Brigitte stood at the door, waiting to help me undress. The rows of tiny buttons, the pins in the bodice, the heavy hooped petticoat were impossible to negotiate alone. At last we were down to the steel corset, the front, flat filigree, hinged in the middle, the back, rods and laces to the neck.

"Brigitte, unlace it. I want it off."

"But, Madame, you have been tightening it every week."

"Off, I say, or I will die. I must be myself again, no matter what it costs." When she had it off, the thin shirt beneath showed the marks of rust where my sweat had eaten at the merciless steel.

"Oh, my God, help me!" I cried, as I collapsed on to the floor. The steady support of the steel had caused the muscles of my torso to lose all their strength. I could not stand or sit upright. I had the backbone of a worm. Brigitte, her eyes wide with alarm, called for her mother, and together the two women managed to drag me to bed. There I lay, staring at the ceiling in the dark, as the fever rushed through my body in fiery waves, and mad images of past, present, and future swarmed like hobgoblins in the air.

"I've seen snails with more backbone." I was having a strange dream. La Voisin, thousands of feet tall, was towering over my bedside in her dusty travelling cloak and wide, plumed grey hat. "No sooner do I return on the diligence from Lyon than I discover that all hell has broken loose. La Filastre has held back money. Guibourg is raising his fee. Who does the man think he is? It is *I* who send him his business! And that ungrateful Le Sage is trying to steal my clients for himself. At least La Pasquier has kept her good sense, I said to myself, only to discover that you are rolled in a ball dying of fever from unrequited love. Surgeon, how many more bleedings to reduce the fever?"

"Another one ought to do it," I could hear the answer from somewhere far away.

"Good. Take it from the heel this time. I don't want her

wrists marked." I could feel the bedclothes being lifted up, and hear other people moving in the room. "And now, Mademoiselle, the name of this *man* who robs me of my investment?"

The dream was very strange. I was not in my bed at Madame Bailly's. "Where am I?" I thought I might have said.

"Don't begin to annoy me with the remembrance of the trouble I have had getting you here without that police snoop of a widow knowing where you were going. The name, the name, Mademoiselle. I know it's André. André what? Speak up. Lamotte? Lamotte, the playwright? Oh, how foolish! You'll build no fortune with *him*! He's a nobody! Listen, you silly, sick rabbit, and take my advice. Brissac is ripe for the picking. He quarrels with Nevers; he has a title; he will advance your interests. And he's hungry. When he sees the money you earn, he'll take up with you in a flash. He can give you as good a tumble as Lamotte, anytime. And he's an alchemist. He can supply us with ... Ha! You've fallen for the most ambitious gigolo in Paris. Fall in love with Brissac, I say. We'll get something out of *that*!"

"Brissac's disgusting," I whispered.

"So you think you can be choosy? Listen closely, little Marquise, there is no room for squeamishness in this business. Once you have entered our world, there is no going back. If you are ever discovered, your closest male relative has a right to everything you own. You'll go straight to the prison-convent on his petition for what you've done already. A girl from a respectable family living on her own? Making money as a fortune-teller? The authorities would be scandalised. As long as they think you're a widow, as long as you have our protection, they'll leave you alone. But don't ever think you can cut and run; once you're beyond our reach, you'll never see the sun again, I can assure you."

As the blood flowed into the surgeon's bowl, I could feel weakness, weakness and sanity filling me. A patch of blue sky shone through a tiny window. A slanted ceiling reached almost to the floor beside the bed. I was in the tiny attic bedroom under the eaves in La Voisin's house.

"And now, I say, you will get up tomorrow, you will lace up that corset again, and you will keep your appointment at the Palais-Royal. Remember this: if you make your fortune, you can buy Lamotte for a toy. If you fail, your uncle will piss on your grave. You have no place to go but up."

"I hate it; I can't wear it any more," I whispered to the towering dream-figure.

"Can't? There's no such word. But from now on, you may take it off at night. You need considerably more spine than you have at present. And you're looking straighter, even now, without it."

Straighter? The room seemed to fall away as my eyes grew heavier. I could see myself like a lady, all straight, in the garden of a château, gathering roses. I could hear a man calling my name. I could be beautiful. I could be rich. I could be beloved. Roses. Yes. I needed the rose-coloured dress.

The light of hundreds of candles multiplied itself in the mirrors and shone again from the gilt panelling of the small reception room in the Palais-Royal. The ranking guests were seated in brocade-covered armchairs; lesser figures had to content themselves with heavy, fringed stools. The small fry stood, or, rather, oozed gently between the armchairs, listening deferentially and offering flattery as required. I could hear the light laughter of the maréchale behind her fan, for, winter or summer, no court lady was without a fan, as she teased, ". . . but, my dear Countess, they say the Marquis de Seignelay is absolutely *besotted* with you!"

"It is not my fault who looks at me. The question is whether I look at him. And you must admit that the marquis has an unmistakable *je ne sais quoi de bourgeois* about him."

"That, of course, is the fault of his father, Colbert. It is such a great shame that the King raises his ministers from *nowhere*. But you can't deny that he is a perfectly darling-looking young man, and of course, exceptionally rich—"

But, of course, the almost invisible stain on his manners, a careless turn of speech, or a tiny flaw in his appearance or dress would deny him entrance to the most exclusive circles. That was the one good thing I had taken away with me from the Rue des Marmousets. The look, the speech of good blood. It couldn't be bought; it couldn't be counterfeited. La Voisin could not do without me. The salons could not uncover me. I felt flooded with satisfaction. I was back at work again.

"Whatever you think of Colbert, you must admit that Louvois is far worse." One minister of state versus another.

"Ah, Louvois!" the lady exclaimed with a laugh. "He has the air of a *valet de chambre.*"

"I hear," said a gentleman in green velvet and the especially high, red-heeled shoes made popular by Monsieur, "that he seeks desperately to repair his appearance, and takes hours dressing, asking advice from men of fashion as to where he should place his ribbons." The ladies all laughed at the image of Louvois before his mirror. Louvois the vengeful, whose word destroyed, and whose minion, La Reynie, carried out the arrests required by the secret *lettres de cachet* Louvois secured from the King. Were he here, with what ironic politeness would he be greeted! How low the bows, how wide the smiles! And how great the laughter when he had made his exit. How could the man not suspect?

But this evening belonged to the occultists, amateur and professional, that had gathered to astonish and amaze one another.

"Why," said an elderly gentleman I did not recognise, "I have even heard of a horoscope being drawn upon handwriting alone!"

"And who could ever have managed such a thing?" The Comtesse de Gramont's accent still betrayed her English origin. Tall and blonde, she moved with the confidence of one who knew that half the men in the room were in love with her. Her husband, they said, was a rake with the nose of a Harlequin, and a bitterly jealous man.

"I do believe it was Primi Visconti," responded the Abbé de Hacqueville.

"Visconti, *bah*. An amateur," said the Neapolitan priest in his heavy Italian accent. "He has no grasp of the sciences of divination. I myself am the fountain and origin of this particular art, as I will demonstrate."

"Bravo, Père Prégnani," called the elderly gentleman. "Demonstrate how your art outshines Visconti's!" So, this was Prégnani, Visconti's rival, and a nasty-looking piece of work he was. The man who was making quite a name for himself predicting horse races for the nobility. I watched his technique with some interest as he called for a handwriting sample and drew up the horoscope, attracting the attention of every soul in the room.

But it was the Marquise de Morville who gained most from the occasion, for the shrewd old lady made enchanted the horoscopic ladies by allowing them to interpret her images with their various methods of divination. Their quarrel over the merits of chiromancy versus palmistry became so interesting that even the Comtesse de Gramont broke off her flirtation with Père Prégnani to join in, and by the end of the evening the marquise had received from her the most coveted invitation of all. The comtesse would curry favour with an increasingly desperate Queen by bringing her yet another of the fortune-tellers Her Highness sought in ever greater numbers. The Marquise de Morville, the most fashionable new *devineresse* in Paris, would go to Versailles.

SIXTEEN

"Your first visit to court," said the sorceress contentedly. Her cats rubbed at her skirts as she sat in the armchair in her cabinet. I had been offered the stool. Moving up, I thought silently. Some day, she will offer the armchair. "I read it in your future. You will climb high. Would you care for another marzipan?" I took a big one. She smiled. At that moment, I would have liked to trade it for the smaller one, but it was too late. Besides, I liked marzipan. "I can, of course, advise you. I have been to the court at Saint-Germain, Fontainebleau, and at Versailles. But the Queen— You have done very, very well so soon. I am gratified." As soon as I had eaten the first marzipan, I started thinking of the next one. I won't look at the plate, I thought.

She got up suddenly and poked at the fire, which had almost extinguished itself. While her back was turned, I took another marzipan. A little one that wouldn't be noticed. The sorceress took out a ledger from the locked cupboard to consult. She turned and looked at me as she replaced the book. "Enjoy yourself among the golden ones, my dear. Learn their secrets, keep their confidences. Remember, I am always here to assist you, and them, with my little 'confidential services'." She sat down again. Her eyes narrowed as she noticed the plate. "Now, when will you be visiting Versailles?" She went on as if she had never noticed the missing marzipan. "I have a little package I would like delivered there. And one thing I must remind you of – why, I think of myself almost as your mother and want only your good – never show weakness to them. They are like gilded wolves. If they sense the slightest hesitation, they will turn on you and eat you in a flash. Audacity! Boldness! They only wish to be dazzled. Rely on your wits. Trust no friendships: a nest of vipers is more generous than the court of the Sun King." Considering the source, I was impressed with the advice.

"You'll need court dress," she announced, "though what you have will do for now, until you earn more money." She laughed. "Would you like to see mine? The embroideries are absolutely exquisite. And well they ought to be, since the gown alone cost five thousand livres." I wondered why she went to court. It certainly wasn't to watch the King dining in public as the tourists did.

Upstairs in her bedroom, La Voisin opened the locked armoire where ranks of clothes were hung, hidden beneath muslin shrouds. She lifted one of the protective sacks to display a silk gown in *aurore* lined with pale green. From another, an array of heavy, brightly coloured petticoats in taffeta burst out.

"Oh, beautiful." I pretended to sigh. I could see her calculating eye. She was whetting my appetite for the grand life.

"Our profession is welcomed at every court on earth – providing we are not uncouth, like the vulgar La Bosse. Mind your manners and remember my lessons, and you will have a dozen gowns like this."

"And that? The red velvet?" I pointed to the corner of a heavy, rich robe embroidered with double-headed gold eagles that was peeping from beneath one of the muslin covers.

"Never," she said, carefully rearranging the muslin. I got a glimpse of sea-green lace before the gown vanished from sight. "This is an emperor's robe. The only way you would ever have one is if you became Queen." She tilted her head and looked at me anew with her black, black eyes. "My, what calculating grey eyes you have, my dear. You certainly have the brains to become Queen – and so few do – but you entirely lack the character to make a good witch. I think I need not stay up at night worrying, eh?" She shut the armoire door and turned the key in the lock with a click.

I thought of the Stoics. I thought of Monsieur Descartes. Here I was offended that I'd been told I wasn't crazy enough to be a *real* sorceress. Father, the lover of ironies, would have laughed.

A knock on the bedroom door broke the moment.

"Madame, the girl you sent for is waiting below, and your husband has returned with the package."

"Oh, excellent, Margot. How many did Samson give him?"

"Four this time, Madame. Will you be drying them here, as usual?"

"Of course. Bring the package in." She turned to me with a cool look, as if she were assessing me. "I have no secrets from the little marquise here," she said in an arch tone. "The coals in the oven have burned quite low enough now." So I was right; I thought I'd noticed an unusual heat from behind the tapestry on the bedroom wall.

As Margot left, La Voisin turned to me. "I've found you a lovely little maid. She's ever so knowledgeable about the court. She can inform you about the people you meet and keep you from embarrassing yourself. Suppose, for example, you knock at a door instead of scratch – you won't live down the disgrace. But she can tell you which doors to knock at and which to scratch at . . . when to open a half-door to a visitor and when to open a full door. It's a matter of precedence. Precedence and court etiquette. It's important you don't go wrong. Oh, yes. And you should start to grow a long fingernail on the little finger of your left hand; all the courtiers do, for scratching at doors." She looked pleased with herself and went on: "How very fortunate I was to acquire her . . . she was in the household of La Grande Mademoiselle until she attracted the notice of the wrong man. A few weeks in the Salpêtrière caused her to repent of her life and send for me. And I, out of the kindness of a too-generous heart, arranged for her departure and am giving her a new start in life."

Interesting. The only way a girl like that could expect to get out of prison was if she was transported for life to the colonies. So La Voisin's reach extended into the jails and "hospitals" of the city. How had she arranged the escape? And now she had another loyal follower, and a spy to report my every movement. Ah, philanthropy. It becomes a way of life. "You are too generous," I said, and she shot me a hard look, before turning to her husband who had entered through the bedroom door.

"So there you are at last – I can't imagine why you've been so slow! How long does it take to go only down the street? It's not as if Samson lives across town, after all!" Antoine

Montvoisin was, for once, not in his dressing gown but in a shabby grey homespun suit and a wide-brimmed, untrimmed felt hat drooping forlornly over a moth-eaten goat's-hair wig.

"He made me ... *hic* ... wait ... for a long time," Montvoisin said in a weak voice. His wife pulled aside the tapestry to reveal the oven door in the stone wall. Montvoisin stood, all drooping, his thin frame occasionally shaken by another silent hiccup.

"Unwrap them and put them on the drying rack – and don't let them drip this time. For heaven's sake! Can't you stop that infernal hiccuping?"

"It's you who ... *hic* ... caused it, so if you're offended, it's ... *hic* ... your own fault. Next time keep your toad powder ... *hic* ... for your clients."

"How dare you insult my profession when you live by it? Oh, those are dreadfully damp; they'll take for ever. Couldn't Samson get us any older ones?" La Voisin was scurrying about like a housewife at preserve-making time. With a rising sense of nausea, I recognised the objects that her lover Samson, the executioner of Paris, had sent her. They were human hands.

"Doesn't the smell offend you – I mean, right here in the house?" I was trying to sound cool, offhand, as if I often saw things like that. But my voice came out smaller than usual. Maybe I really wasn't cut out to be a witch, after all.

"That?" answered La Voisin. "Oh, it's no worse than curing hams. Besides, it's the smell of prosperity. That never bothers me. Pardon, but you're turning green. Do you need to sit down?" I sat down suddenly on the bed.

"Don't you stain my carpet. Use the slop jar. You? At court? You're a weakling still."

"What ... what are they for?"

"Hands of glory. They attract hidden treasure to the owner. Half the court has them. Ladies keep them sewn in their skirts, men in their pockets. Guaranteed to bring luck at the gaming tables. You needn't look so queasy. They're quite compact and free of mess once they're all dried out. They curl up, you see. I buy them from the executioner; the people were already dead. It's not as if I killed them. The King did; the courts did. Why shouldn't someone at least get a little benefit from it? I see myself as creating good from evil. I make money from something that would otherwise go to waste – that's the advantage of understanding housewifery. Nothing should ever be wasted. Learn from me, and you will be able to turn others' wickedness to your own advantage."

I wondered what the Romans did for nausea. They probably never tried vomiting wearing corsets, either.

"Antoine, go hold her head. I won't have her dripping down that good dress I paid for. Nerve! Hah! You haven't got any, Mademoiselle. You? Want vengeance? You couldn't kill a mouse. I don't know when I've met a girl so lily-livered. It's a good thing I've found you a maid who's got more backbone than you, or you wouldn't last a week among the Great Ones."

As she shut the oven door with a clang, Antoine Montvoisin offered me his arm to escort me downstairs.

"She may be the powerful one, but ... *hic* ... no matter what she tries, my soul is screwed fast to my body. There's a virtue in ... *hic* ... sticking power. But I recommend to you ... *hic* ... not to make her angry, or if you do, don't take ... *hic* ... food or drink in this house. And where you're going ... *hic* ... it's useful to know a few things. Keep ... *hic* ... antipoison with you, or failing that, drink a great deal of ... *hic* ... milk if the soup tastes ... *hic* ... odd. I found it ... *hic* ... to be most efficacious, though it's ... *hic* ... left me with these ... *hic* ... *hic* ... cursed hiccups. I'm telling you this because ... *hic* ... you seem to have more of decency ... *hic* ... about you."

That night, I had dreadful dreams. The room turned into a tall, glittering dining room, and I was seated with an elegant company around a great table with a white linen cloth. Silver candelabra stood among heavily laden silver platters, and the talk was witty. There was a lovely pâté on one of the platters. A man reached out to cut it with his knife, to offer some to his lady dining companion. The pâté groaned with a human voice.

"Oh, how offensive!" the lady exclaimed, and as he hastily drew back his knife, I could see the horrid thing was bleeding where it had been cut.

"They should know better than to invite things like that to dinner," observed a lace-bedecked gentleman. A lackey filled my glass full of a rich, green cordial.

"Oh, no more for me," I said. "I've had too much already."

Too much. Too much. Whom did I know at this table? I looked to each side. The three friends of the Rue des Marmousets were seated on either side of me, Lamotte in ribbons, Griffon in fawn-coloured velvet, and d'Urbec, as pale as a ghost, in black silk.

"Tell me," said Griffon, "does the pâté publish?"

"Isn't it sufficient that it speaks?" asked d'Urbec in that pointed way he had. His dark eyes, somehow sunken in his head, glittered with a strange bitterness and mockery I had not seen before.

"Monsieur Lamotte, take me from this dinner party. I am fatigued," I begged. Somehow, he seemed to be the one who had brought me.

"Oh, you can't leave," cried a man eating oysters. "You are supposed to pay for the dinner."

"But I can't—" My desperate protest was interrupted by a woman's indignant shrieks: "You have to. What do you expect?" And with that the company began to argue about who would pay, growing louder and more quarrelsome by the minute.

"Mademoiselle Pasquier, I can't leave just now," Lamotte confided in a low voice. "I'm filling my pockets for tomorrow's breakfast. Poet's privilege." He took more rolls, a dozen or two vanishing beneath the table. Then he folded up a huge soup tureen into a tiny napkin and slipped it beneath his shirt. But d'Urbec looked at me with that strange, intense look that seemed to see everything.

"It offends you," he said, throwing his napkin over the pâté. "Although if you had read the sixth chapter of my *Observations on the Health of the State* more carefully, you would not have been astonished at all. Come, let us leave before their quarrelling sets the hall on fire." And as the first blows sent the dishes rattling to the floor and the lighted candelabra rolling and sputtering across the fine linen cloth, he took my arm and we fled unnoticed into the night.

Sweating and terrified, I lay frozen still, waiting for the dawn. What could they mean, these dreams? Or did they mean anything at all?

And so it was that within the week I found myself hurtling along behind six matched greys in Madame la Maréchale's heavy carriage on the road to Versailles. My new maid, bold and henna-haired, sat across from me on the back-facing seat, clutching my hatbox and squeezed in between the maréchale's personal maid and one of her poor relative lady-companions. Madame herself, and Mademoiselle d'Elbeuf were on the seat beside me. Not so far from the château, where the road divides to go to Marly, we heard the sound of cries and the crack of whips behind us.

"How many horses?" Madame asked, as her maid leaned out the window to see who was coming. We would not defer for a four-horse equipage.

"Six, Madame," responded the maid.

"And what colour are their liveries?"

"Blue and silver, Madame de Montespan's."

"Then by all means, tell my coachman to pull over, or we will be overturned in the ditch." As our coach pulled to a halt on the grassy bank beside the road, a heavy carriage rolled past, the lathered horses at full canter, mud spattering from their hoofs. Inside I could see three women and the pale face of a little boy. We pulled back onto the road behind them only to be halted again a mile farther on. The great coach was stopped in the centre of the road, the blue-and-silver-clad postilions arguing with the coachmen, while in the road, two of the women from the carriage were weeping and exclaiming over the mangled corpse of a poor vine cutter, crushed by the carriage and horses. The huge bundle of sticks with which he had been laden were scattered all about him. Beside the road, members of his family had gathered, staring silently. A plumpish blonde woman with a protruding nose and receding chin leaned out of the carriage window.

"Get back in, I say. What good is your sentimental wailing? Pure hypocrisy! You wouldn't carry on so if it had happened out of your sight! It's not as if my postilions didn't warn him. Everyone knows that a woman in my position drives fast – my equipage cleaves the wind." One woman wiped her nose; the other started to wail even louder at this speech. "Oh, do be quiet!" the woman in the coach shouted at this new impertinence. "It was his own imprudence that he did not remove himself from my path. One has a right to continue in such circumstances."

"That's Madame de Montespan," whispered my maid. Ah, the King's newest *maîtresse en titre*, promoted from her position as *maîtresse en délicat* by the forced retirement of the former official mistress, La Vallière, who had been driven by a thousand humiliations into a convent.

"Your servants are at fault, and you don't even blame them?" one of the women on the ground, the dark-clad, weeping one, said. She stood up beside the body and addressed the blue-and-silver-clad lackeys fiercely. "If you belonged to me, I would soon settle you."

"That's the Duc du Maine, Madame Montespan's oldest son, in the carriage, and that's Madame de Maintenon there, in the black and grey, on the ground. She's the children's governess. And the other woman – she's the Marquise d'Hudicourt." The Marquise d'Hudicourt continued to wail and wring her hands, as the growing crowd applauded Madame de Maintenon's fierce speech.

"*Vive* Madame de Maintenon!" they cried.

"Be good enough to get in, Mesdames. Will you have me stoned?" the woman in the carriage commanded. But the weeping ladies would not be dissuaded until the King's mistress had given them her purse to hand to the poor relations of the dead man. With that, they remounted, and the carriage clattered off in a spatter of spring mud.

"Oh my goodness," said the lady-companion, "the man's eyes were *entirely* out of his head. I shall *require* a cup of chocolate when we arrive; it is simply *too* painful otherwise."

"Surely, Mademoiselle, such sentiment is misplaced on a stranger. After all, it was not a premeditated assassination," said Madame d'Elbeuf coolly.

I sat silently for the rest of the ride.

At Versailles I was shown into the Queen's presence by Mademoiselle d'Orléans, Princesse de Montpensier. "I want to know whether my coming child will be a girl or a boy," the Queen announced in her heavy Spanish accent. I looked at her. She was seated in a large, brocade-covered armchair with gold fringes and gilt-silver legs, a fan of carved ivory half open in her hand. She was about forty, with the prematurely aged look of a weak, inbred constitution. So many lines of princes culminating in this short, sallow blonde woman with the bulging eyes and strange features – almost like a gargoyle – that her flattering portraits never quite recorded. I couldn't but marvel. She had several severe dark-clad Spanish ladies with her, three of her favourite dwarfs – two men shorter than myself but very square, with huge heads, and a perfectly formed, tiny, wrinkled woman – and a good half-dozen flat-faced, hairy little lapdogs of great ugliness.

"I pray daily for another son," she went on. She didn't look pregnant to me, but then, I wasn't experienced in these matters. I'd have to trust the glass. I looked about the immense, airy room for a suitable table. Gold on gold, panels of rare inlaid wood, heavy, elaborately formed furniture of precious metals – despite every luxury, the room seemed cold and devoid of soul. At last I realised why. These were rooms through which wit and learning never passed. The Spanish queen was one of the stupidest women in the entire realm, her conversation dismal and spiritless. My eye lit on a table of solid silver that sat beneath a huge, dark Spanish tapestry. I gestured to it, and they brought a heavy little cushioned stool, made of gold inlaid on silver, for me to sit on. I'd brought one of my nicest orbs with me and requested that they fill it with water. I rolled out my little cabbalistic cloth and set out a nice selection of rods. Her Majesty looked on approvingly as I chanted and stirred with the glass rod. Suddenly I understood why. The ladies that crowded around me were all wearing old-fashioned Spanish farthingales, not unlike my own. Half the people in the room were shorter than I, and the rest not much taller. I fit right in with the freaks of the Spanish court that she still kept around her after all these years in France.

The reflection was clear. She was not pregnant. I didn't dare tell her. I did a second reading and had her put her hand on the glass. I saw an illness and a vase of late-spring flowers in the room. Quickly, my mind worked.

"Your Majesty, I regret to say that in the late spring you will have a serious illness and lose the child."

"Lose the child? Lose the child? I must have another child. That dreadful woman, that odious La Montespan, holds him with her youth, her children. It is I who am Queen, not she, and yet she would rule in my place. Ah, God, too late I regret La Vallière, who was at least ashamed of what she was doing. But now, this sin with a married woman – this shameless harlot with the brazen tongue ... I tell you, this whore will be the death of me—" She broke off into Spanish, which I did not understand, and her ladies rushed to console her. I shall never make my fortune here, I thought. I can't give her good news. With deep curtseys I retreated from the royal presence.

I stalked from the entrance to the Queen's apartments in what I hoped was a dramatic manner, thumping my tall walking stick with each step. My black gown whispered and rustled about me as I descended the extraordinary staircase of multicoloured inlaid marble that led from the Queen's apartments and entered the wide marble corridor beneath it. There I met with a press of lackeys, chairs, and tourists exactly as if I were in the main street of a large town. The only difference was that at Versailles, the avenues were paved with marble and decorated with gold, like the streets of Paradise.

In fact, the palace at Versailles was exactly like a city, with the corridors serving as streets. Porters carried the courtiers in chairs from place to place, for the women, at least, were incapable of walking twenty feet in their heavily corseted court gowns and flimsy satin shoes. Besides, the corridors were not always clean enough to tread safely while wearing a gown whose cost represented the annual income of a thousand peasant families, for impatient courtiers often relieved nature in the corners or against the walls. The chairs threaded their way through a crowd of lackeys of every description, of sightseers and foreigners come to see the public rooms of the château, of petitioners, soldiers, and mountebanks. It was hard to imagine that all of it – the furniture, swarms of courtiers, curiosity seekers, servants, cooks, theatrical troupes – everything, could be packed up in the twinkling of an eye and put on the road for another of the King's palaces whenever he had a mind to change residences. Yet for all his seasonal moving about, he did not return to Paris, the ancient capital, and he had ceded the Palais-Royal to his brother. And so the ostlers of Paris gave special feed to the new breed of vicious, heavy coach horse that could keep the carriages rumbling at top speed to Versailles, to Saint-Germain, to Marly, to Fontainebleau. Grandmother said it was a sin, and Kings should live in the Louvre, among the people of their principal city, as the monarchs of old did. It was a highly unfashionable idea that I did not borrow for the Marquise de Morville.

The marquise was getting to be an old friend of mine. She lived in my head, offering comments on my daily life, bothering me at night when I didn't find sleep easy. A shrewd, sharp-tempered old lady, she coined aphorisms and told lies about her girlhood to me. She bothered me with horrid observations on my character and activities, denounced courtiers with impunity, and cackled at my annoyance. When I was placed into the heavy corset and the preposterous bell-shaped petticoat of hoops was lowered over my head, she shut Geneviève in the closet with a firm "There, now! Waiting will be good for you. In my day, we waited a lot more than young people now – and we were polite about it, too!" And she would stalk off thumping her tall walking stick to tell the world a thing or two, by way of setting it straight.

Now she stalked down the corridors of Versailles, a shrivelled-up, disapproving little figure in the black of a previous century, a mysterious black veil concealing her features. She disapproved of the smell in the corridors, peered through her veil in an offended fashion at the bared bosoms of two ladies-in-waiting who were hurrying past, sniffed at the suit of a rustic-looking lordling fresh from the provinces in a manner that made him blush.

"In my day, a man took off his hat to a lady of rank, not merely touched it as if it had grown into his hair," she said to a slender, olive-skinned gentleman in baggy black velvet trousers and embroidered grey silk jacket. The man looked back at her with a steady gaze. Visconti, the fortune-teller. The marquise was not bothered by other fortune-tellers. Especially Visconti, who lacked at least one hundred and twenty-five years of her experience.

"Good day, Monsieur Visconti. You have fully repaired my estimation of you with your second attempt." Visconti had taken off his hat with several complex flourishes, making an elaborate court bow.

"My dear Marquise, I am delighted to have met you by this happy coincidence. My powers tell me that you have just been consulted by the Queen in the matter of her pregnancy."

"How odd. My powers tell me the same about yourself. I presume you predicted the son she wanted."

"No, because I wish to retain my reputation at court after her miscarriage in April."

"That was wise. You will go far, Visconti."

"I already have, little vixen. Last night I was taken to the King's *petit coucher*. Consume yourself with envy. Though why the greatest nobles in the land would pay a hundred thousand *écus* for the privilege of seeing the King sit upon his *chaise percée* before he retires, I cannot imagine. You French are an insane nation, are you not? And the King is obliged to sit on it whether nature requires it or not because it is expected of him; there he conducts business."

"Monsieur Visconti, you presume upon being a foreigner. Everything our monarch does is perfection itself, including sitting upon his *chaise percée* at the ceremony of the *petit coucher*."

"I never said it was not perfection. Tell me, have you sold any more of your youth ointments now that you have risen to such rarefied heights?" Our conversation had carried us to the corridor before the *cour des princes*. On the far side, great doors opened into the garden. Two lackeys were holding open the door for their master to escort a woman outside to a waiting *calèche* for a tour of the gardens.

"Here I do readings; it is more in demand— Oh, who is that?" I was glad I was veiled. The Marquise de Morville fled in confusion, leaving Geneviève rooted to the spot, her mouth open.

"The Duc de Vivonne, La Montespan's brother. She has made him a powerful man. Surely, you must know him – or perhaps you mean the girl who has just been helped into the *calèche*? She *is* lovely, isn't she? That's La Pasquier, his latest unofficial mistress. Quite a find, isn't she? I hear she came from nowhere – a baker's daughter, some say, but then, they may be jealous. Have you heard how he stole her from the Chevalier de la Rivière? Scandal itself. He won her in a card game – and I know for a fact he cheated! I suppose he's brought her to see the sights. He is renowned as a connoisseur of beauty. They say he's given her a carriage and horses and a little villa in the Rue Vaugirard."

It was Marie-Angélique, my sister. La Voisin had predicted it all that long time ago, that steaming hot summer day in her tall black fortune-telling parlour. But the thing that had shaken me was that Monsieur le Duc had on a sky-blue brocade coat and an immense, curling blond wig.

Now that I had told the Queen's fortune, my readings became all the rage at court. The bored, the worried, the ambitious – they all sought me out, men and women, chambermaids and counts. Their fears, their passions, their avarice – I heard it all. Rumours started that I knew a secret that would cause the owner to win at cards; I was besieged. "The secret has a curse; to reveal it is death," I whispered mysteriously and watched in awe as they promised to pawn their jewellery and face sure death just to own it anyway. Another rumour started that I was in fact immortal and dated from the Roman empire. I suppose I had quoted Juvenal once too often. Now strange whispers accompanied my travels up and down the corridors, and at the sight of my shrunken, black-clad figure and tall walking stick, even battle-tried soldiers drew back. Even my saucy, roving-eyed maid had fallen in with the game, walking deferentially behind me carrying my things, as if my power horrified her. Behind my back, she took bribes from people anxious to gain my secrets. It was a good thing I was at least a hundred and thirty years older than she, otherwise she'd have tried to run everything. My little philosophical notebooks and my cash went into a locked coffer, and I never let the key leave my person. Now the word went around that I kept the key to a secret chamber in a castle in the Holy Land, where the secret of the philosopher's stone was kept.

I kept my secrets to myself. Each night in the tiny rented room in the attic of an overcrowded inn in the village of Versailles, I wrote out my coded list of clients and my predictions, still searching for the true meaning of the pictures in the oracle glass.

"Why do you sit up writing accounts every night?" Sylvie, my maid, would ask when she brushed my hair. "If I had a racket half as good as yours, you wouldn't find *me* sitting up and writing. I'd be dancing, or making the bed bounce with that good-looking fellow that came to you for the secret of the cards yesterday."

"That's just the sort of thing that would ruin my image. My stock-in-trade depends on mystery and terror. People who go dancing and flirting have neither."

"But what do you write?" she wheedled.

"I intend to become very rich some day, and one must start with the correct foundation, records and logic. The Romans—"

"Oh, bother the Romans. Sometimes I actually believe you're as old as they say. Who else but an old lady would come to a place full of beautiful young men and rich old ones and spend her nights *doing accounts*? The best way to become rich is the easy way: marry a man with money. Or find a buried treasure. A woman can't get rich by herself – that's a law of nature."

She unlaced my corset and helped me on with my nightgown. It was exquisite. A waterfall of fine embroidery and lace on linen as thin and pale as if it had been woven of spiders' webs. All my things were nice now. The truth was, I was indifferent to Madame de Morville's clothes, as long as I had my books, but La Voisin encouraged the wearing of luxurious things; it impressed my clients and was supposed to be the lure that drew me deeper into the fortune-telling business. She never understood that for me the best lure was watching the extraordinary assortment of human characters that revealed itself to me each day. It was my reward for a solitary childhood hidden in corners when the guests came.

The only dress I really wanted I was having made in secret; Monsieur Leroux, the draper, had procured the silk for me at a great bargain. But it was not a dress for the old Marquise, and that is why it had to be made secretly, safe from La Voisin's spies. It was a dress for a young girl, not yet twenty. It had a rose bodice and skirts, turned back to show an ivory taffeta petticoat and a stomacher embroidered with flowers like a garden in spring. La Voisin would have hated it. I wanted to walk with André Lamotte in the *orangerie* in it. I wanted to smell the heavy perfumed blossoms and hear him say, "I never understood it before; you are really very beautiful. All that time I was looking at the wrong face in the window." I knew I was a fool, but I couldn't bear not to be. It had to happen. It just had to. With magic, with money, I would make it happen.

"Just how rich do you intend to be?" Sylvie's voice broke into my thoughts.

"Unbelievably rich. I intend to repeal that law of nature of yours." Rich enough to revenge myself on Uncle and the world for making me what I had become, I thought silently.

"Well, you can start tomorrow with the Countess of Soissons. She ought to be a repeat client, the way she runs to fortune-tellers. She sent the most delicious little page, all covered with ribbons, when you were gone this afternoon. If you could have seen him blush when I pretended to pull up my garter!"

Olympe Mancini, the Countess of Soissons – another of the nieces of the late Cardinal Mazarin, and said to be a widow by her own hand.

"Don't get yourself in trouble, teaching pages about nature."

"Trouble? There's no problem with that. Madame Montvoisin arranges everything."

"I hope you don't mean what I think you do—"

"Goodness, where have you been living – the moon? Madame Montvoisin provides the best service in the city. I recommend her to everyone. Safe and silent. Not like those others. They make a mistake, and *voilà*! Your body is dumped in the river. Madame does not make mistakes. You're safer with her than with the King's own surgeon. Her organisation includes all the best ones in the city; they work on commission. All the society ladies go to her. How else could they live the gallant life at court? You ought to know; you've sent her enough business yourself."

Oh, Geneviève, how could you have been so simple? La Voisin is not like you, enchanted with playing the game of deception. How could you have ever believed for a minute she didn't offer real services, not flimflam, for all the money she gets? Here it was, as plain as could be before my very nose, and I hadn't recognised it. She was an angel maker, a high-society abortionist, and the fortune-telling was a cover. The penalty was torture and death – for her, for her associates, for the women who employed her services. Suddenly I saw it all clearly. The secret signals, the terrified faces. A silent network of women, all tied together by fear and the possibility of mutual blackmail, was hidden behind the shining façade of gallantry and jewels, of elegant gowns and velvet masks. Hairdressers, perfumers, ladies' tailors, all organised into a secret business cartel that covered the city like a web. "Have you a problem, my dear? I know the cleverest woman who can fix it. No one ever need know." And I was in the centre of it all. As I blew out the candle, I asked, "And La Bosse?"

"She's a filthy woman. Only whores go to her."

That night I couldn't sleep, despite the medicine. And as I twisted and tangled in the sheets, I felt the eerie warmth of the oven behind the tapestry, and saw the desperate eyes of the women in the waiting room, and heard Uncle laughing, because he was a man, and could do anything he wished.

SEVENTEEN

The meeting of the King's Council had just broken up, and His Majesty had left by an inner door, to avoid the cluster of petitioners at the public entrance of the council chamber. As the dignified procession of ministers of state, in full wigs and wide plumed hats, entered the corridor, there was a murmur of disappointment among the waiting crowd. A delicate jockeying at the door resulted in Colbert's exit being delayed in favour of the Marquis de Louvois – Louvois the merciless, who controlled the King's army and the King's police, whose gaucheries of dress elicited titters from the court, and whose heavy-featured face had the unfortunate look of a coachman.

"Monsieur de Louvois . . ." La Reynie stepped forward as if he had just arrived, rather than having been kept waiting at his superior's request.

"Ah, excellent. You are here," said Louvois in the brusque, commanding tone he habitually used. "I have taken the matter up with His Majesty personally. He commends you and your police for your swiftness in locating her. And His Majesty wants you to know that he takes a profound personal interest in the case. Madame de Brinvilliers must not be allowed to flout the King's justice. She has already been condemned *in absentia*, so it is appropriate that you use all necessary means to bring her back to France for execution."

"That is understood, Your Excellency." The two had drifted away from the crowd, Louvois, with his overdecorated walking stick and ever so slightly vulgar high-heeled shoes, and La Reynie in the sober garb of the chief of police on an official visit to Versailles. In one of the great official antechambers, apart from all listeners, they paused.

"There is something else," Louvois said quietly. "There are persistent rumours that some of the first names in France are involved with an underground traffic in poisons. His Majesty is concerned that such tales may undermine the glory of his reign. So far, the marquise is the only woman of quality who has been connected with such crimes. His Majesty wishes you to conduct an extensive investigation concerning her possible confederates. Only when we have proved to our satisfaction that she is an isolated monster can we put these rumours to rest at last."

"I agree completely, Monsieur de Louvois," responded La Reynie. "But what if she is not?" Louvois turned away, silent.

Even though his carriage did not reach Paris until after nightfall, La Reynie sent a messenger immediately to Desgrez's house.

EIGHTEEN

"Now, you must be very careful of the Countess of Soissons," announced Sylvie as she laced up my corset. "*Oof—* Do you really want it this tight all the way up? You look straight enough to me once it's on . . . Well, you shouldn't offend her, is what I meant to say. Those Italian ladies, they're all poisoners. 'The Italian vice' . . . it's not just a disease, that's what I say! And the Comte de Soissons died just two years ago under *very* mysterious circumstances, to say nothing of others around her. And her sister, the Duchess of Bouillon, she's another one, I tell you. For all her salon is so fashionable, she's still a Mancini, and they say she's just yearning to be a widow. Don't look so surprised. Believe me, I have my ways of knowing. But their custom can be the making of a fortune-teller – not that you aren't all the mode since you read for the Queen. But the Countess – she's a repeat customer. Please her, and you'll make your fortune with all those ambitious, plotting ladies. But if you're dead, you won't do either of us a bit of good, so don't go stepping wrong."

The Comtesse de Soissons, a dark-haired woman with a pointed, crafty face, and an oddly childish, turned-up nose, received me in her rooms at the palace. They were very tiny, by the world's standards, but I now recognised how extraordinarily large and well located they were by Versailles standards, where the courtiers of even the highest ranks are packed in like pickled herring in a barrel. And of course, the gilded and inlaid furniture, the heavy carpets, and the silk tapestries were of a fabulous luxury.

"I want to know whether a . . . supremely noble . . . lover will turn again to me," she whispered, out of the hearing of her attendants. Oh, goodness, I thought, another woman who wants to sleep with the King. They came in the dozens, high and low. Poor provincial nobility would scrape up their last sou to get their prettiest daughter presented at court; great ladies, married or not, would offer bribes to get a place among the maids of honour to the Queen or any other position where they might be seen frequently by the King. They schemed and fretted and bought love charms by the satchelful. Whenever the King's eye wandered, business always picked up. One night with the King was like a lottery prize. Two or three nights with the King, and the court would bow at your approach. "That's the new favourite," they'd whisper, and the other ladies would turn away their cold, powdered faces. It was a kind of magical transformation that lasted only until the gaze of the Sun King shone elsewhere, and the magic vanished. The supreme position, even for a short while, and your family reaped the benefits – pensions, offices, titles. Only an ex-mistress was not to be envied; everyone knew and pitied the fate of La Vallière, once made a duchess but now residing, permanently shaven-headed and divested of her children, within the dank walls of the Convent of the Carmelites. A very edifying change in life, said the preachers.

The image in the glass was very clear, but its significance was ambiguous. "It is unclear to me what this means," I said frankly. "I see you in a carriage drawn by eight horses, travelling at full speed through the dark by the light of torches borne by outriders."

"A night assignation. To Marly, no doubt. I will regain his love." I let it be.

"With such a favourable reading, you might well wish to enhance the image in the glass with something a bit more powerful. I know a woman on the Rue Beauregard who can help you—"

"Oh, my God. You are another one of La Voisin's! To think that I never suspected! What a joke!" She collapsed back in her armchair with a faint laugh, as if the joke were not very funny at all. "It really is too much – her people are absolutely everywhere." She leaned forward again. Her voice was arch with a courtier's self-control. "Tell me, then. What do you see in the glass for Madame de Montespan? I will pay you well for this second reading."

I prepared my things a second time and looked deep into the water. "Oh, this is very interesting," I replied. "I see Madame de Montespan leaving court. She is enraged, travelling in her coach at full speed towards Paris. It is absolutely laden with boxes." I looked at the water-filled ruts on the road and the new spring buds on the trees. "Yes, definitely, she has been sent away, and all the indications are that it will be quite soon."

"Why, this is delightful!" exclaimed the countess. "She will fall, and all her power will be mine." A little half-smile played across her face. "For whom do you read next?" she asked in a casual tone.

Something whispered in my mind, *this means danger*. And to distract her from an interest in my clients, I said, "In this season of holy penitance I have renounced all further readings in order to spend all my hours at my devotions until once again our most blessed Lord is resurrected." After all, we were approaching Holy Week and it sounded like a good excuse. No fortune-telling until after Easter – what could be more admirable? Besides, at court, unlike Paris, it was good form to keep up the appearance of piety just to stay in fashion. Lately I'd found myself sitting through almost as many Masses as Marie-Angélique used to. Very well, the countess's eyes seemed to say. You won't tell me. We understand each other.

It was after Mass the following Sunday, as I followed the crowd of aristocrats and their servants out of the chapel at Versailles, that I was approached by a stranger.

"Madame," he said, as he pressed past a lackey carrying a hassock for the Duc de Condé, "may we speak? I believe I need, ah, a fortune told." I looked closely at him; he didn't seem the type. Besides, he had a provincial accent, complete with rolling southern *r*s. "You have influence: I've seen you with great lords, I've watched you mobbed in the corridors, almost every wretched day that I've spent in this place. And now – your maid tells me you have the acquaintance of the Duchesse de Vivonne." I glared at Sylvie, who paraded behind me with my missal. Influence peddling again. How much money had she taken from this man I couldn't help?

"I am afraid that the Duchesse de Vivonne will not use her influence for anything less than a thousand pistoles, and that only to pass a petition. You have no guarantee that the King will ever receive it. No, you are far better off trying to present it to the King yourself." The man hadn't a chance. He had the rustic, old-fashioned garb of an impoverished provincial noble. His heels were too flat. His buckles were paste. His neck and wrists were without lace. His wig sat ill over his lined, sun-browned face, and the plumes on his hat were sad and shabby. An *hobereau*, a joke.

"There's so little time, and I've waited for days – when the King leaves his carriage, at the entrance to the chapel before daily Mass, at the door of the King's *cabinet de conseil*. I haven't the clothes, the air of a courtier. I can't push through the crowd. I get pushed aside; he doesn't see me. But I must be heard. I must get my *placet* to the King, or my son is doomed."

So he wasn't trying to get an office or secure an inheritance. My curiosity was aroused. Besides, I felt sorry for him. Most people spent months and thousands of *écus* trying to give the King a petition. One bribed lackeys to find out which way the King would pass, one bribed courtiers for their influence, one bought court dress, one hired an overpriced little attic in the town of Versailles, one wore out shoes. Only a provincial could imagine it would be otherwise.

"What is your petition about, M—?"

"Honoré d'Urbec, of the d'Urbecs of Provence, at your service." He took off his hat with a flourish, and bowed deeply. For a moment my breath stopped. Lamotte's friend. There was no mistaking an odd name like that. But Lamotte's friend had a Parisian accent.

"An old family?" I asked politely.

"Our descent is of a most venerable antiquity," he announced with a grandiose flourish of his hands, his southern accent becoming even stronger as he warmed to his subject. "There were d'Urbecs in the time of Julius Caesar, although the name was spelled differently then; there were d'Urbecs with Charlemagne, on the Crusades. Were our goods proportionate to the historical glory of our name, we would rank among the first families of France, as we do, in a moral sense, to those of true discernment..." A dreamer, I thought; a spinner of tales. In short, a Provençal. The elderly gentleman paused, frozen suddenly by my sharp stare. He looked abashed. "I may as well tell you now, Madame, so that you may decide whether or not you wish to continue our conversation, that our family lost its noble standing in my grandfather's time, through engaging in trade. We have been reduced to paying the *taille*, like commoners."

"I do choose to continue the conversation anyway, Monsieur d'Urbec. But not in this corridor. Besides, I have an engagement that I cannot change. Meet me instead in the Grove of the Domes after dinner, where we may be seated and continue at our leisure. It is unattractive to the courtiers in this season, and we will have quiet."

"At what time?" he asked, taking out an immense, old-fashioned, but very elaborate, egg-shaped watch from his pocket. An astonishing watch for one so clad. It appeared to show the phases of the moon as well as the hour.

"At three, shall we say, Monsieur d'Urbec? I am sorry I will not be free before then." And I went off to hunt for an open table for a free dinner, for I had become a shameless *cherche-midi*, like most denizens of Versailles.

A brisk spring breeze was bending the new-budding branches in the Grove of the Domes, and I was grateful for my heavy shawl when I stepped from my chair to find the elder d'Urbec waiting in the marble arch of the first dome. He swept off his rusty black hat by way of greeting.

"I am now ready to listen to everything, Monsieur d'Urbec," I said, as we seated ourselves on a carved stone bench. I must admit I found it interesting, as I did any information that would shed light on some part of Lamotte's life with his friends. Gambling, the old man confessed, was the madness that had cost the family everything, but when the estates were mortgaged and then lost, an eccentric grandfather had turned a passion for telescopes and mechanisms into a prospering business in naval chronometers and fine timepieces for the gentry, to the humiliation of the family's more genteel members.

"My sons all inherited the talent for mechanisms – but in Florent, I saw something more. Was I wrong to think he was the one who would save us? True, he was hot-headed, like all of us, but – to come to this. God, the disgrace . . ."

An uncle had spotted the boy's promise and, because he had only daughters, had sponsored his studies, sending him to Paris to study law.

"My brother-in-law, you must understand, is not like us. He is a crude man but a successful tax farmer, and he craved an heir to whom he could pass on his offices. I was, at the time, much less successful, save in the matter of sons. So I let him have Florent. The opportunities, you see. Education, money. To study in Paris. Why should he be nothing but a clockmaker all his life? I had always" – and here he sighed – "dreamed he might gain rank and fortune enough to petition for a rehabilitation of the family name and standing. What father wouldn't want these for his son? Then I heard that he had fallen into bad company and was neglecting his studies. Women, I suppose, and low-life taverns stuffed full of unemployed writers. His uncle was furious and threatened to break all ties with him. I came to Paris two weeks ago to remonstrate with him, to urge him to obey his uncle in everything – and what do I find? The seals placed on his room. He is under arrest. I went to the police, to the magistrates. I couldn't discover the charges. Then I found a friend of his. Protected by the Duchesse de Bouillon. He told me my son was sentenced under suspicion of writing a seditious book under the pen name of Cato! Totally unlike the boy. He is like me – he would never be ashamed to air his opinions under his own name! A d'Urbec does not hide in the shadows to oppose wickedness! Why, in the old days, my father would—" Here the old gentleman left off abruptly. So, I thought, it does run in the family. A tribe of hot-headed southern crackpots. Revolutionaries. And probably freethinkers, too.

"Clearly," the old man continued, "it was a case of mistaken identity. But I realised that unless I could find the true 'Cato' I could not make a case. Justice moves swiftly in Paris. The inquiry had already taken place. I went every day to the Châtelet. At last I discovered he had been sent to the galleys for life. Monstrous! Monstrous! A miscarriage of justice! Only the King can right this terrible mistake! But each day that true justice is delayed, my son's position becomes worse. The prisoners have already departed for Marseilles. How many will survive the march on the chain? How many will survive the rowers' bench? I have done business in Marseilles, Madame, and I have seen what becomes of *galériens*. They die, Madame. They die like cattle. A law student? He cannot live.

Better if he were a sturdy vagabond or a highway robber. They are the powerful ones in that world; they form alliances at the expense of the other prisoners. You must assist me, Madame. If I could only approach the King, or the Duc de Vivonne, who is Captain General of the Galleys, or even a woman of influence who might intervene with them . . ."

"I am afraid, Monsieur, that at each step of the process you describe, more money than your wealthy brother-in-law collects for the state in a year would have to change hands. You are not very worldly if you think that justice can be got without money." I looked at his petition. It would never move a magistrate who had seen the evidence. What had they found when they searched his room? What had they got from Griffon, or from Lamotte?

"What is the evidence that links your son with this scurrilous work?" I asked.

"Ah, none whatsoever, Madame. That I know for a fact; I bribed a clerk of the court. They had nothing but the book itself, which was banned by the order of the Lieutenant General of Police, a fellow named La Reynie, and a denunciation from a paid informer who lives in taverns. The informer is known to be an untrustworthy fellow, and even the magistrate on the case doubts his word, the clerk informed me. But suspicion is enough, Madame, in cases of treason. And the work, I hear, would merit this. It predicts the fall of the state from fiscal corruption – not, of course, that I have read it, mind you," he added nervously, looking around. Then he looked at me, his face troubled, and went on: "This Lamotte tells me that he managed to see him once in prison. My son never confessed during the interrogation. And Lamotte swears they never found a copy, a note, anything in his possession. So my case is proven. Mistaken identity!"

"No confession? Then perhaps there's hope. Continue with your petition, Monsieur d'Urbec, and I have an idea that I will pursue. And my suggestion is this: take up a position where the King's Apartment connects with the Salle des Gardes, for the Salle des Gardes is wide and long, and the crowd around the King will disperse somewhat, so that you will be able to approach him there."

"A wonderful idea! Why did no one else suggest it to me? A

thousand thanks, Madame! Is there some consideration I may make for your kind intervention?"

"Hardly. I imagine my mercenary little Sylvie has already done you sufficient damage. For myself, I act in the name of justice served." He bowed again deeply and left, trudging through the spring mud, while Syvie summoned the bearers of my chair, who had been throwing dice only a few paces beyond the domed pavilion.

All that afternoon I was in a kind of dreamy daze. André Lamotte and I were sitting at an intimate little supper table, drinking wine.

"That was terribly clever, the way you saved d'Urbec. It's a pity I didn't think of it myself. I admire a brilliant woman. And brains so rarely are combined with beauty. Lackey, pour the Burgundy I've been saving. Geneviève, let's drink to our future." And as we raised glasses, I shook off the dream. Enough of this stupidity, Geneviève Pasquier, I said to myself. Girls who daydream end badly, Grandmother always said. But then, who was she to talk? Hadn't she wept over *Astrée* in her own day?

5 April 1675. What madness makes me want Lamotte who will never have me? It's enough to make a person believe in demons that can seize the soul. Is it because he's beautiful or because he was Marie-Angélique's, and having him would make me as beautiful as she? It certainly isn't his mind. No, it has to be his charm. Even the memory of it warms me through. And he makes the world seem deliciously simple. I want to be part of his easy simplicity— But as I wrote, I started, as if something cold had touched me. I looked up into the dark beyond the candle and saw something hollow-eyed and mocking, staring at me. It looked like the ghost of Florent d'Urbec.

That evening in the town of Versailles, as Sylvie brushed off my clothes in our tiny little rented room under the eaves, I looked up from writing in what she chose to call my "account book". "Sylvie, I want you to take this letter into Paris tomorrow and put it in the confessional box of the Jesuit church on the Rue Saint-Antoine."

"What's in it?" she asked impudently.

"What's in it is a silver louis for you. But if you wish, you may read it. I haven't sealed it yet." Sylvie took the letter and worked her way slowly through it, making her mouth work with each word.

"*Ooo.* This is nasty. A denunciation to the police. Who is this Cato fellow who promised you marriage and absconded with your silver spoons? And you travelled all the way to Paris to find him, and he'd taken up with another woman? He seems pretty villainous— tall, reddish hair with a beard that grows brown, scar on one cheek, makes his living writing *libelles* under false names and takes money from William of Orange. Nasty work!"

"Whoever he is, he is the exact opposite of Monsieur d'Urbec, who is dark and of medium height."

"Oho, you're the sly one. Case of mistaken identity, eh? Delays matters a bit. And if they haven't tortured him to find out who the printer was, why, they might even let him go. That is, if it doesn't hurt their pride too much." She looked at me shrewdly. "But I didn't know you knew this fellow d'Urbec. Are you soft on him?"

"I don't know him at all," I answered hurriedly.

"Then how'd you know what he looks like?"

"Why, I suppose he looks like his father, that's all."

"Too bad for him if he's red headed, then," she answered before she blew out the candle. But her voice sounded cynical.

NINETEEN

The dispatch rider from Paris set out from Fort Saint-Jean early in the morning. Even in the chill air, the stench of the wintering galleys bobbing at anchor almost overpowered him as he rode the length of the Quai du Port to the Arsenal. The pride of the French fleet, the choice assignment for the sons of the highest aristocracy, the low, narrow ships looked nothing like their summer incarnations. The bands of musicians were dispersed, the silk pennants in storage. The gilt and crimson scrollwork was invisible beneath huge canvas tents that stretched from the bow to the stern over the rowers' benches, giving the ships the air of monstrous cocoons. The rider could read the names on the bows: *L'Audace*, *La Superbe*, *L'Héroine* . . .

As the icy pink dawn faded from the sky, the cocoons appeared to hatch hundreds of galley slaves who had been released from the chains that held them to their benches all night. Now chained in pairs, surrounded by armed escorts of halberdiers, they were herded across the quay to various workplaces in the city of Marseilles, to earn their winter keep. The rider hardly noticed this everyday sight, and having made his first delivery at the Arsenal, he headed to the more fashionable section of Marseilles, where the Captain of the *Superbe* had his winter residence.

Breakfast had just been cleared when the lackey showed in the messenger, and the captain was still clad in his quilted silk dressing gown, his wigless head protected by a fur-lined, embroidered cap.

"Well, well," he said, almost to himself as he read the letter from the Captain General of the Galleys, "it looks as if someone has a friend at court. Remind me, Vincent. Who is this Florent d'Urbec? Have I seen him?" Vincent, whose shaven head and eyebrows proclaimed him also to be a wintering *galérien*, thought a moment and answered.

"I think it's that new one on number seven, the one who weeps."

"Oh, yes, the fellow who mends clocks. I like to have skilled trades among my rowers; I'm making a good deal of money from him this winter." He squinted again at the dispatch. *"Pah!* These courtiers – they don't understand necessity. Do they expect me just to throw away the men I need? I must have a full complement for the campaign this summer; I see no reason to let a perfectly good one go just now. Later is good enough to satisfy the captain general." The captain refolded the offending paper and opened the seal on the next dispatch. He waved his hand to dismiss his lackey. "Go see his *comite*, Vincent, and tell him to inform this fellow that when he can provide me with the price of a Turkish slave to replace him, I will let him go."

The *Superbe* spent the first weeks of spring in manoeuvres designed to break the new men to the oar, then joined the fleet on campaign against North African corsairs for the remaining months of summer. Chained around the clock to the benches, the *galériens* sometimes rowed for ten to twelve hours at a stretch, the *comites* feeding them bread dipped in wine to keep them from dropping. Even so, by the summer's end, thirty-six had died and were pitched overboard.

D'Urbec began by assuring himself that in defiance of the galley masters he would at least keep his mind as his own. But as the first week ran into the second and then the third, he realised that pain and hunger, systematically applied, had done their work. His brain could no longer hold more than a minute at a time in focus; his concerns had shrunk to the size of his bread ration. At night he shivered in the open air, sleepless from the rattle of chained men scratching their vermin. And when at last he saw that he had become little more than a beast with arms, no different than the thieves on either side of him, his heart broke. The fever that haunted the oarsmen's benches took possession of him. He had decided to die.

Images moved through his brain randomly. Paris. His friends. A stable yard at home. He could hear voices talking about him.

"Another one with fever, Lieutenant . . ."

". . . the hospital weakens them. Just move him to the end of the oar. He'll harden up . . ."

The rattle of chains and someone saying "Move, you." Other images. A sign over a door, *"D'Urbec et fils, Horlogers."* His father waving goodbye as he left on the diligence for Paris, wearing a second-hand suit. A frail girl with grey eyes, clutching a Latin book. The frightened look on the maid's face at the back door of the great house as she said, "Monsieur, she is dead." ". . . but she was well when I saw her last . . ." "Monsieur, she drowned herself." Let it all go, said his mind as it left him.

The captain increased rations to combat the fever and had meat issued to the rowers. D'Urbec, wasted, blistered by the sun, his eyes burned deep into their sockets, rowed on at the easier end of the oar, his shoulders and arms gradually acquiring the abnormal strength of the *galérien*.

"You speak well," said the ship's *tavernier* when he measured out d'Urbec's watery wine ration. "What were you before?"

"A law student," said d'Urbec, his eyes dull and desperate.

"Ah, just what I could use," replied the *tavernier*, who was also a fence of stolen property when the ship docked for the winter at Marseilles. "I have a client who needs a marriage certificate for his daughter – dated last year, if you know what I mean. Could you draw one up, nice and legal, if I got the right parchment and seals for it?"

"It would not be hard."

"What about wills, deeds? I know people who'll pay well."

"Of course," answered the law student who had once wanted to reform the state.

It was not until the following spring that a filthy, hollow-eyed man in worn, badly fitting government-issue clothes left Marseilles on foot for Paris. A black, shapeless hat hid his shaven head, but nothing could conceal that his face was without eyebrows. A short jacket, sprung out at the seams, and a coarse, patched shirt concealed the GAL branded deep into his shoulder. He was filled with bitter knowledge: how much wine diluted with seawater could be drunk before illness set in, how to bribe a *comite* to spare the lash, how much more easily money could be made secretly forging legal documents than mending clocks, and the exact price of a Turk. Hidden inside his shirt was the document that gave him freedom and a much-refolded, grimy letter from his father that he had paid a considerable bribe to receive. One passage, puzzled over again and again, was burned into his mind: ". . . a generous and titled widow with great influence at court has helped me secure this miracle . . ." Who? Who? he mumbled silently to himself. Those who passed him on the road thought he was insane.

TWENTY

I left court shortly before Easter and returned to Paris, for while the fortune-telling business vanished during Holy Week at Versailles, it remained as good as ever in the city, where the austerities of the season had never interfered with the main business of life, which was to have a good time. The night that we packed, Sylvie got a glimpse of the heap of gold louis in my locked coffer and sucked in her breath.

"Oh my," she said, in her sharp little voice. "That's a fortune. I could retire on that."

"It goes to La Voisin," I replied, locking the box.

"And not a bit to us, for some nice new clothes, or a trip to Vichy to take the waters and meet some good-looking men? She sure has a racket, she does. I wish I was her. I been figuring. I been watching. I calculate, just from what I know about who works for her, she must bring in maybe a hundred thousand *écus* a year – straight profit." Sylvie's eyes narrowed as she savoured the sum. A greater income than all but the mightiest noble families in the kingdom. It dwarfed the modest sum in the box, the annual income of an ordinary family of the provincial aristocracy.

"A contract is a contract," I said, as we departed down the rickety outer staircase.

"Sometimes I think that for an old lady you're kind of simple," she answered, puffing beneath her burden of bundles as she followed behind me.

We arrived after Mass on Easter Sunday at the villa on the Rue Beauregard. The mingled smell of a dozen meat dishes to break the long season of fasting penetrated every room from the inner fastness of the kitchen. The whole house had been newly cleaned for the holiday. The heavy silver plate, all freshly polished, glinted down from the sideboard. The carpets were beaten, the rich, dark furniture dusted, down to the last knob and carving. Marie-Marguerite bustled by in a new dress and cap, with a fresh little linen-and-lace apron that once would have sent my sister into an ecstasy. Only Antoine Montvoisin was not to be seen in new clothes. He was upstairs, sick in bed. Sylvie followed me into La Voisin's little cabinet, carrying the locked coffer.

"You look sour this week. Come, wasn't life pleasant? Imagine, you might live like that always if you are guided by me. Remember that I made you," the sorceress added, counting up the money on her writing desk and opening her great ledger. The little cat's face winked up at me from atop a sheaf of papers with cabbalistic drawings on them. "Is it all here?" she asked in a suspicious voice.

"Everything. I have an accounting, if you wish." Sylvie held out the open coffer. A sudden look of concern crossed La Voisin's face as she snatched up the top notebook, to be replaced with one of relief as she glanced through the pages.

"All in code. Excellent," she said. "Occasionally, you have a sensible instinct after all. I never let my books leave this cabinet, and it is steel lined, with the finest locks in the kingdom. Remember, our first duty is to protect our clients. We go silent to the grave. That is what protects our business."

"The business of fortune-telling or the business of abortions?" I asked.

"My, a taste of the great life, and we become Frondeurs and rebels, don't we? Those who are raised the highest are the most ungrateful, aren't they? Consider this, you are young and without obligations: I support ten mouths."

"You make more than most ministers of state."

"But with much more difficulty and struggle, my dear. Learn from me, and I'll teach you how to become mistress of great enterprises. One day, you'll be as wealthy as I am." She closed her ledger and stood to lock up the money in her strongbox. One of her big cats rose from dozing by the fire and rubbed at her ankles. It was odd, I reflected. She didn't have any black cats. You'd think a witch would have all black cats. Instead she had tabby and tortoiseshell, orange, grey, white, and even one that was sort of pinkish. But the black ones seemed to have vanished, if they had ever been there at all. Then she turned to me, as if she'd just thought of something, but somehow, the gesture seemed contrived. "Now, I've been thinking," she said in a somewhat forced-sounding voice. "You are rising and need a better address. The front room of a cheap boarding-house is hardly the place for the sensation of Versailles to operate her business. What about a splendid little apartment? Or better, a town house? So private, you know. The higher clients like privacy. The greatest of my clients are only content with my little garden pavilion. There is a charming little house coming free in the Marais . . ." So soon, a house? I thought. This is not entirely beneficence. Is she afraid I'm flying so high that I may soon leave her?

"Now the house is a bit narrow," La Voisin was saying, "but it's the best of addresses, and a very private back way out. And a footman – yes, you'll need a footman, and I'm sure I could find you a splendid one. Why, you're almost ready to move up! I'd planned to wait a year, but you're so talented! And Easter, that's sort of the start of a new year, isn't it? So, now, you'll celebrate your new elevation with us, by having dinner here."

Something about her manner sent a shudder through me. I've offended her, I thought. She's angry. I'll never live to see that town house. The whole story is just a ruse to get me to eat here. Didn't old Montvoisin warn me? Why didn't I control myself better and bide my time? Why did I have to blurt out that I knew about those abortions, like a fool? A few years, and I'd have been free. Now, dinner. A cold sweat broke out on my temples as I answered, "Oh, yes, let's celebrate." Easy, easy. Smile and don't show you know anything, Geneviève. Maybe it will go by. Maybe she'll forget what I said, and her anger will pass.

By then the guests had begun to arrive, crowding into the black reception room and the richly furnished dining room beyond, exclaiming and greeting one another. Le Sage, the magician, wrapped in his grey cape, the pharmaceutical specialists La Trianon and La Dodée in bright new gowns that sprouted ribbons at every seam, La Lépère complaining and wiping her nose with a spring cold, the Abbé Mariette, an elegantly dressed young society priest, La Pelletier all in violet taffeta, the same stuff she used for her love sachets, La Debraye, La Delaporte, La Deslauriers, witches all, and more: men and women, priests, tradesmen, *nouvellistes*, diabolists, alchemists, and all sorts of titled folk of dubious origins. Last of all, a strange, hunched-over old man in a cassock, with a debauched face and a swollen nose covered with purple veins, was shown in. He was accompanied by his mistress, a woman with a lined face and hollow eyes. It was the Abbé Guibourg, Master of the Black Mass, who paid in gold for abortionists' foetuses and newborn infants from the orphanages of Paris. At the sight of him, people drew back in the crowded rooms to let them both pass, as if some mysterious cold wind had accompanied them in.

"Has Madame Brunet come to you yet?" La Pelletier said, and laughed. "She wants Philibert, the flute player, at any cost!"

"He's in great demand in this city – I have two clients who want him as well; I imagine we've sold all three the same *poudre d'amour*. Oh well, someone will be happy out of it, so between us, we'll retain partial credit." La Trianon chuckled.

"Either that, or mine will be proved definitively the most powerful," said La Pelletier with a certain professional calm.

"As long as you depend so much on essence of cock's testicles, you needn't count on it," sniffed La Trianon.

"But, my dear, he should have worn a glass mask . . . it's no surprise he was asphyxiated . . . that process creates so many fumes . . ." I could hear from across the room.

"She does such a business in *poudres de succession*, but I don't imagine for long. She is careless. And so vulgar . . ." The words flitted through my head, barely making sense as the terror mounted.

"Well, La Bosse is slipping, you know . . . she really should retire . . ."

". . . so it all goes to show, that strategy is everything, my dear. It's everything—" I realised with a start that La Trianon was addressing me.

"Oh yes, oh yes, I can see that. It's very clever," I answered, hoping I made sense. My voice was thin with fright, and I was sure everyone in the room could hear the pounding of my heart.

The soup was clear. It must be all right. Wouldn't it be cloudy if something were in it? Margot brought it in from the kitchen and served it from a big tureen on the sideboard. How close she was to her mistress. Did I see her hand hover a moment over one of the soup bowls as it passed by her?

"Do eat your soup, dear. You look pale. Soup is good for the pallor," remarked my hostess. Yes, good for it. Eliminates it entirely, along with any other health worries you might have. I took a spoonful.

"Delicious," I said. My sense of taste was abnormally active. Was that a metallic aftertaste? Was it salt?

The first *ragoût* came from the kitchen ready served. Rabbit poached in wine sauce. Onions. And – I could see them – mushrooms. Wasn't there a Roman emperor poisoned by a mushroom? Messalina, that's who did it.

"Oh, the flavour is exquisite," sighed the Abbé Mariette from across the table. "Your cook is truly an artist." I started. La Voisin cast a piercing look at me. All but the mushrooms, I thought. The acute flavouring that fear gives a dish is indescribable. Never in my life have I tasted with such precision the delicately mingled flavours of garlic and herbs, the subtle aromatic savour of wine. The brilliant, heightened flavour was unbelievably delicious. Almost intoxicating. Intoxicating? Something in the sauce? Never mind, it was done now. Enjoy the flavours, Geneviève; you might as well. It's your last dinner on earth.

"The mushrooms ... chanterelles ... so delicate..." someone was saying. Death's heads. Are they what had imparted the subtle and unique flavour to the sauce? No wonder I had never tasted it before.

"Do try the mushrooms, dear Marquise. They are especially in your honour." Did I hear a hint of sly amusement in her voice? Was the little smile too fixed?

"Oh yes, they are lovely." Definitely. It had to be the mushrooms. The taste was exquisite, elegant, incapable of being described. What were those prayers I'd daydreamed through at Mass? They'd flown out of my mind. The Paternoster, was that the right order? It didn't work if it wasn't in the right order. Did I even have a soul? Oh, I wished I had one now, or even that I believed I had one, even if I didn't. I didn't want to die. Wine. A toast. To the arts of Le Sage. To my triumph. Drink, drink. It's your last night on earth.

"My, success has quite gone to your head, Madame. Le Sage, Mariette, carry her upstairs." I was deposited on the bed in the great room with the sinister tapestry. The heavy canopy, draped in rich green and gold brocade, swam in circles above my head. The dark red wall swayed and whirled. Good. Let death come here. I couldn't pick up my head. As my eyes closed and I drifted away, I said the only prayer I could muster. God, if you are, take my soul, if I have one.

I drifted in and out of consciousness as the late afternoon faded into dusk. In a far corner of the now dim room, I could make out whispers.

"Quiet. Is she listening?" A bare scratch of a voice.

"She's dead drunk. She won't hear a thing." Le Sage.

"He grows weaker by the day. His eyes are sunken in. He coughs. I can't bear it."

"Only a short while, then, until we marry, my love."

"I tell you, I can't stand it. It's tearing me apart."

"Love and yearning for me, O sublime queen, or regrets for that miserable weakling you married? What's wrong? Why do you turn coward now? You wanted it; I cast it."

"The spell. It's too ghastly. You must reverse it." At last, I recognised the voice. Hers. La Voisin's.

"Reverse the spell on a ram's head? It's never been done."

"Dig it up, dig it up, I say. I can't stand it any more, seeing him waste so terribly!" The shriek of despair made my eyes fly open. Luckily I had the presence of mind to close them again and lie there, stiff, without moving.

"You don't love me if you dare not risk even this little. I have been loved by greater women than you. Together, we could rule Europe. By yourself, what have you got?"

"Far more than you have ever achieved, you ungrateful, inconsequential man. Whose influence rescued you from the galleys? What convict ever left the galleys except in a shroud? Only you! My high influence at court saw you put ashore at Genoa. Did you think it was an accident? I created you, I can destroy you! Go, go now and dig it up, wherever you buried it out there, and bring it to me in this room! I'll reverse the spell myself. What has he ever done, that man you despise so, but fail me? It's you, you who have betrayed me, time and again – and I come back and beg to be betrayed again. Isn't that love? Love to the point of blindness? Don't try me, Adam, or you'll pay dearly for it." I could hear the scraping of a chair and the sound of footsteps.

"Very well. If you think so little of me, I'll bring it to you. But don't expect co-operation from my associates for your . . . little supplies."

"There are other alchemists in this city . . . I don't need you, you . . . mountebank." My mind was still foggy. The walls turned grey and vanished.

I awoke in the dark. A candelabrum at the opposite end of the room shed a feeble light that did not fill the dark corners. The smell of something rotten being burned came from the oven behind the tapestry. On the table beneath the candelabrum lay an open *grimoire*, the witches' book of spells.

"So, you're finally stirring, are you? I've never seen a human being drunker. You thought I was going to poison you, didn't you? Never fear. The day I decide to poison you, you'll never know it." La Voisin was wearing a sombre black gown that I'd never seen before. The light flickered across her face where she sat beside the candles. Her even features had a frightening beauty beneath the dark coils of her hair.

"You stand to make me a fortune. I never destroy the sources of fortune," she said, folding her hands in her lap. "After that, we will be friends. Only women can be friends. We know how to help each other. When a man and a woman are friends, the man always uses the woman. She must feed his pride, his pocketbook. Not so with us, eh? We who have nothing must raise each other up. But then, only women can be enemies. Men, they don't think a woman is worth the trouble. And that is their weak spot, isn't it? That is how we rule the world of men, we witches. Through their blind spot. Do you have a headache yet?"

The thin coils of smoke above the candles ascended into the eerie darkness that hovered beneath the ceiling. I felt horribly ill.

"I feel as if I'm going to die."

"Good. It will teach you not to drink too much in company. How would you have had the wit to take the antivenom if in fact you had been poisoned? Even a cat has the sense to come in out of the rain." Hearing himself mentioned, the largest of her cats, the grey tom, leaped upon her lap. "You aren't ready yet," I thought I heard her say. The last I remember was the rumbling rise and fall of a cat's purring.

* * *

I awoke the next morning on a cot in the low grey room under the eaves that housed the servants. Sylvie was shaking me.

"Wake up, wake up! All Paris is ablaze with the news. And with your prediction. You're famous! We have three appointments today in the city, and more at court! Oh, there are dozens of hopefuls now, all of the highest rank. What they'll *pay*! Consultations with you, powders from Madame. We'll all be rich!"

"Oh, Jesus, don't shout so. My head's breaking in two. What's the news?"

"How could you not know, when you yourself predicted it? Madame de Montespan has been sent away from court by the King. She's here in Paris, licking her wounds, while her rivals sharpen their claws!"

I groaned and sat up. My head felt like an inflated pig's bladder. Ready to burst. "How . . . what?" I managed to mutter.

"Oh, it was astonishing. Père Bossuet denounced the King's sin with Madame de Montespan from the pulpit on Easter. And he refused the King communion, just on the eve of his departure for the front in Flanders. The King can't go into battle unshriven. They say the King begged for a separation only, as he had done once before as a condition to obtain communion. But that was in the days of Père Lachaise, who was much less exacting. Monsieur Bossuet was adamant. 'Give up the woman,' he said, 'for you are in double adultery, because she is married as well as you.' Now all the unmarried ladies have their hopes up. If I were near the King, I'm sure he'd notice *me*! But I'll not have the chance, well, not unless . . ." Oh my, another consumer of love potions and lucky charms. You'd think the people who sell them would know how ridiculous they are. But they're their own best customers.

But once dressed and downstairs, I noticed that my hostess was not as active an enthusiast as Sylvie. Her two youngest boys, neither yet out of girls' gowns and leading strings, were quarrelling over a ball; their older brother, all of ten years old, was just being sent to pick up a parcel at La Trianon's laboratory. Her stepdaughter, Marie-Marguerite, gave her an evil stare as she passed through the room with breakfast for her father on a tray.

"Well! The *marquise* has finally decided to get up," she said in a sarcastic tone. "Greetings, O illustrious one. Your sun has brightened our horizon at last."

"What's bitten *you* this morning?" Headaches do not make me sweet.

"How *dare* you!" she hissed, her eyes dangerous. "When I sent you out into the world to create new business, I did not mean for you to stir up trouble between my clients." My head hurt too much for tact.

"I did exactly what you said. If you don't like it, then maybe you should keep me better informed, instead of always trying to be so devious." I snapped.

"The Countess of Soissons has been my client for many years. How dare you try to steal her business?"

"I didn't – she called me. When I sent her to you, she just laughed." Madame's mouth was clamped in a grim line.

"You had no business predicting Madame de Montespan's downfall." Well, even with a headache, I knew what that meant. The Marquise of Montespan was her client, too. Not two women one would wish to get caught between.

"She asked, and it was in the glass."

"In the glass, in the glass, was it? Don't you remember any of my lessons? Never read someone else's fortune for a client! You miserable little fool; you'll bring them both down on you!" On yourself, you mean, I thought. But by now La Voisin's rage was billowing like stormclouds. Ordinarily, I would have been frightened, but having already considered myself poisoned once, I had lost all fear. I returned her stare so fiercely that she recoiled from me. "Steal my clients! You set yourself up, don't you! Who pulled you from the gutter, eh? Answer me! Answer me!" Everyone in the room had stopped to stare at the battle.

"It was the river, and I wasn't in it anyway," I said in my most precise voice.

"Oh, yes, we've studied philosophy! We're not a poor woman who raised ourself up. We know Latin, we know Greek, like a man. We're not common! We're almost a *Matignon* on our mother's side. Oh yes, bow to the Matignon blood in the little hussy, if you can find it anywhere!"

"Don't you dare insult my mother, you . . . you dreadful old witch!"

"A witch, eh? There's more honour among witches than among the Matignons, I can tell you that. I *made* you, do you understand, I *made* you! I wanted you, I saved you, I created you, and you're *mine*! Why do you think the door was unlocked the morning you left home? Why do you think I was there to keep you from the river? Your own loving *mother* had better plans than that. Ah, the minute they read the will, she was at my door. 'Why pay for a funeral?' I told her. 'Put her out and you'll be rid of her. She'll never be found, and they'll never trace the death to you.' I could see the glint in her eye. The glint of money. 'Take back your fee,' I said. 'You don't need what you came for. You can have it all without cost.' Without cost – that's what made her eyes shine! Money! That's what makes a *Matignon* act. Money, money, and only money. The money your father left you – she'd stop at nothing to have it. And how much better at a bargain. Oh, what a thrifty little mother you have! An honourable race, the Matignons, like all the other *great ones* who come to see me. Oh, indeed! But you, you've got God-given talent, you eat and drink and clothe yourself at my expense . . ."

My bones felt like ice. It fit, it all fit, like the missing piece of a puzzle. My mind shrank from it.

"Prove it," I said.

The sorceress stood still, looking at me with her dark eyes. "Come with me to my cabinet, and I will show you your mother's entry in my account book," she said in a calm, bitter voice. With a growing numbness, I followed her into her little gilded cabinet room. It was the next to the last entry, at the top of an empty page. "Wishes to purchase inheritance powder for her daughter." The date, after father's death. The last entry, "Sent away without." Mother hadn't been back since.

"I never knew . . . I didn't know . . . any of it . . ." I whispered, as I leaned against the wall to keep from falling. Oh, truth, how ugly you are, when we meet like this, face-to-face. I would rather never know you.

"No," said the sorceress, lowering her voice and inspecting me with her shrewd, almost malignant black eyes, "you didn't know, did you? Tell me—" And her voice became all honeyed and persuasive. "Tell me, what did you read in the glass for the Countess of Soissons?"

"She just . . . asked me what would become of Madame de

Montespan, and I looked and saw her leaving court in a hurry, in her carriage with four outriders, on the Paris road." I felt cold all over. My eyes hurt. My face was wet.

"Which she took yesterday . . . *hmm*. Blow your nose on this, and then read in the glass for me." She extended the embroidered handkerchief she had tucked up her sleeve. She took out a water vase from the cupboard and rang for Nanon to come and fill it up. I looked into the glass that she had set before me. An image formed and shone out of the depths. Madame de Montespan, dressed in cloth of gold embroidered with gold thread, covered with diamonds, sitting regally in an armchair, with other ladies, including the governess I'd seen, standing or sitting on stools about her. A richly dressed man with dark, pockmarked Spanish features entered the room. The King.

"I see Madame de Montespan, all in cloth of gold and diamonds, entertaining the King before the ladies of the court."

"Well, that's better." She looked at me. "Now pull yourself together. You have appointments. And I have business. The carriages are already lining up in the street. Oh, the devil! Lucien is gone; I'll have to send Philippe." And with that she called in her loutish, dough-faced thirteen-year-old son, the one who was far too fat and never did anything, and spoke in a low voice. But I heard anyway, for my ears are good.

"Go to Mademoiselle des Oeillets in the Rue Vaugirard immediately. And tell her that I have means within my power to resolve her mistress's future in the most dazzling way. And if you are not there and back by suppertime, I will stop your sweets for a month." As he left, she said disgustedly, *"That* one is Antoine's. Lazy wretch. My children disappoint me. I expect better from you. Remember, you I chose. And I have made you. You are nothing without me. Go, and wash your face. You look like a fool." As I got up to go, she said calmly, "From now on, pretend you cannot read the futures of those who do not touch the glass. This will keep you from being forced to read the fortunes of distant enemies of your clients. After all, they may become clients in their turn. And you are not clever enough to extract yourself from the intrigues that result from reading the fortunes of third parties. Now, return in a week. I think I will have good news for you. The vengeance that I have promised you will soon be within your grasp."

TWENTY-ONE

"Oh, dear Abbé, you have so relieved my soul on this point."
The fine-boned little blonde in the pale-blue satin leaned closer
to the society abbé who knelt before her, holding her hand to
his lips. The marquise shuddered and pulled her shawl closer
around her with her other hand. Was it the chill of the stone
bench in the convent garden or some premonition, some
tremor of the soul that made the gooseflesh break out on her
arms?

"It cannot be sin if two hearts yearn as purely as ours. How
long . . . how long I have admired you from afar, my dear
Marquise. To save your soul for God, even at the cost of my
own damnation . . ." The abbé rolled his brown eyes heaven-
wards. How attractive his lean, dark face looked in the
twilight. What was the scent that clung about him? Not unlike
incense – it reminded the marquise of heavenly things, and
somehow at the same time of this latest, divine, passion. She
clasped both his hands and pulled him up beside her onto the
bench.

"Must . . . must I confess all?"

"Only before God," whispered the ardent abbé. "No man
alive need know. Write it all down; plead for absolution for your
sins to Him who sits enthroned above. Then seal the document
and bring it to me. We will burn it together, offering up the
very smoke with prayers before the seat of the Supremely
Merciful One." The abbé pressed her hand to his heart. "Feel
my heart," he whispered. "You can never doubt its sincerity; it
beats only for you . . ."

The whites of the marquise's eyes flashed bright, eager, and
insane in the rapidly descending dusk. Her powers of love,
undimmed, even though she had passed forty. Her magnetism, her enchantment, had brought this slender, dark,
worldly abbé to her lonely exile across the miles. The sexual
and divine, all mixed in a mad brew, rose to her head.

"A kiss," he pleaded.

"Yes," she answered, and the embrace sent fire through her. Her youth, not yet spent. Passion, still hers. She felt the old part of her life fleeing from her like a shadow. Yes, she would free herself from it all, confess, and then flee, a new being, washed clean, with this man who made her pulses race like a young girl's.

"Tomorrow," he whispered in her ear, and the soft sensation of his breath made her nerves thrill. "At the Sign of the Castle, on the road from Liège. I cannot live until the moment I hold you in my arms."

That night, the Marquise de Brinvilliers sat up for hours in her convent room. By the light of a candle, she listed the catalogue of her sins: sodomy, incest, murder, attempted murder. She solemnly named the dead: enemies who had offended her, strangers who stood in her way, relatives systematically poisoned for their inheritances. The list covered sixteen pages.

Captain Desgrez returned to the Sign of the Castle.

"So, Captain, how did it go?" asked the policeman disguised as his servant.

"She'll be leaving the convent grounds tomorrow of her own volition, with a written confession in her hand," replied the false abbé. The "servant" whistled through his teeth in appreciation.

"Well done, Captain! Brilliant!"

"I feel like washing," said Desgrez, running his finger under the tight neckline of his *soutane*.

"You *do* smell rather like a gigolo. What is that stuff you've got on?"

"Something my wife picked up in the Rue Beauregard. Supposed to make the wearer irresistible."

"I have to hand it to you, Captain. You don't overlook anything."

"It's my duty," said Desgrez, as he sat down and stared into the fire.

TWENTY-TWO

The news from court had crowded the street outside my house with carriages and chairs. All morning I saw clients, and in the afternoon I made house calls in the more fashionable neighbourhoods. That was when I visited women who were not allowed out of their houses, who feared to be seen at a fortune-teller's – women who were ill, or mad. But wealthy.

My last call of the day was on a new client, a stranger who lived in a little *bijou* town house in the chic new suburban district on the Rue Vaugirard, on the way to Versailles. A maid met me in the street and showed me in by a secret back way, trembling slightly at my gloriously mysterious appearance. Another of those houses where a jealous man fears to let a wife receive visitors, I thought. I followed the maid upstairs to a high, airy bedchamber panelled in white and gold, with an elaborately carved marble chimney, rich hangings, and fabulous carpets. On the immense crimson-draped bed, a woman sat in elaborate négligée with her back to me, her golden hair piled high. In front of one of the windows, a parrot on a tall stand was busily cracking seeds. It looked a great deal like Grandmother's parrot.

"*Awk!*" exclaimed the parrot. "Hell and damnation! Fire and brimstone!" It sounded rather like Grandmother's parrot.

"Be quiet, you dreadful thing!" the woman said, and turned to look at me with red-rimmed eyes. It was Marie-Angélique.

"Oh, you've come at last. You, who have told so many the future, who have saved so many futures. Save mine, Madame, for I am the unhappiest woman in the world."

Silently, I put down my little case beside her dressing table and lifted my veil. She turned and stared a long time. "I know you," she said, looking puzzled. "My God, you look exactly like my dead sister. But she was twisted, and you are straight."

"Unlace this diabolical corset, and I would be twisted again, without a doubt, Marie-Angélique."

"Alive! Oh, I knew it; I always knew it!" She got up to embrace me, then hesitated.

"But just imagine being a hundred and fifty years old! I was quite taken in, as is all of Paris! You're ever so fashionable, you know. It *establishes* a person to have a fortune done by you – just like having the right dressmaker or embroiderer. How did you ever come to this?"

"Why, I studied, Sister – and I took up an apprenticeship."

"Oh, Geneviève." She began to laugh. "How many scrapes I've pulled you out of! And here's another of your pranks— No. I won't tell on you, and that's a promise." She put both her hands on my shoulders, holding me at arm's length to look me over and laughed to see me so odd. But then she sobered, and said, "You haven't been home? You haven't heard?"

"I've not been home since I fled that morning."

"Then you *did* flee. I always suspected that. It was when I saw those little books – the ones you always hid in the attic – were gone, that I thought you might have run away. And I never saw your dress among the clothing of the corpses hung on the hooks above the slabs. I even told the captain there, a Monsieur Desgrez, and he seemed very interested. And I just couldn't believe it was you, no matter what they said. The foot was wrong ... I told the captain that, too. And I always believed I'd see you again. You're that way, you know – you always come back." We sat down together on the bed.

"But how did you come here, Marie-Angélique?" I asked. "Is it true what they say, the Duc de Vivonne himself is keeping you?" Marie-Angélique looked suddenly troubled.

"Oh, Geneviève, it is exactly like when Isabelle was kidnapped by the Sultan of Constantinople and found true love only at the expense of grief." She sighed. "And after I paid all the family's debts, too – or, rather, dear, lovely Monsieur de Vivonne did when I asked him." She shook her head sadly. "And to think I never understood. I have accursed beauty, Geneviève, just like the story. Accursed." She began to wipe away the tears with the back of her hand. "Did you know our brother, Étienne, declared me dead and even had a funeral for me?" She sighed. "It's so *bourgeois* of him, it's just humiliating." She got up and began to pace the floor, wringing her hands.

"Sometimes Mother's maid sneaks away to see me. She says Étienne called Mother a pander and has shut her up in Grandmother's room, just as if she were in prison. He says he'll wash away the stain in blood and a thousand other impertinences to Monsieur de Vivonne. He even sent him an insulting letter! At first, Monsieur de Vivonne just laughed and said if Étienne were a man of the world, he'd be quiet and enjoy the advantages of a high connection. But then last week, when he had a little party of his friends and their lady friends in his box at the opera, *right* in the middle of Mademoiselle Lenoir's aria, I heard one of his friends laugh at him about the fuss Étienne is making, and then he shot me such a sharp glance and said he was growing weary of the whole adventure. Now what will I do, Geneviève? I must know my future. None of my old friends will even speak to me . . . he doesn't want me to go visiting . . . he hasn't bought me even a new pair of shoes in the last month. Even Grandmother's parrot reproaches me—" and she sat down again beside me, dissolving into hysterical sobs.

"Sister, listen to me!" I said firmly. "Listen! Even with all of this, you are not in a totally bad situation. Strengthen your backbone! Even though you are not the *maîtresse en titre*, you are still one of the mistresses of a wealthy man, one of the greatest lords in France. Did you ever imagine it would last for long, with the reputation that he has? Listen to me! You must act charming, demand jewels! Hoard his gifts against the day he discards you. Sell that silly gold snuffbox I see by the bed, those foolish knicknacks on your table, there, which I imagine you took instead of hard coin, and buy an annuity. Then you can become independent when you are old."

"But this is love, Geneviève. It's too sacred to treat like . . . something despicable."

"Don't be foolish, Sister. You are as beautiful as ever. Keep your eyes open. Maybe you'll find someone else."

"Oh, how could you imagine me so *mercenary*? That would make me a— Oh, where would I go? I'm afraid to set foot in the church. The angels, the saints, they reproach me. I can't take communion. If his love fades, I'll be cast out into the street... Who would have me? I'll die without his love..."

"You can always live with me, Marie-Angélique."

"You? And who supports you? Would he have me? Wouldn't you get jealous?"

"I support myself, Marie-Angélique, with my own earnings."

"How is that?" she asked. "With fortune-telling? Aren't you embarrassed at how shameful it is? You have fallen, telling fortunes for a living."

"What is more shameful, Marie-Angélique? Sitting starving in a garret, waiting for a prince to come and rescue me as in a fairy story, or making my own living? It's a hard thing to know that I am the ugly stepsister and not Cinderella, but it has made me more realistic about my chances. There are no princes for me." But even as I spoke, the image of André Lamotte of the gallant moustachios came unbidden to my mind.

"Don't you want jewels? Children?" Marie-Angélique looked puzzled.

"I want to be my own person." My voice was truculent. Marie-Angélique smiled through her tears.

"Oh, Sister, you were always such a little savage. You've never understood what is expected of a girl – or a woman. But me, I've always wanted a home and children." She stood up and went to the parrot stand and put out her hand. The parrot climbed up her arm, making a soft gurgling sound, and nibbled at a curl that lay over her shoulder.

"And jewels," I said.

"I can't help it if I was brought up to like nice things. Weren't you brought up to like books written by dead Romans? Besides, silk feels better than muslin." She felt in her pocket for a sweet, which she offered the parrot.

"Oh, Marie-Angélique, you'll never change. Tell me, do you want me to read your fortune?"

"You? You can't. You must be fake."

"Not so, Sister. Do you remember when we visited the fortune-teller on the Rue Beauregard and she had the little girl read in water? I saw the image, too. I have an unexplained gift. She found me on the Pont-Neuf the day I disappeared and set me up in business." I stood to retrieve my satchel, laid it on the embroidered cushion that sat atop a gilded stool, and opened it.

"Just think, the money I've spent on astrologers and fortune-tellers . . ." She shook her head in amazement. I set up the glass on her dressing table; an image came up promptly.

"Why, Marie-Angélique – I see you pregnant! You look very pretty, too. Your hair is hanging all down your back. Yes, you'll be expecting soon."

"Why, that's lovely!" she cried, clapping her hands with pleasure. "Monsieur de Vivonne will adore me; his love will return! And he'll provide for me better, and be kinder. Oh, what wonderful news! Tell me, is it a boy or a girl?"

I tried again. I saw the water in the little round glass vase turn blood red.

"The picture— It doesn't come. It's— It's too far in the future," I equivocated.

"Oh, who cares? Boy or girl, they're both good." Embracing each other, we took our leave: she swore to call for me again, and as I left I vowed to myself that this time, I would change the picture in the glass.

My little hired *vinaigrette* had been waiting in the street, the man in the shafts renewing himself for the long trip back across the river with a generous portion of cheap wine. By the time we had reached the widow Bailly's, the sun was almost gone. Before my door in the twilight a chair waited, the bearers resting, the occupant not yet dismounted. As I alighted from the *vinaigrette*, a ponderous-looking man in a legal gown and plain linen bands stepped from the chair.

"Madame de Morville? Permit me to present myself. I am Monsieur Geniers, *conseiller au parlement*, and I have come to request a private audience with you." He bowed deeply and handed me a sealed note. I opened it and saw the familiar handwriting of the green ledgers.

Admit this man. Hear him out. He is your vengeance.
                                                    La Voisin

"Come in," I said, as the door was opened from within. The ponderous man with the large nose and heavy dark wig followed me upstairs to my room. I motioned him to sit opposite me in the big armchair before the fireplace.

"Madame, I am a man in deep distress. To make a very long story short, I married a younger wife whom I adored, and who professed to love me. But I find she has betrayed me with an adventurer called the Chevalier de Saint-Laurent." He paused and sighed deeply.

My uncle. "And . . . ?" I prompted him, my voice showing no sign of my emotion.

"I am only a man of law, Madame, successful enough in my own way, but I do not have the rank and favour to risk calling him out. And besides, I am no swordsman. I am old. And a laughing-stock. My daughter's nurse told me there was a woman in the Rue Beauregard who had means to relieve my distress. So I went to see the famous *devineresse*, though I felt like a fool for doing so. The sorceress offered me a powder to regain my wife's love. But when I asked for – you understand – stronger stuff, she laughed. 'Why risk yourself to take a seducer's life?' she asked. 'A slow-brewed vengeance is enjoyed best.' Through her magic arts she had discovered that the Comte de Marsan holds the Chevalier de Saint-Laurent's gambling debts. He is currently pressed by his own creditors and is willing to sell the chevalier's note-of-hand for half its value – five thousand louis, for he knows the chevalier can never raise the money. 'Purchase the note,' she said, 'and put him in debtors' prison with the rats, where he'll never escape. Think of the prolonged pleasure you can have, letting him starve slowly in the dark.' 'Five thousand louis?' I told her. 'That is a fortune. I could hardly raise half that sum.' But the fortune-teller told me, 'I know a woman who has no love lost for the chevalier. She will provide the other half, providing you keep her name secret and her honour safe.' So here I am, Madame, with my proposition. Assist me, and he will never see the light of day again. That I swear."

"If you swear it, I will assist you. I can raise that sum. But only on one condition."

"Yes?" His voice was tense with concealed passion.

"That you inform me regularly of his sufferings. I, too, will enjoy this slow-brewed vengeance," I said quietly.

"Madame, you are an angel from heaven."

"Not precisely," I replied. "But I imagine I will suffice." And when we had set a time and place for our next meeting, he departed, his walk heavy, but his eyes blazing with ferocious purpose. I sat back and slowly let out my breath. Vengeance at last. La Voisin would enjoy advancing the money. It would keep me in her debt just that much longer. Very well, Uncle, I thought. I would have more, but this is enough. May the rats eat you as you sleep.

TWENTY-THREE

"Now," exclaimed La Voisin, "you may take your hands off your eyes and look out of the window. It's the little house in the middle. I want you to be utterly surprised with how perfect it is." Her carriage, which had turned down the Rue Charlot, halted, and I looked out to see a neat little two-storey town house with a stone façade and a peaked slate roof that concealed an attic.

"And it comes already so nicely furnished, too. The owner had to leave town suddenly and was delighted when I could take it off his hands. Of course, I do wish it were on a street with a bit more *tone*; this area has both been built up and come down since old Charlot's day. But no one will deny that the quarter in general is very elegant. So this will have to do for now." La Voisin's footman handed us out of her carriage before the front door. It was made of heavy oak, ornamented and studded with brass, as if to stop a battering ram. An incongruously delicate knocker shaped like a loop of brazen rope between two bunches of preposterous cast-iron flowers sat on this fortress gate. Heavy metal shutters were sealed across the two first-floor windows that faced the street. They were such an odd contrast to the airy lightness of the ornamented yellow stone, high roof, and tall chimneys of the upper floor that Sylvie and I couldn't help looking at each other.

"That knocker, of course, *must* go," announced the sorceress, tilting her head to one side as she inspected it thoughtfully. "It does nothing for your reputation. A dragon, now, would be ideal . . . a skull . . . *hmm*, no, not tasteful. And a hundred conveniences for your peace of mind. The previous owner retired rather suddenly from the smuggling business . . . and you benefit . . . the shutters, for example; some lovely additions to the cellar, an excellent steel-lined compartment concealed behind the panelling in the *ruelle* . . ." She put a huge key into the front-door lock. A smell of dust greeted us. The downstairs reception room showed signs of hasty departure: a rubble of odds and ends, tipped carelessly from drawers, sat in corners and was strewn across the floor.

"There's no carriage gate," La Voisin went on. "That one belongs to the house next door. But there's a scrap of garden in the back. And you should be leasing your carriage, anyway, for the convenience of having the horses stabled for you." A single shoe, a man's, with a hole in the sole, lay on the tiled floor. The sorceress kicked it aside. "You will, of course, have to redo this room. I envision an oriental decor – rich, dark, mysterious. You'll need an excellent carpet. Your clients will notice a cheap one. You can put your reading table . . . there. And . . . *hmm*, black walls, do you think?"

"Blood red, in the ancient style, with gilt stencilled designs," I answered, getting into the spirit of things. Sylvie beamed.

"Oh, what a lovely touch!" exclaimed the sorceress. "How *Henri Quatre*! What a pleasure to work with someone who isn't simple-minded. Yes, I said to myself when I first saw you, that girl has *potential*."

The rooms in the house were few but large and high, even the servants' antechamber. In the half-bare reception room, an immense fireplace with a richly carved mantel that rose to the ceiling formed the chief feature of interest. Light sifted through the back windows from a heavily overgrown, unkempt strip of a garden in back of the house. Behind the great reception room, there was a kitchen with a high hearth and a huge spit operated by a geared wheel with weights like a clockwork. Upstairs, the wide bed-sitting room was in chaos. The dining table was overturned, and the armoire doors hung unlatched. The open blanket chests, pulled from beneath the bed, gaped like hungry mouths. The bed hangings were askew and the featherbed dumped unceremoniously on the floor. Whoever had this house before hid things under the mattress, I thought.

"Now, look at this," the sorceress broke into my reverie. "A perfectly charming *ruelle*." She stood back to look at my face, her black eyes fathomless. The pretty carved wood railing before the bed marked off the space, and the alcove behind the bed, lit by a tall, narrow window, contained not only a writing desk but also a splendid bookshelf perched on the wall above it. A philosopher's study. I was enchanted. I looked at her, holding my face impassive, but I knew she'd known she had me from the minute I'd seen the bookshelf.

"I suppose you'll add it to my contract?" I asked.

"Of course. But at the rate you're succeeding, you'll have it paid off very quickly. After all," she added, smoothing down her skirt, "every woman of business needs a home of her own. And I've found you the ideal footman, quite strong, and admirably silent. I'll lend you Margot for a day or two to help put it right before you move in – all at no extra charge."

"Then it's done," I said. "Let's discuss price. What interest are you charging?" The sorceress's smile was enigmatic.

The actual move did not take long, for I had few possessions to bring from the widow Bailly's. Rendering the house habitable was a considerable task, however, requiring all the extra help that Madame Montvoisin could spare, including the immense new footman that she placed in my employ. From the "philanthropic society", was my first thought as his vast bulk first loomed in the doorway. From the evident strength of his hands and shoulders and the way his shaved head was hidden under an old hat, I could tell that Gilles was an escaped *galérien*, the dregs of the earth. For the rest of his life, he would use every excuse to hide the galley brand under his shirt. No work in the ordinary world for such as he, and a swift return with an amputated foot if he was ever caught. No wonder he could keep confidences. I might have felt nervous about him, but there was something so large and peaceful about the way he lit his long pipe when the furniture had all been moved and moved again that instead I was reassured.

"One's not enough," he observed, as if to no one in particular.

"Pardon, Gilles? What was that you said?" I had just finished arranging my few books on the shelves several different ways, to see which way would show the bindings to advantage.

"One's not enough. I told Madame. One to guard the house, one to travel with you. Two for trouble. A house of women is no good." He sucked on the pipe as if that were the end of it. The bluish smoke rose and encircled his head as he stared out the window.

"Madame, there's . . . ah, someone . . . um, at the door. He says Madame Montvoisin has sent him." Sylvie had come up from her work in recivilising the kitchen. She seemed oddly distracted. Gilles turned slowly, and as he looked at her, a strange, slow smile crossed his face.

"No good," he said.

"What do you mean, no good? Of course I'm good. I'll have you remember that I'm Madame's most trusted confidante and have been with her ever so much longer than you. No good, indeed!"

"Sylvie, I don't think that's what he meant. It has to do with needing a personal bodyguard. Could that be the person whom Madame Montvoisin has sent?"

"I'm not sure, Madame. The man is very hard to explain."

"Then show him up, Sylvie. Madame never does anything without a good reason."

But when at last she threw open the bedchamber door once more, the space behind her, where a massive bravo should have loomed, was empty.

"Madame, this is Monsieur . . . ah . . . Mustapha." I stared in amazement and dismay. Monsieur Mustapha was even shorter than I, a dwarf scarcely three feet tall. He looked like a decayed, perverse, debauched child. Several days' worth of whiskers and a pair of ancient dark eyes were all that appeared to distinguish him from a rather undergrown five-year-old boy. He was holding a bundle on his shoulder, as if he planned on moving in. I couldn't stop staring.

"If you goggle at me any longer, you'll have to glue your eyeballs back in," he said in a queer, hoarse old man's voice.

"Pardon, Monsieur Mustapha. I was told a bodyguard was coming – I expected someone larger." He calmly perched on my best chair and crossed his legs, swinging them because they did not reach the floor.

"I must say, I expected someone larger myself," he answered, inspecting my person with an impertinent eye. "Snuff?"

"You are very rude," I said, not concealing my annoyance.

"My rudeness makes me large. You can't overlook me then."

"Reasonable enough," I observed. "I've tried a bit of that, myself. But aside from rudeness, what qualifications do you have?"

"Qualifications? Dozens. Why, hundreds. I come equipped with a splendid Turkish costume, courtesy of the Marquise de Fresnes, whose train I once carried, when blackamoor dwarfs were all the rage. Ah, those were the days. A little walnut stain, a turban – what a soft job it was. Just eat and drink and go to the opera, the court theatre—" Here he broke off and began to recite verses from Corneille in the voice of a classical tragedian. *"Sois désormais le Cid; qu'à ce grand nom tout cède; Qu'il comble d'épouvante et Grenade et Tolède . . ."* He gestured broadly, extending his arms. "I was meant by the size of my soul, Madame, to play kings on the stage. But my body has led me to other roles. Before the Moorish bit, I made the rounds of the fairs, dressed as a precocious child. Ha! Somewhat the opposite of you, old lady. 'Tiny Jean-Pierre, the child marvel' . . ."

"So why did you quit the marquise?" I stood before him, my arms folded. Sylvie puttered about, pretending to be busy, the way she always did when she wanted to listen in.

"Didn't quit. I was packed off, all of a sudden, by her husband. The Queen had a black baby, and the demand for Moorish dwarfs fell off considerably. All over town, dwarfs were out of work. I suppose I might have turned to drink, like the others – but I had my carnival skills to fall back on."

"Just what are they?" The talkative little creature was beginning to irritate me considerably.

"This," he said. The tiny hands moved rapidly over his body. I hardly had time to watch the hidden knives flash by my nose before they were embedded in the wall in a pattern resembling the points of the compass. "When I wear the turban, I can conceal a half-dozen more," he said calmly. Sylvie's eyes were wide with astonishment. Even Gilles had removed the pipe from his mouth.

"You're engaged," I said.

"Good. I'll carry your train when you go out. I'll add considerable style to your appearance. And when I'm not needed, I'm good at concealing myself in corners and overhearing things. I carry letters unseen and remove the contents of purses from below. All at your service, Madame."

"Mustapha, I apologise for misjudging you."

"A polite marquise? Madame, your origins are showing."

"You are a horrid little person, Mustapha, but then, so am I. I think we'll get on."

The next morning, a page in blue and silver delivered a note on heavy, crested stationery to my door. It was an invitation to attend the Marquise de Montespan, the King's official mistress and La Voisin's prize client, at her house on the Rue Vaugirard the following day. It was a command performance, not to be refused. I dared not tell La Voisin, who might well have exploded with jealousy at the thought that I might steal her favourite client. As Sylvie did my hair, she filled me with information for the visit: the great house on the Rue Vaugirard was where Madame de Montespan's children by the King were kept – for years in secret, and now openly. The widow Scarron, a poor friend of Madame de Montespan's, had been engaged as their governess and elevated to the rank of the Marquise of Maintenon for her service. "But if you can imagine," observed Sylvie, "she had to appear to be living elsewhere, all the time that she was in fact at the Rue Vaugirard raising all those babies." It was there, in her Paris house with her children, that Madame de Montespan had gone to earth when the King dismissed her the month previous. I looked into my dressing-table mirror as my untidy locks were transformed into the ancient hair-style of the Marquise de Morville and pondered my delicate position.

"But, Sylvie, you won't tell La Voisin about this visit, will you? I know that she herself was planning to pay a call on Madame de Montespan, and you know how angry she gets if she thinks anyone is stealing her business. You know I received a summons; I didn't seek this out."

"Oh, she was enraged enough yesterday when I told her, but I said, 'Better my mistress than that horrid La Bosse and her cards, or some palm reader from heaven-knows-where. This way it's all in the family, so to speak, and it will all come back to you.' And she cooled down right away. So, you see? I look after your interests. The higher you rise, the better I'll do. I wish I had a gift like yours. I wouldn't be a maid for another day, I'll tell you. But La Voisin, she read in my palm I'm not destined to stay a servant. Someday I'll be mistress of hundreds, like her, and ride in a carriage, and eat and drink nothing but the choicest things. So I'm helping you now, for the day when I am great. I've learned from her that that is how it's done. Look after people, and they look after you. Do you want the jewelled combs today?"

"Get out everything from the coffer, Sylvie. These court ladies don't believe in modesty. They rank your competence by your clothes. Yes, the pearls, and the brooch, too, along with the silver crucifix."

"My, that does look nice: just like an old portrait." She stood back to admire her handiwork. The Marquise de Morville looked critically in the mirror and snapped: "The lace ruff will do better than the linen one today, Sylvie. I expect you've starched it fresh. That is, if the starch is any good. Ah, in my day, starch was better made . . ."

"I honestly think you enjoy being that horrid old lady, Madame," observed Sylvie.

"Sylvie, I'll have no familiarity. I *am* that horrid old lady. Don't ever forget. The Marquise de Morville is a *formidable monster.*"

A short while later, the eerie old woman who was the fright of the neighbourhood stalked out the door, veiled, her heavy stick thumping on the pavement. A Turkish dwarf held her train above the mud, and her lackey, who looked every bit like the escaped criminal that he was, rushed to open the carriage door, and the unmarked equipage rattled off through the light spring mist to the Rue Vaugirard.

The reception rooms in the house in the Vaugirard district were elegant, as befits a house that might be visited at any time by a king. Even the antechambers were hung with silk tapestries and furnished with chairs and tables of rare inlaid woods. Massive gilt *torchères* that burned a dozen candles at a time stood in the corners. As I was shown upstairs, I took note of the paintings in their heavy, gilded frames that hung on the walls of the principal *salle*: Venus being arrayed by cupids before her mirror, Europa and the bull, a portrait of the King in the place of honour. Beyond, we passed up another marble staircase and through a high-ceilinged schoolroom, where I saw two little boys at writing desks. The older of the two, who looked about six or seven was the boy I had seen in the carriage that day I had first travelled to Versailles. The younger, perhaps only three or four, was already dressed in a miniature version of the embroidered robes and crucifix of the abbé of the great monastery whose income his father had already given him. As the bigger boy got up to show his work to the sombrely clad governess, I could see that he limped.

The mother of these children and the others up in the nursery was lying on an immense gilded bed in a darkened bedroom, the very picture of prostrated grief. A cold compress was laid across her forehead, and her dark blonde hair lay all damp around her neck.

"Madame, it is the fortune-teller."

"Ah, the monster who foretold my banishment. Bring her closer, that I may see her." She had herself propped up, and the compress taken away. She stared at me a long time with her curiously coloured aquamarine eyes. I could see in them a calculating and malicious intelligence, reinforced by the narrow, cold little mouth above the slightly receding chin. I curtseyed deeply, as if to a queen.

"How dare you make me a laughing-stock with the Countess of Soissons." The aquamarine eyes turned hard, like the jewels in the heat of a basilisk.

"I am deeply sorry, Madame. It was never my intention. I only read in the glass and say truthfully what I see."

"The Countess of Soissons is a jealous, scheming bitch. An ugly little used-up Italian who thinks she can win the favour of the King. A Mancini. What are the Mancinis but upstarts? My blood, the blood of the Mortemarts, is more ancient than that of the Bourbons. To my family, the royal family themselves are nothing but upstarts. Do you understand your crime?" She sat up on the bed in a sudden surge of wrath. "You have held a Mortemart up to the ridicule of a *Mancini*." Her voice sneered at the very word. "How dare you play into her hands? How dare you offend me? I still have the power to destroy you. Do you have any idea of my power, you miserable nobody? I tell you, I shall return in gold and diamonds, and I'll have you burned alive on the Place de Grève!" Her face had turned all pink with anger, and her words came faster and faster. Oh, my goodness, I thought. One of Madame de Montespan's notorious rages. She was usually as good as her word, too. My mind began to work swiftly.

"Of course you will return, for it is I who made that prophecy as well. My glass never lies, as every other fortune-teller in Paris knows. Wouldn't it be better to have my glass at your service than my body at the Place de Grève?"

For some reason she hesitated, and her arrogant face paled. "You know La Voisin," she said, raising a heavily jewelled hand to her face. I pursued my advantage.

"Yes, I know her."

"How *well* do you know her?" Her voice was unnaturally calm. I sensed danger.

"I am ... a sort of ... um ... business partner," I answered.

"What was her purpose, then, in revealing this to the Countess of Soissons before she revealed it to me?"

"She had no purpose. I was asked to read in the glass, and I did."

"La Voisin always has a purpose."

"I can read for you now, if you wish it." Madame de Montespan got up and began to prowl around the room, the train of her négligée trailing behind her on the carpet. She turned suddenly.

"That was her purpose! She wished to remind me of her power! Oh, my God, she is subtle. She has cast a spell to make me desire to bring you here. The spell, the spell is powerful. Why else would you haunt my mind, you little nobody? Why would I hear the Countess of Soissons's mocking laughter in my dreams? La Voisin has sent you, sent you with her diabolical enchantments, to read my future. She knows what I know – the dark walls of the prison convent are waiting for me, the discarded mistress!" She paused and looked out of the window onto the street, and her face sagged suddenly, like that of an old woman.

"To never take the air, never ride in my carriage or see my children again. My hair – my beautiful hair – I have made so many elegant hair-styles fashionable – gone. My jewels, my gowns, my cards – the amusement of the theatre. I have embellished his court with my good taste. The Mortemart taste. The Mortemart wit." She turned suddenly on me, as if I were the cause of her misfortune.

"How many poets and painters have I made?" she cried. "How many sculptures have I commissioned? I have surrounded myself, and him, with beauty! All this to vanish! Surrounded by harpies who tell me to repent. Repent! Why should I repent? Why shouldn't he repent as well? Is not our sin double? In our seven years, I have borne him five children. I provided him with other women when he wanted variety. I amused him with my wit when he was bored – which he is most of the time! Has he ever thought that perhaps he is bored because he is boring?" She turned and stared at me suddenly, as if I could understand how she despised men of little wit. "If this were Turkey, and he were the Sultan, I would be the second wife. I would be honoured! I should have known – when he refused to make me a duchess. My future is doomed. I shall be entombed alive, I know it, and La Voisin has sent you to tell me my fate. Take out your glass and read it, read it, you horrible little corpse in black!"

"I'll need to sit," I said. She had not yet requested that I do so. She was famous for that. In a world where the rank of guests was instantly rated by whether they were offered an armchair, a plain chair, or a stool, she had once made duchesses take stools and marquises remain standing. Now she had nothing but her airs.

"If you must. My God, to have a creature like you sit in my presence. I am brought low."

I put my things out: the cabbalistic towel, dragon rod, short candles that gave off a strange aroma, and a round, stoppered jar of water. I had her touch the glass to "bring out the image" and did all the pleasing little tricks I'd devised to make it seem more than it was. But the picture in the glass was hard to make out. A man in full clerical garb was celebrating Mass in an unfamiliar chapel. On the wall above his head was a cross – no – it was upside down. He turned briefly, and I saw his face in profile. The hideous blue-veined nose of the sinister Abbé Guibourg, who had come to dinner at La Voisin's. He set down the chalice on a towel, and by the dim light of the tall, flickering black candles that framed him, I could see that the altar on which the towel was laid was the bare groin of a naked woman. Various figures I couldn't quite make out were clustered around the human altar and the celebrant. A woman stepped from the shadows holding a premature stillborn child. Guibourg slit its throat and drained its blood into the chalice, then gutted it like a fish, reserving its entrails.

"Oh, my God," I whispered softly, "the Black Mass." My breath had stopped at the vile sight. I could hear my heart. The woman in the shadows who had brought the little corpse turned from the altar, and I could see her face. It was La Voisin.

"What is it? What do you see?" The eager, anxious voice behind me interrupted my thoughts.

"Don't breathe on the glass. You'll fog the picture," I snapped, and I could feel her withdraw from her post close by my shoulder.

The hideous abbé was completing the ceremony with an indecent intimacy carried out upon the woman on the altar. As I watched her pale, doughy body writhing in the light of the candles, her hair fell away from her face, and I recognised her. The woman who had commissioned the Black Mass and who lay upon the altar was Madame de Montespan.

I looked up from the glass to see Madame de Montespan's face over mine, trying to peer into the water with me. Her eyes were eager, greedy, her mouth pulled into a right little knot. Her lips seemed redder to me, like a cannibal's who has just tasted blood.

"Madame is taking part in a ceremony . . ." I began.

"Will I be a duchess?" she whispered.

". . . it is a . . . private . . . ceremony leading to her reinstatement . . ." I continued delicately, and Madame de Montespan nodded with understanding. She knew. She had done it before. I took a deep breath. Somehow, fortune-telling wasn't any fun at that moment. I had gotten in too far. Court intrigue, poison, and now Black Masses. The life of a rabbit in a snake pit. Suddenly I wanted to go take a bath.

"Let me view further," I said, and I was sure the pounding of my heart must be heard in the room. Again, I saw Madame de

Montespan entertaining the King, her bodice blazing with diamonds. Then I saw her pour wine from a silver decanter on the sideboard, delicately moving her hand across one of the goblets so that an unknown powder sifted into it. I saw them drinking and laughing together, and the King's face suddenly grow red with desire...

"Madame will regain the full favour of the King. She entertains him in her chambers. He showers her with new gifts and influence. He is mad with desire for her body—"

"Yes, yes," I could hear her sinister whisper. "How soon? How long must I wait?"

"I can only tell from the foliage and flowers I see in the image... Let me stir again... It looks to be ... about midsummer, when the King returns from his campaign in Flanders." Another image rose to the surface: Madame de Montespan in the notorious *"robe battante"*, the elegant waistless gown she had popularised and with which she announced her pregnancies and the renewal of her power to the court. "Never fear," I said. "You shall taste supreme power again, and bear the King a child in token of your reconciliation."

"Ah, little fortune-teller, you are a messenger sent from heaven. My highest desire—"

A messenger from the gates of hell, you mean. The King of France is a poor fool in the thrall of the creatures of night and superstition, who have placed a woman at the height of power through the Black Mass, and who have convinced her to drug him regularly with aphrodisiacs. They have only to say the word and the aphrodisiacs can be replaced by more fatal stuff. The supreme lever of power, La Voisin had said. We rule through their weaknesses. The sorceress of the Rue Beauregard held the entire kingdom of France in her hands.

TWENTY-FOUR

"Who would ever believe it?" said La Reynie, shaking his head. "She is related to half the judicial families in Paris . . . with her birth, her beauty, her delicacy . . . this—" Before him on his desk lay the only evidence against the Marquise de Brinvilliers: a little red coffer containing a few family papers and several vials of white arsenic and the written confession, signed by her own hand, that Desgrez had brought back from the convent in Liège. Randomly, he picked up a page and perused the catalogue of crimes it contained. The midsummer heat lay oppressive in the dark panelled office. Sweat ran beneath La Reynie's collar and trickled down the back of his neck beneath his heavy wig. It stained the neck and underarms of Desgrez's blue jacket, as he stood before the desk of his seated chief.

"Apart from this, Desgrez, we have nothing. After three months' interrogation, she still denies everything. Sometimes I think from the reports that she is a complete lunatic. Abbé Pirot has been with her for the last twenty-four hours, and look at this report." Desgrez took the sheet that La Reynie handed him and read from it:

"'The marquise maintains a cold and arrogant front, but there are moments when her eyes glow like a demon's, and another voice snarls from her throat. She has still confessed nothing to me, though I have assured her it will guarantee her salvation—'" Desgrez broke off reading. "I suppose, Monsieur de La Reynie, that she has had her fill of abbés these days," he added. La Reynie's hard face remained unchanged at the little joke. He leafed again through the pages of the confession, checking again some notes he had taken in his little red leather-bound notebook.

"You needn't worry that she will escape the executioner, Monsieur de La Reynie," Desgrez observed.

"It is not that which worries me," answered La Reynie in a

preoccupied voice. "It is the unanswered questions that consume me. Who supplied her with the poisons she used? Whom else did her supplier supply? What other people have shared in these appalling crimes? Paris is full of rumours. We may only have grasped the tail of a much larger conspiracy. And yet she will not talk, and tomorrow she will be beyond all answers."

"Then I may assume that you will conduct the *question extraordinaire* personally?"

"It is Louvois's express wish. His Majesty takes a personal interest. I have prepared a list of questions myself from this . . . document . . . you acquired so brilliantly."

Deep below ground level, the stone walls oozed damp. Even in July, the room was perpetually cold. A fire burned on the hearth, and next to it was a mattress on which to revive a failing victim for the next round of questioning. A physician sat ready with brandy and restoratives on the bench next to the table at which the clerk made the official transcript of the interrogation.

"*Troisième coin*," ordered La Reynie in a passionless voice, and the executioner's assistant poured the third immense jug of water through a funnel into the marquise's mouth. Stripped and stretched across a trestle, she was already bloated beyond recognition.

"Your lover, Saint-Croix – to whom else did he supply poisons?" asked the Lieutenant General of Police. The clerk's pen scratched as he took down the question. The Marquise de Brinvilliers groaned. The physician took her pulse.

"Continue," he said.

"What other persons, male or female, did he supply with poison?" persisted La Reynie.

"How should I know? I only know that he loved me alone. Oh, dozens. Yes, dozens. But he is dead. He never told me."

"You know the names. Give me the names."

"You'll burst me. So many pots of water for my small body. You disgrace my rank. For that I will never forgive you, *canaille.*" Her voice was weak. La Reynie leaned close to hear her response.

"The names, Madame."

"Oh, I know so many," she whispered. "I could drag half of Paris down with me, if I wanted to. But I'll not give you the names. You police live only to bring your betters down. I'll never give you the satisfaction. Do you know who I am? I am a d'Aubray!" Her eyes lit for a moment with insane fury.

"*Quatrième coin*," ordered the chief of police, his face hard.

By the *huitième coin*, the marquise had still revealed nothing.

TWENTY-FIVE

Since the sensation caused by my prediction of Madame de Montespan's return to favour the summer before, I had been taken up by the most fashionable salons in town. Now for the past year I had hardly ever eaten or slept at home, and hostesses snatched me up to enliven every social event with my now-celebrated wit. And so it was on a bright summer afternoon on 16 July 1676 that I was crammed with a half-dozen others into a window, rented at great expense by one of my patronesses, that overlooked the Place de Grève. It was the execution of the season, and as a result, windows and balconies overlooking the scaffold, or even just along the route of the tumbril, fetched a much higher premium than usual. The square itself and the streets into it were packed solid with humanity, and those of the noblesse who had come too late to rent window space were constrained to watch from their carriages, where the view was not half as good.

"And all for poisoning a tiresome little husband she had," said my hostess with a sigh. "Really, that La Reynie is entirely too savage— Oh, look. There is the Princesse de Carignan in her carriage!" and she waved her handkerchief at her. The Marquise de Brinvilliers had been all the fashion for the last several weeks; the Comtesse de Soissons herself had brought a group of sightseers to the Conciergerie to watch the condemned woman led to her last Mass. But the marquise, still unrepentant, had turned and mocked the comtesse's morbid curiosity before she had vanished again into the prison. Now all of Versailles had come into the city for the edifying spectacle of her beheading and burning as an amusing change from their routine of cards, plays, and water festivals.

"I'll certainly breathe easier when that wicked woman is burned," announced the abbé who accompanied us.

"Actually, you'll be breathing her," I pointed out in a sour voice, for hypocrites annoy me. My hostess let out a little shriek of amusement.

"Ah, what wit, Marquise! Why, we might all take in a little bit of her evil! Even you, my dear Abbé." Oh, bother. Without a doubt, another witticism to go the rounds of the court. How tired I was growing of hearing my own *bon mots* come back to me, all shopworn, with someone else's name attached.

The roar of the crowd beneath the windows announced the arrival of the tumbril at last from Notre-Dame, where the condemned woman had made the *amende honorable*. Weak from the dawn's water torture, the Marquise de Brinvilliers lay back on the piled straw and wood that was to burn her corpse, clutching a crucifix to her bosom, her eyes distended and rolling with terror. She had on the plain, loose shift of the condemned and a little white muslin cap over her loose hair. The executioner stood behind her in the cart, his big two-handed sword hidden from her view. Her confessor leaned over her, exhorting her, though no one could hear his words. A guard of archers surrounded the cart, trying to beat back the crowd, but even so, the tumbril made slow progress. As she rolled her head from side to side, she spied a horseman, half hidden by the archers, accompanying the cart, and started back, making the sign of the Devil's horns at him. Her confessor redoubled his efforts, and she turned her head away from the sight of the horseman.

"Why, it's Desgrez, riding there – he always makes sure to see a case through to the end, doesn't he?" said one of the gentlemen accompanying us.

"Desgrez? Oh, yes, it was he that captured her where she was hiding abroad, I do believe. He tracked her for years. At least, that's what I heard. In disguise. He discovered the written confession she'd made."

"Clever devil, isn't he? It's not many that can catch a poisoner. Most of them get away with it."

"Those and the doctors – otherwise, we'd all live as long as Methuselah, wouldn't we?" My hostess's husband, the Comte de Longueval, laughed too heartily at his own joke.

"Probably so . . . say, do you think he'll have it off at one stroke? I'll lay a wager of five louis it takes him two."

"Done. That's Samson himself down there, not an assistant,

and he could take the head off an ox at one blow. Who am I to turn down a gift of five louis?"

The executioner led her up the stairs of the scaffold, and for a moment she stood, staring up at the crowded windows, and seemed to catch my eye for an instant, before she looked away. Then the executioner cut her long hair away from her neck, and blindfolded her. I closed my eyes, not to open them until a heavy thump told me the thing was done. The archers, striking out with their halberds, cleared a space where wood, straw, and oil could be made into an immense bonfire. The pieces of the corpse were piled on top of the heaped wood and torches applied to the straw.

"That was an easy five louis. You never even saw him hesitate. What did I tell you? Samson never fails. They say he has a Mass said before each execution, to make his hand sure." There was the clink of coin changing hands and a half-annoyed exclamation from Madame de Longueval.

"My dear friends, no differences. I am famished for a bite of supper. And there's really nothing of interest to see now. I suppose she'll burn all night." The comtesse's mind was not of the sort to contemplate anything very long. The last thing I noted from the window was Desgrez, still on horseback, commanding the guard that surrounded the funeral pyre. Already the fickle crowd was proclaiming her a martyr. Now Desgrez would be there all night, too, to keep the crowd from stealing fragments of the body for resale as holy relics. The King's justice required that all the ashes be dumped in the Seine, and Desgrez was not only a persistent, but a literal-minded fellow.

The dispersing crowd kept us from our carriage, which was waiting in a nearby street. Pushing through the press of people, an enterprising printer's boy was selling broadsides in doggerel recounting the day's events and the numerous crimes of the woman whose body was being reduced to cinders in the Place de Grève. Suddenly I remembered Grandmother. In her memory, I'll have one, I thought.

"Hey! You, boy, what have you got there?" I shook my walking stick in the air to get his attention.

"'The Remarkable Crimes and Execution of Madame de

Brinvilliers', illustrated, for only two sous, Grandmother. Guaranteed to give satisfaction," cried the street urchin.

"Oh, I must have one," cried a lady near by.

"Oh, boy! Come here at once," called out a gentleman. The crowd pushed in around him, snatching up the broadsides. By the time he turned to me, the supply in his bag was gone.

"Don't be disappointed, Grandmother. I've got a whole boxful in the doorway over there – I'll get one for you right away." And as he turned to renew his supply, I saw a heavy box of broadsides, cheap pamphlets, and used books set in the arch of a nearby doorway, watched over by a man entirely enveloped in a black cloak with a wide black hat pulled down to cover his face. An odd outfit for a balmy summer evening. Clearly, I thought, he does not want to be recognised.

"Oh, you have books, too?"

"Just a few, Grandmother. Look for yourself." I peered into the box. Several slender volumes entitled *Parnasse Satyrique*, ten sous each. I threw back my veil to see better. Marvellous. A witty rhymed *libelle* on the amours of the court, most magnificently detailed. I could feel myself blushing. The man in the cloak had stepped back into the shadows, and I sensed his stare burrowing into the back of my neck. How embarrassing. I pulled down my veil to hide my confusion and snatched up another book to conceal the malicious little volume I coveted.

"These two, and the broadside," I said hurriedly and threw the boy a gold louis as I fled to rejoin the company with which I had come.

"Oh, how horrid! The ink is smearing on my hands!" exclaimed Madame de Corbon, as she settled into the carriage seat. "Here – fold this broadside up for me, my friend, and put it in your pocket." As her gentleman companion complied, I folded my copy and tucked it away, along with my books, in the little bag I carried. An evening's pleasant reading.

"Why, what a clever idea, Madame de Morville! You have a veritable pharmacy in that bag! What mystical purpose do all those bottled potions serve?" Madame de Corbon was never less than annoying. But when one has just been a guest at a poisoner's execution, it is best not to arouse needless suspicion.

"We ancient people must resort to more artificial aids than you young creatures if we are to get about in society," I said, doing my best to look owlish. "Besides a handkerchief and a bottle of scent, I have here a restorative cordial and a pot of rouge to relieve the pallor that is the result of a tragic life extended beyond the dark and welcome comfort of the tomb." As Madame de Corbon inspected the rouge pot, I offered the company the cordial, which they declined.

"To each their own – eh, Madame de Morville?" said the Comte de Longueval, offering his gold enamelled snuff box around. "Myself, I prefer something a little livelier than an old lady's cordial." The countess took snuff, as did Madame de Corbon. If you knew what was in this cordial, you might reconsider, I thought, as I took a dose while the rest of the company wielded their handkerchiefs.

"You look dreamy, Madame de Morville." The familiar slow, slippery feeling was stealing away the horrors of the day.

"I am reminiscing about my youth. Did you know that I was present at the famous joust where King Henri II died? I was just a slip of a girl. Ah, what a handsome, romantic king – although of course, surpassed by our present monarch..." The conversation turned agreeably to the question of how to measure gallantry in the great figures of history. In my pleasantly drugged state, it seemed to blend in a soothing sort of mindless music. I almost regretted it when the carriage halted in the great *cour d'honneur* of the Hôtel Soissons.

"You do not play, Madame?" the Countess of Soissons raised an eyebrow at me as I offered my salutation. She was dressed in pale blue satin, her *décolletage* ornamented by a quadruple strand of heavy pearls, set apart at intervals with diamonds. She sat at the head of the largest of the ivory inlaid gaming tables in the gilded salon, and around the feet of her brocade armchair, over a dozen little dogs slept or wrangled at her feet. To simplify the accounting, the players were using gold instead of counters, and tens of thousands of *écus* lay heaped about on the tables. As the little piles changed hands, men and women wept or exulted; stoicism was not usually the fashion among gamesters. Only the Marquis de Dangeau sat quietly, his eyes lynx-like as he surveyed the players and shuffled with a practised hand. He was one of those who made his living at the tables, although it was not a thing to be said aloud; he played with strategy, not passion, and needed no ruses, no cards in the sleeves, no marked decks. Here and there men of lesser rank, bankers and financiers, stood beside their patrons, ready to guarantee their bets. Yet a man with good clothes and some appearance of social standing was welcome to sit at the tables if he could wager the immense sums required with the easeful insouciance of a born aristocrat.

"Oh, no, Madame, I enjoy admiring the brilliant new kinds of costumes that people wear nowadays." In the corner, a man shrieked, tore at his hair, and left the room precipitously. "In my day," I observed, "the civility of society was not so far advanced as now; there a man would call out the victor. The streets were slick with blood outside of the card salon of a nobleman of rank."

"How very wise of our King to forbid duelling, in that case," replied the countess, "because in that manner the pleasure of our games is greatly enhanced and the continuity of the players assured."

"Wise, indeed," I agreed in the same bland tone.

"The marquise is being terribly discreet," the Countess of Longueval broke in, anxious to preserve her part in the conversation. "She who can read the future can read the cards ahead of time and wisely refrains from joining our games. Isn't that so?" She turned to me for confirmation.

"It is a point of honour with me." I nodded austerely. As if it would be for anyone else. But the gossip I heard as I wandered among the tables with the other oglers of rank was worth more than a winning bet to me. It helped me elaborate the often-meaningless images I saw in the glass.

Madame de Soissons bestowed an ironic smile on me and returned to her game. Across the room, I recognised the Duc de Vivonne, wastrel, centre of my sister's life. He was resplendent in a heavy green brocade coat, playing *bassette* at the same table with his duchesse.

From the tables floated up a woman's voice: "And then the King was so angry, he called off the party—"

"All because of the favours for the ladies?"

"It was their own fault for rushing to the market stalls in the *palais* to find out how much he had spent on the fans. A king's favour is supposed to be beyond price—"

"Well, *I* heard that he got them very inexpensively, and that they were bone and not ivory." Useless. I passed on. The tall, gilt-panelled room seemed suddenly very hot to me. I'll sweat off my powder, I thought. I can't have them see me all pink. I glanced at my reflection in one of the large mirrors that decorated the room. Something eerie made me feel sick and dizzy inside. The card players in the mirror were not the same as those in the room. The tables were arranged differently, and the men were not in baggy breeches, ribbon-bedecked jackets, and long dark wigs. The women did not have billowing, folded-back sleeves and undersleeves. The strange company were wearing tight, rich clothing, festooned with lace, and men and women alike wore white wigs, the mens' smaller than a lackey's, done up with ribbon at the back. I hadn't called this up. I hadn't felt it come. It was just there.

Shuddering, I averted my eyes from the mirror. A woman with several patches was laughing at one of the tables near by; beside her was a glass of white wine. I could see her face partially reflected in it. Suddenly the reflection became a skull. My breath came fast. What was happening? The alien company looked down from the mirror on the wall. The skull in the wineglass laughed. I felt I was smothering. Snatches of conversation came from the table beneath the mirror:

". . . so Madame de Lionne had no sooner moved into the house than, one day, when she sat to have her hair done, she saw worms falling from the ceiling onto her dressing table. So she had her workmen open up the ceiling, and the mystery was solved."

"And what was it that they found?"

"A decomposing human head. So she notified the police, who paid a visit on the *receveur général du clergé*, the Seigneur de Penautier, who was the last person who had lived in the house."

"That was a waste of time."

"Yes, he just said it was an anatomical specimen that he was studying, and when it tired him, he just sealed it up in the floor of the room above the dressing room. So, of course, they couldn't do a thing. His word is much greater than that of a little upstart like La Reynie. But do you know what they're saying all over town?"

"Could it be . . . ?"

"Indeed it could. When he poisoned the *receveur général* of Languedoc so that he could purchase his office when it came free, the valet who carried the poison disappeared—"

"It was the valet's head, then."

"It does seem probable, doesn't it? After all, the police couldn't identify a headless body, even if it floated to the surface of the river."

I felt I was choking. As I fled from the room, I glanced back: the reflection in the mirror had become a sheet of blood.

"So, Madame, you, too, have found the futility of playing without money?" the lazy sound of a man's voice drawling near me from an alcove made me start. A heavy, saturnine figure emerged from the shadowy alcove. It was the libertine, Brissac. He pushed me against the wall and leaned close. His face, prematurely lined, sagged with debauchery.

"We would make good partners, you and I." His breath smelled like rotten fish. I turned my head away from him.

"What do you mean? We have nothing in common."

"Oh, yes we do. I have a need for money, and you can read lottery numbers in advance." I tried to pull myself up and look disdainful, but I was losing my footing on the slippery marble floor of the corridor.

"If you need luck at gaming, I know a woman who can give—"

"Ha! Do you think I haven't tried it all? The Black Mass, the summoning of demonic spirits?" He laughed and sent a gust of the horrid smell over me. "I'll tell you a secret, Marquise. They are of no more use than the prayers of Père Bossuet at the altar on a Sunday morning. God has abandoned us. So has the Devil. Even Abbé Guibourg can't conjure up the Devil for me, eh? He goes where he wants, His Satanic Majesty. But you, you are genuine. I've followed you, heard your prophecies, and seen them come to pass."

My face showed my disgust.

"Join me, and I will give you pleasure beyond that you've

ever known—" He smashed me against the wall with his body and was about to try to embrace me when the cultivated, oily voice of the Duc de Nevers made him pull free and spin around.

"Madame, you have dropped your walking stick." The Duc de Nevers bowed and flourished his hat, then offered me my stick, which I had dropped during the struggle.

Brissac spoke to his patron just as blandly as if nothing at all had happened: "Madame is considering the advantages to be offered by a partnership with me under your most illustrious patronage."

Nevers raised an eyebrow. "I am so glad, Brissac, that you do not wish to monopolise the future for yourself alone." A condescending smile flickered across the Duc de Nevers's face. His eyes, the treacherous Mancini eyes, were half hidden behind dark, sunken lids.

Brissac smiled his oily, ingratiating smile: "I have offered to resurrect the springtime of Madame's passion, to melt her imprisoned heart with my own ardent flame."

"Monsieur de Brissac," I answered, "a life of love would end the very thing you want most, the prophetic visions. You must offer a different bargain if you wish to attract my favour. Good day and my thanks to you, Monsieur de Nevers." I stalked off haughtily, but not before I heard Brissac say softly to him, ". . . wouldn't want anyone else to have her . . ."

"No . . . absolutely right, Brissac. To see into other lives . . . secrets . . . better that the future remain veiled . . ."

Yet another powerful enemy. Suddenly the air was stifling. I went and stood by the open window, resting my elbows on the sill, trying to breathe again. Outside, in the street, a pack of dogs was foraging in the gutter. A carriage passed, with an old man inside and two footmen clinging on behind. Across the street, standing immobile in a doorway, was a man muffled in a black cloak, his wide, dark hat drawn down to conceal his face. The same man. I saw him glance up at my window, and for a fearful moment, our eyes met. I slammed the window shut and fled back into the gilded *salle*.

TWENTY-SIX

That evening, as the Comtesse de Soissons's carriage left me at my doorstep, I felt an ominous pressure in the air – as if the darkness were going to close in on me. The uncalled vision in the mirror had unsettled me; I couldn't imagine what it meant. Whom was it for? One of the carriage outriders lit the doorway with his torch while the lackeys summoned my own armed groom to escort me in. The shadows seemed alive. Did I see a dark figure move in the street beyond? Someone was watching me; I was sure of it.

"You shudder so, Madame. Are you cold? Here, I'll get your winter dressing gown. You don't feel ill, do you?" Sylvie sounded anxious.

"Sylvie, I think something dreadful is going to happen. I don't know where or when, but it's a terrible disaster. Oh, my God, cover the dressing-table mirror, quickly!" Sylvie tucked one of my petticoats over the mirror's face before figures began to emerge from the sheet of blood that appeared to ooze from its surface. Gingerly, I touched the cloth, to make certain the blood was an illusion, and couldn't seep through.

"What are you doing there? What did you see?" Sylvie sounded alarmed.

"Blood. I saw strange figures at the Hôtel Soissons. I – I didn't call them. Cover up all the mirrors in the house. I can't bear to look in them. And Brissac was there. I think he has a plan with Nevers. I – I'm afraid they might steal me off, do something. And tonight, as I came in, I felt someone following me and watching me from the street . . ." I huddled on the bed, shaking with a strange chill, my arms around my folded knees.

"Brissac, *bah*! He's a sponge, but not dangerous as long as he's kept in line by someone more powerful. The time to fear Brissac is when he has money again. While he hasn't any, he'll fawn all over you. Still, I'll cover the mirrors and make certain the doors are barred and the windows sealed."

"Don't leave me, Sylvie. I'm afraid of being alone." I poured a dose of cordial into a little silver cup that I kept on my dressing table just for that purpose.

Suddenly Sylvie turned on me, her eyes suspicious.

"How much of that cordial have you had already today?"

"Just some after the execution. My back hurt—"

"And some last night to sleep, and some yesterday after a dinner party with bores, and some yesterday morning after a jolting carriage ride from the Marais unsettled your back. Madame, it is the cordial. La Dodée told me to watch you. I'm sure of it. You are hallucinating."

"And what business is it of hers to have you watch me? Everybody watches me! Whom are you working for, anyway? La Dodée and La Trianon? Or me?" I glared up at her from my seat on the bed.

"You, Madame," Sylvie answered, "but you know perfectly well that La Dodée gave you the tincture of opium against Madame Montvoisin's orders, and if you spoil your gift with it, her vengeance will be on La Dodée and me, for not telling her. And if I were you, I'd be a lot more worried about *Madame* than about imaginary things in the shadows. What will you do if she visits and sees your mirrors covered, eh? Me, I want to drink my soup without any worries." She flounced about to the other side of the bed and turned down the sheet, then fluffed up the pillows. I had a lot of pillows – the best goose down. They had lovely linen cases, too, embroidered with the arms of Morville, just like the sheets. The bed curtains were heavy blue brocade, the colour of the sea on a summer day. All paid for by me. They pleased me every time I looked at them.

"I hardly take any. You know it's just for my back."

"*Humph.* I'll believe that when you show me who's been following you."

"You can't see people who follow you secretly." My eyes narrowed. How dare she insult me? She should be the first to understand what care I took with my cordial. I wasn't like those bored rich women who have nothing to do but give themselves opium dreams.

"Especially if they're imaginary. Bloody mirrors, indeed!"

I crossed to the bedroom window and opened the tall shutters.

"So what do you call that?" I whispered. "My imagination?" The black, moonless night had swallowed the city. Here and there, the faint flicker of a candle showed between closed shutters in the tall, sealed stone houses. But in a doorway across the street, half lit by a puddle of faint light beneath one of La Reynie's new street lamps, a figure in a black cloak stood immobile, his wide, unplumed black hat pulled down over his face.

"Oh!" Sylvie was taken aback. "Have you seen him before?"

"This afternoon at the execution. He was watching me then, I'm sure of it. And later, he was standing outside the Hôtel Soissons, staring at me through the window."

"Who do you think has sent him?"

"It might be the Duc de Nevers. He's a ruthless man. Street assassins, bravos, kidnappers – he knows them all. He does whatever he likes, and there's not a law of God or man to stop him."

"But you've left out the Devil. Him, they all fear, those libertines. He'll not risk offending Madame – not directly, at any rate. She is the greater adept. I'll send Mustapha to her with a message tomorrow, and you shouldn't leave the house until he's gone— *Ah*, listen . . . company's coming." There was the crash and tinkle of a street lamp being shattered in the distance, the sound of horses on the cobblestones, and a bawdy drinking song being bellowed by two off-key voices.

"Neatly done! It counts double if you extinguish them with the first blow!"

"Gentlemen," whispered Sylvie, "or they'd flee before the watch arrested them for breaking the lamp."

"Oh, say, look – here's another." The arrogant voice rose from the darkened street. "With a Guardian of the Street Light poised beneath it, just like a gnome. Say, peasant, out of the way, unless you want to be run down. We've got a game going."

"The spirits of darkness tilt against the lamp of civilisation, eh? There is no contest. Louts who put out lights will always outnumber those who light them." The voice sounded familiar, but I couldn't place it.

"How dare you address me that way, you street sweeping!" I could see that the mounted man had drawn his sword as he charged into the lantern's light, but the dark figure had vanished deftly into the shadows.

"Madame, come away from the window, or they will want you as a witness." I could feel Sylvie pulling at my dressing-gown sleeve. The other windows on the street remained resolutely closed.

"*Shh!*" I said as I blew out the candle to darken our window. There was a clatter and an animal shriek as the black-cloaked figure lunged from the shadows and with one arm gave a vicious yank on the horse's heavy bit, causing the animal to rear and fall backward on to its rider. Now something had shattered the street lamp and sent its lighted wick and a shower of flaming candle wax on to the struggling horse and rider. The second rider dismounted and hastened to the aid of the first.

"Philippe, you are on fire – quick!" He batted at the blaze with his hat.

"*Peste* – I'm tangled in the stirrup leather," came the cry.

"Where is he? I'll find him if it takes all night." The first voice sounded menacing in the dark. I could hear the metallic slither of an épée being drawn.

"My plumes . . . ruined. My ankle – *ugh* – it might be broken. But I swear I pinked him. He can't be far . . ." I could hear the grunts of someone attempting to assist another to mount and the clatter of feet.

"Halt, Messieurs. You are under arrest."

"*Ha* . . . the watch . . . no, police archers. Stand your ground, you. It is we who are the aggrieved parties. A knave attacked us here—"

"Madame, where are you going?" whispered Sylvie.

"Sylvie, I think I know that man." I was already half downstairs, with Sylvie and Gilles close on my heels.

At the foot of the stairs, I could hear the sound of laboured breathing even through the heavy door. Someone was hidden in the dark arch of the doorway, leaning against the door itself. I lifted the bar, and he tumbled in. Wordlessly, Gilles dragged him in and swiftly and silently I rebarred the door.

"... breaking three street lamps, that's the charge, as if you didn't know already..." The argument in the street was growing louder.

"... knave, have you any idea of who I am?"

"... if you don't come quietly, you'll be cooling your heels in the Bastille for a good long time, that I promise you..."

"So, Monsieur d'Urbec," I said, leaning over the prostrate figure, "you have chosen an unusual hour to spatter blood on my doorstep." From the dark at my feet came the familiar voice.

"It is clear my injuries have proved mortal, since one encounters the dead only in the afterlife, Geneviève Pasquier."

As the gentlemen, horses and all, were taken into custody, I could hear Sylvie say, "They'll be out and back at it tomorrow." She had poked her head almost between mine and d'Urbec's, the better to listen in.

"Enough of that, Sylvie. Don't lean so close. When you're sure they've gone away, I want you and Gilles to bring a muffled lantern down here and clean up any bloodstains. If they come back in the morning, I don't want them trailing him into this house."

"Understood, Madame."

"So, Monsieur d'Urbec, I knew you were hurt when you pitched a rock at the light. It meant you couldn't get far and needed the dark. So I assumed I'd find you in the doorway. Correct?"

"You always had a superior command of logic, Mademoiselle Pasquier. Though of course I could not be sure you had recognised me." He was struggling to get up.

"Can you mount the stairs unassisted?"

"I think ... perhaps not. I believe I may have hit my head when you opened the door so precipitously."

"Lean on Gilles, here, and be careful of the stairs in the dark."

Upstairs, by the light of new lit candles, Gilles cut away his shirt as I tried to stop the bleeding. He winced as I pressed harder on the wad of rags I held in each hand over the double wound. Even so, the blood kept welling up, running between my fingers, on to my dressing gown, on to the floor. His breathing was uneven, gasping, but still he didn't cry out. The orange light of the candles flickered across the livid galley mark on his shoulder. Had he cried out then? I wondered. I could feel Gilles's calm eyes taking in the whole scene.

"Messy, but not serious. It went in clean and came clear out the other side. The rib deflected it from anything important. I've seen worse when I was in the army. If there's no gangrene, he'll be all right in no time."

"The army? You were in the army, too, Gilles?" I asked. Gilles was certainly a man of surprises.

"Why, any number of times," he answered calmly. "The grenadiers, the musketeers, the infantry. I've been in them all. Mind you, only for a few weeks each. Such dull people. And so stingy with the enrolment bonus. Why, they scarcely keep you drunk for a month. A man's patriotism should be more greatly appreciated, I say. Instead of thanking me for my devotion to the military life, they sent me for a sea-air cure." D'Urbec clutched at his side, his hands over mine in the sticky mess as he tried to laugh.

"You're lucky they didn't shoot you, my friend," he gasped. "That's the new requirement for excessive patriotism of your sort." Gilles chuckled. D'Urbec's eyes hunted around the room, studying the gilded woodwork, the luxurious hangings, as Gilles ran a bandage around his ribs.

"Not so tight," he complained. He had changed greatly. He was thinner, hardened. His jaw was grimmer, his cheekbones prominent, his eyes rimmed with dark circles. His black hair lay close to his skull, and he hadn't shaved for weeks. The student in him had died; in its place was something strong, dark, and bitter.

"It has to be tight, so it won't open up again," said Gilles, inspecting his handiwork. I could feel d'Urbec's eyes on me as Sylvie brought a bowl of water and I washed my hands.

"I must apologise for imposing myself upon you so abruptly," he said.

"It is just as well you guessed correctly about me, Monsieur d'Urbec. What would you have done if you were wrong?"

"I never guess, Mademoiselle. I calculate. Think of it as a proof in geometry." His eyes caught mine. They seemed jet black in the candlelight. I looked away hastily.

"Well, if you calculate so well, why did you need to follow me about?"

"*Ah*. Scientific theory requires verification. And you must admit that it is not often that one sees a decayed body laid in the grave brought back to life under such spectacular circumstances."

"You . . . you saw my funeral?"

"And quite a shabby one it was. You were thrown shrouded into a mass grave for suicides with scarcely a prayer. Only your sister attended – with a rather dubious priest." I was suddenly touched. Why had he, of all people, attended my burial?

"Madame, I knew you were old . . . but you were . . . dead too?" Sylvie shuddered.

"Oh, quite dead," I answered. D'Urbec fixed her with his cynical stare.

"There is nothing beyond the reach of modern alchemy. We live in an age of miracles," he said, but his voice seemed weaker.

"No wonder you conceal your past . . The abbé . . . he must have been a powerful necromancer." Sylvie sounded awed.

"No, in all fairness, it was Madame who brought me back to life, though I don't really like to speak of it."

"Madame," Sylvie whispered, her eyes wide in the candle-light. The pupils were immense, as black as night. Then her eyelids narrowed, and she tipped her head on one side, as if thinking.

"Tell me, is it painful, being dead?"

"The least thing in the world, once the dying part is over . . . no, it is the resurrection that is difficult. And the mildewed grave clothes are so offensively odorous."

D'Urbec's eyes glittered, and one corner of his mouth turned up. But even in the dim light, he seemed to be growing more pallid.

"Monsieur d'Urbec, are you sure you are entirely well?" I ventured.

"The thrill of besting both the aristocracy and the police has worn off, Athena, and I seem to feel the pain more. Tell me, have you room here for the night?" His voice had faded to a hoarse whisper.

"That and more, Monsieur d'Urbec. I have a cordial that will take the pain right off." I retrieved the bottle from my night table, and he took a large dose from the medicine glass I offered.

"Ah, this is excellent stuff," he said, looking at the glass as if it were metamorphosing into a snake. "My mind feels quite woolly, and the walls of the room shimmer. I take it that it mends the undead as well?" I gave him a hard stare, but it was wasted on him. His eyes had shut, and he was slowly slumping in the chair. I suppose I'd overdone the cordial. His face in repose took on an air of deep melancholy. Suddenly, like a fool, I felt terribly sorry for him.

"Gilles?" I didn't need to say more.

"For a fellow *galérien*, yes. Accommodations were no less crowded aboard *La Fidèle*." He picked up the limp figure and laid him in his own narrow bed, foot to head, so there would still be room for himself. As he inspected the body in the bed, he observed, "That cordial of yours felled him like an ox. You must be made of iron, Madame, to go through so much of it in a day."

"I am, Gilles. The undead are more powerful in that respect than the living." He shot me a shrewd glance, then inspected Sylvie's awed face with an odd look and bade me good night.

"Madame, is there something wrong that you still sit up? You're not feeling ill again, are you?" Sylvie's voice came floating out of the dark from her little trundle bed at the foot of my huge curtained one. I was looking at the solitary candle flame in the little silver candlestick on the nightstand beside my bed. An eternity of blackness stretched from the dark shadows of the bed curtains into the sky, the universe. What a tiny circle the light made in that vast dark. A single leaping tendril, as bright and frail as hope.

"My heart's beating too much, Sylvie. I can feel it jumping and pounding. Hand me my cordial."

"You don't need any more. You can't have it."

"But I want it. Who is mistress here?"

"You are, Madame." Then she added brightly, as if to distract a child, or a senile old woman, "But do you know . . . you've forgotten to write in your account books, what with all that's gone on tonight. You always do that – it ought to make you sleepy. If I did accounts, I'd be out like a candle." Again a candle. Why light them at all, when the darkness is so permanent, and we must sleep anyway? There was a rustle as Sylvie got up and searched the room.

"Look, Madame. Here is your coffer and your bag with the key in it. Your account books – you know you never miss a day."

"Very well, then, I'll have them," I sighed, and emptied my bag on to the bed to hunt for the key that never left my person. I could hear Sylvie's breathing grow regular. She was lucky. She could sleep anywhere, any time. She didn't have a conscience. She didn't have worries. I found the string of the key entangled with the little books I'd bought that afternoon. The word *Cato* on the spine of one caught my eye. Sure enough. I had acquired not the work of the Roman but the effusions of Griffon's underground press. *Observations on the Health of the State*, the book d'Urbec had disowned. I looked at *Parnasse Satyrique*, supposedly printed in Rotterdam. The same chipped *e*s and wobbly *f*s. Griffon's cheap type couldn't be mistaken. I opened the broadside. Yes, the same type again. Griffon was still in business, and d'Urbec was writing for him. *Libelles* because they sell better, I thought. No one wants to know about the health of the state. Everyone wants to know about the sex life of the nobility, especially if it's perverse. My mind went back to when I'd snatched up the books. He'd been there, minding the box, ready for a quick retreat. No hope if he'd been caught a second time. This stuff would see him hanged. I'd lifted my veil and he had recognised me and followed me. Why had he done that? D'Urbec never did anything on impulse. And he'd gone to my burial, too. My own brother hadn't bothered. But then, why should he? Monsieur Respectable, the rising *avocat*. My brother wouldn't let himself be tainted by witnessing a suicide's burial. Had my funeral been before or after d'Urbec had turned *libelliste*? His interest had to be professional. That was it. What a silly predicament, Geneviève. You don't even know when your own funeral was. Had he wept? I wondered suddenly. Why did it seem so important to me to know? No, I couldn't imagine d'Urbec weeping. He was probably taking notes, as cold as a clockwork. How stupid you are, Geneviève. He obviously doesn't even see Lamotte any more. Lamotte was fashionable now, too fashionable to be seen with a *libelliste*, an ex-convict, even a pardoned one. Lamotte was the darling of wealthy women; he probably did readings in the salons. I could imagine him drinking wine in the *ruelle* of some modish lady, laughing at her jokes, flattering her friends. Beautiful, charming Lamotte. Forever beyond me.

Sometimes Geneviève, you outsmart yourself. You still haven't got any closer to Lamotte. So much for cleverness and daydreams. And what's more, you have that calculating d'Urbec stuck in your house instead of the gorgeous cavalier. And worse yet, you feel too guilty to throw him out because you're sorry he was hurt on your doorstep. And he knows it, too. Oh, damn, damn. He's managed the whole thing somehow. And for all you know, he was planning another *libelle*. I could see it as if I'd already purchased it from Griffon. Bumpy type with bad *e*s, a nasty woodcut set about with snakes and skulls. *Secrets of the Infamous Devineresse, the Marquise de Morville, Revealed; Hellish Horrors on the Rue Charlot*. He'll up and leave tomorrow, then straight to the printer's. That's what you get for opening doors, Geneviève. And he had it all figured out ahead of time. Oh, damn again! It stung me to be outsmarted. And by a man, too.

The candle was burning lower. I poured myself a bit of cordial and waited for the warm ooze to work its way through my body as I picked up the broadside on Madame de Brinvilliers that had been folded between the books. The ink had smeared, and the woodcut of the execution, depicting Samson in the act of swinging the sword, had doubled itself. Two Samsons, two kneeling women. The scaffold depicted floating, without legs, to make it easier to carve in the figures of the guards on horseback that surrounded it. Two executions, one a ghostly reverse. Reality and dream, face-to-face. Ah, the cordial must be working. The doggerel verses beneath the illustration were scarcely legible. ". . . from grasping pride and greed for gold, poison'd husband, brother, and father old . . ." plus sisters-in-law and her own daughter, rhymed just as badly. Surely not d'Urbec's effort; he couldn't turn a verse that bad. The marquise had had a lover, an alchemist named

Saint-Croix, who'd provisioned her with all sorts of interesting poisons. This fellow Saint-Croix must have been a hardy soul – imagine, contemplating marrying a woman when you knew she'd become rich by dropping your own arsenic in the soup.

A vision floated into my mind. Violins in livery playing at supper. The marquise, tiny, exquisite, in yellow silk cut low on her shoulders, leaning across the table to whisper something tender to Saint-Croix, all splendid in blue silk and lace, an immense curling court wig making his features look narrow and refined.

"Some more wine, precious?" A delicate, pale little finger signals to the lackey at the sideboard. With her own hands she passes him the newly filled goblet.

"It seems to have cork bits in it. Do sip a bit off the top and see what you think." Saint-Croix, with a look of adoration, extends the chased silver drinking cup to her.

"Ah, but I'm feeling a bit faint. The joy of the wedding, you understand. First I must have my drops, my love." A slender white hand fumbles for the secret vial of antipoison.

"How odd; I do myself. It must be the heat in the room. Lackey, open the window." His lace-bedecked hand reaches for an inner pocket.

Grandmother, I would like to tell you about this. I would laugh out loud to hear you cackle as I imitated the voices for you. And then your bird would cackle, too, just like you, and bob up and down shrieking "Hell and damnation! Fire and brimstone!" while you said, "Didn't I tell you, Geneviève? Only the wicked get rich nowadays. It's not like the old days in the Fronde. There were heroes then. Have you read this passage about damnation in Revelation?" And she'd take up her Bible from the nightstand to read about hellfire to the bobbing dance of the parrot crying "Damnation!"

But the parrot had cried, "Drink, drink!" there in the death room.

Suddenly I felt cold. I could see it in my mind so clearly. The thought I had not allowed myself to think. The rolling cordial glass. The heart seizure. The mocking parrot had heard someone shout, "Drink! Drink!" Someone who considered Grandmother a deaf old fool. Someone in desperate haste, who pried open Grandmother's stubborn, hard-clenched jaw to pour the contents of the cordial glass down her throat as the feeble old lady struggled in vain. Someone who snatched a letter addressed to the Lieutenant General of Police from a tightly clenched fist. Someone who knew the carriage was waiting below, who heard my foot on the stair, and hurried away with a rustle of taffeta.

Grandmother, with her shrewd eyes and wizened face, Grandmother, bedridden among her *libelles*, broadsides, and court journals, had discovered what everyone else had missed. Father's illness had been no illness. He must have been slowly poisoned; Grandmother had suspected how and was sending her suspicions to the police. And the proof that Grandmother was right was that someone – someone with a taffeta petticoat, had forced her to drink poison to cover up the crime. My mind fled from the thought. But the image of the death room, the parrot flapping wildly from the curtain rod to the bed canopy was fixed like a mad dream in front of my eyes. How many little vials of white arsenic, of hellebore, of wolfsbane, of *"mort aux rats"* did Mother keep among the rouge pots and beauty powders in the little cupboard in her *ruelle*? Stop, stop. Logic. The rational mind must have logic. But there was only one question that logic was left to resolve. Had Mother procured the poison from the Rue Beauregard? I felt chilled through. I dared ask no one.

TWENTY-SEVEN

"Madame." Sylvie's whisper woke me. It was barely light. "We have the blood off the doorstep. The trail leads from the centre of the street to the corner and vanishes now. You'd think that's where he went, not where he came from."

"Excellent, Sylvie. We'll hire a chair and send him to his people this afternoon, and there's no harm done." My head was beginning to ache, and strange pains seemed lodged in my stomach.

"That's clever – let them call the surgeon and run the risk. Let's hope the police don't listen to those gentlemen they hauled in and conduct a house search of the neighbourhood, or we'll surely be arrested for harbouring a fugitive."

"It's just a pity La Reynie takes his new streetlights so seriously." I sighed. "Though if he didn't, the streets would be as black as pitch before the month was out."

Corseted and gowned in black, I was seated downstairs waiting for my first client when a knock on the door came. Somehow, it didn't seem like the ordinary sort of knock. I heard the scurrying upstairs and realised they had seen something from the upper window. The knock sounded again. "Open, police," demanded a voice. As if I hadn't known the first time.

"Mustapha, open the door to them, but slowly." I composed myself at the table behind my glass and shrouded my face in my veil as Mustapha, resplendent in plumed turban, embroidered Turkish trousers, and purple slippers turned up at the toes, opened the latch.

"Come in," I called in a cold, distant voice, as Mustapha bowed before them. For a moment, they were taken aback. Good, I thought. Every moment's delay is a moment to the better.

"A fortune-teller – he's bound to be in this house," whispered one of the men to the red-stockinged sergeant.

"I am the Marquise de Morville, and this is my house. You are welcome here, but first I beg that you state your business." The coldness, the formality, the lack of fear slowed them. My knees were trembling. It was just as well I was sitting.

"A Marquise— Shouldn't we . . . ?"

"Every house. Desgrez's orders."

"We are searching for a fugitive. There was a disturbance last night – a third man . . ."

"What a pity I heard nothing. But then, it is my custom to take a heavy sleeping potion at eight o'clock every evening."

"Odd, how many residents of this neighbourhood take a heavy sleeping potion at eight o'clock. Would you lift that veil, so that we may identify you?"

"Of course, Messieurs." The flattery of the title I gave them, the curious atmosphere, the Turkish dwarf, the little drama of raising the veil, kept them staring. I could hear the intake of breath at the sight of my white, cadaverlike face. It was, as usual, gratifying.

"I take it, you wish to search my house? I appreciate your protection, Messieurs, because I am a woman alone. Alone for centuries. Any miscreant might creep in through my cellar. But you, you will preserve me from the danger."

They looked at each other and nodded, then approached me. I handed them the key to the cellar from the little purse at my waist. They went out of the narrow side door and I could hear the thump of the cellar door being thrown open and the clatter of footsteps on the narrow stone stairs down into the dusty stone vault beneath the house.

"Mustapha, upstairs, and quickly. I will remain here for them when they emerge from the cellar and see if I can delay them further." Mustapha nodded and went smoothly and quietly up the staircase. I rose slowly and took a deep breath. I had a terrible headache. My stomach was on fire. A cold, shuddery feeling made me tremble. I looked down. There, in the red pattern of the Turkish carpet, I saw it. A splash of dried blood, with tell-tale drops leading in a little trail through the crimson vines and leaves to the stairs, where they stopped short, wiped clean from the floor. Damn. I positioned myself all cold and straight over the most visible of the telltale stains, my veil thrown back. I set my face in an impassive white mask.

"Well, Messieurs? Have you saved me, and this peaceful neighbourhood?" The sergeant looked up from brushing spiderwebs off his cuff and gave me a hard stare.

"Upstairs," he barked. I followed slowly, abandoning the spot only when they were well ahead of me.

"Come in, Messieurs; there are no secrets here." Sylvie curtseyed in respect. I was glad we were not in hired rooms. The house of a marquise, even a false one, is searched with more respect. They prodded in the armoire among the clothes, with a bare *épée*. They opened the bedroom chest to find only folded blankets. They pulled out Sylvie's trundle bed from beneath the foot of the bed and searched beneath the bed hangings.

"What is that I see beneath the bed?"

"Another blanket chest, Messieurs. If you wish, I will have Gilles draw it out for you." Sylvie's eyes were round and innocent. The sergeant tapped the box with his sword. Then he waved his hand as if it were not worth the trouble.

"Look here – the servant's room—" There was a flurry as one of the men produced a bucket of bloody rags from under Gilles's bed. Sylvie rushed into the room, blushing to the roots of her boldly hennaed hair.

"My monthly— Madame has left me no time for the laundry—" The man dropped the bucket in disgust.

"Nothing here . . . Let's try the house at the corner . . ."

"I thank you for your concern, Messieurs. You have been most considerate of my china and furniture." The sergeant pocketed my financial offering so neatly, you could hardly see it vanish. I escorted them downstairs and bid them *adieu* standing over the bloody stain before the stairs.

By the time the door was safely closed, I was shaking all over, pains running inside my bones, deathly ill.

"Madame, they are gone; there's no need—"

"I'm sick, Sylvie – help me upstairs." As I collapsed on to the bed, I whispered, "Where is he?"

"Under the bed, doubled up in the blanket box."

"My God, pull him out; you've killed him."

"Hardly, Madame. But he is gagged, he groaned so. He

refused the opium for fear that it might make him lose his self-mastery. He's a bold soul, Madame. I see now why he pleases a woman like you. I rather like him myself—"

"Don't chatter – give me my cordial and get that man out from under my bed." Shaking, I poured the last dose out of the vial. As the fire in my insides faded, I knew with a certainty that the cordial was more than a convenience. Now I had to have it; now I couldn't live without La Trianon's pharmacy; I couldn't live without the philanthropical society of La Voisin. Logic. I was as firmly in the Shadow Queen's power as La Montespan, or as my Mother, with her failed, greedy dreams. God, I could hear her laugh as if she were in the room. "Little Marquise, why does it take a clever girl like you so long to figure things out?" Oh, damn, damn. A thousand damns. Gilles had drawn the chest out into the *ruelle* and unlatched it.

"Your laces, Madame. Your ruff." I was half undone and the ruff in its bandbox by the time Gilles and Mustapha had pulled the haggard figure to a sitting position in the open chest.

"Well, well," he whispered as they drew my second-best handkerchief from his mouth. "This is certainly a new way to enter a woman's *ruelle*. But I fear the quality of my conversation will not undermine the ever-glorious reputation of the Hôtel de Rambouillet. Oh, damn. I see you've emptied the cordial bottle, Athena."

"Madame has been taken ill suddenly," sniffed Sylvie. D'Urbec had both hands clutched at his side, where the wound had burst open again under the bandages. The blood was running from between his fingers, and his face had turned grey. But his eyes were still fixed on me.

"You skipped your usual dose today, didn't you?"

"None of your business, d'Urbec." I picked my head up from the pillow and glared at him. But my face was sticky with tears and smeared white powder. Another fierce impression, ruined. When would I ever learn to do things right? "Sylvie, get him the brandy. And don't let him drip into my chest like that." My hairpins and veil were strewn across the bed, my dress was half undone and the stays of the steel corset undone. My mouth tasted bitter. I had made a fool of myself in front of a stranger. And not just any stranger. A damned *libelliste*.

"If you write about this, d'Urbec, I swear, I'll kill you," I whispered.

"It would hardly be the way for me to repay your assumption of the risks of hospitality, now, would it?" he answered in a low voice. "Credit me with some manners, even if I have turned to writing *libelles* in my current state of ... er, financial embarrassment. Besides," he added, "I am not actually in a position to remove myself from your chest, let alone rush to the printer's. And you must face facts, Athena. The neighbours are watching the house. They will count every guest and every carriage. A police reward always arouses neighbourly concern. Until I am capable of walking out of here after dark, you have an unwelcome house-guest."

"D'Urbec, you planned it this way, I swear." I sighed, as he was lifted out of the chest and I gave orders to Sylvie to have Madame's network smuggle a mattress and surgeon's supplies into the back of the house under cover of darkness.

"Planned, but as usual, I have overshot the mark," I thought I heard him whisper as they carried him into the servant's room.

"So, Mademoiselle, it has happened at last. I imagine that accounts for your diminished income. I suppose you're buying him gifts on the sly." The Shadow Queen shifted in her big armchair. The faded morning light had made its way through the little window in her study. I could hear the pots and pans clattering in the kitchen and, somewhere, the howl of a baby. She had not yet dressed for the day. The turban over her hair and the painted India-cotton dressing gown lent her an exotic air. Her big grey tom leaped on to the back of her chair, then climbed precariously on to her shoulder. As she pushed him off, I could see that, without her stays, her figure was definitely beginning to spread. But her black eyes were still as sharp as a pair of drills.

"It's hardly at last, because he's not a lover, and so far I've bought him nothing but food and medicine. And I can't really throw him out. I assure you, the only time he doesn't make me furious with annoyance is when he's asleep. The house is too small for an extra mouth. Especially one that talks as much as his."

"And now you're trying to mislead me by denouncing him. Don't think I am so stupid I can be deceived. First Marie-Marguerite, then you. At least I've led her to something a little more profitable than a pastry maker. Her new magician gives me hope for the future. But to move the lowest of the low right in with you – a *libelliste*, a *galérien*, and support him . . . Believe me, you could do better, much better, if guided by me. Well, enjoy yourself, and when you tire of his parasitism, come to me and I'll find you someone who's an improvement, who will make your fortune. In the meantime, don't try to deduct his expenses out of mine." La Voisin shut her big ledger with a snap. "And if you get pregnant," she added, "my standard fee applies. I am displeased with this d'Urbec, but I suppose I must wait until he bores you."

I was well aware that behind all this charade of tolerance lay the fear of the police. An untried stranger had stumbled into her network. If we quarrelled, if he left, if I grew enraged with her and love made me throw aside all caution, or if the neighbours saw him – anything could lead to the police torturer and the unravelling of her hidden kingdom. But she was a cat who had made a career of walking on eggs. I couldn't help admiring the brilliance of her control: her contrived smile, her little tantrum, her show of maternal resignation. I glanced up at the cupboards in her cabinet, where the shelves of neatly labelled poisons lay behind locked doors. Now was not the time. I needed her help with d'Urbec. When I'd sent him off in one piece, I'd face the new battle. Besides, I had to be certain of what was still only a suspicion before I could think about what to do. She knew how to wait. Now I'd learn how, myself. Smile, Geneviève; she mustn't suspect what you know.

"The problem just now is hardly one of pregnancy. He has gone bad in the last two days. Gilles says we need a surgeon. Is there one of us . . . ?"

"Several. Let's see . . . Dubois, no. *Hmm*. Chauvet, I think, would be best. Most of ours specialise in helping people out of this world, not into it, and it would be dreadfully hard to dispose of a body at your house. Your garden is too narrow; the neighbours can see into it. If you bury him in the cellar, the flies will rise into your reception parlour, and that's always so suspicious. Your clients would be bound to think the worst –

that's the way they always are. No, Chauvet. Better that d'Urbec should get well and leave you for another woman."

The surgeon came after the theatre hour, dressed as a dandy, with his assistant in the livery of a valet. A perfect touch. He looked like a customer. Upstairs, he stripped off his coat and good shirt, putting on a heavy apron. He looked at the fevered figure on the mattress and prodded at the wound.

"As I thought," he announced. "It must be opened and the abcess drained to the outside. These illegal duelling wounds – always the same story," he sniffed. Then he looked around. "Has your kitchen a table big enough to accommodate a man, Madame?"

"I believe so, Monsieur."

"Good. We'll operate at once."

He went downstairs in a shower of orders. "More candles, and hurry. Make up the fire; I want it hot in there. Muffle the windows; the neighbours are too close. Hop to it, man. I promised that old witch on the Rue Beauregard I wouldn't kill him."

"Athena, Athena, listen to me." D'Urbec's voice was urgent. I leaned close to him. "Don't bury me in your God-damned backyard, do you hear? Have my ashes shipped home to my family. They always said I lacked a sense of propriety. I want to do something decently, just this once."

"D'Urbec, I swear. By your father, by mine."

"And something else, Athena. I can't go without letting you know the truth. Father told me an influential widow at court had assisted him in getting his petition to the King. I . . . had a long time to wonder about her motives. I followed her, Athena. I followed and observed the Marquise de Morville and found that she was brilliant, calculating, and did nothing without reason. But it wasn't until I saw you, quite by chance, without that ridiculous veil, that I understood who it must have been that wrote to the authorities on the sly, denouncing the fellow who'd stolen her spoons and her virginity."

"It was nothing, d'Urbec."

"Call me Florent, please. I had thought . . . some day . . . to ask you . . . for an entirely different favour . . . if you could bear a man marked for life . . . but now . . ."

"Please ... it will all work out..." I was stricken with shame. How cheap and shallow my motives seemed. He had showed me his heart, and I didn't dare show him mine. It was dirty.

"At least thanks to you I'm not dying on board the *Superbe*. Even if Uncle did disown me. The Bastille, that's respectable, he said. You can meet people from the very best families in the Bastille. But the galleys. No class, Geneviève." His voice had sunk to a hoarse whisper. "He said he'd have sooner hanged me himself. God, I couldn't even get arrested in the right way." He paused. Sweat was rolling down his face from the fever. He looked all greenish grey. "Promise me. No backyard. No cellar. No river. Lamotte is keeping some money for me. Give it to my parents for a memorial service. They don't have a sou. Call him if I don't live through this. He's just moved into the Hôtel Bouillon. Swear it."

"I swear, Florent."

"Oath of a Roman?"

"Oath of a Roman."

When the surgeon's assistant and Gilles had hauled him down to the kitchen, I sat down and cried. I'd only see Lamotte by losing d'Urbec. Everything was so stupid, so ruined.

"Where is that silly old woman?" I heard the surgeon call from below. "I told you; I need both women holding the candles. I need the men to hold him down." I entered the kitchen wiping my face. "Where have you been? Lounging around weeping and wailing? Surely you can't be one of *Madame's*. Why, I've seen them take the head right off a man, smiling the whole while. Take this," he said, grabbing the silver candelabrum he had taken from the little dining table above and shoving it into my hand. By the light of a dozen flames, he peered at my face. "Your powder's running. So's that black stuff around your eyes." He wiped a finger across my face and inspected the residue. Then he leaned close to my ear, so no one else could hear.

"A hundred and fifty years old, eh? I'd be surprised if you were a year over sixteen, myself. Well, keep at it, you little terror; you have my admiration. I've never yet seen a girl make a fortune except on her back. Remember me when you're Queen. I'm competent, I'm silent, and everyone needs a surgeon on occasion." I stiffened with indignation. He laughed. "Old lady, you're holding me up. Time is precious. His hour is running out fast." He ripped off the bandage, and d'Urbec howled. "Shut up, damn you. Want to bring the police on us? Hand me that scalpel. I'm in good practice this week. Three wounds just like this one. I'll be in and out in a minute." The scalpel darted into the oozing mess with the blood. "Good!" pronounced the surgeon, as d'Urbec fainted. The scalpel darted again and then retreated. Monsieur Chauvet wiped it on his apron. Then he sloshed liquid from a bottle into the hole, and the smell of alcohol filled the room.

"What's that?" I asked.

"Brandy. Best quality. Works better than a cautery iron and quicker than hot oil." He spat on his hands, and wiped them on his apron. "And now," he said, as his assistant helped him on with his lace ruffled shirt, "I always take cash. No notes of hand." I paid.

"Will he live?" I asked.

"That I can't say just now. He either will or he won't, but there's nothing more I can do about it. Well, Jacques, let's be off – we've got a full night's work ahead of us."

"More?" I asked, as I handed him his walking stick.

"Next one's easy – a rich woman's secret childbirth. Have to hurry – a carriage is meeting us at midnight on the Place Royale. I imagine they'll take us there blindfolded. That's how it's usually done with the great ones. They strip the linens and cover the crests on the bed hangings so they can't be identified. The next day you see them, all pale, in a carriage on their way to the opera ... and pretend you don't recognise them. It's a strange world, as I'm sure you've noticed by now – eh, old lady?"

"It appears so, Monsieur, though of course, in good King Henri's day, it would never have happened." He shot me a sharp, amused glance and doffed his plumed hat in a formal farewell.

"And to you, too, Monsieur, farewell. And ... be careful tonight."

"Don't worry, old lady. I've been in this business longer

than you have." And he was gone out the door and into the dark
street where his carriage waited.

As I sat up by d'Urbec's bed that night, I wondered over and
over how I could ever keep my promise to him without
arousing the rage of the Shadow Queen. As I watched his
sleeping face, so deeply sad in repose, and listened to his
laboured breathing, I could only ask myself over and over,
Geneviève, what have you done? With all your clever
scheming, all you have accomplished is to bring this ruined man
who has never harmed you to his death. Geneviève, you are
worse than a fool; you are a monster to have made him love
you, I cursed myself and sat there while the tears ran down my
face.

"She's got it bad, hasn't she?" I heard Sylvie whisper as my
eyes closed with fatigue.

"It'll do her good," Gilles answered, his voice so low I could
hardly make it out. "I always thought she was made of ice. A
human heart would improve that little mind-machine. I'd feel a
devil of a lot safer in her service."

He slept for two days, and I thought he was dying. The
surgeon never returned, but I was hardly surprised. I
continued to see clients and attend receptions as if nothing at
all were going on. On the morning of the third day, his eyes
opened and he said in a low voice, "Call Lamotte." I sent
Mustapha in full Turkish livery to the Hôtel Bouillon. In the
afternoon, as I lay resting without my stays in a loose sacque of
embroidered Indian cotton, Sylvie came hurrying up to rouse
me.

"Madame, Madame. The most handsome man in the world
is here, waiting below for you. Oh, if you could only see his
moustachios, his velvet cloak – the elegant way he throws it
over his shoulder. His silk stockings— Oh, his calves alone
give me absolute *palpitations*!"

"That's Lamotte, Sylvie. Help me put on my cap."

"Oh, your curls, I can't get them to lie down here in back!"
she exclaimed, as she pinned my hair into a decent little knot in
back to fit under my low, lace house cap. Then all aflutter, she
hurried downstairs to show him up.

Lamotte had filled out in his prosperity. His early mad

gallantry had been transformed into a glittering, cavalier elegance. He was, if anything, more beautiful than ever. The unconscious charm he had once radiated had become conscious and artful, but nonetheless effective for all that. He paused at the door, his eyebrows raised when he spied me, and a strange smile crossed his face.

"So *you* are the celebrated Marquise de Morville. It makes sense, all the sense in the world, in its own nonsensical way." He bowed low, and flourished his plumed hat. "Greetings, Madame de Morville."

"Greetings to you, Monsieur Lamotte. Your friend Monsieur d'Urbec lies in the antechamber and is in deep need of you."

"D'Urbec the unlucky. But, by God, lucky at last. Would that I had had the foresight and daring to thrust myself upon the Angel of the Window in this manner."

"He lies dying, Monsieur."

"My God, I didn't know. Your message didn't say." Genuine concern flashed for a moment across his handsome features as he rushed to his old friend's bedside. He seemed taken aback as he spied the dreadful transformation in his friend's features. "Have you done nothing at all for him?" He turned on me in a fury. "For God's sake! Send a servant to get him a doctor, before it's too late."

"I can't, Lamotte. Any legitimate surgeon will report the wound. And what's more, you haven't seen me, either. You must swear secrecy, or I'll die twice. You have seen only the Marquise de Morville."

"Mademoiselle Pasquier," he said slowly, looking at me, "just what have you got yourself into?"

"Believe me, Monsieur Lamotte, you don't want to know. Leave it at that. He needs you, and I have risked much." It was all wrong. We'd met again at last, but it was all sad and spoiled.

"Lamotte, you did come after all." D'Urbec could not raise his head.

"Old friend, how could you think so little of me? I came as soon as I heard."

"The money I left with you. You still have it?"

"It has doubled."

"Good. I want you to send it to my parents. Not to the house in Aix. At this season my mother visits her sister in Orléans.

Send it there. Rue de Bourgogne. The house of the widow
Pirot. And see that I have a decent funeral, will you? For
Mother's sake, if for no one else." Lamotte burst into tears.
"Come now, no weeping," whispered d'Urbec. "My bad luck's
at an end. Who would have thought it? A stupid accident. An
encounter with street rowdies. It could have happened any
time. Not even my enemies. Tell Griffon I won't be back. At
least, Mademoiselle Pasquier has seen to it that I didn't die in
the galleys, to the eternal shame of my parents."

"I will tell them all that you died nobly," said Lamotte, taking
his friend's hand as he sat down on the low bed. He sat there a
long time after d'Urbec's eyes had closed, listening to his
friend's breathing, the tears running silently down his face.

For several days, d'Urbec remained much the same, neither
dying nor getting well. Though the fever fell, he lay, hardly
moving, looking at me through half-closed eyes whenever I
came into the room. Then on a sultry August morning, when
business was especially low, as I sat being annoyed that I
couldn't follow the court to Fontainebleau because of d'Urbec,
I heard the sound of battering on the front door. I put the
volume of Tacitus I had been listlessly perusing beneath the
draped table, just in case it was a client at last. I lowered my
veil, hastily dusted off the oracle glass, and sent Mustapha
gliding to the door.

"Get out of my way, little boy— Oh, you horrid thing; you
have whiskers! Ah, there she is, the she-devil, seated there all
in black! You see, Marie-Claude, I told you we should come at
once!"

"Jeanne-Marie, how right you were. I told you I suspected
something. True, all true." The two dusty little women in
travelling clothes, as short and active as shrews, pushed their
way into my reception parlour. The boy servant who followed
them, laden with their baggage, set it down with a plop, just
inside the door.

"Come, Marie-Claude, he must be upstairs, just as the man
said, wounded in a court intrigue...." The two women swept
towards the stair.

"And just what man is that?" I asked, blocking their way
upstairs.

"The Chevalier de la Motte brought to my sister's house a

message that my son was perishing from a fatal wound incurred in defending the honour of a lady of high degree," said the short one. "He brought us money he said was from my son." They both spoke with the rolling *r*s and lazy vowels of the south. Good Lord, it had to be d'Urbec's mother. And his aunt, too. How perfectly awful. Now I lacked only his grandfather and the dog.

"The . . . *Chevalier* de la Motte?"

"Yes. The handsomest man I ever saw. A very important man. A personal friend of my nephew," announced d'Urbec's aunt. "But I knew right away it was one of those court intrigues I've read about. Yes, a plot. Duels, indeed! A plot is much more like him. 'Do you suppose at this very moment he wears an iron mask?' I asked my sister. 'More likely,' she said, 'he discovered who the iron mask was. I know my son; he never leaves other people's business alone. This money can't be his – he hasn't any. It's money to buy our silence. I'll get to the bottom of this,' she said, and so we used the bribe money to take the next diligence to Paris."

"And how, pray tell, did you find my house?" My voice was cool, but I could feel the hot wrath climbing up the back of my neck.

"I recognised the arms of Bouillon on the carriage that brought the chevalier," announced his aunt. "Then we made subtle enquiries at the *remise* of the Hôtel Bouillon when we arrived in Paris." Subtle indeed, I thought sourly.

"And now, you shameless wanton, lead us to him, or I shall report your notorious ways to the police. There's a place for women like you, women of notorious ill life, who draw young men to ruin." D'Urbec's mother looked righteous. I narrowed my eyes.

"If you do that," I said in an even tone, "the man who lies upstairs will die in prison, for his part in the street brawl that took place outside my doorstep, and from which I rescued him."

"Nonsense. Florent d'Urbec lies up there – your lover, whom you have lured to his doom," replied his aunt. In a flash, everything suddenly became clear. Devil take that Lamotte, anyway. That is what you get when you entrust a commission to a man who writes romantic dramas for the theatre. Who knows why he'd done it – to save time, to meet some important obligation in Paris – doubtless some wretched soirée at the Hôtel Bouillon. He had hurried to hand over the money before d'Urbec had actually died. I could see it all as if I'd been there. Lamotte, self-promoted to de la Motte, with his charm, suddenly carried away by a gust of imagination as he strove to leave d'Urbec's mother with a noble memory. He'd brush away one of his easy tears, convincing himself as he spoke that everything he said was true. He'd raised his friend's prospects, added a duel, a love affair, and heaven knows what else. Perhaps a lost treasure and a royal conspiracy as well. And this mess was the result.

"Before we go farther, you must understand a few things. The . . . ah . . . Chevalier de la Motte did not tell you the entire truth."

"They never do, when it's a matter of those high intrigues of court," announced his mother. "I intend to stick like a burr until I have discovered the whole truth." As she wagged her finger in my face, I knew with a sinking heart that she might very well do exactly that.

TWENTY-EIGHT

The Shadow Queen had pulled the curtains against the searing afternoon sun. She had abandoned her stays entirely beneath her India-cotton robe. I could see the sweat running from beneath the turban that hid her hair. She sat limply in her big armchair, her feet, in embroidered Turkish slippers, propped up in front of her on a footstool. She motioned with a listless hand to the chair that stood opposite hers in the tapestried room behind the black reception parlour. Her youngest children could be heard making a racket with a toy drum and tin horn somewhere upstairs. In a corner, old Montvoisin dozed quietly, an open book dropping from between his fingers.

"Orange water?" La Voisin asked, dabbing a little of the sickly sweet cologne on her sweating temples to refresh them, and then handing me the bottle.

"Yes, thank you," I answered, sponging the cool, alcoholic stuff on my face as the sorceress in turn picked up her fan and worked it busily beneath her chin.

"So," she said, "they're in your house ... oh, those children, they have given me a headache— Antoine, Antoine! Yes, you! Wake up and go tell Louise to take the children into the garden. I have business with the marquise, here, and I can't even hear myself think."

"'Invaded' is a better word," I responded glumly, opening my own fan.

"'Invaded'? Just what are they doing?"

"At this very moment? Boiling down calves' feet to make beef jelly. The very day they arrived, they went off and rented themselves furniture and charged it to me. Then they commandeered Gilles and the carriage and filled the kitchen with groceries ... you know I like to send out for meals. Either that or attend open tables. Now my reception parlour smells of garlic—"

"Calves'-foot jelly is very good for sick people. What does *he* say?"

"He's mortified. He said he's perfectly capable of getting well without calves'-foot jelly and it's just the sort of thing that *would* happen to him—"

"When he'd gone to all that trouble to get himself trapped in a fascinating single woman's house, eh?" The Shadow Queen's fan stopped its motion and covered the lower half of her face, but I could hear her suppressed snort of laughter. "So, tell me, why haven't you got rid of them?"

"They threatened to turn me in to the police under the prostitution statutes."

The Shadow Queen looked grim and shut her fan with a snap. "They don't know whom they're playing with," she said quietly. "'Young women of the town who try to entrap men of good family into marriage,' eh?" she quoted. "With a word, I can change that."

"I don't want him destroyed," I said.

"Then you *are* fond of him, despite everything you say."

"I love no man. But I've paid the surgeon, and I don't like to lose an investment." She nodded approvingly. Then her thoughts changed, and she smiled her little pointed smile.

"No man but Lamotte," she observed, just to watch my face turn all red with embarrassment. "Ha! Don't hide your face behind your fan. Every woman in Paris loves Lamotte these days. I wouldn't mind having him myself for a night or two, though there would be no advantage to me in it. Of course, at this point, any woman who crosses the Duchesse de Bouillon would be taking a considerable risk. She's enjoying advancing Lamotte's career, and she's one of my better customers." A warning.

"I imagine Lamotte himself has to be very careful these days, too," I observed.

"It is the price of celebrity. To be loved – passionately – on alternate Tuesdays when Monsieur de Vendôme is at the front. There are many who envy him."

"I hope not all of them are your customers, as well."

"Only some, my dear. But do not pry into what does not concern you. We have business at hand. I think it best for your career to marry." She picked up a little silver bell that lay on the table beside the heavy blue glass bottle of orange water.

"Margot, bring some lemonade for the marquise and me. It is perishingly hot." My stomach made a knot. Whether over the lemonade or marriage, I could not say. "And plenty of sugar," she called after Margot. "You know I like it sweet." She did seem to be putting on more weight these days. She must have a lot of things sweet. "You see, my dear," she went on, "as long as everyone thought you were a hundred-and-fifty-year-old virgin, you ran no risks. As soon as it is known that you have kept a man at your house, you will be open to blackmail, and by far more dangerous sorts of people than these two silly women. But once you are married, you are safe from that and can do as you please."

She dabbed a bit more orange water on the inside of her wrists and on to the back of her neck, reopened her fan with a brisk shake of her hand, poised it at the level of her bosom, and set it in motion once again. "I can arrange you something very advantageous where you can go your own way. Yes, when you decide you need to get rid of d'Urbec would be the best time. A wedding will shed him nicely."

I smiled and nodded. Better to have her think I didn't mind this wedding thing than have her decide to get rid of d'Urbec on her own. I did owe him that much.

"Yes," she went on in a self-satisfied tone, "I think you should marry. Anyone would do. But a woman should not waste herself when there is something to be gained. An alchemist is always a good match for a fortune-teller. Or an ex-priest who's kept his canonicals can be very good for business."

If your business is being a witch, I thought. It's always convenient to have the Black Mass in the family. The silver lemonade cups clinked invitingly on the tray as Margot brought them in. Old Montvoisin, who had completed his errand and returned to somnolence in his chair, sat up and looked about at the sound. Margot served her mistress first, then me, then Montvoisin, who took a large gulp and wiped his mouth on his sleeve.

"But you, you can aim higher." La Voisin's voice, like the lemonade, was sticky sweet. "You should consider a man of position . . . someone like . . . Brissac. Yes, Brissac would be perfect."

"*Brissac?*" My lemonade nearly overturned into my lap. "Why on earth Brissac? What makes you think he would be open to such an arrangement?"

"Brissac has always lived apart from his duchesse. She has cut him off; he is an encumbrance. Do you understand?" She leaned towards me with a strange, intense smile. "Now he is destitute. His attitude softens daily, as he grows more desperate. He has quarrelled with Nevers and is now homeless. Temporarily, he has moved in with *hmm* . . . shall we say, another gentleman . . . who will tire of him soon enough. Just now, however, I have them both in my hand. Their apartment and furniture are rented at my expense. I consider Brissac an . . . investment. And when I consider your future, I see an excellent way to get repayment for my foresight. If you play your cards right, my dear, his cold little duchesse can be made to vanish. And he has, after all, a more or less genuine title, though he is now brought so low he will prostitute it for your money. You could help him at the tables – and, best of all, you do not have to sleep with him. Just as well, for he is said to smell even worse in bed than Louvois. He will go his way, you will go yours, you will grow rich in partnership, and . . . you will be protected from the police. It's ideal."

This is Brissac's idea, I thought. What has blinded her to the danger of this idea? Is it cash? How much money will change hands between them when this marriage is completed? "Brissac . . ." The word tasted nasty in my mouth. "It's such a shock— You . . . you must allow me to think it over . . ."

"Don't think too long. He may not be poor for ever. Just now he has a fancy to win at the tables, so his interest turns to you." I didn't like the sound of it. I don't need the glass to show me how this marriage will work, I thought. Once I make him rich, he'll want another bride, one from a great family. Then he'll visit the Shadow Queen for a little something from her locked cupboard, and I'll have to start watching what I drink. Unless, of course, I move first.

"Don't worry, my dear," La Voisin said, patting my hand almost as if she had read my thoughts. "A titled widow can do almost as well for herself as a wife. And you'd have risen too high through your marriage for the courts to touch you. I always have your interests at heart first. After all, I regard you almost as a daughter."

"I couldn't trust my own mother more," I said, looking at her with innocent, wide eyes over my fan.

The wave of garlic mingled with the steamy smell of boiling beef overwhelmed me when I entered my own front parlour. "Any invitations, Mustapha?" I asked hopefully.

"No, just a visitor with a crate for Monsieur d'Urbec." Mustapha took a fan from his wide Turkish sash and began lazily stirring the sultry air into a breeze about his face. "Enjoy yourself upstairs, Madame," his sarcastic voice followed me up the staircase. Entering my once-beautiful rooms, now crammed with alien furniture, I was entrapped by one of my uninvited guests.

"At last, my poor nephew has spoken from his bed of pain . . ." I had a vision of d'Urbec turning his face to the wall, deadly silent with pure annoyance, for hours at a time. ". . . and the first words through his pale, fevered lips were to exonerate you."

"Exonerate me?"

"Oh, how could I have ever suspected your charity? To risk a woman's most precious asset, her reputation, to rescue a hero from a hideous cabal of assassins. You are a saint." How interesting, I thought. D'Urbec has come to the obvious conclusion that once a story has been started, there is no way to dislodge it except with another, even better, one. "It is exactly like a romance . . ." His aunt clasped her hands before her heart.

"Why, yes, it is, now that you mention it," I couldn't help responding. An irritated growl came from the antechamber, which made us both turn our heads.

"I tell you, Mother, I can't have another sip of it! I'm sloshing in beef broth."

"Florent, what's the big box here by the door? Is it yours?" I poked my head into the antechamber to see d'Urbec propped up on pillows; his mother, with a large bowl of soup in her lap, was sitting on the bed beside him, holding an immense spoon.

An altogether droll situation for the hero of a court cabal to be in. When he spied me, he blushed. Obviously, he'd heard everything.

"You seem embarrassed, Monsieur d'Urbec," I observed rather pointedly.

"Only that I cannot rise to greet you as befits your rank, my dear Marquise," he responded, his voice weak, but ironic.

"Who brought the crate?" I asked. "Is it more food?"

"Griffon came by to see how I was doing – to wish me well, and say goodbye. Didn't he, Mother?" The little woman on the bed looked up with singular annoyance and set the spoon back into the bowl with a clank.

"It is commendable loyalty that you maintain an old friendship, but why you needed to accept as a parting gift a crateful of scandalous publications, I do not know. The bottom of the river is the proper place for things like that," she said firmly.

"Parting gift?" My eyebrows went up.

"Griffon is selling out. Every day, he says, he runs more risks and makes less money. He found a publisher of Jansenist tracts to buy his press and he's emigrating to Rotterdam, where he says a man can print whatever he likes. He brought me a gift – the stuff he can't risk leaving or smuggling over the border."

"Some gift," I said. "I thought he was your friend."

"That's exactly what I said," sniffed Madame d'Urbec, with a righteous nod in my direction. "Imagine bothering a sick man with things like that."

"He meant well," answered d'Urbec, defending his friend. "It's an entire stock-in-trade..." Griffon had left him an income, for when he recovered. My eyes met d'Urbec's. Neither of us could say more, for fear of disillusioning his mother about her son's current occupation.

"I suppose Lamotte... ah... de la Motte told him where to find you."

"He's been very active on my behalf lately," d'Urbec sighed.

"Now *that* is the friend you should cultivate," said his mother. "Someone who can do things for you. You must curb your taste for low company, Florent. As I've always said, it takes no more effort to maintain a friendship with a *significant* person than an insignificant one. I mean it for your good, Florent. You waste your talent. Besides, you have no more room for mistakes."

"Yes, Mother," he said with resignation.

"And don't use that tone with me. You don't know what it is, facing your uncle's stuck-up wife, that barren old stick, after that last little . . . misunderstanding of yours. Her airs, her fancy hat, the way she steps in those silk slippers, as if her feet were too good for the ground, unlike everybody else's! Oh, how I want to see her face when you are great. Why, the last time I saw her at the draper's, even the lackey carrying her train snubbed me! 'I hope you understand, dear sister, that we can no longer associate with your son after . . . what has happened. Believe me, no one regrets it more than I. The years we sponsored his education – a pity – I suppose we had no right to expect *gratitude*. But our position, you know.' Her *position!*—" she snorted indignantly.

But she was cut short by Mustapha, who had barely time to announce "The Chevalier de la Motte" with an ironic flourish before Lamotte himself bounded in, filled with a genuine enthusiasm that seemed altogether unconquered by the oppressive heat and garlic.

"So much joy to see you better, d'Urbec!" he announced. "A mother's love – the all-powerful curative. Why, it's a miracle!" D'Urbec glared up at Lamotte while his mother accepted the compliment with a grateful blush. D'Urbec seemed irritated.

"And what is that that smells so delightfully of garlic downstairs?" Lamotte's charm filled the room like a scent.

"An old family secret – a restorative broth. My children have loved it since they were small. They owe their health to it." She beamed.

"Oh my goodness, my dear Chevalier, how gracious of you to visit." D'Urbec's aunt, not to be left out, had trailed in behind him. Then Sylvie appeared from nowhere and began dusting the furniture – low down, where the view of Lamotte's famous calves was better. "What lovely shoes!" exclaimed d'Urbec's aunt. "Of course, in Orléans, we hardly ever see anything so elegant!" Lamotte's shoes, with their high red heels and silk bows, set off the celebrated calves even more. He was in yellow silk, with a narrow falling band of exquisite lace. A wide plumed hat sat atop his magnificently expensive wig of tightly curled, pale blond human hair.

"I just meant to pop in while I was in town and see how you were doing today – I'm terribly busy just now. So many arrangements . . . They're rehearsing my new play for presentation at court, and I'm off to Fontainebleau to make sure it's done properly. The last light comedy of the season, before the winter of tragedy sets in. Then the stage is ruled by absolutely *dreary* verse and tragic queens. Though they say Monsieur Racine is planning something that will quite overtop the throng. We wait, we wait, but Racine reads bits and pieces at salons, always preparing, never finishing. I say he has exhausted his genius. No, the world awaits my next tragedy without rivals." He glanced at the women to find them staring at him with admiration, and a little smile of self-satisfaction flitted across his face. "Say, d'Urbec, what's in that crate outside? It looks like one of Griffon's."

"It is. He's leaving, you know."

"So I heard, so I heard. Let me satisfy my curiosity and see what he's left you." The train of women followed him into the next room.

"The man's a blasted magnet for women," announced d'Urbec to me, as I lingered.

"Aha, broadsides," we heard coming from beyond the open door. "Madame de Brinvilliers – execrable verse. 'Man slays himself and family in front of tax collector?' – that's old. Oh, here's a new one: 'Infernal Machine Discovered in Toulon Harbour – a Conspiracy of Traitors, Attempts to Explode Flagship, et cetera, Ingenious self-igniting clockwork fuse'—" There was a faint shriek from one of the women.

"Stop him. Shut him up. That busybody Lamotte—" D'Urbec tried to get up. Then he winced and thought better of it. "Go and see to Mother, Geneviève – this is a disaster in the making. Tell Lamotte to keep that thing from her."

I hastened into my own bedroom to find Lamotte sitting on the bed cheerfully reading the details of a conspiracy against His Majesty's fleet at Toulon harbour to the attentive crowd of women. But Madame d'Urbec was deathly pale, her hands clasped tight. Mistaking her feelings, Lamotte cried, "Don't be alarmed, Madame, the King's police will trace the conspirators and execute them without delay."

"Enough, Lamotte. Madame d'Urbec has become ill through overwork. Madame, sit here..."

"Oh, dear Lord, oh, he's done it. He's the only one who could have – my Olivier, my son. Why have my sons been born to trouble? Oh, I must go to him—"

"Why, this is terrible," cried Lamotte. "Hey, lackey, some wine for Madame. She's gone all pale." I took advantage of the moment to snatch up the broadside from where he had set it down and shut it back in the crate.

When Gilles had brought the wine, I said quietly, "Gilles, take this crate and put it— You know."

"Understood, Madame," he said, and hoisted the heavy thing to take it down to the cellar, where there was a secret door hidden behind the wine bottles.

"We must pack at once, Marie-Claude. The next diligence – if only it's not too late." Madame d'Urbec's voice was weak as her sister fanned her where she lay, half fainting, in my best armchair.

"Mesdames, I will offer the use of my patroness's carriage and footmen to see you to the diligence at whatever hour you may wish to depart. The very least I can do for the honoured mother of a dear friend," said Lamotte with a flourish. She looked up gratefully at him, as if half in love already.

"Madame d'Urbec, may I be of assistance?" I asked, suppressing all signs of emotion from my voice and face. The little woman sat down suddenly in her hired armchair and burst into tears. Taking a large handkerchief out of her sleeve, she wiped at her face in between sobs.

"Oh, what can you, with your rank and ease ... and all of this ... a lovely town house of your own ... gowns, nice furniture..." she sniffled and wiped her eyes again, "... what can you understand of the grief of being a mother? Six sons I have, and every one a giver of grief. Taxes! Religion! Politics! The old law! The new law! All the things polite people don't mention. But them – they are human incendiaries, every one. It's a family curse, from their father's side. Oh, God, if they were only daughters, it would be so much easier..."

She sobbed for a while in the midst of the packing chaos, then put away her handkerchief and went into the next room to bid farewell to her son. She emerged dry eyed and announced: "Madame de Morville, I could not leave my son in more capable hands. God bless you for your charitable act. The furniture can be returned to the *tapissier* on the Rue de Charonne just beyond the ramparts. Just send word and they'll remove it. Here's the account; don't let them overcharge you." And she was gone in a flurry of emotion, Lamotte at her elbow, her sister trailing behind, having left the calves' feet still boiling in the kitchen.

"Well," sighed d'Urbec, lifting his head from the pillow, "there goes my mother and my life savings."

"Don't worry, Florent," I said. "I'll see that you're buried properly." He gave me a swift, sharp look.

"I have every intention of living. I wish to erase the memory of this romantic disaster."

"First, tell me what it was all about. Mustapha, if you must listen in, don't be so obtrusive." The curled-up toe of Mustapha's little Turkish slipper withdrew from view behind the half-open door. D'Urbec sighed and looked at his hands.

"Father would be rich, you know, if he had an ounce of sense. He's a first-class clockwork builder and inherited a good business. But he spends his time grieving over lost titles, tracing his ancestors, seeking unwary patrons for his fantastical schemes, and dreaming of being awarded a pension and a title for one of his pet projects. It's Olivier, my older brother, who keeps everything together. In my opinion, he's even better than Father at designing mechanisms and considerably more practical. So, you see, it's only natural that when Mother saw that an infernal machine with an unusual clockwork fuse had been found in the Toulon harbour, knowing the family predilections, she leaped to conclusions. That's all. My mother is one of those who lives for drama. I suppose we all do, after a fashion..."

"But what's all this about a family curse? That is, besides being secret *frondeurs* and, as I gather from your aunt's busy tongue, heretics?"

"I'd hardly count the reformed religion as heresy. Besides, thanks to Uncle, I'm probably a better, or at least a more recent, Catholic than you are. Uncle put the conversion bonus to good work and insisted I do the same."

"And because you don't believe in anything, anyway, it didn't matter either way, did it?"

"I believe in any number of things, Mademoiselle Pasquier. Truth, justice, the powers of the rational mind..."

"Not very popular things to believe in, in my opinion. No wonder you're always in trouble. That's family curse enough, thinking things like that."

He lay back on the pillow, his eyes fixed on me, calculating. He was silent a long time. "Damn!" he said sadly.

"What's wrong?" I asked. "Would you like more calves'-foot broth? It won't jell in this heat."

"You're in love with Lamotte, aren't you? You don't have to be embarrassed about it. Most women are. But ... I had hoped you were above the common taste..." I averted my eyes from his disappointed face.

"I'm not in love with anybody ... and I have important appointments today," I heard myself saying as I fled the room.

The very next day, at the end of another long, sticky afternoon when most of Paris found nothing better to do than to doze behind closed shutters, I returned home from a visit to the suburbs to find an immense sheaf of yellow roses lying in a box on the downstairs table. The whole household was on the shadowy lower floor with the curtains drawn against the all-pervasive heat. Mustapha was fanning himself while d'Urbec, draped in a sheet like a toga, for want of a dressing gown, was seated in my best armchair reading aloud to the assembled company. Gilles was sitting near the kitchen door on a low stool polishing the silver, and Sylvie had laid claim to my second-best armchair, where she sat darning stockings as they listened.

"So, not only does no one see fit to open the door for me, but you all— Oh, what's that?" I broke off the irritated lecture I planned to give when I spied the little mountain of flowers. Sylvie hastily removed herself from my chair and drew out another stool from the kitchen.

"We have refrained from even reading the card until your

return," d'Urbec said. He was looking better, but something inside his soul seemed to have changed. The eyes that followed me about the room were distant and cynical.

"Just as well in this house," I answered, and, putting my gloves back on, I carefully lifted the heavy, engraved card out of the box, shaking it gently before reading it. I could feel d'Urbec's eyes missing nothing. "Oh, ugh, Brissac. The news certainly gets around quickly." I gave Sylvie a hard stare, and she looked as intently at the darning egg as if it were about to hatch. "The lavender ribbons— Looks like La Pelletier's work, doesn't it? Harmless, then. It will be love powder this time." I ran a gloved finger between the yellow petals. A few greenish crystals stuck to my glove. "Bastard," I said. "Sylvie, put a wet kerchief around your mouth and nose and go shake these flowers out the back door before you put them in the vase. I like yellow roses, so I'm not going to throw them out."

"You appear to know a great deal more about the world, Marquise, than the little girl who read Petronius in secret."

"We live and learn, Monsieur d'Urbec," I said as I watched Sylvie flounce out through the kitchen, carrying the flowers. "Love powders, inheritance powders, lovely scented Italian gloves – the fashionable world is not for fools these days – or for cowards, either." I turned to see his dark-rimmed eyes fixed on me, calculating.

"The Duc de Brissac is interested in you, I take it? You must beware of a friendship like that." His voice was even. "Brissac is a ruinous spendthrift who bankrupts his mistresses and . . . other friends. As a professional *nouvelliste*, I will be delighted to provide you with particulars." Something about him seemed to have changed.

"Well, Monsieur le *Nouvelliste*, if I can rely on the laws of hospitality keeping your professional interest quiet, I will tell you that what he wants this time is marriage – a secret marriage of convenience. He has been reduced to owning two shirts and being supported by my patroness. For all I know, he probably even borrowed the money for those flowers from her. He hopes by joining forces with me to regain all his losses at the card tables."

"His current wife proves no deterrent to his plans, eh? And I suppose as the Duchesse de Brissac, you'll have a very fine tomb indeed, once his fortune is mended."

"From him? That stingy bastard? Only if I order it right after the wedding and pay for it myself." I laughed as I took the vase from Sylvie and arranged it on the sideboard. "To what sculptor do you think I should give the commission for my monument? Warin? Or is he falling out of fashion these days?"

"You don't have to accept him, you know, just because I've compromised you," he said quietly.

"I compromised myself when I opened the door. It was my choice. And I choose not to be married. I'll make my own way."

D'Urbec looked at me long and hard, his jaw clenched. Then he announced in a bantering voice that didn't ring quite true, "If a man with no shirt were not even more ludicrous than a man with two shirts in making an offer of marriage, I would propose to undo the damage I have done in the only honourable way open to me. As it is, I must beg your indulgence for a few more days and borrow from you a sheet of paper, pen, and ink."

As I went to fetch the paper and ink, I heard Sylvie ask, "What are you planning?" Her voice sounded shocked.

"This is a historic moment. You are witnessing the foundation of the fortune of the house of d'Urbec," he said in a grim tone, and the tension in the room was heavier than the sultry summer air. He took out the pen and wrote.

"A denunciation," he announced, "from an Italian abbé who has perused a dreadful, irreligious work of scandal that should be brought to the attention of the inspector of the book trade and suppressed. The irreligious and mocking *Parnasse Satyrique*. Griffon has left me two hundred copies of this salacious work as my founding capital. An official condemnation will raise the price from twenty sous to twenty livres. An intelligent man may multiply a stock of two thousand livres through many means in this capital of quick money. The only advantage my life has brought me is that I know where corrupt fortunes are born and how quickly they make one respectable. Madame de Morville, I shall now become rich – rich enough to send my old mother a carriage and horses and a new bonnet fit to cause apoplexy in my uncle's wife. Rich enough to buy back my place in the world." He poured sand on the letter to dry it, then shook it off. "Here, Sylvie, I would like you to deliver this to the police," he said, dripping wax across the folded edge of the letter. "I know you know how." Sylvie looked at me, her eyes questioning.

"Yes, Sylvie, go ahead. It's all right. You can count on our discretion, Monsieur d'Urbec."

"Thank you," he answered. I was suddenly frightened of him, of his determination, of the strange look on his face. He seemed like a man capable of anything.

Watching my face, he handed the ink and paper to Sylvie to put back in the cabinet from which I had removed them. His movement shifted the sheet to reveal the edge of the seared mark on his shoulder. I saw his eyes turn bitter as he caught my quickly averted gaze.

"I can't read pictures in water, Athena, but I'll make a prediction about you. You need to find out Lamotte is not your mental equal before you'll have me."

"What makes you think I want either of you?" I sniffed.

"Have you forgotten I am not stupid? Your eyes betrayed you. Did you have me in only to bring him here? That is not beyond your scheming mind, I know. What is it that glittered so attractively in front of those greedy grey eyes of yours? Was it the silk stockings? Was it his dreadful poetry? Or was it the cow eyes he can't help making whenever there's a woman around? When you grow up, little vixen, you'll know where to find me."

"You're *nasty*, Florent d'Urbec!" I exclaimed, to hide my humiliation at having been seen through so easily. "What is it you want from me? That I should give everything up to go with you and be nothing at all? Haven't I already risked all I have for you? What is enough for a man? Must they own everything they see? Even that ridiculous satanist Brissac offers me a partnership, disgusting as it is."

His face paled, then, eyes blazing with anger, he shouted, "Geneviève Pasquier, you will regret ever saying this to me, I swear." But his anger made me defiant. I stared right back at him and shrugged my shoulders.

"Oh, la, revenge. Everybody wants it these days. It led me to the Shadow Queen, and now I never smell roses any more. Where will it lead you, Florent d'Urbec? But at least I have a monster who wronged me as the worthy object of my revenge, and not a woman who's risked harm to do me nothing but good. Some day you must tell me more about this celebrated brain of yours, my friend, and how you use it to distinguish who's worth taking vengeance on."

He didn't speak to me for the next two days. On the third day he borrowed a needle from Sylvie and, with the finicky exactness of a long-time bachelor, mended his shirt, from which several washings had removed the bloodstains.

"I'll be going now," he said. "I'll send for my box when I've found a place to live."

"You don't have anywhere?" I asked, suddenly anxious. He still looked wasted and feverish. He swayed as he stood in the doorway, and I realised that only pride held him upright.

"I was living in the back room of Griffon's print shop. He and his family lived above. The Jansenists probably won't be as congenial."

"But— Will I see you again?"

"Oh, that? Yes, of course. On the Cours-la-Reine in a carriage and four. Goodbye, Madame de Morville. Don't smell any flowers."

I fled upstairs, weeping stupid tears for no reason at all.

TWENTY-NINE

With the first days of autumn, the court returned. The weather stayed warm, golden and mellow, with that strange luminous calm that vanishes suddenly with the first rain of the season. Lamotte and d'Urbec had disappeared from my life. D'Urbec, true to his word, sent for his box but did not appear in person. I returned the furniture, threw out the soup bones, and plunged myself anew into my work. Business had never been better, for the Sun King was rumoured to be in search of a new mistress, and court intrigue had multiplied accordingly.

"They're all laughing at me, damn them!" Madame de Montespan shrilled at me in her gold-and-white salon. "Out, out, all of you! My fortune is none of your business! Leave, or I swear I'll have you all hanged! I still have influence; don't you forget it!" The King's mistress whirled through the salon like a demon in brocade, took up a little bronze cupid from a table, and flung it at one of her terrorised servants. As her ladies-in-waiting vanished and I took out my glass, she pressed her hands to her temples and sat down moaning. Another of her sick headaches. "Good, they're all out of here. Now, tell me quickly, will that fat, tasteless Madame de Soubise take my place?" Everyone at court knew about the Princesse de Soubise and the secret signal by which the Titian-haired beauty alerted the King to the absence of her husband. When she walked into a room with her emerald earrings on, the murmur of interest followed her, and all eyes went to the King. Those with malicious hearts also enjoyed watching Madame de Montespan's eyes narrow over her fan at the sight of the celebrated earrings. La Montespan's fall was near. Long live the new *maîtresse en titre*.

I assessed her face carefully. Despite the headache, her eerie, aquamarine eyes were still bright with fury. The image came up nicely in the glass this time.

"Your rival's triumph is short-lived, Madame; you may be assured." She leaned closer, trying to peer into the water herself, and her breath fogged the glass. "With her next pregnancy, Madame de Soubise will lose her beauty, and the King will lose interest."

"Lose her beauty?" Madame de Montespan's voice sounded maliciously triumphant. "Just how? Does the glass tell you that?"

"It is plain, Madame. She will lose a front tooth."

"Ah," sighed Madame de Montespan. "My teeth are very strong. What a pity so many women lose their teeth with children. God meant me to achieve power by giving me strong teeth." She smiled. Her teeth looked tiny and white, like those of a child goblin, between her rouged lips.

"Your beauty and good taste are without rivals, Madame," I said soothingly.

"I have sworn no other woman will have him, and I keep my promises." A strange geniality was now hiding the seething cauldron of her wrath.

"Everyone respects you for that, Madame," I assured her.

"I tell you, it is Madame de Soubise's good fortune that she will lose that tooth. I will not have her or anyone else ever be a duchess in my place. Tell me, does your glass tell yet when I will be made a duchess?" This was a sore spot. Everyone knew, but did not dare to tell her, that the King would not give her the title with which he rewarded a royal mistress because he did not wish to make her husband a duke. It was really very simple. But, of course, she believed that it was a test of her power over him – that for love, he would break all precedence and somehow create her a duchess without elevating old Montespan, who still raged in exile in the provinces, where he had been banished by his royal rival. "The Abbess of Fontevrault says I really ought to be made a duchess soon, considering my services to the crown." Her sister. Her only encouragement.

"The abbess is a very perceptive woman."

"But not as perceptive as your glass. Tell me, what does it say about my *tabouret?*" Danger lurked in her smile.

"The glass, Madame, is clear. This is often the case when something is in the future, but not so immediate as to be read.

Perhaps after Madame de Soubise's departure." Her eyes narrowed.

"I tell you, I shall have that *tabouret*, no matter what the cost." I had no intention of telling her that I saw no duchess's stool in her future.

"Madame, your beauty is promise enough of the future." She arched an eyebrow and rose.

"Our interview is at an end, Madame de Morville. Mademoiselle des Oeillets will see you in the antechamber." The fat little silk purse Mademoiselle des Oeillets handed me was still heavy despite the fact that she had already taken her cut. Excellent. At this rate, I would soon be free of the Shadow Queen.

I was the last of the witch's protégées to arrive at the Rue Beauregard that Sunday afternoon. Sitting outside the closed door of her cabinet inspecting the brasswork around the door latch, I was caught by surprise when the door swung open, and I could hear the last snatch of conversation. I caught a glimpse of La Voisin, in a sombre dress, white lace apron, and close-fitting lace cap, escorting La Lépère, all red-eyed and sniffling, out by the elbow.

". . . enough of your whining. You should learn from the little Marquise out there. She has only been in business two years and prospers greatly from heeding my advice." As the old woman shuffled off, looking dejected, Madame showed me into her cabinet.

"Another loan." She sighed. "Ah, me, I support the entire world, it seems. You, at least, are doing well. I hear of you at every turn these days. Have you brought your accounting?"

"Of course, Madame."

"My, my," – she smiled, turning the pages of my little green account book – "you're doing ever so much better since you stopped supporting that menagerie of Provençals. And you're controlling your other expenses well. What nice progress! You'll soon have the house paid for, at this rate. It's all from following my good advice – not like that foolish La Lépère. What a weakling I am, eh, Marquise? But I always look after my people." She's getting ready to tell me something, I thought. "Advice" that I'd better take or else.

"I think so well of you these days." She smiled maternally. "You have a great talent for business. My, such successes! You'll never be a dismal old woman like La Lépère. Now, next week, I'm having a little fête to celebrate the return of the court. Outside, if the weather stays good. I still have so many lovely flowers in my garden! And the new fountain with the little statue does set off my pavilion, don't you think?" She rose and gestured to the little cabinet window. Outside, in the garden, the fountain tinkled amid masses of ferns and the last of the summer lilies. In the centre of the fountain stood a little cupid, holding a water jug that splashed water on his fat feet. The white columns of the classical pavilion glowed golden in the afternoon sun. The chimney of the crematorium stove inside was belching black smoke. "Court business has never been better," she said, gazing fondly at the dark column rising into the blue sky above the city.

"Such a nice party," she said in an offhand way, turning from the window, "a lot of splendid old friends. You'll be getting an invitation in the next day or two – but the engraver has been so dreadfully slow. You'll know most of the people there, I imagine. Many of *us*, some of La Bosse's, and, of course, clients and a few select students of the occult sciences. Violins, of course, and there'll be dancing all night long – oh, don't look so shocked! Where do you think we'd dance? Naked on the Brocken, perhaps? Please, please" – and here she waved her hand in disdain – "I may be a witch, but I am always a Parisian first. My gown is being delivered from the embroiderers' tomorrow evening; my violins will be the best – the band of Monsieur is free that evening. And my guest list – very elegant. Any number of courtiers. Brissac will be here. I do not wish you to miss the opportunity of conversing with him. You'll find him the most elegant figure of a man – most presentable. An excellent husband for a woman who knows how to handle him."

"With all respect, Madame, I want a husband about as much as a frog wants a valet."

"Ha! So very witty! No wonder you're such a success." She laughed a little laugh as she seated herself once more in her brocade armchair, leaving me standing. Her little counterfeit of good humour made my stomach cold. "But, my dear," she went on, looking up at me in an indulgent way, "you may not *want* a husband, but you *need* one. Come now, surely you don't want to be reclaimed by your brother – or your uncle. Remember that I think only of your benefit." And your own, I thought as I tried to make my face look agreeable. "Now, do be good and sit down," she said, gesturing to the narrow, armless chair in front of her writing desk. I sat, bolt upright. "Really, husbands are no trouble at all," she went on, leaning forward in cosy intimacy. "They sit about, they sign legal documents – so important with the laws as backward as they are for us women. I would never be without a husband. All of mine have been a great convenience. Of course, they do need to be fed. Always keep them well sated on heavy dishes. It calms them. You, of course, will have to hire a good cook. But it's a small expense for an unassailable social position."

"I doubt Brissac will just sit around and eat. He's all over the place like a cockroach – popping out of dark corners, scheming, raking lovers, and splashing money all over town whenever he has any."

"My dear," she said, laying a hand over mine, "do you think I would propose an alliance such as this to you, my finest creation, if you were not the sort of girl who had her wits about her? One mounts cowards and old folks on dull old jades, but a thoroughbred – spirited, elegant, half mad – should be mounted by none but the most brilliant rider. Believe me, he is outmatched by you. But the pair – ah! What a pair! Dangerous, brilliant, fashionable – you two will flash across the sky of Paris like a comet! And, in the end, you will have power, which is worth everything!" Her black eyes glittered; and I felt drawn to the idea as a needle seeks a lodestone. As I watched her glowing eyes, a little smile twitch across her lips, the thought came over me: she lives her youth again through you. The Shadow Queen remade, as she would have wished to have been. No poor failed jeweller for a mate but a titled satanist, brilliant and dangerous, a fit equal. Her growing ambition blinds her. Her scheming overreaches itself. Where will it end? Brissac, *ugh*, how filthy.

"I'll do my best with him, but you know I don't know how to

flirt. I can't look up through my eyelashes at a man and pretend he is cleverer than he is. I say what I think. Men don't think I'm pretty."

"Pretty is not what he's after, dear. Just money. Simply drop the name of the last few salons you've been to. Show him how you can read hidden cards in a wineglass. Tell him you're not sure you can read well if you're not happy – that sort of thing. Let him know you're no fool to be won with a few cheap kisses, and he must bargain hard for your skill." I looked dubious. She closed her ledger with a contrived smile. "So clever . . . yes, listen to me, and you'll do well . . ."

That night, my mind ground like a mill, and images, like fragments of the days past, kept me from sleep. The Shadow Queen and her ledger, the repulsive Brissac, the dashing Lamotte, beautiful beyond description in yellow silk, Father on his deathbed with Grandmother's parrot crying out "Justice! Justice! Fire and brimstone!" Marie-Angélique weeping in luxury. The heavy steps on the stair and the echo of Uncle's horrible laughter. And a pair of eyes, hollow, dark, and appraising. D'Urbec's eyes, following me about the way they had in the sickroom. "You'll regret . . . you'll regret . . ." I could hear him saying.

In the morning, Sylvie brought a letter on the tray with my cocoa. The paper was rich and heavy, and the seal had somehow withstood Sylvie's curiosity and remained firmly in place. I could feel her breath on my shoulder as I sat up in bed to read the familiar wide-looped, simple handwriting:

Dearest Sister,

My happiness is complete. I have just returned from Fontainebleau. Never have I been shown such favour and tenderness. My friend has given me a beautiful necklace of emeralds and assures me that I am queen of his heart. What generous condescension from a man so elevated, and of such ancient family! I do not doubt now that despite my lack of rank and lineage, I shall soon be *maîtresse en titre*.

And Sister, because your powers are unfailing, you are the first that I tell: a precious token of his renewed esteem shall soon be mine. I await only the perfect moment to share my cherished secret with him. When you are free, come and share my joy. I am at home on Wednesdays.

Your loving sister,
Marie-Angélique

"Well?" asked Sylvie, having failed to stretch her neck sufficiently to discover the letter's contents.

"Another fortune has come true. Cover my dressing-table mirror again, Sylvie; I've had a bad night."

"So, Madame, will you be wearing the lovely rose dress to the fête tonight? You've never even taken it out of its muslin. And the colour— Oh, it sets you off – you almost look young again, if I may say so. If it's a proposal that I were after, I'd certainly wear it." Sylvie set a half-dozen bone hairpins on my dressing table and took up the hairbrush to attack my wild curls. There are advantages to having a dressing-table mirror draped, I thought. I can't see the disapproving look on Sylvie's face as she tries to create the proper little knot and side curls suited to fit under my cap. The brush seemed impatient, annoyed. I sat straight in the little gilded chair before the dressing table, pondering how best to evade both Brissac and my patroness. How much had Brissac promised her out of my savings for her part in making this match? Madame never did anything for free. And yet, I suppose, there was a certain bizarre honour in her. She never stole, either. That was more than you could say for any number of respectable people. Murder, now, that was different. There she did just as everyone else did. Except, perhaps, more neatly. She would never leave a head beneath the floorboards. It would offend her craft. That is doubtless, I mused, the way one differentiates the professionals from the amateurs in this world.

"Sylvie, the man Madame has chosen cares nothing for youth. He consumes pretty women by the dozen for breakfast. Brissac is a libertine who loves only money and whose only goal in life is to find out where the Devil lives so he can make a pact with him. For this man, I wish to look wealthy, invulnerable, and very mysterious, as if I already had the Devil's address in my pocket. He must be forced to a hard bargain. Madame has said so. I want the grey silk – the low-cut one. Don't get out the partlet. I'll wear it without so my bosom shows. Then I want every jewel I own – the pearls, the ruby crucifix, the diamond earrings, and all my bracelets. Tell Gilles to carry both sword and pistol when he attends me tonight."

"And your hair? The veil?"

"No veil tonight. I want you to do my hair in the new style of Madame de Montespan, with the curls in the back, but ornamented only with a single, blood-red rose. That ought to please Madame."

"A perfect touch, if I do say so. On your black hair, so striking, Madame! Symbols of wealth and passion together. What man could resist?"

"Brissac, who is as conniving as they come. We have our work cut out for us, Sylvie." Excellent, I thought, as she put down the hairbrush. She'll carry a good report of this conversation to La Voisin. "Oh, yes," I added, "I'll want you to wear the yellow silk and carry my handkerchief, just behind Mustapha as he carries my train. And tell him he must wear the diamond and the egret plumes on his turban. I plan to make a grand entrance, after the theatre hour, when most of the guests are there already."

The weather held good, the day of the fête, and so it was one of the last, long violet evenings of the season when my carriage threaded its way through the maze of waiting equipages and chairs clustered around the villa on the Rue Beauregard. There were carriages with the arms of ancient families on them, diabolists or simple amusement seekers, who knew that La Voisin's suppers were always lavish and the company suited to the most jaded tastes. There were flashy carriages hired by the month, like mine, fiacres and chairs hired only for the night by petitioners desperate to make an impression. Fortunes could be made here: the right meeting, the lucky chance, and one's troubles would vanish. We are a nation of courts, I thought: the great nobles who surround the King for favours have little nobles to wait on them; the little ones have still smaller ones to stand around them at their *levées*. And here at the Rue Beauregard is the court of the lewd, the false, the superstitious, who are spinning on their way downwards to perdition. Not so different from the great court, after all.

Every one a parasite. In just what conveyance, I wondered, had the shirtless Brissac arrived?

The queen of the witches of Paris had transformed her house for the evening. The immense double doors between the black parlour and the grandly overfurnished inner rooms had been thrown open, creating a great hall. Banks of candles glittered among the tables piled with delicacies. The sound of the violins penetrated the room from the garden beyond, where the lantern-bedecked striped pavilions sheltered a great artificial dance floor, laid for the evening in the garden between the house and the pavilion. I made a great stir as I was announced at the door. Even the most bored of the courtiers, the most familiar of acquaintances, looked up from the delicacy-heaped tables at the lush, exotic little figure with the tall, silver-tipped walking stick, her train held by a turbaned pagan, her handkerchief-bearing maid followed by a heavily armed human giant of a bodyguard. I had outdone myself.

"Marquise ... you look ... different," stammered La Pelletier, the witch of the lavender-ribboned love-powder sachets. Abbé Guibourg, food dribbling from the corner of his mouth, looked up and grinned a lascivious smile. A space cleared about me as I moved through the crowd. Respect, fear, awe. For I knew the future; I dispensed fate. And, above all, I must be placated – for if I became Queen, who was to say whose fortune, whose life I might some day hold in my hand? La Voisin, brilliant in flame-coloured satin and diamonds, was holding court beneath the striped pavilion roof. Her petitioners and sycophants made way for me as I approached.

"Madame," I said, bowing low, "your evening is most delightful, and I am privileged to be here." She nodded approvingly at my jewels, my entourage, and the red rose.

"My dear Marquise, you have never looked more radiant. I take it, you have already been introduced to the Duc de Brissac?" Brissac, his dark beard showing unshaven, clad in moth-eaten blue velvet and sporting an immense court wig of last year's fashion, doffed his plumed hat and expressed his pleasure and surprise at meeting me again. I shall lead you a merry chase tonight, I thought, as I refused his offer to dance, opening my fan across my bosom to signal in the gesture that means, in the coded language of the fans, "be discreet".

"It is a pleasure I renounced decades ago," I said, closing my fan to display only one compartment, indicating "chaste amity", as, head tilted, I looked at him out of the corner of my eye. "Dancing disperses the mental energies, and I prefer to concentrate my powers." I tapped the fan shut, and held it to the right. "We must talk in security."

"Your powers are only the palest shadow of your beauty," he murmured, as we drifted away from the Shadow Queen. Somehow, we managed to arrive at the grotto. The fountain splashed in an eerily melancholy fashion as we sat on a rustic bench positioned in front of the concealed oven. What a strange place: a white-marble, ivy-entwined crematorium for the use of Madame's "philanthropic society". A fit setting for a satanist's seduction. After a number of absurd flatteries about my white bosom and ivory hands, his fingers crept onto my neck. There is something about a man's touch when he is insincere – his fingers felt like lizards. Revolting.

I pulled away from the warm, rotten scent of his breath, snapped my fan shut, and said, "Let us be frank, Brissac. I get no pleasure from men, and you, I take it, derive little from women. Cease trying to dazzle me with compliments and blind me with your expertise at love. Your rank and your person do not make me shiver with delight. I presume that for somewhat different reasons, you might say the same about me. I do not wish to be your *maîtresse en titre*; I am a woman who can be satisfied only with marriage and wish to know your terms." He seemed shocked at my bluntness. The mask of gallantry fell, revealing naked avarice, snobbery, and the male rage at being thought less than charming.

"Marriage? To a monster? What leads you to think that a Brissac would stoop to such a shameful misalliance?" He looked as if he might strike me. I drew away from him and fixed him with a commanding stare.

"Why stoop to me at all, then? Surely not to gain pleasure from my seduction. Wouldn't your reputation suffer then, too? 'Brissac sleeps with a deformed, centuries-old woman,' they'd say. Or were you planning that the high and mighty of the court should whisper instead, 'Brissac has driven the ancient sorceress mad with desire – she gives him everything. What a clever fellow!'"

"You – you savage!" he exclaimed. No one likes his plans uncovered, I thought. She has mistaken him; he has deceived her. He drew himself up to his full height, which was modest, for a man, and his face froze in an aristocratic sneer.

"Evidently, Madame, no one has taken the trouble to inform you that you lack all desirable qualities for a wife: unblemished lineage, youth, that soft sweetness in the midst of innocent desires . . ."

". . . and a handsome dowry, without which all the rest is dross," I finished up.

"Yes, a family of standing – of fortune . . ."

"And perhaps, Monsieur, no one has bothered to tell you that even with rank, should you become available, you are still tarnished goods, unlikely to appeal to any family of standing. Your personal habits make you unlikely to produce heirs; add to this that rumour has it you have already tainted half the little ice sellers in town with the Italian disease – hardly an affliction one wishes to see in grandchildren. You spend money like water, especially that of other people, and have caused at least one lover to leave this earth under questionable circumstances. You have fribbled away your patrimony and alienated your connections at court. These things would weigh yet more heavily than your satanism with even the most grasping family of the petty bourgeoisie, let alone one of high lineage. No, Monsieur de Brissac, even those beneath you will not have you. I suggest you keep the wife you have. Perhaps if you are gracious, she will grant you an allowance."

"I do not have to listen to this," he said, rising.

"No, but before you go, you should recall that not only do I come with a fortune greater than all but a royal dowry, but that, unlike a dowry, this fortune of mine is renewed and grows daily. I wish to be a duchess; you wish to be rich – it is entirely rational to form a business partnership in the guise of marriage."

"You – you are not a woman; you are a cold-blooded monster."

"And you a hot-blooded one."

"I could destroy you for these insults."

"Why, yes, and then you'd lose your last chance at a fortune."

"I can find a dozen better brides."

"Good. Go try, and when you are tired of being rejected, return to me. I will of course be richer then. My terms may not be as easy."

"Your terms? *Your* terms? How dare you! It is *my* terms you must deal with, you unnatural crone. Brissac's terms!"

I found it hard not to laugh at him as he turned on his heel and stormed out, the very picture of deflated pomposity. An excellent outcome, I thought. I've made the offer that will please La Voisin and he has declined it, thus displeasing her. And while she has hope of him, she cannot rage at me. My soup remains wholesome, and I am unbothered by Brissac. An excellent outcome.

"Ah, there you are, after your little *tête à tête*. Tell me, how did it go?" The rustle of my patroness's taffeta underskirts had announced her presence long before her voice did so.

"He did not want marriage; I let him know that marriage was the price of my fortune. He said I was too deformed and obscure for a duchess. He will seek elsewhere, fail, and then return. That I can predict without the glass." Her mouth drew into a grim line.

"If he has been playing with me, I swear—"

"Oh, take into account that he is a man and, therefore, hot-blooded, illogical, and changeable. He must be handled delicately if you want him to . . . behave."

"Ha! You are coming along nicely, my dear. Your brain is developing admirably." She looked almost benign as she accompanied me out through the now-crowded dance floor.

At the refreshment table, we met La Lépère, who was putting candied fruits into the sagging pockets of the old jacket that she wore over her shabby gown.

"Do take some of the rolls, too, my dear; they will make a lovely breakfast," said La Voisin as the old woman whirled around and tried to conceal what she was doing.

"You – you smile at me so. Your guests would not be so content with you if they knew what makes your garden so green," she said, thrusting her hands into her pockets as if to prevent anyone from snatching back the concealed delicacies.

"So now you begrudge me my gardeners? Come, come. There was a time you thought more generously than that."

There was a shrill laugh from a masked court lady who had overheard us. "Oh, my, yes, your gardeners are miracle workers! I begrudge you them myself. Look at those roses, still blooming so lushly, and those lilies! And chrysanthemums! Twice the size of mine! Oh, what is your secret?" The chemists of the Rue Forez, La Trianon and La Dodée, who had stopped at the wine fountain, turned their heads toward us and nodded and smiled.

"It's what you feed them," La Voisin said archly.

"And what is that?" the masked court lady asked.

"Have your gardeners compost spoiled fish from the market. They work miracles," replied the sorceress with her strange, pointed little smile, and she turned away. La Lépère followed us into a grape arbour lit with hanging lanterns and draped with lush vines, heavy with fruit.

"Catherine," she said, "it was not always like this. Take my advice as an old friend – get rid of this garden full of bones."

"Get rid of it? Ridiculous! I'm very fond of it. They keep my oven running day and night, these courtiers, in the good season, and my garden – exquisite. And I like them there – all those little marquises and counts and chevaliers and whatnot who make my flowers bloom. And how delightful a spectacle to see their high-born parents dancing on them without a care in the world— Oh, Margot, what? The wine fountain needs renewing already? Use the cheaper Bordeaux. They've been drinking long enough not to know the difference. Yes, do hurry along now. Where was I? Oh yes, my garden. I like it this way. I have no intention of digging it up." Insects swarmed around the lanterns, battering themselves on the glass.

"Catherine, it cannot end well. This . . . this . . . the way you mock the world. You should give it up."

"And be poor? *Va, va,* I have ten mouths to feed . . . and I do it rather well, too, not even counting the fact that I'm supporting people like you. My business is no different from half the world's. I just do it better, that's all."

"Better – or worse – depending on how you look at it," muttered La Lépère, as the violins struck up a pavane.

It was on the Wednesday following the party that I received a note from Monsieur Geniers, my silent partner in vengeance.

My uncle, the Chevalier de Saint-Laurent, had refused, it seems, to make good on his debts and, after the appropriate legal processes, had been thrown into debtors' prison, where he wrote pitiful letters begging Monsieur Geniers for money to pay the jailers for food and blankets. Good, I hope he stays locked up for ever, I thought, and felt indescribable relief that I no longer risked crossing his path and being recognised. Things seem to be working out for me, for Marie-Angélique. Now I'll end my day by dropping in on Marie-Angélique to see how she is. I wonder what would be a nice gift for the baby? Half daydreaming, I mounted into the carriage, hardly noticing that it had pulled out into the street. Perhaps the baby will be a girl. That will be easy to choose for. I'll get her a dress and a little silver spoon with her name on it. The carriage paused, halted by a crowd of pedestrians, chairs, and a dray wagon at the corner of the Rue de Picardie. An aunt? That will be odd to be an aunt. All memories of Uncle flew out of my mind with the agreeable notion of aunthood. Outside, my driver was shouting insults, but I didn't really notice. Suddenly I thought of d'Urbec's busybody aunt and how her mind was all formed by romance novels. Perhaps the brain softens when one becomes an aunt. I'll borrow Marie-Angélique's copy of *Clélie* and see if it seems any less silly. Then I'll know. The odd notion amused me, and I laughed out loud. I could feel the stares of strangers at the eerie old crone who laughed alone in the carriage caught in the midst of a street quarrel.

THIRTY

"I declare, Sister, I will never get over the new way you look,"
exclaimed Marie-Angélique as we kissed each other in
greeting. "My, my, haven't we come a long way from the time
we'd peek from behind the curtain at the cavaliers in the street!
Remember the one with the mandolin? And the poor fellow with
all the ribbons, who brought his friends to give him courage?"
The silk of her gown rustled as she poured a cordial from an
ornate crystal-and-gold decanter. Her face looked puffy under
its layers of rouge and powder. But not a hair was out of place
beneath her elegant jewelled combs.

"You look tired, Marie-Angélique. Is something wrong?"

"Oh, Geneviève," she said, sitting down and wiping her
eyes, "I told Monsieur de Vivonne last night about the baby. He
. . . he doesn't want it. He looked so cold, Sister. He said there is
something ugly and puffy about pregnant women, and that
explained why I'd had a . . . a distinctly *lower-class* look about
me lately. He said . . . if I truly loved him, I'd keep myself
attractive for him."

"But, Marie-Angélique, you're beautiful! You haven't
changed at all!"

"He says I have. And I've heard he's seeing Madame de
Ludres, that awful, rich, snotty little canoness. She's ambitious, she has the rank . . . the elegance. And . . . and she's not
. . . puffy. I have to keep his love, or I'm ruined, Sister."

"Marie-Angélique, this doesn't sound very honest to me. He
just doesn't want to acknowledge the child and end up
supporting it. If you want your baby, you should just have it."
Marie-Angélique bowed her head and wiped her eyes with the
back of her hand, smearing black eye shadow and white powder
together in a muddy trail. Her voice was low.

"He said that if I didn't care enough for our love to please him
and get it taken care of, he'd sooner see me in a convent – or in
the Salpêtrière like a common prostitute – than flaunting his

bastard around town. He has power, Sister, great power. I'd never see my child again— What would happen then? Oh, God, Sister, what shall I do? The cast-off little mistress, locked up for life to pray for forgiveness for her sins! And my baby— Without a mother, what would happen to my poor child? I can't live; I swear, I can't! God wishes me to die for my sins—" I held her to me as she doubled over with weeping.

"Don't cry, Sister, Don't cry," I pleaded. "It will all be all right. God means you to live and have your baby and be happy." Strands of Marie-Angélique's hair came loose from her combs, shining all golden. A trail of light across the sombre black silk of my dress. Even with her beauty, she, too, had been betrayed by Mother, just as surely as I had been.

"Marie-Angélique," I said, "I've got a house, I've got money put away. You could stay with me and have your baby secretly. He'd never know. You could fool him. Tell him you can't make up your mind. Tell him it's risky early on. Then when it's time, tell him you're visiting an abortionist. I'd keep the baby for you, and you could visit. It . . . it would be nice for me. And it would be almost like keeping it yourself."

"Oh, Geneviève, if I only could. But he won't wait any more. If I put him off, I'll lose him. There are dozens of women who want him. Women of rank, women of wealth and beauty. I've . . . I've stepped into a world that's beyond me, Sister. All I have is my beauty. I must renew our love before it is lost. It is the only way open to me. I must." Her eyes, as she stared at my face, were full of desperation. Her face was pale and twisted with anxiety beneath the gaudy spots of rouge and muddy splashes of smeared powder. "Tell me," she whispered, "in all your, ah, business, have you ever heard of the Comte de Longueval?"

"Longueval?" I asked again just to make sure. My heart stood still for a moment. I knew Longueval all too well.

"Yes. Longueval. I have . . . been given his name. He . . . he can fix things."

"Longueval has a poor reputation, Sister. He's ignorant and money hungry."

"He says he'll pay . . ."

"You mean, the duke will pay Longueval for you to . . . ?"

"Yes," she whispered and averted her face from me. "Don't

hate me for it. I already hate myself." Her voice was sick with shame.

"Marie-Angélique, Longueval has his servants dump the bodies of his mistakes in the back alleys behind the Bicêtre and the Hôpital de la Charité."

"Don't shame me more, my poor child..."

"Marie-Angélique," I said as gently as I could, "do you think I'm speaking of infants here? Most of the time, it is the women who see him who end up in the alley."

"But Monsieur le Duc said—" Her eyes opened wide. "Geneviève, what proof have you?"

"Sister, I live a different life now. So different you can hardly imagine it. I know the secrets of the world. The women who rise high on men's favours, the unfaithful wives, they pay a visit... sometimes several a year, to... well, a place that I know. It doesn't give them a pin's worth of worry, and they live to return the next time that love inconveniences them. In the right hands, it's far safer than being cut for the stone. Believe me, I've seen them all – actresses, noblewomen, unfaithful wives. Women like that, they know how to take care of themselves. Marie-Angélique, let me arrange it for you. But don't go to Longueval. Swear to me you won't."

"I... I don't know," she answered. "I wasn't raised to know these things," she equivocated.

"Listen to me," I said firmly. "Promise me you won't go to that man. I'll fix everything for you. You're all I have left in this world. You can get another child, but I can't get another sister. And if the duke demands to take you, tell him you insist on seeing La Voisin."

"The fortune-teller..." She drew in her breath. "So that was her real business all along."

"One of them," I answered, thinking of the garden of bones. "But she's quick, quiet, and safe." But Marie-Angélique had begun to tremble all over.

"I'm so afraid, Geneviève. I'll burn in hell for this."

"Then you'll have the most fashionable people at the court for company. Goodness, the Princesse de Tingry alone could keep Madame in business with her annual... offerings."

"Annual? Oh, I could never— Dreadful!" Marie-Angélique looked shocked.

"Marie-Angélique, you want to keep this man. That is the price. If you weep and mope, you will bore him. Whatever you do, do it boldly."

"But I have to keep him, I have no way to live otherwise. And . . . and he loves me. He says so. Our love is precious, he said. This is the only way."

With regret I felt the state of aunthood slipping away. No knitting, no visits, no silver spoon. The oven still warm with incinerated hope. All for this worthless old roué. What liars men are, and here's the proof. Marie-Angélique promised me so many times, first with tears and then with renewed resoluteness, that I believed her. And though it was not my day to visit, I went straight to the Rue Beauregard.

Antoine Montvoisin, in his old, food-stained dressing gown and moth-eaten wool slippers, let me in by the side door.

"They're all upstairs. They've got business," he announced, as if that explained everything. "I'm drinking her Beaujolais," he said, and a conspiratorial tone entered his voice. "She forgets to lock it up when they're all upstairs with a client. Do you want some?"

"Not just now; my stomach's weak today. But thank you, anyway," I added, noting the dejected look on his face.

"Oh, there you are, Antoine. Into my good wine again, eh? Well, pour yourself another drink and then get dressed. I have a delivery for Guibourg today." Margot came downstairs with a wrapped package neatly tied with string. I knew now what was in them. This one was big, near term. Madame might well have had to drown it in the big brass bowl she kept at the bedside in case the foetus emerged living. "Oh, good—" La Voisin turned and spied me. "Why, Marquise, to what do we owe the honour? It's not even your accounting day."

"I've come to arrange for your . . . services for . . . female embarrassment—"

"Ha! Not you? Who on earth was it? D'Urbec, after all?"

"Not for me, for my sister."

"Oho, the beautiful Marie-Angélique Pasquier. She's flown high. But Vivonne is changeable. You'd be surprised who's been purchasing love powders to sprinkle in his food. She'd do well to consult me in other matters, too, your sister. Who is paying? Vivonne?"

"I am. Vivonne wants her to go to Longueval."

"Then, in my opinion, he's either a fool or wants her out of the way. Knowing him, the latter. Longueval is an incompetent."

"That's what I told her." As I negotiated the price, I felt deadly calm.

"Come, sit down, Marquise. Just how far along is she?" We sat together on two big brocade armchairs, and she propped her feet on a stool. Her ankles, in scarlet silk stockings, looked more swollen than I remembered.

"It doesn't really show yet," I answered.

"Oh, a pity. If it were big enough to send to Guibourg, I could offer a discount. There's a shortage these days, and he pays well."

"Pays? For what?"

"Oh, don't be so particular. They're already dead when I send them over. He baptises them, of course, though he says it's second rate if they're not alive. And then he . . . reuses them. After all, they would just go to waste otherwise."

"Oh yes, of course. It's silly to waste," I said in a distant manner. The only use for a dead baptised baby I could imagine was in the Black Mass, one of Guibourg's specialties. The Shadow Queen's jet-black eyes looked inscrutable as she watched my mind absorb this information. She seemed businesslike, calm, as if she were testing me. We watched Antoine, all wrapped in his rusty old cloak, stump out of the door with the package, and I turned to her. Marie-Angélique betrayed to this. Knowingly. By her own mother, who had used her salon to launch her into this life just as clearly as if she had auctioned her off. Should I add the baby to the list of deaths Mother had to her account? The Shadow Queen must have seen the look in my eye. She stared back evenly at me. Now, somehow, when I had placed my sister and myself in her hands, it was time to ask the question I had not dared to before.

"Tell me," I said, my voice calm and precise, "did you sell my mother the poison with which she killed my father?"

"I wondered when you'd be asking that. You certainly took your time figuring it out."

"It only just now came to me," I lied.

"Really, for a person who reads the future so well, you are a bit dense in reading the past. The answer is no. I didn't. La Bosse did."

"Then it's true. He was murdered, and you knew all along." She leaned back in her chair and looked at me a long time.

"You must understand, there are certain types of women to whom I do not sell poison. I am an artist. I create death in undetectable ways. The laughing death, oil of vitriol, distillation of toad – they are not for me. I require a customer who is brave, patient, and subtle. Someone who has suffered great wrong and is willing to follow my instructions exactly to even the score. You, for example, would be ideal." She paused. I didn't say anything. "This little . . . business of mine was built by the revolutionaries of the Fronde. No, not in the way you think, by political conspiracy, but by women who had managed households while their husbands were away at war. They return, those lords, they take away the purse strings, they are brutal; they leave bruises, they threaten with imprisonment in the cloister. Poison – it evens the score. My little services, they keep women from slavery. Isn't that so? In a better world, I would have to sell perfume and beauty powder. But this wicked world of ours needs its witches, and so I am wealthy."

"My mother—"

"Your mother was a poor client. Vengeful, rageful. Such women do not spread out the dose. In their haste, they give it all at once. Then they are detected. Under torture, they name the source. Then I couldn't give my lovely garden parties, could I? I sent her to Notre-Dame de Bonne Nouvelle with powders passed under the chalice. When she became dissatisfied with masses to Saint-Rabboni, I turned her away. Besides, I did not like her." I could feel the coldness stealing towards my heart.

"Then she did do it, after all. Why? It has brought her nothing."

"That is what I told her. 'Never poison a perfectly good husband on a promise of marriage alone,' I advised her. 'At the very least, find out what your husband's true finances are and the amount you can expect in widowhood, and don't just go burbling on about hidden wealth abroad, or you'll end up worse than ever. Poor, and without your lover as well, for a man like the Chevalier de la Rivière will leave you if you have no money.'

The woman was incapable of seeing logic. She left in a rage, and I sent to La Bosse to warn her. La Bosse . . . forgets herself sometimes. She's getting old. Her good sense leaves her when she sees gold. And if one of us is lost, all will be lost." La Bosse. The archrival but a collaborator, too. And La Voisin. Her hands were not clean of this thing, either. Through her, Mother's flowing river of resentment had found an outlet.

"What did La Bosse sell her?"

"La Bosse was crafty. She sold her a very weak compound. But your mother was shrewd. She tried it out on the patients at the hospital and came back shrieking she'd been cheated. 'You see?' I told La Bosse. 'You should never have entangled yourself with a woman like that.' So La Bosse followed my suggestion and sold her arsenical soap for washing his shirts in. It sets up skin sores like the Italian disease. Then the physician is called and usually finishes the job by bleeding the person to death, all the while speaking Latin. So, properly speaking, your father was killed by his doctor, thanks to a process set in motion by your mother. Remember that and beware of physicians." She laughed, a sharp little laugh.

The laughter rattled in my head like stones in a bottle. Her words rushed all around me. 'Arsenical compounds', 'laughing death', 'bleeding to death', 'too rageful'. I looked at my hands. They were clenched so hard the knuckles were white.

"Tell me just one thing more," I asked very quietly.

"Yes?" Her face was positively maternal.

"Will you sell me poison for my revenge?"

"Oh, good. I have waited a long time for this moment. At last, my dear, you are one of us."

La Voisin rose, and I followed her into her little cabinet. Her face had a strange, impassive calm as she unlocked the first door of the tall, gilded cupboard opposite the fire. "Sooner or later, no matter what her condition, your mother will send for you. She has never yet failed to seek out the most fashionable fortune-tellers. At that time, you must be ready to be the avenging arm of God," she said quietly. She took down one of her ledgers from the shelf. It was all bound in dark green leather with gold stamping. She set it on her writing desk and opened it up. "Let us see," she said, running her finger down the rows of neat writing. "Pasquier . . . *P* . . . no, this is *R*. My goodness, not only is my waist spreading, I do believe my eyes are fading. I suppose I shall soon be wanting glasses. No matter how we hide, age finds us at last." She put back *R* and pulled down the correct ledger.

As she leafed through the book, pausing occasionally, I could read some of the entries upside down: *Pajot*, wishes to make a pact with the Devil. *Pardrière*, Madame, purchase of powders to soften behaviour of husband. *Vicomtesse de Polignac*, poisons for La Vallière, assorted sorceries for holding lovers, for finding treasure; a formula for breast enlargement. *Poulaillon*, *Madame de*, regular purchases of slow poison. Names, desires, numbers: poisons bought, amount, kind, and price. Aphrodisiacs purchased, powders passed under the chalice, White Masses to Saint-Rabboni, the mender of marriages, said over shirts, Black Masses done with infant's blood in the chalice. How many. The price. The purpose. The secrets of the monstrous world of the Sun King, written in a heavy green ledger.

"*Pasquier*. Yes. Here it is. Wishes for a youthful skin . . . no, skin cream is too slow. You will have only one chance, and it must not be traced to your visit. Something she must take in weekly doses. Cumulative. Delayed action, so her suspicions won't be aroused." She shut the book. "A youth restorative . . . a tonic syrup to enhance the beauty . . . I think it will do nicely." She replaced the ledger on the shelf and locked the door. The green wood hissed on the hearth between the cat andirons. Her old grey tom roused himself momentarily from sleep to stretch and yawn before the fire. La Voisin searched briefly among her big bunch of keys and found the one for the second set of doors in the cupboard. She inserted it in the lock and flung both doors wide to reveal a set of shelves with rows of bottles of different sizes, all neatly labelled. Most were the tell-tale green of La Trianon's laboratory, but there were others. Boxes of hair and nail clippings, jars of strange oleaginous substances. A box of black candles. Several wax figurines. Larger jars with glory hands and other indescribable body parts, black and shrivelled like old mushrooms. Dried toads, cocks' testicles. In the stillness, I could hear my heart beating.

"Grenouillet . . . the laughing death . . . so obvious, wolfsbane . . . no . . . distilled toad . . . no, too characteristic . . . powder of diamonds . . . too unreliable. Hemlock . . . vipers' venom . . ." She selected two bottles and set them on a low shelf that topped a set of drawers at the base of the cupboard. "For this job, white arsenic is best, I think. Arsenic and syrup of roses – a poetic touch." She took an unlabelled green bottle and with a tiny funnel filled it from the first two bottles. Then she corked it and sealed the cork with wax by holding a dripping candle over it. "Let's see. A touch of luxury . . ." and she snipped a bit of gold thread from a narrow wooden spool and wound it into the wax about the neck and cork of the little vial to make a seal. "Very elegant," she pronounced it, as she put it into my cold, trembling hand. "Remember," she added, "this is justice. You can expect it nowhere else. I will wait for the news that the job is finished."

I left the sorceress's house, still weak with the shock of my new knowledge. La Voisin was no amateur, no housewife with an unpleasant relative and a jar of "*mort aux rats*" in her cupboard. She was a professional poisoner of the highest rank, perhaps the greatest in Europe. As I summoned my waiting carriage, I felt suddenly lost. See where vengeance has led you, Geneviève Pasquier, a voice said in my head. Through righteousness, you have descended into evil. I seated myself and inspected the vicious little bottle in my hand. "Justice," she had said. Yes, it had to be justice. "For you, Father," I whispered, as the driver cracked his whip and the carriage rattled into the misty autumn evening. That night even the cordial couldn't put me to sleep. I took dose after dose, and even then, sleep was filled with monstrous dreams. Above the horrible shapes and strange, distorted faces I could hear the Shadow Queen's ironic laughter. "One of us at last, at last, at last . . ."

I woke the next morning sick, and the morning after that too. The hours slipped by like green eels, all tangled and slippery, one very much like another. But even the most terrible of thoughts soon becomes ordinary with repetition; eventually I became well again and the green bottle in the dressing table drawer became a common thing, no different than a thimble or a box of *mouches*. And so it was that I emerged a week later, all hollow eyed from days with no food but opium, for an evening of amusement at the Duchesse de Bouillon's, where I had been invited with a Spanish horoscopist. There amidst brilliant gossip and much discussion of the occult I read fortune after fortune until the horoscopist, with a malicious smile, led the Duc de Vivonne to me and, amidst the laughter of the company, asked what I saw in the future of a man so gallant. But as his shadow fell across the oracle glass, the water within turned blood red.

"You will soon have a new mistress," I said quietly. Luckily that, too, passed for wit, for Vivonne was a well-known rakehell, and the company laughed again. But I knew that moment in my heart that she had gone to Longueval despite every promise, and now I needed only to know where they had left her.

On the way home, I kept peering from the carriage window into the alleys as we passed, as if I might see something; but it was a foolish idea, because the maze of dark alleys behind the principal streets would never admit a carriage, nor would they be safe for any night wanderer on foot. The night has made you stupid, Geneviève, I cursed myself. Tomorrow morning I will make a plan, and begin my search of the hospitals.

But the next morning, before I was even out of bed, Sylvie showed in Marie-Angélique's little maid. She was carrying a large bird cage, and her eyes were swollen.

"You know where she is," I cried, setting aside my cup of chocolate and throwing back the covers. "Quickly, Sylvie – my clothes. We'll go to her; we'll get her back!" Sylvie hurried to the armoire to fetch my dress and petticoats.

"She said to bring you the bird if she didn't return by last night, and she hasn't."

"But where is she now?" I asked. At the armoire door, Sylvie paused.

"I don't know; nobody does. They either come back, or they don't— That's all." The little maid rubbed her eyes with her knuckles.

"Just what do you mean by 'they'?" I asked slowly, the horror of the thing beginning at last to fill my mind.

"She's not the first, you know. But I liked her, I did. Mademoiselle Pasquier was not made for the life – I could tell. She was different, kinder. But what could I do? She went to him, all a-tremble, to tell him she would find a woman to do it. But I saw him just sit there behind his big writing desk without looking up from his papers and say, all smooth and cool, 'I hope you don't mean La Voisin. I have no intention of allowing you to set me up for blackmail.' 'In the name of our love,' she said, 'I could never even imagine such a thing. I could never stoop to such dishonour.' 'In my experience, there is no dishonour to which a woman cannot stoop. You can hardly admit you have not stooped yourself more than once.' She got all stiff and clenched her hands. 'Now, now,' he said, 'if your love was true, you would not question my choice in this matter.' She bowed her head and left, like a lamb to the slaughter. 'God wishes me to die for my sins,' she said, as I saw her to the carriage. 'Give the bird to my sister. It will live longer than both of us.' She knew, Madame. God knows how, but she knew."

"I am going now to search the hospitals and the basement of the Châtelet. Will you come with me?" I asked her.

"I dare not, Madame. I can't be gone long. I could vanish, too, and he'd just tell everyone I went home to my relatives in the country." I remembered the head beneath the floorboards.

"I'm sorry," I said softly, and she looked shocked at the unexpected apology as she set down the bird cage and fled.

"Sylvie," I asked as I heard the back door slam downstairs, "can you accompany me?"

"Madame, your logic has deserted you. If you are seen making enquiries, it will tie the abortion to us, and to La Voisin. I have learned a charm to prevent talking under torture – but you, how could you bear the water torture or the boot? No, every one of us will be lost because of your foolishness over a friend that is lost. Let her be. I don't wish to be executed for an abortion some stranger botched." Sylvie's face looked hard and shrewd, the face of a country woman calculating whether to wring an overaged laying hen's neck.

"Sylvie, she's my sister."

"Your *sister*? Why, she's no more than twenty, I'd imagine. Your mother certainly couldn't have taken that alchemical stuff ... or is that just your way of talking?" I slumped over, still sitting on the edge of the bed, and held my head in my hands.

"She's my full sister, Sylvie. My older sister. Don't tell Madame I told you. She'll never forgive me. Just help me, please. She was more to me than any mother on earth." I could hear Sylvie's foot tap impatiently.

"My goodness, little Miss, you certainly had me fooled. A

hundred and fifty years old! I thought you were lying. Maybe sixty or seventy, with that sharp tongue and those old-ladyish ways. There's got to be something to that wrinkle stuff, I thought. I'll be wanting it myself someday, it works so fine. Next thing you'll be telling me is that you don't actually read fortunes in the glass."

"I do read fortunes," I said in a small voice. "I'm just not very old. Only my heart's old – before its time." I could feel her studying my face and looked up to see her standing over me.

"Madame, let me make a suggestion. Leave the Marquise de Morville at home today. Everyone in Paris recognises her. We'll take up the hem on my Sunday dress, and you can go as a maid. Not hers. Any servant of hers will be thought to be a conspirator, too, and interrogated. They need to think you're ignorant of everything. You're clever enough to play an old lady. Think of a disguise, a good story."

And so that is how that very day a bartered fiacre disgorged a crippled servant of the house of Matignon at the Châtelet, where she was shown by the police to the dank cellar where all the bodies that turn up in Paris lie for three days before burial. The stench of the place nearly drove me away, but I pushed forward to the slabs. Above them on hooks hung the victims' clothes, to aid in the identification of the bloated, putrid bodies.

"This servant girl, she was well dressed when she disappeared?"

"Yes, in my mistress's clothes, the hussy. But my mistress is a Christian woman and forgives her. She'll have her back with a good beating to teach her a thing or two."

"More than she deserves, I say. Was it yellow hair?"

"Yes, yellow . . . but not like that one . . . that's dyed."

"Then she's not here . . . probably left town with a lover by now. Your mistress will have to find another maid, I fear."

By the time the fiacre halted at the Parvis Notre-Dame, before the main door of the Hôtel-Dieu, my back, unsupported by my steel corset, was aching dreadfully with each swaying step I took. I suppose it's a kind of progress, I thought, that I can't slide back into my old bobbing, crab-wise walk without this much agony. A beggar on the street made a sign to avert the evil eye. That had never happened in the old days. Then I remembered. I had left behind the marquise's posture, gown, and walking stick, but I had kept her commanding, shrewd eyes. Oh, goodness, I must look like a witch, I thought, hastily lowering my eyes and assuming the sly, apologetic look of a household servant.

I had not expected to find what I sought so soon. The novice pointed from the door of the women's ward down the long, medieval stone hall lined with curtained beds. "She's there," she snapped, "the one on the right side of bed number four. Though why her family would want her is beyond me; better to let her vanish. She's lucky she's dying – it's the sort of thing they do to escape the punishment for infanticide. But she'll not escape God's punishment, that I can assure you." I'd rather deal with witches any day than this nasty woman, I thought.

Marie-Angélique lay crowded into a bed with four other women, one of whom seemed already dead and another raving with the fever that follows a bad childbirth. A man in the blue suit and wide, white plumed hat of the police was leaning over the bedside with a notebook.

"No farther!" A burly sergeant, unshaved and menacing, stepped from an alcove. "She's being questioned; you'll have to wait. Are you her maid?" I sensed the danger in the question.

"No, I'm from the family, sir. She was lost to us through sin, but when she vanished, her brother sent us all out in search of her so that he could forgive her; he's that good a Christian, he is."

"Brother, eh? And who might he be?"

"Why, Étienne Pasquier, the avocat, at the House of the Marmousets." Ah, lovely. I shall entangle my respectable brother in a horrid scandal. How he'll puff and pose when the police arrive at his door and go through the house questioning everyone to try to find out who procured the abortion.

The sergeant turned to see what progress the policeman at the bedside was making with his inquiries. Marie-Angélique's lips did nor seem to be moving. The man shook her shoulder to try to rouse her; her eyes opened momentarily and rolled with terror, but not a sound escaped her. Honour I thought. That worthless Vivonne's honour. How wasted your love was, Sister. Tell it all, tell it all.

"I know it's wrong, but I can't help feeling sorry for them," the sergeant muttered. "Poor little girl. That one was beautiful, too. And now she won't live out the day. Don't think we're being rough – it's the only chance we have to get the name of the abortionist. We execute swine like that."

"God grant you find him, the dreadful murderer," I agreed. The man at the bedside sighed with disappointment and stood up, looking in our direction. He never changed his expression as he stared directly into my face. It was Desgrez. I couldn't start or flee but stood as still as a bird that is paralysed by the snake's gaze. Courage, I said to myself, and, making my face look stupid, I shuffled with an exaggerated limp towards the bedside.

"Don't I remember you from somewhere?" he said blandly.

"A servant of the family, sent to search her out, though why they bothered, I can't say," interrupted the novice, who had returned with a pitcher of water and several towels over her arm.

"Christian forgiveness is to be commended," replied Desgrez, but his eyes, which never left me, seemed to cut through to my backbone.

"Let me go closer; I must see her face to know for certain," I said in the thick, lower-class accent of the Parisian streets.

"I do know you – the *lingère*'s apprentice."

"I got me a better place now – plenty better food and less work." Damn his excellent memory. A walking police-records office.

"With the house of . . . ?"

". . . Pasquier," interjected the sergeant. Desgrez raised an eyebrow.

"Interesting, Sergeant. That explains the lace on the linen. I am surprised she was ever found at all. Tell me, little *lingère*—'

"Annette, sir—"

"Tell me, Annette, would this woman here be the celebrated La Pasquier?"

"I don't know nothing about that. She's just my master's sister."

"And how, pray tell, did you end at the house of Pasquier?" I didn't like his questioning at all. It was taking a wrong turn.

"My fiancé . . . he knew someone and fixed it for me to get the place—" I winked. Desgrez looked at me a long time, up and down. I could see his eyes taking in the gaudy, cheap trimmings on the lower-class dress. A fastidious look of disgust crossed his face. Evidently, sexual social climbing among the lower elements didn't please him. I wonder what you think of the same thing among the rich, I thought. Did you bow to La Pasquier when she passed you in her carriage? Do you bow to La Montespan?

He drew the sergeant aside, and I could hear him say softly, ". . . not a word about today . . . this case involves bigger game than we thought . . . dangerous to meddle, must go to La Reynie . . ." I took advantage of their inattention to slip to Marie-Angélique's bedside.

"Did she tell you anything?" The sergeant's question to Desgrez carried in spite of his whisper. I knelt down beside her and put my hand on her forehead. She was burning up with fever. Desgrez's voice was low in response, but I could catch a few words from my place by the bed.

". . . incoherent since the priest sent for me . . . not a word since the confession of abortion . . . he couldn't get the name from her, either . . . but now she's identified, I have my suspicions . . ."

"It's me, it's me," I whispered urgently to Marie-Angélique. "I've come for you. Don't die, please. You must get well. How can I live if you die?"

"You, there!" Suddenly I heard the voice of Desgrez above me and looked up with a stare of pure fear. Suppose he had been there awhile, silent, and heard the shift in my accent? "Maybe a woman can get it out of her." His voice was brisk. "Ask her who the abortionist was."

I embraced the sweating body on the bed and whispered in her ear the one thing I knew she wanted to hear above anything else. "God has surely forgiven you, Marie-Angélique." Her eyes half opened. "Live for my sake, for those who love you." For a moment, she seemed to speak. I put my ear close but couldn't hear a thing.

"Well?" Desgrez's voice above me sounded harsh.

"Oh, Sir, she says a name sounds like 'Longueval'."

"The Comte de Longueval, eh? Well, well. The old pander. I thought he was confining himself to alchemy since his last interrogation. Lebrun, we need to pay a call on the comte as soon as possible." He strode from the bedside and was on his way, but not before I'd heard him take the sergeant aside and whisper, "Follow that servant girl when she leaves here. I want to know where she goes, whom she sees." My heart stopped nearly as still as Marie-Angélique's.

"You needn't sit there any more. She's dead." The voice of the old-woman attendant roused me. She leaned over me and whispered confidentially from between rotted teeth, "Now, if the family wants to claim the body to save themselves from the disgrace of having it exposed on the street, I can arrange for it to disappear for a consideration..."

"Of course they will want it— Are you sure you can?"

"It's not easy, you know... the body of a criminal... there's lots as has a claim on them... the surgeons, for example..."

"For God's sake, how much?"

"Not a sou less than twenty *écus*." The old woman looked sly.

"You'll have it. Just swear you'll keep her safe 'til they return for her."

"Oh, I does it often enough... I have my ways. Don't let them dillydally, though. Tell them to send to old Marie before tomorrow night. Remember, old Marie in the Salle du Rosaire."

As I left the hospital ward on to the Rue du Marché Palu, I heard the sound of footsteps behind me. Alarmed, I fled on foot towards the Parvis Notre-Dame, and the sound of the following footsteps was lost in the street cries and noise of carriages. But the eerie pricking in my scalp still told me that someone was behind me. There was no doubt about it; I was being followed.

THIRTY-ONE

I knew I couldn't run, so instead I walked confidently through the crowd of shouting bearers on the square before Notre-Dame to the spot where the drivers of fiacres lounged, waiting to hire their little carriages. Loudly, I engaged the driver with the sturdiest-looking horse for the long trip to the Faubourg Saint-Honoré. My voice carried well, though I could barely hear it over the thumping of my heart. I've misled that policeman, I thought; now he'll go back and report. But as I mounted the little fiacre, I turned to see the red-stockinged sergeant of the Salle du Rosaire mount another carriage. My driver passed rapidly enough to the Pont Notre-Dame, only to be entangled there among the crowd of chairs and foot travellers in the narrow way between the elegant shops that lined both sides of the bridge. I peered out behind us to note with relief that the pursuing carriage was equally entangled in a knot of dandies leaving a gallery of paintings.

"Driver, I have changed my mind. Take me to the Hôtel Bouillon, and I will pay you the same. Get me there in half the time, and I will double your fare." The long whip cracked to the left and right of us, sending a crowd of apprentices fleeing, as the driver urged his nag to a swift trot. Again I peered back behind us. My enemy was making no progress against the crowd. I saw him shake his fist at his driver. Good, he's lost, I thought. But I did not breathe easily until I had mingled with a crowd of market women bringing provisions into the kitchen entrance of the vast hotel and crept invisibly by back ways to the apartment of the one man in Paris who might help me.

I found Lamotte in a red silk dressing gown and Persian cap, giving orders to an assistant cook.

"Now, remember," he was saying, "shellfish gives Monsieur

L'Evêque a rash, but the nature of the entertainment is such that Madame will wish something light, terribly light, to be served. We must not weigh down the spirits of our audience, eh?" He was waving his fingers in the air to symbolize the lightness desired. Interesting, I thought. From pet poet and playwright to designer of entertainments and general factotum. A man with a good profile certainly can go far in the right circles.

"Monsieur de la Motte, a servant girl demands to see you with a message from a Mademoiselle Pasquier." The lackey did not seem altogether respectful. Lamotte glanced up and saw me waiting at the tall, double doors of the salon, only one of which was thrown partially open.

"Oho, I know this servant girl, Pierre. And don't go making surmises about Mademoiselle Pasquier that would disturb the idol of my heart. La Pasquier is one of numerous women foolishly and uselessly in love with me, whose favours I scorn for a higher, brighter, nobler flame. No, Pierre, let Madame know that she alone commands my heart, her stellar radiance alone inspires my muse." He accompanied these words by striking the embroidered silk directly above his heart. He had been putting on weight. Even in a few months, he had contrived to look sleeker, and his mustachios had become even grander, if possible. I could not but admire the catlike grace with which he had climbed from one society boudoir to another, until he had arrived at the very highest level, moving into the Hôtel Bouillon itself. Only two things seemed to have suffered: his name, which had come apart and added a syllable, and his passion for writing tragedy. Since his triumph with *Osmin*, he had written nothing of note for the Paris stage. But the Chevalier de la Motte was all the rage for his light verse and the charming little scenes that he wrote to be set to music for the ballet. Now he dismissed both the cook and the valet, but I saw his eyes take note of the fact that the latter stood behind the double doors to listen.

"What message have you?" he asked casually, his voice loud so it would carry behind the door.

"Monsieur de la Motte, Mademoiselle Pasquier lies dead in the Hôtel-Dieu, victim of a dreadful accident. By all that you once held sacred, I beg you to return with me to help claim the body." We both heard the rustle from behind the door as the valet departed. Good. A dead woman was no rival to even the most jealous beauty. The airy complacency fell away from Lamotte's face, and his eyes were suddenly troubled.

"What . . . what has happened?" I spoke swiftly and softly now. Who knew how long we would be alone?

"Not really an accident . . . a . . . a botched abortion. Can you forgive her? She said God wished her to die." As I wiped my eyes, Lamotte took out a large handkerchief and sneezed noisily into it. "I need you, Monsieur Lamotte; she needs you, for this one last service. I've made arrangements to bribe an attendant for the body. They won't question a man, not if he says he's from the family. But me . . . they might take me for an accomplice of the abortionist." Lamotte's eyes were troubled. Transporting criminals' bodies was not the work for a rising favourite of an arbiter of artistic taste.

"Her family?" he asked. "What kind of inhuman family is yours, that they won't even bury her?"

"My brother declared her dead years ago. He'll never try to claim her. He's so stingy, he'd begrudge the money for a decent burial even if it wouldn't bring disgrace to him. He's very fond of appearing respectable, Lamotte. But I've got money; you know that. I'll see her remembered, I'll have a stone made – but you must assist me. Think of what she once meant to you . . ." At this his face crumpled, and he suddenly looked old.

"My youth is gone, Geneviève. The man I once was has died there with her. My dreams of achieving immortal greatness, of winning the angel in the window – gone, dead, lost. Do you understand? I write poetry for ballets."

"And much acclaimed you are! I saw *The Princess of the Enchanted Castle* myself at Saint-Germain."

"But my tragedy – I could never finish it. My *Sapho*. Gone, dried up. And this end . . . how sordid, how ordinary . . ." He rubbed his eyes fiercely and blew his nose again. "If *I* had written of her, she would have stabbed herself nobly with a silver dagger on a precipice above the sea, reciting classical verse. Nothing less was worthy of her. But this – bleeding to death in a filthy charity hospital . . ." He put his head in his hands for a long time, sighing. Then he looked up at me. "What must I do? Become an avaricious little bourgeois for the afternoon? Very well. For you, it is done." He hitched his dressing gown tighter around his embonpoint and stood up. "Pierre! Pierre!" He clapped his hands. "Where is that rascal when you need him?" He went to the double doors and shouted; I could hear the patter of feet. Eventually the lackey returned, breathless.

"Pierre, my smallest day wig. And a suit of mourning. No funeral bands. I go to assist at a bourgeois funeral. You understand." He waved his hand carelessly, as if annoyed by the dull and trivial duty. Then he vanished into the small cabinet behind his reception room, which I took to be his bedroom, or his dressing chamber. I could hear his voice through the open door. "Tell that servant girl to wait here to show me the way." Always, Lamotte was a man of the theatre. If anyone could play a bourgeois *avocat* to perfection, it would be he.

I shivered as I sat huddled alone in one of the light carriages from the *remise* of the Hôtel Bouillon. He had left me in the Rue du Sablon, a street away from the entrance of the Hôtel-Dieu. It wasn't that cold outside, though it was not warm. The autumn winds had blown away the dank grey clouds to show patches of blue mingled with the rosy pink of the dying day above the pointed slate roofs. The sort of day Marie-Angélique had liked. She always said weather that made your cheeks look pink could not be spoken ill of. Ahead of us on the Rue du Sablon, the horses of the hired hearse waited listlessly, while the driver dozed, his reins knotted to the box.

"Don't fret indoors on weather like this, Sister! Winter will be here soon enough." I could hear her voice in my ears as if she sat next to me. "Why, we'll go take the air at the Palais-Royal gardens, and you'll shake off that bad mood. Besides, we might very well see someone interesting . . ." Marie-Angélique, we'll take the air one last time, and I'll see you home.

Around the corner, the figure in black had emerged from the hospital. Even though his head was bowed, he had not forgotten the stolid walk of the bourgeois. He walked slowly, so slowly past the carriage where I waited to the waiting hearse. I could see him talking at length with the driver, who gesticulated wildly. He pressed money into the man's hand. Then the driver cracked the whip and the hearse departed down the Rue du Sablon.

"What has happened? Why didn't he go in by the carriage gate?" Lamotte seated himself wordlessly in the seat opposite me and didn't answer my question.

"Don't ask," he said at last. His face was like iron.

"But you did pay the attendant, didn't you? What's gone wrong? Why couldn't you get her right away?" Lamotte gave orders to the coachman. He closed his eyes and remained silent for a long time before he spoke again.

"Someone sent word to your brother," he said, and the words came out like heavy stones. "Luckily, my wits were about me, and I said I was a cousin on your mother's side."

"But . . . what?"

"Your brother told them they had made a mistake. He had once had a sister of that name, but she had died years ago."

"No less than I expected." Who had gone to him? The police. It must have been. Only they could be that swift. But Lamotte had put his hands over his face and begun to sob. I grabbed his arm and tried to shake him.

"You must tell me what happened," I whispered fiercely.

"The body of a criminal . . ." I heard him say. I shook him again. "Don't ask me. Don't ask me to say," he mumbled.

"But I must know – I can't go on without knowing," I cried. He picked his head up and looked at me with his eyes all red.

"The anatomy theatre at the Collège Saint-Côme. They found the idea of a septic abortion . . . interesting. My God. Interesting. And I still see her looking down from the window – her beautiful blue eyes. Laughing. Do you understand now? There's nothing left of her – nothing. Cut up, dispersed, for the advancement of the study of the science of anatomy. I grabbed the ward surgeon by the throat. 'She's not a machine! She had a soul! You can't do this!' 'I'm sorry, Monsieur, what's done is done,' he said, and pulled himself away as if I were a madman. I'm afraid I made a fool of myself. I had . . . I had conceived a fantasy of kissing her once in farewell – just once. The only time. To bid my youth adieu, you see. Was that too much to ask? Only once, not much. But this is the modern era. There is no place any more for gestures – romantic gestures – foolish, hopeless gestures. The men with the knives, the scientists, they got there first." My beautiful sister, butchered like a pig. No tomb, no place for me to weep. I felt as if my bones had cracked open and the marrow run out.

Lamotte was still incoherent when they opened the great carriage gates of the Hôtel Bouillon. Hearing the shouting and rattling, he pulled himself together, wiped his face, and smoothed his once-jaunty mustachios with his fingers. "And tonight I dine with the swine, face in the trough, no better than the rest." His voice was quiet, his eyes bitter.

"Are you all right, Monsieur de la Motte?"

"Not now, not ever," he said, as the carriage left us at the foot of the broad staircase that rose from the *cour d'honneur*. He looked up to the carved balustrades and gilded doors above as if surveying the gate to Gehenna. "Come with me a moment, Mademoiselle Pasquier. Talk to me about her. I . . . I feel as if I cannot breathe." His face was so devastated, I could not refuse. He led me through the long corridors and open state apartments to his own tiny set of rooms in the back of the great house. Entering by the main way and winding through to the back as we did, it became clear how many retainers, pet writers and artists, orphans, distant cousins, and hangers-on were housed in the vast mansion. A mini-society, with its own levels, its own court, a tiny imitation of the great one at Versailles. A life of flattery, back stabbing, and climbing, and they counted themselves fortunate. Better to be a society sorceress, I thought. One enters and leaves by the front door as one chooses.

Passing through his reception room, he took me into a low, gilt-panelled room, lined with books. A writing desk and two comfortable armchairs were crowded amid the clutter of manuscripts and theatrical souvenirs. His dressing gown, abandoned so hastily, was flung untidily across a narrow, cluttered, brocade-hung bed stuffed into an alcove.

"My hiding place," he said, with a gesture about the stuffy little chamber. "Even *she* must leave her beast his den." He rummaged in a little cupboard and brought out a decanter and two glasses.

"I have not a soul but you to tell about her," I said, taking the glass. "Who else could understand her goodness, her sweetness? Her beauty was her curse." The brandy was strong and made me cough. He refilled my glass, and his own as well.

"Not her beauty, no. Her family. Your brother, if you will pardon me, Mademoiselle, is an unnatural monster with a stone for a heart." He looked into his glass, as if he could see images in the bottom of it. "There are many such, nowadays. If I had the pen of Molière, I could make him comic. That is the role of art, is it not? To make monsters comic, so we can bear them, and our own cheap griefs into grand tragedy, so that others will weep with us." He swirled the remaining liquid in the glass and then, as he took up the decanter, again, stared long into my face. Then he looked away at the tiny window, as if he were seeing into another time, and his voice was low. "Two sisters, like white roses, blooming in a dark, unnatural place. I can still see your faces peeping from the window, pulling the curtain back, just so. I always imagined her high in the tower, reading romances, waiting for her prince." He sipped again from his glass and poured more for me, too. "Mademoiselle Pasquier," he said in a low voice, "I dreamed of being that prince, even though I was only the son of an upholsterer."

The strong brandy made my broken bones melt into his soft armchair. At last, I could feel the tears running down my face. He handed me his handkerchief and poured himself another drink.

"I wrote her . . . my dreams. Poetry. I schemed, I plotted, I wrote all night by the light of my only candle, to make myself great enough to be received in her home . . . your home . . ." Lamotte had poured himself several more drinks. He sat on the bed, amidst the rubble of discarded shirts, open books, and rumpled nightclothes, bent almost double, his head buried in his hands, speaking between sobs. "I was different then. I could have been anything for her, anything. And now . . . she hasn't even a tomb." He looked up at me, his face tear-stained. "Tell me, did she read my letters?"

What could I say? André, my sister was trained from birth to want more than you could offer? It was I who saved your notes from the fire? I would have given everything I had if one line of that poetry had been written for me. Which of us, André, was the greater fool? But crushed by his grief, and mine, I lied.

"She always kept them in her bosom, so she could read them over often."

"I knew it. The cynic was wrong. 'The heart of a lover has eyes to see the truth,' I told him, and he laughed. He told me I was a fool for not seeing reason, and I hated him for it. 'If I were choosing,' he said, 'I'd take the younger sister. She has the better mind and the faithful heart.' But he was wrong, and now I can forgive him utterly. He poisons his world with reason and has suffered terribly for it. I cannot resent him any more."

The cynic. He could only mean d'Urbec. Why did the thought of him bring with it a pang of guilty sadness, even here, when my heart was drunk with loss, with brandy, with the intimacy of hearing Lamotte's secrets? And yet even deeper in me was the long-suppressed voice of desire. Like a demon emerging from a subterranean cavern, it was battering its way out from some hidden place within, shaming me even as it made my mind crafty. I want him, it said. Not now, not at a time like this, I said to it. Betray her, it said. She's dead anyway. Get away from me, you disgusting thing, I answered it. I got up to pour myself more from the decanter on the little table. I could barely stand.

"Console me, Geneviève. I am as cold as if I were already in the tomb with her." Lamotte shivered violently as he reached up and grabbed my free hand, causing me to lose my balance and sending the glass crashing to the floor. He caught me as I fell towards him on the bed and set me on his lap, his arms around me. I put my head on his shoulder. I could feel him stroking my hair, as if consoling a child. His tears were damp on the back of my neck.

"Console me," he said. "Console me." His hand had moved down the front of my neck to my bosom. It felt warm, human.

"Not that way," I said in a faint voice, still battling the demon. Now his face was at my bosom; his rough cheek against the tender skin made me weak. The beautiful cavalier of the window. Mine. At the most terrible price in the world. I shivered.

"Feel my tears," he said, as the warm damp spread across my bosom. Some tiny something in the tone of his voice seemed to hint of the professional persuader. He's using you, I thought. But the demon said, have him. When else will you have a man like this?

"I ... I can't do this. For God's sake, stop. I can't bear getting pregnant. Not when I've seen—"

"So smooth, so white. Like cream." His hand had worked its way beneath my skirt. "Warm. Human. Alive."

"No," I said, But my leaping heart battered at my ribs. The demon, triumphant, flew free. My body shuddered with passion as his hand reached its goal.

"Beautiful," he mumbled as he laid me backward, and I felt his weight on me. "Don't fear anything ... in all this time ... since I lost her ... I've learned a thousand tricks ... to please the ladies. They run no risks with me. You needn't fear ... anything ..." The pins of my bodice had been scattered to the floor. My skirts and petticoats lay crumpled about me like a bank of multicoloured flowers. The fear dissolved in the heat of new joy. But even though his hands and lips roved everywhere, his eyes remained closed. And I knew, even as he entered the last stronghold, that he was trying to reassemble Marie-Angélique with his hands, his mind, his passion. His face, damp with tears and sunken with grief, was still beautiful.

"André," I whispered as the frenzy overtook us both.

"Angélique!" he cried, as he withdrew and the wasted seed stained the bedclothes. He had been as good as his word. He would not leave me pregnant. But it was my sister that he had possessed, not me. Even so, as I looked at his face, all relaxed and full of gratitude as he began to sink into sleep, I felt no regret at all, not a bit. The afterglow of warmth still coursed up and down my body. Uncle, I thought, you were wrong. The most beautiful man that ever haunted my dreams has wept with me, has begged for me, has fulfilled me, and is grateful to me. I was happy at that moment, terribly happy. Burn in hell, Uncle, my mind whispered softly. At this moment, André Lamotte is mine. No other moment matters. I don't care.

"André, André," I whispered. "Don't sleep. Your entertainment. The duchesse. You must be up." I shook him by the shoulder. His eyes flickered open.

"Oh, it's you. Geneviève." A long look passed between us. Both of us knew everything. "I am grateful. What can I do for you now? What can I give you, poor as I am, to repay you for saving what is left of me?"

"You can help me brush off this dress and put it on and summon a chair to take me home. Then you must be a monument of wit at your supper party tonight."

"Oh, my God, the entertainment! The duchesse!" he cried, as if the whole situation had suddenly sunk into his mind at last. I smoothed out Sylvie's bright Sunday petticoats.

"Surely, even she doesn't begrudge you a tumble with the servants on your day off. I'll go out by the back way, and no one will suspect that anything more than that has happened." He looked horrified.

"You . . . you think of everything. So self-possessed . . . it's unnatural. It reminds me of the way that blasted d'Urbec calculates. Always rational." Again, d'Urbec. Why did my insides twist so?

"André, I know it was Marie-Angélique you wanted. I lay no claims on you; I'll not embarrass you. Just remain my friend. That's all I ask." He looked at me, stricken. In that moment, his face looked old. There were circles under his eyes. The gay mustachios were limp. He sagged with the weight of good living that had encumbered him. The ponderous middle age of the idle was not far off.

"You have the honour and heart of a man," he said. "In a world of false, envious, malicious women and treacherous, smiling courtiers, I will treasure your friendship. D'Urbec was a wiser man than I. I go to dance attendance on a selfish rich woman . . . and you, I hope you find a man worthy of your heart, Geneviève."

Only a poet would wish such a silly thing, I thought as the bearers set me down before my own front door. Still, the moment of sentiment pleased me. And I had kept his handkerchief.

A morbid sadness clung about me like mist all that long autumn. Wherever I turned, I saw Marie-Angélique's face. I fled from the shops and fairs; the spending of money lost its pleasure. I'd see a display of lace, a silver brooch, a sumptuous length of brocade, and I'd think, before I could stop myself: My, wouldn't Marie-Angélique like that – I must tell her about it. Her ghost seemed to haunt the *galerie* of the Palais, the walkways of the gardens. I could see us again, two girls in springtime, pretending to admire the roses but admiring the elegant strollers more. "Look, Sister, do see that lovely bonnet; when I'm rich, I'll have one just like it. Oh! Do you suppose that dashing young officer with the crimson cloak is staring at me?" "When I'm rich, I'll have one just like him," I'd conclude her sentence in my sour little voice. "Oh, Geneviève," she'd say with a laugh, "you are so droll! Let's have one each!" And I could hear the echo of her laughter as I stumped along the rain-washed paths, searching among the dead leaves and empty pavilions as if I could find her hiding somewhere there.

I took to sleeping past noon; my servants turned away clients whispering that Madame was very ill. In the afternoons, I wandered aimlessly in the gardens of the Tuileries or the Palais-Royal. When I'd tired of walking, I took the carriage and drove mindlessly about the city or took the road to Versailles, only to return without accomplishing any business. Even the bird, my one consolation, moped on his perch on the tall stand that stood by the table in my upper room, his feathers puffed up, saying nothing and refusing bread crusts from my hand. Once, heavily veiled, I hired porters to carry me through my old neighbourhood. We went the length of the Rue des Marmousets, but I made them stop at so many places that they thought me mad, and I had to double their tip. Our house still looked the same, tall and dark, the little gargoyles crouched on either side of the ancient Gothic portals. I saw my brother at a distance, walking from the house towards the Palais de Justice with a portfolio under his arm. The porters set down the chair at the very place where Lamotte and his two friends had stood, and I looked up, half expecting to see the heavy curtains part and our two white faces peep from the corner of the dark window.

"Go by the Three Funnels, then double back past the Pomme de Pin," I said, "but don't stop there; I just want to see the open door." The door where I had first seen them, the three friends, young, full of hope, and laughing. One of the porters gestured towards his temple with a forefinger before picking up the shafts.

Then one day, after nearly two weeks had passed, the inevitable happened. Shortly before noon I felt myself being shaken awake. I looked up to see the witch of the Rue Beauregard towering above the bed like an evil dream, with Sylvie hovering guiltily in the background.

"Get up, get up, there's business to be done! Do you think I established you so that you could lie in bed all day? The King's attention wanders like a weathercock; every woman at court is running to have her fortune told. It's high tide, and you catch no fish!" I mumbled something, but that only set her off worse.

"It's the height of stupidity to mope about what can't be undone. Make money, buy her a monument, and get on with it. You have servants to pay, a household to run, and a debt to *me*! And as far as I'm concerned, if you've gone and rotted your brain out on that wretched opium elixir of La Trianon's so that you can't work any more, why, then, you might as well make an end of it, you little fool. Drink down the whole bottle, I say!" Sylvie, her eyes wide with horror, tried to grab the bottle, but La Voisin froze her with a single stare.

"My brain is not rotted, you – you witch! It's twice what anyone else's is, even if I drank a hundred bottles!" In a rage, I pulled myself up to sitting.

"As you probably already have—"

"I'll have you know, I'm tapering off! And at least I don't sit up every night drinking wine until I'm red in the face, singing filthy drinking songs with the executioner!"

"So now you're claiming opium is more genteel, eh? My lovers are my own choice; I've had comtes and vicomtes, I'll have you know. If a man pleases me, I take him. I am powerful enough to make my own choices. Whereas you are too cowardly to make yourself a duchess. But oh, I forget; you're an *aristocrat* . . . I suppose that's why you keep your sexual adventures in the family?"

"I'll kill you for that!" I shrieked, and leaped out of bed to attack her. She stepped back and pulled a vicious little knife from her sleeve.

"Ha! Come closer, sweetheart, and see who kills whom," she said, her black eyes commanding.

"I swear, I will."

"An entire waste of time," she announced calmly. "You'd do better to kill your uncle, who introduced your sister into the life she led for his pocket money and tried to destroy you to get his hands on what your father left you."

"How do you know about Uncle?"

"You forget, little ferret, that he's a client, too. I know all my client's secrets. But he paid badly. I don't miss him. Send him a charitable basket of my little pâtés in prison and be done with it." She put the knife back in her sleeve. It made an odd sound as it slid home in the hidden sheath. A businesslike sound. Damn, I thought, as my head cleared. Once more, I've just danced like a puppet on her string. She knew exactly how to get me up and working again. She must have planned it all, the confrontation, the quarrel, before she came. When will I learn not to be used by her?

"You . . . you're horrible . . ."

"And you are not?" she taunted, as she cocked her head to one side and put her hands on her hips. "But at least now you're out of bed. Sylvie, get her dressed – the grey silk – while I see if Nanon is finished in the kitchen." As I watched her vanish through the bedroom door, I felt totally annoyed. Damn her, anyway. Oh, damn again; I forgot she was already damned. Double damn, then.

A curious odour of burned cork was wafting upstairs. "Sylvie, what's that I smell . . . is it coffee?" A rustle of taffeta petticoats announced the return of the sorceress, and her voice answered from beyond the dressing screen.

"Turkish coffee. I've been much taken by it lately. I have brought Nanon along to brew you a potful. You are going to drink it. I may have a little myself. I am very fond of it."

"But . . . but isn't it expensive?" I asked. She had come behind the screen now to inspect the progress Sylvie had made with my stays and petticoats.

"Of course it is. But it makes the mind powerful. Yours is pretty much reduced to mush. I've used an entire quarter pound. Don't worry, I'll just add it to your bill." Sylvie was now engaged in hooking the dozens of buttons on my grey silk dress.

"My hair . . ." I said, clapping a hand to the disaster on my head.

"For now, just knot it in back, Sylvie," La Voisin commanded. "The lace cap is sufficient. The marquise does not need to go out today; she will be receiving callers at home . . ." The taffeta bustled officiously as she left us alone behind the screen to complete my toilette. I could hear a clatter as La Voisin's chambermaid, Nanon, set down a little tray on the table beyond the screen. I emerged to see two steaming pots, two white china cups, and La Voisin, who had just seated herself in my best armchair.

"You don't understand," I said as I seated myself opposite her. "My sister's dead . . ." Nanon poured hot milk and hot coffee together from the little pots with a practised hand. ". . . my beautiful sister. And she was killed by—"

"I know, I know. The Duc de Vivonne. Not the first, not the last. Don't imagine you can take vengeance on him – he's not only powerful, he knows too many people of the wrong sort." Odd words from La Voisin, considering she wasn't exactly the right sort herself.

The sorceress set her coffee cup back on the saucer with a clatter. The noise made the parrot poke his head out of his feathers. He made a soft noise, like *"Urk, urk, urk . . ."* He stretched out first one yellow foot, then the other. Then he tilted his head and peered at La Voisin with his ancient black eyes, and she returned the stare with black eyes that suddenly seemed just as ancient. "Drink, drink," said the bird. La Voisin looked amused, stood up suddenly, and flicked a few drops of coffee into the little water bowl at the end of his perch. The bird stretched out his green head and put his heavy orange beak into the water. The witch queen chuckled, "Leave Vivonne to his wife, my dear. She has been wanting her liberty for some time." I stared at the sorceress with new eyes. She smiled benignly and folded her hands across her stomach. I took another cup of coffee.

"So now," she announced briskly, "on to business. You'll find it's mightily restorative. The news at court is that the King is feeling old, now that he is nearly forty. He thinks a change of women will restore his vanished youth. Most men do at that age. So his attention wanders once again from La Montespan. Until now, she has maintained her hold by keeping his affairs within her household. But now her lady-in-waiting, La des

Oeillets, has come to bore His Majesty. No, no, she's nothing
– he hasn't even acknowledged his children by her."

"Hellfire and damnation!" announced the parrot, bobbing up
and down on his perch. The sorceress smiled approvingly at
him.

"So now he is fascinated by Madame la Princesse de
Soubise. Her family is poor; she repairs their fortunes with
the collusion of her husband. The prince goes out for the
night; she wears her emerald earrings to signal the King that
he will be gone. But lately the earrings have not been seen. It
is clear: either the King or the husband is tiring of the affair. So
the game begins afresh – you may expect a number of
consultations."

"You didn't read this in the cards."

"No, I didn't. But this afternoon Madame de Ludres will be
consulting you. Sylvie, who looks after both our interests,
took the precaution of accepting for you and notifying me. I
want you to tell me exactly what you see for Madame de
Ludres."

"In short, she is a leading contender and La Montespan is
consulting you."

"Good. Your brain is working again. The stars tell me
that this is a critical time, and there is an immense sum
of money to be made if we triumph. And if Madame de
Montespan comes to you, I must know her reading immediately. Now, admit this is amusing, and your mind is now
occupied fully with calculations."

"My mind is, but my heart isn't."

"Then discount the heart," she said, leaning forward and
depositing her empty cup on the saucer with a clatter. "It's
only excess baggage in today's world. Here. I will leave you
the two pots and the cups. Take my advice and take up coffee
drinking. Give up opium before it kills you. Only coffee is brain
food."

"Coffee! Coffee!" gurgled the bird, marching up and down
his perch with his big yellow claws. The sorceress flicked
another drop into his water dish.

"I suppose you've already added the crockery to my bill as
well?"

"Of course. What else? Goodbye. And remember, I want a

complete report this evening. I'll be expecting you after the theatre hour. I'm going to the Hôtel de Bourgogne tonight. While you've been mooning about, Lamotte has surprised us all with a new tragedy. Some Greek woman who stabs herself on a precipice overlooking the sea, they say. There wasn' t a dry eye when he read the last act at the Duchesse de Bouillon's salon. So she has hired a claque to support him, and I have taken a box to go incognito with the Vicomte de Cousserans, Coton, and a few other friends. The Comte d'Aulnoy, whose wife, they say, was once seduced by Lamotte, has hired a claque to shout down the play. It promises to be an amusing evening."

Lamotte. And he hadn't even invited me to a reading. Damn La Voisin, anyway. She certainly knew how to keep me irritated.

THIRTY-TWO

Madame de Ludres was not married but an unmarried demoiselle of the court, who had the title of "Madame" because she had taken religious vows as a canoness, which gave her a considerable income from a distant convent to spend on pleasure and amorous dalliance. The minute her arrogant little satin-shod feet crossed my threshold, I hated her. I hated the way her powdered little nose turned up; I hated the way she covered the spots on her complexion with tiny black velvet crescent *mouches*. I hated the footman who carried her train and the waiting woman who carried her little lapdog. Marie-Angélique's little finger was more beautiful than her entire body. For her ambition, my sister's bones were on display at the Collège Saint-Côme. Vivonne's *maîtresse en titre*; what a pretty and convenient step up for her. But it was only a footstool to poise her for the higher climb: to the supreme power of *maîtresse en titre* to His Majesty, the Sun King. I'll see you in hell first, I thought.

The reading was clear. I saw her at court in an antechamber I did not recognise. The courtiers rose to her as she entered the room. Though the women were in the glistening summer dress ordered by the King, I could tell by the way they shivered, and the heavy wool uniforms of the lackeys, that it was midwinter. In the shimmering reflection, Madame de Montespan, in her notorious "floating gown" of advanced pregnancy, raged soundlessly behind the wall of courtiers, whose gaze was fixed on the new favourite.

"You will not attain the supreme favour immediately," I said calmly. "Madame de Montespan has been reconciled with her august lover and will soon become pregnant by him. When the pregnancy is advanced, his fancy will stray again, and you will achieve the highest recognition."

"When?" she asked, her hard little eyes intense with avarice and ambition. I wished that I, too, had a garden of bones and that she were its chief occupant.

"It looks like midwinter," I answered. "Possibly the beginning of the New Year."

"And Mademoiselle de Thianges, what of her?"

"That will require another reading," I said in a bland voice. "It is very difficult to read for a person not present in the room. I require a double fee and can guarantee nothing." Grudgingly, she doled out the money. "Have you brought me anything that belongs to her?" I asked.

"I have bribed her maid for a rosette from her shoe," she said, producing a limp pink satin rosette. Clearly, she had heard of my methods. So what if I'd promised La Voisin to avoid these third-party readings? I consulted the oracle glass again, with great show, holding the rosette against the glass.

"Mademoiselle de Thianges is negligible. She will never enjoy more than passing favour and will soon be married off."

I was happy to be rid of the despicable little canoness and her entourage.

La Voisin was right. The next week was full of hopefuls, and of their mothers, their brothers, their fathers, and even husbands, all seeking information from the glass. For those who wished a more active form of intervention, I sent them to La Voisin for *poudres d'amour* and whatever else they thought might improve their chances. The witches of Paris did a ferocious business in wax manikins and spells in those weeks. Bold new hats and silk-lined mantles were in evidence on Sundays at Notre-Dame de Bonne Nouvelle, one could hear women's voices singing raucously from the back rooms of certain taverns in less savoury neighbourhoods, and the black market price of abandoned infants rose to two *écus*. Myself, I bought several curious old books I had long coveted and an Italian painting of Susanna and the Elders for my reception room, but I had not a moment left in the day to enjoy them. I felt as if I were in the very centre of a storm of greed, my work at the glass by far the most honest undertaking in a society hell-bent on sucking away the resources of the crown through the King's philanderings. Just as the storm would abate, some new piece of news would set it off. Now the Prince de Soubise was rumoured to be planning a new town residence built with the King's gifts to his wife, setting the court ablaze with envy. I glimpsed it once briefly, shining in the depths of the water vase, an immense palace in the heart of the city. Not bad payment for the uncomplaining loan of a wife for a few nights' adultery.

It was at the very height of this frenzy that I encountered d'Urbec again, purely by chance, in the public rooms of an inn on the way to Versailles. As usual, I made a tremendous stir as I alighted from my carriage and made my way through the crowded room to the fireplace. Only a group of card players, hard at it, did not look up. I had barely settled myself by the fire when one of the players, with a cry of despair, stood up and threw his hat on the ground.

"What will you have of me, Monsieur, the coat off my back?"

"Your note of hand is sufficient," said a familiar voice in cool, even tones. The transaction accomplished, d'Urbec stood and turned from the table around which the players were gathered.

"Good day, Madame de Morville. I regret that we have not met on the Cours-la-Reine after all," he said.

"He knows the fortune-teller . . . yes, that is his secret . . . the Devil assists him . . ." the room was abuzz.

"My condolences on the death of your si— ah, Marie-Angélique," he said. He must have seen Lamotte, then. Did he know everything? He must. Yet even so, he hadn't betrayed my identity. Why did seeing him again disturb me so?

"I tried, but I couldn't save her," I said, trying to hide my discomfort.

"People often cannot be saved from themselves," he answered, and turned on his heel, leaving without another word. Cut dead, I thought, and looked into the fire so that no one could see my eyes.

"To what do I owe this honour, Madame?" Once again, La Voisin had invaded my house. The sorceress handed her wet cloak to Sylvie to dry before the fire and then seated herself in my best armchair to warm her red boots on my hearth. It must be important, I thought, to bring her out in this weather.

"Do you still see Monsieur d'Urbec?" she asked abruptly.

"No, Madame," I answered, still trying to anticipate what

she was doing here. She disliked d'Urbec and knew that I knew it.

"Well, I wish you to take up his acquaintance again," she announced, her face firm.

"Madame, I cannot. I believe he hates me."

"After you saved his life and fed his relatives into the bargain? I hope you are not deceiving me."

"About what, Madame?" I must have looked innocent of whatever plot she suspected me of. Her face relaxed.

"Little Marquise, that no-account *galérien* is everywhere these days. I've made inquiries, but whatever he is up to, he's kept it well hidden. All I know is that he bought a vial of quick-acting poison from La Trianon and that he has travelled twice to Le Havre. But what is more important, he wins at cards as if he had made a pact with the Devil himself. I have had nearly a dozen clients come to me for the 'secret of d'Urbec'. What is this secret? As far as I know, he has bought no glory hand. He has visited no one I know to have a spell cast. I believe he may have developed a new way of marking the deck. Either that or he has purchased some secret abroad. I must have that secret, little Marquise, if I am to keep my reputation long in this town. I want you to get it for me."

"Madame, the man will not speak to me. He cut me in public the last time we met."

"I think, perhaps, you still do not appreciate my powers. The man confides in no one. That means he is lonely. I will cause him to fall in love with you. He will be able to deny you nothing. Not even his secret of the cards. Tell me, do you have anything he left in the house, anything he used? I will need that, and a lock of your hair." The memory of d'Urbec's public insult made up my mind for me. I'll get back at him, I thought. With La Voisin's sorcery, I'll flaunt Lamotte in his face. That will show him.

"I think I do— Sylvie, go upstairs and get the handkerchief that is folded in my dressing-table drawer." Sylvie returned with Lamotte's handkerchief, all folded and perfumed.

"A handkerchief? My goodness, fussy manners for a *galérien*," she said, turning it over and inspecting it. Fortunately, it had no monogram.

"Well, he was a law student before . . ." I said.

"Then that accounts for it," she said, as she wrapped the lock Sylvie had cut off in the handkerchief and rose to depart. As she left with Lamotte's handkerchief, I felt as if I should begin a new notebook. *Trial No. 1: Can La Voisin's sorcery make Lamotte love me back? We shall see.*

"That ragbag! That piece of garbage! How dare she think she can threaten me!" La Montespan's shrieks of rage could be heard even through the half-opened doors of her vast twenty-room apartment on the ground floor at Versailles. I had cleared my schedule and travelled at full speed in her own heavy carriage over icy roads to wait like a lackey while she gave vent to her spleen. Oh well, I thought, better outside the room than inside it, as I heard a piece of china crash against the wall. I peered in to watch her pace the length of the blue-and-gold Savonnerie carpet like a tigress, kicking her train out of the way as she doubled back to advance towards the window. "I swear, she'll never have him," she shouted, raising her fist to the window. "Never!" Even the glass panes seemed to shudder at her wrath. Her stays looked looser to me. Her latest pregnancy was beginning to show. The brief reconciliation was over, and the King was on the prowl once more. "I'll not lose everything for that mealy-faced, conniving, simpering canoness!"

"Madame, the fortune-teller," one of her ladies announced tentatively, afraid to approach her. She turned suddenly.

"Oh, it's you! The black-clad doomsayer." Her face was distorted with rage and, beneath it, fear. "Why do I always turn to you, eh? Because you tell me the truth. The others, they all lie. It's truth I need now, to lay my plans." She seemed suddenly quiet and menacing. She advanced midway across the room and addressed her waiting lackey. "Bring a stool and water for the Marquise de Morville. Then clear the room. I want to be alone with my grief." Her maids fled as leaves blow before a storm, leaving the room silent. The light from the window caught on the immense table of solid silver that stood, flanked by elaborately cast silver chairs, in the centre of the carpet. A sculptured table clock, its face supported by nymphs, ticked slowly as I unrolled my cabbalistic cloth beside it. A servant brought a gilded stool with a blue-and-silver tapestry cushion to the table, as another filled my water glass from a silver pitcher with a long spout. Noiselessly, they retreated, sealing the great double doors behind them, and I sat to read the water.

"Madame has the honour to be expecting His Majesty's child," I said quietly, so the ears pressed to the closed door would not overhear.

"Yes, yes, of course. That's no miracle of prediction. That's when he strays, as every cur at court knows. I give him my maids, I give him my nieces, but now even that is not enough for his endless appetite. He wounds me. He destroys me." I wondered if she had already turned to the Rue Beauregard for a method of removing the canoness.

"No interpretation," she ordered. "Just what you see. I must know. I will not fail. If he is not mine, he will be nobody's. That I swear. How many years have I put up with his stinking body in the bed? I am owed, owed, I tell you. He'll not lock me away when he's done with me. I can play as deep a game as he does." She drew up one of the silver chairs and seated herself among its brocade cushions. I could hear her breathing heavily, and I saw as I glanced away from the glass that her hands were shaking.

"I see Madame de Ludres entering the *appartement*. She is in midnight blue velvet and is wearing a heavy diamond necklace with matching bracelets—"

"My necklace, damn him. I am the one who should have that necklace."

"The court rises—"

"Damn! Damn! The diabolical little bitch. What spell did she use to attain the supreme favour? I'll undo it. I'll finish her."

The King's mistress leaned forward in the silver chair and spoke low, her voice quiet and threatening. "Tell me, is she the one? Look again. Is she the one who steals my just reward, the position of duchess?"

I stirred the water again. The glass bowl glinted with the reflections from the gold ribbon on Madame de Montespan's gown as she leaned forward in her armchair, trying to peer into the depths. Beyond the closed double doors I could hear the rustle of clothing and the muffled thump of shifting feet. But Madame de Montespan was oblivious. Her strange aquamarine eyes glittered in her haggard face, bloated with the first signs of pregnancy.

"You are smiling. What do you see?" she whispered.

"Madame, something that will please you. Madame de Ludres is entering a convent ... I can't tell which. She is before the altar, and they are clipping her hair." Madame de Montespan laughed out loud and pressed her hand to her heart.

"Then mine is the triumph," she said happily.

"It would appear so, Madame."

"You appear rather pleased yourself. Tell me, have you found the little canoness offensive?"

"Madame de Ludres is not celebrated for her graciousness."

Madame de Montespan stood, whirling about almost like a girl. "Your news has made me young again, Madame," she cried. She ran to the tall mirror that hung opposite the window and peered closely at her face. "Ah! I look younger already! Look! The lines are fading!" She stood back and turned before the mirror, twisting her hips sideways to create the greatest illusion of slenderness.

"Oh! If only I didn't grow so stout!" Madame de Montespan smoothed down her dress to make her waist look narrower. "He told me I was growing too heavy. 'Thick legs are so unattractive,' he said. Imagine how it stung me to the heart! Six living children I've borne him, and my waist as slender as ever, and he says my legs are thick! His stomach is not exactly slender, either, you know. And it's begun to droop like an old woman's breasts. A convent! Her! You'll never find *me* locked in a convent, I tell you." She turned from the crimson-stained mirror. "Open the doors, Madame. Let the air in again! I'll send for my masseuse. By the time the child is born, my legs will have regained their youth, just as my face has today!"

Servants and attendants poured in through the open doors with a suspicious rapidity. The anxiety on their faces shifted almost in an instant when they saw their mistress's merriment. I left richly rewarded and with the promise of a thousand favours when the fall of Madame de Ludres should come to pass. But best of all, I thought, as I sat listening to the crunch and rattle of the carriage and the steady beat of hoofs on the frosty road, I can bear any slight from Madame de Ludres now. It would be a pleasant amusement to observe over the coming months exactly how her fall would be engineered by the vicious souls at court. This time, little satin slippers, you have stepped into a game too deep for you. I wished I could tell Marie-Angélique.

It was hardly a week later when a boy left a note at the door that nearly stopped my breath.

"Mademoiselle," it said, "I no longer sleep at night for the dreams that haunt me. Again and again I relive that sweet moment of sympathy we shared. I must see you again at any cost. André."

"Tell him yes," I said to the boy. And before the day was done, Sylvie had come from the front door with his answer.

"Meet me masked in the pavilion of the Tuileries garden tomorrow at three o'clock. I will wear a military cloak with gold braid facings. A."

"Surely Madame will not go alone?" said Sylvie, all aflutter at the thought of seeing Lamotte again herself.

"Of course not. Suppose it's a trap? Not everyone loves me in this city, you know. I'll have you with me, and Mustapha can hover invisibly about. He's something of a specialist at hovering."

"He hovers like the dragonfly, blends like a shadow, and stings like the serpent," observed Mustapha about himself cheerfully. "I think I'll dress as an apprentice boy— Devil take it! That means I'll have to shave tomorrow morning. It's a good thing I'm such an artist about my work."

"I am always grateful for your artistry, Mustapha," I answered as I sat for Sylvie to undo my combs and brush my hair. Outside, I was as cool as ice, but my heart was pounding. I was haunting Lamotte's dreams. Had La Voisin done it, or was it truly because he had discovered love in our moment of shared grief? The charming cavalier, mine at last. A bit the worse for wear, but still well worth having. The miracle had happened. It was me, me he wanted, though surrounded by all those aristocratic beauties. After so long, so very long. We would talk. We would remember Marie-Angélique together. And then he would tell me that it was me he had loved all along but hadn't even known it himself. After all, what are blonde curls compared to a serious mind and a warm, womanly sympathy?

I found it hard to sleep that night, and the next day it took me an eternity to select my clothes. I paused for a long time before the rose satin, still virginal new in its muslin shroud. But it was not the gown for a damp garden in fall. He'll ask me someplace elegant later on, and I'll dazzle him in it. But for today, something warm, friendly, serious-looking. A colour. Oh, why do I have so much black? I need young dresses, pretty things with flowers on them, I thought as I pawed frantically through the armoire, checking and rechecking each dress while Sylvie tapped her foot impatiently. At last I settled on the dark green wool with the black ribbon trim and added a costly white lace fichu to give it a younger look. My sombre grey cloak, an anonymous-looking plain, wide-brimmed hat, and a black velvet mask completed the picture.

"Your walking stick, Madame?" Gilles was already holding open the door of the carriage when Sylvie came racing out with my tall, silver-headed stick.

"I'm not taking it, Sylvie."

"But . . . you'll limp more. With the stick, one can scarcely see the limp."

"With the stick, I look like the Marquise de Morville, Sylvie. We're going early, so that I'll be seated in the pavilion waiting to meet him."

The previous night's rain had wet the gravel paths of the gardens and left dead leaves strewn in soggy clumps beneath the still-dripping trees. But as I was assisted from my carriage at the gates, the grey clouds parted to show the blue sky, and the sudden light reflected from the dozens of little puddles on the ground, converting them instantly to dazzling fragments of silver. A sign, I thought. After all these trials, I am meant to be happy.

Lamotte was late. When I heard his footsteps, I sent my servants away from the little pavilion hidden among the trees.

"Mademoiselle, a thousand pardons," Lamotte swept off his scarlet plumed hat in greeting. My face felt hot beneath my mask.

"I was delayed by the duchesse. Such errands, such foolish tasks she has for me! And yet my career prospers; I am fortunate in my patronage. Who can create without patronage? The fine fever of the mind ... does not thrive on bread and cabbage—" He broke off and looked a long time at me. "I dream of you at night. That day, that terrible day ... and you ... haunt me."

"I ... I have thought of it myself." Where was my self-possession, my wit? I was dissolving into a total idiot. He sat down beside me on the marble bench.

"Everything is pale since that day. The insincerity and shallowness of my world are everywhere apparent. For one moment, I thought, I have shared truth." The words I'd always dreamed of hearing. I tried to answer, but nothing came out of my mouth. "You must have felt it, the perfection of that moment," his voice resonated like a hero in the theatre. "Sincerity, that is what I have been lacking, I told myself. In all the world there is only one woman with sincerity, and that is why I am haunted by the memory of that moment of mad, exquisite passion." He moved closer. I could feel his warm breath on my neck.

It is not sincerity, whispered my cynical mind, all tight and clever with too much Turkish coffee, it is something else entirely. Don't believe him. But my heart, all swollen with the frenzy to think that I was at last beautiful and beloved, told my mind to be quiet.

"Don't you feel it?" he asked, his arm slipping around my waist. "Two hearts that were meant to beat as one?" He took my hand and pressed it against his heart beneath his heavy cloak. My bones went limp when I felt the beating of his heart. "That moment of tenderness – I must, we must, repeat it."

"Not now, not here. It's indecent," I managed to croak out.

"Indecent? This pavilion could whisper a thousand secrets if it could speak. Where there is love, there is no indecency."

"Please, André, I don't dare ..." I wanted to push him away, but I hadn't the strength. Was this the kind of love that witchcraft had brought me? Hollow words and selfish passion? And yet still I wanted it. His touch thrilled me; it made me feel beautiful. Was this part of La Voisin's ghastly spell, or was it me, made stupid by a child's silly passion clutched too long?

"You will join me tonight," he murmured, as his hands made my body weak. "Dismiss your carriage and servants and we will go to a quiet little auberge I know of on the road to Versailles."

"I . . . I can't," I whispered. A kiss, and then another. My will was paralysed. "Oh yes," I said, almost faint. But even as my mouth was agreeing, my mind was crying, say no, you idiot. Don't let him. You'll get pregnant and die. Never mind, let it be, rejoiced my heart; he wants you, the handsomest man in the whole world. Who cares why? A disaster, whispered my mind. You'll lose your living and die in the gutters behind the Hôtel-Dieu. But he loves you, cried my stupid, exulting heart. He must love you. What else matters? Fool, fool, sighed my brain, as I let him take my arm to escort me to his carriage.

The candles were burning low over the remains of a little supper in the tiny room under the eaves. Through the open window, we could hear nothing but the sound of crickets in the dark.

"Mademoiselle, such perfection of love is rarely achieved," he announced, buttoning up his baggy wool breeches. Somehow, the gesture suddenly looked too professional to me. "I thought I might never find happiness such as this again," he said in his warm baritone as he tucked in his shirt with a practised gesture. "My love, my gratitude, are immeasurable." What was it in the tone of his voice? Now that the heart was sated, the mind was running things again. Listen to him, said the mind. He was using you. He'll walk off, now. Aren't you sorry?

"Will we . . . meet again?" I asked in a small voice.

"My dear, my precious thing, I intend to sweep you off your feet. My muse is at your service." Why did it suddenly sound so false to me? He had never sounded false long ago, before the Maison des Marmousets. Fancy, yes; false, no. But then he smiled his charming smile at me, and I felt all doubts vanish. He loved me. He was just afraid to say so. At least for now, he was the duchesse's creature. But his heart was mine.

"My heart is yours, and yours alone," he said, almost as if he could read my thoughts. "My patroness is a powerful woman, though. We must be careful, circumspect. When we meet in public, as we surely will, you must pretend not to know me."

"I know . . . André," I hesitated at the name. The dear name I'd so often dreamed of saying under exactly these circumstances. "I understand."

"Ah, you are a treasure. The philosopher was right on that point, and wrong on the rest." The philosopher? D'Urbec. Always d'Urbec. Even *in absentia* he had a way of coming in where he wasn't wanted.

"The philosopher?" I asked, as if I hadn't guessed.

"The sincere woman is best, he always said. But he never understood that passion is more important than the meeting of minds, for a woman."

For a woman? I was beginning to be angry. "And not for men?" I asked.

"Oh, yes . . . of course for men," he said, with a condescending smile, as if he didn't quite mean it.

"I thought you two were friends."

"Of course. D'Urbec and I are the best of friends. Old chums from school days, even if he did insist on rating his brain above mine."

"D'Urbec rates his brain above everyone's," I answered.

"Ha! That he does. But what annoys is when he twits people about it. That satire he wrote on the suicide scene in my *Osmin* . . . ah, it's a bother, sometimes, knowing a *libelliste* . . . but still, a friend is a friend . . ."

"Satire? You mean that bit in the—"

"The *Parnasse Satyrique*, damn him, as if I didn't know who had written the wretched thing the minute I laid eyes on it. There's no mistaking his style. I know the lion by his claw. Of course, I'd never betray him. But it's all over town. An underground classic, ever since it was banned by the police. Why, the Bishop of Nantes had to pay thirty-five livres for it. The minute he showed it to me, I knew. Everywhere I go, people quote the damned thing at me, and I have to pretend to laugh." Lamotte stood up suddenly from the bench and began to storm, back and forth. His fists were clenched, the veins in his temples stood out. "Can you imagine? He's gone nowhere! He's accomplished nothing! And yet he *dared* to mock my creation! Does he think I have to accept an insult like that?"

Suddenly he turned back and looked at me sitting there, and his face softened.

". . . Ah, but enough. I am a new man now. You have renewed me, inspired me. My next masterpiece, far greater than my *Osmin*, more exquisite than my *Sapho*, will be drawn from life. *Théodora* – and you shall be the model for the heroine. You, and only you, O divine inspirer of passions." I could feel myself blushing with pleasure. I didn't care if I were pregnant. I'd manage somehow. Me, an inspiration for the poet's muse! I could hardly breathe for joy. But even as my heart expanded, the mean little voice in my brain said, Well, well. He thought d'Urbec was in love with you, that he had claims on you, when he saw him there in your house. So now he's just using you to get back at d'Urbec. Witchcraft, indeed! All that spell stuff with the handkerchief didn't do anything except make you silly! Aren't you ashamed to be caught this easily? And on a mistake, too. Lamotte doesn't know you've quarrelled with d'Urbec, and he doesn't even like you any more. Never mind, glowed my heart. Before Lamotte finds out, I'll win him over truly. And meanwhile, his *amour* will be flaunted all over the city; the gossip about the secret inspirer of his work will penetrate every *ruelle*. His masterpiece will be mine. Just think, me – a reigning beauty, the inspirer of the Muses, the envy and admiration of the salons of Paris. My brain tried to say, Do you think he doesn't know that would be a plain girl's dream? How many other women does he say exactly the same thing to? But my heart drowned out the voices in my head. It always was a rather noisy and stupid organ.

The rest of the autumn passed by in the shimmering light of romance. The shifting grey clouds, the damp chill of the wind blowing the dead leaves in swirls down the gutters, the melancholy dripping from high slate roofs – all was infinitely exquisite to me, now that I was a poetical inspiration. How pleased I was with myself as I leaned out of the upstairs window watching for him, or sat by the fire reading Horace and waiting for a message from the handsomest man in Paris. I didn't see him much. He snatched only a moment or two from his duties, his patroness, his writing, his necessary attendance at this or that salon. Sometimes our paths crossed at a dinner or a reading in some aristocrat's hôtel.

Then we'd pretend we didn't know each other, and I would hug to me every overheard word: "My dear, that's the Chevalier de la Motte . . . Isn't he good-looking? They say he's creating a masterpiece to rival his *Sapho*. *Officially*, of course, it's dedicated to the *duchesse*, but I hear that there's a woman he's secretly enamoured of who serves as the model—"

"Do you know who?"

"No, she's very mysterious, though some say she might be Ninon de Lenclos."

"Ninon? She's much too old, I think. The woman who inspires him is said to be a great beauty."

Music could not have sounded more lovely to me.

Once he came secretly at midnight to my little house on the Rue Charlot and by the light of candles declaimed his latest verses, the tragic empress's *tirade* in stately alexandrines. The wineglasses winked and shone in the candlelight as he assumed a stately pose and his resonant baritone lovingly caressed the lines.

"Why, That's inspired! Your gift rivals Racine's – puts the great Corneille in the shade." The truth was, his work seemed on occasion a bit pedestrian, but because it was about me, it acquired infinite charm. I couldn't have enough of it. When my monthly came and went without skipping a day, I felt quite disappointed. I'd decided a baby would be very nice to have, even if it did cut into business. Besides, it might keep him at my fireside longer, reading poetry for ever.

"'Rivals Racine's'? Why, I am much better than Racine. He creates a thousand enemies with his pen – besides, I sense a certain coarseness in his portrayal of people of aristocratic breeding. The scene where Alexander comes from the stables after feeding his horses, for example. No gentleman would ever feed his own horses. It reeks of the bourgeois – totally lacking in refinement."

"Dear André, what would you think of a child of our love?"

"Wha—? A child? You're not pregnant, are you? For God's sake—"

"Not yet . . . but suppose I were?"

"Oh, you're not?" He looked relieved and took his

handkerchief out of his sleeve to mop his brow. At the time, I was touched by his concern.

"Madame, you are looking entirely too rosy these days." Sylvie's voice was disappointed and curt. She had been very snippy lately. "I've sent to La Trianon for a heavier white make-up."

"The one she sells to women who've had the smallpox? It's like plaster!" I laughed.

"Laugh away, but if you don't look like a corpse you'll lose half your income, and Madame will want to know why. Oh, Mustapha, who is at the door now? I hope it's a client and not another tradesman with a bill."

"This time, a client. A servant girl with a request that Madame de Morville pay a house visit. Tomorrow, in the afternoon, when the man of the house is out."

"And the house?"

"On the Rue des Marmousets on the Ile de la Cité. The Maison des Marmousets." It had come. At last.

"Who is the woman, Mustapha? I do not know this house."

"Oh, I do, Madame," broke in Sylvie. "She used to be a good customer of Madame Montvoisin, but now she's ill and housebound. She's especially taken by astrology. The widow Pasquier. Surely, you must have heard of her. She was once fashionable, though never of the court."

"I think I might have heard that name before." Yes, indeed. Mother. Betrayer of daughters, husband poisoner. Monster. "Tell the servant I will be there promptly at two in the afternoon tomorrow." Yes, I will be there, I thought. With the very stuff with which you stole my father's life away. Justice. Justice and damn the costs.

THIRTY-THREE

Heavily veiled, I was shown in from the carriage entrance in the courtyard by a subdued Suzette, Mother's maid, who seemed to have grown, in only two years, much older and more sombre. The house looked so much smaller than I remembered it. It seemed dank and old to me now, a house that hid dreadful secrets. I could never imagine the laughter of children in these cold, airless rooms. Could Marie-Angélique have ever stood there at the window, her golden hair shining in the spring light, blushing and giggling at some pretty young man with a guitar in the street beneath?

"Madame is indisposed; her son is out today. She has heard that you have made wonderful predictions for the Comtesse du Roure and the Duchesse de Bouillon. She has had a difficult life lately, a strange illness that comes and goes. Even the visits of the physician and the priest bring no relief. Only astrologers and chiromancers give her peace of mind now." Suzette's voice was bleak and tired.

As we climbed the stairs to Grandmother's room, a wave of the old fear passed through me. Although Suzette hadn't recognised me, I feared Mother's sharp eyes. The case with my glass, rod, scarf, and the tiny green glass vial seemed to become suddenly very heavy. My heart pounded beneath the heavy black gown of the Marquise de Morville.

"Is that you, Suzette? Have you brought the *devineresse?*" I scarcely recognised the woman who sat on the bed, staring out of the window. In the time since I had last seen her, she had crossed from well-preserved middle age to blowsy decay. Something – a disease of the body or soul – had eaten away her former beauty. Mother's body and features had swollen strangely; her once-ivory complexion had grown sallow and greasy. She turned her head towards us when we entered. Her eyes, watery and distended, sat above drooping swellings. They looked in our direction, those lost, rolling eyes, but not at us. The eyes of an insane woman, I thought – the eyes of someone nearly blind.

"Madame does not see well; you will have to go closer."

"I see very well, Suzette. I see the light at the window. Show the *devineresse* in."

The room was cluttered and dusty. Grandmother's things had never been moved out, and Mother's had been moved in: a second armoire was crammed in beside the first; the doors had burst open with the burden of old clothes that had been stuffed inside it. Another dressing table crowded with porcelain jars, bottles, and little boxes was pushed against a wall; and a little cabinet from father's study had been shoved into a corner, its shelves laden with trinkets, porcelain figures, and a half-dozen dusty books. The sickly sweet smell of illness filled the room and hung from the dusty old bed curtains. The blood-red walls had grown brownish, and the gilt pattern stencilled across them had faded to a blackish grey. I found it hard to imagine that Grandmother, with her neat little cap and her linens that smelled of lavender, could ever have lain in that sagging, filthy old bed.

"Sit down over there – not the armchair, the stool," the cracked voice said. One thing about Mother was still unchanged: her snobbery. I took the armchair.

"I did not hear you move the stool," the voice said suspiciously.

"Madame, I am the Marquise de Morville; I have taken the armchair."

"Morville? I have not heard of that family. By blood or marriage?"

"By marriage. I am, however, a widow."

"Only a widow? What was your maiden name?" I recited the false genealogy prepared by Monsieur Bouchet. I had become, through my experience at court, an expert in battles of precedence.

"I am a Matignon by birth. A great family among the *noblesse d'épée*."

"I, however, hold a title. Also *noblesse d'épée*. Your armchair is most comfortable and well appointed."

"My dear Marquise, it is such a pleasure to hold a conversation with a woman of rank once more. So much

greater delicacy of sentiment can be expressed by those of
gentle birth." She tilted her head and rolled her eyes sideways
in a mockery of her old flirtatious gesture. Her silver
"company" laugh, now cracked and tarnished, clattered
through the room.

"I believe you wished to consult with me about the gifts that
fate has in store . . ."

"Oh. Oh, yes. That's it." She looked confused. "You read
the future in cards, do you not?"

"No, Madame Pasquier. God has granted me the gift of
seeing images in water."

"Suzette, leave us now," ordered Mother, as she smiled a
nervous half smile of anticipation. Her eyes shifted conspiratorially, and she ran her tongue around her lips. Just as
well. Suzette might recognise my voice if she were there any
longer.

"I was not always as you see me now," said Mother,
". . . this old gown, these reduced circumstances." She ran her
hand across her ravaged cheek. "See how white my skin is? I
was always a beauty. I might have been a duchess. A gypsy
woman read it in the cards for me. But before my good fortune
came, my parents arranged a match with a man of no rank, for
money. This dreadful house" – she gestured scornfully around
her – "I brought it light, culture, style. One does what one can,
even with a nobody. Tell me, is that your glass you are putting
on the dressing table?"

"Yes. I have several things to prepare. Can you see them
here?"

"Oh, yes. I see very well. Light and shadow. I see you as a
dark silhouette. There's a glint of light from your glass. But I
can't distinguish small things any more. Like letters. Do you
know what my son did? Shut me up here with a lot of books.
Prayer books. 'You little bastard! You know I can't read a
word!' 'Then pray for the edification of your soul, Madame,' he
said. But I fixed him. Oh yes, I did. 'Uphold the honour of the
Pasquiers,' he said, '. . . an important juridical family,' he said.
'And just because your name is Étienne Pasquier, what makes
you think you were got by that fool husband of mine?' said I.
'You're made of better blood than that. Act like what you are.
Put on a sword and go and gain favour at court.' Ah, he was

shaken. But now, now he's worse than ever. He won't even let me meet his fiancée. But *I* know, *I* know what he's saying." Mother looked sly. Her head turned towards the door as if she were listening.

"He says I'm mad," she whispered. "Mad. His own mother. Can you imagine? Ungrateful monster. I should have strangled him in the cradle."

"Many things are regretted in hindsight, Madame."

"Your voice sounds familiar. Marie-Angélique, have you brought me money? I'm sadly lacking in money. Now that I've established you so well, you should think of me."

"Your fortune, Madame. I have come to give you a reading."

"Oh, yes. The Chevalier de la Rivière is coming for me. How much longer must I wait? He swore he would marry me once I was a widow. Tell me, is that he I hear in the street? Is that his carriage? I need to refresh my complexion, I want to be at my best. He is coming with a carriage and six. I sit in the window every day and watch. If I only knew the day! Tell me – you fortune-tellers always have a little something – have you brought me something? Something to set off my beauty? He always said he loved me in yellow silk. But now I need something, something..."

It was now. I could give her the little vial. Drink it for a youthful complexion. Your eyes will sparkle. My father lay in his grave because she had planned to marry her lover. It's fair, Geneviève, it's justice. Give her the vial. The vacant, mad eyes searched my face. Her lip trembled expectantly.

"I only read fortunes, Madame. You must send to someone else for beauty aids. There is an excellent *parfumier* on the Pont Notre-Dame."

"It is fortunate I still retain my beauty after all my sufferings. But he is surely coming. I have waited here at the window a very long time, you know. He'll be here shortly now. That's what he said. Just a bit of time to wind up his affairs in Poitiers. That's not far. Oh, yes, it's an excellent fortune you've told." Her confused mind seemed to think she had already heard her fortune. Just what did she imagine it was? Your lover is coming to take you away at last. How clever it was of you to poison a nobody husband for a somebody lover. She looked around slyly, as if evading some invisible watcher, then rose and went to the corner, bumping into the stool on her way. "You know," she whispered, "my son doesn't give me any money. I've already spent enough, he says. But when did I ever spend anything that wasn't for the good of this house? Money. Oh, yes, money. I can't offer you anything. I'm poor now, so poor. Ah, it is the lot of women to be poor. I cashed my annuity. What sacrifices I made for him – all in secret, all in secret. But I had to, you see. Étienne is such a naughty boy! I'll tell La Reynie he's a bad boy. La Reynie knows who's good and bad. The old lady wrote to him. Wicked old thing – but she won't write any more. See these books? You'll have to take them instead of money. They're very valuable, I'm sure. I can't read them anyway. Read and pray, he said. What does he know? A dried-up little stick at twenty – maybe he is his father's after all. Prig! What does he know of how things are done at court. *We* know – don't we, Marquise?"

"We certainly do." I had covered my glass. I had no desire to see what was in it.

"Those are the books. Can you reach them?" She put her hand out towards the cabinet shelf, and a china cupid crashed to the floor. "Yes, I have them. Here. There are six of them." They made my heart freeze. Grandmother's Bible. A theological tract called *La mystique cité de Dieu*. Three odd volumes from father's library, all bound in identical calfskin with gold tooling: Aristotle's *Ethics*. Seneca. Descartes. And my Petronius. An odd set of books for a blind woman locked up to meditate upon. They smelled of dust and mildew. I put them in my satchel, along with my glass.

"It is me the chevalier is coming for, not Marie-Angélique," announced Mother. "I am still a beautiful woman, don't you think?" She glanced coquettishly from the corners of her ruined eyes. The whites shone yellowish, the watery colour of a frog's belly. An old gesture, once charming, now terrifying.

"Yes, of course."

"Of course. Yes, you're right. Marie-Angélique's hair is not the colour of mine. Pure gold. And blue eyes are much more common than green. But she's younger, you know. Men of rank like them younger. But then they see me and are dazzled. But my husband punished me, you know. He complained of having them in the house." I felt I was smothering. I had to escape. But she grabbed my sleeve and whispered confidentially in my ear. "That is how these little bourgeois husbands are. 'No matter how you dress a monkey in silk, he's still a monkey – and *you* are still a bourgeois,' I told him. And then he went and gave the ugly little one everything in revenge. Revenge, I say. How did he know she was the only one that was his? The Devil must have told him. He gave her everything. Bastard. But she was dead, so it didn't do him any good. They read the will, and I laughed. 'To my daughter Geneviève,' he said, and I laughed. The lawyers tell me a man cannot leave anything to his wife, only to his children. Ha! Nothing to nobody. A joke, a joke, Madame. The hand from the grave – foiled." She laughed uproariously. Then she lowered her voice conspiratorially. "So the lawyers got it all for my son. And what has he done? Ungrateful." She shook her head. "Ungrateful." Her wandering mind horrified me. She was insane.

Shifting images of my childhood formed in my mind, like the pictures in the oracle glass. Mother's strange glances, her curious cruelties, the theft and sale of little things, the attempts to purchase the notice of persons of rank. Then the calculated poisonings, at the hospital, in the family, without remorse. Could the worm of insanity have begun eating out her mind long ago? Perhaps Father had always known. Perhaps that is why he did nothing. Father. Dead at her hand. Waves of nausea and hatred washed over me. I started to shake uncontrollably.

"I must go now, Madame," I said, with every ounce of control that was in me. The old woman bumped about the room again, feeling for something. She was blocking the door.

"You *have* come. I know your voice well. Marie-Angélique, have you brought the money?" She felt her way about the room, towards the sound of my voice, whimpering.

I turned back. "Yes, Mother, I've brought the money." I turned out the contents of my purse and pressed them into the yellow-stained, cracked palm. Five louis d'or. She felt them carefully and held them up to the light from the window.

"What's this? Only five louis? Marie-Angélique, I found you a wealthy lover; I have made you rich. You are a wicked ungrateful daughter. You were a good girl once. Where is your gratitude? You are a wicked, wicked girl to bring your mother only five louis! After all she's done for you . . . ah, it's fortunate that I am still beautiful. I'll make my own way without you . . ."

I fled to the waiting carriage. On the Pont-Neuf, I had the coachman halt. Shaking all over, I pressed between a sweet seller and a beggar woman to the bridge rail and flung the vial of poison into the rushing green waters of the Seine.

I stood there watching the swirling waters long after the bottle had disappeared. In the midst of a crowd of beggars and vendors, a psalm singer loudly proclaimed the Lord's way before a display of holy pictures. There was a clink as someone dropped a coin into his cup. The shouts of the bearers and coachmen crowding past seemed to fade and I stood as if in utter solitude, imagining the progress of the little green vial to the river's bottom. Had I done right? What was Right, anyway, or Justice? How much does Revenge weigh against Pity in the scales of logic? Monsieur Descartes, you have given me no answers.

"Madame, it is a crime to jump, and a waste to merely stand still in the cold. Send away your carriage, and I will see you home." I turned. A man in a crimson wool coat cut in the new style and a heavy mantle faced with gold embroidery stood behind me, studying me. Beneath a blazingly new plumed hat, a dark wig fell to his shoulders. Familiar dark eyes were looking at me with a mixture of distaste, pity, and some hidden grief. It was d'Urbec.

"Monsieur d'Urbec, I cannot walk that far in these clothes," I said.

"I have an equipage these days – hired by the month from the same establishment yours comes from." His voice was ironic as he swept off his hat in formal greeting.

"Did you follow me here?" I asked suspiciously.

"Follow you? No. But admit that a woman dressed in widow's weeds of the period of Henri Quatre does not draw the eyes of the curious. Especially when she looks to be throwing a rather expensive perfume bottle to the fishes and then stands staring morosely at the water for rather longer than is decent. Tell me, had you planned to drink it yourself?" His voice was quiet.

"No, the scent was too vulgar to bear, that's all."

"There are better ways to escape the contract of the Queen of the Shadows."

"The Shadow Queen? Then you call her that, too?"

"It's a term that occurs naturally to the intelligent observer. The Goddess of the Underworld. The Empress of the Witches. The Queen of the Sorceresses. This realm of the Sun King has its dark places, and I am well acquainted with them. How many years did she demand of you for this ... ah ... prosperity?" He gestured to my black silk dress, the waiting carriage. "Twenty? Seven?"

"Only five, and it's fair, considering what she's done for me."

"Five? And what happens at the end of five?"

"You think, perhaps, that she collects my soul, like Beelzebub? No – this is a business relationship. We're done, and we go our own ways."

"Are you so sure? All over town *parfumiers*, hairdressers, fortune-tellers, and even less-savoury occupations are tied to one or another of the powerful ladies of the underworld, of whom yours appears to be the chief. And they give every sign of being tied for life."

"That's just friendship and mutual assistance. These are business friendships, no different than that of the King's pastry maker. Powerful patronage is a convenience in business just as it is at court."

"Hey, there – move that carriage. You are blocking the equipage of Cardinal Altieri."

"So," he said, handing me into his carriage and turning to offer a tip to my driver for returning home without me, "we must continue our discourse on business methods elsewhere or risk dismemberment for the convenience of the cardinal." In very little time we were entangled in a mass of drays, labourers, and market women near the Quai de Gèvres.

"Tell me, now that we are alone, while you look me in the face, that that vial was not poison." He leaned back on the carriage seat to look at me, where I sat opposite him, through half-closed eyes.

"It was," I said simply. He looked quiet and grim. "I didn't want to have it any more," I added. Seeing the look on his face,

I tried to be light. "It's simply not the appropriate thing for philosophers."

"Just how much of you is still philosopher, and how much is witch, these days?" he asked, in a deceptively lazy tone of voice.

"Too much philosopher, too little witch," I answered.

"In short, small witch, nothing has changed."

"I suppose you could say so."

"Except that you are having an affair with Lamotte." I must have looked surprised. "Come now, you didn't expect me not to know immediately the secret that half of Paris is trying to guess? How flattered you must be to be such a Muse of inspiration, and how pleased he must be when applying his moustache wax in the morning to look in the mirror and exclaim, 'Who's cleverest now, d'Urbec? Even philosophy pays homage to charm.'" His bitterness frightened me.

"But you . . . you've changed too. You're so . . . so prosperous."

"Merely an application of science to the art of card playing. Having suddenly seen the necessity of becoming extremely rich, I decided to apply a geometric formula I once devised concerning the likelihood of a given card coming into play. I bet accordingly. Sometimes I lose, mostly I win. The ignorant think I have made a pact with the Devil."

"So your Devil is Reason. How disappointed they would be if they knew."

"Even if I were to publish the formula on the front page of the *Gazette de France*, there are only a half dozen men in Europe intelligent enough to use it, and the majority of them are not interested in cards."

"You still set a rather high value on intelligence, Monsieur d'Urbec."

"As well I ought to. The world, society, all are amenable to geometric analysis. I now climb high in society by the simplest of formulae: high-stakes gamblers are welcome everywhere. When I have accumulated enough I shall purchase a couple of tax-farming offices and then enter the greatest gambling salon of all: high finance."

"I thought you hated people like that."

"Hate or love will not change the fate of this nation. In the meantime, I know every low byway where the quick money hides. That seems to be the chief advantage of the study of political economy." He sounded so hard and bitter that even I was shocked.

"Something is wrong with you, Florent. Has something happened to you? What has become of your brother Olivier?"

"As perceptive as ever, Mademoiselle." His face looked hard. "Olivier is dead. The cleverest of us all. Executed in Marseilles this week past despite every appeal I could mount. His legacy, a cabinet full of plans for new inventions in clockwork, including a new self-lighting fuse for infernal machines. They hanged him like a peasant." I put my hand to my mouth.

"Oh, I'm sorry." I could understand now the circles under his eyes, the new gauntness in his face. He sat silently for the rest of the trip, his thoughts in some faraway place, while I looked at my knotted hands. As the carriage drew to a halt before my door, I asked, "Will you come in? Is there something you'd like?" His calculating eyes fixed on me for what seemed like an eternity. His gaze seemed to go straight through me and bite into my backbone.

"There *is* something I'd like, and you've made up my mind for me. I'll not come in. I'm off to the south for a while. Mother needs me. Father has become useless, work flounders without Olivier to direct it, and the entire family is in turmoil. Enjoy Lamotte – at least until you become bored with that turnip he calls a mind." With cold certainty, I knew that once d'Urbec was gone, Lamotte's interest in me would vanish. Vain, selfish, changeable, charming Lamotte. He had cut his friend to the bone to avenge a slight, and he had used me to do it. My weakness, my foolishness, my illusions. And d'Urbec saw it all.

Silently, he handed me out of the carriage. "Please . . . please don't think ill of me . . ." As I looked up at his grim face, I could feel my eyes pricking.

"Surely, Mademoiselle, you who have known so much despair could not fail to recognise it in another." He ducked his head away from me without a farewell. I stood a long time at the doorstep, watching while his carriage slowly vanished down the Rue Charlot.

* * *

That evening Sylvie brought my books to me as I sat in bed.

"You left these on the seat of your coach this afternoon, Madame, and the stableman's boy brought them over. Do you want me to put them on the shelf?"

"No, give them here, Sylvie. I'll put them on my nightstand." I picked up the Petronius, but as I began to leaf through it, my eyes began to sting again, and I sniffled.

"Oh, they *are* dusty old things. Here, let me fix them so they won't make you sneeze." Sylvie picked up Grandmother's Bible and brushed off its covers with the edge of her petticoat. Then she shook it so the pages spattered open and a cloud of dust flew up from the abused book.

"Oh— *Achoo!*— What's this that's come out?"

"Sylvie, plague take you, you've dropped a page out of my grandmother's Bible."

"Oh no I haven't, Madame. It's got writing on it, not printing." She handed it to me, and I saw a sheet of grandmother's letter paper. In her shaky hand, written across the centre in black ink, were the words "Cortezia et Benson, Banquiers à Londres."

THIRTY-FOUR

"Aha, my dear Marquise, come in, come in – there is someone here I would like you to meet," the witch queen's voice called from the depths of her brocade armchair. Nanon, wearing a fresh new apron and house cap, had shown me through the front door into Madame's black parlour. The curtains let the pale winter sunshine in through the windowpanes, to impose little rectangles of light upon the fanciful gargoyles in the dark crimson carpet. The entire cabinetful of china angels and cherubs, all freshly dusted, observed the scene with rank upon rank of painted eyes. Two magnificent armchairs, all gold fringe and brocade, were pulled up at the gilded table where Madame read cards, opposite her own dark, carved armchair. The sickly, heavy smell of incense overpowered the pale, sweet beeswax of the eternally lit candles in front of the statue of the Virgin in the corner. Two lanky men in blond wigs and expensive, provincial-looking clothes were seated in the armchairs opposite her gilded table, their legs crossed, sipping wine from silver goblets. What rustics, I thought. Swedish, perhaps – or English. Fresh off the boat, or surely they would see a tailor and have something decent made for their court appearance.

"Milord the Duke of Buckingham and Milord Rochester, allow me to present the Marquise de Morville." The odd pair rose and bowed in acknowledgment of the introduction.

"The immortal Marquise, eh? I heard of you by reputation on my last visit, Madame. I am enchanted to meet you in the flesh. Let me compliment you on the remarkable state of your preservation." As Buckingham's head rose from bowing over my hand, he inspected my face with a pair of ravaged, debauched blue eyes. I could not determine his age: his own face was a ruin of premature decay, ghost-white, lined, set off by a moustache so thin as if drawn on by a child with a pen. His companion took out a lorgnon with which he inspected my complexion. I was careful to remain serious at the droll sight of one peering blue eye, immensely magnified, at the end of a stick. My face never even twitched. Madame smiled maternally all through this process.

"Remarkable! Remarkable!" He walked entirely around me for a better look. "Pity the secret of that compound was lost with the alchemical abbé. You might re-create it in your chemical laboratory, my lord." Milord, who had seated himself again in the largest armchair, nodded thoughtfully.

"Milord is an alchemist and seeker of some renown," explained La Voisin to me, looking as contented as the cat that twined itself around her ankles. "He extends his patronage and protection to the most distinguished alchemists and herbalists of Europe."

"Of whom Madame Montvoisin is one," observed the duke's companion in a flattering tone, bowing slightly from the waist in her direction.

"I say, we must be going," observed the duke, rising, as Nanon hastened to bring his heavy mantle and stick. "And you, Madame, do give consideration to my proposal." Standing, he looked about the black parlour appreciatively, with the eye of a connoisseur. Madame Montvoisin rose with a rustle of silk.

"I have indeed considered and could not fail to accept such a gracious and generous offer of patronage," she said. "However, I have business I must complete here first." – The two men eyed each other knowingly – "after which, well, I have long craved a healthful sea voyage and a change of climate. Then I will be delighted to reestablish myself in England under your sponsorship." The duke turned then to me, with a look of polite interest.

"And you, Madame de Morville, are a curiosity of the first order. Should you ever journey to England, be assured of my favour and patronage." I thanked the duke as graciously as I knew how, as he left in a flurry of courtesies. After all, he meant well. Foreigners never seem to understand how little attraction an island of damp fogs, cut off from civilisation, and a provincial little court has for us Parisians, who inhabit the most cultivated, powerful monarchy in the world. The English, after all, know so little of how things are done properly and are so backward in dress and manners. Besides, it is hardly safe there, among those turbulent regicides. Absolutely anything could happen. But then, the thought flashed through my mind, What a delightfully perverse place to conceal good French gold from Colbert, the King's ever more greedy finance minister. A dismal little island where one couldn't even get a proper loaf of bread. It suited Father's sense of humour. Yes, it all made a certain kind of sense. Cortezia et Benson, Banquiers à Londres. When he lay dying, he told Grandmother, expecting she'd outlive him and tell me, no doubt. But she had died first, and the news had been kept from him. I wondered if anything was left of his hoard. Doubtless confiscated or embezzled by now. A joke. Fate is always a joker.

"So that's that until the next visit," announced La Voisin, turning from the door. "Come into my cabinet, Marquise, I have business with you that must not be overheard. Tell me, how did you get Lamotte to come to you instead of d'Urbec? Have you seen someone else in secret?"

"No, Madame. And I saw d'Urbec last week. He stopped his carriage for me." I could see her searching my face, trying to tell if her potion were working.

"And I suppose you haven't asked him for the secret of the cards?"

"No, Madame, he boasted about it right away – the secret is mathematical. He says only six men in Europe can understand it, and they aren't interested in cards." La Voisin looked relieved, as if her supernatural powers still acted with the same force. Then she frowned.

"Mathematical. Damn. Then it is closed to us. I always knew I distrusted that man. Well, never mind. I shall tell my clients it is a pact with the Devil and sell them a Black Mass instead." As she closed the door of the black parlour behind us, she turned and squinted suspiciously at my heavy, satin-rimmed velvet dress, my new shoes, and the new sapphire ring that nestled next to the heavy, carved gold one on my right hand. "And has your income fallen off with all this scandalous romancing of yours?" she asked, like some shrewd housewife assessing the fat on a chicken in the market. She took my little account book from my hand, pausing beneath the tapestry of the repentant Magdalen to leaf through it. "I see here a new court dress. New gloves. A velvet cloak. Hat and plumes – rather costly ones – to match. I do hope they are black."

"My income is better than ever, if you're worried about your share. Besides, I have to keep up appearances, with the sort of people I'm seeing these days. Nobody believes the advice of a poor-looking fortune-teller. It's as if she can't even predict her own fortune."

"I'm concerned about more than that, my dear," she said, suddenly leading a rapid pace through the great room behind the parlour. Antoine Montvoisin sat at the dining table in his dressing gown working over a necklace with a pair of tweezers and tiny pliers, removing the stones. With a "click" he dropped one into a tiny metal box. His fat son stood beside him, eating a bun. Marie-Marguerite, his daughter, visibly pregnant, sat knitting, her feet propped up on a stool. She hadn't bothered to marry the magician; that wasn't how things were done in this household.

"Don't breathe on me," Montvoisin snapped at the boy, who bit into the bun again.

"And now," said La Voisin, shutting her cabinet door, "the real business." I didn't like the look on her face as she sat, then motioned me to the stool.

"The Duchesse de Bouillon has paid a visit to me," she said significantly.

"So? What did she want? A fortune? A love powder for the King?"

"Don't be pert. She wants poison for a rival: the mysterious inspiration of the Chevalier de la Motte's new play. And she is coming to you for a reading to help her determine who the woman is. This time, my dear, you are in even deeper trouble than when you insulted the Duc de Brissac in this very house."

"Insult? I was very polite. But I did speak the truth."

"You *are* a fool, then. To Brissac, the truth of his situation from the mouth of a woman is an insult. It was a great deal of trouble restraining him from having you assassinated after that trick. And now, you flaunt one of the duchesse's little toy lovers all over Paris. I tell you, you do not need an enemy of this power." She stood up suddenly and stared down at me with hard eyes. "She will finish you with no more emotion than she would squash a bug. Remember this, Marquise, that for all you mix in the grand world, you count for nothing in it. No one would even inform the police if you were to vanish tomorrow." I could hear the blood beating in my ears.

"He's mine. I won't give him up to that pretentious old cow."

"Listen to me, for a change," she sat back down again and looked at me intently, as if her black eyes could command my secret will. "You must give him up. Now. And when she comes to you, give her the description of Mademoiselle de Thianges. She knows La Thiange's ambitions lie at the throne. Therefore the duchesse will assume the whole affair is one of Platonic devotion. A certain amount of flattery of the ladies is expected from a man in his position. You will be saved – and so will he. And if you don't care for yourself, at least give a thought to his career, and the perpetuation of those celebrated calves you appear to be so fond of."

"I'll think about it." Give André back to the duchesse? When it was *I* who was his inspiration? La Voisin was just jealous, too, now that I was an important beauty.

"You'll *think* about it? Jesus and Mary, you are even stupider than that idiot stepdaughter of mine! I tell you, you'll do it! I won't have my investment spoiled for a ridiculous love affair!" She stood again and went to the locked cabinet where she kept her great green ledgers and her grimoires. "And now, for your accounts – and quit looking at me that way. You can't outplot a Mancini, any more than that English milord can."

"He's plotting?" She took my curiosity for acquiescence. Good. André would stay mine.

"Oh, he schemes constantly. Ever since he fell from favour with the English king, he plots with the French court. Now here, now there. He flits all over Europe, trying to get his power back." She turned and fluttered her fingertips as if they were bird wings and she were a disgraced courtier fluttering like a migrant swallow over the cities of Europe. Madame did have a sense of humour, even if it was not the ordinary sort. "Every so often, he stops by for a Black Mass to assist him. This morning I read his cards and told him he'd land in jail if he didn't restrain himself. But of course, dukes don't listen to good advice any more than girls do." She took the *P* ledger from the cabinet, set it on her desk, and sighed. "But I keep him happy. He's my retirement, if things become uncomfortable here. Though they'd have to be uncomfortable indeed for me to wish to live in such a damp, backward place as England."

I left with my accounts settled and my mind made up. I had not the slightest intention of giving up Lamotte. After all, I'd got him the hard way, by sacrificing my honour on several levels altogether, and he was mine at least until he found out d'Urbec had left town. The more I thought about it, the more reasonable it seemed. He made my insides race. I'd wanted him for years, and there was no reason to cut it off now. I would defy the world with my passion. That was, after all, what Théodora would have done. Who knows? Perhaps some trace of the blood of the ancient empress really did run in my veins.

"Your mask again, Madame? Don't you ever grow weary of defying fate? I saw in the cards that you are crossed by the Queen of Swords. Give up this insane passion. A man who makes love to older women for their money is not a proper lover for you."

"Fortune-telling again, Sylvie? I thought that was my speciality. Or does Madame pay you to issue dire warnings at two-week intervals? Hand me my walking stick. Did you call my carriage, or must I ask Gilles?" My toilette was magnificent. Amber silk pulled back to expose a petticoat of deep brown taffeta whose folds glittered with a sombre gold light. A wide-brimmed hat in the cavalier's style, lavishly trimmed with green and brown plumes sat rakishly above my dark curls. I didn't look in the least like the Marquise de Morville in her antique black brocade and tiny veiled widow's cap. The stiff, domineering little lady couldn't be seen at all in the glass before me. Even through the crimson stain across the mirror's face, the masked woman in the glass looked young, elegant, rich and raffish. I liked the look.

"At least have Mustapha follow you at a distance. If you are slain, there'll be hell to pay with Madame."

"Slain? *Phoo!* Who'd assassinate a woman in the street? Queens of Swords are more subtle than that. Besides, if I'm dead, I'll hardly have to worry about Madame, will I?"

"Then at least use a taster at your rendezvous. Powerful women have friends everywhere, especially in kitchens."

"I'll think about it. Now, the carriage?"

Sylvie sighed. "It's at the door, Madame."

Her warnings only increased my zest for the adventure. My skin tingled; my pulse drummed in my ears. Twisted motives, madness, danger – none of it mattered. A moment's pleasure snatched with the handsomest man in Paris made me feel like the most beautiful woman in the world. I loved that feeling. I cared about nothing else.

My equipage rattled past the flickering lamps of the Marais and onwards, then plunged into the maze of narrow unlighted streets near l'église de la Merci, a district of all-night gambling dens, flashy bordellos, and home of every vice for a price. Here the members of the Shadow Queen's philantropic society plied their trades without hindrance. Here also, the silent partners of great financiers and nobles operated money-making establishments in a totally discreet fashion. Lamotte, who understood almost nothing of this world, had made arrangements for our meeting in one of the private upper rooms of Mademoiselle la Boissière's fashionable establishment at the corner of the Rue de Braque and the Rue du Chaume. Here, in what the police so unkindly called *"un lieu de débauche"*, out-of-town dandies, businessmen and officers on the prowl, and the slumming sprigs of the aristocracy could find music, women, and cards at any hour of the day or night. And among all the mysterious, beautiful women, I felt myself the most beautiful and mysterious of all. It was intoxicating.

"My love," the man in the black silk mask whispered, as he helped me from the carriage and sent it on its way, his hand never far from his sword hilt. Lamotte's voice resonating softly in the dark, the rough feel of the wool of his heavy cape, the unmistakable scent and feel of his presence in the dark made my pulse speed. The light of hundreds of flickering candles gleamed through the closed shutters enough to guide us to the secret entrance, and the shouts and din within covered the sound of our footsteps in the alley behind the Rue du Chaume. Forbidden music, sounding in the depths of a winter's night. Even now the memory of it sears me. Fleshly lust has been entirely underrated by the sentimental devotees of the *Carte de Tendre*, that old-fashioned map of the stages of gallantry that was once so popular in the salons. And André was the high priest of pure carnality. I never even asked him how many other women he had led to the secret room – I didn't care. This moment was mine.

"A little wine?" he whispered, indicating the decanter that stood on the little round table by the bed.

"I want only one kind of wine tonight," I whispered back.

"The wine of Venus," he said, and, his soft voice oozing over me like syrup, he recited the celebrated couplets he had dedicated to my breasts as he reached beneath my stays. He buried his face in my newly freed bosom; his hand pushed up my skirts to search out the pale flesh beneath my tumbled petticoats. His lovemaking was slow, refined. He seemed to touch every nerve in my body. And I, at long last, felt beautiful – so beautiful I could hardly bear it. The letters, the love poetry, the months of adoration beneath the window, they seemed as if they were all mine now. The treasure had never been thrown away. I had caught it, the wasted dream. Now I was the beloved of the window. It felt just right.

"Oh, damnation, I've turned over the decanter," he exclaimed as he reached lazily out of bed towards the cup that stood beside it on the nightstand. Was it imagination, or was there something annoying about André when he was sexually sated? Then he rolled over to look at me again. "Never mind. I will drink only from your lips tonight." He kissed me, his kisses progressing up my face and around my ear. What is it about a woman's ear that connects it so intimately to the body? The warm, soft feel of his breath made my skin feel like quicksilver, molten and trembling around every limb. But at the same time that I shivered with the sensation, a tiny voice inside said to me, My, he certainly is practised, isn't he? How many other women's ears has he breathed on? Do we all behave in exactly the same way? Yet even as my mind was becoming vaguely annoyed with his professionalism, my body, which had no judgment at all, adored it. Ah, Lord, even when I think back on it, I can see the usefulness of being all body and no mind. But the mind insisted on interfering during the second encounter. Even while the body was thrilling with each new touch, the mind said, Goodness, he takes you through all these stages of ecstasy like a horseman over the jumps; how much does it really mean to *him*? Troublesome mind. It quite took the edge off. That is the

problem with women, I guess. Something in the mind, not just
the body, has to touch when one is lovemaking. And, what was
more irritating, for some reason I couldn't help thinking of
d'Urbec's sarcastic eyes as Lamotte rolled off me with that
conceited self-satisfied look of his. His eyes heavy lidded, his
voice low and contrivedly thrilling, he looked at me and said,
"My precious, even the most perfect moments must end, and
this is not a place where it would be wise to spend the night."

"You are a man of the world, André," I agreed. For I knew
even better than he did that to sleep in such a spot might lead to
permanent rest, stripped and unidentifiable, in the river.

"Let me help you dress," he offered gallantly. "I love the feel
of ladies' clothes – the little buttons, the delicious pressure of
the stays, the scented silk . . ." He knelt to put on my stockings
as if he had done it for hundreds of other women, passing his
fingers up my thighs so nonchalantly it appeared almost
accidental. Then I felt him hesitate. His eyes, which had fallen
on my deformed foot, were averted.

"Never mind," I said, "I can do that." He looked relieved and
rose to put on his own breeches as I finished fastening my
garters and laced on the padded, built-up shoe.

"Have you seen d'Urbec recently?" he remarked in an
offhand way. How curious. He'd been thinking of d'Urbec, too.
"He appears to be fabulously wealthy these days. A while back I
ran into him at my tailor's, ordering a suit of cut velvet. Imagine!
D'Urbec in velvet! 'No matter how much you comb the dog, he's
still a dog, eh?' I said to him. He had the effrontery to ask me
whether the rumour that the duchess has a mole on her behind
was accurate. Damned embarrassing, in front of my good
friend, Pradon."

"Monsieur d'Urbec is not generally praised for his tact," I
answered. But what had Lamotte expected? Of course d'Urbec
would mock Lamotte for making a career as a lover of
aristocratic women. D'Urbec made his living in the salons. He
didn't dare have an affair with any respectable woman, for fear of
revealing the galley brand that could get him barred from polite
society. Lamotte ought to hire a dray cart to carry his vanity
around in.

"Ah, but enough of these things . . . let us talk only of us. We
have been too furtive, my love. And when I am with you, I feel I

must proclaim our passion from the housetops! Ours is a love that laughs at conventions. We must defy the world! Yes, we must appear in public; we must tantalise the gossips!"

"André, think of your career – we can't appear in public. Your patroness . . ." But even as I spoke, I reflected that his tone sounded contrived. What did he have in mind?

"A flash, a hint – a tidbit for the *libellistes* – it can only enhance my reputation. What better way to keep my name on every tongue in preparation for the reception of my *Théodora*? Incognito in a box at the theatre on my dear friend Pradon's opening night. A mystery woman in the party of the Chevalier de la Motte – could it be she, the inspiration, or some other? It will be an *occasion*." Ah. That was it. Who could recognise me, masked and out of my widow's weeds, except d'Urbec? And d'Urbec never missed an opening night. Lamotte plans to return d'Urbec's insult by flaunting me, I thought. I would have felt mean about hurting d'Urbec, except that I knew that he had left town. Perfect. I'll have a lovely time being a glamorous woman of mystery and watching the look on Lamotte's face as he scans the theatre, looking for d'Urbec.

Is it so wrong to have wanted so desperately to be beautiful, to be like other women? It was having André that proved to me that I was not the lost, ugly little monster of the Rue des Marmousets. His lovemaking made me feel the equal of the beautiful, aristocratic women who advanced his career and paid him handsomely for his services. And I never gave him a sou. So didn't that make me even better than they? Why should I care about his motives? And yet, even while I was enjoying the ridiculous extravagance of his lovemaking, I felt that I had somehow betrayed myself. And d'Urbec, too, though I was not his, nor he mine.

When we were at last ready to leave, I leaned over to pick up the decanter. It was only then that I noticed the curious bubbles that the spilled wine was making as it ate its way through the finish on the floorboards and deep into the wood.

"Now, Madame, admit the new make-up is very effective."

"Not bad at all, Sylvie. I look like a well-preserved corpse." For once, I was pleased with the effect. Goodbye, tell-tale flushed cheeks and bright eyes. I would have been even more pleased if I could have worn a sack with eye holes over my head. Shivering with the cold, I had risen before dawn to prepare for the Duchesse de Bouillon's *levée*. I'd never want to be a courtier, I thought. They do this every day. The candles still flickered on my dressing table, competing with the first faint light of dawn. Somehow, on a cold winter's morning, the idea of defying the world with one's passion did not exercise the same magnetism as on a wine-scented evening spent in anticipation of a splendid sexual encounter. The question that haunted me was this: had she known with whom Lamotte's rendezvous was? Did he know she knew, and had his carelessness in knocking over the decanter been feigned – or was he ignorant? And yet there was a certain fascination with the idea of perishing in the midst of an affair, having excited the envy of half the women of Paris, immortalised, as it were, at the very moment when everyone would remember me as a fatal beauty. It was the sort of idea that appeals to a plain girl. After all, Lamotte's interest couldn't last. And nothing like this might ever happen again.

But cold dawn was different. It reminded me of Lamotte's shallow motives and of the pleasures of much smaller things: breakfast, slippers, chocolate, warmth. It made me want to live as a plain, comfortable girl rather than dying as an Aphrodite.

"More shadow under my eyes, Sylvie. I want to look more haggard." Sylvie finished up the job and added a dusting of faintly green face powder, before taking the cloth from my shoulders and fastening the antique ruff around my neck.

"You look dreadful," she announced cheerfully, "just like some horrid sorceress."

"Perfect," I responded, as I rose and let her put my heaviest cloak over my shoulders.

I took a certain pleasure in the *frisson* of horror that went round the duchesse's bedchamber as I was shown in. The flute player's breath lapsed for a fragment of a moment, but the two violinists covered the bad patch in the music. The ladies-in-waiting cast glances at each other. The gentlemen petitioners moved uneasily. Pradon, who was reciting from his latest work, stopped dead to stare. The maid's hand stopped midway in the air, still holding the hairbrush above her mistress's dark, tumbled hair. Only the duchesse's eyes, black stones at the bottom of a black pond, those cold Mancini eyes, remained unchanged as she turned her face towards me, then turned again to the tall mirror on her dressing table. Among the perfume bottles on the table, Madame Carcan, her favourite cat, contentedly preened her long white fur, deigning to look at me only briefly with her enigmatic yellow eyes.

"Very good, Pradon; you may continue," said the duchesse. He looked confused. The manuscript from which he had been reading rattled in his hand. "You had just finished Phèdre's response," the duchesse prompted. Pradon continued reading his verses in a hesitating tone. They seemed well-enough rhymed but somehow mediocre, elegant without substance and power. But the play – how curious – it was the very subject on which the Sieur Racine was known to be composing his long-awaited masterwork.

"Pradon, it is the very thing. You must read at my *salon* tomorrow so that all Paris can acclaim your talent. Admit now, I was right to suggest this topic to you. I myself am a better judge of Pradon's mastery than Pradon himself." Pradon bowed deeply, humbly.

"Madame has a perception that is more than human. She can see into the soul."

Madame's hairdresser had now replaced the maid. With the singeing smell of curling irons, he was creating a symmetrical array of curls, set off at intervals with tiny diamond-studded combs. The petitioners began to advance, but Madame, seeing their movement in the mirror, waved them back.

"First," she said, "I will have a fortune told. Madame de Morville, I have need of your celebrated skill. Someone has annoyed me; someone who dreams she can be a rival to me. I wish to know who her lover is." Her gaze did not move from the mirror.

"Madame, a true image in the water does not arise unless the person whose fortune is to be read puts his or her hands on the glass. I would not have your patronage on a falsehood." The duchesse laughed – a high, cold tinkling laugh.

"Why, how unusual! Surely, Madame, you do not set yourself above the rest of humankind? Tell me, could you attempt it with an article belonging to the person?"

"I could try, Madame," I announced in a sombre tone. She

opened a drawer in her dressing table and took out a man's glove. Then she turned to me. "I have been offended by the man who wore this glove. Tell me what you see in the glass." As she spoke, a lady-in-waiting took the glove from her hand to hand it to me, and two lackeys brought a low stool and little table for my equipment. She did not ask for a screen, or to have the room cleared. She wants everyone in the room to carry the tale, I thought. It is her way of sending a warning.

I put André's glove across the narrow opening at the top of my round glass vase. I chanted. I removed the glove. It still bore the shape of his hand. I longed to pick it up and tuck it into my bosom, but I kept my face unchanging and set down the glove beside the glass as if it were a dead frog.

An image was forming. Water, greyish green. Above it an endless horizon, grey and cold. A face. With a shock, I recognised it. The image I had first seen in La Voisin's black parlour, all those years ago. The woman at the ship's rail, staring out to sea. I gasped. This time, I recognised the stranger's face. It was my own. I peered closely; tears ran down the woman's face. What was going on? Was I dreaming, or was fate changing before my very eyes?

"Well, what is it? What do you see?" The duchesse's voice broke into my thoughts. I looked up to see that everyone in the room was waiting, silent and breathless, for the reading.

"Madame, I saw a crowd of courtiers leaving Madame de Montespan's apartment at Versailles. Among them is a beautiful young woman, short, with dark hair. She is flirting with several men. The owner of the glove approaches her as the crowd thins, stepping before her waiting woman to hand her a folded piece of paper. She laughs, takes her fan from her waist, and taps his wrist with it to show her displeasure at his rudeness. But she keeps the paper."

"Mademoiselle de Thianges," I could hear a voice whisper behind me. The duchesse looked straight at me.

"Yes, it appears to be Mademoiselle de Thianges," I answered her unspoken question.

"And the gentleman?"

"The gentleman appears to be the playwright, the Chevalier de la Motte," I said. The duchesse's face never changed.

"Then you have read truly. I would have been displeased at a deception," said the duchesse. She may be a Mancini, I thought silently, but I have a few tricks left myself.

"So," she asked, almost nonchalantly, "did the woman go to an assignation incognito?"

"That, Madame, the glass does not say. For all I could tell, the folded paper might simply be a verse of admiration."

"If that is the case, then there are two . . ." she mused to herself. I could feel my heart pounding. "Never mind," she said aloud. "It does not take much to bring a little poet to heel. You may go, Madame de Morville." She made an almost imperceptible gesture, and a lackey showed me to the door, pressing a brocade silk purse heavy with coins into my hand. Just so it's not thirty pieces of silver, I thought. I have betrayed André, fool that he is.

Outside, a light snow was falling, dusting the carriage, the coachman's hat and cloak, and the horses' backs with white powder. No, I haven't betrayed André, I thought, as I huddled under the fur carriage robe, staring at the tall, white-powdered houses that lined the street. She already knew about him. Then I remembered the way he averted his eyes from my foot. All this whole seduction—he had only done it to hurt a friend for mocking his play, *Osmin*, in the *Parnasse Satyrique*. He must have thought d'Urbec and I were secretly affianced after what happened there at my house. But I couldn't really blame d'Urbec for insulting him. After all, I might call somebody a few things too, if he'd managed to waste my burial fund. Besides, if a person isn't very bright, he shouldn't be insulted if someone tells him the truth. For example, the death scene in Lamotte's *Osmin was* rather overwritten, and there were times his verse was rather feeble. He should be pleased to receive honest criticism. And anyway, Lamotte didn't ever really care about me. I was just a symbol of the big house he couldn't get into long ago, the house of *Osmin*. He had used me. It was fair, then; he had earned whatever he would get.

But I had wanted to be used. I had adored his lies, his amazing charm that he could turn off and on like a spigot, his easy tears, his romantic posturing. What did that make me? Never mind; he would get what he deserved. But then, I thought, what was it that I deserved? The fast-falling veil of white seemed to hide all the answers from me.

THIRTY-FIVE

There was still a crowd in the street, even after the body had been removed. Desgrez pressed through the motley assortment of lackeys and passers-by to where the elderly servant woman sat on the front step weeping into her apron, surrounded by the mournful household staff.

"I saw it all, I saw it all, Monsieur," she responded to Desgrez's questions. "Good, kind, generous Monsieur Geniers had just given something to a beggar, when a hideous man, his face all wrapped in a scarf, stepped out from the alley over there—" she pointed, and all eyes turned to the narrow alley, its gutter running with filth.

"And then?" pressed Desgrez, his voice low and sympathetic.

"Monsieur, the fiend beat my master to the ground right there, where the bloodstain is. He smashed in his head with a big metal-tipped walking stick he was carrying."

"Can you describe the man you saw?"

"He was a beggar in a shapeless grey coat. But he had a gentleman's accent. There was no mistaking that."

"He spoke? What did he say?"

"He shouted something like, 'Here's your repayment, you bastard—'"

"Monsieur, the scarf fell off . . . and . . ."

"Yes?" Desgrez was attentive.

"Monsieur, the man had no face."

"A faceless man, Desgrez? This should not present much of a problem of identification. Did she say if he were a leper?" La Reynie was inspecting the murder report that lay before him on his desk.

"I think it more likely that it was a criminal whose nose and ears had been cropped," answered his subordinate.

"And yet with a gentleman's accent. An impossibility, I

think. This presents a puzzle, Desgrez." He shook his head. "A man of Monsieur Geniers's position, respected, of unblemished reputation, murdered on his own doorstep. It is a scandal. Louvois will doubtless take a direct interest, and possibly even His Majesty. We must give this case the highest priority. Search his house again, Desgrez. Interview his colleagues. Go through his correspondence. There is not a man alive that does not have some hidden enemy."

THIRTY-SIX

"Madame, you make a fool of yourself staring out of the window. He won't come back, and you know it. Men always vanish when they've had their pleasure." Outside, the white curtain of falling snow hid the tall, slate rooftops of the city, covered the black icy mud of the Rue Charlot, and changed everything inanimate into curious mounds and shapes of shining white.

"I just like looking at the snow. Some people find that poetic, you know." If was the eve of the new year; tomorrow would be 1677.

"Poetic, ha! That man's afraid of losing the duchesse's patronage. Men always look to their own convenience first. He may be a ladies' man, but he knows which side his bread is buttered on."

"Men this, men that! Who made you the philosopher of men?"

"Men did, Madame. And I say that when one of them walks out, you should do as they do, and take another lover. Brissac, for example. Myself, I think a man of rank is better than a nobody scribbler, even if he does have absolutely lovely calves." I turned on her fiercely.

"Sylvie! Who has paid you? Brissac or La Voisin?"

"Oh, both," she said calmly. "But as I'm loyal to you, I won't hide it. My own opinion is, take Brissac, have a good time, and forget about the rest."

"I thought Brissac was angry at me."

"Oh, that was before. Now he tries to creep back into Nevers's favour. But he needs to be seen at the right places, you know. He has to look good, craft some new *bons mots*, provide little services..."

"All of which require money. So, if I buy him a new suit of clothes, hire a poet, and cover his gambling debts, he'll escort me about to places I don't want to be to associate with people I dislike. It's no bargain, Sylvie."

"But . . . a duchesse . . . you could have a grand title, even if he is bankrupt."

"Don't fool yourself, Sylvie. As long as he has a hope of prying a sou out of the current duchesse's family, she'll keep her health. And once he's free, the only use I would have is to provide money for him to chase another pedigree."

"But Madame says he has weakened. He confessed to her that he would consider a secret marriage."

"And what good would a secret marriage do me? That's for silly girls who want to pretend they haven't been seduced. It's the protection of an acknowledged marriage that I need – that, and his title, dubious as it is. He must think I'm a simpleton."

"But at least say you'll give the idea consideration. Then I don't have to lie to Madame." Her face was serious.

"Well then, I've considered it. There. Now tell me who'll be at La Voisin's New Year's celebration tonight. Brissac?"

"Of course. But Madame has also hired the most splendid violins. And there'll be partridges and suckling pig, as well as mutton and ham."

"Oh, if there'll be partridges, then everything will be perfect, won't it?"

"That's what I told Madame, and she said I was a greedy wench, and she was surprised I hadn't eaten you out of house and home already. She also said wear the antique black with the jet-beaded bodice. You might get some important new customers. The Marquis de Cessac and his friends will be coming. Also some Italian bishop who's in town. Madame says you must develop foreign connections if you wish to prosper."

The evening was already well under way when I arrived. Through the frosted windows, bright lights blazed, and one could hear the clatter of conversation and laughter each time the door opened on to the snowy street. I picked my way through the crush of carriages at the door just behind a masked actress and her latest escort. The sound of violins and laughter could be heard in the black parlour.

"Ah, here is the ever charming Madame de Morville, whom the centuries cannot spoil..." Brissac, pushing his way through the crowd to greet me at the door. How offensive. But with La Voisin and Brissac's creature de Vandeuil hovering in the background, I smiled, but not too much. He bowed an elaborate greeting. He had a new hat but the same velvet coat with the tarnished gold braid and the singe marks from standing too close to the fire during one or another experiment in diabolism.

"Monsieur de Brissac, I am so enchanted to see you once more." I removed my mask.

"Ah! I am overwhelmed. Your features are more radiant than ever, my dear Marquise." Brissac stepped back, as if dazzled by some overbright object. How long will this go on, I thought, as I smiled an arch little smile at him.

"My dear friend," announced La Voisin in tones of false warmth, "Monsieur le Duc has the most splendid idea for a charming little evening that we cannot but enjoy immensely." We. Oh, damn, I couldn't wiggle out. La Voisin had accepted for us both.

"Ah, it is nothing – a trifle – but one that I lay at your feet, gracious lady." Get on with it, Brissac, you toad. I tilted my head and tapped my cheek with my closed fan, to show my interest. La Voisin beamed.

"The Duc de Nevers has entrusted me with a little commission. A delightful one. He has joined with the Duchesse de Bouillon in purchasing a number of boxes for the performance of the rarest effusion of Monsieur Pradon's genius, *Phèdre et Hippolyte*, and wishes, as a mark of his favour, to distribute the places to those connoisseurs of art who can truly appreciate such a masterwork." Ah, another Mancini cabal. This time with Brissac as the agent. What a pretty little plan of his to regain Nevers's favour! The Duchesse de Bouillon had bought and left empty all the boxes at the theatre to destroy Racine's premiere and now she would raise up her pet, Pradon, with the assistance of a claque recruited by Nevers. The way of the artist certainly isn't simple. For a moment, the memory of Lamotte so long ago, hollow cheeked and idealistic, flashed into my mind. Then I thought of Racine. What had he done to offend them, these

Mancinis, that they would destroy his masterwork as casually as one would crush a fly?

"Surely, you are not proposing that I, a widow of antique reputation, attend the theatre?"

"In disguise, masked, with a party of ladies and gentlemen of rank. Such a lark, to witness the triumph of Pradon. And, after all, true souls grow in understanding in the presence of great art. Give me hope, Marquise, that in securing your enjoyment I can hope to enjoy your favour." I opened my fan one compartment and moved it languidly. "Maybe," it signalled.

"Madame Montvoisin has offered her kind consent to accompany my dear friend, the Vicomte de Cousserans." La Voisin's latest lover. Damn. There'll be no backing out of this one.

"Who am I, then, to refuse the promise of such a delightful evening?" La Voisin's eyes glittered. Lamotte and d'Urbec had been vanquished. Her project was under way.

"Tell me, Madame," I asked lightly, as if it were nothing to me, "why do you favour Pradon, when the common opinion is for Racine, and he has as his patroness Madame de Montespan?" Her face grew dark with remembered hate.

"In this, I am with the Mancinis. Out of envy he poisoned his mistress, the actress La Du Parc, who had been my friend since childhood. Her children are being raised at the Hôtel Soissons. I still visit them on occasion, but thanks to the generosity of the countess, they lack for nothing. The Mancinis, they have long memories; just as I do." She swept off to oversee the dancing, which had begun. As I turned to watch the figures in graceful motion before the wide tapestry of the Repentance of the Magdalen, Brissac, standing behind me, spoke softly into my ear.

"You do not dance, do you, Madame?"

"No, Monsieur, it is an old infirmity with me."

"Well then, Terpsichore's loss is my gain. I will offer you one of those lovely little sweet pastries there, and we shall discourse on philosophy, which I hear is an interest of yours." The confident, intimate tone disgusted me. That old witch has prompted him on how best to approach me, I thought. She has assured him that he will win in the end. The laughter and music rattled shrilly in my ears as he found me a place on a narrow love seat and sent Monsieur de Vandeuil threading through the crowd to the refreshment table.

The masked woman behind me laughed again as she recounted a tale of amatory adventures. A cavalier with a star-shaped patch laughed with her. Brissac was silent, but his eyes rolled with amusement as he took in the conversation. He was seated so close as to be repulsive.

"Why do you hesitate, my dear Marquise?"

"Oh, a sudden faintness. The heat in the room. We are so close to the fire here. Tell me, how go your researches in the ... ah ... occult sciences these days?"

"By a most extraordinary coincidence, that old alchemist, the Comte de Bachimont, has revealed to me an entirely novel method for calling up the demon Nebiros to reveal hidden treasures."

"Nebiros? But he is only of the rank of field marshal. Surely, you should deal only with infernal spirits of higher rank. Now Astaroth, for example, has the rank of grand duke and is the commander of Nebiros . . ." We continued in this vein until the great amounts of wine he had drunk caused him to need to absent himself temporarily. The moment he got up, I fled, my train clutched in my hand, with Gilles close behind. Mustapha and Sylvie had brought up the carriage to the front door, as if they had read my mind. Inside the house, the crash of bottles and snatches of drunken song signalled that the party was growing wilder. Outside, in the dark, the snow had begun to fall again. Sylvie brushed the melting flakes off my cloak as I seated myself in the safe darkness of the carriage.

"Madame, what is wrong?"

"Brissac – I think he's going to propose, and I don't dare refuse."

"Oh, think of the advantages, Madame. And besides, there are plenty of people in this city worse than Brissac."

THIRTY-SEVEN

A closed, brass-bound coffer, the lock smashed open, lay on La Reynie's desk. Desgrez stood beside the desk and watched as La Reynie opened the box and leafed through the papers inside. He picked out from the rubble of receipts and memoranda a bundle of greasy, unsealed letters written on cheap paper. He read one or two of them through.

"Interesting, Desgrez. A correspondence between Monsieur Geniers and this Chevalier de Saint-Laurent, who appears to have been consigned to debtors' prison by Monsieur Geniers. He complains of the food, he asks for blankets, for money, for wine . . . he begs, he blusters, then threatens . . ."

"I thought you would see it immediately, Monsieur de La Reynie. Our suspect."

"And . . . ?" the Lieutenant General of the Paris Criminal Police raised an aristocratic eyebrow.

"We have made inquiries about this Saint-Laurent, Monsieur de La Reynie. His last address was the House of the Marmousets in the Quartier de la Cité. Madame de Paulmy paid for his release last month with her lottery winnings." La Reynie's curiously sensuous smile showed Desgrez that he had caught his chief's interest.

"I am surprised the Marquis tolerated this, Desgrez. His temper and his jealousy are both notorious."

"You are, of course, entirely correct. According to the servants of the de Paulmy household that I interviewed, he hired bravos to waylay the man and crop his nose and ears."

"Well done, Desgrez. We have our man with no face. But what is this I see here?" From the bottom of the sheaf of letters and papers, he removed a slip of paper.

"The address of the Marquise de Morville, written in Monsieur Geniers's hand. I thought you might find that interesting, Monsieur."

"The Marquise de Morville – have you any idea how much

that woman irritates me? She swept past me at the
maréchale's reception last month in the most offensive
manner, almost daring me to uncover her charlatanry. I
suspect her . . . I don't know what of, but I suspect her. Follow
this up, Desgrez; bring her in and question her about this
murder."

"Monsieur, she has protectors in the very highest circles."

"Then proceed carefully, but proceed. I mistrust mountebanks – especially of the female variety."

Desgrez's expression never changed from the eager,
attentive look he wore in Monsieur de La Reynie's presence,
but inside, he concealed a certain amusement. It took a great
deal to irritate the impeccably controlled Lieutenant General of
Police. He wondered exactly what the impertinent little
marquise had said to his chief.

THIRTY-EIGHT

"Take them out and lay them on the bed, Sylvie. I just can't choose." I've always found it hard to select a gown when I am going out with someone I don't like. A person wants to look devastating but still not spoil a favourite dress with a bad association. Which gown would I sacrifice to this evening with Brissac? I inspected the embroidered mounds of silk and velvet on the bed. Too nice, all much too nice for that grotesque Brissac, duke, or not.

"Madame, someone is at the door. Brissac is early. He must be eager."

"Eager to see me in my dressing gown, you mean. Have Mustapha go down and make him wait. Don't show him up until you've finished my make-up."

"Very well," answered Sylvie as she tied my hair away from my face with a wide blue satin ribbon, and began to apply the heavy white cream that gave my face its unique ghostly pallor. But she had hardly finished when the bedroom door was flung open with a crash.

"Madame, I swear, they wouldn't wait," cried Mustapha. I turned to face Brissac, eyes cold, eyebrows raised. But it was not Brissac who stood in the doorway. It was Captain Desgrez, with two assistants in the baggy blue breeches and plain blue wool jackets of the police. Desgrez himself, his narrow face unshaven, bowed and removed his white-plumed hat. Thank goodness my face is unrecognisable, I thought.

"Madame de Morville, I am Captain Desgrez of the police," he said.

While my mind raced through a list of reasons he might be there, I could hear my voice saying, "Monsieur Desgrez, please pardon my *déshabillé* and do me the honour of taking the armchair over there." He sat, his assistants standing on either side of the armchair that stood outside the screen in my *ruelle*.

Somehow he managed to make himself look like a magistrate, finding me guilty even before I had opened my mouth.

"Hellfire and damnation!" announced the parrot. Desgrez looked towards the bird's perch, and the bird looked back, fixing him with a beady eye. As his assistant stifled his amusement in a cough, Desgrez looked suspiciously at me.

"Curious vocabulary for a bird."

"I got him from someone else who taught him to speak. I am thinking of hiring a tutor to teach him better manners," I answered.

"Madame, I have come to ask you a few questions," he said, while the man standing beside him took out a little notebook.

"I will be delighted to answer any of which I have knowledge," I responded, with a condescending nod of my head.

"Your dressing-table mirror is shrouded in muslin, Madame de Morville. Why have you hidden the chief delight of women?"

"Monsieur, I have the unfortunate gift of seeing images of the future in reflections. My own future is a skull. I do not wish to see it."

"You are aware, of course, of what they say about those who sell themselves to the Devil. They have no reflection. Would you mind, Madame?" As I nodded silently, one of his assistants drew off the muslin shroud. I turned my head away from the mirror, hiding my eyes with my hands.

"You have a perfectly normal reflection, Madame," he announced, sounding vaguely relieved, "so why do you hide your eyes? What is it you see?"

"Blood, Captain Desgrez. Blood like a river, dripping across the face of the mirror." He got up, came close, and passed his hand between me and the mirror.

"Whose blood?" he asked softly.

"I don't know, but it's very bad. Sometimes I see it seeping between the stones of the Place Royale. Blood and more blood, enough for all of France," I answered, looking down at the floor, away from the mirror.

"It's about blood that I have come, Madame de Morville." His voice sounded lulling, disarming. "Tell me, did you know Monsieur Geniers, the magistrate?"

"Monsieur Geniers?" I looked up with a start. "Yes, I do know him. Why do you say 'did'?"

"He is dead, Madame – murdered. And your name and a receipt for money were found among his papers— Why, your hands are trembling. Tell me, what do you know about this crime?"

"The Chevalier de Saint-Laurent. It must be— Oh, God, he is vengeful!"

"The Chevalier de Saint-Laurent? How, Madame, do you come to know these men? Have you told their fortunes?" He sounded bland, but somehow beneath the gentle voice was something sinister. *You are in too deep already, Geneviève; the truth will have to do. Or at least, part of it.*

"Monsieur Desgrez, I was a silent partner of Monsieur Geniers. I lent him money to buy up the Chevalier de Saint-Laurent's gambling debts, so that Monsieur Geniers could put him in debtors' prison. Monsieur Geniers wanted vengeance for the seduction of his wife. And I, I had been cheated in an investment by the Chevalier de Saint-Laurent, so assisting Monsieur Geniers served my vengeance too, while preserving my reputation." The two men behind Captain Desgrez looked at each other as if something significant had been said. Suddenly I felt anxious. "Tell me, Monsieur Desgrez – have you taken the Chevalier de Saint-Laurent yet?" I asked. My body felt cold. *Either he was on the street, and I must pray he never connected me with Monsieur Geniers, or he was in prison, undergoing the question, and I must pray he did not connect me with his vanished niece. They'd bring me in. They'd question me.* The words of La Dodée echoed in my mind: "You can't withstand police questioning. You can't even withstand the pain of a tight corset."

"Unfortunately, he has eluded us," answered Desgrez.

"Does he know . . . ?" My voice was faint and hoarse.

". . . that you are the other one upon whom he must visit vengeance? Possibly not. The paper was locked in Monsieur Geniers's cabinet, and Saint-Laurent beat him to death with a heavy walking stick in the street before his own doorstep. The magistrate's servants raised a hue and cry and pursued him for some distance before he vanished." I put my hand to my heart.

"Then perhaps, Monsieur Desgrez, the blood is not mine – at least not yet." Desgrez looked avuncular.

"Then you wouldn't mind coming with us to make a statement before a police notary." Danger, my mind cried. Once there, they might keep me for forcible questioning.

"Monsieur, I am not dressed."

"Then get dressed. I can wait."

"But, Monsieur, I have an engagement this evening."

"Surely, you owe it to the peace of His Majesty's realm to assist in the apprehension of a murderer. It will only take a moment of your time – besides, a little lateness is fashionable." He settled deeper into the armchair as if he owned it. Delay him, my mind hummed. Delay him until Brissac arrives. That will at least complicate matters.

"Would you like refreshments while I am dressed?"

"I am content to wait for you, Madame." Oh. Horrid Jansenist. Duty before all. I began a lengthy conference with Sylvie about my toilette. My hair, what a complexity: should I use the jewelled combs or have it sprinkled with brilliants like the night sky? My hands: should I set them off with bracelets, or were the rings sufficient? I watched his bored gaze scan the room, taking in the tall carved and painted screen by the armoire, the little desk in the *ruelle*, the shelf of edifying classical works above it. With a sly sideways glance at the now-fidgeting assistants, Sylvie launched into an inventory of my box of *mouches*.

"The crescent moon is not so much in fashion since Madame de Ludres was seen wearing it. I would suggest the butterfly, Madame," she concluded.

"It is winter; I find butterflies inappropriate." A corset lace had snapped and had to be replaced. My green silk stockings were exceedingly difficult to locate. Once behind the screen to dress, we rearranged the order of petticoats several times and changed the bows on my shoes. Every so often I would peek at the back of the armchair, which could be seen through the joint of the screen. There sat my unwanted guest as stiff as a statue. But the back of his neck appeared to have turned red. His men were inspecting the furniture and peering out of the window.

"The green taffeta, Sylvie."

"Oh, Madame, with the lilac underskirt? Surely the blue satin would be so much more striking."

"It still has creases from the last time I wore it. You are so careless, Sylvie."

"Oh, please, Madame, please – I'm sure I can take them out in only a moment," Sylvie wailed in her finest imitation of a mindless lady's maid.

"Tell her to wear the god-damned green taffeta," came a growl from the main room beyond the screen.

"Duval, you exceed yourself," responded Desgrez's voice, taut with suppressed irritation.

"Captain, a carriage has drawn up before the house." Sylvie and I looked at each other behind the screen.

"I think I'll have the blue satin after all. The creases are not as bad as I thought," I announced.

"Oh, yes, Madame. Didn't I tell you it would be lovely?" Sylvie's whining, apologetic tone was fit for the theatre. I found it hard to keep a straight face. But it would never do for Desgrez to hear women's laughter from behind the screen.

"Duval, who is it?" Desgrez's voice was crisp.

"The carriage is unmarked. The people inside are very well dressed, but masked." I emerged from behind the screen.

"My theatre party, gentlemen. What do you think of the blue satin? Will it please Monsieur le Duc?" Desgrez's face was set like iron. But Duval and the other assistant gave each other a meaningful glance.

Desgrez rose as Brissac was shown in, and the police captain bowed low, removing his hat, as he was presented to the duke. Brissac, a man practised at evading bailiffs and bill collectors, took in the situation at a glance. Slowly, he lowered his black velvet mask to stare at the lower order of humanity displayed there before him. His face was cold and haughty as he informed Desgrez that it would be a pity if he interrupted plans for an evening devised by the Duc de Nevers himself. It was canny, the delicate way he injected the name of the all-powerful Nevers into the discussion and suggested that, lover of justice that he was, a notary might be sent to the house at my convenience at some later time. A malignant little half-smile crossed his face as he watched Desgrez bow himself out of the room backwards. Brissac then turned to me and bowed, flourishing his hat in a manner that said, You see the advantages of an alliance, Madame. But I was not pleased with the look I had seen on Desgrez's face. Hooded, hidden rage. He hated the great: their money, their immunity. He would wait until he found me alone and unprotected, this man who had tracked the Marquise de Brinvilliers across Europe for years, this man who had managed to acquire a confession from which even a title could not protect her. Brissac knew that, too. Now I must have Brissac, just as he must have Nevers.

THIRTY-NINE

Brissac had served his patron well; the boxes above the stage were crammed with masked men and women of the demi-monde, chattering loudly, displaying their finery, and peering about to see if they could determine who else of interest was there. Our own box was filled with a satanist abbé and his mistress, ourselves, and La Voisin and her current lover, the Vicomte de Cousserans, a debauched gentleman with purple veins on his nose. In the ripple of conversation the name "Pradon" could be distinguished, as well as rumblings of Racine's failure – the dreadful blonde actress, too coarse for the part, the common verses, the vulgar treatment of a subject that must be handled with the utmost delicacy if it is not to become, well, indecent. Thus can the opinion of the world be purchased, I thought. In the pit beneath, soldiers, students, and riff-raff paid for the evening set up the cry "Pra-don, Pra-don!" as if rehearsing for the rolling cheers with which they would greet every line of the work as it was presented.

"*Oooo!*" I heard a woman squeal. "That is definitely Mademoiselle Bertrand, the comedienne. I'd know her *hair* anywhere. And that dress!" I looked to see exactly what sort of hair this prodigy possessed. Blonde. Dyed. Mountains of it, all done up with brilliants and bows. Not as nice a box as ours, I sniffed to myself. And public lovemaking with that over-dressed fellow in the crimson velvet. Actresses have no taste. It is, after all, a profession without respectability, scarcely better than prostitution. A vast, powdered bosom heaved up above tight stays. Her ungloved hands seemed rather entangled in the gentleman's clothing. He laughed, and the way he tilted his head seemed familiar.

"Why, that is indeed Mademoiselle Bertrand. And who is her latest moneybags?" The vicomte leaned forward to look more closely, applying a lorgnon to the eyehole of his mask.

"Well, I'll be damned! It's that wretched upstart who finished me off at *lansquenet* last week. What was his name?"

"D'Urbec," prompted La Voisin with a sideways glance in my direction. I looked again. This time his face turned fully in my direction. Unlike the occupants of our box, he was unmasked. D'Urbec, in an immense black wig, with a massive silver-knobbed walking stick leaning beside him, a comedienne draped over him, and a boxful of raucous companions. I wanted to think he looked lonely in the midst of it all. But he didn't. He radiated smugness, satisfaction. He was taking in the scene as if he owned it. He didn't even look a trifle wistful, damn him. Just arrogant and pleased with himself. La Voisin's eyes were watching me from behind her mask.

"I loathe upstarts," announced Brissac.

"The man comes from nowhere. Everything he gets is at the tables. He wins as if he's made a pact with the Devil. Tell me, my dear; you are an expert. Has he made a pact with the Devil?" asked the Vicomte, giving La Voisin a squeeze around the waist.

"Not with the intervention of anyone I know of," announced La Voisin. "Though I have heard he has gone abroad to a foreign adept."

"I've a sure test of that." Brissac laughed. "Tell me, what would you say if I ruined him publicly?"

"Why, that the Devil wasn't his patron ... shh ... the curtain's going up." Brissac leaned towards the vicomte's ear and whispered something. They both chuckled. "Done!" said the vicomte, as the first of Pradon's dubious verses rolled across the stage.

I returned home with a dreadful headache. The play, perhaps, the crowded box and the stench from the pit. Or was it the lemonade Brissac had purchased for me? I remembered the yellow roses. Definitely, something in the lemonade. Damnation. And La Voisin's maternal look of approval as he offered it. Another love powder. Powdered cockscomb, desiccated pigeon hearts, and who knows what other rot. No wonder I had a headache. I thought of Brissac. As repulsive as ever. Madame's love powders were about as effective as that irresistible perfume my mother used to use. How can I turn this to my advantage? I deserve revenge for this headache. I will pretend that it has worked; first, I'll show a growing tenderness for Brissac – I'll buy him a new suit. That will put them off. Then I'll act as if the stuff is fading and watch their contortions as they try to slip me another dose. I'll lead them a merry dance.

My head throbbed terribly. The love powder must have had some damned drug in it. Images flitted through my mind, and my stomach felt ghastly. I seemed dimly to remember some sort of conversation with the vicomte about – yes, d'Urbec. Ruining him. Wasn't he ruined already? I lay down on the bed, trying to decide which part of me felt the sickest. D'Urbec had sat on the edge of my armchair, as if he feared to spoil it, and inspected his hands, all torn and callussed from the oar. How many times can a man be ruined and still press on? There was, after all, a sort of perverse gallantry about it. And bitter determination. I saw again the scene in the box; now I understood it. He had hired a woman, the same way he'd leased a flashy carriage and bought all those showy clothes. He was thumbing his nose at the world, as if to say: You think money is important? I'll give you money. Quick, loud, vulgar money. The man with a mind mocks money, too. I couldn't help liking his mockery, for I knew it well – the mockery of the arrant stupidity, of the cold heart of society.

I broke into a cold sweat as I lay there, my mind a riot of strange memories. D'Urbec had a whole vocabulary of mockery: There was the funny tenderness beneath the mockery in his voice when he called me "Athena", knowing that I could barely make out Greek, and his mockery of Lamotte, as sharp as a sword run through a friend that had become a rival . . . A rival? For what? Not . . . no, it couldn't be – not for me. Oh! What was the odd feeling that was coming over me? Horrible. Not sensible. D'Urbec, he was filling my mind, making my heart hurt. What a stupid heart I have, I thought. Runny, like a half-boiled egg. Why is my heart like this? I don't want a heart. I'd cut it out if I could. But then my chest would ache as much as my head.

That night I lit the candle in my *ruelle* from the fire and sat thinking before my open book. I could see d'Urbec, in that ridiculous Brandenburger overcoat he used to wear, his dark eyes glowing and his arms gesticulating as he explained his theory of the fiscal incapacity of the state. *What has happened to me?* I wrote. *Have I been drugged? Is it La Voisin's spell at work? Or is it something in me that has always been there? Is it only sympathy that has grown to overwhelming proportions, or was it always more, and I was afraid to recognise it? Why did it frighten me so? Why does it frighten me now? God help me. I am in love with Florent d'Urbec, and I have made a mess of everything.*

I blotted the page and shut the book. Then I took out a fresh sheet of paper and wrote: *Beware Brissac. He has made a scheme to ruin you*, and signed it, *A Friend.* D'Urbec was still too angry with me, I judged, not to throw it out if he knew where it came from. I'll trust it to Mustapha to deliver it. At least he won't take it straight to La Voisin. Even so, in this city of intrigue, d'Urbec might well never receive it. Yes, Mustapha. Sylvie takes money from too many people. Putting the letter under my pillow, I fell into a troubled sleep.

"So, Mustapha, did he get my letter?" Mustapha, heavily bundled up against the cold, had returned, ostensibly from his mission to purchase more cordial from La Trianon's ever-busy laboratory. As I hurried downstairs to open the door for him myself, Sylvie didn't even look up from her mending, assuming my eagerness was related to my lust for opium.

Mustapha's voice was low. "Yes and no, Madame."

"What do you mean? Didn't you see him get it?"

"I found his rooms by enquiring at the Théâtre Guénégaud and sent an old friend of mine, a dwarf who begs on the Pont au Change, to deliver the message so that he wouldn't recognise me. My friend, who is trustworthy, was shown in to find him at breakfast with La Bertrand, the comedienne. He was wearing a silk dressing gown and a brocade fur-lined cap. Evidently he has shaved his head like an aristocrat these days and hired the services of a rather exclusive wig maker."

"I don't care about his wig. Go on." Mustapha hesitated.

"Madame, he recognised the handwriting. He tore the letter up unread." He shook his cloak off before the fire. "And

. . . that's not all. When La Bertrand asked what the letter was, he shrugged his shoulders and said it was just another *billet doux* from one of the many women who were mad for him."

"Mustapha, no one paid you to tell me this, did they?"

"On my honour, Madame. I've told you just as it was told to me." I took a deep breath and let it out slowly.

"Then, evidently, there is nothing more I can do for him."

"Evidently. But what was in the letter, Madame?"

"A warning, Mustapha."

"I myself would never discount a warning from the celebrated seeress Madame de Morville," observed Mustapha. "Among other things, you are never wrong."

"I wish I were this time," I said. How could I blame d'Urbec for hating me? What more had I a right to expect? If only I could at least win back some small part of the friendship I had thrown away so foolishly! How was it that in my mad dash after the trivial-minded, empty hero of my childhood I had missed the fact that I possessed something as precious as d'Urbec's regard? Suddenly I felt old and sad. I went to stand by the fire, extending my hands before the leaping flames that looked so much like glowing salamanders among the logs.

"Still, in my search about town I have found other scandals that may amuse you, Madame."

"Oh, do tell. I am in need of amusement."

"There is a new sonnet attacking Monsieur Racine's *Phèdre*, said to be penned by Nevers himself – or at least one of his camp. It is so vicious that Racine will have to answer."

"And then, of course, Nevers will have licence to counterattack," I pointed out.

"Exactly," agreed Mustapha. "Then it is the end of Monsieur Racine's masterwork, and possibly of Monsieur Racine himself. I've never heard of anyone yet who has outsmarted a Mancini cabal."

They were playing *bassette* at the Hôtel Soissons, and the money fever was high. At the principal table sat the countess in her great armchair, a dozen or so of her little dogs clustered about her feet. Madame de Vertamon was cutting the cards, while the Marquis de Gordes observed them all through the lorgnon in his hand. At the other tables one could see the players exulting as fortune turned their way or tearing at their wigs and beating the tables with their fists as thousands of pistoles vanished at a turn of the cards.

"My friend, I am short of money. Have you five hundred pistoles?" Madame de Rambures turned to the gentleman standing behind her, who was obliged to supply them. The requirements of male gallantry were such that few men who won ever left with their winnings; one must assist the ladies' play. And the ladies did lose. They lacked strategy, I observed, and let themselves be carried away by the emotion of the moment.

I drifted through the room, picking up gossip: the new styles, news from the front, the personalities of military commanders dissected, ditto ladies of fashion, society physicians, and magistrates. Through the gabble of voices I heard a woman laughing: "Oh, my dear, you hadn't *heard*? The Sieur Racine has fled to the Jansenists. He wrote a sonnet accusing Nevers of incest. And Nevers has made it clear Racine's life was worth nothing if he stayed."

"Nevers is entirely within his rights. I say, it warrants a thousand cuts with a stirrup leather . . ." I moved on, not wishing to be caught listening in.

"So, Primi, you do not play?" Visconti had appeared at my shoulder, ever the bored observer.

"I ventured a single pistole the day before yesterday, Madame de Morville, and within an evening had won a thousand. Then the ladies all said, 'Visconti the magician will win for us' and had me play for them as their champion. This evening I was wiped out and withdrew before I went into the kind of debt I could not repay."

"Eminently sensible, I think."

"Ah, but it harms my reputation. How can a prophet fail at cards? Perhaps it is wiser never to play, as you do."

"Primi, who is the dark fellow holding the bank at the table over there? I don't believe I've seen him here before."

"Oh, him? That's Monsieur d'Urbec. Not a very distinguished-sounding name, but they say he's connected with foreign banking interests. There are rumours of a foreign title, but as the possessor of one myself, I can assure you that it counts for little. No, it's the money he has that makes him welcome. He's very generous with the ladies, he knows how to get a gentleman out of an embarrassment, and he has the Devil's own luck at cards."

"Oh, he cheats?"

"No, he's like Dangeau. He plays with strategy, not emotions, and so has become Fortune's favourite. He comes from nowhere and is invited everywhere. They say he may be negotiating to buy an office – some provincial tax farmership, I think. A parvenu, but not without wit. Ah, there's Monsieur Villeroy – look how he dissembles; he thinks he conceals from the world that he is the countess's lover, but it is written clearly on his face. The science of physiognomy, it is infallible."

"How would you read Monsieur d'Urbec, Primi?" He shot me a quick glance.

"He's not for you, little vixen, unless you want to live a life in exile, shuffling between the courts of foreign princes. You are too much a Parisian, I judge, to want that. He has the face of a born adventurer. Bitter, intelligent. He owns too many secrets. He lays plans like a chess master in a world of fools and amateurs. He will counsel kings; but they will not love him."

"Bravo, Primi. And the physiognomies of the others he plays against?"

"Brissac, our old friend – a delicious monster, a master of débauche. See the slant of the forehead and the way the eyelids droop? Perverse. And the ambassador Giustiniani— Oh, look—"

At the table, some sort of drama was taking place. Giustiniani had laid his cards face down on the table. Brissac tipped his head back and laughed madly. D'Urbec stood up suddenly, his hands flat on the table, his face white.

"Come, let us not miss the excitement," said Visconti, taking me by the arm.

"A hundred thousand pistoles. I want them immediately, *Monsieur* d'Urbec."

"Surely, you do not expect Monsieur d'Urbec to leave town tomorrow—" Giustiniani broke in, ". . . among gentlemen . . ."

"'Gentlemen'? And who says Monsieur d'Urbec is a gentleman?" Brissac's voice was cold and taunting.

"Oh, la, dear Monsieur d'Urbec, I would repay your favour

of last night, if only I hadn't lost so heavily this evening. My husband will be so annoyed with me," Madame de Bonnelle said with a sigh.

"Gentleman?" said d'Urbec between his teeth. "Gentlemen do not cheat at cards."

"I could run you through for that. You insult the oldest blood in France, Monsieur Nobody." Brissac stood up suddenly. The press of people around the table had grown as players left their own games.

In a moment, d'Urbec had seized Brissac by the coat and shaken him in his powerful grip as a terrier shakes a rat. A shower of cards fell from Brissac's sleeves.

"Why, what's this?" cried Madame de Bonnelle. "Monsieur Brissac, you naughty man!"

"*Canaille*," snarled Brissac, as he dealt d'Urbec a blow across the face, as one would to a lackey.

"Monsieur de Brissac, the dignity of my house..." the Countess of Soissons's high voice cut through the astonished murmur of the crowd. I watched d'Urbec flush, then grow white. He had nearly given himself away, through the unnatural strength of his arms and hands. And to engage in an illegal duel with a man of such rank as Brissac would expose him and cause his ruin. But the worst that Brissac could expect for offending the King with a duel was to cool his heels in the Bastille for a few weeks. Brissac laughed. The countess looked at d'Urbec as she would a mongrel that had somehow slipped in among her lapdogs. It was a long look, humiliating even to witness.

"How dare you embarrass Monsieur le Duc in my house?" she said in an icy voice. "You may go at once—"

"Not without paying his debt to me," Brissac broke in, his harsh voice devoid of all courtesy. "I want it now, d'Urbec. Your carriage, the coat you're wearing, everything."

"My bankers will deliver it to you tomorrow morning, Monsieur le Duc."

"Monsieur de Brissac, I do not want this quarrel. I want him removed immediately. Do not risk offending me with your delays over trivialities," the countess said.

"The scoundrel may flee – I want it now, or I want him in prison."

"A point in your favour, Monsieur de Brissac. But you should understand I do not appreciate sordid things happening in my house." The countess looked about her. "Who will guarantee this man's debt until tomorrow morning?" Not a soul answered. The press of bodies drew back from d'Urbec, who stood like a wounded beast before a pack of encircling hounds. In the silence, I heard my own voice speaking, as if from another place.

"Madame, last night I had a terrible vision, that came unbidden as I looked into my mirror. Blood dripped across the face of the glass. I took it for an omen of the day to follow."

"Listen to the prophetess," a man's voice said behind me. The countess, a veritable well of superstition, recoiled slightly. I saw several ladies crossing themselves. "To spare your gracious house, your illustrious personage, and your distinguished guests from this ill omen, I will stand security for this man's debt until tomorrow morning." Brissac's eyes looked hatred at me. D'Urbec turned, slowly, to look at me. His face was impassive. He bowed in my direction.

"My thanks, Madame de Morville," he said. And with an obeisance to the countess, he walked out through the hall alone, never looking back.

"He gets off too lightly," growled Brissac to a gentleman in his service, Monsieur de Vandeuil. "Have my lackeys thrash him on the way home." As I watched Monsieur de Vandeuil vanish, I recalled that d'Urbec was not wearing a sword. Silently, I turned to follow Vandeuil out past the lackey picking up the fallen cards. I could hear the countess admonishing Brissac as I went to seek my cloak and hat. "Remember, Monsieur de Brissac, what happens in my house is my affair . . ." Mustapha saw me depart and followed at a distance. On the stair outside, I paused. De Vandeuil had stepped in front of d'Urbec, barring his way.

"The Duc de Brissac is offended by your presumption, lackey." Four men armed with heavy sticks seemed to detach themselves from the shadows and stood silently in the blackened, churned-up snow of the courtyard within the carriage gate.

"For what? For making him the laughing-stock of Paris? Cards up the sleeve – bah! Little cur, your master cheats like an old woman." D'Urbec stepped away from the blow. The sound of his laughter, mad and bitter, echoed in the darkened courtyard. A half-dozen guests and a cluster of servants had gathered on the stair behind me to watch. There was the metallic slither of a sword being unsheathed.

"You know I am unarmed," I heard d'Urbec's voice, steady and calm.

"I wouldn't dirty my blade with you, Monsieur d'Urbec from nowhere. Lackeys, ho!" The thugs encircled d'Urbec from behind. Somewhere behind me, a woman's high-pitched laughter sounded.

"Enough, Monsieur de Vandeuil," I called in a commanding tone, and as he turned to see where the voice was coming from, I advanced down the wide staircase. There was no sound but the thump-thump of my tall walking stick on the frosty stone. "I do not wish to see my investment spoiled." I stopped directly before his drawn blade and stared coldly at him. My ghoulish white face and eerie antique black had made him pause for a moment.

"Madame de Morville, kindly remove yourself from this quarrel. I would rather that Monsieur de Vandeuil suffer the consequences of his acts." D'Urbec's voice was level.

"Well, here's a change. I thought someone like you would prefer to hide behind a woman's skirts," Vandeuil sneered.

"He does not need to, Monsieur de Vandeuil," I said in what I hoped was a sinister and meaningful tone. "*He is one of us.*"

"One of you? The society of old ladies?" De Vandeuil's high-pitched giggle betrayed his nerves.

"Astaroth never fails to repay. Tell Brissac." I watched as de Vandeuil's sword point quivered and lowered slightly. "Astaroth dislikes waiting for your answer, Monsieur. I must warn you that to him, delay is an insult." De Vandeuil sheathed his sword, and I stepped aside.

"I would not insult the paving stones of this great house by allowing your blood to fall on them, Monsieur d'Urbec . . . out of consideration for our hostess, and for this old dame here, we will meet elsewhere." In a show of bravado, de Vandeuil flourished his hat as he bowed.

"Very well, Monsieur de Vandeuil, at our next meeting I shall take the precaution of wearing a sword." D'Urbec bowed in response. As he turned, he saw for the first time the armed lackeys behind him. His face was impassive.

"Monsieur d'Urbec, are your porters here? I suggest you dismiss them and escort me home in my carriage. The streets are so full of ruffians these days, it's dangerous for an old woman." D'Urbec took my arm with a formal gesture.

"I am at your service, my dear Marquise." But as he handed me into my carriage and Gilles got up behind, he hissed, "Again you interfere with my life. When will you tire of meddling? What is it you want, anyway?"

"Certainly not gratitude, Florent," I answered as I leaned back against the cushions and put my hands in my muff. "I don't want them waylaying my investment on the way home."

"Your 'investment' was not required. You could have withheld your idiot desire to interfere in my business. Now, you compound the trouble you've caused."

"If you'd read the warning I sent you, you'd have had no trouble at all."

"Hardly. I needed to be at the Hôtel Soissons tonight." His voice sounded distant, hard. This man was not acting like any professional gambler that I knew.

"Only if you had other business than gaming, I'd say. You've lost a fortune tonight, and you do not turn a hair. If I were more interested in you, I would ask who's backing you. About the only person I'm certain it's not is Astaroth."

"Your mental powers, like your malice, are undimmed, Madame de Morville. My compliments." I was sure of it now. A *nouvelliste* who knew everyone and everything in a wartime capital. One with a grudge. One who, with only a little sponsorship, could worm his way into any circle. He must be selling information to some foreign government. I wondered if his family had been offered asylum in return for his espionage. Where had they fled? Amsterdam? London? But why did he let me suspect? Somehow, I felt he was testing me.

"It is only common logic, Florent. Astaroth is too capricious a demon to suit most men, and, of course, he is such a tyrant."

"No greater a tyrant than the King who believes he is the sun," said d'Urbec quietly.

"Daedalus paid with his life for going too close to the sun," I answered.

"And Persephone, tempted by a feast of six pomegranate seeds, was condemned to the underworld."

"Ah, but she was Queen of Hades. There are those who believe that social rank is always worth something, even in the underworld." D'Urbec remained silent until the carriage pulled into the street where he had his rooms. In the chill dark of the carriage, I could feel his warm breath. The small space seemed somehow filled up with him, with a sort of powerful, animal tension. Suddenly I was jealous of the woman in his bed. As I bade him good night, I couldn't help adding, "Is that actress waiting up for you? Or do you just lease her along with your carriage?"

"Geneviève Pasquier," he hissed, "have you ever believed that love is not something that can be bought and paid for?"

"Of course, Monsieur d'Urbec. Love has many motivations. Revenge, for example."

"And cruelty, Mademoiselle. That innocent cruelty that leads cats to dismember mice as toys and children to pluck the legs off living insects. The need of a clever monster to see how things work."

"And what if she knows how they work?" His silence in response was brutal. I could feel him looking at me in the dark. I could almost feel his thoughts as they flowed from violence into understanding.

"And so you have tried to buy me, haven't you, little Athena?" he said softly. "Will you ever be capable of believing that a man could be interested in you for any other reason than money or revenge?"

"God did not make me a lovely person, Florent. I am brave enough not to deceive myself. One must be rational."

"Yes, always rational, aren't you? Perhaps some day you will learn that you must accept love that is a free gift, instead of putting it out with the trash. Until then, goodbye, little fortune-teller."

"Florent, wait—" But he had already dismounted from the carriage.

"Don't worry, Madame de Morville. I'll send you a message tomorrow when I have discharged the debt. I thank you and owe you my gratitude." My heart turned into a knot, there in the dark, and I did not know if I hated him or not. I think maybe I did – the way we hate things that are for ever out of reach.

The following afternoon, a boy came with a letter from d'Urbec. The arrangements to transfer the money had been accomplished, and he was leaving Paris on business that might take several months.

"It strikes me that I was perhaps ungracious after your intervention in the most delicate situation of yesterday evening. With your permission, I will call on you after my return, to offer my thanks in a more creditable manner." I read it over several times. I was not sure what I felt. Perhaps the *grippe*. After all, the weather had been exceptionally nasty lately.

That night I wrote in my notebook: *10 January 1677. Could d'Urbec have ever cared for me once? It must have been. And now that I have found him, I have lost him. He will never come back. And not only that, but in going, he has made Brissac rich again. Brissac is now free of his need to deal with me, and as full of hatred as a toad. All I have done with my life is trade away love for shallow and trivial desires.*

Several salty drops fell on the page, smearing the ink. What could I have ever wanted with Florent d'Urbec anyway? Logic said it could only have ended badly. Logic said he couldn't like me long, once he'd seen me as I really was. I'd been a fool. It was over.

FORTY

"Oh, Sylvie, look outside for me – I've had a dreadful dream." I sat up in bed to see that Sylvie had brought my morning chocolate and bread bought fresh that morning. She pulled the heavy curtains and looked out into the spring morning. "What do you see out there in the street?" I asked anxiously.

"A big dray cart, Madame, the woman who just sold me the milk for your chocolate . . . she's dipping some out from her bucket for the woman across the street. There're two cats, a yellow dog . . . and someone's pig has got out."

"No one else? Are you sure?"

"Oh yes, Madame. There's a boy selling little pastries on a tray. Do you want me to get some?"

"Don't go. Look again – you don't see a . . . a man without a face, do you?"

"Of course I don't. We live in a nice neighbourhood. What on earth is wrong with you?"

"I dreamed he was outside, waiting for me, looking up at the house. It was as real as real— Then I woke up when you came in."

"Madame, it is the opium again. How much cordial did you take before you went to sleep last night?"

"Hardly any, see?" I said, holding up the bottle from my nightstand. "I'm cutting down."

"You've cut down before, and you always go back to it. It's not doing you any good, I can see that."

"Sylvie, you go beyond your place."

"Madame, what do I care? Listen to me – times are hard and places are scarce. It won't do me any good to be working for a corpse."

"It's not the cordial this time – look again." Something in my tone of voice made her look intently at my face, then go again to look. The pale light of early spring poured in through the tall window, making a shining rectangle across the heavy brocade bedspread and dark-patterned carpet. The scent of blooming narcissus from bulbs forced in a pot on a side table filled the room.

"I see the first carriage in the street – your customers are coming. You'd best dress quickly."

"Very well, Sylvie, but—"

"Don't worry, Madame, I won't let in any faceless men." Sylvie's voice was ironic.

The morning was unusually full: I divined the fate of a son at the front and a lover at sea, advised on an engagement, and referred an artillery officer to La Voisin for an ointment to make him impervious to bullet wounds. By late afternoon, business had dropped off. Mustapha had brought a copy of *Le Mercure galant*, which he began to read aloud for my amusement.

"Listen to this, Madame. The fashion is changing again: ribbons are to be removed from the rest of the costume, and the mode for men will be for 'more sumptuous materials, elegance residing in the *coiffure*, the shoes, and the beauty of the linens and the vest'. Just as well my own costume has timeless elegance, isn't it? The truly fashionable man is above the mode," he announced, inspecting the turned-up toes of his embroidered Turkish slippers.

"One might as well say the same for me." I laughed as Mustapha gave me the paper and glided to the door to admit another client. Only his cough reminded me that I should give up the paper, for the client was waiting, and I looked up to see a demobilised soldier, his back to me, inspecting my furniture. He had on a wide hat and carried a heavy metal-tipped walking stick in one hand. With the other, he stroked the silver vase on the sideboard with a possessive air that I did not like. I sat up straight, tucked away the *Mercure galant*, and pulled the veils of my mourning headdress back down so my face was again hidden in mystery. All was in order: the round globe of the oracle glass shining on its stand of entwined silver dragons, the rods, the cabbalistic cloth. Mustapha looked uneasy.

"Monsieur," I said, "with what business may I assist you?"

The man turned and walked across the room with an arrogant air. I could see him staring at the heavy rings on my right hand as it rested on the black velvet that covered the table. He seated himself opposite me without my invitation, laying his walking stick against my table. I drew back with a start. It was not the false nose he wore or the stench of the infection from his cropped nose and ears. It was that I had recognised the faceless man.

"I have come to inquire after a missing relative," the faceless man said. His voice was low, menacing. I could hear the breath hiss in and out of the mangled holes in his face beneath the artificial nose that was tied to his face with a silk cord. Yes, the voice was his, too. The voice of my nightmares. The Chevalier de Saint-Laurent. Uncle.

"I cannot see the past. Only the future. There will be no fee if I cannot obtain a reading on this missing relative." My voice was calm. I am no child now, Uncle; I am strong. And even as I feared it, I craved this moment, when I could confront you and tell you what you are.

"Oh, I think you will succeed in finding her. Lift up that veil, Geneviève Pasquier."

"So, Uncle, we meet again at last. What excess of family devotion has brought you here? Would you like me to read your future?" I lifted the veil and stared directly at his hideous face without flinching. He sucked in his breath. The change that artifice, money, and love had brought to my face could not be mistaken.

"You have changed," he said, regaining his calm. "You're not a bad-looking girl these days."

"Geneviève Pasquier is dead. I do not appreciate your familiarity. State your business or leave."

"Come, come now," he said, leaning across the table in repulsive intimacy, "you should be a little more friendly. Family is family, eh? Consider your duty to your elders." He got up suddenly and paced around the room. "I've done a great deal for you. Look at you! You're rich." He gestured around him at the opulent furnishings of the room. "That desk, inlaid . . . and the tapestry . . . a Gobelin, isn't it? And that carpet – it looks Turkish." Turkish – Mustapha had vanished silently to fetch Gilles, as he did whenever a client looked troublesome.

"It was hardly your doing, Uncle. I owe you nothing." His sly, foxy eyes darted sideways at me. He smiled that wide, confident grin that had once so entranced the ladies. It was hideous now. It distorted the scarred face and set the artificial nose off centre.

"I think you do," he said.

"I imagined that's what you would think. You've never been more than a parasite. It would not be true to character for you to come for any other reason than money," I answered.

He sprang forward with a growl and put both hands upon my desk. "Be careful of your tongue, you little bitch, or it will cost you everything."

"Everything, Uncle? Didn't you take that from me already? And see what good it did you. Be warned, Uncle, I will never be robbed again." Hard and invulnerable in the iron garments of the Marquise de Morville, I felt exalted by the rising ferocity that came like the smoke of a raging fire deep inside me. I stood. "Beware of what you ask, for I will pay you in exactly the coin you deserve." I felt that if he came even an inch closer, my rage would spill over him and dissolve him like vitriol. And facing me as he did, Uncle could not see Mustapha return with Gilles, silently motioning him to hide behind the screen that hid the kitchen door.

I could see the blood twisting the arteries in Uncle's neck. His breath came hard. "I could wring your neck right here, you smiling, deformed little monster."

"Hardly as deformed as you," I laughed. "Whoremonger, betrayer of innocence, poisoner of old women. What do you intend to do? Blackmail me by threatening to inform the police about me? I'll have a good bit to tell them about you, myself." I stepped back from behind my table. He picked up his heavy walking stick from the floor beside the chair.

"You'll stop laughing when I identify you and, as head of the family, put you in a convent and lay claim to everything you possess," he hissed.

"You? The heir of the Pasquiers? Hardly, Uncle. I'm not an ignorant girl any more. Anything you do will only enrich my brother, who will take everything. How silly of you not to settle for mere blackmail. How much you could have sucked from me under the threat to tell my brother where I was! And how unlikely for you to miss such an obvious source of money. Clearly you, too, are afraid Étienne will find you. No, you've been a fool, Uncle. Your threats have lost you everything. You won't get a sou from me."

"You stand there so cool, so arrogant. Who do you think you are? You're nothing! I've had you, you're nobody – and I can have you again. And what you have, I'll take, just as I take whatever I want, now." His fierce, wolfish smile showed his curious pointed eye-teeth. Like fangs. They seemed somehow as if they were dripping blood from a recent kill. What had he been doing since the police had last heard of him? He seemed ruthless with some recent evil. Careful, careful, I told myself. Don't set him off by showing fear. Paralyse him with your coldness, as the viper does with his staring, venomous eye. I stood up, smiling, and strolled calmly around the table past him, stroking his arm with my jewelled fingers as casually as I would a cat, until I stood a foot before the screen where Gilles and Mustapha were concealed. He started and swore at my touch, his eyes following my hand. I knew how much he valued jewels.

"'Nobody', Uncle? No, I am somebody. It is you who have become a nobody. A leech without prospect. It's really quite pitiful, wouldn't you agree? Tell me, which of your besotted lady friends paid to get you out of prison this time? Did she turn away when she saw what her husband had done to you, Monsieur Lover of Women? And have you now added her to your list of female enemies? It strikes me that you hold too many grudges, Uncle."

"I do not keep them long, dear little niece. The woman who scorned me is dead. So is everyone else who stands in my way. What have I to lose? I will take your money, your jewels, to flee the country. I will buy the women I want with the rings on your fingers, when I have sent you to keep your mother company. She tried to hide her money, too, but I knew she had it. She dared to call me a monster – she who outdid every monster living. My stick convinced her. What a fool she was. And all for five gold louis. But I wasn't disappointed, for she led me to you. And now, Niece, I want to know where your cash box is . . ." He smiled, showing a large number of teeth, and tapped the heavy stick on his open palm. Mother. How on earth had a blind, insane woman led him to me? And what had he done there in the Rue des Marmousets?

"You're a clever man, Uncle, to find me here. Surely, Mother did not give you the address." He smiled again, temporarily distracted by the contemplation of his own brilliance.

"You were a fool, Niece. You let slip your mask. What fortune-teller gives away money rather than takes it? She said she didn't have anything more for me – Marie-Angélique had visited and had given her hardly anything. But the stable boy had seen the celebrated Marquise de Morville leave by the back way. It would have been clear to a fool. The blind woman knew her daughter's voice. Only it was the wrong daughter." I could hear the breathing behind the screen. Mustapha, silent as a cat, peeped out. I must keep Uncle's eyes only on me.

"What did you do to Mother?" Uncle came closer, his eyes sly and triumphant. Mustapha crossed behind him, his Turkish slippers making not a single sound on the heavy carpet.

"Helped end her misery on earth," answered uncle, "as I will now ... help ... you—" His remnant of a face distorted with rage, and the nose fell away, revealing two raw and oozing holes. His teeth were like a wolf's, his eyes insane with evil. I saw the stick lash out and instinctively raised my arm before my face, screaming and falling to the ground as the bone snapped under the heavy blow. In another moment, the breath went out of me as Uncle's body fell on mine. The screen overturned with a crash as my servants rushed to my aid. The ghastly dying thing sprawled across me, suffocating me, its touch filling me with horror.

"Don't pull my arm!" I cried as Gilles rolled the body off me and Sylvie pulled at me, trying to right me. "He's broken it. I swear I heard the bone break."

"Well, he won't be breaking any more, that's for certain," said Gilles with calm distaste, as he turned over the body with his toe. Two sharp little knives were sunk deep into the Chevalier de Saint-Laurent's back, soaking in black blood that was oozing onto my dress, into the carpet, everywhere. "I think the second knife was entirely superfluous, Mustapha. The first seems to have gone to the heart." Gilles looked at the little man with admiration.

"Oh, God, you've killed him." I was shuddering all over. Uncle's hideous face had touched mine, his filthy blood was staining me. His stink was in my nose, rising to my brain.

"Surely Madame is not sorry for him," said Sylvie with some astonishment.

"No, Sylvie," I answered, clutching my arm and lying absolutely still on the floor. Gradually, I was regaining control of myself. The pain in my arm seemed to spread all through me. "It is the problem of getting rid of the body."

"What problem, Madame? We'll simply bury him in the garden tonight."

"And arouse the neighbours? The garden is too narrow, and the wall is directly beneath the windows of the house next door."

"Madame is right," said Sylvie with a sigh.

"And, Gilles, don't imagine I'll let you risk trying to dump him in the river tonight. You know the police are uncommonly interested in who goes in and out at night, ever since d'Urbec bled all over the neighbourhood." Gilles looked annoyed, but he knew I was right, too. I sat up gradually, clutching my arm, and made my way to my armchair. "Oh, Lord, my arm hurts," I said as I settled into the cushions. "Sylvie, go upstairs and get my cordial. Something . . . something is coming to me. A very good idea." The idea continued to form as Sylvie pattered off upstairs. "Cleopatra . . . Ha, there are virtues to a classical education, after all. Gilles, would you and Mustapha be so kind as to roll up my former uncle into the rug? I think we need to have it sent out for cleaning. I want it out of the house before Chauvet comes to set my arm."

Late in the afternoon, the neighbours all observed a cart draw up to the front door and a pair of lackeys, directed by a servant maid, load up a heavy, rolled carpet to be sent out for cleaning. The gossips of the neighbourhood carried far and wide the news of the good fortune by which a terrible accident had been prevented. A *torchère* overturned, and a dreadful stain and burn mark had to be cleaned up and rewoven.

"Can you imagine the expense? It is a terrible pity; the carpet looks so costly!" Voices were rising to my open bedroom window, where I lay nursing my arm.

"It's just the intervention of God that they didn't set fire to the house. The whole neighbourhood might have gone up in flames." Excellent, I thought, as I heard them make way for the surgeon, whom they took for a gentleman from his dress and the liveried lackey with him.

Once shown upstairs, Chauvet had his lackey unpack an assortment of splints and bandages while he inspected my arm.

"Of course," he observed in a voice that dripped irony, "there's no telling how long it takes bones over a century old to heal."

"I'll just put some of the alchemical formula on it," I replied blandly. He chuckled appreciatively as he tied on the splint.

"But next time, pick your clients more carefully... Oh, don't look so surprised. No fall I've ever seen broke a wrist that far towards the elbow and left a welt, to boot. I'd say a cane, or a walking stick, or the flat of a sword. Your hand up so – across the face. It must have been a man. If it had been one of your witches, now, you wouldn't have lived out the week, and there wouldn't be a mark to show. Take a leaf from their book, sweetheart, or he'll be back." He finished by taking out a large square of black silk for a sling.

"I don't need your advice," I told him.

"Sorry, dear. But it's not good, your living alone and known to have cash on hand. Whatever happened to that fellow with the duelling wound? There's a solid fellow – plenty sturdy, and he's stuck on you, too. You should marry him and give up this dangerous business. I'd marry you myself if you weren't too old for me – and if I didn't have two wives already. Both happy enough, they are – but, Lord, the expense."

"Monsieur Chauvet, that's not decent!" I exclaimed. I heard his laughter echoing down the stairs until the door was shut behind him.

I sat on the edge of the bed thinking. My right arm ached horribly. It was hard to believe that Uncle, the inhabitant of my nightmares, was dead. How formidable, how destructive he had seemed. A force of nature, brought down in retribution. And led to me by an old, blind woman who was trying to protect my gift of five gold louis. He must have gone to her for money to flee the country, after the first murder. And if she had had nothing at all, he might have believed her. But the little sum, in gold, convinced him there was more. How desperate, how crazy he must have been: he had beaten Mother to death to get her to reveal the hiding place. If I had walked out without giving her anything, she might still be alive. But instead, I had felt sorry for her. My pity had killed her more surely than the poison that I had thrown away unopened. My mind felt numb with the sadness of it. All at once the world seemed so desolate, so wicked, that I could not bear to live. No wonder people believe in the Devil, I thought. How else could you explain the conversion of a fleeting moment of grace into evil?

"No, it's all logical," I said firmly to myself. "Everything works by logic. The world is made according to rational law – no more, no less. There is no grace and no evil; everything follows the objective laws of nature."

"Madame, I thought the surgeon had left. Oh, I see. You're talking to yourself. Well, the carpet's been sent off and Gilles with it. Mustapha has gone ahead and will meet them there, and I've ordered the carriage. My, that does look neat – the sling matches your gown. What a touch! That Chauvet is an artist!" Her voice seemed to come from a thousand leagues away. "Goodness Madame, what is wrong? I thought you hated him, and yet you sit there mourning. Or have you gone and taken too much cordial again? Not that I blame you this time." Sylvie bustled to the armoire to fetch my light travelling cloak, laid it on the bed, and then got the footstool to reach down the hatbox.

"Sylvie," I said dully, not moving, "Mother's dead, too. I killed her." With a gift compounded of guilt and good intentions. How stupid. How sad. A waste. It was all a waste.

"Killed her? Why of course you did. Madame will be delighted to hear that the poison finally took effect. It's been such a long time! Why, she's had Antoine down to check your parish death register three times already. Oh, I've never seen her so anxious to make someone one of us. But you lacked the basic requirements – and now, at last, you've done it! You're fortunate, you know. She sets great store by you." She got out the wide-brimmed black hat and blew on the black plumes to get the dust off them. "Now, don't go moving that arm. Ha, and it's your right one, too. How will you write your accounts now? What a nasty fellow. We're well rid of him."

* * *

The pharmacological laboratory in the Rue Forez was all abuzz with activity when I stepped over the threshold from the black parlour that formed its antechamber.

"Ah, dear Marquise!" cried La Dodée, perspiring from the fire she had built up under the great kettle that sat on the hearth. "You look so well, all things considered. My, I can't help but remember the first day you stepped into our workshop. You're so changed, so elegant now!" I must indeed have looked different from the lost girl in the torn dress. The mirror told a new story these days: it showed me a tiny, straight figure in a black cloak and an old-fashioned, wide-brimmed, high-crowned hat over a lace cap. A nice face except for being all white with a bit of green under the eyes, just like a corpse. A tall walking stick topped with a silver owl's head and decorated with black satin ribbons. Really, not too unlike the pictures of witches in certain engraved picture books. Altogether delicious, it seemed to me. I was fond of dramatic entrances, predictions made in a thrilling whisper, and curious accoutrements that set people talking. Oh yes, I was different. Well played, Geneviève.

Above, the familiar harpy, her wings outspread, sailed serenely. A series of large, empty jars stood on the worktable, ready to receive the product of the night's labours. One of the little girls, grown larger now, was making labels for them. "Brain of a criminal," "heart of a criminal," and so forth, written in a clumsy hand. The other was brewing coffee on the strange brick stove, which I now knew for an alchemist's athanor. Mustapha had pulled up a stool and was kicking his heels while he criticised her labours.

"Not so much water – you'll steal the essence. Don't you know anything about making Turkish coffee?"

"How would you know, since you're not Turkish, anyway?" responded the girl.

"I'll have you know I'm an honorary Turk. Look at my turban. Anyone who wears a turban like this is an expert on coffee," Mustapha replied in his strange old-man's voice. The smell of the coffee, all hot and heavy, filled the room. In the centre of the floor, rolled tight, lay the rug.

"We've put the coffee on. It will be a long job tonight. La

Voisin may drop in to see us a little later," announced La Trianon wiping her hands on her apron. "So kind of you to think of that empty space in our reception parlour. Are you sure you don't want to charge anything for him?"

"No. He's absolutely free, and good riddance."

"An old lover?"

"Hardly," I answered.

"Oh, I see. A relative. Well, he's certainly handy. We've had a bit of a dry spell lately. So many customers, and the executioner raising prices every day! Livers are so scarce. You swear he's a criminal? I don't want to give false value to my clients when they come in for their formulas."

"Absolutely. He's killed off his mistress and has just bludgeoned an old blind woman to death this very day."

"Why, excellent! That's almost as good as if he'd been executed. Marie, get those two layabout men to unroll the carpet. They're looking a bit pale – a little exercise ought to bring the roses back into their cheeks." Silently, Gilles and Mustapha unrolled the carpet. Uncle's blue-grey body flopped out like a fish at the market. "Goodness!" exclaimed La Trianon. "Knives right up the hilt! Whoever threw them was a real professional." Mustapha bowed to her without a word. The girls got a pair of scissors and a little knife and began to remove Uncle's clothing, clipping off the buttons for later use and then throwing the cloth into the fire as they finished. The wig sizzled and stank as it burned smokily next to the false nose.

"If you'll pardon, I think I'll wait in the next room," I said faintly. Sylvie shot me a withering glance.

"Oh, la, what delicacy!" exclaimed La Trianon. "I suppose philosophers have no stomach for real work. Truly, Marquise, we'd thought you would have outgrown your squeamishness by now."

"Oh . . . it's my arm that makes me feel faint. He broke it, you know, when he tried to . . . to . . ."

"Marquise, you shouldn't feel bad. After all, everyone has a worthless relative or two," broke in La Dodée. Sylvie had donned an apron and poked up the fire around the smouldering clothes.

"Yes, but I seem to have so many," I murmured.

"Well, he'll certainly be worth something now," announced La Trianon. "Enough of this and that to keep us in business a good long time, to say nothing of the improvement in the decor of our parlour."

"My dear," said La Dodée comfortably, putting her arm around me, "perhaps you'd like to take coffee and wait outside in the parlour, after all. You look pale."

"Why yes, I believe I would, thank you," I answered. I felt suddenly very drained.

"I will carry the cup for Madame," announced Gilles, "because she has only one good arm." Mustapha swept up my train as if it were what he had been planning to do all along. As I left, from the corner of my eye, I could see La Trianon sharpening a set of knives on a whetstone. I could hear her voice; she was humming.

In the long silence, I could see Gilles surveying the black parlour from his seat in the corner. Mournfully, he eyed the portrait of the Devil partially concealed by the half-drawn curtain in the alcove. He shook his head, then turned his eyes up to the black ceiling, then looked at me, where I sat in the little armchair poised near the shuttered window. I could hear the faint clatter of the cup and saucer as they rested on my trembling knees.

"The river is neater," announced Gilles slowly, staring at the toes of his worn shoes.

"I'd not have you take the risk," I answered. The coffee made my stomach hurt.

"They appear to enjoy their work," said Gilles, after another long silence. He got up and walked silently around the room, inspecting the astrological charts, fingering the cat's-skull candle holder, picking up a little drop of black wax that had fallen on the table. Mustapha's intelligent little eyes glittered with amusement as he watched Gilles's mournful examination of the black parlour.

"Obviously, Gilles, you have not worked for witches very long. Now me – I've seen all types. Dwarfs have a wider experience of life than *galériens*. You can't deny that these ladies have a certain fascination. Work, after all, is always better accomplished when done with enthusiasm."

"When they're done, will they burn the remains?" asked

Gilles, plucking at the buttons on his jacket, one by one, with his fingers.

"Oh no," I answered. "They've been wanting a skeleton for the parlour for ever so long. It all came back to me when Uncle, ah, inconvenienced us so. They'll mount it over there, in that empty space beside the curtain that's over the picture."

"Oh, I see," said Gilles, looking unhappy.

"You must admit it's brilliant. Concealed in plain sight. Our mistress is an extraordinarily intelligent woman. All that, and they'll clean the rug in the bargain." Mustapha's hoarse young-old voice sounded admiring.

"I suppose it's education that does it," muttered Gilles.

"That, and a wide acquaintance," said Mustapha. "Marquise, you have an unequalled mind. I am yours for life."

"Thank you, Mustapha. Your service is equally appreciated."

"Madame," interjected Gilles, who appeared to have been silently ruminating over some idea, "may I dare to ask one question?" I nodded silently in response. "You aren't one of them – a witch, too, are you?"

"No, Gilles. I hope it doesn't disappoint you. I only know how to tell fortunes. I've never boiled anyone down before and haven't the slightest idea how to mix poison. I'm accounted pretty much a failure in these circles. I lack character, they say." Gilles seemed relieved. I inspected the pattern in the carpet beneath my feet with a morbid eye. It looked cheap. Not nice, like mine. Black and blood red is so garish in a carpet.

"It's a lot easier makin' corpses than gettin' rid of 'em," Gilles mumbled under his breath.

The bell attached to the front door tinkled, and La Voisin, looking busy, stood before us in her wide dark cloak and untrimmed black felt hat over the lace cap that hid her hair. A housewife on a shopping trip. As if to complete the illusion, Margot followed with a basket on her arm. Only the red boots peeping from beneath La Voisin's heavy green quilted petticoat added a jarring note to the pattern of bustling bourgeois efficiency.

"Well, well, the smell of prosperity! And here you are sitting in the parlour sipping coffee instead of helping out. Ah, philosophers! Always so bloody tongued and lily handed! I never thought the trait would infest the female half of humanity! My dear, you should be celebrating – savouring – not just lounging about. Today your long-awaited vengeance is complete! A burial scheduled across town – no, you can't deceive me – she used it at last, you little charmer . . . and an enshrinement about to take place. Rise and I will embrace you, dear little philosopher, for you have proved you are worthy to be one of us, for all your milk-faced looks and pale, useless hands." I had already put down the coffee cup at her jibe. Now I rose and was clasped to her ever more capacious orange-water-scented bosom.

"Ah, you are a picture!" she exclaimed, extending me at arm's length to admire me a bit. Under her gaze, I could feel how dark and picturesque I had become. I lack only a monkey in silk on a chain, I thought. "My most exquisite creation!" she exclaimed happily. "And writes Greek, too! That is an elegant touch, if I do say so! Come, my dears, all of you, and you shall see how a skeleton is mounted tonight. I stopped by to pick up the wire and bolts on the way. Not just any will do, you know."

The basket, much too immense for only a scrap of wire and a few screws, also contained provisions for the long night: cakes and wine, roasted capons stuffed with chestnuts, and a string of steaming sausages garlicky enough to make one weep. As darkness fell, La Trianon had the two great wrought-iron chandeliers under the high roof of the laboratory lowered and the candles lit. In the light of the dozens of flickering candles and the orange glow of the fire beneath the great kettle, the ladies worked indefatigably until the jars were filled with pickling solution and sealed. While I looked on morosely, what remained of Uncle was deposited in the great kettle.

"There," announced La Voisin as the lid clanged down on the pot, "almost as good as a parricide."

"Cat food," said Mustapha knowingly to Gilles, who turned pale at the thought. "Waste not, want not," he added almost maliciously, just to see the look on Gilles's face.

Their pickling done, the witches stacked the jars neatly on the shelves, wiped their hands on their aprons, and spread out the feast. Sausages and crusty loaves, chicken and cakes were demolished with gusto.

"My," said La Dodée, wiping the grease off her face, "this

work certainly does give one an appetite." La Trianon began a drinking song, and the others joined in. Not to be outdone, La Voisin countered with a lewder one involving a priest and an abbess, while the others joined in the chorus. The lid on the huge kettle rattled and leaped over the fire in the great hearth, keeping time to the songs they sang as they passed the bottles around. By the time the first pink stains of dawn were visible in the eastern sky, I had learned not only how a skeleton is mounted but also that La Voisin had an even greater store of filthy ballads than is possessed by the grossest-minded sailors. As we prepared to depart, with the new accessory, still damp, hanging in the niche by the curtain, La Trianon sighed happily. "Ah," she exclaimed, rolling her eyes to heaven, "at last my deepest desire – to have an image of death constantly before me for the edification of my soul." La Voisin rolled her eyes in an even more exaggerated imitation of piety and crossed herself; then the two witches burst out in raucous laughter.

"My, my," exclaimed La Dodée, wiping her hands on her apron, "I'm sure he's never looked better."

"Pretty is as pretty does," I answered, picking my cloak and hat from the peg on the wall. That morning I went home to bed and slept for the entire next day and night, and didn't have any dreams at all.

FORTY-ONE

Several months passed. Then, on one of the hottest days of summer, just as suddenly as he had vanished, d'Urbec appeared again. The city seemed bereft of all but the poor: those of the fashionable who were of a warlike disposition were at the front, the rest had left for their country estates. This time, he sent a note before he appeared at my door.

"Good day, Madame de Morville, and how is the fortune-telling business?" The man that Mustapha had shown in was dressed like some sort of Jansenist divine, in a broad felt hat, his clothes dark, unadorned, and travel stained.

"Very slow, Monsieur d'Urbec. La Montespan reigns supreme once more over the King's affections, so court business has fallen off sadly. Allow me to offer you some lemonade – or wine, if you'd prefer. Have you travelled far?" I rang for Sylvie as we seated ourselves in my two best armchairs. Something about him seemed to fill the room, even when he was silent.

"I've been abroad," he answered slowly. "It's good to hear French properly spoken again." Mustapha fanned himself busily, pretending not to be listening. Why had he come? I knew whatever sentiment he had had for me had vanished the night of the confrontation with Brissac. Perhaps it was information he was after, because of my knowledge of the court.

"You will be pleased to know that no one of standing will play with Monsieur Brissac any more. He has been reduced to the lowest gaming houses."

"So I have heard, Madame. I also heard that there was an attempt on your life." His eyes were on the black silk sling that held my arm.

"It was nothing. A man wanting money. But my arm's very near well now; you needn't trouble yourself. Besides, everything turned out well in the end."

"May everything always turn out well for you in the end." He half bowed from his seat as he spoke. His impassive manner, impeccably polite, told me nothing. Yes, it must be information, I thought. The court news. War. Politics.

"But Monsieur d'Urbec, what of yourself? Have you accomplished a great deal abroad?"

"A great deal," he answered softly. To break the uncomfortable silence that followed, I chattered on:

"They say you are with international banking interests, these days, Monsieur d'Urbec. I have need of someone who knows about foreign bankers. What can you tell me of Cortezia et Benson, the London bankers?"

"That's a curious firm for you to mention. What is your interest in them?"

"There was always speculation in my family that my father concealed funds abroad before he died. My suspicion is that he intended me to inherit them."

"Ah. You have read the will?"

"No. But I came to hear of its contents from . . . someone in the family. Father wisely refrained from telling me before his death." D'Urbec leaned back in his chair, fixing me with a calculating stare.

"And thus he secured your inheritance from your grasping relatives. He was an intelligent man, your father."

"But inadequately suspicious. He did not count on Grandmother dying with unusual suddenness before she could oversee the arrangements for the transfer of funds."

"Why do you tell me this, Athena?"

"Because you are a man of secrets, who is interested in mysteries." How clumsy I was – I, who prided myself on my witty conversation! Something about him unnerved me. In the silence that followed, my heart sounded too loud. Can he hear it beating? I wondered.

"And for other reasons, too, I suspect. To remind me of days long gone by, I suppose, to soften my hardness of heart. And because you still think what interests a man is money— Now, now, don't cry; you'll run all that dreadful white powder you're wearing." I felt humiliated when he offered me his big handkerchief. It was as if he had re-established our ages. He's older, the handkerchief said, and you are still an infant. Even so, I took it.

"Everything's spoiled," I said, wiping my eyes. "You don't have to stay."

"I didn't have to come back, now, did I?" he said gently. "But when I heard . . . it made me think . . ." I looked intently at him. Could it truly be? I was terrified of disappointment.

"Your arm, Athena, who broke it?" His voice was soft but had a vaguely menacing sound to it.

"A . . . a blackmailer. But you needn't bother with him. He's gone. Oh, Sylvie, do please refill Monsieur d'Urbec's glass – it's quite empty." Sylvie, who had been hovering within earshot, took the glass and the hint, and removed herself to the kitchen.

"Gone for good, I imagine, knowing the crowd you're with. Blackmailers, poisoners . . . Has it ever occurred to you that you know the wrong sort of people?"

"You sound just like my sister. She associated only with gentlefolk, and they killed her."

"I never said aristocrats can't be blackmailers and poisoners, too. I just said that blackmailers and poisoners make poor associates."

"Oh, you still talk like an idealist. It's a fantasy, Florent. We live in a wicked world."

"That we do, Geneviève. But have you considered it might be more bearable if we were together?" I stared at him. He looked uncomfortable, stood up, and walked to the window, staring out as he spoke in a low voice. "Why do you think I returned here? For the weather?" He turned to look at me. His face was dark and sunburned, unshaven, and his eyes, sunken with weariness, held a kind of deeply hidden sadness. "On sea voyages, a man has time to think," he went on. "The air cools the brain, I suppose. There was a time when I was all aflame to create a fortune to offer you. Then I was equally on fire to see you dead and damned. I suppose that is the flaw in the southern character – too much heat. Lately I have associated with the congealed thinkers of the damp and foggy north. It has made me think through my life. I am approaching middle age – in two more years I will be thirty. I am weary of games. I cannot court a woman on lies. I am a marked man, without a social position or even a home to offer you. Tell me now, Mademoiselle Pasquier, whether you will accept me as I am or whether I must leave for ever."

My good hand was knotted tight on my lap, clutching his handkerchief rolled into a soggy ball. I could hear my heart thump in the long silence while I studied him as he stood there before the window. He looked careworn, and the mockery and malice had gone from his dark eyes. Around them were the first fine lines of the approaching age that he feared. Suddenly, I wanted his old self back, the impudent, innocent cynic who had been on fire to reform the world. And I wanted to be the girl I had once been, who had never seen anything worse than the naughty works she read in secret and whose only plans were to read Herodotus to her father every evening. Now we had both seen too much, and done too much, and each of us knew that about the other without a word exchanged.

"Yes, Florent, I will accept you as you are, provided you can do the same for me." Could he know everything? Did he understand the whole of what he was promising? Suddenly, I was terrified of losing him all over again.

"That was always part of it, Geneviève."

"You . . . you might take my hand," I said in a small voice. He came and stood before my chair, taking the hand that I extended.

"It's all damp," he said tenderly, looking down at me.

"Florent . . ." I managed to stammer. I wanted him so. Was it real? Could he care for me this much, in spite of everything? I couldn't bear for love to come and then vanish. Gravely, he knelt on one knee before me, not letting go of my hand.

"Would you consider marriage, Mademoiselle Pasquier? I am not sure to whom I should apply – your brother, who has the legal right to dispose of you in marriage, but who believes you dead, or your patroness, who seems to have a certain . . . moral right, if witches can be said to possess such a thing."

"More to the point, Florent, she will regard it as an attempt upon her income and act accordingly."

"Then I shall have to buy out your contract, won't I, little witch?"

"I shouldn't try that just now, if I were you. Business is slow and Madame is irritable. Besides . . . I . . . I have difficulties with the idea of marriage. So many couples seem to poison each other . . ."

He laughed and got up, dusting off his knee. "You certainly are far from the common ... most women think only of marriage, no matter what the price. But then, that's part of your charm: you've always been completely eccentric. You could never bore me, Athena. And if this is how you want things to be for now, who am I to say no?" Then he pulled the footstool close to my chair, sat down, and took my hand in both of his.

"Seriously, Geneviève, consider this: my parents are still quite pleased with each other, despite everything they have been through – it's quite possible, you know." His face was amused and tolerant, his voice drolly self-mocking. I looked at him and I knew he was the only man I'd ever want. I couldn't help smiling.

"I like your parents, Florent. I imagine I'd like your brothers, too. I hope to meet them all some day. But I'm not sure I'm prepared to travel abroad just yet."

"What? You imagine I would dare to defy Colbert and smuggle them across the border?"

"It's something I thought of. After all, I had a father who defied Colbert. And, knowing you, you probably managed to get their last franc out as well as the entire household down to the dog and cat."

"No, the cat we had to leave. It was not Protestant. But the dog, seeing no future for the Reformed Religion in France, was happy enough to go." I laughed out loud. I'd judged his character right. He was the one, and only he.

"Colbert and Louvois are fools, I think. If they want to preserve the skilled workers of France, the state should offer incentives to stay, not punishment for flight."

"And so we talk politics instead of making love." He sighed. "I should have known this would happen. Mademoiselle, at what level of amity shall we agree to, since you seem so uninterested in marriage? 'Constante Amitié', 'Tendre-sur-Estime', or shall we rush on to the 'Tendre-sur-Inclination'?"

"Oh, the *Carte de Tendre*. You are a wicked fellow, Monsieur, to tease me so."

"Tease you, Mademoiselle? How so?"

"Well ... you know..." and here I paused as I felt my face turn hot, "...I didn't have in mind a ... *platonic* friendship..."

"Mademoiselle Pasquier," he said, his face full of happiness, "may I have the honour of inviting you to supper?"

The summer heat in d'Urbec's rooms had not fled with the evening. It made my bones feel loose and my mind languorous. I was intoxicated with food and drink and the nearness of him. Entering the bedroom, I spied in the shadows behind the closed shutters a curious clock of great antiquity on an inlaid table. His books were in a corner cabinet, in neat rows like soldiers, evidently arranged by subject. The heavy curtains on the bed were pulled back. For once, I didn't want to read the spines of someone else's books.

"That's a strange clock you have there, Florent," I said as he closed the door behind us. He had taken his coat off in the heat, and the neck of his shirt stood open.

"It's quite old; it tells the movements of the planets as well as the hour. Lately I have not been able to resist the urge to collect a few rarities. Some of them have to be put in working order again. It amuses me, I suppose." A thin sheen of sweat stood on his face and shone on the muscles of his neck and the little hollow between the collarbones.

"What is the box there?" I asked, pointing to the night table by the bed.

"It plays music," he answered, opening it up to show the mechanism within — a row of tiny bells and hammers entangled in clockwork. His hands were wide and muscular; I was surprised at the delicacy of their movement as he showed me the working parts of the little box. ". . . or, rather, it will play soon," he went on. "It needs a new mainspring and a part I am having made to order across town." I sat down on the bed; he sat beside me and put his hand around my waist. I could feel the heat of his body and smell the soft animal scent of a man in desire.

"So much steel," he murmured, as his hand encountered the heavy corset stays.

"It's an easier mechanism than the box," I answered. He said something soft, rhythmic, his voice like dark smoke. "What is that language?" I asked, looking up to see his dark eyes fixed on me.

"It is the old language," he said, but he seemed to mean more. The language of the conquered south, of the vanished

troubadours. All that was Parisian, cosmopolitan, seemed to
have been stripped away like some false skin. Slowly and
precisely, he undid the pins on my bodice, smiling as he
translated the old *chanson*, his voice sensual. ". . . good it were,
I count it, naked to hold her and behold . . ." The corset stays
loosened, he peeled away the shift beneath. "Beautiful," he said
softly. But he had left his shirt on. With my good hand, I began to
unbutton it.

"All of you, exactly as you are . . ." I repeated my promise,
stroking the livid mark. His bare torso shone with sweat; the
black hair on it felt damp on my breast. "Just as you are,
forever . . ," I whispered.

"My love," he said, but it was in the old language.

"I don't see why you're annoyed with me, Madame. *Someone*
was bound to tell Madame Montvoisin you'd taken up with
d'Urbec again, and if it hadn't been me, I'd have been in a lot of
trouble." Sylvie shook the featherbed viciously and then
pounded the pillows until wispy bits of down floated in the
morning air. I sat at the small writing table in my *ruelle*, quill in
hand, writing up my accounts for the weekly reckoning with
Madame. Zero, zero, zero. Nothing at all. Twenty-five per cent
of nothing is nothing. A splendid week it had been, full of lazy
breakfasts in bed, the *Gazette de France* crumpled among the
rumpled sheets, and an open volume of Ovid still lying beside a
burned-out candle on the nightstand.

"Why do you look at me that way?" I asked, as he lay
contented on the pillows, his hands behind his dark head, the
noonday sun picking a bright pattern across his wide chest and
the crumpled coverlet that was spread over far too little of us.

"Because you are so beautiful," he said happily. "Your face,
the way the dark curls fall over it, the way your grey eyes shine,
your body, your mind, your soul . . ." Then I could feel the
warmth of love welling up again to fill everything in me, even my
fingertips and the ends of my hair. I thought my heart would split
apart with the flood of it.

"When I first saw you there, in the window of that great, dark
house, you were like the light of a little candle, flickering bravely
in the gloom. Now you shine like the sun."

"Yours forever, Florent. No matter what." I put my head on

his heart to hear it beat while he stroked my hair. "Always and forever." I sighed again.

"And I," he answered, "no matter what comes."

What did come was soon enough, although we knew it had to be. He left on another of his mysterious trips, and I did not ask where he was going, or who his patron was, although I had my suspicions. After all, what one doesn't know one cannot be forced to tell. And in the meantime, although his entrée with the Mancinis had been spoiled by the Brissac affair, his welcome at the enemies of the Mancinis had become all the warmer, especially because he dressed well and made a point of losing large sums to the proper people, recouping from those who were out of favour.

"It is the last day before I must leave," he had said only the day before, as he buttered a roll at breakfast. His dark eyes amused, he extended a bit of crust to Grandmother's parrot. The bird snatched it and converted it to crumbs, which dribbled down his feathery front.

"Pretty bird, pretty bird. Clever d'Urbec. Clever d'Urbec. Geneviève, doesn't your bird ever learn anything new?"

"Only when it pleases him."

"He's a stubborn creature – not unlike myself, I suppose. Come now, Lorito. Say 'pretty bird'. It's high time you quit spouting Protestant hellfire and damnation."

"Fire and brimstone!" announced the bird and went back to cracking seeds.

"Hardheaded bird. Will you miss me when I'm gone?"

"Hell and damnation!"

"Well, that's sort of an answer," I offered. It was in the air, though the days were still warm.

"Let us do something splendid, Geneviève. Let me take you driving on the Cours-la-Reine this afternoon, and then we'll go incognito to the opera. One of Lully's new operas is playing. They say the stage machines are a marvel. Would this please you, do you think?"

"Oh, divinely, Florent, and I have the perfect dress to wear. I've been saving it a long time – everyone said I was foolish, but now it's just perfect." But when I saw Sylvie's eyes narrow as she took the rose silk dress from its muslin, I knew that, within the day, she would betray me to the Shadow Queen. It didn't matter at all to me, for something very strange had happened when I put on the dress. As I stood before the mirror admiring the embroidered flowers and the glistening rose and ivory silk, I realised suddenly that I was seeing the true colour, not through a wash of crimson. In the mirror I saw nothing. Nothing, that is, but a girl with a neat waist and dark, tumbled hair, looking back out of the mirror at me with shining grey eyes.

The rest of the day, bright with summer sun, had passed in a daze of happiness. As the carriage rattled past the Tuileries Palace and its gardens to mingle with the fashionable equipages on the wide, scenic avenue of the Cours-la-Reine, Florent had no eye for the scenery. Instead he took my hand.

"You said we'd meet again, driving on the Cours-la-Reine, and you were right, Florent. Now will you steal my fortune-telling business?" I teased.

"On the contrary. I said I'd meet the Marquise de Morville – and look! She's nowhere in sight," he said, his arm around the rose silk.

The next morning, when d'Urbec had departed and I spied the new paste buckles sparkling on Sylvie's shoes, I knew she had done the deed and the witch knew everything. Accounting day. It always comes. But I had the memory of his face when he first saw me come from behind the screen in the dress I now knew I'd been saving all along for him. And I could still feel his kisses on my neck as he muttered, ". . . too young and lovely to wear black . . ." Accounting day didn't matter. I felt like another person altogether. I could manage anything. Besides, I had a card up my sleeve. In the last days before d'Urbec had left, I had received the ultimate invitation. Who had informed him of me, I do not know. But Louis Quatorze himself had summoned me to Versailles to read the oracle glass.

I took a hired chair to the Rue Beauregard that Wednesday afternoon, for I had dismissed my leased carriage for the weeks I had been with d'Urbec in order to save money. That afternoon, Madame was engaged in the placement of a new tall clock, which depicted the phases of the moon as well as the hours, in her black parlour. As the sweating workmen set it down in the corner by the china cupboard, she said, "No, I've changed my mind. Not over there, after all. Across from the window is better. Here it detracts from my *objets d'art*." The heavy shutters were closed against the heat and dust, enshrouding the room in twilight. The musty smell of scented candles perpetually lighted around the feet of the statue of the Virgin reminded me of funerals and things long dead. Madame, however, was very much alive, the sweat rolling down from beneath her white lace cap as she fanned herself with one hand and gesticulated with the other.

"Oh, there you are at last, Madame Stay-Abed," she called to me. "You'll have to wait. I'm expecting Madame Poulaillon for her weekly . . . ah . . . consultation." So I wandered off to the kitchen, account books under my arm, to see if there were any pastries left over from the previous day's open house.

"There're none left," said old Montvoisin, greeting me at the kitchen door with the crumbs dribbling down his half-open, tobacco-stained shirt. His baggy old breeches looked as if he'd slept in them. He still had on his slippers and a napkin in place of the glossy horsehair wig he'd taken to wearing on weekdays. "Here, have some snuff instead." He reached into his pocket and pulled out a cheap tin snuffbox.

"No, thank you; it makes my nose tickle," I answered, and he shuffled off through the double doors to the black parlour.

There I heard him say as the front door was opened, "Ah, good day, Madame Poulaillon. And how's the husband these days? Quite reformed?"

"Antoine, remove yourself," I could hear Madame hiss. "You interfere with my business." The double doors slammed behind him, and he meandered out to seat himself in Madame's favourite armchair and set his slippered feet on her footstool.

"Marquise," he said, pausing to take snuff and sneeze into a vast, filthy handkerchief, "has my daughter sent you word yet? I said to her, I said, 'Marie-Marguerite, try the Marquise. She has ready cash and doesn't carry tales.'" I looked up at him, puzzled, from where I sat on the smaller armchair opposite, and folded my fan.

"I've been busy," I said. "I haven't heard anything."

"Go by La Lépère's new place then, and don't take Sylvie with you. She meant to send for you, I'm sure." He looked around as if the world were all too complex for him, his faded blue eyes all runny. Then, as if it could resolve everything, he took more snuff. "Get off me, you fool cat," he said, as the grey tom leaped from the chair back to his lap. The tom looked at him briefly with hooded eyes and bit his thumb before he managed to sweep the cat off him with a series of nervous, unhappy gestures. "I hate them, too. I hate it all," he said and then lapsed into a somnolent silence while I wondered what to make of it all.

One of the parlour doors opened suddenly, and I knew that Madame Poulaillon must have departed out of the front door with her week's instalment of arsenic. But the sorceress lacked the pleasant air of contentment she usually had after such transactions. She appeared irritated as I scrambled to stand, and she took the armchair that old Montvoisin had suddenly seen fit to vacate with a snort of annoyance. She tapped her fingers on the arm of the chair and did not invite me to sit. The sight of me seemed to enrage her further. Cautious, Geneviève, I said to myself.

"So, there you are, the second little ingrate. I suppose you know where Marie-Marguerite is. Everyone knows but her own mother!"

"Marie-Marguerite? What's happened? I hadn't heard."

"Ha, I suppose you hadn't. Too busy disporting yourself with that gutter-crawling *galérien*, downing wine and oysters at my expense. I make you a marquise and you throw it away on a branded criminal."

"He's not a criminal," I answered, my voice cold.

"Might as well be," she sniffed. "Anyway, Brissac will probably slit his nose for him before the month is out." I changed the subject, in order to channel her rage in another direction.

"Isn't Marie-Marguerite's baby due soon? I thought she'd be home at a time like this."

"That hussy! That ingrate! I offered my dear friend Romani ten thousand francs to make an honest woman of her, and she spurned him." In a sarcastic high voice she imitated an adolescent's whine. "'*I'm* not going to marry a professional poisoner, Mother.' 'So, young lady, what do you think keeps putting the food in your face, eh? Especially now that you're bloated like a pig and do nothing but lie around! Romani is a genius, a man of a thousand disguises.' 'I don't care if he's a genius; I want a nice man.' Nice, bah! A pastry cook! And not even with his own shop! A *journeyman* pastry cook! I'll not have my daughter marrying riff-raff like that! So now she's run off and hidden herself, although where a girl as big as a sow and as slow as a snail could hide herself in *this* city, I do not know! I tell you; I'll find her, if I have to have my people search every house in town!"

"My, my, what a pity," I responded. "She really ought to listen to people who have her good at heart." The Shadow Queen glared suspiciously at me.

"I do hope you are not being sarcastic, Mademoiselle. When have you ever listened to me? And I imagine you've not a sou to show me after your recent debauchery."

But here I played my winning card. "For the past two weeks there's nothing, but I've been invited to appear before the King when he returns to Saint-Germain-en-Laye next week. He's fond of novelties, they say, and my reputation has finally reached him." La Voisin drew in her breath.

"Buckingham must have told him," she whispered.

"Either him or Primi."

"No, not Visconti. He's a rival. He'd not promote you so high. Ah! So high! I knew it! Your accent! Your manners! There's no substitute for the real thing, I've always said. And who groomed you to fly so high?"

"You did, Madame, and I am grateful. I intend to make the best of the opportunity."

"Ah! That's my girl, my darling girl! Truer than my own daughter – or rather, stepdaughter. Tread carefully, my dear, and you may yet replace Visconti at his side." There's a fantasy, I thought. A king who prided himself on never taking advice from women certainly didn't want a female fortune-teller.

But, buoyed up by her imaginings, the Shadow Queen had become expansive. Nothing would do but to have a bottle of excellent wine brought from her cellar, and even old Antoine and her oldest son were offered a glass.

"Oh, yes, and the marzipan. I know what a taste you have for it, little Marquise!" And with a sly, sideways look she went to unlock the secret cabinet where she kept it hidden. And, bother her, she gloried in the fact that in nearly five years of acquaintance, I still hadn't found out where she got it. The best in Paris. I could get opium, I could get arsenic, I could get pigeons' hearts and toads' toenails, but I couldn't find out where she got that marzipan. She always smirked when she went to fetch it. But then, I reflected, it's better to leave her mellow. Besides, I loved the stuff – so lovely, sticky, sweet, and rich, with the perfumed flavour of almonds and a hint of something else mysterious. I stayed until I had consumed several pieces and a glass of wine, leaving when I knew she was at last in a good mood.

La Lépère, the abortionist, had moved up in the world, both literally and figuratively. She had two rooms on the fourth floor of a narrow, shabby building that housed a ribbon maker's establishment on the first floor. At the tiny balcony at the top of the outer staircase, I found she had already opened her door, having heard my painful progress up the many rickety flights of steps.

"Antoine Montvoisin sent me," I said to the old woman.

"I know," she answered. "Marie-Marguerite is here. The baby was born safe and sound last night. Come in."

We entered the darkened room to find Marie-Marguerite, her curls dank and matted to her head, sitting up and nursing the baby. "Now see here," announced La Lépère, "don't she look good? And it's a fine boy. The live ones do give more satisfaction, though I do more of the others these days. Oh, what a world! I must have done maybe ten thousand in my lifetime!" Ten thousand? Even in her lifetime, which must be nearly eighty years by now, that seemed like quite a lot of abortions. I rapidly multiplied one-half that figure times the number of other "businesswomen" I knew worked on contract for La Voisin. No wonder the chimney in the garden pavilion smoked all the time.

"See how lovely he is," said Marie-Marguerite, looking pleased with herself. And though I thought him rather too small and red, I agreed. "I've named him Jean-Baptiste, after his father." She did make a pretty picture there, with her small Jean-Baptiste. *Hmm*, I'd call it *"The Little Madonna of the Poisons"*, I thought.

"Madame de Morville, Madame," Marie-Marguerite said, "I need to borrow money. I need a plan. You are clever; you have to think of something. I want to put my baby out to nurse secretly, where Mother can't find him. You're the only one who has the wit to deceive her. Help me."

"Marie-Marguerite," I said, sitting down beside her on the bed, "your mother isn't going to stay mad at you for ever for not marrying Romani. Sooner or later she'll hatch another scheme and decide it's all for the best that it turned out this way."

"That's exactly what I'm afraid of. She'll think of the money and *poof*! I lose my baby. She's capable of anything when she gets in that greedy mood, or an important client wants a Mass. It's not wise to leave a new baby in Mother's house."

"Surely not . . . her own grandchild?" I asked.

"Why not? That ugly old Guibourg uses his own children by his mistress when he runs short. And they're short now. When the court comes back, business picks up. They've bought up everything in the orphanages. You haven't seen the Black Mass, Marquise, but I have. Several times. Madame de Montespan, she's done several, and I helped get the room ready for all of them. And she's not the only one. Mother does a lot of business. I'll not have my beautiful baby's throat cut just because some fat old whore wants to hold on to her pig of a lover."

She looked down to admire the little, mewling thing at her breast. The pastry cook's baby, eyes closed, sating himself all oblivious of the storms around him.

"Don't send him by common carrier," I said. "So many don't survive the trip, you know. I'll hire a carriage for you in secret and give you a year's fees. Baby-farmers respect payment in advance."

"I knew you'd help. I don't know why; it just seemed like you would," said Marie-Marguerite.

That evening, when Sylvie made several pointed comments about my lateness, I announced that Madame, rather than berating me, had ordered up a celebration on account of my invitation to appear before the King. It was that that had delayed me considerably.

"The King?" gasped Sylvie. "Why, I never knew! You are the sly one!"

"Fortune-tellers have to have some secrets," I announced, as I put away my account books and flung my hat upon the bed.

FORTY-TWO

Again and again the mass of women surged into the main street of the Faubourg Saint-Antoine. "Witches, witches, cannibals, baby thieves!" they cried. "Kill them; kill them all!" There was the sound of shattering glass, of stone against stone, the screams of people trampled by the crowd. A lone *avocat*, his clothes nearly torn from him, emerged near the police barricade, the rioting women screaming in hot pursuit.

"Back, back!" cried the sergeant, pulling in his sweat-stained bay mare. Raising his arm, he again ordered the mounted archers to charge the swarming, maddened women, who retreated shouting curses and dragging their injured with them.

"How goes it, Sergeant?" La Reynie himself, immaculate in high boots, a gold-braided jacket, and wide plumed hat, had ridden his big grey up to the barricade. "I want this whole quarter under control by nightfall," he added.

"I think this is the last of them," the sergeant replied, as they trotted the length of the street amidst the rubble that is always left by a riot: wood and junk from the pried-up barricades, loose stones, odd wooden shoes, and here and there a crumpled apron or an old kerchief torn loose from its owner in the struggle. And there was red in the dust. "We're just lucky they set no fires."

"How many dead?" asked La Reynie.

"Of them, we don't know. But they have killed a midwife, a shoemaker, and severely battered an *avocat* whom we have taken into custody under suspicion."

"I'll be wanting a full report when you have suppressed this disturbance. What, in your opinion, set them off this time, Sergeant?"

"You know the common people, Monsieur de La Reynie. It's another witchcraft scare. These women claim that babies are being stolen for resale as sacrifices in the Black Mass.

Right off the street, in some instances. They claim the going price is two *écus* these days, and that's a temptation to just about everyone. And now, every stranger that's seen in the district is taken for a baby-thief."

"Insane superstition. Would that education could cure them of it. But the common mind, Sergeant – it's peasant thinking, and beyond the reach of rationality."

"Quite so, Monsieur de La Reynie," agreed the sergeant, who wore a charm against the evil eye under his shirt.

In the dark quiet of the nave, two Jesuits opened the poor box to count the daily offering. Among the coins was a sheet of folded paper. The first Jesuit unfolded the sheet and read it by the light of the hundreds of flickering candles set at the feet of a statue of the Virgin. His face froze in shock.

"What is it?" asked the second Jesuit.

"The denunciation of a conspiracy to poison the King and the Dauphin. It gives names, places. It seems there is a massive trade in poisons in Paris, about which the police know nothing." Within the hour, the two Jesuits were waiting in the antechamber of the Lieutenant General of the Paris Criminal Police.

The records clerk had left La Reynie alone at his desk, where he sat silently, thinking, making notes to himself in his little red notebook. Paris was awash in conspiracies and foreign intrigues against the King. Everywhere in Europe, His Majesty's glorious conquests had made enemies who sent their agents to his chief city to plot and organise cabals. La Reynie's agents discovered them, rooted them out, and he sent them to their deaths without a qualm. But this new conspiracy that the Jesuits had reported was different. It indicated that Paris was the centre of a vast web of professional poisoners far greater than anything they had suspected before. Even more dangerous, the conspiracy involved the principal nobility of the King's own court. Everything was tied to it: mysterious deaths, the recent riots. Could it be a fantasy? If the great aristocrats discovered he was gathering evidence against them, they could convince the King to have him destroyed. His career, even his own liberty, were at risk. Fouquet had been a powerful minister in his day, far greater than La Reynie, but he would never see the light again. And yet, if the conspiracy were real, La Reynie knew his duty was to inform the King. Unless the King, too, were involved ... La Reynie frowned and wrote out a list of the logical possibilities in his notebook, indicating the necessary course of action in each case. The affair would have to be handled with the greatest delicacy, with incontrovertible evidence gathered from the smallest conspirators, before he moved against the great ones. He leafed through the list on his desk. It was a job for a man of the greatest discretion. He summoned Desgrez.

"Desgrez, I have here a list of all the alchemists, fortune-tellers, and *parfumiers* in the city. I want your people to pay every one of them an inconspicuous visit. Keep your eyes open for anything suspicious. It seems we have not spread our net wide enough in times past." La Reynie passed a sheaf of papers with hundreds of names to his associate. Captain Desgrez shook his head.

"This is a considerable list. It may take a while."

"Start with the ones you consider most suspicious," suggested La Reynie, returning to the report he was finishing for the King on the suppression of the most recent riots in the city.

Desgrez leafed through the list. At the top of the third page, he saw "Marquise de Morville. Rue Charlot." He smiled. He knew exactly what would please La Reynie most.

FORTY-THREE

At the end of September, the autumn rains came; the gutters ran deep with filthy water, and cold and damp seemed to penetrate every corner of the house. Florent's departure had taken all warmth and joy from my hearth; yearning for him made me grow so thin, I could count my rib bones. I got sick and went to my readings wrapped in a heavy shawl, feeling every bit as ancient as I claimed to be. Then at last a letter came, all covered with seals and battered with the signs of foreign travel, bringing his love and saying he would be back some time soon. I took to peering out of the upstairs bedroom window at the carriages and passers-by in the street, searching for his dark hat and cloak, his deliberate, sturdy walk, hallucinating that I saw him in doorways or in crowds, on horseback or passing incognito in a coach.

Then one afternoon, when the sharp wind was driving the fine drops of a light rain like icy needles, I looked out and saw a heavily cloaked figure getting out of a little fiacre in front of the door. Him! Thank goodness I hadn't seen clients today. I didn't want to look like a corpse for him. I was wearing a simple blue wool dress with lace at the collar and a pink satin ribbon in my hair. I could feel my blushes as I pushed my curls behind the ribbon and smoothed down my skirts. I hurried downstairs. He stood with his back to me, facing the fire, his dark wig shining with the damp, his hat and cloak still on.

"Madame," said Mustapha quickly, as if to stop me from saying something, "it is Captain Landart of the musketeers to see you for a consultation." As he spoke, the man turned. A stranger, whose gold-braided military coat and wide, ornate baldric were visible beneath his half-open cloak. His smile, as he saw my confusion, the pink flush on my cheeks, was knowing and wolfish. Suddenly I knew him. The man of disguises. Not Captain Landart of the musketeers, but Captain Desgrez of the police. And I was undisguised.

"Oh, my pardon, Captain Landart; I was not expecting any business this afternoon, or I would have dressed more properly to receive a man of your rank."

"Evidently not, though I must say you look most charming as you are, Madame de Morville."

Oh, damn. He'd seen everything. God help me. The servant girl, the old crone – he knew they were one. For a moment I fantasised fleeing. A minute, Monsieur, I'd say – then run out the back door and take the diligence to Calais. Buckingham, he'd take me. He'd said so at Madame's. I could start over. If he does not know I recognise him, he might leave and give me time to flee, I thought frantically. But then I smiled as if nothing were wrong and answered, "You flatter me, Captain. It is clear you know how to enchant the ladies. But tell me, how can I help you?"

"I have come in search of a weapon salve, Madame, which has miraculous properties. Several reputable physicians I have spoken to swear by it."

"There are a number of varieties compounded by persons I know, though I myself do not know the secret. I could obtain two kinds for you, but in both cases you would do better to go to the source: the instructions for the care of the wound vary with the formula used to anoint the weapon. Let me give you the address of Monsieur Jordain, the pharmacist." Monsieur Jordain, distributor of so many of La Trianon's more questionable products, would place his order with her little laboratory when he delivered the toads.

"You do not sell compounds, then, Madame de Morville?"

"My dear Captain, if my late husband, the Marquis de Morville of sainted memory, knew that I had sullied his name with shopkeeping, he would not rest in his grave. I use my gifts to advise ladies of good family what the future holds for them. Ah, me," I said, fluttering my hands before my face, "once a harmless parlour game in my youth, now, sadly the mainstay of my old age. And yet, as I can tell you are calculating when you look around you like that, through the kindness of these very ladies, I can afford enough of the simple decencies to avoid descending beneath my station." His head turned back to me with a swift motion – he had thought I hadn't noticed him surveying my paintings, the furniture, the silver on the sideboard, with the eye of a professional appraiser.

"All this . . . is from fortune-telling alone?" he asked.

"Captain Landart, you have obviously been at the front a very long time, or you would know that the incredible vogue for fortune-telling grows every day in Paris. I am summoned to find lost objects, discover the hiding places of lovers, consult on engagements, and a thousand other things. I would have to be a fool to waste my time on anything less lucrative or more risky." He came closer, as if he were about to ask me a question, but another knock sounded at the door.

"I am so sorry – my visiting hours appear to be more crowded than I thought. Did you also wish me to consult the glass for you, Captain?" Mustapha returned from the door, announcing a lackey in anonymous grey livery. Desgrez seemed disturbed, unsettled.

"Madame de Morville," announced the lackey, "my master sends this jewel with his profoundest apologies, and his most fervent hope for a renewal of that tender sentiment once shared." Before I could even tell the man that I wouldn't accept the time of day from the Duc de Brissac, the lackey had unwrapped an oiled silk from around an exquisite inlaid rosewood coffer, set the object on my mantelpiece, and departed hastily. I noticed that he had never touched the box with his bare hands.

"Oh, damn, another one," I muttered to myself. "The man must think I'm an idiot."

"You spoke, Madame de Morville?" The voice directly behind me came as a shock, breaking my thoughts. Now it was my turn to be distracted. I whirled around from contemplating the box to confront Desgrez. "Just thinking aloud, Captain . . . uh, Landart. Tell me, did you want me to read your fortune in the glass?" I knew my question might well drive him off. Many men hate having their fortunes told; they believe it is female superstition of the worst order. Physiognomy, graphology, and weapon salves, however, count as "science" and are therefore suitably masculine, not being superstitions at all. Desgrez was obviously a man of science. He looked rather red in the face and ran his finger under his collar, as if he were choking with annoyance. Ah, if you were truly a scientist, Desgrez, you'd ask for your fortune in order to entrap me, just as you made love to Madame de Brinvilliers.

"*Ahem.* Not now. No, the address is sufficient. Will you want a fee?" No, he was poised between superstition and science. He wants me to tell his fortune, and he doesn't dare ask. He wants to try me, prove that I'm a fake. But what if I'm not?

"I require a fee only for the fortune, Monsieur." Casually, as if to conceal his feelings, he walked to the mantel and fingered the box, looking as if he might open it.

"For God's sake, don't touch it!"

The ring of fear in my voice made him turn and, sensing vulnerability, he said, "Madame, it is an exquisite offering. Pardon my curiosity. Surely the jewel within must be a fabulous object."

"Fabulous indeed, Captain. Like so many gifts of the great." Something in my voice made him stare at my face. It was as if something he had decided about me was suddenly thrown in doubt. "Let us both satisfy our curiosity about Brissac's treasure," I said and crossed to my table and opened a drawer for my gloves and one of my rods – the steel one. Putting on the gloves, I lifted the box carefully from the mantel, reversing it so that it would open away from me. Then I set it on the stones of the hearth, and with the tip of the rod flipped up the catch.

"Curious precautions, Marquise. Especially in dealing with a gift from someone of such high rank – Brissac, did you say?"

"Did you see the little steel point beneath the catch? Stand back." As I opened the lid with the rod, there was a sudden *clack* and a clatter as a little bolt, almost as fine as a needle, flew into the stones of the fireplace. I stopped him as he reached for the box. "Don't pick it up without gloves. You don't know if the box is poisoned as well as the dart." From his pocket he drew a pair of heavy leather gloves and, putting them on, retrieved both dart and box.

"Ingenious," he said. "The principle of a crossbow, made small. Tell me, Marquise, have you received such gifts before? How did you suspect?"

"It was either a mechanism or a live viper, knowing the source. I'm glad it wasn't the viper. I can't abide snakes."

"Would you mind if I took this box with me?" he asked casually.

"Surely, it does not fire at a great enough distance to be of use on the front, Captain Landart."

"Madame de Morville, cease play-acting. You know me just as I know you. In the name of the police, I request that you give me that box. I also wish you to tell me your connection with the Duc de Vivonne's late mistress and why you visited her deathbed in disguise."

"Oh, very well." I sighed, collapsing in my armchair as if beaten. But beneath the limp look my mind was speeding like a racehorse.

First I bought time to plan my strategy: "Mustapha, go get Captain Desgrez something to wrap the box in. I don't wish to be blamed if it gives him a rash." As he left, I turned to Desgrez and said, "Mademoiselle Pasquier was a good client of mine – and a friend. Fortune-tellers know many secrets, Captain Desgrez, and I knew hers. I advised her not to go to Longueval, but Monsieur le Duc found her pregnancy ... inconvenient and consulted with him anyway. When I did not hear from her, I went to the Châtelet and to the hospitals—" I couldn't help it; at the thought of Marie-Angélique, my eyes filled with tears.

"And the disguise?" Desgrez's voice sounded almost tender. Beware, my mind shrilled, he wants to use your weakness to lure you into saying too much.

"Captain Desgrez, I feared to be suspected of procuring the abortion. It is a suspicion that always falls first upon women in such cases, and doubly upon a woman such as I – a widow, alone . . ." I sighed melodramatically. He looked unconvinced. I went on, "Follow me for a week, Monsieur Desgrez, as you most probably will, and you will see that my clients are so great that I have no need of shady business. My reputation is dear to me, and I go to great lengths to protect it." Yes, do it, you police snoop, and you will follow me to Saint-Germain, where I shall entertain the King and you will not even be admitted to the antechamber if you wear your Sunday suit. Then realise what you are entangled with, and back off. I looked him in the face. I accept the challenge, his eyes said.

Then he stood up, looking around as if he had it in mind to depart. He paused briefly, looking down at me. "Only one more question, Madame de Morville. Just exactly how old are you?" If I persist in lying, he will not believe the rest, I thought. The truth must do, though it opens new risks.

"Eighteen, Captain Desgrez."

"You are a formidable woman, Marquise. You have deceived half of Paris." I did not like his tone.

"I beg you not to reveal it. My custom depends on my antiquity, you understand."

"Police records are not published on the streetcorner, Madame. The gullible will continue to be convinced." As he was shown to the door, I was glad there were no laws against fortune telling. He would be the first to propose my arrest if there were. And worse, his curiosity had been piqued. When a tenacious man like that fails to prove one pet theory, he'll search in the records until he concocts another. Now that he couldn't sustain his theory that I was an abortionist, he'd try to find out what I really was – an associate of poisoners, of abortionists, of foreign spies, who had failed to report them to the police. That, of course, was just as bad and equally fatal. A cold shudder passed through me. I wished I could read my own fortune in the glass.

Grand occasions often do not turn out to be as anticipated, and certainly my appearance before the King was an illustration of this principle. It was clear there would be trouble as soon as I was ushered into the immense, high-ceilinged salon, with its huge, dark old tapestries and glittering chandeliers. I spied the King across the room, laughing with his "Monsieur Primi". A dozen or so courtiers were standing near by and laughing in imitation of the royal mood. Their women tittered behind their fans. At the centre of the room was a curious object. I recognised it immediately: Maestro Petit's magic clavecin from the Foire Saint-Germain. It had made quite a stir there; without visible levers or the touch of a human hand, it played airs on the command of the maestro alone. He had a good living, taking it on tour of the various fairs of the kingdom, and no one could divine how it worked. That is, until now. A red-faced maestro was bowing sheepishly before the King. Beside him bowed a tiny little boy who had crawled from the innards of the instrument. The King walked over to the instrument to inspect the system of internal levers by which the little boy, the maestro's precocious son, had played the tunes. The courtiers, following the example of His Majesty, jockeyed for a better position and remarked, "Ingenious!" "Oh, how shameless!" "The impudence!" and the like. An evening of amusement and unmasking, doubtless concocted by Primi. It certainly had his mark on it. I always suspected he saw me as a rival; now he could put me out of business all at a stroke, just like poor Maestro Petit, with a harmless joke.

I curtseyed deep as Primi presented me to His Majesty, and I rose to see that the Sun King was inspecting me quite closely. He himself was wearing a *justaucorps* in heavy blue velvet, embroidered with gold and diamonds, a deep blue hat bordered in gold and covered with red plumes, fawn-coloured velvet breeches, red silk stockings, and shoes with high red heels and red silk bows. The lace at his neck and wrists fell like waterfalls.

"Our Primi tells us that you are over a century old, Madame de Morville. Surely, as a service to improve the beauty in our kingdom, you might share your secret with those unfortunate ladies who are only a third of your age."

"Your Majesty, I am honoured at the great compliment you pay to my state of preservation, but regretfully the alchemical formula by which my life and youth were prolonged has been lost."

"A great pity, because we hear both from Monsieur de Nevers and Milord Buckingham that you also possess the secret of the renewal of virginity. That alone should secure your place among the history of the wonders of the world." I could feel myself blushing under the layers of heavy white make-up. It was not going well.

"In a kingdom where family virtue is as well ordered as Your Majesty's, it is, for the most part, a superfluous talent" – The King's eyes glazed over with boredom at the flattery – "though perhaps if I travelled abroad, it might make my fortune." His Majesty's eyes lit briefly with malicious amusement.

"Primi, where would you suggest this secret might be sold at a greater profit? Milan?"

Primi, standing at His Majesty's shoulder, smiled pleasantly and answered, "Better Rome, Your Majesty." The crowd of watchers was silent at this audacity. The King, however, chuckled appreciatively. At the sound of the royal vocal cords, the courtiers all produced similar sounds of amusement. Seeing the rapidity with which the courtiers changed their mood, the King laughed again, this time at them, and then observed as the circle of laughter travelled ever wider in the room, even to those who could not possibly have overheard the exchange. His Majesty was amused. All was well.

"So, Madame de Morville, Primi tells me you can predict what card will fall and other wonders of the future."

"I can, Your Majesty; it is why I never play at cards, though it cuts into my amusement sorely."

"Think of that, no cards! Should you ever remarry, Madame, your husband will think you a treasure. Consider the savings, Primi! Perhaps we might start a fashion among the ladies."

"Ah, but Your Majesty, there are those who would say it is the most harmless of the amusements indulged in by ladies," Visconti replied with a sly smile.

And so, amid general hilarity, I read from the vase and predicted what card would fall, a trick I had perfected over the past several years in the salons of Paris. I let one man shuffle, another deal, and the King himself inspect the cards. There was applause, amazement, and I was pronounced even better than the magicians at the Foire Saint-Germain, and me only a woman in the bargain.

"Primi entertains us by reading character from handwriting," said the King. "I propose a contest in graphology between the champion and the new female contender." He turned a bland face on Visconti, who was red with annoyance.

"Monsieur Primi will have the championship," I answered, "for I am not a graphologist. However, I propose a partnership for the evening. On occasion, I can see in the glass the image of the writer of a letter even when it is sealed and no writing is visible. I propose to take a sealed piece of writing and describe the writer, then Monsieur Primi can open it and analyse the character of the writer."

"Splendid, splendid – a wonderful game," murmured the courtiers. The King looked amused and turned to one of his aides, asking that he bring some letters from his cabinet.

His Majesty himself handed me the first letter, having first read it himself, smiled, and then folded it closed again.

This was a more difficult game than the cards. I held the letter in place on the vase with one hand, and curled the other hand around the base of the glass. I breathed deeply to calm myself and looked deep into the water, with that curious sense of relaxation that lets the image come up. I saw a dapper little man in heavy make-up with an immense, elaborately curled wig. He was wearing red high-heeled shoes of an astonishing height. He seemed to be engaged in the selection of a ball gown from a ladies' tailor who was holding up a series of drawings. It was Monsieur, the King's brother.

"Your Majesty, the writer of this letter was Monsieur, the Duc d'Orléans." There was an awestruck murmur. Primi Visconti opened the letter. He looked annoyed.

"Since it is signed, Your Majesty, there is no doubt about the origin of the letter. My analysis would be superfluous. Let me take the next letter." The King, with a strange smile, handed him the next letter, having first folded the bottom half of it so that the signature was not visible. Visconti squinted at the writing, peering this way and that. He was certainly a showman.

"This is the writing of a vain old man who considers himself to be far grander than he is," announced Primi.

"See the signature, Primi," urged the King. There was a gasp of horror in the room. It was the King's own signature.

"Let us see what Madame de Morville makes of it," proposed the King. Oh, nasty, I thought. The King has tricked Primi into the crime of publicly insulting him. But Primi is his jester, and a man, so he will forgive him as part of the joke. It will not go so well with me. But I laid the letter on the glass and waited for the image.

"An elderly gentleman – in plain black, without a moustache. He has an immense but unfashionable wig and badly fitting false teeth . . ."

"The King's secretary!" shouted one of the courtiers. "Why yes, that's him to the life!" exclaimed another. "He prides himself on imitating the King's handwriting perfectly," announced a third. I glanced up at Primi. He looked quite relieved. But the King's dark eyes were trained on me. His face was immobile with suspicion and a certain quiet horror. This is bad, I thought. He sees that either his deepest superstitions are true, and that his secrets may be found out by magic, or that I, an outsider, have a network of spies that have penetrated his inner circle. I couldn't tell which.

"So, Monsieur Primi, have I bettered you?"

"Hardly," announced Visconti, with a melodramatic sniff.

"Ah, but she's saved you from the crime of *lèse-majesté*, hasn't she?" said the King, distracted from his sudden suspicion and amused by Primi's discomfiture. "Tell me, Madame de Morville, do you ever make more . . . serious . . . predictions?"

"Sometimes, though I always warn clients to be careful. I do not believe the future is inevitable, but only what might happen, if things continue as they are. And the farther away from the present, the more it is only a probability."

"So the cards are the most accurate, being the closest in the future."

"Exactly, Your Majesty." He took a letter from his pocket and placed it on the table before me.

"Tell me what will happen to the writer of this letter."

"Your Majesty, I cannot tell you anything but the image. The whole of the writer's future is hidden even to me."

"Proceed," said His Majesty, making an impatient gesture with his ringed hand. The picture came up unusually clear.

"The writer of this letter is a short man, almost hunchbacked, with an ill-fitting wig and clothes that seem very expensive, but of a provincial cut. He has an extremely large, aquiline nose, and a small, tight mouth set back in his face. Not much chin, either." The King smiled at my description. Evidently others recognised it, too, for they smiled as well. "He is apparently standing in a private chapel . . . he is . . . appears to be . . . getting married."

"To whom?" whispered His Majesty.

"I don't know the woman, either. She is evidently a very

wealthy lady, quite young, pretty to look at, dark haired, and extremely tall. The man is hardly up to her shoulder. But she towers over her ladies-in-waiting and several other men in the room." The King looked furious.

"Your impudence, Madame de Morville, exceeds even Monsieur Primi's."

"I am deeply sorry if I have offended Your Majesty, but I have no idea of who the people in the image are."

"No idea at all?" The King fixed his eyes on me – he was doubtless accustomed to shocking the truth out of people with that fixed stare.

"None whatsoever," I answered.

"Then perhaps, Madame de Morville, I need to speak to you apart from the others – Primi, quit following me; I would speak to Madame de Morville alone." He led me behind an immense, ornate screen that sheltered the room from breezes that would blow through the double doors when they were opened. "My secretary tells me that the Marquisate of Morville is extinct these last two hundred years." A test of truth.

"It is, Your Majesty."

"Your lineage, then, is it genuine?"

"It was drawn up by Monsieur Bouchet, the genealogist. It is as genuine as many others at court."

"I did not ask that, Madame. Come, I will have the truth. Answer me honestly, and I will give you a pension of two thousand livres. Try to deceive me, and I'll have you burned alive in the Place de Grève." I looked at him. Two thousand livres was not an amount to sneeze at, but I was clearing better than two thousand livres a month. Accepting his generosity seemed like a rather extravagant sacrifice. Still, the alternative was worse. "How old are you really?" he asked.

"Your Majesty, I am eighteen years old." He looked deeply relieved.

"And your true name and origin?"

"My name is Geneviève Pasquier, and I was born here in Paris. My father was the financier Matthieu Pasquier, who was ruined in 1661. He died without leaving me a dowry, and I have since made my living by my wits." His eyes narrowed. He did not approve of nobodies. "On my mother's side, the family is related to the Matignons." At this news, his eyes changed, filling with genuine curiosity.

"Why doesn't your Mother petition for a pension, to prevent her daughter from sinking into dishonour?"

"Your Majesty, she is dead." The King pondered a moment.

"Tell me, who is your informant about my letters and my affairs?"

"No one, Your Majesty. In the course of my fortune-telling, I learn many secrets from women, but they are about love, not statecraft."

"Yes, yes, that must be so," he strode about and muttered. "You still say you have no idea who wrote the letter?"

"None, Your Majesty."

"Then see this." He held the letter up briefly so I could see the signature. It was from the Protestant prince, William of Orange, the Stadtholder of Holland, Louis XIV's greatest enemy and rival. I had only a glimpse of it before he put it back in his pocket, but it was clear it was a refusal of the King's offer of his illegitimate daughter by Madame de Montespan as a bride. The phrase that caught my eye was this: *The Princes of Orange are accustomed to marry the legitimate daughters of great princes, and not their bastards.* Oh, my.

"The woman you describe could be no other than the Princess Mary of England, who is as well known for her beauty as for her height." Oh, dear. Even worse. Gossip was that the King had intended the English princess for his own heir, the Dauphin, thus securing another kingdom in his orbit and returning it to the Catholic fold. I could not have made a more insulting or dangerous prediction. The King was watching my face. "So, now you appear to understand. Either you are the most impudent woman in this kingdom, or you have correctly predicted that my worst enemy will become, some day, King of England." And either way I'm in trouble, I thought. "Either way," he went on, "you deserve to be shut up for life. But I have promised you a pension. Now, tell me honestly, do you make up what you claim to see in the oracle glass?"

"Your Majesty, most water diviners are false. It is easy to post a confederate who gives secret hand signals concerning the persons who lay their hands on the glass. In my own case, however, the images come up from the water like little dreams made up of fragments of reflections. I interpret them as best I can, just the way you can see pictures in the clouds. And I must tell you, too, that for me, the images are enhanced by opium." He nodded as if that last bit of information explained everything. "Mostly, the images are meaningless, and I interpret them to please my clients."

"And did you make this particular prediction by interpretation?"

"No, Your Majesty. I saw the scene: the man, the woman, the priest, the witnesses."

"Then you have earned your pension, Mademoiselle Pasquier, for you had my promise, the promise of a King. But if at any time I hear that you have ever again made any political predictions by looking in water, I will have you shut up for life in the Pignerol. Incommunicado. And that, too, is the promise of a King."

The evening was over. But as I was escorted from the hall, Primi stopped me.

"Out of my way, Monsieur Visconti. You have set me up for this," I snapped.

"Ha— He offered you the fortune-teller's bargain, there behind the screen, didn't he?" I tried to push Primi aside, but he evaded me and reappeared in my path.

"I don't know what you mean," I answered.

"He offered me eight thousand livres to tell him how I did my handwriting analysis."

"Eight thousand? He only offered me two thousand!" I was indignant.

"That's because you're a woman, Marquise."

"It's all very well for you to gloat, you wretched Italian; you've put me out of business."

"Why, that's entirely unfair. After all, it's an honour to be put out of business by the King himself."

"I don't want to see you again, Primi." I stalked past him to the chair that waited for me in the outer corridor. Quite an honour, I thought, as the bearers took me to my waiting carriage. The cold wind of an autumn night hit my face as I mounted into the carriage to return to my inn. First he ruined Fouquet and Father, now he has taken my living. For the second time in my life, I have been ruined by Louis Quatorze, I thought.

A new thought: *one must beware the generosity of kings nearly as much as their wrath.*

But by far the greater surprise was waiting for me when I returned home, almost as pale with sleeplessness as if I had used a double layer of my white make-up. The police seals had been placed on my front door. And as I inspected them, unbelieving, Captain Desgrez stepped out from a sheltering doorway near by with three quite large-looking foot sergeants.

"Madame de Morville, we would like you to come with us," he announced. And before I knew it, I had been hurried, satchel and all, into a waiting carriage for the trip to the Châtelet.

FORTY-FOUR

Desgrez sat silently observing me as I sat between the two sergeants on the seat opposite him. Facing backward, I could not see the *boucherie* as we approached the Châtelet, but I could smell it. Piles of offal, the alleys running with animal blood and filth – the slaughterhouses of Paris made bad neighbours, except for a prison. I started counting the possible reasons for being detained. They certainly were numerous, now that I thought about it. What I hadn't done, I'd seen or heard about. I knew enough about the underground life of Paris to vanish for life. And they'd sealed the house. I doubted they'd find my coffer and cache of forbidden books in their hiding place behind the wall panels. But the last of my coded "account books" had been left in the drawer of my nightstand. I racked my brains trying to remember what was in it. Had I been careful enough? And then there was all that dreadful business with the King. Suppose he'd decided to put an end to my political fortune-telling by imprisoning me for life with a *lettre de cachet?* In that case, I'd never even know why I was held. I'll be silent until they read the charges, I thought. Then perhaps I can think of something.

A covered cart – the Châtelet hearse – passed us going in the opposite direction. The smell of it was so foul that the driver and attendants had tied kerchiefs over their faces. The unclaimed dead, being hauled to the order of Les Filles Hospitalières de Sainte-Catherine, where the nuns as a holy duty prepared the rotting bodies for burial in the Cimetière des Innocents. An image arose in my mind – d'Urbec, following my coffin, and my eyes stung. Would he ever find out what had become of me when he returned? My nose seemed runny, and my hands were unsteady. Desgrez had taken out his hand-kerchief to cover his face. Even the man who could sit impassively all night by a burning corpse was choking on the stench of the lost souls of Paris. My mind seemed to flicker like a candle in a draught. Perhaps I'm getting sick, I thought.

I had expected the carriage to enter the dark underpassage and deposit us by the prison entrance. But instead we turned, passing by the twin towers and their central arch, incongruously surmounted by a statue of the Virgin, and entered the judicial side, where the courts and guardrooms for the watch and the *huissiers* were located. I staggered as I got out of the carriage in the courtyard. Desgrez smiled as the sergeants had to steady me on our march up the stairs into the cavernous old fortress. Our war of nerves has begun, he seemed to announce, and you are losing.

After passing through a long, dank corridor, I was shown into an antechamber where several clerks sitting at high desks were transcribing records into ledgers. Rows of muskets and pikes were mounted on the walls, and men in the blue suits and white-plumed hats of the police were lounging on wooden benches. The centre of the police hive, I thought. But there was a centre within a centre. We passed through a hidden corridor into a narrow room, richly panelled, with a high seat and heavy table behind a low wooden barrier. The secret interrogation chamber for suspects of high degree. "Wait," said Desgrez. "The session in the chambers is not yet finished."

A moment later, an inner door opened, and La Reynie himself appeared, wearing the pale, heavy wig, long red judicial robe, and white linen bands of a Lieutenant General of the Police. He was followed by a clerk.

"Monsieur de La Reynie." Desgrez took off his hat and addressed his chief, who looked at me a long time with his hard, intelligent eyes. The man who had supervised the torture of the Marquise de Brinvilliers. Not someone to play games with, especially on his own territory.

"Captain Desgrez – I see you have brought the so-called Madame de Morville. Excellent," La Reynie replied, motioning Desgrez to sit on one of the armless chairs that lined the room, but leaving me still standing. As I stood there, I realised I was developing a splitting headache, so bad that I could hardly think. I could feel the cold sweat starting to run down my temples. Then a fine tremor began to run down my limbs.

Damn, damn! I wasn't ill at all. I'd missed my dose of cordial. And here I needed all my wits about me. I could almost see the lovely little green bottle lying there in the bottom of my satchel, in the grasp of that big lout of a sergeant.

"Madame, you look pale," said La Reynie. "Do you need to sit?" I didn't like the tone of his voice, all that false sympathy that shrouded something quite the opposite. Tell him you want the stuff, cried my body, shouting through the throbbing headache. Keep quiet, shouted my mind. Do you want to put yourself entirely at his mercy? I sat down suddenly on the little wooden stool reserved for those being interrogated. The body, which usually tends to win these internal arguments, set my mouth to talking:

"Monsieur de La Reynie, Monsieur Desgrez, your pardon, but I am suffering from an old infirmity and must have a few drops of my, ah, heart medicine, which is in my satchel over there." By now the tremors were visible. The two of them looked at each other, then at me. La Reynie made a gesture to one of the sergeants, who began to unpack my bag onto a nearby bench. As the cabbalistic cloth, the rods with the strange figures, the round glass vase were unpacked, Desgrez could not resist picking them up and inspecting them. Then the sergeant handed him the green glass bottle and the tiny cordial glass.

"Poison?" Desgrez asked, turning to La Reynie.

"Hand the bottle to me," answered the Lieutenant General of Police. Unsealing the bottle, he ran it under his nose, and a strange little smile crossed his face.

"Not poison, Desgrez. Madame is an opium eater. Look there, at how eagerly she pours the precise dose. This makes our job even easier." La Reynie's voice was even, his faint smile ironic. Body, you do it to me every time. Now he has you, I thought. But the trembling was fading, the pain passing, and I felt self-possessed again.

"Madame de Morville, we have had our eye on you for a long time. You are a charlatan; you are posing as a person of aristocratic birth, and you have grown wealthy on deception – No, don't protest. We have the records. The Marquisate of Morville is long defunct. The only way you could lay claim to the title is if you were, in fact, over a century old. Do not take me for a superstitious woman, Madame. I find your claims to longevity preposterous, although not illegal. However, your other activities, Madame de Morville, are a different matter altogether." The clerk handed him a little green notebook, the one I had put in my own nightstand drawer the night before. La Reynie took it up in his hand and, with a pleasant expression, leafed casually through it, well aware of the desperate search I was now conducting in my mind, trying to remember what was in it: clients' names, dates, fees – a calculation of La Voisin's percentage . . .

"French written in Greek letters – not difficult for an educated man to penetrate, though doubtless confusing enough to the kind of people you associate with. Why do you keep your book in code, Madame?"

"To protect the names of my clients from gossip and my, ah, personal observations—"

"Personal observations that might be construed as heretical in some quarters, eh?" La Reynie set the book down on the table and smoothed down a page, reading aloud: "'If the nature of God is both all-powerful and good, then why would He create a world so full of evil? Either He is not all-powerful, or he is not good. In the first case, He could not then be God as defined, or, in the second case, in the creation of evil, He would be difficult to distinguish from the Devil. Therefore, a geometrical proof of the existence of God must depend first upon the precise definition of evil—' Have you heard enough?"

"My thoughts were not for publication."

"Ah, but they are written evidence of a most impious state of mind. Are you aware of the penalties reserved for freethinkers? I could send you to the block. Good. Shall I go on to other matters? Murder, perhaps?" He paused and stared into my eyes. Now I know how a bird feels when it is frozen in the stare of a viper, I thought. He wants to know about Uncle, or the procurement of abortion. Either one could be my death, even if he didn't have proof of freethinking. He knows everything. But I'll give him nothing. I won't let him startle a confession from me. He'll have to go the whole way to get any information from me.

"Why are you playing with me like this?" I asked. "You want something of me. What is it?"

"Ah, very clever, Madame de Morville. I felt your reputation as a fortune-teller must rest on a certain native intelligence. And somewhere you have been tutored, though I found many errors in your Latin. Yes, I want something of you. And I want you to understand that your life is in my hands, so that you will not hesitate to provide the information I seek."

"What information is that?"

"Madame de Morville, it is my job to secure the tranquillity of this tumultuous city. I deal daily in cabals, conspiracies, assassinations. For this I need information about the actions of suspicious persons." He paused and leaned back in his chair, the better to inspect my reactions. "I have a number of informers among the confessors of this city, but their information is so often after the fact – the deed has been done, the crime committed, the criminal eventually feels guilt and runs to the confessional to confide in God. But a fortune-teller" – he leaned forward across the table and stared at me— "a fortune-teller hears the secret desires of the city before they become deeds, at the very moment of their planning. A fortune-teller with a high clientele is perfectly placed to find conspiracy *before* it is enacted."

He paused and turned the pages of my account book. "Here" – and he again began to read aloud, hesitating only slightly over the alien letters – "'Madame de Roure wishes for the return of her lover, visit on 13 April last, v. prediction, 100 francs. Madame Dufontet desires the Duc de Luxembourg to give a position to her husband, n.v., she vows she will have it anyway. The Countess of Soissons desires a lover of the highest rank—' The King, I believe? The writing of this alone could send you to the Bastille for life, if it were made known in the correct circles. Need I read more?" I was silent.

"Not only do you know the secrets of the city before they become action, you can, by your predictions, shape action," he went on. "'v.' stands for 'I see,' doesn't it? And 'n.v.' for 'I don't see'? *'Non video,'* or *'ne vois.'* Transparent." He raised a supercilious eyebrow. "Your predictions in each case, aren't they? I want to know these passions, these predictions, these vendettas." I didn't like the look on his face. Hard, unpleasant, superior, as if he held a spider in his hand and would as soon smash it as anything else. I looked about the dark panelled room with the unlit candles in the heavy iron sconces on the walls. I could see the same expression on the face of Desgrez, the clerk, and the sergeants.

"You want me to become a police informer? And if I don't?"

"Then you will find the punishment for murder is very swift and sure here. I pride myself on the fact that my reforms have made justice a matter of days in this city."

"And just what murder is that?" I asked. Best to know how far they've gone, and what they know.

"Ha, I see you require a tight leash. You are bold as well as intelligent. But I think we are coming to understand each other. From this moment on, if you try to deceive me even once, I'll see you hanged for the murder of Geneviève Pasquier." He paused for effect. Desgrez's eyes narrowed. I couldn't believe it. Of all that I'd done, of all that I'd witnessed or been a party to, they wanted me for the murder of myself! I began to laugh. The sound of it clattered eerily in the near-empty chamber. I doubled over, and tears ran down my face. I was nearly choking with hilarity. I could feel my face all hot and fevered with it, and could hardly breathe. La Reynie stood up, furious, and clenched his fists.

"Madame, if you cannot control yourself, I'll shut you up in La Griesche until you can."

As the fit passed, I wiped my eyes with the back of my hand. The laughter had turned into hiccups.

"Your pardon . . . M. de La Reynie . . . *hic* . . . you see, it's not possible . . . *hic* . . . because I myself . . . *hic* . . . am Geneviève Pasquier."

"This changes nothing," snapped Desgrez. Ah, Desgrez, so *that* was your pet theory. Too bad, I thought.

"Of course, Desgrez, though it complicates things slightly. Tell me, Madame, what proof do you have of your claim?" La Reynie's voice was bland, sinister.

"Proof? Why His Majesty himself knows. When I appeared before him he demanded to know my true identity and then promised he'd have me executed if he ever heard of me reading fortunes in water again. You're too late, Monsieur de La Reynie. The Sun King has already put me out of business." La Reynie looked annoyed.

"I am afraid we shall have to hold you until we have verified what you have said, Madame, or Mademoiselle, as it may be."

"Leave me my cordial then, I beg you."

"Your cordial, and a volume of Père Clement's excellent sermons, to mend your fractious spirit. And I assure you, if you have practised the least deception, I will have your opium taken away and let you writhe until you've revealed the entire truth to me. In fact, it's not a bad idea to do that anyway. Take her away, Desgrez. I want her in solitary confinement, with orders that she is not allowed to speak to anyone."

I emerged two weeks later considerably lighter of purse, for it is the custom of Parisian jails to charge for accommodations, just as if they were a sort of diabolical inn. My only company was an eye that peered in from time to time through a peephole in the door, a sliver of sunlight that crept along the floor during the afternoon hours, and an assortment of insects. Alone and silent, my mind was haunted by terrible thoughts. Suppose I was never released? What if Florent never found out what happened to me? Would he think I had abandoned him? Would he hate me then? Then a new thought crossed my mind. Suppose when they verified my identity, the King ordered that I be returned to my family? God knows what Étienne would do. Would a prison-convent be worse than this? Could Florent find me there?

Huddled in a corner, shaking and sweating, I was ravaged by my lack of opium. The eye came and went. But when I began to vomit up blood, a bottle of tincture of opium appeared on a plate with the bread that I was too sick to eat. I took it as a sign that La Reynie planned to release me eventually and wanted my co-operation. I sat up to look at the book he had left me with. Père Clement's sermons turned out to be of an extraordinary dullness. La Reynie's little joke. Now boredom became my enemy, as La Reynie softened me up with waiting and more silence. I leafed through the book from front to back and back to front again. Then I treated the odious sermons as if they were a code, using different mathematical methods of skipping words and letters to create new and fascinating messages from Père Clement's vapid, pompous prose.

Trapped with his sermons, I grew to hate the man, although I had never met him.

When at last I was brought again into the secret hearing room, there was very little left of the Marquise de Morville. My clothes were crumpled and my hair undone. The heavy white make-up had been worn away by my tears. Humiliation and uncertainty had done as neat a job of breaking me to La Reynie's will as the police torturer would have, and without leaving a mark. That was La Reynie's way. Always efficient. But he had also given me plenty of time to ponder my situation, and I had come to the conclusion that the Lieutenant General of Police needed me more than he had revealed. I would play along with him, then flee the city at my own convenience. As soon as I was home again, I'd begin laying plans. First a bank transfer abroad, preferably through a middleman, the conversion of some of my holdings and larger *objets d'art* into highly portable jewellery...

"So, Mademoiselle Pasquier, did you find the sermons enlightening?" La Reynie looked up from his work. A curious expression crossed his face as he spied my disarray, as if even he had not expected what he found beneath the disguise of the immortal marquise. He had been signing papers brought to him by his secretary while he waited for me to be led to him. I could read them upside down. It appeared to be his daily report to the King on conditions in the city of Paris. Crimes, gossip, plots – even upside down, it seemed calculated to arouse the interest of a man habitually bored.

"Tremendously enlightening, Monsieur. They are written in a code based on the number six." La Reynie's eyebrows went up. "If you look at the sixth line of the sixth paragraph in the sixth sermon, and skip every sixth word, you will find the author's true meaning." I extended the book to him. He opened to the correct page and ran his finger over the line.

"... the ... Devil ... rules ... France ... rebel ... against ... sin ... crush ... viper ... tyrant."

"Quite easy to decode, really. As everyone knows, 666 is the number of the beast in Revelation. The good father is a conspirator sending secret messages to the other Frondeurs and assassins of his gang." I watched La Reynie as he carefully marked the place and set the book aside. It heartened me to imagine the pompous Père Clement being put to the question. "*Huitième coin*, please. Now, tell us again just why did you hide the message in a sermon?" It would serve him right.

"But we are not here to talk about sermons," La Reynie said. "We are talking about an impudent nineteen-year-old girl who has run away from home to consort with criminals and amass an illicit fortune under an assumed name. In quieter times, you would deserve nothing better than to be turned back to the head of your family for a good spanking and consignment to a convent to repent at leisure. But your crimes are such, Mademoiselle" – and here he smiled in anticipation – "that His Majesty has instead turned you over to me to do whatever I wish with you. So now, Mademoiselle Pasquier, let us talk about your future . . ."

The fire leaped between the black cat andirons, and the driving rain rattled at the window of the Shadow Queen's little cabinet as she got up and poured another glass of sweet wine. Her smile was sticky sweet, too, as she offered it to me. Her informers among the jailers had told her when I was to be freed, and her own carriage had delivered me from the Châtelet directly to the Rue Beauregard. Now I sat, still damp and crumpled, beside her little writing table.

"So now, have a little more, my dear . . . just precisely what did you tell La Reynie about me?"

"Only that you were my teacher in the art of fortune-telling and that the fees in the book were apprenticeship fees—"

"They got your books?"

"Only the last one – it didn't have anything in it . . . I've been careful . . ." She waved her hand to dismiss my excuses.

"And why did he let you go?"

"Well, he couldn't very well prosecute me for murdering myself," I said lightly. I couldn't let her know the truth. La Voisin's eyes narrowed. "So he had to let me go, even though it didn't please him." La Voisin's mouth clamped shut, and she tapped her fingers on the table as she looked out the rain-splashed window.

"Damn!" she said. "He'll plant an informer in your household, just to be on the safe side. Someone easily convinced by a little cash . . ." Sylvie, her lips seemed to say soundlessly, as the name popped into my own brain at the same time. The sorceress broke off and looked at me a long time, shaking her head. "Are you sure there's nothing else?" she asked suspiciously.

"Well, he's given my description to the watch. I can't pass the customs barriers to get out of the city without his written permission. I'm trapped here."

"But the King – your great triumph . . . surely you must pass out of the city if you are called to court again . . ."

"He knows if he lets me out of the city to follow the court, I'm as good as gone. And I'm sure he has seen the King. After all, he reports to him daily. My identity was established too quickly for him not to have seen the King. And I'm allowed to use the glass again, providing I report all requests for political readings to him and make no political predictions of my own."

"Thus the King keeps the letter of his word," muttered La Voisin.

"Exactly," I agreed.

I did not dare to tell her what information the police had asked me to bring them: information about people in debt, people desperate for a legacy, who might turn to poison to improve their situation. Their questions had led me to suspect that the confessors of Paris had done their job all too well and that the police had at last discovered the trade in "inheritance powders". It was only a matter of time until some other informer led them to La Voisin. My plan was to drown them with trivia until such a time as I could flee safely. I would not betray the queen of the witches. Ghastly as she was, I owed her that much.

FORTY-FIVE

There is something depressing about cleaning up a house that the police have searched. Papers, books, and clothing were strewn everywhere. The wine cellar was a jumble and half the bottles missing. We threw out the broken china and sent the slashed tapestries out to be rewoven.

"Don't sigh so, Madame. The chair can be re-upholstered."

"I think I'll just have it patched, Sylvie. And I'm going to sell my paintings. We aren't going to be nearly as well off, now that I can't travel with the court." The grey day suited my grey mood. The year had already turned, but spring seemed very far away. I'd managed to sell my ivory-inlaid end table and the biggest pieces of silver and convert them into two diamond bracelets. But La Reynie, when I had visited him in the gown of a fishwife from Les Halles, had wrinkled up his nose and said, as he read my report, "Ah, excellent, just what I wanted. So tell me, what does a fishwife want with diamond bracelets? I do hope you aren't thinking of leaving us. My Desgrez is a bloodhound who laughs at borders." Sylvie, I thought, as I watched him fan away the scent of dead fish with his hand. She's on the police payroll, too. I must be more careful.

"Oh, look, Madame, a carriage is stopping before the house. It's a sign. Your grand clientele is returning." I looked out the window and saw a familiar figure in a heavy, gold-braided cloak and wide plumed hat descend from the carriage.

"No – It's Florent! He's back!" I cried joyfully as I rushed to open the door for him. His face lit up at the sight of me, and he embraced me so tightly that my feet didn't even touch the ground.

"Oh, God, I was so hungry for you," he said. "It's been so long, and I thought you might not . . ."

". . . not wait for you? Florent, how could you? There's no one for me but you . . ." His rough cheek against my face felt so good. His warmth went through me. The sunshine of the south seemed to fill the house. He set me down and sent Gilles upstairs with his trunk.

Then he looked around, quietly noting the vanished silver and furniture, and remarked mildly, "Things seem to have changed around here, haven't they? Ah well, they are changing throughout Europe as well. Have you heard the news about the Prince of Orange's wedding to Mary, the English princess? Quite unexpected. Now he is heir to the English throne. They say that they hurried to the chapel with only a few witnesses. But it makes sense. The King had launched a plot to have the Princess kidnapped, brought to France, and forcibly wedded to the Dauphin."

"Actually, Florent, I predicted that wedding ages ago. That's what started all my troubles." D'Urbec looked indulgent, as if he didn't believe a word, but he owed me a hearing anyway.

"You know," he said, "what surprised half of Europe was how calmly the King took the news, almost as if he knew already. 'The beggars are well matched,' he said, and that was all. Quite astonishing, really, considering how disappointed he must have been. He had planned to gain favour with the Holy Father by reconverting England to Catholicism. Amazing" – and here d'Urbec shook his head— "the King must have spies everywhere. The Prince of Orange hiccups in his own cabinet, and the King gets the news within the week."

"That's part of the problem, too, Florent. The King has taken my living, and the police are after me." Florent looked deeply troubled, but I put my finger across his lips to silence him. "Not here, not here," I whispered. "Let me tell you all about it over supper."

In one of the curtained assignation rooms in the back of a fashionable restaurant, I laid out the problem over supper. The very mention of my predicament cost me my appetite, but Florent ate like a wolf, finishing my portion, too, while he listened.

". . . so you see, Florent, I've never been in more of a mess. La Reynie has threatened to have me condemned for freethinking, *lèse-majesté*, treason, and God knows what else if

I don't turn police informer. If La Voisin finds out that's what he wanted, snap! She'll get rid of me just like that! Poison in the soup, an accident, who knows what? Besides, I don't earn enough money to tempt her to leave me alive, now that the King has undercut my business for fear my political predictions could be used in plots against him. And oh, Florent, I *hated* jail! I was all alone . . . I thought you'd think I left you . . . and La Reynie locked me up with nothing but a horrid book of . . . sermons!" I started to cry, remembering, but Florent just tipped his head back and began to laugh.

"A feast of moral masterworks? Now *there's* what I call real torture."

"It's not funny, Florent; they were *ghastly*," I said, wiping my eyes.

"So," he announced cheerfully, polishing off the last bones of the capon and wiping his fingers on the napkin, "there is really only one way out of your problem."

"Yes, out of Paris, and I'm trapped here like a dog on a leash."

"No," he said, "first of all you need to get married – preferably to me."

"How would that solve anything? I thought you were brilliant, Florent, but now you turn out to think just like a man."

"And very good thinking it is, too." He laughed. "Consider my reasoning. First point: if you are married, your brother, as head of the family, no longer has a claim on your property – nor does he have the right to confine you in a convent for a scandalous way of life, which, by the way, you lead. So La Reynie loses this implicit threat over you. Second point: as your spouse, I can pursue your inheritance, since it becomes mine. In France, this would mean years of litigation and bribery. But abroad, it would be much simpler, because your brother does not have possession – indeed, he does not even know about Cortezia et Benson."

"But . . . but—"

"No, hear me out. There's a third point. The officers at the barriers give their chief attention to goods being smuggled in, not criminals being smuggled out. You could flee the city any time if you were content to go in disguise with only what you could carry concealed on your person. It is Madame de

Morville, her carriage, her servants, that are notorious. Geneviève Pasquier on foot would be almost invisible, especially if she could restrain her desire to wear two rings on every finger. But you shrink from the gypsy life, Athena; you entertain a most understandable fear of dying in a ditch in some foreign country."

"So what if I do?"

"Love of material things has closed your escape route, Athena. You should have considered more closely the excellent spiritual materials offered you by Monsieur de La Reynie."

"It's not that ... but my books, my silver ... why, the furniture alone is worth—" Here he shushed me by putting a finger across my lips.

"Point proven, my sweet. Now, you must remember that I am a specialist in transferring resources abroad in secret. I am exactly what you require. I cannot make a move, however, unless I have a legal right to handle your property." He cocked his head sideways and looked out of the corner of his eyes at me, his face amused.

"Florent..."

"Yes, I know what you meant to say. You'd have to trust me. And it's one thing to love a man but quite another to trust him, especially in your book – not so, little sorceress?" He smiled, finished off the last of a half-empty wine goblet, and waited to hear what I would say.

"No, that's not it. It's that you'd risk your life..."

"Risk? That's nothing to me. Geneviève, I have trusted you, even though you tell me you are a police informer." He saw the shocked look on my face and went on. "What you do not know is that I have a vial of poison sewn in the hem of my coat. In my work, it is best not to be taken alive. The risk to me, these days, is being in Paris at all, and the main reason I am here is you. But with you ... life seems ... too precious to throw away. I have high connections abroad these days. We could start again overseas, have a home together, everything we can't have here. So you see? I have just trusted you with my life. The least you can do is trust me in return."

"Florent, you're trying to trick me into marriage." I could feel my hands shaking.

"Of course I am. And what is your answer?" I looked into the bottom of my wine goblet, trying to decide, and I could feel the fear welling up in me like a fever.

"I . . . I need to think. Let me tell you tomorrow."

"And I knew that would be what you would say. Send me word when you have made up your mind, won't you? But don't delay too long; we don't know how long you have. Weeks, months – think about that when you ponder the terrifying issue of marriage." That night I woke up what seemed like dozens of times, trembling all over.

It was Grandmother's parrot that made up my mind for me. The damp thaws that come just before spring had given it a chill, and it sat huddled up on its perch, its feathers all fluffed up in a dismal ball, its black eyes mournful. As I set it by the fire to warm, it gurgled unhappily.

"Lorito, you and I feel the same," I told it.

"Hell and damnation," it croaked dolefully.

"Exactly. What a mess. Tell me. Should I leave or stay?"

"Sodom and Gomorrah," announced the bird, poking his head up hopefully.

"What do you know about marriage, anyway? Me, I know too much. Lorito, I make my living from marriages where love has turned to poison. Suppose I marry him and he quits loving me?"

"Fire and brimstone," replied the bird, agreeably.

"Oh, what help are you? I have to decide whether a fortune-teller in trouble with half the world should marry an adventurer in trouble with the other half. To marry d'Urbec – it can't work out."

"Marry d'Urbec," the bird said, peering at me with one eye. "Clever Lorito. Pretty Lorito." Something about the bird's face reminded me of Grandmother in her little cap. I took out paper and ink, sat down, and wrote a letter. It contained only one word.

Yes.

"My love!" he cried when he saw me, his face eager and boyish. "I'll arrange everything. You won't have a worry in the world." I loved to see him that way, his eyes bright, his mind busy. His embrace was rapturous, but I could feel something cold stalking my heart. It was fear. They all begin this way, I thought, with pledges of love.

"The chief thing for the moment is to keep everything secret – both from the police and from that old witch on the Rue Beauregard. We don't want either of them to think the bird will fly. Don't let Sylvie know. I'll get witnesses and a priest who are on no one's payroll; that will buy us time, though how much I don't know." He looked down at me suddenly. "You are happy, aren't you? As happy as I?"

"Oh, yes, Florent," I said, as I took his hand.

"You aren't . . . having second thoughts, are you? Forgive me if I am terrified you might escape when I have waited so very long."

"When I give my word, it is given; my heart will never change. Remember that, and . . . and be kind."

"You mean if I should ever change? Don't think it of me, not ever."

The next day, under the pretext of a supper party, I dressed gaily in my rose silk gown, and we drove through the grey mist to a remote parish in the suburbs, where we were met by a half-deaf old notary and two dark-cloaked, masked witnesses. It was already dusk, but even the newly lit candles in the nave revealed the ruinously needy state of the building. In the darkening arches above, there was movement and a shrill whistle: bats had made their home in the crumbling masonry. Dust sat heavy on the chipped, ancient paint of the statues of the saints. The nicked wooden panels of the confessional had cracked with age and lack of paint. Battered iron grilles sealed off the private chapels. Clearly a parish where the priest might stand in need of ready cash.

In the side chapel, the witnesses unmasked. Lucas, the underground poet, and . . . Lamotte. Florent's smile was ironic, as he saw me start. There are certain things one doesn't want to remember on one's wedding day, no matter how informal the occasion.

"You'll find these to be men you can trust, Geneviève. We have been through too much together for it to be otherwise."

". . . but the Duchesse de Bouillon . . ." I managed to say.

". . . will be delighted, should it ever come to her attention," finished Lamotte. "She loathes La Reynie and all his works."

"An old family feud between the La Reynies and the Bouillons – over taxes, I believe," added Florent, smoothly. Lamotte, his figure even fuller than I remembered but still resplendent in a vast pair of heavily embroidered petticoat breeches and a heavy blue velvet mantle with flame-coloured satin lining, advanced several steps.

"And . . . ," he said, hesitating, "I owe you an apology. Both of you. It is the least I can do to make amends. Envy, d'Urbec, it makes a man a fool. And I have paid . . . many times over, a terrible price, beyond even that imposed by my conscience." His face, in the fast dimming light, looked drawn and sad. "All I ask is that when you count up my sins, don't include hard-heartedness among them."

"Enough of this soul-searching, my dear chevalier," announced Florent. "We have business under way, and Père Tournet does not like being detained." Being detained from his bottle, I thought, as the old priest stumbled over the service. I could feel the panic rising as the words droned on. My mouth was too dry to make a sound as I mouthed the responses. The priest's odd, bulbous nose and moth-eaten vestments, Florent's dark, anxiety-ridden face in the flickering light, the glitter of candles reflected on tinsel and gilt – all seemed to whirl together in the strangest way. My stomach felt awful and my knees weak.

The next thing I remember is choking on brandy. "Ah, her eyes are open now," someone said. "You fainted, Madame d'Urbec," came the voice of the priest, "a not uncommon occurrence at weddings. Though it is of course more embarrassing if it is the groom."

"Married? I'm married?"

"Of course. Completely. Legally. Every *i* dotted." Florent helped me from the floor. His expression was concerned. "Geneviève, are you well?" he asked softly.

"Oh, Florent . . . married . . . it can't be . . . I care for you too much . . . Now what will become of us?"

"Why, I can look after you and we'll be happy, that's all," he said, as he brushed away the curls that had fallen into my face.

"But . . . but that's not how it works."

"It's how it can work if you wish it to, Geneviève. Try it,

won't you? For my sake, let us try to be happy." But I could only clutch his coat and weep.

And as he put his arms around me I could hear Lucas remark, "Without a doubt, my dear de La Motte, that is the oddest bride I have ever encountered."

D'Urbec's manservant set out supper for us with the neat, small movements of someone who had long been crowded in close quarters at sea and then withdrew. How quiet he was, and how discreet. The fraternity of the damned, I thought. One grew to recognise them by their eyes, by the way they'd lift a heavy chest or chair like a feather, without giving it a thought, by their strange and random silences.

"You still look pale," said Florent, his face knotted with worry. "And still you don't eat. Are you well?" I could hear the clocks in his room tick, each one at its own rate, like different heartbeats. My hands felt cold. "Look here," he said. "I've ordered all your favourite dishes. Try this wine – it's splendid. Fit for our wedding night." I sipped it to make him happy, but it was as dry as dust. Florent's dark eyes were troubled as he inspected my face. "What is wrong? Have I lost you by marrying you? Have I asked too much of you?"

"Too much?" I repeated, frightened suddenly at the look on his face. "What do you mean?" It's already happening, I thought. So soon after the wedding, he's stopped loving me. I could feel my eyes grow large as I stared at him. Yes, I could see it. He was already tiring of me.

"Are you frightened of me? Was my love good enough for you, but not my name?" he asked in despair.

"No, no – that's not it. That's not it at all." Tears I couldn't stop ran down my face. "You can't love me any more, now that we're married," I said, weeping. "I knew . . . I knew it would happen this way. Marriage makes people cold and hateful, but . . . but you said I had to . . . and . . . I wanted to make you happy . . ." I put my head down on the table and sobbed as if my heart would break. I could hear the chair scrape as Florent got up from the table I could feel his hand stroke my head. With his big handkerchief he tried to wipe my eyes.

"It's not the disgrace?" he said softly, brokenly. "It's not . . . what I am?"

"Never, never. You are the only man I will ever love. Your love is the only good thing I have . . . but now you can't love me, and I only wanted to make you happy—"

"Happy?" he said. "You mean, you thought you were sacrificing love for my happiness?" He sounded taken aback, puzzled. "You would do that? Give up everything? For me?"

"A hundred times over," I said in a low voice, clutching at his hand and holding it to my face.

"Geneviève . . . love," he said softly, "don't you know what you are to me? I thought . . ." I wiped my face and looked at him. His love was my joy, but it was his need that cried out to me.

". . . that I would be ashamed to be Madame d'Urbec? Florent, I have many causes for shame, but wedding you is not one of them."

"Geneviève!" he cried out, and I could see his face shine with new light.

"Madame d'Urbec," I corrected him, my heart beginning to hope again. The curve of his cheek, the wide, strong line of his neck, his eyes, his lips, his hands were beautiful. I could see the pulse of blood beneath his ear when he turned his head away to brush a hand across his eyes.

"Madame d'Urbec," he said, turning back to me with great courtliness, "let me show you that married love is the truest of all." And with that, he scooped me from the chair as if I were no heavier than his handkerchief. I felt drunk with his body. I twined my arms around his neck and he kissed my face, my hair, my neck, as he carried me through the open bedroom door.

FORTY-SIX

"Gossip, tittle-tattle, and stale intrigues. That brazen girl drives me mad. The secret life of Paris turns out to be a veritable web of amorous conspiracies. Look at this stuff, Desgrez! Repulsive! There's hardly a so-called respectable name in France absent from this trash!" La Reynie, pacing before the table in his study, flung the latest report from the Marquise de Morville down in disgust. He looked out of the narrow, diamond-paned window into the courtyard of the Hôtel La Reynie. It was the spring of 1678. His wife's carriage was departing to take her on a call to her cousins; he could hear the shouts as lackeys opened the heavy wooden gates of the porte cochère. The architect Fauchet was getting out of his chair with yet another sewer-drainage plan rolled up under his arm for the Lieutenant General of Police to review. Inspectors of books and weights, police, servants, stable boys, and informers all mingled, coming and going across the cobblestones on their various errands. La Reynie's face was bitter as he surveyed them. He spoke so softly towards the window that Desgrez almost couldn't hear him. "Sometimes," said the chief of the Paris police, "I wonder just what it is that I am protecting."

"The state, and the honour of His Majesty," responded Desgrez. La Reynie turned from the window.

"Yes," he said slowly, and his eye returned to the discarded document on the table. "So what is that blasted female up to these days, anyway?" he asked.

"According to her maid, she is chiefly engaged in a most shameless and open love affair with Florent d'Urbec, the gambler."

"Another one! The two most irritating people in Paris have formed an alliance. How appropriate."

"Your pardon, Monsieur. I have come to make a suggestion. You need to use La Pasquier to discover the facts about this latest intrigue of Buckingham's."

"You know how I hate to depend on her. And I swear, she wears that fishwife disguise solely to offend me with its odour."

"She is our only conduit to Buckingham's occult activities. He is believed to have enlisted the satanists in support of this new attempt."

"I'm afraid, then, I shall have to put duty before aroma."

"Exactly, Monsieur. Wittily put," answered Desgrez.

The next day, two red-stockinged sergeants showed Madame de Morville into La Reynie's reception room. La Reynie, in a plain suit of tawn-coloured velvet with lace at the throat and sleeves, paced up and down impatiently, while the celebrated fortune-teller, in the discarded apron, cap, and gown of a fishwife, inspected the jumble of nymphs and other half-robed mythological beings that adorned the ceiling of the long, high room.

"I would think, Mademoiselle, that one of your origins would tire of the smell of that abominable costume." La Reynie spoke impatiently. Brushing some invisible dust from his sleeve, he ordered a lackey to open the window in an irritated voice. "And kindly do not sit on the up-holstered chair," he added. Madame de Morville smiled secretly and, with exaggerated humility, took the plain wooden stool without a cushion that was reserved for low-ranking visitors.

"The English Milord Buckingham has arrived in Paris with two companions. I have been informed that he has made a number of contacts throughout the city. This evening, he goes to get a reading from the spirits." The two sergeants took up their post at the white-and-gold panelled door to the antechamber.

"Yes, at Madame Montvoisin's. I have been invited. Spirits, as you know, are not my specialty."

"Lately, your specialty seems to be predicting gambling winnings and loose living," La Reynie observed drily. "This time, I expect a full report: what Buckingham desires, who joins him there, and what the spirits promise. A *full* report, do you understand?"

"Yes, of course, Monsieur de La Reynie." Was her tone a shade too sarcastic? La Reynie had learned over the course of several encounters that Madame had a decided bent towards sarcasm. But he didn't take the bait this time and remained dignified, looking down his long nose at her with a fixed expression of disdain. "Then you may go, Mademoiselle Pasquier," he announced. "Latour, open the other windows before I smother in the smell of rotted fish."

FORTY-SEVEN

It was already late in the afternoon by the time I had bathed away the smell of fish and had myself laced into my most impressive antique court dress for my appearance with the sibyls. Sylvie accompanied me, also dressed in her best, and Mustapha carried my train. I had promised Florent that I'd be back before dark, because the spirits don't usually take more than an hour. Madame burns incense and chants, and Nanon whispers from behind the tapestry in the next room through a speaking tube into the black parlour. The client is awed, the spirits equivocal, and Madame well paid.

I found the milords already arrived and drinking wine at the dining table in front of the tapestry, while Madame, sitting with them, gave orders to Nanon and Margot, who were scurrying back and forth into the black parlour.

"Ah, there she is – the dear marquise. Now our number is complete. Sylvie, you must join Nanon in front. Margot, I'll be wanting the cordial glasses in my cabinet. Mustapha, wait in the kitchen; our mysteries are only for initiates."

"I must say," giggled Milord's plump blonde companion, "I am dreadfully partial to demonic seances. Tell me, will there be a virgin sacrifice?"

"Our mysteries are not to be revealed carelessly," answered La Voisin in a deep, thrilling-sounding voice. "You have requested the aid of one of the most powerful of the princes of Hell. It is enough for you to know that the sacrifice will be entirely appropriate. Astaroth does not serve without the payment of a human soul." The milords shuddered deliciously, and even the jaded face of Buckingham seemed to come alight with new interest.

"Tell me, does it involve . . . orgiastic excesses?" asked the second milord, and the bizarre lust in his eyes unsettled me. "I am especially fond of ceremonies performed . . . without clothing." Oh, goodness, I thought, the things La Voisin does for money. Money and a refuge abroad. You'd think, with her passion for elegance, she'd manage to conduct a ceremony with dignity.

"Oh, *you* may be undressed if you wish." La Voisin chuckled. "But as for me, I am Empress of these shadows and dress accordingly."

"Silly French biddy," whispered the milord to Buckingham. But only I heard him.

"Then it's settled – the three of us will witness, and I will make the request to the demon. What must we do first?" asked Buckingham.

"First we must have a brief protective ceremony in my cabinet, because my lackeys are already preparing the parlour for the ceremony." At that moment, two servants carrying a rolled-up carpet appeared in the door of the black parlour. "Then I must robe in my vestments of power. That is a ceremony you must not witness. Purification, dedication. They must be absolute, if we are to retain power over the demon."

"*Hmmm* – a genuine Turkish carpet. Your business must be very good, I assume," observed the second milord.

"Of course. I am aided in every project by infernal powers, as you yourself will soon be," answered La Voisin, unperturbed. Then she turned to me with a curious smile. The little V, all pointed, with the eyes caressing. "My dear Marquise, could I impose upon you to supervise the labours of those simpletons in my parlour? The windows must be sealed tight with pitch. I want no forgotten corners. Make sure the servants don't nick my desk when they bring it through the door – replacing gold leaf is costly. The braziers must be exactly equidistant in the corners of the room, and the black drapes over the statues and the face of the cupboard with the figurines. Ah, good – I am so grateful, Madame." She summoned Marie-Marguerite to her, and I heard her say as they vanished into the cabinet: "My daughter, an adept of superior powers . . . long ago dedicated to the demon in just such a ceremony . . . wealth and power . . . your request is simple for such a high prince of hell . . ."

"Yes, yes . . ." I could hear him agreeing as they vanished in the direction of her cabinet, but the rest was lost. What request? I needed to know. I'll have to sit through the whole wretched ceremony now to find out, I thought. Damn that troublesome policeman, anyway. This was obviously going to take half the night, and I'd rather be home with Florent.

But at last, under my supervision, the room, stripped and sealed, was ready. The preparations seemed a bit elaborate for an ordinary spirit reading, but, then, impressing milords requires more show. The candle sconces on the walls were filled with black candles, and the heavy black brocade curtains were pulled across the tall windows. The remaining furniture, shrouded with black cloth, took on strange, eerie shapes like ghosts, while the faces of the Virgin and all the little cherubs on the shelf had been hidden away under black drapes. The black-tiled centre of the floor, ordinarily hidden under the rug, reflected the glitter of candle flames in its clean-scrubbed surface. Marie-Marguerite, strangely subdued, appeared at the open door to tell me that I was wanted in her mother's cabinet.

In Madame's cabinet, I found three shivering milords with cabbalistic signs painted on their foreheads; the pupils of their eyes were large and glittering. Drugged, I thought. They certainly will see things. A little dish of something burned to ashes sat on the writing table beside the inkstand. There was a parchment with odd figures drawn in black. A bottle of cordial, some little glasses, and a plate of marzipan, all in little coloured shapes like fruit and toys, sat in the midst of all this. Madame was sitting in her brocade armchair like an empress. A robe of scarlet velvet lay over her shoulders. It was heavily embroidered in gold, with hundreds of double-headed eagles, their wings spread. Beneath was a skirt of sea-green velvet, heavily trimmed with lace. On her feet were scarlet velvet slippers, embroidered in gold with the same double-headed eagles. On her head rested a crown of lead, ornamented with death's-heads.

"Sit down, my dear. We have a long night's work ahead of us, and you know I hate to proceed without a little refreshment." I watched carefully as she poured the cordial into the glasses. Each was clean; there was one for her as well. Good, it wasn't drugged. You always had to check these little things when drinking with La Voisin. The milords raised their glasses to her. So did I. The marzipan went around, my favourite thing. I took the one shaped like a little cottage, which looked a bit larger than the other pieces.

We sat in silence for a while, which was just as well, because I suddenly felt very tired.

"It is time," the Shadow Queen announced, her voice deep and strong. "My powers are at their height. The moon has risen. My blood is inflamed with the powerful seed." The milords shuddered. "I will draw the circle." As if through a haze, I saw her take from the cupboards boxes and jars and mix the contents in careful proportions in a big brass bowl. "For the braziers," she said. Opium, St John's wort, mandrake, and who knows what else. Then she took out chalk, a knotted cord, and five candles from a special box. In a strange metal box she had a mummified head. "The head of a parricide," she announced.

"Th-those candles are made of human fat?" asked one of the milords.

"Of course. I would use nothing else for such a powerful ceremony," she answered. His companion shuddered. She picked up her little silver bell and rang it. Her two lackeys, now clad in black, appeared at the door. "Take the offering into the chamber," she said, with a single, commanding gesture in my direction. It was at this time that I discovered I could not stand. I felt odd all over; I tried to turn my head to see what was happening, and it wouldn't move as I wished it to.

"How much did they pay you for this?" I tried to croak, before my tongue itself thickened and refused to do its duty.

"Don't struggle too much against the drug, my dear. You'll just overburden your breathing, which is much weakened just now." I couldn't move to see her. She leaned in front of me. "They are paying me quite a lot, Marquise. And you really have to understand that my investment in you was spoiled after that business with the King. And, too, how could I trust you once it was clear you'd become a police informer – no, don't look so annoyed. I guessed it right away. I'm not stupid, you know, and La Reynie never lets people go without some little bargain or other. Never mind; it will all work out for the best." She patted my hand and smiled. "Besides, once

Astaroth has taken possession of your mind, you will be entirely reliable again. One of us – you really ought to be pleased." Your daughter was right, I thought. You'd sacrifice anything if it were convenient.

"Oh, yes, I can see it in your eyes. You're wondering how I administered the drug, aren't you? So cautious, you are. Well, it wasn't in the wine; it was in the marzipan. You always *will* take the largest piece." She chuckled, and the view shifted crazily as the lackeys picked me up and deposited me in the black chamber, propping me up limply against the wall under the window.

"I beheld Satan as a bolt falling from heaven. It is thou who hast given us power to crush dragons, scorpions . . ." La Voisin was tracing the outer circle counterclockwise – the direction of the Devil – with the point of the great sword as she chanted. Marie-Marguerite and Sylvie, dressed in close-fitting blood-red robes, their hair unbound beneath circlets of lead, both stood behind her, holding something. Then followed the inner circle, traced in chalk, and the cabbalistic signs, the triangle, the seal of Solomon. The Shadow Queen's two adepts lit the chemical mixture in the braziers and the brass bowl, and a fetid smoke began to fill the room. Then La Voisin placed the contents of the other bowls, a cat's head and the mummified head, outside of the circle as offerings to tempt the demon close.

"The cat must always be black?" murmured one of the Englishmen.

"Yes. And fed on human flesh."

"Must blood be shed?"

"Yes. Keep your hands close to you. If you extend them beyond the circle, we may lose you." The milords drew their hands close to them in horrified silence. The Shadow Queen resumed chanting, reading from her open grimoire while her two red-clad adepts lit the human candles and placed them within the circle. Meanwhile the room filled with the stifling smoke from the braziers. The milords were sweating and choking. Astaroth, however, stubbornly refused to put in an appearance.

"Mother, you must conjure him by Lucifer, his master—"

"Not yet. It is too dangerous. One more time." The Shadow

Queen read again, "I invoke and conjure thee, O spirit Astaroth and, fortified with the power of the supreme majesty, I strongly command thee by Baralamensis, Baldachiensis, Paumachie, Apoloresedes, and the most potent princes Genio, Liachide, Ministers of the Tartarean seat, chief princes of the seal of Apologia in the ninth region..."

I felt violently ill. A dreadful sense of pressure and foreboding filled me. Marie-Marguerite fell to her knees. La Voisin's hair seemed as alive as snakes, all spread out over the crimson robe as she raised her hand, holding a rod, in a commanding gesture.

"Appear!" she cried.

"Oh, my God, I see it!" cried the plump blond milord. "It's an infernal woman! Blood drips from her fangs!"

"Monstrous. Oh, monstrous – the horror—" The second milord fell to all fours in the circle and began clawing at his black robe.

"A king – a king in a chariot of flames ... hung about with human heads..." whispered Buckingham.

"Appear in comely human form..." La Voisin went on chanting.

"Mother, Mother, the circle – he's broken it, crawling about like that—" Marie-Marguerite's voice was urgent. But La Voisin chanted on, exalted, oblivious.

I thought I could make something out in the shadows. My limbs prickled and ached. The drug was beginning to wear off. But I was sweating, my head throbbing. I felt violently nauseated. Oh, Lord, get me out of this stuffy room with these lunatics. If only I had my cordial... As the thought crossed my mind, I realised I hadn't had any cordial since last night. Oh, damn. All this and sick, too. I lifted a weak hand and felt my face. My head hurt hideously. The occupants of the circle were writhing around on the ground at the feet of the Shadow Queen, who still stood upright, rod in hand.

"Reveal yourself, demon. Enter the body of the woman outside the circle and speak your name."

The smoke had sunk down to the floor level now, where I could breathe it in. Opium smoke, charged with the bitter odours of foul herbs. As I took it in in great breaths, I thought, not enough, damn it all. Enough to make everyone else in the room as mad as hatters and not enough to stop this blasted headache.

"... take her, enter her, possess her, rule her. Accept this sacrifice, O Astaroth. Take her mind and soul, give her the power, give her—"

"*No!*" A great cry came from within the circle. La Voisin looked horrified. She had at last spied the break in the circle. A low, demonic snarl sounded from within the circle. Sylvie, her hair wild, was writhing on the ground. From her lips, a bass voice growled, "I am here. What is your wish?"

"Take possession of the soul dedicated to you, and leave this circle," commanded La Voisin, taking up the sword to retrace the broken portion.

"I don't want it."

"What do you mean, you don't want it? It was perfectly prepared for you. Demons always want souls." La Voisin was incensed.

Buckingham had regained his composure. He fished underneath his black robe and found his lorgnon. "Marvellous," he said as he inspected Sylvie through it.

"What worthless, slippery rag of a soul do you offer me? A silly, snobbish girl who doesn't believe in the Devil and keeps *account books* instead of lovers?" Sylvie's voice was deep and resonant. Unfair, I thought. That's what Sylvie *would* think. The demon in Sylvie went on: "I'll have this fine figure of a woman here, who knows what to ask for when the Devil woos her: palaces, clothes, lovers, damnation! I have taken the real woman, not the cold-blooded lady philosopher who hasn't enough blood and bone for a decent meal."

"I say," interjected Buckingham, "take the demon's advice and quit bothering him. That's quite a woman, heh, heh—" He peered again through his lorgnon. "The demon has good taste." I couldn't believe how offensive I found the milords, as they goggled at the latest novelty they had financed.

"I conjure you in the name of the archfiend Beelzebuth, leave the circle—"

"The archfiend has left on business for Constantinople," announced Sylvie in her new, deep voice. "It is I who rule Paris. I have taken this woman. Hers is the power. Worship her. I am in her." I had to admire Sylvie's audacity. La Voisin saw what she had done, too. Raging, the Shadow Queen began to cough. Overpowered by the fumes, the milords weakened, and one of them passed out. Desperate, La Voisin began to chant the demonic dismissal, but Sylvie stood her ground, snarling like an enraged wolf.

". . . I permit thee to retire wheresoever it may seem good to thee, so it be without noise and without leaving any evil smell behind thee . . ."

"Never!" shouted Sylvie. "I, Astaroth, have chosen!" La Voisin sprinkled something into the burning mass in the brass bowl that gave off heavy white smoke. Sylvie, breathing heavily, passed into a stupor on the floor, and my own eyes started to stream. The last thing I remembered before I lost consciousness was La Voisin leaning over me, her black eyes raging.

"How *dare* you, how dare you! Even the demon won't have you, you dreadful . . . cold-blooded . . . *machine*, you! You're not even a snake in my bosom – I've nurtured a damned *clockwork*!"

FORTY-EIGHT

"It's really very simple," announced Florent as he poured coffee into two cups the next morning. "You have accustomed yourself to opium the way the Italian princes accustom themselves to poison – a drop at a time. They cannot be assassinated, and you cannot be possessed. Everyone else was seized with hallucinations, and you simply sat there annoyed with the poor quality of the drug." His eyes were sunken with fatigue. He seemed relieved that I was up and listening.

I sat there huddled in my dressing gown, still nursing a dreadful headache. I had black circles under my eyes and strange bruises all over me, as if I had been bitten by invisible animals. Despite a great deal of washing, I could still smell the reek of Paris mud on me and feel the panic engendered by the rolling clouds of suffocating smoke in the sealed room. Florent had found me in the small hours of the morning, wandering demented in the gutters of Bonne Nouvelle. They say I was howling like a wolf, but I can recall only a pair of strong arms carrying me home and wide hands cutting off my filthy clothes, wrapping me in heavy blankets as convulsions twisted my body. But coffee, coffee mends everything. Morning and sanity had come. I thought about Florent's explanation. It had its points.

"I don't think opium is the whole story, Florent. I think that possession is a matter of the desire to believe. After all, Montaigne says that belief can make the body well or ill. I don't see why one could not add 'possessed' to that list, do you?"

"*Hmm.* That makes sense, too. But what person would be so silly as to wish to be possessed? I find it hard to discern a motive."

"I don't," I answered, as he poured more coffee.

"Mustapha," he called, "you have made a mistake – you

brought only two cups. You must bring a third and drink with us. If you had not fled that house and found me, your mistress might be dead."

"Drinking with servants breeds familiarity," said the little man as he brought the third cup and clambered up onto the empty chair.

"Coffee does not count, Mustapha. Besides, what else would you expect from a man of such questionable social origins as I?" There was something strong and refreshing about Florent. The way he poured the coffee with a flourish, the way he got up to open the window himself and let the cold, fresh air in while I coughed last night's filthy smoke from my lungs.

"So, Mustapha, what has happened to Sylvie?" I asked.

"Gilles found her at Madame's, flung her over his shoulder like a sack of grain, and brought her back still raving. Several buckets of cold water seem to have put the demon to flight, at least temporarily."

"He is in love with her, isn't he?" said Florent. I looked up, astonished. I'd never even suspected.

"Hopelessly," replied the little man. "But she wants that Romani, the poisoner. She told Gilles that she wants to better herself. I am grateful I have been spared the vicissitudes of unrequited love."

"I think perhaps not," said Florent quietly. Then he looked at me and back at the little man with a strange, deep sympathy. "But it is part of the human condition, isn't it?" he went on. "God spares none of us." I looked at the grounds in the bottom of my coffee cup.

"Pardon," said Mustapha, changing the subject as he put down his coffee, "I think I hear someone at the door."

But there actually was someone at the door. As I heard the noise downstairs, I called, "Show whomever it is up, Mustapha; I am in no condition to come downstairs."

When the cloaked woman was shown into the bedroom, she threw back her hood and took off her mask, looked about her, and said, "My, your upper chambers are nicely furnished, Madame de Morville. I've never seen them before." It was Mademoiselle des Oeillets, Madame de Montespan's lady-in-waiting. "And who is this gentleman?" she asked, spying

Florent, who had risen to greet her. "A magician?" Florent gravely nodded assent.

"I'm sorry I could not receive you downstairs. I was present at a demonic possession last night, and I am still quite exhausted."

"Oh, yes. Those can be tiring. Was it a major or a minor demon?"

"Major. Astaroth. And someone broke the circle."

"Oh, my goodness! I'm surprised you're receiving *at all!* I'm sure I should have been in bed for a week, if I had been there!" Pleasantries exchanged, Mademoiselle des Oeillets drew me behind the screen in my *ruelle* for privacy and came straight to the point.

"Madame de Montespan needs you to consult the glass for her – in strictest confidence."

"But I thought Madame de Montespan was at court. I can't travel to Saint-Germain, you know, since ... uh, the incident. And I am forbidden to do any readings that might be political."

"Madame arrived in the city last night, and will be returning as soon as her business is done. She wants you to meet her at her house secretly. No one must know she is consulting you."

"Then it is politics."

"Oh no. It has only to do with love."

"With Madame de Montespan, love is political." I was calculating which was worse: Madame de Montespan's certain vengeance versus the King's probable punishment. There was, in addition, the hope she could keep quiet and produce another cash payment that I could convert into jewellery. The jewellery won.

"So, I take it, you are going to give a reading to Madame de Montespan?" asked Florent with a smile, as the door closed behind Mademoiselle des Oeillets.

"Yes. She probably has another rival on the horizon."

"She should quit looking at the horizon and start looking within her own household. I'd put money on the governess."

"Madame de Maintenon? She's far too old – the King likes little blonde girls. What makes you think the governess has a chance?"

"You forget. It is my business to play cards with the greatest gossips in the kingdom," answered Florent, laughing.

"Astaroth wants to know why you are not wearing the excellent fishwife's disguise," announced Sylvie, as she brought me the drab habit of a *dimesse*, the collector of contributions for convents.

"Tell Astaroth that La Reynie hated the smell," I snapped. There is nothing more annoying than a maid who considers that she has been occupied by one of the ranking powers of Hell. I put on the heavy gown, coarse shawl, and long white apron and attached the large, plain rosary to my waist – and found it really wasn't bad at all. Of course, what Astaroth didn't know was that I was going to Madame de Montespan's.

"Astaroth says when you return from the Châtelet, you must go to Madame, his faithful servant."

"Tell Astaroth that Mademoiselle Pasquier has no wish to be poisoned again. Madame may come here, if she has business."

"Astaroth has told Madame she must receive you graciously. Astaroth will accompany you to see to your safety. Astaroth senses great changes in the world. Great danger for the faithful."

"Sylvie, when will you tire of this Astaroth and evict him?"

"Astaroth would be angry, except that he knows you are a fool. *Obey Astaroth, mortal, and then Sylvie may have the body again.*" Sylvie's voice took on a deep bass growl as the demon spoke directly through her. Her eyes looked quite odd. Insane, really. But crazy people have never bothered me. After all, I grew up with one. It was Gilles who was bothered. He looked as if his heart would break. Once he came up to me quietly and said, "This Astaroth, he is worse than a lover. Do you think an exorcism would help?"

"Doubtless, Gilles," I had told him, "but remember Astaroth is quite canny. You'll have to deceive him to get her to the exorcist."

"I'll remember that, Madame. It is good advice." But so far, Astaroth had bullied us all, even La Voisin, who was doubtless heartily sorry she'd unleashed him upon the world.

I had to wait in the antechamber to Madame de Montespan's

bedroom while her masseuse finished. It was a long time. Some things never change, I thought. Even in disfavour, that woman would keep everyone waiting. At last the masseuse departed, and after a decent interval, I was shown in. Madame de Montespan had grown immense since the birth of her last child. A billowing *robe de chambre* of gold-embroidered green velvet covered the vast rolls of fat that shrouded her once-famous waist. Her face was drawn, lines had formed in the celebrated ivory complexion, and her eyes were sunken in the middle of dark circles. She sat on the edge of her bed and looked at me, her aquamarine eyes dull with months of despair and an ocean of hate.

"I have a rival," she said.

"So I suspected," I answered.

"Mademoiselle de Fontanges. She is nineteen, fresh and new, and has never borne a child."

"I have been away from court. I really don't know anything any more," I said.

"It appears to have done you good. You're not so pale, and you look younger than ever. Oh, God, that I could be young again! I spend three to four hours a day with my masseuse, but nothing seems to work. It is over. My reign of wit and taste. He has found a ridiculous little upstart with the brains of a donkey." She shook her head despairingly. Then she looked at me and said, "But he'll never imprison me. I have sworn it. He won't live to do it. I am a Mortemart. Compared to Mortemart blood, the Bourbons are upstarts. Shall an upstart imprison a Mortemart? Never, I say! The gods themselves are against it!" She got up and went to her armchair that sat beside her little writing table. "Pull up that stool, put out your glass. There is only one more thing I must know. Does this miserable, provincial know-nothing steal my rank of duchess?"

I set up my things as she had requested, and Mademoiselle des Oeillets herself brought the pitcher of water.

"Here," said Madame de Montespan, "I took this from her as I laced her up last month. I prepared her for the King. Just as La Vallière once had to lace me up, now I must lace up the odious little Mademoiselle de Fontanges. Things come full circle, don't they? When my star was rising, I enjoyed humiliating La Vallière. And I would enjoy it still, if it were to happen all over again. She was a simpleton who did not deserve the exalted honour she received. She had no wit and taste to hold him with. She got brown in the sun. She did trick riding – can you imagine? What man can stay in love with a woman whose greatest achievement is to stand on the back of a cantering horse? But to have this new little country bumpkin lord it over me, a woman of mind, culture, breeding— Tell me, tell me: will she commit a social *gaffe* like La Ludres and destroy herself?" Madame de Montespan extended to me a tiny rosette, snipped from an embroidered chemise. Dutifully, I pressed it against the glass.

"Madame, I see a young girl with blonde hair, a small mouth, a straight nose like a statue, and simple blue eyes – is that she?"

"Yes, to the life."

"Her eyes are sunken in . . . she looks tired, or ill—"

"Good," interrupted Madame de Montespan.

"She is riding in a pearl-grey carriage . . ."

". . . with the King?"

"Alone." Madame de Montespan let out a sigh of relief.

"But how many horses?" she asked.

"Let me see . . . they are rounding a curve in the country . . . trees are in the way . . . they are approaching a group of buildings . . . a convent? I can't tell, I've never seen them before. One, two, three . . . yes, four pairs of horses. Eight horses pull the carriage, Madame."

"Eight, eight! I knew it. Then it *is* she that will be the duchess. I swear here before you, she won't live to enjoy it!"

"Madame, please contain yourself. Remember, you promised secrecy."

"Secrecy?" and her voice became sly. "Oh, yes. Strictest secrecy. For you, and for me, too, because for you to tell of this meeting is death. Yes, we shall be very, very quiet, won't we? Adieu, Madame de Morville; I will see you well rewarded for this." I left hoping the only reward she meant was the fat purse I was handed in the antechamber.

The trip to the Rue Beauregard was less than pleasing. I sat in glum silence while Astaroth carried on about what an indignity he found it to ride in a carriage behind only two horses, whereas in Hell he was carried on an immense gold-and-jewelled throne on the backs of a thousand fiery imps, et cetera, et cetera.

"Sylvie," announced Mustapha, "if you do not get rid of that boring devil, I will start attending Mass again."

"Astaroth hopes you are joking."

"Of course, of course, Astaroth. Just make sure Madame doesn't play any nasty tricks on us, won't you?" I always believe in conciliating lunatics.

"Madame is an underling. Astaroth can make her vanish with a snap of the fingers."

A faint, lingering smell of the foul black smoke still seemed to cling to the curtains and the upholstery in the black parlour. It inflamed Sylvie, whose nostrils spread wide to catch the scent and whose eyes darted about as if seeing invisible things in the air. Myself, it made my stomach churn.

Nanon showed us into the back room where old Montvoisin shuffled out from the kitchen with a roll in his hand and said, "Well, how's the King Devil today, feeling fine?"

"Astaroth greets the husband of his devotée." Montvoisin chuckled at the greeting and sat down to consume his roll, brushing the crumbs off his lap. Sylvie sat down in Madame's best armchair to wait, and I took the plain-backed chair. Nanon's eyes narrowed as she saw Sylvie sit, and she went off into the bowels of the house to summon her mistress. Soon after, La Voisin appeared, her black taffeta petticoats rustling beneath her dark green satin gown, which was fastened up at the hem to show a pale green satin lining. Her braids were knotted up beneath her lace house cap, with curls hanging down in front over her ears, almost concealing her heavy emerald earrings. Her dark eyes flashed annoyance as she spied Sylvie.

"Astaroth takes the armchair," announced Sylvie, her eyes alight with a strange fire. La Voisin seemed taken aback, looking first at one of us, then at the other. Then she shook her head slowly.

"Damn," I heard her mutter to herself. "Well, my dears," she went on in a voice oozing cheer, "let's let bygones be bygones. Would you like a glass of wine?"

"Astaroth doesn't drink," announced Sylvie. I bit my lip to

keep a straight face. Astaroth was good company. From the corner, I heard old Montvoisin's high-pitched giggle.

"Antoine! Enough! Mademoiselle, I have business to discuss with you in my study."

"Astaroth's mighty power controls all business." Madame glared at Sylvie as she led the way to her cabinet and took her own large armchair behind the writing desk before Astaroth could get at it. I took the plain chair on the other side of the desk, and Sylvie, her eyes blazing, the armchair by the fireplace.

La Voisin looked across the writing table at me, and her face sagged with weariness and disgust.

"I still have need of you – and yet the demon rejected you. Why? You were fully prepared. I myself led you to the required deed of power. I put the vial of poison in your hand myself. You were the perfect offering: brilliant, educated. You would have been one of us. The greatest among us. Merciless. And yet the demon wouldn't have you." She shook her head slowly in disbelief. "What is it that is wrong with you? Something lacking – it must be because you are one of *them*," she said softly. "An enemy of our kind. One of La Reynie's betrayers." She tilted her head and looked slyly at me out of the corner of her eye. "Tell me why I shouldn't get rid of you," she said.

"Because I didn't betray you. It was you who tried to betray me to the demon. Besides, you wouldn't have asked me that if you intended to kill me." La Voisin sighed.

"You grow too old. You grow too clever. I needed your mind, your position, your access to society for my great work, but now it has all slipped beyond me. Have you never understood why I created you? You could have been the mightiest of our queens in your turn. Now who will you be? A gambler's fleeting *amour*. Dead. Wasted."

"I'll be my own person."

"Then you are truly lost. No human can live without a master, and you serve neither heaven nor hell. What power is it that has stolen you from me? What is it that rules you?"

"Truth. Reason. Whatever is beyond cannot be found without them. I am still searching."

"Pure lunacy," she said, sighing. "All this has cracked your mind. No wonder the demon didn't want it. Still, you are the best water reader in the kingdom, and I need your glass. The great work I have planned must go forward, with or without you, and with all my powers, I cannot see its end. Read here for me," she said, indicating a tall water vase that sat among the curious objects on her desk.

"Concentrate," I said.

The sorceress began to speak in a low voice, almost to herself. "I am engaged in a mighty deed. The powers of the earth assist me. When I am finished, I will sit beside kings, the equal of princes. The shadows will rule the sun." I looked up from the water to see that her eyes had grown strange. What did she mean? She must have breathed too much of her own smoke last night. Whom was she plotting against? Who were her allies? No wonder La Reynie had acted so strangely. "What is the future of this kingdom?" she asked. I looked at the vase; it was drenched in blood.

"Blood," I answered. "Blood and more blood, running like a river over the stones in the Place Royale. An ocean of blood."

"Good," she said, in a voice almost as if she were in a trance. "This is La Voisin's revenge."

"Madame, you go too far. Give up vengeance. Ignore the glass. You don't know when it will happen, or if you yourself will be pulled into it. Let it go."

"Oh, yes," she said in a mocking voice. "Do good, love God, bless those who push you into the mud, die poor, and go to heaven. Little Marquise, I will let you leave with your life because I now know you are too much of a fool ever to betray me." The last thing Sylvie and I heard as the door closed behind us was the sorceress's bitter laughter.

FORTY-NINE

As the wine went around the table again, Maître Perrin, *avocat* and dabbler in the occult, helped himself to another immense slice of the leg of lamb. "And some more of that excellent sauce, please, Madame Vigoreux!" he exclaimed happily, patting his mouth with his napkin. A splendid supper, the guests pronounced it, uniting good food, good wine, and those intelligent souls who had an interest in treasure hunting by occult means. So many fortunes, buried in the earth and forgotten during the *Fronde*, just waiting for the correct incantation, magnetic dousing rod, or diabolical assistance to cause them to rise to the surface! It was a topic of near-universal interest. Maître Perrin himself, although an *avocat au parlement*, expected to enrich his patrimony considerably during the next few months, but by means of a rare parchment recently purchased from a woman called Marie Bosse, who seemed to have many valuable connections.

La Bosse herself had become quite red in the face with wine, and her son the soldier was becoming ever more raucous. The little tailor who was his host was quietly drunk at one end of the table, humming a tune to himself. Even Maître Perrin was decidedly more mellow than usual.

"Ah, Madame Vigoreux, what a wonderful table you set!" he cried. "Who could be a finer hostess than you. Such lavish hospitality! I bow to your knowledge of the occult!" He stood and bowed to the accompaniment of much laughter.

"Here's to wealth without work!" Monsieur Mulbe raised his glass.

"What do you amateurs know about that?" La Bosse said, to the general amusement of the guests. Someone had spilled wine on the white tablecloth; the candles were burning down. It had been a long night already. "Why, if you knew what a racket I've got!" boasted the old witch. "And what a classy clientele! Duchesses, marquises, princes! Why, only three more poisonings and I plan to retire with my fortune made!"

La Vigoreux cast a warning glance across the table, which Maître Perrin intercepted. A convulsion seemed to pass through his midsection. With whom, and with what, had he become associated? All thought of buried treasure fled from his mind. The company laughed heartily, as if it were all a joke, and Maître Perrin laughed too. When the party ended, he departed in a flurry of cheerful compliments. And even though it was past midnight, he went directly to the house of Captain Desgrez of the Paris Police. As Desgrez's wife and servants bustled about lighting candles, Desgrez himself, still clad in nightshirt and slippers, showed Maître Perrin to his private study. He did not seem to mind being awakened at all.

"Well," said Monsieur de La Reynie the following morning, "I find your scent much improved. To what do we owe this honour?" The Marquise de Morville, clad in black silk and onyx mourning jewellery, had taken an armchair at the far end of a table in the Lieutenant General of Police's book-lined study. With a flick of her wrist, she snapped open her ebony and black lace fan. Somehow, the gesture irritated La Reynie. Maybe he preferred the fishwife disguise after all.

"To your sergeant there, who dragged me from a card reading at the maréchale's in the most precipitous manner," she answered in a sharp-edged tone.

"Our business would not wait," said La Reynie, gesturing to Desgrez and two grim-looking undercommissioners who sat at the other end of the table. "We have a few questions about the, ah, fortune-telling industry, if we may call it that." The Marquise de Morville nodded slightly, as if to say, Go ahead, if you are capable of asking anything intelligent.

"Let us skip the preliminary formalities. First of all, who is the finest fortune-teller in the city?"

"Myself, of course." The jewels on the marquise's hand caught the light as she gave her fan a little flourish.

"Ah, of course. And where would you place Marie Bosse?"

"La Bosse? She is a dreadful, vulgar, illiterate woman who

has a certain skill at deceiving people with cards. That is all. Nice people don't go to her." The undercommissioners leaned forward with uncharacteristic interest.

"A rival," muttered Desgrez.

"Evidently. That's good – we'll hear more," responded an undercommissioner in a low tone.

"And who is the woman known as La Vigoreux?"

"Another fortune-teller – her specialty is reading palms."

"Do you know her?"

"Yes, of course. She is the wife of the ladies' tailor where I'm having a dress made up. But I wouldn't associate with a woman like that professionally. She's an amateur." A narrow smile appeared beneath La Reynie's moustache when he caught the condescension in the marquise's voice.

"Well, well, it seems that every housewife with a need for pocket money tells fortunes." La Reynie's voice was vaguely genial, but his eyes were cold and probing.

"That's about right," answered the marquise, resetting the train of her long black gown around her feet with a rustle of expensive silk. "But most of them are no good. Washerwomen taking in each other's laundry." La Reynie looked at Desgrez, and Desgrez nodded grimly.

"Do La Bosse and La Vigoreux know each other?"

"Of course. They are good friends." The marquise appeared utterly calm.

"Do they dine often together? Who, would you say, attends their typical dinner parties?" Behind the marquise's cool grey eyes, the watchers at the table could sense a strong intelligence working. They looked at each other. No, she could not be allowed to leave the building until the business was done.

"I'm sure they do dine often together, but I'm not acquainted with the others of their set: second-class magicians, card sharks, forgers, false coiners – that sort of people. Not the sort I wish to associate with." The marquise's answer was clear and without hesitation. No, she could not be one of those involved, thought La Reynie. But still, he distrusted her command of herself. That alone was suspicious. One of the undercommissioners leaned forward across the table with his own question:

"Would you say that fortune-tellers have ... ah ... corporations, like the more respectable trades?"

"More or less; the trade tends to be passed down in families, exactly like any other. The difference is that there are even fewer outsiders taken as apprentices, and also, the association is run by women."

"And what, Madame de Morville, do you know about *poudres de succession?*" Desgrez broke in smoothly. The marquise, entirely self-possessed, answered without turning a hair.

"What all of Paris knows, that they are rumoured to be everywhere." Her voice was calm and even. "Whenever a death is unexpected, it is said to be caused by poison. I do a good trade in discovering enemies for people fearful of poison, as you know from our ... ah ... previous discussions. I believe, of course, that this fear is entirely exaggerated, but I certainly would never say so to my clients." The men at the table looked at each other again.

"And what would you say about the character of La Bosse?" La Reynie continued. "Would you say she is ... boastful?"

"I don't know much about it. Occasionally I see her on the street, but she is not of my type. She is, after all, the widow of a *horse dealer.*" The marquise's voice dripped snobbery.

"Has this horse dealer's widow a taste for the bottle, or for something a little more genteel – say, opium?" La Reynie asked smoothly. He was rewarded with an irritated glance from the marquise. Her fan snapped shut. La Reynie's eyes glinted with secret pleasure: at last he had broken through that damned woman's iron self-control.

"If she is like the rest of her type, she probably drinks like a fish." The marquise bristled.

"That is all, Madame de Morville. I am afraid we will have to ask you to remain in my reception hall with the sergeant here for the rest of the day. But perhaps I can find another volume of edifying sermons to help you pass the time."

"Monsieur de La Reynie, you are always so graciously hospitable," replied the marquise.

"And as usual, you may speak to no one about this," La Reynie responded.

"You know I can't. Not if I wish to stay in business," the

marquise snapped. La Reynie's smile was strangely sensual, his eyes caressing.

As the marquise was shown through the door, Desgrez said in a low voice to his chief, "Yes, Monsieur, immediately. I'll have Lebrun send his wife to her." Madame de Morville paused in the hall, then continued as if she had heard nothing. That afternoon, as the marquise stared out of a back window in the Hôtel La Reynie in utter boredom, Marie Bosse sold a vial of white arsenic to a policeman's wife who had come to complain of her husband's brutality.

"You say they were all in bed when you arrested them? How convenient for you, Desgrez." La Reynie looked up from his desk, where he had just put his signature on his weekly report to the King. Desgrez was standing, holding his hat.

"In the *same* bed, Monsieur. La Bosse, her grown son, the whole lot of them. It proves—"

"That the race of sorcerers is perpetuated by incest? Desgrez, I do not care in the least about sorcerers; it is poisoners I am seeking. I wish to get to the root of this conspiracy."

"You will find a good beginning in the contents of these women's cupboards. There is hardly a poison they don't possess. That does not even count the black candles, wax figurines, a medallion of the King—"

"The King?" Even La Reynie was taken aback. In this setting, an image of the King could be used for only one purpose. A sorcery to encompass his death.

"Desgrez," he said quietly, "I believe we have found them."

FIFTY

It was not until late afternoon that I was able to send for my carriage and escape my afternoon of unwanted hospitality. I was not much concerned about La Bosse or La Vigoreux, who surely were intelligent enough to recognise a policeman's wife, but La Reynie's insult rankled and festered for hours. Once free, I went straight to La Trianon's little laboratory in the Rue Forez. I was fired with fury and resolve. In the street, a group of giddy girls in aprons and wooden clogs had just left the shop, giggling to each other and hiding something. A love potion, no doubt.

The little black reception room in front was more magnificently decorated than ever. The ladies were clearly prospering. On the mantel, a candle on a cat's skull stood before a complex drawing of the circles of heaven and hell, and the consultation cable held several mysterious bottles, as well as the coffer with the tarot cards and a book on the science of physiognomy. In the alcove, the curtain was discreetly drawn over the portrait of the Devil, and Uncle was getting a nice patina where he hung, suspended from a wire. There is something impersonal about a skeleton; I had found in the course of many visits here that I could view him without any feelings whatsoever, except, perhaps, a vague sense of contentment.

"Ah," said La Trianon, summoned by the shop bell from her laboratory, "it's the little marquise! My dear, to what do we owe the honour? Surely, you are not out of nerve medicine yet?"

"It's about the cordial I needed to see you. I need to give it up."

"Oh, you've said that before. What's happened now? Another physician says you'll die of it? We told you as much ourselves, you know. You take more of it than any living being I've seen."

"It's a weakness. It makes me vulnerable. Times are dangerous. I don't want to be vulnerable." La Trianon's eyes narrowed.

"You *know*," she said. Know what? I thought. This must be something quite bad. "Has *she* told you?" asked La Trianon in a whisper. "I should have known it couldn't be hidden from you – not while you read the oracle glass." I acted smooth. If I asked questions, I might reveal my ignorance.

"I don't pry," I answered, "but I can't help knowing *something*. Still, I'm here for other business. I want you to dilute the opium in my cordial, but make the solution taste just as strong. I'll pay you the same, but each week you reduce the opium by a quarter. That way I can deceive myself as I cut down." La Dodée, having come to fetch some papers from the front room, smiled in greeting as she saw me seated with her friend before the fire. She had obviously overheard my proposal.

"Just so you don't end up vomiting blood, like last time. Madame will think we've poisoned you," she broke in cheerfully. I noticed that La Trianon became very quiet in the presence of the younger woman. So, she hasn't even told her partner about this. La Voisin must be up to something very serious indeed. As La Dodée left, La Trianon stood and put one hand on the mantel, motioning me close with the other.

"I need to talk to you – confidentially," she whispered. "I cannot get La Voisin to understand me, and she has always had a weak spot for you. Maybe she will listen to a warning, if I say it comes from you."

"Tell me everything. I swear secrecy."

"Last week she came to me for a poison that could penetrate material. She wished to poison a footstool so that whoever rested their feet on it would die. I told her it was impossible. 'Don't sell it in Paris, if you want to keep your reputation. Sell it to someone who is leaving the country,' I advised her, 'so if it fails, you won't have an infuriated customer returning for revenge.' 'I need it for here,' she said, 'I mustn't fail.' She sounded remote, strange – almost mad." La Trianon's voice was soft, hurried.

"This could only be for La Montespan," I whispered.

"I cast the cards yesterday. The Queen of Wands was

crossed by the King of Swords. I cast death, and the shattered tower. I am sure it is Montespan. She wants revenge."

"I know that; I've heard it from her own lips."

"But what you may not know is that since the King has withdrawn his favour from Madame de Montespan, La Voisin has put Romani on the trail of Mademoiselle de Fontanges, the new mistress." La Trianon's voice was low. Suddenly, I could see the whole pattern of the plot. La Voisin's greatest conspiracy. There must be money in it, too. Immense sums from foreign treasuries, more than just La Montespan's money. It was clear to me at that very instant that it was not a woman that the sorceress intended to pursue to the death.

"But the King, though he no longer eats or drinks with Madame de Montespan, still pays her a brief formal visit each week, surrounded by his courtiers. In her apartments, he sits in the big armchair she keeps for him, and puts his feet on the special footstool that is reserved only for him," I said to La Trianon.

"Exactly," she whispered, "and the cards say that if La Voisin continues on the path she has chosen, she will die, and bring everything down with her. The only question in my mind is whether the shattered tower is our own 'society' or the entire kingdom."

"I suppose you want a water reading."

"Yes – your best. Absolute truth." Motioning me to wait, she went into the laboratory and returned with a clear glass vessel of water.

"I don't really need all the other things," I said. "That was just for effect."

"I know," said La Trianon, sitting down at her card-reading table where she had set the water vase. "She taught you well. It's a pity, you know. Even if you had never read again, you could have been queen, the greatest queen of all. But you've wasted yourself on the wrong things: men, for example."

The dizzy, weak feeling that accompanied the rising image swept over me. But the image that came glittering up from the bottom of the water was the old familiar one: the girl with the grey eyes, whom I now recognised as myself, looking out to sea. But the cloak she clutched around her shoulders was entirely different. A heavy cloak in blue trimmed with gold braid, with a crimson lining that flashed brightly as the wind tugged at it. I knew that cloak well. I watched for it in crowds, from out of my upstairs window, from the carriage window as the driver coaxed the horses through the crowded streets. The image, for many years the same, had changed! Behind the girl, another figure was forming. The wind tore at the plumes of his hat, and he put a hand on it to keep it in place. The other arm he put around the girl who was wearing his cloak. She looked up at him, and they smiled.

"My God," I whispered. "Causality. Free will. We are all fools, we fortune-tellers. Fate and creation. But how, when did this happen?"

"What are you talking about? What do you see?" La Trianon whispered anxiously.

"We shape our own fate, but . . . I can't understand how . . ."

La Trianon sighed. "At last I see what she meant. Too many books. What a gift to be squandered on a pedant. And a female pedant at that. Who ever heard of such a thing? Just tell me the image."

"It's just the ocean. I get the same image every so often when I'm looking for something else. I'll try again." My knees felt watery, and my essence seemed drained. I dipped my finger into the water to shatter the image and looked again.

"I see Madame in full court dress – her dark green silk. She is wearing a great emerald ring . . . and holding a little vial, one of yours, I believe. She is scratching at a double door . . . white wood panelling with the carving picked out in gilt . . . at the end of a marble-floored corridor. Ah, I recognise it now – it is the entrance to Madame de Montespan's rooms at Saint-Germain. The door opens half-way. Mademoiselle des Oeillets stands there, gesturing silence. La Voisin gives her the bottle, and Mademoiselle des Oeillets closes the door quickly."

La Trianon suddenly looked shrivelled, as if she had aged a hundred years. "I saw it when I cast the cards," she said. "This is death. I will go and beg her to give it up. What prideful demon leads her to this madness?"

"You know that it is Montespan," I answered.

"If she were not of a mind to, even La Montespan could not move her to this. It is suicide, and they both know it."

"You know as well as I do, she will be second to no one –

now she feels her time has come. She will open the gates of hell and rule chaos alone, as queen."

La Trianon sighed. "And she was always such a *practical* person – it's this mysticism thing. It gave her vision, you know. Who else could have dared dream that our profession could become so great? She created an empire with her dreams – but now . . ."

"Now they will destroy her," I finished.

"More to the point, they will destroy us," said La Trianon, getting up briskly from the table. "If the police ever get hold of her ledgers, that's the end of me – and you, too, little Marquise. I'm going to have a talk with her. There are safer ways of making money than feeding La Montespan's hopeless dreams of revenge."

"But is there any better way of feeding Madame's itch for glory? That's your problem." Glory, yes, I thought. But not just glory. This was La Voisin's revenge, a revenge so formless, black, and absolute that it could pull down the world, dragging us all with her into death. As I got up to leave, I felt my mind working like an overwound clock. Somehow, I had to get hold of my contract and the *P* volume of the Shadow Queen's ledgers. Without them, no matter where I fled or how I changed my name and appearance, I might some day go to the door to find Desgrez standing there. Where couldn't he follow me? Only the New World, I sighed to myself. But then I thought of music, the theatre, my books. How could I ever live among savages, even if I had a taste for it? Ah, me, better the savages that I know than the ones I don't. One thing was sure: I couldn't tell Florent. The knowledge of what was in the ledgers would make the magic leave his eyes. He'd see me as I really was. If I told him about the ledgers and what was in them, he'd abandon me.

FIFTY-ONE

"Pretty bird! Clever Lorito! *Awk!*" Grandmother's parrot paced up and down, inspecting himself in his New Year's gift: a little mirror attached to the end of his perch. Trust d'Urbec to know what a bird would like for a present. He had come back so laden with good things from his latest trip abroad that even Astaroth had vanished for several days after Sylvie had tried on the pretty new cap with silk ribbons on it.

"Florent, since you've returned, that bird has become as vain as a peacock! Aren't you even ashamed, for having corrupted him so?"

"Vain bird. Pretty bird," announced the parrot, preening before the mirror.

Still in his dressing gown, with his feet propped up in front of him on a footstool, d'Urbec set down his cup on the table beside him and looked up at the parrot with a self-satisfied, proprietary air. "Parrots and lapdogs – they can't resist me. Only cats and I have difficulties. Don't you find that significant?"

"Do you mean that's why you and Madame can't stand each other? I think it's more than cats. And you still haven't told me why she had you thrown out of her house right in front of Madame de Poulaillon."

"I was hoping you wouldn't hear about it. That shows I should never underestimate you."

"I want to know, Florent. I need to know just in case I get any strange gifts. Perfumed gloves, for example, or a bottle of wine. And you might have to send your shirts to another laundress."

"Oh, don't worry so. I just showed her my hand, is all. I tried to buy out your contract. You'd think she'd want to sell it; after all, the value has declined recently. But then, she does blame me. She refused, and there was quite a scene. She warned me I'd better not be entertaining any notion of marrying you. But I talked legalities until my mission was accomplished. She got the contract out to show me that it was legitimate. And I found out where it was kept."

"Florent," I said, shocked, "for God's sake, don't try to break in to get it – it's worth your life. It's bad enough that she thinks we are having an affair."

"Sylvie, more chocolate please – the first was excellent." D'Urbec gave the order nonchalantly and, as she left the room, signalled caution. "Now," he said quietly, "you will have to take it on faith that I can outwit the Shadow Queen. If I can fool Desgrez and those police hounds and get you beyond the ramparts of Paris, I can certainly retrieve a few papers."

"Florent, I beg you, don't do rash things – it's not important."

"On the contrary, it's quite important – and you know it. It is the only written connection between you and La Voisin. The rest is all rumour. Half of Paris has been to her house, and even La Reynie will not track down half of Paris. I want the contract, and I want the ledger I saw on the shelf above it – the one labelled *P*." I was horrified. How could he love me any more if he saw what was in it?

"You know about the ledger?" I gasped.

"It's my business to know things that might lead to losing you for ever, Geneviève. I have waited too long to lose everything."

"But see here; it can't be urgent. La Bosse and La Vigoreux were taken over a month ago, and they haven't even bothered Madame, or any of hers. It's like when they took the Chevalier de Vanens for false coining two years ago. They found he was a poisoner, but it went no further. The cloud passes, Florent. It would be better to sell my paintings than waste time trying to get your hands on a book she won't give up." Florent nodded, and I thought he'd forgotten.

February passed, and even though the first winds of March were raw, one could feel a hint of spring in the air. Not long, not long, said the wind, and soon there will be flowers, and fish will be banished to its proper place of exile on the menu. Florent was progressing handsomely with the sale of my paintings, which I did regret, and with the disposal of a rather large and heavy sideboard which had no more purpose since it no longer contained silver plate.

Late one morning, when my only client had departed, I noticed Sylvie dusting and humming. It was a salutary change. Astaroth didn't like dusting because he refused to bend over.

"Sylvie, you are very cheerful this morning. Where's Astaroth?"

"Astaroth? Oh, he's gone off to visit his family."

"Demons have families?"

"Of course. If you were possessed by one, you'd know. Astaroth has dozens of wives, and even more mistresses, to say nothing of children, cousins, brothers, uncles, and aunts, and, of course, he has a very important position to maintain – he is master of absolute *legions* of devils. You can't keep up all that without work, you know – even if he does prefer Paris."

"Everyone sensible prefers Paris," I answered. "Have you got the black taffeta laid out? This afternoon I go for a private reading at the Hôtel Soissons."

"It's a sign of spring – everyone will be wanting a new lover and a reading. You'll grow prosperous again. You'd be prosperous now if you'd quit supporting that professional gambler – not, mind you, that I don't like him. But *really!* Your painting that you liked so well! You've become a regular love slave. If Madame weren't so busy, she'd have words."

"Well, *I* shall have words if you don't answer the door. Mustapha! Where is he when I need him?" I turned back from the kitchen door to see that Sylvie had shown in a pair of sober-looking citizens, lawyers, by the look of their long gowns and heavy wigs. One of them had his back to me; he was evidently inspecting the furniture. The other was running his fingers along the faded spot where the painting had hung. He turned his hand to inspect his fingertips for dust.

"There seems to have been a painting removed from this spot. Evidently, you were informed just in time, Maître Pasquier." At the sound of the name, my blood froze. The second man turned from his appraisal of the furniture to look at me. After only five years, he looked much older. His face was fatter, his eyes quite dead with righteousness, like two turnips that have been too long in winter storage. His complexion reminded me of those bloated pink worms that one finds drowned above ground after a rainstorm. Evidently his profession had agreed with him.

"Well, well, it is Étienne, the bloodsucker. To what do I owe the honour of this visit, Brother? Have you run through your profits from your sale of our sister?" I enjoyed watching the rage rise in him.

"At least, she didn't deny her identity," said his companion, as he restrained him.

"You always had a shrewish tongue, Sister. I'd recognise you by that even if no other part of you were the same. Enforced silence in a solitary cell in a convent will do your soul good. Doubtless you will even come in time to thank me for saving you from a life so disgraceful."

"Thank you? For what? For interrupting my business and inspecting my house like a pair of pawnbrokers?" Now it was Étienne's turn to restrain his companion.

Behind me, I could hear Sylvie whisper, "Mustapha, run to the art gallery on the Pont Notre-Dame and get Monsieur d'Urbec. Tell him there's terrible trouble."

"Leave her alone. We've proved that our informant was right. She can't go anywhere. And soon enough, I'll be able to conceal this . . . this horrible disgrace to the family honour."

I took a step forward and stared into his corrupt face like a basilisk. He took a step back. "Who informed you I was here?" I said, in a cold voice.

"I have my means. Informants among the police. La Reynie protects you, but La Reynie has enemies." Yes, I thought. Enemies among the great, who don't want him discovering their corrupt activities with the occultists of the city. Someone on their side with access to police records had wanted me quietly put away to cut off La Reynie's investigation. They must have passed my name to my brother. "And of what did these informers inform you? That Mademoiselle Pasquier lived in the Rue Charlot, that she was rich, and you owed it to your honour to seize her goods and lock her up in a convent?"

"I was informed that my runaway sister had disgraced the family name by setting herself up as a fortune-teller and was now engaged in a ruinous affair with a gambler."

"And spending everything before you could get your hands on it, eh? What unseemly haste, Brother."

"Your insults only dig your own grave, Sister." He folded his arms and stared at me arrogantly.

"And my marriage means nothing either, I suppose?" He drew back. Sylvie seemed shocked. Her eyes got a strange, faraway, calculating look in them.

"Marriage? You lie. Who would have a disgraceful monster like you?" Safe in my fashionable gown and costly lace, I laughed at him.

"Why, any number of fortune hunters would. Didn't your informant tell you that? I think he owes you a refund on your bribe. Poor Brother, you came at the end of the line. You're too late. My fortune has escaped you. And now you insult a married woman in her own home." I sat down in my own crimson-brocade cushioned armchair, barricaded behind the big gilded desk that held my water vase in the dragon stand.

"You little shrew," he cried, approaching the desk, "you'd say anything just to put me off, wouldn't you? But you can't deceive me. I'll believe you the day I see the marriage contract, and no sooner. I'll get an order to have you seized, and as for that adventurer, I'll have him arrested—" He had begun to shout, as if loudness could make up for lack of logic. Gilles had moved to stand behind them at the foot of the staircase, his immense arms folded, in case of trouble.

"And interfere with the sanctity of the family so beloved by our monarch?" I answered, my voice dripping sarcasm. "Perhaps you do not know; I have read for him personally . . ." At the very mention of the King, the second lawyer got a strange, deferential look in his eyes, but nothing stopped Étienne, so fiercely did he desire the furniture he had been stroking. "Be careful, you hypocrite," I hissed. "If you continue to bother me, there will be questions raised about your own conduct that you will not enjoy answering—"

But both men turned suddenly at the sound of the front door opening and heavy boots at the entrance. Étienne's companion pulled at his sleeve, trying to get him to leave.

"Oh, do stay, gentlemen. I'd so like you to meet my *husband*." I said, rolling the word around in my mouth with suppressed triumph. Sylvie ran to take Florent's cloak, and I noticed she had the oddest expression on her face. Mustapha was behind him. Florent's dark, intelligent eyes took in the entire scene in a moment. A strange smile crossed his face.

"My, what an honour," he said mildly. "Lawyers. Could they be relatives? I think not. There is no family resemblance. If they claim to be of the family, they must be illegitimate." He paused to enjoy the effect. Étienne's face turned most satisfactorily red.

"You lying bastard—" Étienne exclaimed. Mustapha's hand went unobtrusively to the sash at his waist, but I stopped him with a glance.

"My dear husband," I addressed Florent, "my brother has been so kind as to bring a witness with him. Sweetheart, what would you say to owning a distinguished residence in the Cité? My inheritance, now that my brother has so kindly confirmed my identity."

"The Hôtel Pasquier? But isn't it a little dreary, my love?" answered Florent, fully in the spirit of the thing.

"Never mind, precious. We could redecorate it with the money from the sale of the lovely little country property my grandmother left to me. I do hope you have looked after it well for me, Brother."

"You bitch!" Étienne exclaimed. I looked at Florent, and he looked at me. The thought flashed through both our minds. Check and mate in two moves.

"Maître Pasquier, is this true?" asked Étienne's companion.

"Never . . . I . . ."

"Étienne," I broke in, "you cannot have it both ways: either I am your sister, and you conspired to rob me of my inheritance, or I am not your sister, and you are attempting to rob me now of my property. Do, please, decide in front of this obviously respectable witness whom you have so conveniently brought with you."

"Maître Pasquier, my reputation – you have deceived me . . ."

"So you still can't make up your mind, Brother dear? Then let me help you. The police are fully informed of this case. Perhaps they even suspect you of having murdered that poor girl you went and identified as me. Mustapha, I would like you to take a message to Monsieur de La Reynie . . ."

"Come away, come away – you can settle the claim later," Étienne's companion tugged at his sleeve.

"What, going so soon? Just when our conversation has become so charming?" asked Florent as Étienne's companion dragged him to the door. "What a pity. Perhaps another time? Farewell, gentlemen."

As the door shut behind them, Sylvie applauded and exclaimed, "Bravo, bravo! Just like at the theatre, magnificent!" Florent and I grinned at each other.

"But unfortunately, unlike the theatre, in real life the curtain does not come down," announced Florent. "He may be back. And if he investigates your claims, the very least that will happen is that our marriage will be revealed to the wrong parties. It's not good. I hadn't planned for this." He began to pace up and down, and his brow was drawn up in a frown. "Damn him! Damn him! If he'd come a month later . . . ! Now I'll have to think of something else."

"Astaroth says he will arrange everything," Sylvie announced.

"Will you and that wretched demon shut up? I'm thinking!" exclaimed d'Urbec in pure annoyance. Sylvie burst into tears.

"Now, now, Sylvie," I consoled her, "Monsieur d'Urbec is just upset. He didn't mean any insult to the Prince of Demons, I'm sure." Suddenly, I needed to sit down. Étienne had brought a train of ugly memories with him, memories of Uncle, of Father dying in his great bed, of Mother, blind and insane, staggering into the furniture. I did not dare to speak of them, or even to think of them for long. I wanted to hide from memory. I sat, putting my hands to my face. I felt transparent with exhaustion. A wraith, a wisp of vapour. "Oh, how will I manage the Comtesse de Soissons's reading this afternoon?" I leaned my head on the back of the chair. "I'm simply too drained to read in the glass."

"What?" asked Florent. "The comtesse is in town? Why isn't she at court in this season? Everyone who is anyone is at Saint-Germain. Something serious is going on. I only wish I knew what."

"Oh, I don't think so. With that woman, it could be anything from indigestion to a new lover," I answered.

* * *

But I was wrong. As I was helped out of my carriage at the foot of the great stairs in the carriage court at the Hôtel Soissons, I saw Primi Visconti descending them. He was hunched against the sharp March winds, his cloak pulled tightly around him, his head bent down, the picture of despondency.

"Hey, Monsieur Primi!" I called into the wind, and he tilted his head up and assumed a jaunty expression as if he hadn't a care in the world.

"Why, hello, Madame de Morville. My congratulations: you look younger every day."

"No thanks to you, Primi. Tell me, what is it today? Another duel of the fortune-tellers? Or shall I be put on exhibit with a clockwork figure and a dancing bear?"

"I suppose I should apologise, Marquise. The King's favourite sport is unmasking fortune-tellers, magicians, and mountebanks."

"Next time unmask yourself, Primi, you charlatan. I've half a mind to curse you, to burn a faggot against your body just to teach you a lesson."

"Ah, I always said you were a witch – not that it matters any more," he said, sighing.

"So what have you to be sad about? He made you a favourite . . . but he ruined me."

"We are all ruined now, little Marquise. I would flee, but I am in love . . . so I'll stay, and risk everything."

"I'll be frozen long before I'm starved. Let's stand in the doorway."

"Better to freeze, in this case. We shouldn't be overheard." He gestured to the Swiss guard in livery standing at the great double doors of the mansion. The cold wind seemed to want to blow us apart as we stood together on the wide stone staircase. "The rumour has been about town in the last few days that the fortune-tellers of Paris have enhanced the quality of their predictions by poison. Some dreadful old woman I never heard of was arrested. Marie Bosse, they called her. She implicated a fortune-teller called La Vigoreux. I met this woman once at Madame de Vassé's – she read my palm. Now she is at the Château de Vincennes, and they say she is giving the names of her accomplices under torture."

"Primi, you are morbid – one little palm reading? They'll find you innocent, just like all the other silly women who had their palms read by her." But the barb went wild. Primi was too upset to notice.

"If that were only so," he said, looking frantic. "But Marquise, for me it is worse than you can imagine. The woman I love – oh, Marquise, you should see her! She is a divinity!" his mood shifted just as suddenly as it had collapsed. He kissed his fingers at the mere thought of this woman, then went on. "We met when she called me to read her palm. One look, and I was immediately in love. Those eyes! That adorable waist! I just had to win her! I read her fortune. I predicted that she would soon fall passionately in love with me and be my bride. Unfortunately, she was already married. Doubly unfortunately, her husband has fallen ill and died, putting me under suspicion that I poisoned him with the aid of this La Vigoreux."

"So you have given her up?"

"Give her up? What madness! Of course not. We make passionate love every evening. I am bound by Cupid's chains – it is my destiny to perish of love . . ."

"Primi, you are a madman."

"Of course. What other way is there to be in this insane world? Adieu, Marquise. We may only meet again in the next world—"

"Primi, wait—" I cried into the wind, as he started down the stairs. He turned, and the wind blew his words back to me.

"No more; it's all finished, our world. Over. Go console the countess, but be sure you get your payment on the spot." I watched the slender figure of the Italian as he climbed into the waiting carriage. As the coachman gathered the reins and drove off, I could see Primi slumped in the back, his hat pulled over his eyes.

I waited for a long time in the cold, marble-floored antechamber of the countess's rooms. The glass panes rattled in the tall windows, and I could feel the draughts blowing under the gilt-panelled doors. What could she want, the countess? She was consulting fortune-tellers – something must have happened at court. She'd heard something that had sent her once again to the occult. Either something she wanted, or something she was afraid of. But what?

The countess's face was drawn; she had tried to conceal the
new lines that crossed her ravaged cheeks with heavy white
make-up. Her eyes darted from side to side in her narrow little
face; her smile was so strangely pulled out that it looked like
some sort of soundless scream. This time, it isn't because she
wants the King for a lover, I said to myself. This is fear.

"Madame de – well, whatever you call yourself now, I know
you read true. Visconti, he saw a break in my line of fate; he
saw disgrace, a fall, in the cards. A secret of my past will
emerge from darkness into the light." Ah, that was it. The
rumours swarming around the arrest of La Bosse and La
Vigoreux that Visconti had warned me about. But he didn't
know what I knew, that the investigation had stopped short.
The arrests had gathered in only La Bosse's people, and no
one had touched La Voisin or her close associates. Had the
countess procured from La Bosse the poison with which she
had removed her husband? If so, she had a right to be worried.
La Bosse had been under torture for several weeks now and
might well have been made to produce a list of her clients. And
now through the gossipy magistrates, some sort of news had
escaped La Reynie's secret inquiry into the families of the
robe, and thence to court. And if it wasn't a matter of her
husband, what other persons had left this earth by the
countess's little white hand? Perhaps enough to condemn even
a woman of her rank.

"You wish to know your future," I announced, unrolling my
cloth.

She leaned over the glass as I stirred, the diamonds on her
bosom reflecting little rainbows into the water.

"Madame, please – the colours of your gown, your jewels,
they interfere with the image."

"I must know," she said, moving back slightly.

"I see the same image I saw for you many years ago: your
carriage at night, your footmen in plain grey, your horses at full
speed, hurrying through the dark. The Marquise d'Alluye is
with you. You are not speaking . . . your faces are tense."

"Not an assignation after all – no, flight. And to think that for
years I have supposed that reading to be your one failure! Oh,
how bitter! You saw it all along. Why didn't you warn me?"

"Wait, Madame, another image is coming up. You are— It

must be a foreign place, the clothes are strange . . . they don't seem French. You are at Mass in a strange church . . . "

"Then I am saved—"

"Wait! Two men are in the back of the church, one with a large sack. The first – I believe I recognise him – signals by dropping his hand. The second . . . Oh, and there is a third, on the other side of the church . . . open their sacks. Goodness! The sacks are full of black cats. They run pell-mell through the church. The crowd is turning on you – they appear to think the cats are devils brought by you . . . They are shouting, threatening. They drag at your gown, trying to tear you to bits . . . your lackeys beat them off as you flee to your carriage outside."

"The man who does this – you say you recognise him?"

"An agent of the Paris police, Madame." To be precise, Desgrez. The man who had lured Madame de Brinvilliers out of her sanctuary in a foreign convent.

"They will kill me! They incite the mob against me! Oh, what a convenient death – and no one is to blame! The low-born villains dare not attack a Mancini directly, so they use craft. I swear it is Louvois. He hates me. He hates us all, we who are above him in breeding. I know him; he will use his creature La Reynie to pursue his vengeance under cover of law. That is how he is – devious – and he bides his time. No one is safe, not even the Mancinis. Tell me, my death . . . "

"That will require payment in advance, Madame." I took the fee and looked again. "You die old," I said. The air in the chilly room was shattered by the countess's mad laughter.

She stood up suddenly, stretching her arms above her head, shrieking, "Old, old, I shall live despite you, Louvois!" Then she remembered I was there and, looking at me with glowing, insane eyes, she said, "Louvois, what do I care for him? Ha! He is nothing, not even this—" She snapped her fingers to show his insignificance. "Oh, the ugly little bourgeois man; I swear, I'll have my vengeance on him!"

As my carriage pulled into the Rue de Picardie I leaned back into the cushions, nearly ill with the fatigue that comes from too many readings close together. A few more like that will kill me, I thought. I think I might even have dozed off, for I felt as if I awoke with a shudder when the carriage stopped in the Rue

Forez. My final errand of the day. To get my last cordial made up at one-quarter strength.

La Dodée met me at the door. Her ordinarily cheerful face was long with worry beneath her white linen house cap. She wiped her damp hands on her apron as she said, "Oh, you've come, after all! It's all made up, your order, but not in the bottles yet. La Trianon wants you in the back. She's been worried to death and needs a reading." I groaned.

"I don't have it in me. I've been doing readings all afternoon and feel as if I will faint if I even look at the glass again."

"Come into the laboratory and put your feet up. We'll make you coffee, and your strength will come back. Terrible things are happening. The lightning is striking all around us, and we must know where it will fall next."

They put an armchair by the fire, and as I sank back into it, my eyes closed. One of the girls must have brought a footstool, for the last thing I felt before oblivion was someone propping up my feet.

"Wake up! Wake up!" La Trianon's voice was urgent. She was shaking my shoulders.

"Why, I wasn't asleep at all – just resting my eyes."

"A curious way of resting. It must be your eyes that snore, then."

"Me? Snore? Never!" I sat up straight. La Trianon stood beside me, hands on her hips, the sleeves of her black dress rolled up to the elbow as if she had just left her worktable.

"I thought that would rouse you. Now, restore your strength with this – we must have a reading. It is life or death." The Turkish coffee was heavy and sweet, better than medicine. I held the little cup in my hands, warming them, as I breathed in the dark, strong scent.

"Ah, excellent. You definitely look more alert. We have the water set up on the worktable by the athanor." I looked across the room to see the water vase shimmering in the fading light from the window. One of the girls was sweeping the floor; a cat was nursing its kittens in a box behind the athanor. La Dodée and another girl were finishing pouring the last of my cordial into bottles with a funnel and sealing the corks.

"Oh, look at that; your harpy is coming unravelled – it must be the moths," I observed.

"More than the harpy is coming unravelled these days. Those who can are going into hiding. But we can't hide – our livelihood is here. But all may yet be mended. Madame has planned a great *coup* that will save us all. She is taking a petition to the King. But we must know how it goes, so we can lay our plans."

"A petition? Whatever for?"

"It is poisoned," whispered La Trianon. "Even La Dodée does not know. Next week she goes to present it at Saint-Germain. She was overwhelmed by the crowd around the King last time and returned with it. But next time she will not fail. And now, now . . . it is essential to us that she succeed."

"But how can poison go from paper to the eyes of a reader?"

"Not to the eyes, to the pocket. The petition is covered with a fine powder. The King habitually places petitions, unread, in the pocket where he keeps his handkerchief. When he is dead, his ministers will fall; no one will think to pursue this case in the turmoil and this dreadful inquiry will stop before we are all implicated."

"And if she fails?"

"Then we are all dead – you, me, Madame de Montespan, the Mancinis, and all the rest."

"Very well, then, let me do the reading." I pulled a stool up to the high worktable. La Trianon shooed away the girls, and even La Dodée, with a tense, "Later . . . later. You mustn't disturb the little Marquise. It must be a perfect reading."

The water seemed to darken, as if it were absorbing the falling dusk from outside. Then in the centre, I could see an orange glow, first small, then larger, until it filled the vase.

"What is it you see?"

"A fire— Wait, I see something more." Above the flames, the end of a heavy stake. In the centre of the flames, a living figure, chained sitting. A face, distorted, screaming silently in the orange heart of the fire.

"Sitting . . . someone who has been tortured . . . legs broken – it is . . . Wait, I can't quite make out . . ." I peered closely, so closely my breath dimpled the water. The image wobbled and swayed. I pulled back. It was certain.

"It is Madame, being burned alive."

"Are you certain?"

"Certain. Her hair is a cinder. Her face is black – but I would know it anywhere. The executioner's assistants . . . are pulling the body apart with hooks – but . . . I don't think she's dead . . . the limbs are moving. . ." The weakness was terrible. I swayed as the ceiling, harpy and all, began to rotate above me.

"Come quick! Come quick!" La Trianon held me up as the others came back to help me into the armchair. "It is the worst, the worst. Marie, call a vinaigrette from the corner. I must go to Madame tonight. I must dissuade her. She must not go to Saint-Germain next week; she must flee—" One of the girls had already brought La Trianon her wide black felt hat and her dark cloak, but as another went for the door, I called out to her to halt.

"My carriage is waiting outside. We'll go together. If Madame is to be stopped, I must tell her myself. Just send a message to my house that I shall be late. They are expecting me." La Trianon wrinkled up her nose.

"You mean that *man* you're sleeping with is waiting there. Let him wait – it's good for them."

"Not him – he'll go in search of me; he may uncover your plans."

"Not only a man, but a clever one. You have let yourself in for trouble," announced La Trianon.

"Enough, enough. There's not much time." And I had just enough presence of mind to scoop up my bottles from the counter before we hurried to my waiting carriage.

FIFTY-TWO

"Well, well," said the Shadow Queen, "to what do I owe the honour?" She stood before her great tapestry of the Magdalen, her hands on her hips, regarding us with her head to one side, as if we were a tradesman with a late delivery. Near the hearth, a nursemaid held her youngest child on leading strings while he played with a little wooden bird on the end of a stick, making its wings flap up and down with a clatter in imitation of flying. One of Madame's tabby cats was rubbing itself on my ankles. Old Montvoisin and his daughter stared suspiciously at us from the corner.

"Catherine, we must speak with you alone." La Trianon's voice was urgent. I noticed Antoine Montvoisin's eyes follow us as La Voisin led the way to her cabinet, and I heard the creak of a floorboard behind us as he trailed behind to try to overhear our business. La Voisin shut the cabinet door behind the two of us, then lit the candles in the wall sconces from the glowing embers in the grate. Then she pulled the heavy crimson curtains across the narrow little window.

"Now," she said, "we are entirely private. I hope you have not come to try to dissuade me from my great work." In the light of the candles, her black eyes glowed like burning coals. The glow made my skin crawl. It seemed like madness.

"Catherine, the little marquise has seen a vision in the glass. You will burn."

"A vision? You miserable little thing, who told you to interfere with my business?" Her face shone with the flickering rage of insanity.

"No, no, Catherine. It was I. It is your interests I have at heart. I am your oldest friend."

"Were, you mean. You have always wanted me to stay small and safe. Within your reach. When have you failed to warn me against becoming great? Remember the first Black Mass I did for La Montespan? It gave her the King – and founded my fortune. It was you who tried to hold me back – from glory."

"Madame, I beg you. Preserve yourself. Preserve us," I broke in.

"And now speaks the devotée of featherbeds and linen sheets, fine wines and easy lovers. You were never destined for greatness. I was a fool to have taken you in out of the snow."

"Madame, I saw you in the flames."

"But when did you see me in the flames? Tomorrow, next year, or perhaps a decade from now? Your visions are flawed – they show too much and too little all at once. For all you know, I won't be burned for this great undertaking at all, but for something entirely different. Why should I fight my fate? No, I embrace it, and my eternal fame."

"But, Madame, the pictures can be changed. Take a new path. God does not only give us fate but free will; there is a choice—"

"Bah! What is this drivel? No wonder the demon wouldn't have you. You live in books, Mademoiselle, and not in life. God, indeed! And now you are an expert in theology, as well as everything else! No, I will press on with this great deed, and I will have—"

"Death, Madame."

"No, you little fool. *Respect.*" The sorceress stood at her full height, head thrown back, her nostrils flared and eyes glowing. The word resonated in the stillness.

"'Respect'?" broke in La Trianon. "For *that* you risk us all?"

La Voisin smiled conspiratorially and waved her hand as if to dismiss our doubts. "Come, come, there's a fortune in it as well." Once again she sounded like her old self, a practical, mocking housewife turning a penny on soap or candles bought at a bargain. "Times are hard – I have ten mouths to feed. Do you think I can feed a family on air? On philosophy? On good intentions? No, I'll look after them – and you, too. The milord waits for me when this is done. La Montespan's money will smooth my exile—"

"You mean, you will flee when we cannot?" La Trianon's voice was horrified at the betrayal.

"Please, I think of it as retirement. They will send their hounds after me when I flee and never notice you, crouching in the burrow. But the foreign king and his great nobles will protect me. Then the police will give up. The Dauphin, that great, stupid mound of lard, will reign, and the investigation will end. Politics will change. No, I will not burn for this. And besides, once I'm retired abroad, there will be plenty of time to change the image." She looked pleased with herself. Then she looked at me and shook her head. "Once again," she said, "the little marquise has made a hash of things."

"Then there is nothing more I can say to persuade you?" La Trianon's voice was plaintive.

"Nothing. Go home, go to bed. Your nerves are overwrought. You were never one to have the strength of mind to plan great enterprises. And you, Mademoiselle – go home to your opium and your soft featherbed with that useless gambler and quit bothering me with your visions. Now out, both of you. I have plans to make." She opened the door of her cabinet and shooed us out as one would chase away chickens. Then she shut the door behind us and remained alone in her cabinet.

"You didn't convince her," whispered old Montvoisin, pulling at my sleeve from his hiding place outside the door of her cabinet.

"No," I answered. La Trianon looked annoyed at the crumpled little man and sailed out to the great parlour to wait for me.

"Then we are lost. My daughter, my grandson. I haven't a sou of ready cash. She has locked up everything for fear we will betray her to the police and flee. Betray her? How could I think of it? But flee, yes I would. With my child, to a safe place in the country. My wife is a madwoman who will destroy us. Are you sure you don't have money? One hundred livres? I'll borrow it from you – I have unset jewels as security. Emeralds, diamonds. They're worth more than the cash, I assure you." Something about him, his pitifulness, made my skin crawl.

"I haven't that amount now, but I'll see if I have it when I go home. I'm not as prosperous as I used to be—" I had to get away from his whining. Anything, just to get him to let go of my sleeve.

"You will? Oh, bless you, bless you. Come to the house

tomorrow. Sunday morning – she'll be at Mass. She'll never know." I pried his dirty old claws off me and fled to the carriage with La Trianon.

"*Oof*; you were so late, Madame. Your . . . er . . . husband was going to send us after you. But we told him you usually know what you are doing." Sylvie had finished undoing my corset and was now brushing my black gown before putting it away. D'Urbec lounged on the bed, pretending not to listen, while he read Tacitus by the light of a candle.

"Oh, Sylvie, I have such a headache! It was horrid. I saw Madame being burned alive, as clear as clear. We went to warn her, La Trianon and I, but she said, 'nonsense' and shooed us out. And that horrid old Antoine, he held me by the sleeve so I couldn't leave. He wants a hundred livres to leave her and take his daughter and grandson into the provinces to hide. I told him I'd think about it just to get rid of him, and he slobbered on my dress, kissing my hand in gratitude."

"Well, no wonder you washed your hands so when you got home."

"So," spoke up Florent, putting down his book and rising from the bed, "you persist in claiming you see visions? Geneviève, Geneviève, give up that dreadful opium. If you're not afraid of death, at least stop and think: it will steal your mind long before it takes your life." He stood beside me, put his hands on my shoulders, and stared directly into my face. His eyes were pleading. "Remember whom you would leave behind. If you can't think of yourself, think of me."

"Florent, I'm trying – for your sake, for mine." He looked dubious.

"These headaches of yours, they get worse all the time . . . and you see things, you act frantic—"

"Florent, I had to fool even myself. I've been having the formula made weaker each time I replenish my stock. I'm down to a quarter strength now. In a month, perhaps, I'll be free of it. But the headaches – cutting back just spreads out the pain, so I can bear it." His face was tender, concerned.

"Why didn't you tell me? Why did you try to bear it all yourself, in secret? Why didn't you ask me to help you?"

"I . . . I was afraid you'd quit loving me if you knew how

much I was taking – I knew you hated it. La Reynie, he mocked me for it. A genteel vice, he called it. He took it away and nearly killed me – that's ... that's how..." I was overwhelmed with shame at the memory of how quickly La Reynie had broken me. Florent put his arms around me.

"And so now you think I'm La Reynie? What an insult," he said, but his voice was kind, and the warmth of his body comforted me. I put my arms around his neck and rested my head on his wide shoulder.

"Florent, I love you so much. I wish I were perfect, just for your sake. I'm crying..." He kissed me gently, as if to tell me that words weren't necessary.

"You are perfect, for me," he said softly.

"Good night, Monsieur, Madame," said Sylvie, and the door closed as Florent blew out the candle.

The next morning Florent rose and dressed early, as the sound of Sunday bells rolled across the city. It was 12 March 1679.

"Florent," I called lazily from the bed. "Mass? I thought twice a year was enough for you."

"Not Mass, business," he answered. "I have a few things in my rooms, and some errands for my valet." Somehow, I didn't believe him. Still, it was not my habit to question his odd business. Sometimes he burned letters to ashes after receiving them. And he had a curious brass wheel with two rows of moving letters that he sometimes set on the desk when he was writing. The less I know, I thought, the less I can tell. But as he approached the head of the stairs, I heard Sylvie call to him in an odd, deep voice:

"Stay, mortal. Astaroth has plans for you."

"Oh, bother," I heard him respond. "Just a moment, you tiresome old devil. I'm in a hurry."

"You will be in even more of a hurry, once Astaroth has advised you." I was annoyed. It was all very well for Florent to hurry off without breakfast, but I wanted some, and Astaroth might just be too snobbish to bring it up.

That, of course, turned out to be exactly the problem, so I summoned Gilles and went downstairs in my robe to see what was in the kitchen cupboard. No butter. Yesterday's bread. A half a cheese turning mouldy. A dried sausage. A pot of preserves with a suspicious-looking scum across the top. I scraped off the scum, scooped out a dollop of the preserves, and cut a piece of the bread.

"The coffee, Madame. I'll grind it." Gilles looked at me mournfully.

"And no milk? Very well, then, I'll have it Turkish style."

"Astaroth is a great trial," said Gilles.

"You'd better check the cistern, too," announced Mustapha from his seat on the kitchen bench. "Astaroth doesn't haul water, either." I lifted the lid on the kitchen cistern and peered down into its green depths.

"There's plenty—" But even as I spoke, I could see an image coming, all slippery and dark, in the water.

"Madame, I have the dipper—"

"*Shh*, Gilles. Look at her face. It's another image," Mustapha whispered.

A black carriage stood by the open double doors of a church. Notre-Dame de Bonne Nouvelle. A woman was being forced into the carriage while a half-dozen archers kept the crowd away. As the man pushed her in and sat down opposite her, I saw their faces. Desgrez. And La Voisin.

"It's today," I whispered. "I must warn her. She must not go to Mass. They're waiting for her at the church." I stood up suddenly, all thought of breakfast forgotten. "Bring the carriage. Sylvie! I need to dress!"

"Madame, Monsieur d'Urbec has taken the carriage."

"Oh, damn! Then call me anything you can find. Oh, it's Sunday! It's hopeless. Find someone; do something! I must get to Notre-Dame de Bonne Nouvelle before late Mass!" Gilles disappeared out the kitchen door.

"Astaroth does not lace up women," came the impudent voice from the next room.

"Plague take you, Sylvie, and Astaroth, too!" I shouted as I hurried upstairs. I struggled into my shift and buttoned on a loose *sacque* of indigo wool that I wore only indoors. Then I pinned my hair back untidily and hid the mess under a white linen cap.

"There," I said as I settled my wide-brimmed hat over the cap, "at least it *appears* decent." I fastened my heavy cloak and fled to the front door, where I found a vinaigrette waiting accompanied by an apologetic Gilles.

"I told them it was a holy duty to take a poor, infirm woman to Mass," he said.

"Notre-Dame de Bonne Nouvelle," I told them. "If you get me there before the late Mass, I'll double your fee."

But we reached the Rue de Bonne Nouvelle just as the bells were pealing. As I paid the man and told him to wait, the doors of the church were thrown open, and the first Mass goers strolled out, talking. But as I tried to pass by them into the church, the black carriage drove up and halted in the street before the church door. I shrank back behind an immense woman in half-mourning as the archers stationed themselves near by and Desgrez and a companion strode purposefully towards the doors.

Madame was elegantly dressed in her green gown, covered by a fur-trimmed mantle and hood. Her hands were concealed in a matching fur muff, and she wore a pair of cleverly made wrought-iron pattens to save her handsome kid shoes from the mud. She never paused when she saw Desgrez but raised up her chin and looked down her nose as a housewife might when she sees a mouse run through another woman's kitchen. The crowd had stopped to watch the scene unfolding before us.

"Madame Montvoisin, I believe?" asked Desgrez.

"I am she," responded La Voisin.

"I arrest you in the name of the King," announced Desgrez.

But the crowd began to mutter. Then a woman's voice cried, "What are you doing? She is an honest woman!"

"Yes! Yes!" shouted someone else. "She supports her old mother!"

"Arrest your own mother, police dog!" cried a man.

"Archers!" called Desgrez. "Disperse, all of you, before you are shot as rebels. You interfere with the King's justice!" As the archers forced the crowd back, Desgrez and his companion forced La Voisin into the carriage. I stood paralysed. How could it all end so quickly, so surely? La Reynie had won. Montespan had lost. There would be human bonfires on the Place de Grève. Desgrez, his face like cold iron, would sit on horseback beside them until the blackened cinders floated away on the wind. The greatest sorceress the world had ever known was finished.

Suddenly fear seized me. The account books, the thought burned through my brain. I fought my way through the crowd and found that my conveyance had vanished at the first sign of the police. Limping rapidly through the spring muck, oblivious of my shoes, I raced for the house on the Rue Beauregard. Too late. The seals had been placed. Two guards stood at the front door. As I tried to go round to the side door, someone powerful grabbed me from behind, covering my mouth and dragging me into an alley.

"Quiet, you idiot. I knew you'd be here."

"Florent," I tried to mumble, but his hand stopped me.

"Don't mention my name," he hissed. "The police are everywhere. The carriage is hidden in the next street. This way, and quietly."

We hurried through the narrow alley and out on to the Rue de la Lune, where he pushed me into the carriage and swung in beside me.

"The books, Florent . . . the contract . . . I'm lost."

"Never mind. We'll leave anyway."

"I can't, Florent. The police know me; my description is at the barriers. For all I know, they have orders to arrest me already. There's only one way. Take everything, and go without me. God knows, I won't be needing any of it any more."

"Geneviève, what are you saying?" I clutched at him and wept.

"Go right away. Don't lose your life for me. And when you marry again, name a daughter after me, and remember that I loved you—"

"Geneviève, my darling," he said tenderly, embracing me, "I couldn't, I wouldn't, leave without you. I have the contract, and the *P* volume of her account ledgers. I went away this morning to buy them from Antoine Montvoisin for a hundred livres. When I heard you talking last night, I knew it was my best chance."

"You *bought* them? You *have* them?" My heart began to beat hard, and I looked up at his face, unbelieving.

"Well, more or less bought. I bribed him and then broke into the cupboard. The locks weren't hard – remember, I'm a clockmaker's son, and have plenty of experience with mechanisms."

"Then Montvoisin – he's fled? And Marie-Marguerite?" He shook his head.

"Both taken, I'm afraid. He was keeping watch outside her cabinet. When I heard the knock at the front door, I tied the stuff into my shirt and dropped out the window. I barely fit – and nearly broke both legs in the bargain. But it was just as well. It turned out the police were at the front, back, and side doors. The place was surrounded. I climbed over the neighbour's garden wall and left through the alley. See here? I've ruined my breeches."

"Oh, Florent." Even hearing of his narrow escape made my heart stop.

"Then as I was about to depart, I reflected: The way you've been claiming to see things lately, you might well try to come to the house to talk her out of the contract yourself—"

"I came to warn her – I saw her taken after Mass—"

"Same thing. Two equally foolish endeavours, and both the sort of thing you'd try, if you flew into a panic. What would have happened if you'd kept her from Mass? They'd have just arrested her at home. You can't change fate— Oh, look at this; we're almost home."

Upstairs, I found Sylvie packing, while Mustapha sat in my big chair and criticised: "Too much, Sylvie, too much. We're not taking a wagon."

"Two small trunks only, and the little chest with Madame's jewels. You need to leave room for the bird cage," announced Florent.

"But Madame's dresses—"

"Leave all the Marquise de Morville's things, Sylvie. Just pack my linens, my court gowns, the rose dress, the crimson velvet, and the new one with the pretty blue stripes and flowers. I will just have to leave my old age behind me."

"Very well, Madame." She began to unpack the widow's weeds, the Spanish farthingale, the ruffs, and black veils. She shook her head; a pity, she seemed to say. All that money.

"Sylvie, has the message come from the Chevalier de La Motte yet?"

"Not yet, Monsieur." Florent began to pace and fume.

"Florent, what's wrong?" I asked him.

"Nothing, nothing. Come away and I'll explain." He took me into the antechamber and shut the door. "My plans have been disrupted, but Lamotte has vowed to do his best."

"Lamotte?"

"Yes, Lamotte, who rises in favour daily, and who owes me rather more than he can repay. Oh, he had tears in his eyes when he promised. It's just that Lamotte's tears are plentiful and dramatic, but never quite reliable— Damn! If we could have waited until Easter, it would have been easy. His new play will be presented at court. He will have to leave Paris to supervise the arrangements, and he has been granted the use of one of the carriages from the stable of the Hôtel Bouillon for the trip to court."

"Why, it's perfect. Carriages with the arms of great houses are never stopped or searched like common vehicles. They wouldn't even think to ask that the window curtains be opened. They never ask who's inside."

"Exactly. But we have bought only a few days at best by absconding with La Voisin's records. We need to be far gone from here before her interrogation under torture begins."

"But it's Lent – there are no plays."

"Exactly. I have begged Lamotte to think of an excuse, and now I wait for his answer." But that evening, a boy arrived at the door with a letter.

My friend, I have tried everything I can think of, but I can do nothing. I have gone to light a candle for you at the cathedral. May God relieve your troubles with all speed.

"Oh, that wretched André!" exclaimed Florent, crumpling up the letter and throwing it into the fire. "Everything his minuscule brain could think of! In short, nothing at all!" He paced ragefully up and down on the bedroom carpet. "Geneviève," he announced at last, "there is only one way out. We must pass out of Paris separately, in disguise, and meet again in Calais."

"But what about my servants, Florent?"

"You have to leave them behind, I'm afraid. They would identify you." Then he saw my face and paused. "Or perhaps they could leave later, in disguise, too," he added to mollify me.

"Florent, it's very hard to disguise Mustapha – or Gilles, for that matter. And Sylvie's always spouting off in that demon's voice at unexpected moments. She'd give herself away. You know if I leave them behind they are as good as dead." Florent looked ashamed.

"I'm sorry," he said. "I know it's selfish, but it has to be done. I can't bear to lose you."

I thought, and I thought again. I remembered the basement of the Châtelet. Betray them to that for my own convenience? It would make me no better than La Voisin. At last I said, "I think I have an idea, Florent, but it's not very honest." I went to the little desk in my *ruelle* and wrote a letter. "How soon can you get to Versailles to deliver this to Madame de Montespan?" I asked.

"I can take a horse tonight and ride by moonlight," answered Florent. "But what makes you think that Madame de Montespan will assist you?"

"Oh, she will be assisting herself," I said, somewhat evasively. "I tell her of La Voisin's arrest in this letter and offer the assistance of my oracle glass. Once I see her in person, I am sure I can convince her." Florent called for his hat and cloak and vanished into the gathering dusk.

By the next morning he had returned and fallen fully clothed across the bed, where he went to sleep instantly. He was still asleep when Mademoiselle des Oeillets, dressed in travelling clothes, was shown in to my downstairs reception room. She removed her mask as Sylvie took her cloak. "Madame de Montespan has just returned from court to her house in Vaugirard. We travelled at full speed, as soon as she heard the news of La Voisin's arrest." I acted calm, though I didn't feel that way at all.

"And how may I serve her?"

"She needs a reading." Sylvie vanished from the room.

"Her future?"

"That – and she needs to find something that is lost."

"What sort of thing? I don't have good luck with all lost things. Jewellery, corpses, I do better at those." I feigned ignorance to draw her out.

"This would be well, ah, papers. A book, perhaps. Madame needs to know where they are." Ah, good. The fish had taken the bait. Madame de Montespan wanted La Voisin's records of her ghastly commerce in poison and witchcraft. She had to know if the police had them.

"I will return with you immediately," I answered. "Just let me retrieve my cloak from upstairs." Upstairs, I found Florent lying on the bed, still only partially awake.

"Florent, Florent. Listen." He groaned. "I will need your help in a deception." His eyes flicked open. "Madame de Montespan has arrived from Versailles just this morning. I am going to promise to retrieve the *M* ledger from the police for her in return for smuggling us all out of Paris in her carriage. I want you to go ahead of us, so that in case anything happens, you will not be lost. I'll tell her I have bribed the police through one of La Voisin's contacts and have stolen it out of Paris. That way she won't have me waylaid and searched."

"The *M* ledger?" said Florent, rubbing his head and sitting up. "But I have it, Geneviève." He looked puzzled, the way people do when they are still half asleep.

"You *have* it, Florent? However did you get it?"

"When I broke into La Voisin's cupboard, I not only brought away the *P* volume, I took the *M* as well."

"What on earth made you think of it, because only now did I think of asking for her help?" I fastened my cloak and pulled my hat on over my house cap.

"It was Astaroth's idea," he said simply.

"*Astaroth?*" D'Urbec looked amused at my amazement. He seemed fully awake now and was rebuttoning his shirt.

"That Astaroth is one smart devil – smarter even than Sylvie, who guessed where I was going yesterday morning, and who never lets a chance go by for getting money. Once he had spoken, I saw his point immediately." He got up and went to the mirror to inspect the stubble on his jaw. He poured a bit of water into the basin and then splashed it on his face.

"How should we do this, then?"

"Tell Madame de Montespan to send a trusted agent with you, or better, come herself to the Inn at the Sign of Saint-Peter, which is two leagues out of Paris on the Calais road. There you will meet a man who has her papers, and she can burn them with her own hand, if she wishes." Florent's mind was so swift and sure, I admired him utterly. His eye caught mine, and a look of appreciation passed between us, as quick as thought. Two halves of the same mind, working at full speed, in perfect co-ordination. "Remember," he said, "don't let her think that you have them on you." I took the key from my neck and opened the secret compartment behind the bookshelf in my *ruelle*.

"Of course not. But I'm sure I'll sound much more convincing now that I know it's true." I stuffed my collection of little notebooks into the bag that I carried my oracle glass in. Last of all, I put in Father's little brown leather one.

"Good. I'll take my valet, the chest with your dresses, and the trunk with the silver out right away. Remember, Sign of Saint-Peter. I'll expect you there with your people. I'll be waiting for as long as it takes." I locked the cupboard, replaced the bookshelf, and headed for the stairs.

I returned with Mademoiselle des Oeillets to the mansion in the Rue Vaugirard and was shown into Madame de Montespan's presence immediately. She was pacing beneath an immense tapestry of Joseph and his Brothers in her green *salle*, wringing her hands. Strands of her usually flawless coiffure were flying loose about her forehead. Her clothes were dusty with travel. So tightly did she clasp her hands together that I feared her rings would cut her fingers.

"Madame," I said, bowing low, "I believe I can help alleviate your troubles. You seek, ah, lost papers?"

"Yes, very special ones. They say you can find lost things. I need to know . . . where something lost is—"

"Could these papers be La Voisin's account books?"

She came close to me and grabbed my shoulders fiercely with a clawlike grip. "Yes," she whispered.

"I can get them for you on certain conditions," I said softly, so that we would not be overheard.

"I'll go myself," she whispered, having heard me out. "I can't risk anyone else getting their hands on them."

Her eyes looked calmer now, calculating.

"You are shrewd, Madame de Morville."

"No, just fortunate in my, ah, connections. And I have now a powerful desire to retire peacefully in the country. I am planning to buy a little cottage and raise bees." Let her think my connections were with the magistrates who kept the evidence sealed. They sold the stuff often enough. Why not let them take the blame this time? She laughed – a short, sharp little sound.

"I think you love beekeeping as much as I do, Madame de Morville. But, at any rate, I wish you good luck in your true plans – whatever they are. And . . . I want one more thing."

"Your future?"

"My death, Madame. How will it be?"

"I always charge in advance for that."

I seated myself before the water vase with some fear, for if her death were grievous enough, she might not want the papers any more. But I needn't have worried. She appeared very old in the image that arose.

"You will live a long life," I said. Her famous complexion was in ruins: it looked like crumpled paper that children have played with and discarded. She appeared to be dozing on a great, canopied bed.

"You are in a bed with rich hangings in the great room of a château that I do not recognise. A portrait of the King hangs opposite the bed." A château of exile.

"Ah!" she exclaimed. "Then he is still mine!"

"You have plenty of company: ladies are playing music and singing. There are others – yes, sewing and talking." It was a strange scene, late at night. The room was full of blazing candles, as if Madame de Montespan was afraid of the dark. The ladies' heads were nodding. Suddenly Madame's ancient eyes opened with a look of panic – she shrieked soundlessly at the women, who resumed their singing. Paid companions, to frighten off the night with cheerful noise.

"Then I am beloved," said Madame de Montespan.

"Evidently so," I agreed.

"Then your plan must work. I'll waste no time. Mademoiselle des Oeillets, call my great carriage. I want four footmen, three postilions, in the blue and silver livery. And my mounted guard – quickly! And dress in your best. I have an important errand in the country, and I will need your company."

"Tell me," she said as we mounted into her carriage and

settled into the heavy velvet cushions, "how did you know what I wanted and prepare to have it so soon?"

"The glass," I said. "It showed your salvation and mine." She nodded as if she believed every word.

We stopped briefly before my house in the Rue Charlot and were immediately surrounded by little boys, shouting to see the grand equipage and attendants in their bright silver and blue. The postilions warned them away from the immense, vicious carriage horses as the lackeys helped Gilles bring out my trunks. Sylvie, clutching a satchel, handed the bird cage in to me while Mustapha, in full Turkish regalia, turned the key in the front-door lock. As the carriage rattled towards the ramparts, Madame de Montespan overcame her distaste of the bird enough to ask, "Tell me . . . does that . . . creature . . . talk?"

"Hellfire and damnation!" announced the bird, as we were waved past the customs barrier and into the suburbs.

"Unusual vocabulary," observed Madame de Montespan. She pulled back the carriage curtains to let in the light and air. The carriage swayed and rattled as the horses broke into the fast trot that took us into open country.

"What else would you expect of a bird that knew La Voisin personally?" I answered. But inside, my heart was singing "He's waiting for you" and my mind was fixed on the remembrance of his dark eyes.

A HISTORICAL NOTE

La Voisin and the witches of Paris were real historical figures, whose lives and deeds are preserved in the testimony they gave, under torture, during the celebrated *"Affaire des poisons"*. These records have generated a great deal of controversy, as various historians have sought to prove the participation or nonparticipation of some favourite figure in the web of poison, conspiracy, and witchcraft. Evidence of classic coven structure is found by some authors; others disagree. To me, the organisation looked more like a cross between the "corporations" that organised the trades of the day and a sort of franchise structure, and so this is how I have depicted it.

The evidence against Madame de Montespan, along with that implicating other persons of quality, was kept in a separate sealed coffer and burned by the King himself. Madame de Montespan did, however, definitively lose favour after the Affair of the Poisons and died in exile from the court. Madame de Maintenon, the new favourite who succeeded her, is thought to have been secretly married to the King after the death of the Queen. Her rise to favour inaugurated a reign of piety, conformity, and vicious religious persecution.

Mademoiselle de Fontanges died shortly after giving birth to a child who also died. To still the rumours arising from the accusations of the witnesses before the commission that Madame de Montespan had engaged Romani to poison her, the King reluctantly agreed to an autopsy. The doctors, who had no effective means of detecting poison anyway, declared her death to be from natural causes, thus saving a great deal of trouble.

The Comtesse de Soissons was warned by the King of her coming arrest and fled in the night. Thereafter she wandered across the face of Europe, leaving a trail of mysterious deaths in her wake.

The Duchesse de Bouillon brought twenty carriages full of

aristocratic supporters to her trial. Having been accused of wanting to poison her husband to marry her lover, she appeared with her husband on one arm and her lover on the other, to announce that she had indeed seen the Devil, and he looked exactly like La Reynie. The King exiled her with a *lettre de cachet*.

Primi Visconti survived the scandal to write gossipy memoirs of the court.

La Trianon and La Dodée committed suicide in prison.

La Bosse was burned alive, but La Vigoreux died during torture.

Marie-Marguerite Montvoisin, the Abbé Guibourg, Le Sage, Romani, and others who were witnesses to the activities of Madame de Montespan were not brought to trial, where their evidence might become public, but were imprisoned for life, incommunicado. Also imprisoned in this fashion were all those unlucky enough to have temporarily shared a cell with them.

Gabriel Nicolas de La Reynie is considered to be the founder of the first modern police force.

William of Orange and the Princess Mary were brought to the throne of England after the Catholic monarch, James II, was driven into exile in the Glorious Revolution of 1688.

King Louis XIV died in 1715, having outlived three throne heirs. He was succeeded by his great-grandson, who became Louis XV.

The fiscal collapse of the state, projected by the great patriot, soldier, and administrator Sébastien le Prestre de Vauban in 1709, was complete before the end of the century.